'WHO ARE THESE PEOPLE?
WHAT DO THEY WANT FROM US?'

It was, Han Solo thought, a reasonable question Badure was asking the 'droid Zollux. Their party had stumbled across what looked like a used-spaceship lot, then discovered that all the craft on display were crude mockups – and then been captured by men speaking a long-forgotten language and imprisoned deep beneath the planet's surface. There were, it seemed, a lot of things that needed explaining ... but Zollux, who had established a queer kind of rapport with their captors, didn't seem too happy with the answers he had come up with.

Sounding dismayed, the 'droid said slowly, 'I know it sounds absurd in this day and age, sir, but unless we can do something, you're all about to become, er, a human sacrifice.'

D0544332

Han Solo and The Lost Legacy

From the Adventures of Luke Skywalker

by BRIAN DALEY

Based on the characters and situations
created by George Lucas

SPHERE BOOKS LIMITED
30-32 Gray's Inn Road, London WC1X 8JL

First published in Great Britain by
Sphere Books Ltd 1981
Copyright © Lucasfilm, Ltd. (LFL) 1980
TM: A Trademark of Lucasfilm, Ltd
Sphere Books authorized user
Published by arrangement with DelRey/Ballantine
Books, a division of Random House, Inc.,
New York, N.Y., USA
Reprinted 1983 (twice)

TRADE
MARK

Set in Baskerville

Printed in Great Britain by
Cox & Wyman Ltd, Reading

A book for Linda Kuehl
and, with particular gratitude,
for John A. Kearney

I

Han Solo nearly had the control-stem leads hooked up, a sweaty job that had him stuck under the low-slung airspeeder for almost an hour, when there was a kick at his foot. 'What's holding things up?'

The leads, now gathered together in precise order, sprang free of his fingers, going every which way. With a scalding Corellian malediction, Han shoved against the machine's undercarriage, and his repulsor-lift mechanic's creeper slid out from under the airspeeder.

Han leaped up instantly to confront Grigmin, his temporary employer, the colour on his face changing from the red of frustration to a darker and more dangerous hue. Han was lean, of medium height, and appeared younger than his actual age. His eyes were guarded, intense.

Grigmin, tall, broad shouldered, handsomely blond, and some years younger than Han, either didn't notice his pit-crewman's anger or chose not to acknowledge it. 'Well? What about it? That airspeeder's an important part of my show.'

Han attempted not to lose his scant temper. Working as pit-crewman to Grigmin's one-man airshow on a circuit of fifth-rate worlds had been the only job he and his partner, Chewbacca, had been able to get when they found they needed work, but Grigmin's unrelenting arrogance made the task of keeping his outmoded aircraft running nearly unbearable.

'Grigmin,' Han said, 'I've warned you before. You put too much strain on your hardware. You could stay well within performance tolerances and still complete every manoeuvre in your routines. But instead you showboat, with junk heaps that were obsolete when the Clone Wars were news.'

Grigmin's grin grew even wider. 'Save the excuses, Solo. Will my airspeeder be ready for my afternoon show, or have you and your Wookiee sidekick decided you don't like working for me?'

Masterpiece of understatement! Han thought to himself, but mumbled, 'She'll be in the air again if Fadoop gets here with the replacement parts.'

Now Grigmin frowned. 'You should have gone for them yourself. I never trust these useless locals; it's a rule I have.'

'If you want me to use a starship for a crummy surface-to-surface skip, you'll have to pay the expenses – up front.' Han would sooner trust a local like the amiable, gregarious Fadoop than a shifty deadbeat like Grigmin.

Grigmin ignored the invitation to part with some cash. 'I want my airspeeder ready,' he concluded and left to prepare for the next part of his performance, an exhibition of manoeuvres with a one-man jetpack. *Manoeuvres any academy greenie could do*, Han thought. *These backwater worlds are the only place anyone would pay to see a feeble act like Grigmin's.*

Still, if it hadn't been for Grigmin's needing a pit-crew, Han Solo and the Wookiee, Chewbacca, freelance smugglers, would have been on the Hurt Vector. He adjusted his sweatband, toed the mechanic's creeper over to him, settled onto it, and pulled himself back under the airspeeder.

Groping half-heartedly for the control leads, Han wondered just what it was that made his luck so erratic. He had had strokes of good fortune that rivalled anything he had ever heard of, but at other times ...

He barked his knuckles, swore a mighty oath, and mulled over the fact that only a short time ago he and his Wookiee partner had held the galaxy by the tail. They had defied a slavery ring in the Corporate Sector, held the Authority's dreaded Security Police at bay with a Territorial Manager as hostage, and come out of the deal ten thousand credits richer.

But since then there had been needed repairs for their starship, the *Millennium Falcon*, and monumental celebrations on a dozen worlds as they put the Corporate Sector behind them. Then there had been ill-fated smuggling ventures: a ruinous try at clotheslegging in the Cron Drift; a failed Military Script – exchange plot in the Lesser Plooriod Cluster; and more, each adventure bringing a little closer that day when they would find themselves among the needy.

So they had ended up here in the Tion Hegemony, so far out among the lesser star systems of the vast Empire that the Imperials didn't even bother to exert direct control over it. In the Tion tended to congregate the petty grifters, unsuccessful con-artists, and unprosperous crooks of the galaxy. They ran *Chak*-root, picked up R'alla mineral water for the smuggling run to Rampa, swiped, ambushed, connived, and attempted in a thousand ways to fuel careers temporarily at a standstill.

Han considered all this, as he carefully gathered the leads, once again separating them delicately. At least with Grigmin, Han and Chewbacca were paid, once in a while.

But that didn't make it any easier to take Grigmin's high-handedness. What particularly irritated Han was that Grigmin considered himself the hottest stunt pilot in space. Han had entertained the idea of taking a swing at the younger man, but Grigmin was a former heavyweight unarmed-combat champion ...

His musings were interrupted by another kick that jolted his boot. The control leads sprang from his hands again. Furious, he pushed off against the airspeeder's under-carriage, jumped off the mechanic's creeper, and, combat champion or no, launched himself at his tormentor ...

... and was caught up instantly against a wide shaggy chest in a frightfully strong but restrained hug and held a half-metre or so off the ground.

'Chewie! Let go, you big ... all right; I'm sorry.'

Thick arms muscled like loops of steel released him. The Wookiee Chewbacca glared down from his towering height, growling a denunciation of Han's manners, his reddish-brown brows lowered, his fangs showing. He shook a long, hairy finger at his partner for emphasis and tried straightening the Authority Security Police admiral's hat perched rakishly on his head, his lush mane escaping from beneath it.

The admiral's hat was just about the only thing the two still had from their adventures in the Corporate Sector. Chewbacca had taken a fancy to its bright braid, snowy-white material, glossy black brim, and ornate insignia during an exchange of hostages just before their hasty departure from that region of space. In his people's tradition of counting coup on their enemies, the Wookiee had demanded the hat as part of the ransom. Han, pressed by events, had indulged him.

Now the pilot threw up his hands. 'Enough! I *said* I was sorry. I thought you were that vapour-brain Grigmin again. Now what?'

Han's giant copilot informed him that Fadoop had arrived. Fadoop stood nearby on her feet and knuckles, an unusually fat and outgoing native of the planet Saheel-indeel. A short, bandy-legged, and densely green-furred primate, she was a local wheeler-dealer who flew an aircraft of sorts, an informal assemblage of parts and components from various scrapped fliers, a craft which she called *Skybarge*.

Pulling off his sweatband, Han walked towards Fadoop. 'You scrounged the parts? Good gal!'

Fadoop, scratching behind one ear with a big toe, removed a malodorous black cigar from her mouth and blew a smoke ring. 'Anything for Solo-my-friend. Are we not soul-sealed buddies, you, me, and the Big One here, this Wookiee? But, ahh, there is a matter –'

Fadoop looked away somewhat embarrassed. Working the quid of *Chak*-root that swelled her cheek, she spat a stream of red liquid into the dust. 'I trust Solo-my-friend, but not Grigmin-the-blowhard. I hate to bring up money.'

'No apologies; you earned it.' Han dug into a coverall pocket for the cash he had got in advance for the airspeeder parts. Fadoop tucked the money away swiftly into her belly pouch, then brightened; a twinkle sparkled in her close-set, golden eyes.

4

'And there's a surprise, Solo-my-friend. At the spaceport, when I picked up the parts, two new arrivals were looking for you and the Big One. I had room in my ship, and so brought them with me. They wait.'

Han reached back under the airspeeder and drew out his coiled gunbelt, which he always kept at arm's length. 'Who are they? Imperials? Did they look like skip-tracers or Guild muscle?' He buckled the custom-model blaster around his hips, fastening the tiedown at his right thigh, and snapped open his holster's retaining strap.

Fadoop objected. 'Negatron! Nice, peaceful fellows, a little nervous.' She scratched her verdant, bulging mid-section, making a sandpaper sound. 'They want to hire you. No weapons on them, at least.'

That sounded reassuring. 'What do you think?' Han asked Chewbacca.

The Wookiee resettled his admiral's cap, pulling the gleaming brim down low over his eyes, and stared across the airfield. After a few seconds, he barked a syllable of affirmation, and the three started off for Fadoop's ship.

It was high festival on Saheelindeel, formerly a time of tribal reunions and hunting rituals, then of fertility and harvest ceremonies. Now it incorporated elements of an airshow and industrial fair. Saheelindeel, like so many other planets in the Tion Hegemony, was struggling to thrust itself into an age of modern technology and prosperity in emulation of the galaxy at large. Farming machinery was on display as well as factory robotry. Vehicles new to the wide-eyed Saheelindeeli but obsolete on more advanced worlds were in evidence, along with communications and holo apparatuses that delighted the touring crowd. In an exhibition game of shock-ball, the charged orb sizzled between players wearing insulated mitts; the winning team was using a zoned offence.

Off in the distance, Grigmin was looping and diving in jetpack harness. Just seeing him again put Han in a more receptive frame of mind to meet Fadoop's passengers. Passing by the reviewing stand, he saw the Saheelindeeli's grizzled matriarch holding the elaborate trophy she was to present that afternoon for the best thematic float or exhibit. The fair's theme was *Fertility of the Soil, Challenge of the Sky*. Favoured heavily to win was the opulent float entered by the Regional Fork-Pitchers' Local.

At last Han and his companions arrived at Fadoop's slapdash cargo ship. Despite her reassurances, Han was relieved to see the new arrivals were not Imperial stormtroopers – 'snowmen' or 'white-hats,' as they were called in slangtalk – but an unassuming pair, human and humanoid.

The humanoid – a tall, reedy, purple-skinned type whose eyes, protruding from an elongated skull, held tiny red pinpoints of pupil – nodded at Han. 'Ah, Captain Solo? A pleasure to meet you, sir!' He stuck out a thin arm. Han clasped the long, slender hand, trying to ignore its greasy skin secretions.

'Yes, I'm Solo. What can I do for you?'

The human, an emaciated albino wearing a sun-proof robe, explained. 'We represent the Committee for Inter-institutional Assistance of the University of Rudrig. You've heard of our school?'

'I think so.' He vaguely remembered that it was the only decent advanced school in the Tion Hegemony.

'The university has concluded an Agreement of Air for a fledgling college on Brigia,' the albino continued.

The humanoid took up the conversation. 'I am Hissal, and Brigia is my homeworld. The university has promised us guidance, materials, and teaching aids.'

'So you should be contacting Tion Starfreight or Interstellar Shipping,' Han noted. 'But you came looking for us. Why?'

'The shipment is completely legal,' the gaunt Hissal hastened to add, 'but there is opposition from my planetary government. Though they can't contravene Imperial trade agreements, of course, we still fear there might be trouble in delivery and –'

' – you want someone who can look out for your stuff.'

'Your name *had* come to us as a capable fellow's,' Hissal admitted.

'Chewie and I try to avoid trouble – '

'The job pays rather well,' interposed the albino. 'One thousand credits.'

' – unless there's some profit in it. Two thousand,' Han finished, doubling the price automatically even though the offer had been more than fair. There ensued a few moments of haggling. But when Han pressed the university representatives too sharply and their enthusiasm began to waver, Chewbacca issued a howl that made them all jump. He didn't much like crewing for Grigmin either.

'Uh, my copilot's an idealist,' Han improvised, scowling up at the Wookiee. 'Luckily for you. Fifteen hundred.' The albino and the Brigian agreed, adding that half would be paid on consignment, half on delivery. Chewbacca pushed his gaudy admiral's hat back on his head and beamed at his partner, overjoyed to be lifting off again.

'So,' said Fadoop, slapping her belly merrily with both hands and one foot, 'that only leaves telling that fool Grigmin good riddance.'

'It does, doesn't it?' Han agreed. 'He'll be doing his big stunt display any time now.' He rubbed his jaw and studied the ungainly, stubby-winged vessel that stood nearby. 'Fadoop, can I borrow old *Skybarge* for a few minutes?'

'No questions asked. But she's got cargo onboard, several cubic metres of enriched fertilizer for the agricultural pavilion.' Fadoop relit her cigar.

'No problem,' Han told her. 'Warm up your ship. I'll be right back.'

Having already amazed the unsophisticated Saheelindeeli with his hover-sled, jetpack, and repulsorlift swoops, Grigmin began his grand finale, an exhibition of stunt flying with an obsolete X-222 high-altitude fighter. The triple-deuce looped, climbed, dived, and banked through textbook manoeuvres, releasing clouds of colourful aerosols at certain

7

points to the delight of the crowd.

Grigmin came into his final approach, putting the limber and lean ship through a fancy aerobatic display before coming in towards a precise landing. He didn't realise, however, that a second ship had come in after him on the same approach his fighter had taken. It was Fadoop's cumbersome *Skybarge* with Han Solo at the controls. To show what he thought of Grigmin's flying ability, Han took the tubby ship through the same display the exhibition flier was just completing. But, coming into his first loop, Han feathered his portside engine.

The green-furred Saheelindeeli gasped collectively and pointed the second ship out to one another with a great commotion, forgetting to watch Grigmin's landing entirely. They expected to see *Skybarge* plummet from the air. But Han completed the roll, deftly working with the nearly empty craft's stubby wings, control surfaces, and chugging engine. On the second roll, he feathered the starboard engine, too, and went into a third with zero thrust.

Shrieks of fright from the crowd and their tentative race for cover abated as they saw the unwieldy aircraft was still under control. Jumping up and down, pointing with fingers and toes, they sent up a ragged cheer for the mad pilot, then a more forceful one, reflecting the Saheelindeeli affection for grand gestures, even insane ones.

Grigmin, who had exited from his ship virtually unnoticed, threw down his flight helmet and watched *Skybarge* in mounting fury. Han coaxed the third roll out of the homely vessel and waggled her down towards the strip.

But only one landing wheel emerged from its bay. Grigmin grinned at the prospect of a crash; but unexpectedly the ship bounced off the single wheel, trimmed handily, and settled a second time as another landing wheel lowered. She bore on the reviewing stand with surprising grace and rebounded from two wheels.

As *Skybarge* neared the reviewing stand, the crowd parted before her, clapping their hands and feet in high approbation. The ship waggled her tail in midair, extended her third and last landing wheel, and rolled cleanly for the

8

reviewing stand. By that time Grigmin was so distracted that he didn't notice the cargo ship heading directly for his precious triple-deuce fighter.

Too late! Slam! He could only dodge out of the way as *Skybarge* rolled by. Han threw a wicked grin at him from the cockpit.

Skybarge's high, heavy-duty landing gear permitted her to pass directly over the low, sleek fighter. With consummate skill, Han flipped open her cargo-bay doors and suddenly an avalanche of enriched fertilizer dumped directly into the fighter through the open cockpit canopy.

The Saheelindeeli began applauding madly. *Skybarge's* overhead cockpit hatch popped open, and Han's happy face appeared. He inclined his head graciously to acknowledge the ovation as Grigmin was being elbowed farther and farther away by the press of the crowd.

From the reviewing stand the matriarch's voice wheezed through the crackling public address sytem. 'First prize! Trophy to *Skybarge* for best exhibit, *Fertility of the Soil, Challenge of the Sky.*' She waved the tall loving cup as her advisers whistled and stomped their feet in glee.

II

The *Millennium Falcon* rested on Brigia's single spaceport landing field. She looked very much like the battered, much-repaired, and worn-out stock freighter she was, but there were incongruities. The irregular docking tackle, oversized thruster ports, heavy-weapons turrets, and late-model sensor-suite dish betrayed something about her real line of work.

'That's the last of the tapes,' Han announced. He checked the offloading on his hand-held readout screen as Zollux, the labour droid, stumped past, guiding a repulsorlift hand truck. The automaton's green finish looked eerie in the glow of the irradiators with which the ship was now rigged. Brigia was flagged in all the standard directories, thus requiring phase-one decontam procedures. The ship's environmental systems circulated broad-spectrum anticontamination aerosols along with air. Han's and Chewbacca's immunisation treatments would protect them against local maladies, but they were nonetheless eager to be away.

Han watched Zollux head for the steam-powered freight truck parked near the ship. The glare of the landing field's illumigrids showed him the Brigian workers, all volunteers from the budding college, arranging crates, packing canisters and carry-cases that the *Falcon* had delivered. They conversed animatedly among themselves, thrilled with the new broadcasting equipment and especially with the library of tapes.

Han turned to Hissal, who had accompanied him on the flight and who was to be the college's first president. 'The only thing left to get outboard is your duplicator.'

'Ah, yes, the duplicator, our most-awaited item,' commented Hissal, 'and the most expensive. It will print and collate material at speeds our own presses cannot match and synthesise any paper or other material from the raw constituents it contains. This, from a device that fits into a few crates. Amazing!'

Han made a noncommittal sound. Zollux was returning, and Han called down the curve of the passageway, 'Chewie! Secure the main hold and crack open the number two; I want to get that duplicator off and raise ship.' From aft echoed the Wookiee's answering growl.

'Captain, there's one more thing,' Hissal went on, drawing a pouch from beneath his lateral folds. Han's right hand dropped immediately to his blaster. Hissal, sensing his breach of decorum, held up a thin hand in denial.

'Be of tranquil mind. I know that among your kind it is customary to offer a gratuity for a task well done.' Hissal plucked a curl of bills out of his pouch and extended it to the pilot.

Han examined the bills. They had a strange texture, more like textile than like paper. 'What *is* this stuff?'

'A new innovation,' admitted Hissal. 'Several Progressions ago the New Regime replaced bartering and local coinages with a planet-wide monetary system.'

Han slapped the sheaf of minutely inscribed bills against the palm of his flying glove. 'Which gives them a hammerlock on trade, of course. Well, thanks anyway, but this stuff isn't worth much off-planet.'

Hissal's elongated face grew even longer. 'Unfortunately, only the New Regime may hold off-world currency; thus, all equipment and materials for our school had to come by donation. The first thing the New Regime did when it accumulated enough credits was bring in a developmental consulting firm. Aside from the currency system, the firm's main accomplishment was to profit from a major purchase of military equipment, which included that warship you saw.'

Han *had* noticed the ship, a pocket-cruiser of the outmoded Marauder class surrounded by worklights and armed guards.

'Her main control stacks blew on her shakedown cruise,'

11

Hissal explained. 'Naturally, there are no Brigian techs capable of repairing her, and so she remains inert until the Regime can muster enough credits to import techs and parts. That money could have brought us commercial technology, or medical advancements.'

Han nodded. 'First thing most of these boondock worlds do – no offence, Hissal – is pick up some toys to build their image. Then their neighbours run out and do the same.'

'We are a poor planet,' the Brigian told him solemnly, 'and have more important priorities.'

Han declined further comment on that subject. Zollux had returned and was waiting for Han's next order, when suddenly there was a distant screeching of steam sirens.

Han walked down to the ramp's hinged foot. Closing in from all sides were rows of lumbering metal power wagons, petro-engines chugging, sirens ripping the night, high wheels making the landing field tremble. Arc-spotlights swung to converge on the *Millennium Falcon* and the freight truck.

Han shouldered past Hissal and dashed to the ramp head. 'Chewie! We've got problems; get into the cockpit and charge up the main guns!' He rejoined Hissal halfway down the ramp.

The college volunteers stood surprised and unmoving on the bed of their truck, unsure of what to do. In moments the cordon of power wagons had been drawn tightly. Doors flew open and squads of figures came leaping from the vehicles. They were obviously government troops, carrying old-fashioned solid-projectile firearms. But something about their uniforms seemed odd. The troops wore human-style military regalia ill-suited to the gawkish Brigian anatomy. Han surmised that remnants and leftovers had been foisted off on the unsuspecting New Regime as part of their overall military purchase.

The soldiers marched in badly fitting battle harness, far-too-loose helmets perched precariously on their heads, filigreed epaulettes sagging forlornly from their narrow shoulders, embroidered dispatch cases flopping against their skinny posteriors. Their legs and feet were too narrow

12

for combat boots, so the warriors of Brigia wore natty pink spats with glittering buttons over bare feet. Among what Han assumed to be their officer corps were an abundance of medals and citations, one or two ceremonial swords, and several drooping cummerbunds. A number of troopers with no detectable talent were blowing bugles.

In moments, the soldiers had taken the shocked college volunteers captive at bayonet point. Other units advanced on the starship.

Han had already grasped Hissal's thin arm and was dragging him up the ramp. 'But, this is an atrocity! We have done nothing wrong!'

Han released him and plunged through the main hatch. 'You want to debate that with a bullet? Make up your mind; I'm sealing up.'

Hissal hurried up the ramp. The main hatch rolled down just as the troops reached the ramp's foot; Han heard a salvo of bullets ricocheting off it.

In the cockpit, Chewbacca had already activated defensive shields and had begun warming up the engines. Hissal, trailing Han, was still protesting. Han couldn't take the time to reply; he was completely absorbed in readying the ship for takeoff.

The volunteers were being dragged, pushed, and thrown into confinement in the waiting wagons. The few who protested were summarily struck down and towed off by their slender, strangely boned ankles. Han noticed that the Brigians' war-bannered personnel carriers were, in fact, garbage trucks of an outdated model.

Chewbacca made a grating sound through clenched teeth. 'I'm mad about our money, too,' Han replied. 'How do we get the other half if we can't get a delivery receipt?'

The troops were taking up firing positions in ranks around the starship. 'They couldn't have waited another ten minutes?' Han muttered. A Brigian stepped out in front of the firing lines. Because of the glare of the spotlights, Han had to shield his eyes with his hand to see that the Brigian held a loudhailer in one hand and an official-looking scroll in the other.

13

Han donned his headset and flipped on an external audio pickup in time to hear '– no harm will come to you, good friends from space! The peace-loving New Regime requires only that you surrender the fugitive now onboard your vessel. The Brigian government will trouble you no further.'

Han keyed his headset mike over to external-speaker mode. 'What about our pay?' He avoided looking at Hissal, but kept one hand close to his side arm.

'Agreements can be reached, honoured offworlder,' the Brigian below answered. 'Allow me to come onboard and parley.'

Han keyed his mike again. 'Pull the soldiers back and turn those spotlights off. Meet me at the ramp, no weapons, no stunts!'

The Brigian passed his loudhailer to a subordinate and motioned with the scroll. The ranks fell back and the spotlights flickered out; the martial garbage trucks withdrew. 'Keep an eye on things,' Han instructed his first mate. 'If anyone moves wrong, let me know.'

Hissal was outraged. 'Is it your plan to treat with these hoodlums? Legally speaking, they haven't got a *crowbt* to stand on, I assure you. The courts –'

'– don't concern us now,' Han interrupted, motioning him aside. 'Go find a seat in the forward compartment and don't worry; we won't hand you over to them.'

With great dignity Hissal corrected him. 'My concern is for my friends.'

Zollux, the labour droid, was waiting in the passageway, the crated duplicator components loaded on his handtruck. In his measured drawl the automaton asked, 'What are your instructions, Captain?'

Han sighed. 'I don't know. Why is it I never get the easy jobs? Go up forward, Zollux. If I need you, I'll holler.' The machine's heavy feet clattered on the deckplates. Chewbacca yeowled that the area was clear.

Han pulled his blaster. The main hatch rolled up, and at the ramp's foot waited the Brigian. He was taller than Hissal, broadly built for his species, his colour a little darker than average. He wore a chrome-studded battle harness,

14

rhinestone shoulderboards with dangling brushes at the ends, several colourful aiguillettes, a salad of decorations, and impressive, red-sequinned spats. A plume bobbed from his tilting helmet.

Han beckoned warily. The creature marched up the ramp, the scroll tucked under one arm. Han stopped him at the head of the ramp. 'Shuck the harness and the tin lid and toss them back down.'

The creature complied. 'Welcome to our fair planet, fellow biped,' he said with an effort at heartiness. 'I am Inspector Keek, Chief of the Internal Security Police of the very progress-minded New Regime of Brigia.' He cast his harness and helmet away with a racket of clanking metal.

'I figured you weren't the Boosters' Club,' Han said wryly, making the inspector raise long, skinny arms high. He cautiously poked at the security chief's lateral folds to make sure he had no hidden weapons there. Keek wriggled. This close, Han could read Keek's medals. Either these, too, had been obtained secondhand, he thought, or the inspector was also spelling champ of the planet Oor VII.

'All right, into the forward compartment there. Best behaviour now; I've had all the games I'm going to play today.'

Entering the forward compartment, Keek gazed without comment at Hissal, who was seated in an acceleration chair near the holo-gameboard. The inspector found his own seat by the tech station. Zollux had seated himself on the curved acceleration couch behind the gameboard.

Han rested one hip on the gleaming gameboard. 'Now, what's the hitch? I've got my clearances. The Imperials aren't going to be too happy about you local enforcers trying to hijack an authorised shipment.'

Keek spoke with forced jocularity, 'Ah, you scaredy-*norg* human. Nothing's wrong! The benevolent Inner Council held an emergency session when word of this transaction reached them and placed all teaching materials and off-world literature on the restricted list.' He waved the beribboned scroll. 'I have here the Edict, which I am to present to you.'

'And just who's the flaming Inner Council? Listen, slim, no little slowpoke world alters Imperial trade agreements.' That he himself had often broken Imperial laws – shattered them to fragments would be more accurate – was something he chose not to mention.

'We are merely here, my troops and I,' Keek replied evenly, 'to take temporary custody of the cargo in question, until a Tion representative and an Imperial adjudicator can be summoned. The arrests were strictly an internal matter.'

And the Tion representative and the Imperial adjudicator would undoubtedly come with price tags attached, Han reflected. 'So who pays me?'

Keek attempted to smile; he looked preposterous. 'Our supply of Imperial currency is depleted just now, due to repairs to our spacefleet. But our Treasury's note, or our planetary currency –'

'No play money!' Han exploded. 'I want my cargo back. And besides, one run-down gunboat is no *spacefleet*.'

'Impossible. The cargo is evidence for the trial of certain seditionists, one of whom you've been deceived into sheltering. Come, Captain; cooperate, and you'll be well received here.' Keek winked, with effort. 'Come! We'll pass intoxicating liquids through our bodies and boast of our sporting abilities! Let us be jolly and clumsy, as humans love to be!'

Han, who hated being played for a sucker worse than anything, gritted his teeth. 'I told you already, I don't want any of your homemade cash –'

A sudden thought struck him, and he jumped up. 'You want part of my cargo? Keep it! But I'm going to come across to Hissal with what's left.'

The security chief seemed amused. 'You seek to extort me with educational materials? Come, Captain; we're both worldly chaps.'

Han ignored Keek's attempts at flattery. Carrying a power prybar, he began breaking packing straps from a crate on the hand truck. 'This is a duplicator, just the thing to set up a college press with. But it's a top-of-the-line

16

model, and it's versatile. Hissal, I'll take that tip after all.'

Confused, Hissal handed over the Brigian currency. Han showed them one of the duplicator's components.

'This is the prototyper; you can programme it for what you want or feed it a sample. Like this.' He inserted a Brigian bill and punched several buttons. The prototyper whirred, lights blinked, and the original bill reappeared together with an identical copy. Han held it up to the light, eyeing the duplicate critically. Keek made choking sounds, comprehending now that the pilot was holding his planet's entire monetary system hostage.

'*Hmm.* Not perfect,' Han noted, 'but if you supplied the machine with local materials, it would work. And for different serial numbers on each bill you just programme that into the machine. That consulting firm must've been a cut-rate operation; they didn't even bother to set up a secure currency.' The New Regime had obviously been the victim of aggressive salesmanship. 'Well, Keek, what you do –'

Keek had snapped the end off his scroll's wooden core and pointed it directly at Han, who didn't doubt for a second that he was looking down the barrel of a gun.

'Lay your pistol on that table, alien primate,' hissed Keek. 'You will now have your automaton take the hand truck and he, you, and the traitor Hissal will precede me down the ramp.'

Han gave Zollux the order as he carefully put his blaster on the gameboard, knowing Keek would shoot him if he tried to warn Chewbacca. But as Keek reached to take possession of the blaster, Han inconspicuously touched the gameboard's master control.

Miniature holo-monsters leaped into existence, weird creatures of a dozen worlds, spitting and striking, roaring and hopping. Keek jumped back in surprise, firing his scroll-weapon by reflex. A beam of orange energy crashed into the board, and the monsters evaporated into nothingness.

At the same instant Han, with a star-pilot's reflexes, threw himself onto the security chief, catching hold of the hand holding the scroll-gun. He groped for his blaster with his free hand, but Keek's shot had knocked it from the gameboard.

The security chief possessed incredible strength. Not stopped by the pilot's desperate punches, Keek hurled him halfway across the compartment and brought his weapon around. Just then Hissal landed on his shoulders, making Keek stagger against the edge of the acceleration couch. The two Brigians struggled, their arms and legs intertwining like a confusion of snakes.

But Keek was stronger than the smaller Hissal. Bit by bit he brought his weapon around for a shot. Han got back into the fight with a side-on kick that knocked the scroll aside so that the charge meant for Hissal burned a deep hole in one of the safety cushions.

The scroll-gun was apparently spent, and Keek began to club Hissal with it. Han tried to block him, but Keek knocked the pilot to the deck with stunning force, then turned to grapple with the other Brigian, their feet shuffling and kicking around the downed human. Unable to get around them and recover his blaster, Han tripped Keek. The inspector sank, taking Hissal with him.

Suddenly the scroll, which Keek had dropped, rolled into Han's palm. As Keek was kneeling over the fallen Hissal, Han swung the scroll, connecting solidly with the security chief's skull. Keek's lank body shook with spasms and stiffened. Hissal merely pushed him, and the security chief toppled to the deck.

A roar came from behind them. Chewbacca, seeing his partner unharmed, was visibly relieved. 'Where were *you?*' Han cried. 'He just about put out my running lights!' Rubbing the bruises he had received, Han recovered his pistol.

Hissal, collapsed in an acceleration chair, tried to catch his breath. 'This isn't my usual line of endeavour, Captain. Thank you.'

'We're sort of even,' Han replied with a laugh. Keek began to stir, and Chewbacca the Wookiee snatched him to his feet with one hand. Keek, strong as he was, had better sense than to resist an enraged Wookiee.

Han covered Keek's small bud of a nose with the muzzle of his blaster. The security chief's bulging eyes crossed, watching the weapon. 'That little trick of yours wasn't nice, Keek; I hate sneaks even more than hijackers. I want Hissal's people and my cargo back onboard this ship in five minutes or else you're going to have the wind whistling through your ears.'

When Hissal's freed colleagues and the controversial cargo were back onboard, Han brought Keek to the ramp's head. 'The Empire will hear of this,' the Brigian vowed. 'It's the death sentence for you.'

'I'll try not to lose sleep over it,' Han replied dryly. With the ship's forged papers he had used this trip, he doubted any law agency would be able to trace him. Moreover this would be, by the preoccupied Empire's lights, a very minor incident. 'And do yourself a favour: don't try anything funny when you get clear. There's nothing on this planet with enough fire power to take this ship, but you might make me mad.'

Keek looked at the other Brigians. 'What of them?'

Han sounded casual. 'Oh, I'll drop them off somewhere away from the noise and the crowds. It's legal; a spacer can contract for a surface-to-surface hop if he wants. We're going to take a long orbit, so Hissal can try out his broadcasting rig, hook it into ship's power systems.'

Keek was no fool. 'With that much altitude and power, he'll be reaching every receiver on the planet!'

'And what do you think he'll say?' Han asked innocently. 'Something about what the New Regime's pulling? It's nothing to me, of course, but I told you pulling a gun on me would be a mistake. I'd be thinking about early retirement if I were you.'

Chewbacca gave the security chief a shove to start him on his way. Han closed the hatch. 'By the way,' he called over to Zollux, 'thanks for handing me that scroll during the fight.'

The droid replied with characteristic modesty. 'After all, sir, the inspector had said it was for you. I can only hope there'll be no repercussions, Captain.'

'What for?'

'For destabilising a planetary government to get even for having your ship shot up, sir.'

'Serves them right for cheating!' Han Solo declared.

III

Han stepped into the sunlight of Rudrig's brief afternoon with the balance of his pay safe in his pocket. Around him the spires, domes, towers, and other buildings that housed this part of the university stood in harmony with the lacy flowers, thick-boled trees, and purple lawns.

The university made use, in one fashion or another, of the entire planet. Its vast campuses and housing, recreation, and field training sectors were scattered over the globe. Students from all over the Tion Hegemony were compelled to come here or else leave the Tion entirely if they wanted advanced education of top quality. Centralisation wasn't the best method of offering schooling, Han supposed, but was symptomatic of the languid, inept Hegemony.

He idly studied passers-by for a moment, noting many species flocking between classes, holding conversations, or playing assorted sports and various instruments. Stepping gingerly across a broad boulevard between rolling service automata, quiet mass-transit vehicles, and small ground-effect cargo transporters, he ascended a low access platform and boarded a local passenger beltway. It zipped him along between huge lecture halls and auditoriums, theatres, administrative buildings, a clinic, and a variety of classroom configurations.

Reading the glowing route markers and recalling the coordinates he had memorised from a holo-map, he stepped off the beltway again at that sector's spa, an annex of its sprawling recreation centre. He had just started for the spa when he heard a voice. 'Hey there, Slick!'

Han hadn't gone by the nickname in many years. Still, as he turned he kept his right hand high and near his left lapel. Though the carrying of weapons was prohibited on this quiet world, having one, Han's pragmatic philosophy ran, was a risk he was willing to take. His blaster was suspended slantwise, grip lowermost, under his left armpit and was concealed by his vest.

'Badure!' His right hand moved away from his blaster and closed in a grip on that of the old man who had called him. He used Badure's own nickname, 'Trooper! What are you doing here?'

The other was a big man with a full head of hair going white, a sly squint, and a belly that had come to overlap his belt in recent years. He stood half a head taller than Han, and his grip made the younger man wince.

'Looking for you, son,' Badure responded in the gravelly voice Han recalled so well. 'You're showing up good, Han, real good. It must be a Wookiee's age since I've seen you. Which reminds me, how is Chewie? I was trying to find you two, and they said at the spaceport that the Wook rented a groundcoach and left word for it to be dropped off here.'

Badure – Trooper – was a friend of long standing, but he seemed to have come on hard times. Han tried not to take notice of his faded, patched labourer's tunic and trousers or the scuffed and torn work boots. Still, Badure had held on to his old flight jacket, covered with its unit insignia and theatre patches, and his jaunty, sweat-stained beret with its fighter-wing flash. 'But how'd you know we were here?'

Badure laughed, his belly rolling. 'I keep track of landings and departures, Slick. But in this case I knew you were coming.'

Much as he liked this old man, Han was suspicious. 'Maybe you'd better tell me more, Badure.'

He looked pleased with himself. 'How do you think those university types got your name, son? Not that it doesn't get around as is; I heard about that stunt at the Saheelindeeli airshow – and some rumours from out in the Corporate Sector, and something about water smuggled down the Rampa Rapids. I was here tracking down a few things on my own and heard someone was asking about capable skippers and fast ships. I passed your name along. But before we go into that, shouldn't you be saying hello to my business partner here?'

Han had been so preoccupied that he had ignored the person standing beside Badure. Chiding himself silently for this unusual lapse in caution, he looked her over.

The girl was short and slender, not long into womanhood, with a pale face and disorderly red hair that hung limply. Her brows and lashes were so light that they scarcely showed. She wore a drab, baggy brown outfit of pullover and pants, and her shoes appeared to be a size too large. Her hands had seen hard work. Han had met many men and women just like her, each bearing the stamp of the factory drone or mining-camp worker, lowest-echelon tech or other toiler.

She in turn studied him with no approval whatsoever. 'This is Hasti,' Badure said. 'She already knows your name.' Indicating the flow of beings moving around them to and from the busy spa, he gestured that they continue towards the entrance.

Han acceded, moving slowly, but a sideways slide of the older man's eyes confirmed something. 'What do I watch for?' he inquired simply.

Badure laughed and said, more to himself than to Han or Hasti, 'Same old Han Solo, a one-man sensor suite.'

Han's thoughts were on Badure. The man had been his friend many years before and his partner on various enterprises a number of times since. Once, in an uncomfortable situation stemming from an abortive Kessel spice run, Badure had saved both Han's and Chewbacca's lives. That he should have sought them out here could mean only one thing.

'I won't waste your time, kid,' Badure said. 'There are some that would like to see my hide hung out to dry. I need a ship with punch, and gait to spare, and a skipper I can trust.'

Han realised that Badure wasn't going to be the first to mention the life-debt the two partners owed him. 'You want us to put our necks in the slot for you, is that it? Trooper,

23

saving someone's life doesn't give you the right to risk it again. We're finally ahead of the game; do we owe it all out again this soon?'

Badure countered in neutral tones. 'You're answering for the Wook, too, Han?'

'Chewie'll see it my way.' *If I have to reason with him with a wrench!*

Hasti joined the conversation for the first time. '*Now* are you satisfied, Badure?' she asked bitterly.

The old man hushed her gently. To Han he went on, 'I'm not asking you two to work for nothing. There'd be a cut –'

'The thing is, we're flush. Uh, in fact, we can cut some loose to see you through for a while.'

He felt he had gone too far and thought for a moment that Badure was going to swing at him. The old man had made and spent a number of fortunes and had always been open-handed to his friends; but the offer of charity to himself had the ring of an insult. Favouring Han with a venomous look, Hasti put a hand on Badure's arm. 'We're wasting time; our luggage is still at the district hostelry.'

'Clear skies, Han,' Badure said in a quiet voice, 'and to the Wook as well.'

Han gazed after the two long after they had disappeared on a passenger beltway.

Determined to put the incident out of his mind, he entered the spa. It offered specific creature comforts to a huge variety of human, humanoid, and nonhumanoid species. There were zero-gee massagers, ozone chambers, effluvial rinses, and many other options for humans; mud tanks for visiting Draflago; dermal autostrippers to service a Lisst'n or Pui-Ui; gill-flushes for any of a number of piscine or amphibian life forms; and as many other ablutive and restorative amenities as could be packed into the huge complex.

Inquiring at the central information area, Han discovered that Chewbacca was still enjoying the pleasures of a full-service grooming. Han himself had meant to take a leisurely cycle of soaking, sauna, massage, and pore cleansing, followed by a visit to the tonsorial centre. But his encounter with Badure and Hasti left him feeling in need of a more active and distracting programme.

He undressed in a private booth, storing gun and other valuables in a lockbox and feeding his pleated dress shirt, clothes, and boots to an autovalet. Then he dropped several coins into the slot of an omniron and stepped inside, keying it for maximum treatment.

In fifteen-second cycles icy water sprayed at him, sonics vibrated his skin and flesh, waves of heat lashed and nearly seared him, needle-streams of bio-detergents lathered him, walls of swirling foam broke and surged through the cubicle, air nozzles hosed their blasts, and emollients were rubbed on him by vigorous autoapplicators.

He withstood the brunt of these processes and took on more cycles, finding he couldn't shake the image of Badure. Telling himself he had done the shrewd thing did no more to improve his state of mind than did the elaborate bubble bath he was taking, he concluded. So he terminated the omniron's programme short of its allotted time, recovered his cleaned clothing and shined boots from the autovalet, donned his blaster, and resettled his vest. Then he set off to find his partner.

Chewbacca was in the portion of the spa reserved for its more hirsute clientele. Following the light-strip directory system helpfully placed along the floors, Han found his friend's treatment room. Checking the room's monitoring screen, he saw the Wookiee floating in a zero-gee field, arms and legs splayed. He was near the end of his session; every individual hair had been given a light mutual-repulsion charge to separate it while dirt, particulate matter, and old oils were being removed. Now new oils and conditioners were being gently applied. Chewbacca wore a toothy grin, luxuriating in the treatment as he floated like a tremendous stuffed toy, his billowing pelt making him seem twice his normal girth.

Turning from the screen, Han noticed two very appealing young human females who were also waiting. One, a tall blonde in an expensive jumpsuit, spoke into the ear of her companion, a shorter girl with ringlets of brown hair. The second girl wore a sportier outfit of shorts and singlet; she eyed Han speculatively. 'Are you here to meet Captain Chewbacca, sir?'

Mystified, Han repeated, '*Captain* . . .'

'Chewbacca. We saw him walking across campus and we had to stop him and talk. We're both taking courses in nonhuman sociology, and we couldn't pass up the chance. We've studied the Wookiee language tapes a little, so we understood a bit. Captain Chewbacca told us his copilot would be coming by to meet him. He invited us to go with you on a groundcoach ride.'

Han smiled in spite of himself. 'Fine with me. I'm Captain Chewbacca's first mate, Han Solo.'

He had just established that the brunette's name was Viurre and her blonde girlfriend's Kiili when Chewbacca emerged from the treatment room. The Wookiee, settling his admiral's hat on his head at a rakish angle, wore a beatific grin; his shaggy coat, now glistening and lustrous, floated lightly on stray air currents.

Han sketched a sarcastic salute. '*Captain* Chewbacca, sir, I've got the whole crew standing by for orders.'

The Wookiee *wuff*ed in confusion, then, remembering his assumed role, rumbled a vague reply that none of them understood. The girls promptly forgot Han and closed in on the Wookiee, complimenting him on his appearance. 'I believe you ordered a groundcoach, *Skipper?*' hinted Han.

His partner *awoo*ed confirmation, and they all set off. 'What have you found to be the essential differences in the life-experience on Wookiee worlds?' Viurre asked Han earnestly.

'The tables are higher off the floor,' the pilot replied without expression.

When they arrived at the carport, Han goggled and shouted, 'Tell me this is the wrong slip!' Kiili and Viurre 'oohed' in delight, while Chewbacca beamed fondly at the vehicle he had selected.

It was over eight metres long, wide and low to the ground. The groundcoach's sides, rear deck, and hood were panelled in dazzling scarlet *greel* wood that had been lacquered and polished and lacquered over and over until its metallic gleam seemed to go on forever through the fine grain. The coach's trim, bumpers, door hinges, latches, and handles were of silver alloy. It boasted an outlandish crystal hood ornament – frolicking nymphs in a swirl of gauzy, windblown veil-dresses.

The driver's seat was open to the weather, but just behind it and a luggage well was an enclosed passenger cab, also panelled in *greel* wood, complete with elaborate, hanging road lamps, tasselled bunting, and running boards and handrails on either side for footmen. Astern the cab was another luggage well between a pair of ludicrous metre-high tail fins bejewelled with all manner of signalling and warning lights. From the coach's primary and secondary antenna whips fluttered two pennants, several streamers, and the furry tail of some small, luckless animal.

'Too austere,' Han muttered sarcastically, but he couldn't resist popping the coach's hood. A massive, fiendishly complicated engine squatted there. But Chewbacca quickly silenced Han's denunciations and amazed the two girls by throwing open the cover of the midship luggage well. It contained, due to his thoughtful arrangement, a heroic picnic lunch.

Kiili and Viurre had piled into the driver's compartment, investigating controls, dials, the sound system, and stowage drawers. Chewbacca was running an adoring palm over a quarter-panel when Han blurted out, 'I bumped into Badure today, just as I was coming into the spa.'

Forgetting everything else, Chewbacca barked a question. Han glanced away. 'He wanted to hire us, but I told him we didn't need the work.' Then he felt compelled to add, 'Well, we don't, do we?'

Chewbacca howled furiously. The two girls studiously ignored the argument. '*What* do we owe Badure?' Han hollered back. 'He made a business offer, Chewie.' But he knew better. *Wookiees will honour a Life-Debt over anything else; he'll never walk away from it*, Han thought. Chewbacca growled another angry comment.

'What if I don't want to? Are you going to go after him

without me?' Han asked, knowing what the answer would be.

The Wookiee regarded him for a long moment, then uttered a deep *Uurrr?*

Han opened his mouth, closed it, then finally answered, 'No, you won't have to. Get in the bus.'

Chewbacca yipped, knuckled Han's shoulder, ambled off around the coach's stern, and climbed in. Han slid into the driver's seat and swung his door shut.

'*Captain* Chewbacca and I have to go track down a pal,' he told Kiili and Viurre brusquely. Then to himself he added, *I knew this would happen; I never should have told Chewie. So why did I?*

Kiili, twirling blonde hair around one finger, smiled. 'First Mate Solo, what should we talk to the captain about?'

'Anything. He just likes to listen to people talk.' Han gunned the engine and expertly pulled the powerful coach out of its parking slip. 'Tell him how he's ruining a great afternoon,' Han encouraged her, then smiled. 'Or sing some off-colour ditties, if you know any.'

Kiili eyed the contented Wookiee uncertainly. '*He likes those?*'

Han smiled engagingly. 'No. I do.'

IV

Remembering that Hasti, the young woman with Badure, had mentioned the district hostelry, Han zoomed off in that direction. The scarlet monstrosity of a coach, riding its low ground-effect cushion, handled smoothly and responded well for its size.

One long arm along the back of the driver's seat, Chewbacca tilted his admiral's cap down and listened while Kiili and Viurre described the life of an undergraduate student of nonhuman sociology.

They didn't have to enter the hostelry. Badure and Hasti were waiting at an intercampus shuttleskimmer stop near the building. Han pulled over to the curb with a belch of braking thrust, and he and Chewbacca jumped out, followed by the two girls. The Wookiee hugged the old man, giving out joyous sounds. Hasti regarded Han coolly. 'Attack of conscience?'

Han angled a thumb at the Wookiee. 'My partner's a sentimental fellow. Do you feel like telling us what we're getting into?'

Indicating Viurre and Kiili with a slight nod, Badure cleared his throat meaningfully. Viurre took the hint and, dragging the tall blonde with her, was suddenly inspired to inspect some nearby foliage. In confidential tones Badure asked Han, 'You must've heard of the ship called the *Queen of Ranroon?*'

Chewbacca quivered his nose in surprise, and Han's eyebrows shot up. 'The treasure ship? The story they use to put kids to bed?'

'Not story,' Badure corrected, '*history*. The *Queen of Ranroon* was crammed full with spoils from whole solar systems, tribute to Xim the Despot.'

29

'Listen, Badure, crazies have been hunting that ship for centuries. If she ever existed, she was either destroyed or someone plundered her long ago. You've been watching too many holo-thrillers.'

'When did I ever go chasing vacuum?' the old man countered.

A good point. 'You know where the *Queen* is? You've got proof?'

'I know where her log-recorder is,' Badure announced so confidently that Han found himself believing it. The vision of a treasure arose, a treasure so stupendous that it had become a synonym for phenomenal wealth, more than a man might squander in many lifetimes ...

'Let's get going,' Han proposed. 'We're not getting any younger.' Hasti's derisive look didn't faze him. Then he noticed that Badure's face was drawn with tension.

Following his gaze, Han turned to see a black groundlime slowly cruising towards them. Han drew Badure over to the coach, encouraging Hasti to move as well with an inclination of the head. Chewbacca, who had already thrown Badure's and Hasti's light baggage into the passenger cab, was also on the alert.

Someone in the limo had noticed their reaction. The black groundcar accelerated sharply and veered straight at them.

'Everybody into the coach,' Han yelled as the limo jumped the curb and screeched to a stop, blocking the coach's front cowling. Badure began pushing Hasti into the coach's front seat as Chewbacca, unable to carry his bowcaster on this peaceful world, glanced around for a makeshift weapon.

Figures tumbled from the limo as Han drew his blaster. The blue concentric rings of a stun charge reached out and caught Badure, who had just propelled Hasti out of the way. She fell backwards across the seat; Badure staggered. She managed to grab him and pull him onto the driver's seat just as Han fired an answering shot.

By then a half-dozen beings had emerged from the limo with weapons of one kind or another. Han's hasty return

30

shot caught the stun-gunner, a red-beaked humanoid, in its long, feathered arm. Two male humans armed with needlebeamers ducked as Han's shots shattered two of the limo's windows. The assailants, seeing that they had a fight on their hands, made a general migration towards the ground.

Chewbacca was clambering over the midship luggage well to help Hasti when she, hanging on to Badure with one hand, kicked the engine over and threw the scarlet coach into reverse. Two of the attackers who had been closing in found themselves pouncing on empty air. With a tremendous bump, the coach climbed the curb in reverse. Chewbacca had to cling to a decorative lantern to save himself, and Han jumped aside to keep from being run down, as Hasti hit braking thrusters, kicking up clods of purplish turf and exposing the rich grey soil of Rudrig.

'Well, pile on, Solo,' she shouted at Han. He barely got to a running board, seizing a footman's handrail, before the coach surged forwards.

Hasti didn't quite clear the end of the obstructing limo. The coach bashed it aside, half-rotating the black vehicle and crunching in its own nose cowling with a shower of *greel* wood fragments. Chewbacca cried out at the damage. As they lurched past, Han directed a suppressive barrage at the limo and its passengers, more intent on clinging to his life than on accuracy.

Hasti swerved to avoid a robo-delivery truck, thereby slamming Han up against the cab and nearly wrenching Chewbacca from the lamp, flipping him over with a snap that twisted his neck and sent his prized admiral's hat flying in the breeze. The Wookiee keened, grief-stricken, for the lost headgear.

Over the howl of the coach's engine and the blast of its slipstream, Han yelled, 'They're coming after us!'

The black limo was already slewing around to give chase. Han brought his blaster up. At that moment Hasti, ignoring a traffic-robo, tore into an intersection directly towards a slow-moving maintenance hauler that was towing a disabled freight droid. The girl set all her weight against the steering-grip yoke and hit the coach's warning horn. The first two bars of the Rudrig University Anthem sounded majestically from the coach's fractured hood. The maintenance hauler dodged with a bleep of distress and barely missed taking the driver's side off the coach.

The coach streaked straight down the thoroughfare now. Holding his abused neck stiffly, Chewbacca began inching forward again in order to take over the driving duties. A double column of students and visitors on an orientation tour chose that moment to enter a crosswalk, and Hasti hit braking thrusters.

Chewbacca flew head-first into the driver's compartment and hit the floor, his feet sticking up into the air. But even under those conditions, he had the presence of mind to notice that Badure wasn't completely aboard, and he clutched the stunned man's clothing to tug him into the coach. Hasti noticed her companion's dilemma and gave the coach a snappy cut so that the passenger door swung shut. Though hampered by wires of pain lancing through his neck, the Wookiee began extricating himself.

Just astern, Han had managed to pull himself inside the passenger cab and saw that the limo was closing in rapidly. He smashed the cab's crystalline rear window with a hard blow from his blaster. It cracked in webs, split, and fell away. Clearing away the shards, Han leaned his forearms across the empty sill. The coach's bouncing made the macro-sights useless, so he waited for a clear shot.

Chewbacca had hauled himself up and was yelping loudly at Hasti and gesturing madly. She somehow understood his meaning and hit the couch adjustment controls, which started up the servo-motors. Hasti held tightly to the control stem as the couch moved from under her, leaving her in a tense stoop. The Wookiee slid in behind her, whisked her out of the way, then took over the controls. Hasti turned at once and saw to her relief that Badure was unhurt. He was already stirring, throwing off the stun charge's effects.

The Wookiee proceeded directly through an intersection without benefit of right of way, aware that the limo, still chasing the coach, was zooming along between towering buildings.

Taking a fast curve, Chewbacca came abruptly up to a road-repair site. Far back in the mirror's reflection he could see the limo closing in. He gunned the engine, bursting through illumi-panel markers, smashing warning light-banks aside, and hurling two robo-flagwavers, still diligently waving their flags, several metres into the air. But his hopes for a safe route through the site were dashed when he rounded the turn; the roadbed had been excavated completely, side to side, the shoulders torn up right up to the building faces.

Chewbacca slowed, calmly considered his options, and decided he would have to offer his pursuers a head-on challenge. He hit the accelerator and swung the steering grips over for a smuggler's turn. The long coach leaped forwards into a precise end-for-end spin, destroying several more danger indicators, its lift cushion kicking up dirt and debris. Then it sped off in the direction from which it had come.

Han leaned out a side window. As the limo bore down on them he propped his forearm through a handrail and opened fire, scoring hits on the limo's hood and one in the centre of its windshield. Prepared for a terrible impact, Chewbacca uttered a piercing cry and Hasti began hugging Badure. Han could make out terrified expressions among the limo's occupants.

At the last moment the limo driver wavered, declining the imminent head-on, and the black vehicle swung aside. Ripping through a dense Mullanite lattice-sculpture of thick creepers, slewing across a stretch of purple lawn, and – after bowling aside several long planters and snapping support columns – the limo ended up on a portico outside the local Curriculum Committee headquarters.

Chewbacca brayed his delight, but Han called a warning as the limo started up again. Chewbacca, glancing at the several rearview mirrors and single aft viewscreen, made a hard right turn to high speed by dint of sheer strength applied to unwilling controls.

The coach's left side rose, and the Wookiee took advantage of his momentum to snag another quick right into a side avenue, hoping to break off the chase. Unfortunately, he had swung the long coach onto the up-ramp of a major ground-transport artery. But he had the presence of mind to apply a Han Solo adage: when it won't help to slow down, pour it on! So he slapped toggle switches for full boost and auxiliary guidance thrust.

The immediate problem was a refuse-collection robo-dumpster making its way up the ramp. Its cyber-pilot system was in a quandary over this unusual obstruction. Chewbacca, still exploiting centrifugal force, hit his offside thrusters and took the groundcoach full tilt against the ramp's safety fence.

The fence, part of a traffic-control design scheme based on very forgiving systems, gave and bent outwards as the Wookiee barrelled along with half the coach on the ground, half up on the wilting fence. Han, dragging himself up off the cab floorboards, took one look ahead and hit the deck again. The robo-dumpster edged towards the opposite side of the upramp and the two weighty vehicles passed each other.

The coach had lost its outermost rearview mirror post and part of the picnic lunch, and debris from the jostled dumpster was splattered across its metre-high red tail fins. Chewbacca was baying in utter exhilaration, an ages-old Wookiee war cry.

Hasti had just finished fastening a seatbelt across herself and Badure when the coach roared onto the main artery. Seeing that he was heading the wrong way on a high-speed road, the Wookiee hugged the outside wall while he assessed the situation. He kept one finger on the horn button, sounding the first two bars of the anthem over and over. All factors considered, Chewbacca felt, things were going fairly well.

Han, back in the passenger cab, held a somewhat different opinion. The black limo had taken advantage of Chewbacca's descent and was still on their tail. The intercom wasn't working, so Han pushed up the cab's forward window and shouted, 'They're still on us!'

The Wookiee growled an irritated reply, then spotted his opening. He turned the steering grips with such emphasis that the yoke groaned on its stem, threatening to snap. But the coach managed to fishtail across three lanes of oncoming traffic, and Chewbacca hung in the centre lane while awaiting shifts in the configuration of the traffic.

Automatic safety systems had taken notice of the potential massacre, and suddenly sequential warning lights began to flash, cautioning other drivers where the danger lay. Overhead illumi-markers and danger panels began flashing along the way, and those vehicles operating under autocontrol were brought to a halt at the shoulder by Traffic Central Override.

Meanwhile, Han, clinging to the rear window frame, saw the limo coming on. Its driver was having an easier time, following the trail the Wookiee had blazed. Han braced his right shoulder against one side of the frame and his left hand against the other to draw a steady aim. Just as he fired, Chewbacca, having lined up another gap in the oncoming traffic, hauled at the steering grips and cut hard for the centre divider. Han's shot went wild, blowing a small hole in the tough fusionformed road.

Chewbacca came at the divider as directly as he could, aware that it was built to resist collision. He hit it with the coach's accelerator open, keeping his enormous foot down hard on emergency-boost auxiliaries. The engine wailed. Hasti clung to Badure.

The coach burst through a double retaining rail, taking two lengths of railing with it. Chewbacca then swooped up the sloped centre abutment; two lanterns fell from the coach, and its curb feelers, he noticed, had been sheared off. Han tangled both fists into embroidered safety belting and set his feet against the cab's front wall.

The coach shot through the fence at the top of the abutment, the durable links stretching, then bursting with a titanic jolt that sent the remainder of the picnic lunch arcing into the air. Crashing down the abutment and through a second section of railing, they bounced into the traffic lanes now headed in the appropriate direction, if at illegal velocity.

Manoeuvring smartly, the Wookiee avoided any other collisions. The coach sped along, intermittently shedding trim and pieces of smashed *greel* wood. Glancing out a side window, Han found himself the object of the surprised scrutiny of a gowned senior professor, a stalk-eyed creature in a robo-hack. Chewbacca accelerated and left the hack behind.

Less than a minute later, the black limo appeared at the crest of the abutment and descended through the swath of destruction left by Chewbacca. It, too, slid into the traffic lanes. A man, holding a long needlebeam rifle in his hands, stood up and poked his head and arms through the sunroof.

Han left the cab, swung from the handrail with one foot on the running board, and dived into the driver's compartment. 'We've gone and made them mad,' he hollered. 'Escape and evade, old buddy!'

But even as Han exhorted his partner, Chewbacca was throwing the coach through zigs and zags, ignoring lane divider illumi-strips, applying full power though a disconcerting black smoke had begun to roil from the vehicle's engine. At last, the rifleman, his eye at his weapon's scope, fired.

A needlebeam sizzled at one of the scarlet tail fins, setting the lacquered wood afire and shearing off its tip as taillight circuitry blew. Han stood up, one hand firmly on the windshield and blaster gripped in the other. He replied with a hurried shot of his own; the bolt splashed harmlessly onto the pavement.

A second rifle beam hissed through the cab. 'Get us out of here before they cut us in half!' Han yelled to his first mate.

Smoke from the hood now rolled more thickly. The Wookiee spun the steering-grip yoke, veering and putting an enormous robo-freighthauler between the coach and the limo. Another needlebeam, missing them, burned across the freighthauler's rear end. The last view Han had of the limo was of its driver trying to manoeuvre for another clear shot.

He shouted to Chewbacca, 'Pump your braking thrusters!' The Wookiee did so without question, accustomed to his friend's mad inspirations. When the freighthauler outstripped the coach, they found themselves even with the limo.

The surprised rifleman started to bring his weapon up, but Han fired first. The marksman, clutching his smouldering forearm, dropped back through the sunroof. Han's second shot blew out a piece of the limo's door. Two or three beings were trying to elbow their way up through the sunroof to set up a rocket launcher. If they couldn't stop the coach, they'd settle for blowing it all over the landscape.

Han felt the coach surge and looked around. Directly in front of them was the freighthauler, its long rear gate bouncing on the road. Its bed was half empty, a pile of construction rubble heaped against the front wall. An overpass loomed in the distance; Han quickly grasped his first mate's plan, holstered his weapon, and clung to Badure and Hasti for his life.

The coach jumped up the hanging rear gate, engine pouring black smoke, auxiliary thrusters overloading. Chewbacca pumped braking thrusters once to time his manoeuvre, then hit full power and the front-lift thrusters designed to help the coach negotiate low obstacles. The coach shot up the pile of rubble at the front of the cargo bed and soared into the air, the Wookiee plying his controls frantically.

Then the overpass was beneath them, and through some miracle it was unoccupied just then. The coach hit with an impact that collapsed its shock-absorption system, burned out its power routing, broke all the remaining lanterns, and shattered the cab windows. It slid, then ground to a halt against the overpass sidewall, crumpling its hood and popping its doors.

Coughing, Han and his first mate pulled Hasti and Badure from the wreckage. The black limo was already far down the road, forced along by the flow of traffic. Chewbacca, surveying the demolished groundcoach sorrowfully, sniffled and moaned to himself.

Wiping her eyes and choking, Hasti wanted to know: 'Who ever told you two morons you could drive?' Then, noticing Chewbacca's gloomy look, asked, 'What's wrong with him?'

'He figures he'll have a hard time getting his deposit back,' Han explained.

Police groundcruisers and aircraft, converging under Traffic Control's direction, were already beginning to gather farther down the highway. Since Chewbacca had elected to leave the road in a unique manner, it would probably take the local authorities some time to piece together what had happened.

V

'Quiet down and sit still.' Han took a firmer grip on his first mate's head.

The Wookiee, seated in a rump-sprung, sweat-stained acceleration chair in the *Millennium Falcon*'s forward compartment, stopped squirming but couldn't stifle his whimpers. He knew his neck injury had to be tended right away. Han, standing behind him, shuffling for a better stance, held his friend's chin clamped in one elbow. He pushed the palm of his hand against the Wookiee's skull.

'How many times have I done this now? Stop complaining!' Han began to apply pressure again, twisting Chewbacca's head up and to the left. The Wookiee dutifully fought the urge to rise, crimping his long fingers on the arms of the acceleration chair.

Meeting resistance, Han drew a deep breath and, without warning, yanked the thick-maned skull with all his might. There was a cracking and popping; Chewbacca yipped and snuffled pitifully. But when Han ruffled his friend's fur compassionately and stepped back, the Wookiee rubbed his neck and moved his head without pain. He immediately went off to prepare the starship for liftoff.

'If you're through ministering to the afflicted, Doctor,' Hasti said from her seat by the gameboard, 'it's time we got a few things settled.'

Leaning against the tech station, Han agreed. 'Let's put them on the table and see what we've got.'

Badure, fully recovered from the stun charge, was sitting next to Hasti. To avoid conflict, he took over. 'I met Hasti and her sister, Lanni, at a mining camp on a planet named Dellalt, here in the Tion Hegemony. It was a small plunder operation; I was contract labour there.'

He ignored Han's surprise. *Things have been worse than I*

39

thought for him, the pilot realised.

'And things weren't too much better for them,' Badure went on. 'You know how those camps can be, and this one was about the worst I've seen. We three sort of watched out for one another.

'Lanni had a Pilot's Guide book and flew a lot of work runs, surface-to-surface stuff. Somewhere she had picked up a log-recorder, one of the ancient disk types. No ship has used one in centuries. She couldn't read the characters, of course, but there was a figure most beings in this part of space know, the *Queen of Ranroon*.'

'How'd a log-recorder get to Dellalt?'

'That's where the vaults are,' Badure said, and that brought some history back to Han. Xim the Despot had left behind legends of whole planets despoiled, of mass spacings of prisoners and other atrocities. And Xim the Despot had ordered that stupendous treasure vaults be built for the tribute to be sent him by his conquering armies. The treasure never arrived, and the vacant vaults, all that remained from Xim's reign, were a minor curiosity generally ignored by the big, busy galaxy.

'Are you telling me the *Queen* made it to Dellalt after all?'

Badure shook his head. 'But somebody made it there with the log-recorder disk.'

'The disk is in a lockbox in the public storage facility that set up operations in the old vaults,' Hasti told him. 'My sister was afraid it would be taken from her, for the mining company runs surprise inspections, barracks searches, and sensor frisks. So she diverted course on a freight run and made the deposit.'

'How'd she get it in the first place? And where is she now?' Han saw the sobering answer on both their faces and wasn't surprised. The opposition, he had already learned, was in deadly earnest. He abandoned the subject.

'So, off to Dellalt before that rental agent comes looking for his groundcoach.'

But Badure, slapping his ample belly, announced, 'We have one more crewman coming. He's on his way now. I cancelled our public-carrier reservations so the line will refer him directly here.'

'Who? What do we need him for?' Han was reluctant to involve too many in this treasure hunt.

'His name is Skynx; he's a ranking expert on pre-Republic times in this part of space. And he reads ancient languages; he's already deciphered some characters Lanni had copied from the log-recorder disk. Good enough for you?'

Conditionally. Somebody, Han saw, would have to decipher the disk to find out what had happened to the *Queen*. Removing his vest, Han began disencumbering himself of the shoulder holster. 'Next question: who's the opposition?'

'The mine operators. You know how the Tion works. Somebody pays someone in the Ministry of Industry and gets a permit. The mining outfit carves up the terrain any which way, grabs what it can, and gets out long before any inspectors or legal paperwork catch up with them. They usually get their financing from some crime boss.

'This outfit's run by twins. The woman's name is J'uoch and her brother's R'all. They have a partner, Egome Fass, their enforcer. He's a big, mean humanoid, a *Houk*, even taller than Chewie there. All three came up the hard way, and that's how they play.'

Han had buckled on his gunbelt and holster and transferred his blaster. 'So I saw. And all you want is for us to get you to Dellalt and get you off?'

Just then the intercom carried the Wookiee's news that someone was signalling for permission to board. 'That'll be Skynx,' Badure told him. Han passed word to admit the academician.

'If you'll get us to the vaults and off Dellalt again,' Badure resumed, 'I'll pay you twice your usual first-asking price, out of the treasure. But if you throw in with us, you and the Wook can split a full share of the take.'

Hasti cried, 'Half-share!' just as Han protested, 'Full share each!' They glared at each other. 'Wound up a little

41

too tight are we, sweetheart?' Han asked. 'How're you going
to get there without us, flap your arms?' He heard
Chewbacca's footsteps moving towards the main hatch.

Hasti's temper flared. 'For one hop, you and that furbal
want a full cut?'

Badure held up his hands and bellowed, '*Enough*!' They
quieted. 'That's nicer, kiddies. We are discussing major
cash here, plenty for everybody. The breakdown's this way:
a full share for me because I got Hasti off Dellalt alive and
Lanni passed what she knew along to both of us, equally.
Two shares for Hasti, her own and poor Lanni's. And for
you, Skynx, and the Wook, half-shares each at this point.
Depending on who has to do what in the course of finding
that treasure, we renegotiate. Agreed?'

Han studied Badure and the seething red-haired girl.
'How much are we talking about?' he wanted to know.

The old man inclined his head. 'Why not ask him?'

Badure indicated the individual who had come onboard
and was following Chewbacca into the forward compartment. *Now why did I assume he'd be human?* Han wondered.

Skynx was a Ruurian, of average size – a little over a
metre long – low to the ground, his natural coat a thick,
woolly amber with bands of brown and red. He moved on
eight pairs of short limbs with a graceful, rippling motion.
Feathery, bobbing antennae curled back from his head.
Skynx had big, multifaceted red eyes, a tiny mouth, and
small nostrils. Behind him rolled a baggage-robo with
several crates and boxes on its flatbed.

Skynx paused and reared up on his last four pairs of
extremities. The digits on his limbs, four apiece, were
mutually opposable, deft, and very versatile. He waved to
the humans. 'Ah, Badure,' he called in a rapid, high-
pitched voice, 'and the lovely Hasti; how are you, young
lady? This fine Wookiee I've already met. So you would be
our captain, sir?'

'Would be? I *am*. Han Solo.'

'Delighted! I am Skynx of Ruuria, Human History sub-
department, pre-Republic subdivision, whose chair I
currently hold.'

'What do you use it for?' Han asked, eyeing Skynx's strange anatomy. Seeing no reason to delay where cash was concerned, he inquired, 'How much money are we after?'

Skynx poised his head in thought. 'There's so much conflicting information about the *Queen of Ranroon*, it's best to say this: Xim the Despot's treasure vessel was the largest ship ever built in her day. Your guess, sir, is no less plausible than my own.'

Han leaned back and thought about pleasure palaces, gambling planets, star yachts, and all the women of the galaxy who hadn't been fortunate enough to make his acquaintance. Yet. Chewbacca snorted and returned to the cockpit.

'Count us in,' Han announced. 'Tell the baggage clunker to leave your stuff right there, Skynx. Badure, Hasti, make yourselves at home.'

Hasti and Skynx both wanted to watch the liftoff from the cockpit. When they were alone, Badure spoke more confidentially. 'There's one thing I didn't want the others to hear, Han. I had my ear to the ground, heard about some of the crazy jobs you've pulled. Word's out that somebody's looking for you. Money's being spread around, but I haven't heard any names. Any idea who it might be?'

'Half the galaxy, it feels like sometimes.' There had been many runs, many deals, jobs, and foul-ups. 'How should *I* know?' But his expression hardened, and Badure thought Han had a very good idea who might be seeking him.

Han stood in the middle of the forward compartment, listening. The tech station and most of the other equipment in the compartment had been shut down to lower the noise level. He could feel the vibrations of the *Millennium Falcon*'s engines. He heard a quiet sound behind him.

Han spun, crouching, in execution of the speedraw, firing from the hip. The target-remote, a small globe that moved on squirts of repulsor power and puffs of forced air, didn't quite dodge his beam. Its counterfire passed over him. Deactivated by his harmless tracer beam, the orb hung immobile, awaiting another practice sequence.

Han looked over to where Zollux, the labour droid, sat; his chest panels were open. Blue Max, the computer module installed in the droid's chest cavity, had been controlling the remote. 'I told you I wanted a tougher workout than that thing's idiot circuitry could give me,' Han reprimanded Blue Max.

Zollux, a gleaming, green, barrel-chested automaton, had arms long enough to suggest a simian. The computer, an outrageously expensive package built for maximum capacity, was painted a deep blue, whence came his name. Part of Han's post-Corporate Sector splurge had included the modification the two mechanicals had requested, because without them he and the Wookiee might never have survived. Zollux now contained a newer and more powerful receiver, and Max had been provided with a compact holo-projector.

'That *was*,' the little module objected. 'Can I help it if you're so flaming fast? I could cut response time to nil, if you want.'

Han sighed. 'No. And watch your language, Max; just because I talk like that doesn't mean you can.' He took the combat charge his weapon usually carried from its case at his belt.

Badure was reclining in one of the acceleration chairs. 'You've been practising all through this run. You're beating the ballie every time. Who's got you worried?'

Han shrugged, then added as if by afterthought, 'Did you ever hear of a gunman called Gallandro?'

Both of Badure's thick eyebrows rose. '*The* Gallandro? You don't bother yourself with small-timers, do you, Slick? So that's it.'

Han looked around. Hasti, at her own and Badure's insistence, had commandeered Han's personal quarters – a cramped cubicle – for some secret purpose. Chewbacca was at the controls, but Skynx was present. Han decided it didn't matter if the Ruurian heard.

'I backed Gallandro down a while back, didn't even realise who he was. See, he had to let me do it at the time because it was part of a bigger deal he was working. Later

44

on, though, he wanted to settle up.'

Sweat gathered on his forehead with the memory. 'He really *moves*; I couldn't even follow his practice draw. Anyway, I pulled a stunt on him and got out of the mess. I guess I made him look pretty bad, but I never thought he'd go to all this trouble.'

'Gallandro? Slick, you're talking about the guy who single-handedly hijacked the *Quamar Messenger* on her maiden run and took over that pirate's nest, Geedon V, all by himself. And he went to the gun against the Malorm family, drawing head bounty on all five of them. And no one has ever beaten the score he rolled up when he was flying a fighter with Marso's Demons. Besides which, he's the only man who ever forced the Assassins' Guild to default on a contract; he personally cancelled half of their Elite Circle – one at a time – plus assorted journeymen and apprentices.'

'I know, I know,' Han said wearily, sitting down, '*now*. If I'd known who he was then, I'd have put a few parsecs between us, at least. But what does a character like that want with me?'

Badure spoke as to a slow-witted child. 'Han, don't make someone like Gallandro back down, then walk away making a fool of him. His kind live on their reputations. You know that as well as I do. They accept no insult and never, never back down. He'll make you his career until he settles with you.'

Han sighed. 'It's a big galaxy; he can't spend the rest of his life looking for me.' He wished he could believe that.

There was a sound behind him, and he threw himself sideways out of his chair, firing in midair, rolling to avoid the remote's sting-shot. His tracer beam hit the dodging globe dead centre. 'Good try, Max,' he commented.

'You strike me as being very adept, Captain,' Skynx said from the padded nook over the acceleration couch.

Han climbed to his feet. 'You know all about master blastermen, don't you?' He appraised the academician. 'Why'd you come on this run anyway? We could've brought the disk to you.'

The little Ruurian seemed embarrassed. 'Er, that is, as

45

you probably know, my species' life cycle is –'

'Never saw a Ruurian until I met you,' Han interjected. 'Skynx, there're more life forms in this galaxy than anyone's bothered to count, you know that. Just listing the sentient ones is a life's work.'

'Of course. To explain: we Ruurians go through three separate forms after leaving the egg. There is the larva, that which you see before you; the cycle of the chrysalis, in which we undergo changes while in pupa form; and the endlife stage, in which we become chroma-wing fliers and ensure the survival of our species. The pupae are rather helpless, you'll understand, and the chroma-wings are, um, pre-occupied, caring only for flight, mating, and egg-laying.'

'There better be no cocoons or eggs on this ship,' Han warned darkly.

'He promises,' Badure said impatiently. 'Now will you listen?'

Skynx resumed. 'All that leaves for us larval-stage Ruurians is to protect the pupae and ensure that the simple-minded chroma-wings don't get into trouble – and to run our planet. We are very busy, right from birth.'

'What's that got to do with a nice larva like you raising ship for lost treasure?' Han asked.

'I studied the histories of your own scattered species, and I came to be fascinated with this concept, *adventure*,' Skynx confessed as if unburdening himself of some dark perversity. 'Of all the races who gamble their well-being on uncertain returns – and there aren't that many, statistically – the trait's most noticeable in humans, one of the most successful life forms.'

Skynx tried to frame his next words carefully. 'The stories, the legends, the songs, and holo-thrillers held such appeal. Once, before I spin my chrysalis, to sleep deeply and emerge a chroma-wing who will no longer be Skynx, I wish to cast aside good sense and try a human-style adventure.' Saying the last, he sounded happy.

There was a silence. 'Play him the song you played for me, Skynx,' Badure finally invited. In the upholstered nook he had occupied for most of the trip, Skynx had set up his species' version of a storage apparatus, a treelike framework used in lieu of boxes or bags. From its various branches hung Skynx's personal possessions and items he wished to have close to him. Each artifact was an enigma, but among them was apparently at least one musical instrument.

Han had heard enough nonhuman music to want to forgo listening. Though he might be passing up decent entertainment, he might also be avoiding sounds resembling somebody's unoiled groundcoach. He changed the subject hurriedly.

'Why don't you show us what's in the crates instead?' Han looked around. 'Where's Hasti? She should be in on this.'

'We'll be making planetfall soon, and she has preparations to make,' Badure said. 'Skynx, show him those remains; they should interest him.'

Skynx rose, shook out his amber coat to fluff it, and flowed smoothly out of his nook. Hoping that 'remains' didn't refer to the sort of unappetising objects he had seen in museums, Han stepped up to the crates with a power prybar. At Skynx's direction, he opened a container and whistled softly in astonishment. 'Badure, give me a hand getting this thing out of the crate, will you?' Between them they strained and lifted out the object, setting it on the gameboard.

It was an automaton's head. More correctly, it was the cranial turret of some robot out of ancient history. Its optical lenses were darkened by long radiation exposure. It was armoured like a dreadnought with a coarse, heavy grey alloy Han didn't recognise. The assorted insignia and tech markings engraved into its surface were still visible but readable. Han expected the speaker grille to spew a challenge.

'It's a war-robot. Xim the Despot built a brigade of them to serve as his absolutely faithful royal guard,' Skynx explained. 'They were, at that time, the most formidable human-form fighting machines in the galaxy. This one's remains were recovered from the floating ruins of Xim's orbital fortress, possibly the only one that wasn't vaporised in the Third Battle of Vontor, Xim's final defeat. There are more pieces in these other crates. There were at least a thousand just like this one travelling onboard the *Queen of Ranroon* and guarding Xim's treasure when the ship vanished.'

Han opened another crate. It contained a huge chestplate; Han knew he would never be able to uncrate the thing without Chewbacca's help. In the plate's centre was Xim's insignia, a death's head with sunbursts in the eye sockets.

Zollux entered, chest panels open wide to let Blue Max perceive things as well. These two machines had been combined by a group of outlaw techs and had been instrumental in Han's survival at an Authority prison called Stars' End several adventures ago. Zollux and Max had elected to join Han and Chewbacca, exchanging labour for passage, in order to see the galaxy.

'Captain, First Mate Chewbacca says we'll be reverting to normal space shortly,' the droid announced. Then his red photoreceptors fell on the cranial turret, and Han could have sworn they abruptly became brighter. In a voice more hurried than his usual drawl, Zollux queried, 'Sir, what *is* that?' He went over to examine the thing more closely. Max studied the relic as well.

'So very old,' mused the droid. 'What machine is this?'

'War-robot,' Han told him, sifting through the other crates. 'Great-grandpa Zollux, maybe.' He didn't notice the droid's metallic fingers quizzically feeling the shape of the massive head.

Han was mumbling to himself. 'Reinforced stress points; heavy-gauge armour, all points. Look how thick it is! You could run a machine shop off those power-delivery systems. Hmm, and built-in weapons, chemical and energy both.'

He stopped rummaging and looked at Skynx. 'These things must've been unstoppable. Even with a blaster, I wouldn't want to mix with one.' He slid the lid back on the crate. 'Find yourselves a place and get comfortable, everybody. We'll revert from hyperspace as soon as I get to the cockpit. Where's Hasti? I can't hold up the whole –'

His jaw dropped. Hasti – it had to be her – had just swept

into the forward compartment. But the factory-world, mining-camp girl was gone. The red hair now fell in soft, fine waves. She wore a costume of rich iridescent fabrics in black and crimson; the hem of her ruffled, wrapfront gown brushed the deckplates, and over it she wore a long quilted coat with voluminous sleeves, its formal cowl flung back and its gilt waist sash left open. Her steps revealed supple, ornamentally stitched buskins.

She had applied makeup, too, but with such restraint that Han couldn't tell what or how. She was cooler, more poised, and seemed older than Han recalled. Her expression dared him to make a crack. One side of him was trying to tally how long it had been since he had seen anyone this attractive.

'Girl,' breathed Badure, 'for a second there I thought you were a ghost. It might've been Lanni, standing there.'

An hour ago I'd have said she couldn't find romance in a prison camp with a jetpack on! I'm slipping, Han thought. Then he found his voice. 'But why?'

While Hasti inspected Han distantly, Badure explained. 'When Lanni diverted course on a freight run to store the log-recorder disc at the vaults, she changed into this local outfit Hasti's wearing so word wouldn't leak that a woman from the mining camp had been there. Fortunately she gave us the rental code and retrieval combination before she was killed by J'uoch's people. Hasti must look as much like poor Lanni as possible, in case any of the vault personnel happen to remember her sister.'

Hasti motioned back towards Han's quarters. 'Nice wallow you have there; it looks like the end of a six-day sweepstakes party.'

His reply was cut short by an angry caterwauling from the cockpit. It was Chewbacca insisting that Han come up for the reversion to normal space. 'I wonder if I wouldn't be asking too much to view the procedure from the cockpit?' Skynx said to Han.

'Sure; we'll find some place for you.' Han met Hasti's aloof gaze. 'How about you? Care to watch?'

She pursed her mouth indifferently. Skynx left off observing what was, as far as he could conclude, a variation

49

on human preenings/courting rituals and excitedly hurried towards the cockpit, followed by Badure. Han, weighing Hasti's expression, decided neither to offer his arm nor to touch her in any ushering-along gesture.

None of them noticed Zollux, who remained behind, contemplating the war-robot's head, his cold fingers resting on the imposing armoured brow.

VI

Dellalt had, in its heyday, been a prominent member of a strategic cluster during the pre-Republic phase known locally as the Expansionist Period. That importance had run its course. Altering trade routes, increased ships' cruising ranges, intense commercial competition, social dislocation, and the realigning power centres of the emergent Republic – all had long since converted the planet to a seldom taken side trip, isolated even from the rest of the Tion Hegemony.

Dellalt's surface boasted far more water than soil. The treasure vaults of Xim were located near a lake on the southernmost of the planet's three continents, a hook-shaped piece of land that crossed Dellalt's equator and extended almost to its southern pole. Around the vaults stood Dellalt's single large population concentration, a small city built by Xim's engineers. The travellers studied it during their approach.

Heavy weapons emplacements and defensive structures around the city were now gutted ruins filled with crumbling machinery. Broken monorail pylons and once grand buildings, falling back to dust, were over-grown with thick dendroid vines. Recent construction was sparse, poorly planned, and done with crude materials. There was the wreckage of a sewage- and water-treatment plant, indicating just how far back Dellalt had slipped. Badure mentioned that the planet harboured a race of saurop-teroids, large aquatic reptiles that lived in a rigidly codified truce with the human inhabitants.

Port officialdom was nonexistent; a bureaucracy would have been an unprofitable expense, something the Tion Hegemony avoided. Han and Badure, intending to attract attention, made a show of stretching and pacing as they came down the ramp to a landing area that was no more than a flat hilltop showing the scorches of former landings and liftoffs. Their breath crystallised in the cold air. Han had donned his own flight jacket. Glossy, cracked, and worn with age, it showed darker, unweathered spots where patches and insignia had been removed. He pulled his collar up against the wind.

Below them the decaying city spread out along slopes leading down to the long, narrow lake, part of Dellalt's intricate aquatic system. Han estimated from the condition of the landing area that it saw no more than three or four landings per Dellaltian year – probably just Tion patrol ships and the occasional marginal tramp trader. The planet's year was half again as long as a Standard one, with a shorter-than-Standard mean day. Gravity was slightly more than Standard, but since Han had adjusted the *Millennium Falcon*'s gravity during the flight, they scarcely noticed it now.

People came running up from the little city, laughing and making sounds of greeting. The women's attire was like Hasti's, with variations of colour, layering, and cut. Male dress tended towards loose pantaloons, padded jackets, all manner of hats and turbans, and pleated, flowing cloaks and robes. Children copied their parents' appearance in miniature. All around these humans were packs of yipping, loping domestic animals, grainy-skinned quadrupeds with needlelike teeth and prehensile tails.

Han asked who owned the single building on the field, a decaying edifice of lockslab that might be used as warehouse or docking hangar. The owner appeared quickly, making his way through the mob with curses and insults that no one seemed to take personally. He was small but heavily built, and his scraggly whiskers failed to hide pockmarked cheeks and throat that had been ravaged by some local disease. His teeth were yellow-brown stumps. Crude or nonexistent medical care was too common on fringe worlds for Han to feel disgust anymore.

He inquired about the building. The language of Dellalt

was Standard, distorted with a thick accent. The man insisted that rental terms were so minor a problem that there was no reason to waste Han's time, that the outloading of cargo could begin at once. The pilot knew that to be a lie, but confrontation was a part of Badure's plan.

Zollux appeared and began making trips between the starship and the building. At first the perplexed droid found himself surrounded by screaming, laughing children and snarling, snapping domestic quadrupeds. But the cousins of the building's landlord threatened, cursed, and slapped them away, then formed an escort to see to it that the labour droid could work in relative peace. Still, many eyes followed the gleaming Zollux; such automata were unknown here. The landlord's cousins opened one of the building's doors just wide enough for the droid to enter and leave. He began stacking crates, canisters, pressure kegs, and boxes inside.

The crowd milled around and under the *Millennium Falcon*, timidly touching her landing gear and gawking up at her in amazement, yammering among themselves. Then someone noticed the Wookiee, who sat looking down from the cockpit. Shouts and shrieks went up; hands were thrust at the Wookiee in gestures meant to repel evil. Chewbacca gazed down on all the activity impassively, and Han wondered if it had occurred to any in the crowd that his first mate was manning the freighter's weaponry.

A considerable pile of cargo containers had already accumulated in the building when, with his cousins stationed around its main doors, the landlord abandoned his effusive welcomes and named an enormous rental fee. Badure shook his scarred fist under the landlord's nose, and Han shouted a threat. The landlord threw up his hands and besought his ancestors for justice, then insulted the offworlders' appearance and the circumstances of their birth. His cousins let the droid continue stacking cargo in his building, though.

Each time Zollux left the outbuilding, one of the cousins swung the door shut with a creak of primitive hinges. Waiting until she had heard that sound for the third time to

53

be certain of the routine – and having timed the droid's purposely slow trips – Hasti pushed the lid off her shipping canister and stepped out, lifting her hem carefully and rubbing her cramped neck.

Anyone seen leaving the starship would have been trailed all over town by the crowds. That in turn would have made recovery of the log-recorder impossible. Badure's plan had circumvented all that.

The building had a small rear door. Everything was as Badure had predicted – on a backward world like Dellalt, the landlord could ill afford expensive locking systems on each door. Therefore, this rear door and the larger hanging door were secured from the inside, with only a smaller door set in the larger one equipped with a lockplate. Not that that mattered. Han Solo had given Hasti a vibrocutter in case she had needed to force her way out. But she needed merely to move the bolt and then emerged into the light behind the building, shouldering the door closed again.

Peering around the corner, she could isolate at least three different centres of furor. In one, Han Solo and Badure were squared off with the landlord, insulting one another's antecedents and personal hygiene in best Dellaltian haggling style; in another, people were pointing at and debating hotly over Chewbacca's origin; and finally, the landlord's cousins were battling the crowd so Zollux could keep filling the building with the containers they would later confiscate if the offworlders didn't meet the exorbitant rental fee. All the Dellaltians seemed quite happy with their unscheduled holiday.

At that juncture another distraction, also planned by Badure, occurred. Skynx ambled down the ramp, ostensibly to confer with Han and the old man. An astonished shout went up from the crowd, and most of the people tagging along after Zollux went at a run to see this new wonder.

Making sure her compact pistol was safe in an inner pocket, Hasti set off, keeping the building between herself and the field. She had draped the cowl over her head and went unnoticed. She had been in the city before, sent from the mining camp with Lanni to make minor purchases. Recalling the layout of the place, she set out for Xim's treasure vaults.

Pavement laid when the vaults were new had been chewed and disintegrated by use and time. The streets were rutted and hard-packed in the middle and muddy along the sides where slops had been dumped from overhanging windows. Hasti prudently kept along the middle way. Around her people ran, limped, or were carried towards the landing area. Two cadaverous oldsters, members of the local aristocracy, were carried past in an opulent sedan chair borne by six stooped bearers. A buckboard drawn by two skeletal, eight-legged dray beasts followed.

Three drunks lurched out of a drinking stall, arms around one another; they were waving ceramic tippling bowls in the air, sloshing liquor. They regarded her for a moment, then elbowed one another. Under the native code of ethics a woman was fairly safe, at least in town, but Hasti kept her eyes to the ground and her hand near her pistol. But the celebrants decided that the starship merited their attention first, or they would be excluded from an event the rest of the city would talk about all year.

Picking her way through a city that seemed to be falling apart before her eyes, Hasti at last came to the vaults of Xim the Despot. The vaults were contained within a sprawling, cameral complex of interlocking structures, immensely thick-walled and, in its day, impervious to forced entry. Still, thieves had got in over the years and, finding only empty vaults, yawning treasure chambers, and waiting bins and unoccupied shelves, had soon departed. Only the occasional wanderer or scholar of the obscure came here to tour Xim's barren edifice now. The galaxy was rich in sights and marvels worth the seeing and easier to reach; there was little of allure in the haunted emptiness here.

In the vaults' worn and pitted facade were engraved Xim's insignia of the starburst-eyed death's head and characters from an ancient language: IN ETERNAL

HOMAGE TO XIM, WHOSE FIST SHALL ENCLOSE THE STARS AND WHOSE NAME SHALL OUTLIVE TIME.

Hasti paused for a glimpse of herself in the gleaming stump of a fallen column, hoping she resembled her sister sufficiently. She fumed at the memory of Han Solo's sudden change of attitude towards her – first fussing over the buckling of her seatbelt and then his reckless – but expert – planetfall, done to impress her. Either the oaf couldn't see how much she disliked him or, more likely, refused to accept it.

At the top of the steps she crossed the wide, roofless portico and passed through the vaults' single, gigantic entranceway. The interior was cool and dark. There was a vast circular chamber under a dome half a kilometre in diameter, a mere vestibule to the huge vault complex.

But this outermost chamber was the only part of the vaults in use any more. Hasti's eyes adjusted to the light of weak glow-rods and tallow lanterns guttering smoke into the cavernous room designed to be lit by monumental illumi-panels. Farther in towards the centre of the place was a small cluster of work tables, partitions, and cabinets – the administrative annex for the minor activity the vaults still housed.

A few Dellaltians, carrying data plaques, old-fashioned memo-wire spools, and even a few sheafs of paper computer-printout, passed by her. Hasti shook her head at the primitive operation. But, she remembered, the vaults had very few tenants. The Dellaltian Bank and Currency Exchange, a minor concern, was one, while the Landmark Preservation Office, charged with looking after the abandoned labyrinth with almost no resources, was that grouping of desks and partitions.

A man approached her from the semigloom – tall, broad-shouldered, his hair as white as his forked beard. He moved briskly; at his heels was an assistant, a smaller, grimmer man whose long black hair was parted down the middle and showed a white blaze.

The tall man's voice was hearty and charming. 'I am steward of the vaults. How may I help you?'

Holding her chin high, Hasti answered in her best approximation of a local accent. 'The lockboxes. I wish to recover my property.'

The steward's hands circled one another, fingers gathered, in the Dellaltian sign of courtesy and invitation. 'Of course; I shall assist you personally.' He spoke to the other man, who departed.

Remembering to walk on his right, as a Dellaltian woman would, Hasti followed the steward. The vaults' corridors, musty with age, displayed mosaics of coloured crystal so complicated that Hasti couldn't interpret them. Many of the pieces were cracked, and whole stretches were missing; they arched high overhead into shadow. Here, their footsteps resounded hollowly.

At last they came to a wall, not the end of the corridor but a partition of crudely cut stone that had plainly been mortared into place after the original construction. Set in the wall was a door that looked as if it had been scavenged from some later, less substantial building. Next to it was an audio pickup. The steward pointed to it.

'If the lady will speak into the voice-coder, we can proceed to the lockbox repository.'

When Hasti's sister had told her and Badure about depositing the log-recorder disk she had told them the box-rental code and retrieval combination, but had mentioned no voice-coder. Hasti felt the pulse in her forehead and the thumping in her rib cage quicken.

The steward was waiting. Leaning to the audio pickup she said, as if in mystic invocation, 'Lanni Troujow.'

'My last offer,' Badure threatened for the fourth time, resorting to hyperbole common on Dellalt, 'is ten credits a day, guaranteed three-day minimum.'

The landlord shrieked and tore hairs out of his beard, beat his chest with his free hand, and vowed to his ancestors that he would join them before letting plundering offworlders steal the food from his children's mouths. Skynx took it all in, amazed by the carefully measured affrontery of the hagglers.

Han listened with one ear, worried that Hasti might not have been able to get away from the landing area undetected. There was a tug at his shoulder; it was Zollux. 'I noticed this altercation, sir. Shall I continue to outload our cargo?'

That meant Hasti was away. Badure heard and understood. 'Get everything back onboard until this son of contaminated genes, this landlord, bargains reasonably.'

'Unthinkable!' screamed the landlord. 'You have already made use of my precious building and diverted me from my other pursuits. A settlement must be made; I hereby hold your cargo against the arrival of the Fact-Finders.' He and Badure swapped deadly oaths.

The landlord called the old man a horrible name. Skynx, quivering in excitement, immersed himself in the spirit of the thing, antennae trembling. 'Devourer of eggs!'

Everyone stopped, glancing at the diminutive Ruurian, who swallowed, appalled at his rash outburst. The landlord departed, along with much of the crowd, hurling back epithets and leaving his cousins to guard the outbuilding. From somewhere, the cousins had produced bolt-operated slug rifles with hexagonal barrels and long, lens-type scopes.

Back onboard the *Falcon*, Badure threw himself into a chair. 'That landlord! What a freighter bum he'd have made!'

Han grabbed Zollux. 'What happened?'

'The men guarding the building entrance kept looking through the door after me as I deposited the cargo. It was some time before they became bored and gave all their attention over to Badure's performance and Skynx's appearance. Hasti was no longer in her crate, and the inner door was unbarred. At Blue Max's suggestion I resecured the door.'

'Tell Maxie he's a good boy,' Badure said. 'I like you two; you've got a touch of larceny in you.'

Zollux's chest plastron swung open, the halves coming apart like cabinet doors. Blue Max's photoreceptor lit up. 'Thanks, Badure,' he said, sounding smug. Han told himself, *I should keep an eye on that computer or he'll end up wearing juvie-gang colours and packing a vibro-shiv.*

Just at that moment, Skynx appeared with Chewbacca, who had just left the cockpit. The Wookiee was holding the metallic flask of vacuum-distilled jet juice the partners kept under the control console for special occasions. 'Skynx,' Badure said, 'I think it's time to strike up the band.'

Skynx flowed to the acceleration couch and on up into his nook. He began taking objects from his tree-like storage rack. 'If you have no further tasks for us, sir,' Zollux told Han, 'Max and I would like to continue our study of Skynx's tapes.'

'Whatever you want, old-timer.'

Zollux crossed to the tech station, where he and the computer resumed their perusal of the ancient records Skynx had brought along. The labour droid, who had worked his way across the galaxy and had already outlived one body, possessed an almost sentient streak of curiosity, and Blue Max was always ready to absorb new information. The two mechanicals were particularly interested in technical data and other references to the giant war-robots of long-dead Xim.

Skynx, sitting up on his rearmost two sets of limbs, took and held a miniature amplified hammer-dulcimer in the next set and two hammers in each digital cluster of the next. He strapped a pair of tympanic pulsers around himself, tapping experimentally with the digits of his next-higher limbs. Above those he fastened a pair of small bellows to pump air to a horn held in his uppermost-but-one set of extremities. In the uppermost he took up a flute of sorts and tried a few runs. The sound was like the wind-cones Han remembered from his own homeworld. He wondered what kind of brain could coordinate all that activity.

Skynx launched into a merry air, full of sudden runs, bright interplay and humorous progressions, and impudent catches made to sound as if the instruments or Skynx's limbs were getting out of hand and taking their own course. The Ruurian made a great pretence of distress and bewilderment and a desperate effort to bring his extremities under control again. The others laughed, particularly Chewbacca, whose Wookiee chortles made the bulkheads ring. Badure rapped time on the gameboard and even Han was tapping a toe or two. He opened the flask, took a swig, and passed it to the Wookiee. 'Here, this'll put some curl in your pelt.' Chewbacca drank, then sent the flask along. Even Skynx accepted a drink.

They demanded another number after that, and a third. Badure eventually jumped up, both hands over his head, to demonstrate the Bynarrian jig. He capered around the compartment as if he were twenty kilos lighter and as many years younger.

At the height of the Bynarrian jig the ship's hatch signalled. Badure and Chewbacca rushed off, eager to see what Hasti had brought back. Zollux and Blue Max looked up from the strobing rapid-readout screen, and Skynx began extricating himself from his instruments.

'Step one completed!' he said in his quick fashion. 'Skynx, of the K'zagg Colony, off on a treasure hunt! If my clutch-siblings could see me now!'

But when the Wookiee reentered the compartment, he slumped dejectedly over to his partner and sank into the couch, head in hairy hands. *Bad as that?* thought Han. Badure followed, one arm clasped around a despairing Hasti. She took a sip from the flask, coughed, told her story quickly, then took another.

'Voice-coder?' Han exclaimed. 'Nobody said anything about a voice-coder.'

'Maybe Lanni never realised her voice was being printed,' Badure replied.

'That steward,' Hasti muttered. 'I should've jabbed my gun into his bellybutton and offered to glaze his gallstones for him.'

Han handed the half-empty flask to his copilot and rose. 'Now we do it *my* way.' He headed for the cockpit, pulling on his flying gloves. Chewbacca fell in behind. 'Want to know how to make a withdrawal? Stick around.'

Badure hurriedly interposed himself between the two partners and the main passageway. 'Steady there, boys. Just what've you got in mind?'

Han grinned. 'Swooping down on the vault, blowing the doors with the belly-turret guns, going in, and taking the disk. Don't bother getting up, folks; it'll all be over in a minute.'

Badure shook his head. 'What if a Tion patrol cruiser shows up? Or an Imperial ship? Would you care to have a hunter-killer team on your neck?'

Han made a move to step around him. 'I'll chance it.'

Hasti jumped up. 'Well, I won't! Sit *down*, Solo! At least consider the options before you risk the death penalty for all of us.'

Chewbacca awaited his friend's decision. Zollux watched impartially and Blue Max with a certain excitement.

'Some forethought might not be out of place here,' Skynx contributed in a very subdued voice.

Han disliked complications and subterfuge, but his hasty action was stayed, for the moment, by the conviction that being dead was the least interesting thing in life. 'All right, all right; who's hungry?' he asked. 'I'm sick of ship's rations. Let's go see what kind of meal we can get in town. But if nobody thinks of a new one, my plan still goes.' He clipped the flask to his gunbelt while Chewbacca gathered up his bowcaster and bandoleer of ammunition. Badure found the small purse of local currency he had brought, and Zollux shut his plastron halves on Blue Max.

Hasti saw Skynx shedding his instruments. 'Hey, I never got to hear anything.'

Badure looked around. 'Bring them along,' he bade Skynx. The Ruurian began tucking his instruments into carrying cinches he fastened around himself.

Pulling on his flight jacket, Han shut and sealed the hatch behind them. Storm clouds had moved in, and electrical discharges illuminated the clouds in strange flashes of red. Badure pointed out that the landlord's cousins had disappeared. 'They probably figured out they were guarding empty boxes.'

'More likely they didn't want to sit around in that leaky barn,' Hasti reasoned. The rest of the onlookers who had been watching the starship from a distance, mostly children and the domestic yappers, were gone as well.

They set off downslope with Zollux bringing up the rear. Up this high, away from the docks, the streets were poorly maintained and lighting was unknown. They didn't get far.

Han was first to sense something wrong – everything was too quiet, too many ramshackle windows were shuttered. No lights were showing and no voices could be heard anywhere nearby. He grabbed Chewbacca's shoulder, and the bowcaster came up, the blaster appearing at the same time. By instinct, they stood back to back. Hasti had her mouth open to ask what was wrong when the spotlights hit them.

Han recognised them as hand-held spots and, figuring that a right-handed man would be holding the spot as far out with his left as he could, took an estimated aim.

'Don't!' a voice ordered. 'We'll cut you all down if anyone fires a shot!'

They were surrounded. Han holstered his side arm, and the Wookiee lowered his bowcaster. Humans and various other beings appeared in the glare waving rifles, riot guns, slug-shooters and other weapons. Han and his companions were easily disarmed and their equipment examined. Skynx chittered in terror while their captors pawed his delicate musical instruments, but he was allowed to retain them.

Three individuals strode forward to search the captives. The smaller two were mainbreed human – twins, a young man and woman who shared traits of thick, straight brown hair and widow's peaks, startling black-irised eyes, and thin, intense, pale faces. The third personage hung back, a looming hulk in the light backwash of the spots. Han remembered the name Badure had mentioned: Egome Fass, the enforcer.

The twins approached them, the female in the lead. 'J'uoch,' murmured Hasti, shivering.

The twins' faces held the same rigid, lethal composure. 'That's it,' J'uoch replied quickly. 'Where's the disk, Hasti? We know you went to the vaults.'

She gave Han a chilly smile. Then the smile vanished and she turned again to Hasti. 'Give it up, or we burn down your friends, starting with the pilot here.'

Chewbacca's great arms tensed, fingers curling. He prepared to die as he would be expected to, head of a Wookiee Honour Family, his life so intimately intertwined with that of Han Solo that there existed no human word for the relationship.

Han, in turn, was choosing among several tactics, all of them suicidal, when Zollux spoke. 'Captain Solo mustn't come to harm. I will open the *Millennium Falcon* for you.'

The woman eyed him. It hadn't occurred to J'uoch that the droid would be cleared for ship access. 'Very well. All we want is the log-recorder disk.' Han, in the grip of adrenal overload, stared at Zollux and wondered what was going through the old labour droid's logic stacks. One fact did not escape him: he had heard high-pitched communicaton bursts exchanged between Zollux and Blue Max.

Their captors herded them back towards the *Falcon*. Too late, Han understood why the Dellaltians had scattered. He just hoped the two machines had a workable plan.

Zollux, climbing the ramp, was at the main hatch lock with several of J'uoch's people near. Strangely, just as the main hatch rolled up into its recess, the droid chose to swing his chest panels open. Then Han and the others heard Blue Max's high-speed burst signals.

An ear-splitting hiss of a hurtling object echoed through the air. One of the men who was guarding Zollux was lifted off his feet by terrific impact, and in the next moment was stretched headlong on the ramp. Another captor, farther down the ramp, was slammed in the shoulder and knocked through the air.

'Run for it!' Blue Max shrilled. As suddenly as that, chaos broke loose.

VII

The two strongarm specimens still standing at the top of the ramp ducked instinctively. Something small and fast swooshed past Han, knocking the humanoid who had been guarding him off his feet. Zollux pivoted to follow the action.

From the now-exposed Blue Max more high-pitched beeps issued forth. Han realised with some amazement that the computer module had managed to summon the remote target-globe from the *Falcon*'s interior and was using it as a weapon.

Before J'uoch's people could react, Han yelled, '*Hit 'em!*' He grabbed the nearest opponent's weapon, a slug-shooter carbine with a drum magazine and, twisting his leg behind the other's, toppled him over.

Badure rammed his elbow back into the face of his guard and turned to grapple with him. Chewbacca was less fortunate. Preparing to enter the fray, he was unaware that the massive Egome Fass had stolen up behind him. The enforcer's hard fist crashed into the base of the Wookiee's skull.

Chewbacca staggered, nearly falling to his knees, but his tremendous strength bore him up again. He turned groggily to give battle, but Egome Fass's first blow had given the enforcer a formidable edge. He avoided Chewbacca's slowed counterpunch and landed another blow, bringing his fist down on the Wookiee's shoulder. And this time the *Falcon*'s first mate went down.

Badure was having a difficult time with his second guard, who was young and fast. They struggled, feet shuffling in the dry dust, but just as the older man was gaining the upper hand by dint of weight and reach, he was tackled low around the knees and went down.

The tackler was Hasti. She had seen that J'uoch's men on the ramp were about to open fire on Badure. Propelled by its repulsor power and forced air, the remote globe had taken two more antagonists out of the fight. J'uoch was shooting at it with Hasti's confiscated pistol, missing, and screaming orders that her troops ignored.

Han had retrieved the carbine, knocking his opponent away with a stroke of the weapon's butt. He spotted his partner struggling to rise as Egome Fass hovered over him. The enforcer's hood was thrown back, and in the light spilling down through the hatch, Han saw the humanoid's huge, square jaw and tiny, gleaming eyes set far back under thick, bony ridges of brow.

Han clamped the carbine stock to his hip and squeezed off a burst. The weapon stuttered with a deafening staccato and reeked of burned propellant. A stream of slugs plucked at the enforcer's chest but only ripped away fragments of cloth. Egome Fass was wearing body armour under his outsized coveralls. Before Han could adjust for effect, the humanoid lunged for cover.

A wash of white fire flared on Han's right. Turning, he saw that it was a power-pistol shot aimed at Badure by a man on the ramp who missed because Hasti had just tackled the old man. But it hit the man with whom Badure had been struggling. He shrieked once and died as he fell.

Han grabbed Chewbacca's elbow as the Wookiee struggled to his feet, shaking his head to clear it. Retaking the *Falcon* was impossible; the two remaining guards at the ramp head were kneeling in the shelter of the hatchway and firing into the night. 'Get back!' Han hollered to his companions. He moved back, firing in brief bursts, followed by Hasti and Badure with Skynx scuttling rapidly behind.

The spotty return fire, hasty and poorly aimed, never came close. But one guard, a leather-skinned creature with a horny carapace, blocked Zollux's retreat. Blue Max beeped, and immediately the remote flashed out of the darkness, striking the creature from behind and knocking it over. Since the remote couldn't operate at any great distance from the starship, Max gave the signal that sent it jetting back onboard.

The labour droid hurried after the others, bounding in long strides made possible by heavy-duty suspension. The group ran, bounded, and scuttled to the edge of the landing area. All the while Han raked the field behind them to keep J'uoch's people pinned down. Then the carbine went silent.

'Drum's empty,' he said. Off in the night he could hear J'uoch railing at her followers and calling for a comlink.

'She's posting a guard on the ship and calling for reinforcements,' Badure announced. 'We'd best lose ourselves in town for a while.'

The group descended through the city in an informal race, past shuttered shops and locked doors. No lights could be seen; the Dellaltians who had seemed so curious earlier wanted no part of this lethal dispute among offworlders. Leading the others, Han plunged into an alley, followed it to a market plaza, and hurried down a trellised side street that smelled of strange foods and fuels.

They came to a factory district. Pausing in the shadows, the humans and the Wookiee leaned against a wall and fought for breath while Zollux waited impassively and Skynx, with a superior respiratory system, checked his carrier cinches to make sure that none of his precious instruments had been damaged.

'You should've snagged a gun,' Han puffed, 'instead of worrying about that one-man band of yours.'

'These have been making music in my family for a dozen generations,' Skynx replied indignantly. 'And I'm sure I don't know how I could've wrested a weapon away from some malodorous ruffian four times my size.'

Han gave up the argument and checked the nearby rooftops. 'Can anybody spot a ladder or staircase? We have to see if they're trailing us.'

'Now I can be of help there, I believe,' Skynx announced. A nearby pole supported fibre-optic cables for in-town communications; wrapping himself around it, Skynx spiralled up the pole, protecting his instruments carefully. Since all the buildings were one-storey affairs, he had a good view of the surrounding area.

Having reconnoitred, Skynx corkscrewed his way down the pole again. 'There are search parties working their way down through town,' he told them. 'They have hand-held spotlights; I assume them to be using comlinks.' He tried to hide his fearful quaking.

'Did you see their ship?' Han asked eagerly. 'It must be around here somewhere. Perhaps we could pick up some fire power there.'

But Skynx hadn't spotted it. They decided to try to skirt the search parties' pattern and see if they couldn't get back to the *Millennium Falcon*. Skynx's feathery antennae wavered in the air, attentive to vibrations. 'Captain, I hear something.'

They all held their breath and listened. A rumbling swelled until it shook the ground. 'Looks like J'uoch got through on the comlink,' observed Badure over the tumult. An enormous vessel mounted with heavy guns was hovering above the landing area, its floodlights playing over the city. The fugitives pressed back into the shadows.

The ponderous lighter couldn't hover and search for long; instead she descended. 'There'll be more manpower onboard her,' Badure warned. 'Skynx, shinny up and take a look. Be careful.'

The Ruurian went up a nearby line-pole and was down again almost at once. 'The big ship must have dropped off parties down in the lakeside area,' he told them urgently. 'I saw them spreading out, coming up the hill. And there's a group of three coming down this way from above. One of them is carrying Chewbacca's bowcaster.'

The Wookiee growled ominously. Han agreed, 'Let's take care of them, but *good*.' No one mentioned surrender; it was plain J'uoch would do anything to get what she wanted.

The search party flashed hand-held spots into alleys and doorways. Teams were being organised to scour the rooftops; virtually every trustworthy being who could be spared from the mining camp had been armed and brought to the scene.

The man leading this particular party, the man whose

carbine Han had appropriated, carried Chewbacca's bowcaster and had tucked Han's blaster into his belt. He had seen a Wookiee bowcaster used in the holo-thrillers and was determined to get even with the two by downing them with their own weapons. He was delighted, therefore, to see a looming, shaggy shape step out of the darkness before him.

Blocking his companions in the process, the man with the bowcaster took a stance and fired. But Chewbacca ducked at the last instant, knowing that the man's unfamiliarity with the feel and aiming characteristics of the bowcaster would cause a first-round miss. In a flash the Wookiee hurled himself forward.

The man gave the bowcaster's foregrip a yank to recock it and strip another round off the magazine for a second shot. But he got nowhere; the weapon's mechanism was set for a Wookiee's brawn and length of arm. Before he could cast it aside and pull out Han's blaster, a mountain of angry brown fur descended upon him.

The other two searchers fanned out to either side. One was felled immediately as Han Solo stepped out of the shadows and knocked him out with a swipe of the carbine's butt. The other was stunned by masonry brickbats flung by Hasti and Badure.

Han adroitly snatched his victim's pistol and fired at the brickbat-stunned searcher. Yelling, the man clenched his calf and fell. Meanwhile Chewbacca had separated his man from the bowcaster and thrown him against a wall. The man crashed with an impressive thud and slid to the ground.

'You'll live,' Han decided, toeing over the man he had shot and waving his recaptured blaster, '*if* you make some worthwhile conversation. How many guards on my ship?'

The man licked his fear-parched lips. 'Ten, maybe twelve. A few actually onboard, the rest around her.'

'What about the ship you came in?' Hasti asked their captive. 'The first one, not the big lighter.'

Han slightly depressed the blaster trigger.

The man gasped. 'Backslope of town, below the landing area, in the rocks.'

Badure came up, having collected the comlink dropped by the bowcaster thief. 'Sonny boy, you just bought yourself a future.' Then he told them that J'uoch's spaceboat was grounded on an expanse of flat stone, with only two men guarding her. 'I've grown to dislike unnecessary killing,' Badure explained, setting an appropriated stun-gun for maximum dispersal. He squeezed the trigger, and blue rings of energy leaped outward. Immediately the two guards collapsed. Badure and Hasti patted them down for whatever weapons or equipment they might have, then Han climbed into the boat and moved to the pilot's seat. 'Fuelled and ready!'

Chewbacca, examining the copilot's side of the board, *woof*ed a question.

'No. We won't leave Dellalt without the *Falcon*; we couldn't get out of the system with this baby carriage anyway,' Han replied. 'We'll jump out of their search locus, then work out our next move.' He began throwing switches and punching instructions into the flight computer.

A warning sounded and the board lit up. Chewbacca threw his head back and yeowled his frustration. From the console rang J'uoch's voice: 'Attention landing boat, attention! Why are you attempting to violate instrument lock? Guard detail, answer!'

'I need tools; they've got the board locked down,' Han said urgently. Chewbacca dug long fingers around the edges of the utility locker's door and ripped it away. Han was busy unfastening the console's housing latches. The Wookiee grabbed some implements from the locker and handed them to Han, and soon the partners were attacking the lockdown mechanism, ignoring J'uoch's vehement transmissions that crackled in the background.

Chewbacca howled in triumph, neutralising one security circuit. 'Got the other,' Han crowed. But their elation disappeared as they heard the thunder of mass-lift thrusters.

'She's coming after us in the lighter!' Hasti yelled from the hatchway. 'How soon can we lift off?'

'She's too close with those heavy cannons,' Han rasped. 'But at least we'll have a diversion. Get clear!'

The others ran for it. There was a chart readout on the console; Han slipped it into his vest and, with one foot out the hatch, inserted a series of instructions into the console. Automatic sequence cycled the hatch shut, and the boat lifted off.

Han hurdled a rock and crouched in its shelter with the others, and they watched the spaceboat rise into the night sky. The lighter was already on a close interception course; it seemed to Han a good time to get as far as possible from the liftoff site. Having distracted those on the lighter, the fugitives moved off in a ragged line. Chewbacca kept rearguard and, wielding a clump of dry red shrubbery, eradicated the few prints they'd left on the rocky terrain.

The spaceboat picked up speed, following Han's programming. The lighter's heavy artillery spoke, and tremendous spears of green-white energy made a brief noon in the Dellaltian night. The first salvo missed but gave the gunners their registration. The second hit dead centre, several beams converging on the small boat at once. It exploded in a fireball, leaving a few scraps of burning wreckage to flutter from the sky.

'Capturing us wasn't such a big priority after all,' Badure observed.

They had barely reached the temporary shelter of a rocky outcropping and hidden themselves among the boulders when the lighter returned with a rumble of brute thrusters and settled in where the boat had lifted. In moments the area was swarming with armed searchers sweeping hand-held spots. The stunned guards were quickly discovered, the ground examined.

'They're buying it!' Hasti whispered with muted elation. The searchers noted the prints left by Han and the others when they had approached the boat but missed any sign of departure, thanks to Chewbacca's painstaking work. The dozing guards were lugged aboard the lighter and the rest of J'uoch's employees embarked. Thrusters flared again.

Han's mind was racing. Now that they were armed and J'uoch apparently believed them dead, they had a chance of retaking the *Millennium Falcon*. Han expected to see the

70

lighter land next to his own ship, to take away the guards onboard. Instead, the larger vessel hovered above the freighter. The *Falcon*'s ramp was up, her ramp-bay doors closed. Han suddenly understood what was happening.

He threw himself forward at a flat-out run, bellowing at the top of his lungs, with Chewbacca only a step behind. No one on either ship heard them, of course; the lighter, its hoisting gear making loud contact with the freighter's upper hull and achieving tractor-lock on the smaller ship, lowered her mechanical support booms. In the same manner as she transported mining equipment, the lighter lifted off with the *Millennium Falcon* tucked up tightly to her underside.

The lighter veered south, gathering speed and altitude as she went. Han slowed to a stop. In despair he and Chewbacca watched their ship being borne away across the lake and over the mountains beyond. The others caught up.

'They think the log-recorder disk is onboard, isn't that it, Captain?' Skynx asked, somewhat in shock. 'They searched us and didn't find it and tried to kill us, so they must assume we left it onboard the *Falcon*.'

'Where are they headed?' Han asked tonelessly.

'Straight for the mining camp,' Badure answered. 'They'll have all the time and privacy they need to tear – to search her thoroughly.'

Han pivoted on his heel and walked off towards town. A drizzle was starting.

'Where are you going? Where are *we* going?' Skynx yelped as the others hurried after.

'I want my ship back,' said Han simply.

VIII

'It's a lamebrained scheme, even for you,' Hasti was saying. Han peered into the greyness and wished Badure would return.

The drizzle had become a freezing-cold downpour during the night, then slackened to a drizzle again. Han and the others, awaiting the old man, had taken shelter under a tarp behind piles of cargo in a broad-eaved wooden warehouse by the docks. They were sipping sparingly from the flask, which had remained clipped to Han's gunbelt throughout the night's action.

They were damp, bedraggled, and miserable. Han's hair was plastered flat against his skull, as was Hasti's. Drops fell from Skynx's matted wool, and Chewbacca's pelt had started exuding the peculiar odour of a wet Wookiee. Han reached out and patted his friend's head in a gesture of consolation, wishing there were something he could do for Zollux and Max. The two automata, abiding patiently, were worried that their moisture-proofing would fail.

'You haven't got a prayer of pulling this off, Solo,' the girl finished.

He swiped a damp strand of hair off his forehead. 'Then don't come along. There'll be another ship through here any year now.'

A man in a shabby cloak appeared, splashing through the puddles, bearing a bundle on his shoulder. Han, his blaster's scope set for night shooting, identified Badure. The old man crouched with them under the tarp. Having acquired a cloak from an alley-sleeper, he had contrived to buy four more. Han and Hasti found that two fit them passably well and even Zollux could don one stiffly, unaccustomed as he was to the extraordinary feel of clothing. But the biggest cloak Badure had brought could barely contain Chewbacca; though its hood managed to cover his face from casual observation, his shaggy arms and legs stuck out.

'Maybe we could wrap him in bunting, like mittens and leggings,' Badure suggested, then turned to Skynx. 'I didn't forget you, my dear Professor.' With a flourish he produced a shoulder bag, which he held open invitingly.

Skynx shrank back, antennae wobbling in dismay. Surely you can't mean. ... This is unacceptable!'

'Just until we're out of town,' Han coaxed.

'Um, about that, son,' Badure said, 'maybe we should lie low awhile instead.'

'Do what you feel like; this could be a bad hike. But they're probably tearing the *Falcon* apart at that mining camp.'

'Then what's the point in going?' Hasti remonstrated. It's a couple of hundred kilometres. Your ship'll be in pieces.'

'Then I'll put her back together again!' he near-hollered, then calmed. 'Besides, how did J'uoch and company show up so fast, unless she's got contacts here? We'd be sitting targets, not even to mention the average citizen's dislike of offworlders. We could end up bunking in the local slams.'

Badure looked resigned. 'Then it's the Heel-and-Toe Express for us.'

The rain was letting up, the sky lightening. Han studied the chart readout he had picked up. It turned out to contain a complete survey map of the planet, dated but in exacting detail. 'At least we had the good luck to get this.'

Hasti sniffed. 'You spacers and mariners and aviators are all alike: no religion, but plenty of superstition. Always ready to invoke luck.'

To forestall another verbal skirmish, Badure jumped in. The first thing is to get across the lake; there are no connections south on this side. No air service anywhere, but there's some ground transport over there somewhere. The only way across is a ferry service run by the natives, the Swimmers. They're jealous of their territory and they charge a fee.'

Han wasn't sure he wanted to be transported by one of the sauropteroids, the Swimming People of Dellalt. 'We could hike around the lake,' he proposed.

'It would take us five or six extra days unless we could negotiate a vehicle or get our hands on some riding animals.'

'Let's check the ferry. What about food and equipment?'

Badure looked askance. 'What about lovely ladies and hot food? There'll be settlements along the way; we'll have to improvise.' He blew his breath out, and it crystallised.

'Are you coming or staying?' Han asked Hasti.

She gave him a scalding glare. 'Why bother asking? You'll lean on people until there's no choice left.'

The moderately safe and comfortable adventure envisioned by Skynx had become a very real struggle for survival, but his Ruurian practicality made his decision simple. 'I believe I'll remain with you, Captain,' he said. Han almost laughed, but Skynx's simple tone of pragmatism and self-preservation lifted his opinion of the Ruurian a notch.

'Glad to have you. All right; down to the docks and across the lake.'

Skynx crawled unwillingly into the bag, which Chewbacca then shouldered. They proceeded in a tight group, with Badure in the lead and Hasti and Han on the flanks. The Wookiee and Zollux kept to the middle of the group in hopes that in the poor light and rain they would be mistaken for humans, one extremely tall, the other barrel-chested.

Skynx poked his head out of the bag, feathery antennae thrashing. 'Captain, it smells awful in here, and it's cramped.' Han pushed him back down, then as an afterthought gave him the flask.

The docks and their moored embarkation floats were already busy. Leaving the others in the partial concealment of stacks of cargo, Han and Badure went to inquire about passage.

Though the docks had space for many of the towrafts used by Dellalt's native sauropteroids, only the middle area seemed busy. Then, scanning the scene, Han saw one lonely raft off to the right. Though Badure had briefly described the Swimmers, Han still found them a startling sight.

Men were loading cargo aboard the tow-rafts, which were tied at the embarkation floats. Tow-lines and harnesses bobbed as the rafts waited in the water. Beyond them lazed twenty or so sauropteroids, circling or treading water with flipper strokes of immense power. They ranged from ten to fifteen metres in length, their heads held high from the water on long muscular necks as they moved in the lake. Their hides varied from a light grey to a deep green-black; lacking nostrils, they had blowholes at the tops of their long skulls. They idled, waiting for the men ashore to complete the manual labour.

One of the men, a burly individual with a jewelled ring in one ear and bits of food and droplets of breakfast nectar in his beard, was checking cargo against a manifest. As Badure explained their needs, he listened, playing with his stylus.

'You will have to talk money with the Top Bull,' he informed them with a smirk Han didn't like, then called out: 'Ho, Kasarax! Two seeking passage here!' He returned to his work as if the two men no longer existed.

Han and Badure went to the dock's edge and stepped onto an embarkation float. A sauropteroid approached with a few beats of his flippers. Han surreptitiously moved his hand closer to his concealed blaster. He was ill at ease at seeing Kasarax's size and his hard, narrow head with its fangs longer than a man's forearm.

Kasarax trod water next to the float. When he spoke, the blast of sound and fishy breath made both men fall back a bit. His pronunciation was distorted but intelligible. 'Passage is forty *driit*,' the creature announced, a hefty sum in Dellaltion currency, '*each*. And don't bother haggling; we don't fancy that down here at the docks.' Kasarax blew a spout of condensing moisture out the blowhole in his head to punctuate the statement.

'What about the others?' Han murmured to Badure, indicating the rest of the sauropteroid pack.

But Kasarax caught Han's query and hissed like a

pressure valve. 'They do as I say! And I say you cross for forty *driit!*' He feinted, as if he were going to strike, a snakish movement that rocked the float with turbulence. Han and Badure scrambled onto the dock as the men there guffawed.

The man with the manifest approached. 'I'm chief of Kasarax's shore gang; you may pay me.'

Han, red in the face, was growing more furious by the moment at this high-handed treatment. But Badure, glancing toward the lone raft they had noticed earlier, asked, 'What about him?'

A lone Swimmer was down there, a big, battle-torn old bull, watching events silently. The shore-gang chief forgot his laughter. 'If you enjoy living, ignore him. Only Kasarax's pack plies this part of the lake!'

Still fuming, Han strode down the dock. Badure followed after a moment's indecision. The shore-gang chief called, 'I give you fair warning, strangers!'

The old bull reared up a bit as they approached. He was the size of Kasarax, his hide a near-black, networked with scars. His left eye was gone, lost in a long-ago battle, and his flippers were notched and bitten. But when he opened his mouth his tremendous fangs gleamed like honed weapons. 'You're new faces to the docks,' he said in a whistling voice.

'We want to get across the lake,' Han began. 'But we can't meet Kasarax's price.'

'Once, human, I'd have towed you across as quickly as you please and carefully, too, for eight *dritt* each.' Han was about to accept when the creature cut him off. 'But today I tow for free.'

'Why?' Han and Badure asked together.

The bull made a burbling sound that they took to be a laugh, and shot a blast from his blowhole. 'I, Shazeen, have vowed to show Kasarax that any of the Swimming People are free to work this dock, like any other. But I need passengers, and Kasarax's shore gang keeps those away.'

The shore gang was gathered in conference, grouped in a knot of perhaps twenty, and shooting murderous looks at Han, Badure, and Shazeen. 'Can you meet us somewhere farther down the shore?' Han asked the native Dellaltian

Shazeen reared, water streaming from his black back, looking like some primitive's war god. 'Boarding here at the dock is the whole point! Do that and I will do the rest, nor will any of the Swimming People meddle with you; it's Shazeen they must deal with, that is our Law, which not even Kasarax dares ignore!'

Badure pulled thoughtfully at his lower lip. 'We might go around the lake.'

Han shook his head. 'In how many days?' He turned to Shazeen. 'There are a couple more passengers. We'll be right back.'

'If they menace you on the docks, I cannot interfere,' Shazeen warned. 'That is the Law. But they won't dare use weapons unless you do for fear the other humans, the ones who've been driven from their jobs, will have cause to intercede.'

Badure clapped Han's shoulder. 'I could stand a little cruise right now, Slick.' Han gave him a wicked grin; they started back.

The others were standing where they had been left. Hasti held a large cone of plasform that contained a mass of lumpy, pasty dough, which she and Chewbacca were eating with their fingers. She offered some to Badure and Han. 'We were starving; I picked this up from a vendor. What's the plan?'

Badure explained as they shared the doughy stuff. It was thick and gluey but had a pleasing flavour, like nutmeat. 'So,' finished Han, 'no shooting unless we have to. How's Skynx?'

The Wookiee chortled and held open the shoulder bag. The Ruurian lay in a near-circle, clutching the flask. When he saw Han, his faceted red eyes, which were somewhat glazed, grew wider. Skynx hiccupped, then chirped, 'You old pirate! Where've you been?' He flicked an antenna across Han's nose, then collapsed in chittering laughter.

'Oh, great,' said Han, 'he's tight as a scalp tick.' Han tried to recapture the flask, but Skynx curled into a ball and was gripping it with four limb-sets.

'He said he's never metabolised that much ethanol

before,' said Hasti, looking slightly amused. 'That's exactly how he said it.'

'Keep it then,' Han told Skynx. 'But stay down; we're going for a ride.'

Skynx's muffled voice came from the shoulder bag, 'Perfect idea!'

They made their way back to the dock. Men from Kasarax's shore gang blocked their way to the embarkation float. Others, not of the gang, had appeared and leaned against walls or stacked cargo, carrying spring-guns, firearms, and makeshift weapons. Han remembered what Shazeen had said: these people had been forced out of a living by Kasarax's racket. None had been willing to risk riding with Shazeen, but they would see to it no weapons were used to keep Han's party from doing so. The rest of the shore gang was scattered around the docks, holding weapons of their own. As Han understood it, any shooting would trigger a general bloodbath, but anything short of that was allowable.

When Han was within a few paces, the shore-gang chief addressed him. 'That's close enough.' Several of his men were whispering among themselves, seeing the size of the cloaked and hooded Chewbacca.

Han moved closer, giving out a string of bland cordialities. He had the impression that the man was a good brawler and thought: Victory first; questions later! The chief reached to shove him back, with a warning. 'I'm not telling you again, stranger!'

How right, agreed Han silently. He speedrew, blindingly fast, and placed his gun against the chief's head. The man was shoving and warning one instant, falling the next, with a look of surprise on his face. Han had time to backhand another man and give the shore-gang chief a stiff shove, such was the surprise he had generated. Then he had to duck a truncheon, and the scene erupted.

One young shore-gang member swung an eager one-two combination at Zollux, a short set-up jab and a long uppercut that would have done considerable damage to a human. But the youth's fist gonged off the droid's hard midsection and rebounded from his reinforced faceplate. As the boy cried out in agony, Hasti stepped around Zollux and brought the barrel of her gun down on his head.

Another shore-gangster reached for Han, who was otherwise occupied. So Badure stopped him with a forearm block and lashed out with his foot, kicking high and hard. His antagonist dropped. They had done well enough for the moment, but now the rest of the shore-gangsters pressed in vengefully.

Then Chewbacca joined the brawl.

The Wookiee had stepped back to shuck the shoulder bag and put Skynx out of danger and to lay down his bowcaster. His hood still pulled low, he selected two men, shook them hard, then hurled them up and back in either direction. A swing of one long arm brushed another man back off the dock; Chewbacca kicked out in the opposite direction, connecting with a man who had lunged at Hasti. The man flew sideways, tumbled twice, and stretched out full length on the dock.

Two men tackled the Wookiee from either side. He ignored them, his legs as sturdy as columns beneath him. He struck out all around him, felling opponents with each blow.

The fight raged around Chewbacca, a flock of flailing, desperate shore-gangsters swarming at him. Spoiling for a fight since he had been downed by Egome Fass's treacherous attack, the Wookiee obliged them. Bodies flew back, up, over. The *Millennium Falcon*'s first mate restrained himself to spare needless bloodshed. His companions found themselves left out of the riot with only occasional assistance to be rendered in the form of a tap on the head, a shove, or a shouted warning.

Chewbacca found time to give each of his legs a shake, and the men straining at them were flung loose. Those who remained standing made a concerted charge. The Wookiee spread his arms, scooped up all three of them, and dashed them against the dock. One of them, the gang chief, who had recovered from Han's blow and reentered the fight, pulled a punch-dagger from a forearm sheath.

Han angled for a clear shot then, whatever the

consequences. But Chewbacca caught the chief's movement. The Wookiee's head snapped around, his hood falling back for the first time, and he unleashed a full-throated roar into the shore-gang chief's face, drawing his lips back off his jutting fangs. The chief turned absolutely white, eyes bulging, and managed to produce the smallest of squeaks. His punch-dagger fell from limp fingers. The snarling Wookiee, having attended to all the others, set the man down and put one forefinger against his chest. The chief fell backwards to the deck, trying to draw breath.

Hasti grabbed Chewbacca's bowcaster and her dropped cone of dough; Badure held the sack containing Skynx, from which emerged chitters of hilarity. Han grabbed his partner's arm. 'Gangplank's going up!'

They dashed for the embarkation float, hopping one by one to the tow-raft. Shazeen, who had watched the whole encounter, loosed a blast from his blowhole. Closing a nictitating membrane over his eye, he ducked beneath the water to reemerge with his head through the tow harness, commanding, 'Cast off!' Badure, last in line, brought the raft's painter with him.

They had expected Shazeen to move off quickly, but the Swimmer warped the raft out slowly. When he had put a few dozen metres between the raft and the dock, he slipped the tow harness by submerging, then resurfaced to nudge it to a stop with his rocklike snout. 'That was some fine thumping!' he hailed. Throwing his head back, he issued an oscillating call that rolled across the water. 'Shazeen salutes you,' he clarified.

'Uh, thanks,' Han replied dubiously. 'What's the holdup?'

'We wait for Kasarax,' Shazeen answered serenely.

Han's outburst was forestalled when another sauropteroid surfaced next to Shazeen, whistling and hissing with mouth and blowhole. 'Use their language, woman,' Shazeen chided the newcomer, who was smaller and lighter of hide but nearly as battle-scarred as the big bull. 'These are Shazeen's friends. That pipsqueak there with the hairy face can really *thump*, can't he?'

80

The female switched to Standard. 'Will you really oppose Kasarax?'

'No one tells Shazeen where he may or may not swim,' replied the other creature.

'Then the rest of us are behind you!' she answered. 'We'll keep Kasarax's followers out of it.' The lake water swirled as it closed over her head.

'Drop anchor!' shouted Han. 'Cut the power! Cancel the reservations! You never said anything about a faceoff.'

'A race, a mere formality,' assured Shazeen. 'Kasarax must pretend now that it's a right-of-way dispute, to conform with the Law.'

'*If* he can get passengers,' Hasti broke in. 'Look!'

Kasarax was having trouble getting any of his shore gang aboard his tow-raft. The clash at the dock had put doubt in them; now they were having second thoughts about being dragged into the middle of a Swimmer dispute. Their chief, too, hesitated.

Kasarax lost his temper and thrashed himself up over his tow-raft, half onto the dock. Men drew back from the enormous bulk and the steaming, gaping mouth. Kasarax bent down at the chief.

'You'll do as I say! There's nowhere you can hide from me, even in that shelter you built under your house. If you make me, I'll dig you out like a stone-shell from the lake bottom. And the whole time, *you'll hear me coming!*'

The shore-gang chief's nerve broke. White-faced, he scurried aboard the tow-raft, pulling along several unwilling followers and browbeating several others to accompany him.

'Mighty persuasive lad, that nephew of mine,' reflected Shazeen.

'*Nephew?*' Hasti burst out.

'That's right. For years and years I whipped every challenger who came along, but I finally got tired of being Top Bull. I drifted north, where it's warm and the fish are fat and tasty. Kasarax has been running wild too long; partly my fault. I think shore folks put this takeover nonsense into his head, though.'

'Another victory for progress,' Badure murmured. Kasarax was nudging his tow-raft up even with Shazeen's.

'Anyway, don't worry,' Shazeen told them. 'The Swimming People won't attack you, so don't use your weapons on them, or you turn it into a death-matter. That's the Law.'

'What about the other humans?' Han called, but too late; Shazeen had gone to confront Kasarax. The shore-gang members had brought along their harpoon spring-guns and a variety of dockside cutlery.

The two bulls churned the water, trumpeting to one another. At length Shazeen switched to human speech. 'Stay clear of my course!'

'And you from mine!' Kasarax retorted. They both plunged for their tow-rafts, flippers beating with full force, diving for their harnesses and creating rolling swells. They reemerged with heads through harnesses and snapped the towing hawsers taut. The hawsers creaked with the strain, wringing the water from them. Water gushed up from the rafts' blunt bows, breaking in spray and foam. Everyone on both rafts fell to the deck, snatching frantically for a handhold.

Kasarax and Shazeen breasted the water neck and neck, shrilling challenges to one another. Han began to wonder whether a hike around the lake wouldn't have been a better idea after all. *Why do I always think of these things too late?*

IX

Towing hawsers thrummed like bowstrings. The rafts moved forward with surges matching the Swimmers' rhythms.

Han clasped the low deck rail. The water teemed with sauropteroids, both Kasarax's cronies and Shazeen's supporters, who had been kept from work by Kasarax's alliance with the shore gang.

Long, scaled necks cut the water; rolling backs and broad flippers showed with each dive, and the spray of swimming and blasting blowholes made it seem the rain had resumed.

'Chewie!' shouted Hasti, who was hugging a rail stanchion, 'the bag!'

The shoulder bag containing Skynx was sliding aft. Badure rolled from a stern-rail corner and caught it, wrapping his legs around a stanchion. Skynx popped out of the bag, his big red eyes more glazed now than before.

Taking in their situation unsteadily, the Ruurian scuttled up halfway onto Badure's head, his antennae bending in the breeze, clinging resolutely with every digit he could spare, and hurled the empty jet-juice flask into the air, cheering, *'Weee-ee heee-ee!* I bet five *driit* on us!' Spying Kasarax's raft, he added shrewdly, 'And five more on them!' He sank back down into the bag, which Badure closed over him.

The rough ride didn't trouble Han nearly as much as the fact that this was no ordinary race. The two bulls were straining, neither able to gain headway against the other. Kasarax made a bid for the lead, then another, but Shazeen matched his spurts and held the pace. Han could hear their booming grunts of effort over the rush of the wind and the slapping of water against the rafts.

Kasarax changed tactics, slackening his line. Shazeen

followed suit. The younger creature changed course in an instant, cutting across Shazeen's path just behind his elder. He ducked under Shazeen's towing hawsers and pulled hard. His tow-raft came slashing after, hawsers brushing at angles under Shazeen's.

Han saw the shore-gang chief hoist a broad-bladed axe; Kasarax's men obviously intended to sever Shazeen's hawsers when the hawsers came up against Kasarax's raft's bow rail. The pilot drew without thinking; a blaster bolt flickered red across the water, and the axehead jolted, sparks arcing from it, a black-edged hole burned through it. The shore-gang chief dropped it with a cry as his men ducked.

Someone else grabbed the axe and swung it as both rafts and the Swimmers towing them were dragged and slewed around by each other's momentum. Han's aim was spoiled and the axehead descended. Perhaps it was an off-world product with an enhanced edge; in any case the axe parted a hawser with one blow and bit into the bow rail. Shazeen's raft swung, coming nearly side-on, with the unbalanced pull of the remaining hawser.

The chief had the axe back, ready to chop the other hawser. Han was aiming carefully at the axe when Shazeen changed course in an effort to see what had happened. The remaining towing hawser dragged across Kasarax's raft's rail, catching the shore-gang chief and pulling him overboard. At the same moment Shazeen's manoeuvre bumped his own raft into a trough. Han lost his footing, slipped, and fell, whereupon the blaster flew from his hand.

The chief was still clinging to Shazeen's remaining tow-hawser, lower body in the water, sawing at it with a knife. Han couldn't spot his blaster, but was determined not to let that second line be severed. The gang chief was working at the hawser, Hasti was shouting something about not starting a firefight, and Badure and Chewbacca were yelling something he didn't want to take time to listen to, being in no mood for a debate. Losing patience, he threw off his flight jacket, stepped over the bow rail, sprang, and began drawing himself down the hawser, hand over hand, his legs wrapped around it, the higher swells wetting his back.

The shore-gang chief felt the vibrations in the hawser, saw Han, and sawed more furiously at the tough fibre. The chief took a moment to slash at the pilot. Han suddenly realised how impetuous he had been, as if another man entirely had occupied his body for a moment. He didn't quite avoid the stroke and the knifepoint cut across his chin. The water pulled at them both.

But Han avoided the back-slash with dexterity gained in zero-gee acrobatics drills. He lashed out flat-handed in a disarming blow, and the knife plunked into the water. As the knife fell, the shore-gang chief began to lose his grip on the hawser. He grabbed at Han, and both men plunged into the water. The lakewater was agonisingly cold and had a peculiar taste.

Han dived as deeply as he could, his clothes dragging at him. Underwater he heard the thud of the raft's bow striking the chief's head. Cheeks puffed, the pilot glanced up through the icy, dark water as the raft passed over him, and then surfaced just behind it. He grabbed for the stern rail, missed, and was himself grabbed.

Chewbacca pulled his partner over the stern rail in one motion just as the raft began drifting to a halt. Shaking wet hair out of his eyes, Han gave an involuntary cry of surprise, seeing why they had stopped. Kasarax's manoeuvre had been Shazeen's needed provocation for combat under Swimmer Law. Both the monstrous bulls had ducked out of their tow-harnesses; now they met in resolute battle.

They charged into collision, a butting of great heads whose report sounded like the crack of a tree trunk, and an impact of muscular necks and broad chests that sent waves racing outwards. Neither seemed hurt as they circled for position, flippers whipping the water into foam. The shore-gang boss was paddling towards his raft, eager to be out of the behemoths' way.

Han felt Zollux's hard finger tap his shoulder. 'You'll no

doubt be wanting this, sir. I caught it before it could go overboard, but you didn't seem to hear me call you.' He passed over Han's blaster.

Without taking his eyes from the battle, Han promised, 'I'm doubling your salary,' ignoring the fact that he had never paid the droid a thing.

Kasarax wailed; he had been too slow on the withdrawal after nipping Shazeen. The older bull hadn't got a full grip with his fangs, and Kasarax had got away, but now blood flowed down his neck scales. Kasarax, wild with rage, charged again.

Shazeen met him head-on, each of them trying to butt and bite, to press the other under the surface, shrieking and trumpeting. Shazeen failed to repel a determined assault by Kasarax and slid back as the younger creature surged up over him seeking a death grip on his uncle's throat. But he had been too eager. Shazeen had drawn him out and now the older bull dropped his pretext and dived, rolling. His blunt tail slammed Kasarax's skull, and the younger combatant fell back in pain. They resumed butting heads, biting, thrashing flippers, and colliding with one another.

'Hang on!' warned Hasti, the only one who had thought to watch for other danger. The raft shuddered and timbers splintered as the bow was tipped into the air.

It was one of Kasarax's followers, a very young bull from the looks of him. He had closed crushing jaws on the raft's stern, shaking it, spouting wrathful blasts from his blowhole. He tore a metre-wide bite out of the raft, spat the wood aside, then came at them again. Han set his blaster to maximum power.

'Don't kill him!' Hasti shouted. 'You'll have them all down on us!'

As the sauropteroid butted the raft, nearly capsizing it, Han bellowed. 'What do you want me to do, sweetheart, bite him back?'

'Leave it to them,' she answered, pointing. She meant the other Swimmers, who were closing in. Kasarax's overeager follower had ignited a general fray. One – Han thought it was the female who had surfaced at the dock and offered support to Shazeen – kicked up an impressive bow-wave, making straight for the raft. But once again the creature closed jaws on the raft's stern.

The trick's to keep on breathing till help arrives, Han told himself. He spied the cone of gooey dough Hasti had brought, still more than half-full. He reached for it, calling, 'Chewie! Lock hands!'

Han got to unsteady feet. The Wookiee reached out his long arm and caught Han's free hand, steadying him. The young bull had seen him coming and opened its maw, but when he pulled up short it closed its jaws with a crash and blew a geyser of spray through its blowhole.

When he saw the edges of the blowhole vibrate with the indrawing of breath, Han jammed the cone of dough down on it as hard as he could. It landed on the sucking blowhole with a peculiar *shloop!*

The Swimmer froze, its eyes bulging. Into what air passages and chambers the dough had been drawn, Han couldn't begin to guess. The creature shook, then exploded in a sneeze that convulsed him, kicking up a fountain of water and nearly blowing Han off the raft with the fish-scented gust.

At that moment Shazeen's friend arrived. She hit the younger creature and they battled furiously. All around, pairs of the creatures rolled, ducked, bit, and butted in pitched combat. Scaled hides took tremendous punishment and the sound threatened to deafen the humans; the turbulence promised to capsize the raft.

Han kept his attention riveted on Shazeen and Kasarax, thinking, *If that old bull loses, it'll be a wet stroll home. And the fish are biting today!*

Both bulls were torn and injured, chunks missing from each one's hide and flippers. The older one moved slowly, worn down by his nephew's youthful endurance. They rammed together for another fierce exchange. Surprisingly, Kasarax went under.

Shazeen sought to follow up his advantage but failed to keep track of his antagonist and circled aimlessly. The air was so full of pealing battle cries that Shazeen took no notice of his passengers' warnings. Kasarax had slyly and quietly surfaced behind his uncle and to his left, in the blind spot resulting from his missing eye. The younger Swimmer lunged with jaws gaping for a lethal grip at the base of his uncle's skull.

But Shazeen moved with abrupt speed, coming around and bringing his head up sharply, tagging Kasarax's chin with the boniest part of his foreskull. The crack echoed from the opposite lakeshore. Dazed by the terrible blow, Kasarax barely had time to wobble before Shazeen had his throat tightly between black jaws.

'That old con artist!' Badure whooped. Chewbacca and Hasti hugged, and Han leaned on the rail, laughing. Shazeen was shaking his nephew's head mercilessly, side to side and forward and back, but refraining from the death bite.

At last Kasarax, head bent back at a painful angle, no fight left in him, began a pitiful croaking. All around him, combat ceased at the sounds of ritualistic surrender. When all the others had separated, Kasarax was released and allowed to tread water meekly while his uncle stormed at him in the sibilant language of their kind.

With a final piercing rebuke, Shazeen sent his nephew off with a hard butt of his head. Kasarax submitted, then stroked slowly away to haul his tow-raft back the way he had come. His followers trailed him in disarray, convoyed by Shazeen's victorious supporters.

Shazeen moved to his own raft, feeling the pain he hadn't allowed himself to show his enemies. Bleeding from fearsome wounds, his scarred, one-eyed head battered and torn, he asked, 'Now then, where were we?'

'*I* was in the drink,' Han reminded him. '*You* were hauling the raft around to take out the shore-gang boss. Got him right in the bulb, too. Thanks.'

The old bull made a gurgling sound resembling a chuckle. 'An accident, peewee; didn't I tell you it's un-Lawful to meddle in a human squabble?' He gurgled again, bringing his wide chest against the raft's stern and shoving towards the opposite shore.

'What about your nephew?' Hasti wanted to know.

'Oh, he's through trying to make the lake his own pond. Fool idea would have got him killed sooner or later anyway, and he's too valuable to waste. I'll need a deputy soon; haven't got many more scraps like that one left in me. These youngsters always think they're clever, going for my blind side.'

'I still wouldn't trust him,' Han warned.

'You don't trust *anybody*,' Hasti chided.

'And you don't see me getting my flipper bit, do you?' he retorted smugly.

'Oh, Kasarax will be all right,' Shazeen said. 'He just thought he wanted us to fear him. He'll like it better once we respect him; all but the worst ones come around, given the chance.'

The far shore had come up quickly. Shazeen propelled them towards it with a few more hard strokes, then flipped over and shoved them on with a sweep of his rear flippers. The raft nosed onto the strand, lifted on the crest. Han stepped onto the damp sand.

The others followed him. Badure had a rather sick Skynx slung over one shoulder. The female who had saved Shazeen's passengers surfaced next to him, obviously concerned.

But her eye fell on Hasti, whose cowl had fallen back to display her red hair. 'You had a rougher ride this time, human,' the Swimmer observed.

Hasti registered confusion. 'Wasn't that you,' the Swimmer female asked, 'back before Kasarax took over? Sorry; the hair and, what do you call them, the clothes, are just the same.'

Hasti whispered, 'Lanni! These are her clothes!'

Badure asked the female what this passenger had done.

'Just came across and asked people questions about those mountains there, waved a little machine in the air, then went back,' she replied.

Han, pouring water from his boot, looked up at the mountains rearing to the south. 'What's up there?'

'Nothing,' answered Shazeen. 'Humans don't usually go

up there. Fewer come back. They say it's just desolation up there.' He was studying Chewbacca, who had doffed the hated cloak, Zollux's gleaming form, and the now-reviving Skynx.

'I'd heard that,' agreed Badure. 'The mining camp lies on the far side of the mountains, Han, but I'd reckoned we'd go around. Why should Lanni have been interested in them, I wonder?'

Han stood up. 'Let's find out.'

X

The terrain lifted away from the lakeshore in a series of rolling hills carpeted with soft, blue moss that cushioned their steps. Han was gratified to see the moss spring back when they had passed, thereby obliterating the group's prints.

Supplies were no problem. The workers on this side of the lake, all members of Kasarax's shore gang, had departed in haste on seeing their leader defeated, fearing the blood-vengeance of the non-gang members. Calculating a ten-to-twelve-day march through the mountains, the party had carefully picked through the abandoned storage buildings for provisions and equipment.

They had filled their packs with jars of lake crustaceans marinated in syrup, plastic cartons of the doughy stuff Hasti had first sampled, tubes of pickled vegetable slices, bags of meal, smoked fish, cured meat, and some hard purple sausages. Even though they carried capacious water bladders, they were relying on finding more water in the mountains. According to the survey map, there were abundant run-offs and fresh springwater throughout the area. Those who wore clothing had gathered cold weather gear. Han had pulled off his wet clothes, settling for a Dellaltian outfit until he could dry his own, and contrived a bandage for the knife cut. Practicality had made Hasti exchange her robes and gown for an outfit suitable for an adolescent boy. They had also found thick, insulated bedrolls.

There were no riding animals or power vehicles to be found. But Han didn't mind, trusting unfamiliar beasts no more than he did the aged and breakdown-prone Dellaltian machinery. Zollux, who could bear a heavy pack and yet

consumed no water or food, found that his popularity ha
increased. They felt lucky to have him along, knowing non
of the local domesticated animals or ground vehicles wer
suited to the mountain terrain and aircraft were few and fa
between on Dellalt. They had found some lengths of rop
but no other climbing gear. Neither had they foun
medicine or a medi-pack, additional weapons or charge
commo or navigational gear, heating unit, or macro
binoculars or tele-eye, though the scope on Han's blaste
would be some compensation for the last. For shelter, the
had brought along a wagoner's tent they found in one of th
abandoned buildings.

And they were armed. In addition to Han's side arm an
Chewbacca's bowcaster, they also had the weapon
captured from J'uoch's forces. Badure carried the stun-gu
he had already used and a brace of long-barrelled powe
pistols. Hasti had a compact disruptor, a dart-shoote
loaded with toxic missiles, and a blaster, but the latter wa
nearly exhausted because Han had used it to recharge h
own. Skynx declined to bear arms, which his species neve
used, and Zollux's basic programming, the droid sai
prohibited him from using them as well.

Ascending the foothills, they kept the ridge lines betwee
themselves and the region behind, though Han doubte
anyone was taking time to try to spot them. The collapse
Kasarax's racket was probably occupying everyone's atten
tion. Gusting winds tore across the open hills, pressing at th
resilient moss and stirring the travellers' hair, clothing, an
fur. The country was stark and vacant. Lacking a secon
comolink, they decided not to put out a point-walker, b
rather to rely on the wide field of surveillance they coul
maintain.

Chewbacca took the lead, treading the blue moss light
for all his size, testing the air with black nostrils flaring. H
blue eyes moved constantly, his hunter's senses keen
attuned. A dozen paces behind trudged Zollux. The labo
droid had opened his chest plastron a crack at th
computer's demand, and Max was taking in the view.

Next came Badure and Hasti side by side. Skynx followed after, carrying only his musical instruments because none of the packs fit him and he couldn't have borne much weight anyway. Undulating along, he kept pace without difficulty.

Han brought up the rear, frequently casting glances behind, making minute adjustments in the balance and shoulder-strap padding of the makeshift pack he had thrown together. He lined up prominent terrain features and did his best to keep track of their direction and course, since that was the only way they would have of orienting themselves to the surveying map. From time to time he thought about the treasure, but the open countryside and the brisk wind made him happier than he would have admitted. In a way, they reminded him of the freedom of space travel.

The group moved on throughout the morning with deliberate speed, Han stopping frequently to scan his blaster's scope for some sign of pursuit. But as Dellalt's blue-white primary climbed the sky and none appeared, they slowed a bit, saving strength for the long journey.

Skynx dropped back to talk to Han. The Ruurian had a rapid metabolism and so had recovered from his bout with the flask. Han, who had been walking backward for a few paces while he checked the rear, pivoted around in step. It occurred to him that Skynx must be thoroughly dis-illusioned with human-style adventuring.

'Hey, Skynx, break out that hip-pocket orchestra of yours. We're out in the open anyway, like a bug on a canopy. A little music won't make things any chancier.'

The Ruurian complied eagerly. Using his lowermost four sets of limbs for locomotion without decreasing speed, he took up the tympanic pulsers, bellows-horn, and flute. He began a human-tempo marching tune, one for marching overland rather than for a parade.

The small pulsers held a catchy beat, the bellows-horn tootled, and the flute skirled. Han resisted the quickened pace, but enjoyed the music.

Badure squared his shoulders and fell into energetic

stride, sucking in his overhanging stomach and humming with the music. Hasti smiled at Skynx and strode along more quickly.

Chewbacca tried to stay in step, although Wookiees don't generally take to regimentation. The process was awkward for him. He achieved a kind of animated swagger, though not even remotely in time. Zollux, however, fell right into step, mechanical legs pumping precisely, arms swinging, chin held high.

They trod blue moss; cold wind made the landscape seem barren and free. In this manner they proceeded over the hill.

They were well up into the heights when the blue-white sun set. The few lights of the city came on, far below and behind them. Outcroppings of rock had begun to appear, rising from the blue moss. They camped at one of these ledges, under an overhang that would afford some protection from wind. There was no fuel for a fire.

As they settled in, Han established priorities. 'I'm going to check the area with the scope. Chewie will take first watch, after he eats. Badure, you take second and I'll take third. Skynx can have the wake-up duty. Is that all right with everybody?'

Badure didn't mention Han's assumption of leadership, being content with the arrangement. 'What about me?' Hasti asked evenly.

'You can have first watch tomorrow, so don't feel left out. Would it be straining our bonds of affection to ask to borrow your wrist chrono?'

Teeth clenched, she threw it at him, then he and Chewbacca set off. 'You're welcome!' she called after him. 'Who does he think he is, anyway?' she said to the others.

Badure answered mildly. 'Slick? He's used to taking charge; he wasn't always a smuggler and a freighter bum. Didn't you notice the red piping on the seams of his shipboard trousers? They don't give away the Corellian Bloodstripe for perfect attendance.'

She considered that for a moment. 'Well, how did he get

it? And why do you call him Slick?'

'You'll have to get that first part from him, but the nickname business goes back to the first time I met him, way back.'

In spite of herself, she was curious. Skynx was also listening with interest, as were Zollux and Blue Max. The two automata decided to hear Badure out before shutting down for the night; their photo-receptors glowed in the dusk.

It was becoming colder fast, and the humans pulled their cloaks tighter, Badure closing his flight jacket. Skynx curled his woolly form to conserve body heat.

'I'd been a line officer, had a few decorations myself,' Badure began, 'but there was the matter of a floating Jubilee Wheel I was running onboard the flagship. Anyway, they reassigned me to the staff at an academy.

'The commandant was a desk pilot, off his gyros. His bright idea was to take a training ship, an old U-33 orbital loadlifter, and rig her so the flight instructor could cause malfunctions: *realistic stress situations.*

'"Enough can go wrong without building more into a ship," I said, but the commandant had pull. His programme was approved. I was flight instructor, and the commandant came along on the first training mission. He gave the briefing himself, playing up the wise old veteran act.

'In the middle of it a cadet interrupted. "Excuse me, sir, but the U-33's primary thrust sequence is four-stage, not three." The kid was gangly, all elbows and ears, and had this big chow-eating grin.

'The commandant was cold as permafrost. "Since Cadet Solo is such a slick student, he will be first in the hotseat." We all boarded and took off. Han handled everything the C.O. threw at him, and that grin grew bigger and bigger. He really had put in a lot of time on that kind of ship.

'That crate had checked out one hundred percent, but something went wrong and something blew; a second later we had all we could do to keep her in the air. I couldn't get the landing gear to extend, so I raised ground control and asked for emergency tractor retrieval.

'And the tractors failed, primaries and secondaries both on the approach run. I just managed to get us up again. The commandant was white around the eyes by then; the crash wagons and firefighting machinery were deploying onto the field.

'Which was when Cadet Solo announced, "The reservoir locking valve on the landing gear's stuck shut, sir; these U 33's do it all the time."

'And I said, "Well, do you feel like crawling down into the gear bay and taking a wrench to it right this second?"

'"No need," the kid says, "We can joggle it with a couple of manoeuvres."

'The commandant's teeth were rattling. "You can't take a bulk vessel through aerobatics!" Then I said, "You hope to sit in your mess kit *I* can't, sir, because I don't know which manoeuvres Slick over there is talking about. He'll have to do it." While his mouth was hanging open, I reminded him he was ranking officer. "Either you land this beast or let the kid try out his idea."

'He shut up, but about that time there was a rumpus in the passenger compartment. The other cadets were becoming nervous. So Han opened the intercom. "By order of the commandant, this is a full-dress emergency landing *drill*. All procedures will be observed; you are being graded on your performance."

'I told him he was playing fast and loose with what might be somebody's last moments, and he told me to go ahead and tell them the truth if I wanted a panic in the hold. I let it ride. Han took control back.

'The U-33 isn't designed for the things Han did to that bird. He took her through three inverted outside loops to free up the locking claws. Our vision began to go. How Han coaxed lift from those inverted wings, I'll never know; but he was smirking, hanging there from his harness.

'He went into barrel rolls to build centrifugal force in the reservoir. I thought he was going to rip the wings off and almost took control back, but just then I got a board light. He had forced the valve open.

'But gravity could've swung it shut again, so he had to fly

upside-down while the landing gear cranked out. The ship had begun losing altitude and the commandant was sort of frothing at the mouth, babbling for Han to pull out. Han refused. "Wait for it, wait for it," he said. Then we heard this long grinding sound as the landing gear seated, and a clang as it locked.

'Han snap-rolled, hit full reverse thrusters, and hung out all the hardware. We uprooted two stop-nets and only lived because we landed into the wind. Jouncer landing, I tell you.

'They had to help the commandant off the ship. Then they deactivated that ship for good. Han locked down his board, just like the rule book says. "Slick enough for you?" he asked. I said "Slick." That's how the nickname started.'

It was fully dark now. The stars were luminous overhead, and both of Dellalt's moons were in the sky. 'Badure, if it happened today,' Hasti asked quietly, 'would you tell those cadets they might die?'

He sounded tired. 'Yes. Even though they might've panicked. They had a right to know.'

The logical next question, then, was, 'Well, what're *our* chances, the truth? Can we get the *Falcon* back, or even survive an attempt?' Skynx, and the automata, too, hung on his reply.

Badure remained silent. Through his mind passed the options: lying, telling the truth, or simply rolling over and going to sleep. But when he opened his mouth to answer, he was interrupted.

'Depends on what we run up against,' Han Solo said from the darkness, having returned so quietly that they hadn't heard him. 'If camp security's loose, we could get away without losses. If it's tight, we have to tackle them somehow, maybe draw them out. Anyway, it means risk. We'd probably have casualties and some of us might not make it.'

'*Some*? Admit it, Solo; you're so concerned with getting that ship of yours back that you're ignoring facts. J'uoch's got more hired killers than –'

'J'uoch's got portside brawlers and some small-time muscle,' Han corrected Hasti. 'If they were quality, they

97

wouldn't be working for a two-credit outfit like hers Handing some clod a gun doesn't make him a gunman.'

He stepped closer and she could see his silhouette against the stars. 'They have the numbers, but the only real gunman within light-years is standing right in front of you.'

The craft was trim, sleek, luxuriously customised, a scoutship off the military inventory. Her approach and landing were exacting, and she set down precisely where the *Millennium Falcon* had landed several days earlier. Her lone occupant emerged.

The man was limber, graceful, though his movements were at times abrupt. Although he was tall and lean, his form seemed compact. His clothes were expensive and impeccable, of the finest materials, but sombre – grey trousers and a high-collared white shirt with a short grey jacket over it. A long white scarf, knotted at his throat, fell in soft folds, and his black shoes shone. He wore his greying hair cropped short, but his moustachios were long, their ends gathered and weighted with two tiny golden beads, giving him a subtly roguish look.

Townspeople appeared and clustered around him, just as they had greeted the *Falcon*'s passengers. But something in this stranger's blue, unblinking eyes, something penetrating and without mercy, made them wary. He soon obtained from them the story of the *Falcon*'s arrival and removal by the mining-camp ship. They showed him the spot where the spaceboat had been destroyed by the lighter. Even scavengers had avoided the bits of wreckage, fearing radiation residues.

The stranger told the townspeople to disperse, and seeing the look in his eyes, they obeyed. He carefully removed his jacket and hung it inside his ship. Around his waist an intricately tooled black gunbelt held a blaster high on his right hip.

He brought certain sensitive instruments from his ship, some on a carrying harness, others attached to a long probe, and still others set in a very sophisticated remote-globe. Loosening is scarf, he made a patient examination of the area, working in a careful pattern.

An hour later he returned the equipment to his ship and rubbed the dust from his gleaming shoes with a rag. He was satisfied that no one had died when J'uoch's spaceboat had been destroyed. He reknotted his scarf while he considered the situation.

Eventually, Gallandro drew on his jacket and locked up his ship, then made his way into the city. He soon heard rumours of bizarre goings-on down at the lake and battles among the natives. He couldn't verify much about the outside humans involved, though; the only close-range witnesses, the shore gang of the sauropteroid Kasarax, had gone into hiding. Still, he was willing to credit the story. It was in keeping with Han Solo's wildly unpredictable luck.

No, Gallandro corrected himself. 'Luck' was what Solo would have called it. He, Gallandro, had long ago rejected mysticism and superstition. It made it that much more frustrating to see how events seemed to conspire to impel Solo along.

Gallandro intended to prove that Solo was no more than he appeared to be, a small-time smuggler of no great consequence. That the gunman had doubtless given the matter far more thought than Solo himself was a source of ironic amusement to him. Using the vast resources of his employer, the Corporate Sector Authority, he had tracked Solo and the Wookiee this far and would, with only a little more patience, complete the hunt.

XI

'There's something wrong,' Han said, peering intently through his blaster's scope in the morning light. 'I'm no sure, but – Here, you look, Badure.'

'It just looks like a landing field to me,' Hasti commented

'Just because it's big and flat and has ships parked on it?' Han asked sarcastically. 'Don't jump to any conclusions after all, we may've stumbled onto the only used-aircraft lo in these mountains.'

A stiff breeze at their backs blew down the narrow valley towards the field. It had been snowing heavily in the region at the far edge of the flat area below, a snowfield slope sharply downward towards the lowlands.

'It's not on any map I ever saw,' declared Badure squinting through the scope.

'Doesn't mean a thing,' Han replied. 'The Tio Hegemony's survey-updating programme is running some thing like a hundred and eighty years behind schedule and getting worse. And these mountains are full of turbulence and storm activity. A survey-flyover ship could've missed that place altogether. Even an Alpha Team or a full Bet Mission might not have caught it.'

Thinking it over, Han rubbed his jaw, feeling his growth of beard. He, like the others, was drawn and haggard from the march and had lost a good deal of weight. The knife cu across his chin was healing well enough in the absence of medi-pack.

'Badure's right,' Hasti said, holding the survey-ma reader up close to her face! 'There's nothing on here at all And what's it doing out here anyway? Look, they had t have carved away half that cliff to build it.'

Han was concentrating on the field with his remarkabl

acute vision. There, guidance lights and warning beacons were dark, understandable at a hidden base; but they seemed to be of a very outdated design. He could make out several craft that appeared to be about the size of spaceboats, and five larger ones. It was difficult to see any details because their tails and afterburners were pointed in his direction. Then he knew what was bothering him.

'Badure, they've got those ships parked and tied down with their rear ends into the wind.' Since the craft on the field followed common aerodynamic design principles, the sensible way to position them would have been with their noses into the prevailing air currents.

Badure lowered the scope and handed back Han's blaster. 'The wind's been steady, at least since last night. Either they don't care what kind of knocking-around their ships will take if a storm kicks up, or the place is deserted.'

'We haven't seen a soul down there,' Hasti said.

Han turned to Zollux. 'Are you still getting those signals?'

'Yes, Captain. They originate from the antenna mast down there by the field, I would say. They're very weak. I only picked them up because the summit we climbed was close on a direct line of sight.'

Han and Zollux had ascended that summit, a laborious session of trudging and scrambling and occasionally climbing, because of a suspicion of Han's. In the mining camp, Hasti and Badure had heard rumours that J'uoch and her partners were increasing camp security. Adding to that an apparent interest in the mountains on the part of Lanni, Hasti's late sister, Han thought it possible the mountains were seeded with antipersonnel sensors that were somehow tied in with the treasure. On the chance that, if there were sensors, they would be active rather than passive and therefore detectable, Han had taken the futilely protesting labour droid up to see if, now that they were approaching the lowlands, they could detect any signals. Using his built-in command-signal receiver, Zollux had tried all the standard calibrations and, when those yielded nothing, sampled others. Finally he had picked up a signal of a long-outmoded sort, and Han had taken a rough fix on it. The signal had led the group to this narrow valley, and the morning revealed what was apparently a landing field bracketed in stone.

They had been marching through the mountains for days; songs and high spirits had given way to sore feet, overworked servo-motors, aching muscles, and shoulders chafed by pack straps. The visit to the spa at the University of Rudrig seemed to Han like a dream of another life. According to the map, they were very nearly through the mountains.

That map had turned out to be their most important piece of equipment, allowing them to choose the easiest course. Nonetheless, they had hit a number of places where they had to climb, where Skynx suddenly became a major asset. The Ruurian could scale or descend sheer rock faces, carrying one end of a climbing rope with him. Without Skynx, Han knew, they would still be somewhere far back in the mountains. As it was, their food was running low. Fortunately they had managed to find water on their route.

But even after they left the mountains they would still have to cross an expanse of open plains before reaching the mining site. A common thought was running through the group's respective biological and synthetic synapses: acquisition of a ship, even an atmospheric craft, would mark an end to their walking days. In addition, the field might offer supplies as well as transportation.

'Could this be what Lanni was curious about?' Badure wondered aloud.

'We'll see,' Han decided. They had concealed themselves behind some rocks within a kilometre of the field. 'Chewie and I'll go first. If we give the all-clear sign, come on down.' He demonstrated a broad waving motion, left to right. 'But if we don't signal you within half an hour, or we give you any other kind of signal, get yourselves out of here. Write us off and try to reach the mining site, or double back to the city i that's what seems best.'

Han and the Wookiee started shedding their extra gear 'I'm not so sure we shouldn't have stayed in the city,' said Hasti.

Han tried to reassure her. 'You would be if you'd ever done any time swabbing out the plumbing in some local lockup, doll. You ready, Chewie?'

He was. They moved out, taking turns advancing from cover to cover. Each awaited the other's hand motion before moving; they had done this sort of thing together before.

They observed no sentries, patrols, watchtowers, or surveillance equipment as they approached; but they felt no less uneasy. When at last they reached the edge of the field, they held a brief but heated debate conducted entirely in hand signals, over who would be first to step into the open. Each insisted that he should be the one. Han cut the dispute short, just before it developed into an exchange of angry gestures, by rising and stepping out from the cover of the boulder.

Chewbacca, eyes roving the scene, bowcaster raised and ready, immediately shifted to a position from which he could give supporting fire. Han slowly moved across the open area, blaster out, nerves taut.

No shot or outcry came – and no alarm. The field was a simple expanse of flat ground – partly smoothed soil and partly rock that, from the looks of it, had been levelled a long time ago. Han wondered why somebody hadn't done a complete job and paved it over with formex or some other surfacing material.

He saw no buildings of any kind – only the primitive antenna mast, ground beacons, ground-control light clusters, and area illumination banks. He skirted the edge of the field, darting in among the rocks without warning to make sure no one was waiting in ambush.

He reemerged and continued working his way towards the parked ships. When he was satisfied that nobody had a gun turret or missile tube pointed at him from one of the craft, he approached them. And when he had come close enough to make out detail, he had difficulty speaking for a second.

What the flaming – 'Hey, Chewie! Get over here!'

The Wookiee was out in the open instantly, racing towards him, bowcaster held high. His charge slowed to a distracted lope, then immobility as he saw what Han was talking about. He gave a bemused, lowing sound.

'That's right,' Han agreed, slamming the side of one of the ships with his fist. It gave, leaving a deep indentation. 'They're phonies.'

Chewbacca came up slowly, shouldering his weapon, and took a firm grasp on the hatch of the next ship in line. He tore it off easily: it was merely a mockup constructed of treated extrusion sheeting and light structural alloys. He cast the hatch aside with a brayed Wookiee imprecation and leaned into the open hatchway. Light came through the clear pane used to simulate the cockpit windshield. The dummy ship, ribbed by support members, was gloomy, stale-smelling, and empty.

Han, examining the ship and the general layout of the field, was stumped. Nonetheless, he kept his pistol in his hand. The mockups were crude but had been made with obvious attention to details of landing gear, fuselage, propulsors, and control surfaces. They were copied – at least, he presumed them to have been copied – from models he didn't recognise and secured in place with lines of some artificial fibre.

His first thought was that this was a decoy base, part of some military campaign or defence system. But there had been no organised conflict on Dellalt or, for that matter, in this sector of space for years and years. Furthermore, this fake landing field must demand a certain amount of upkeep to be in the shape it was. A trick of J'uoch's? No logic sustained that.

Chewbacca was more instinctive. In his mind the place conjured images of some malign force using the field as a sort of trap, like those of the webweavers on the lower tree levels of his home planet. Nervously glancing around, eager to be away, he set one paw against Han's shoulder to get him moving.

The pilot shrugged off the paw. 'Take it easy, will you? This place might still have some stuff we can use. Take a quick look around while I check out that antenna mast.'

The Wookiee shambled off unenthusiastically. He made

a rapid, thorough sweep of the area, discovering no watchers, no tracks, nor any fresh scents.

When Chewbacca returned, Han straightened from his examination of the instrument pods at the mast. 'It runs off some kind of sealed power plant, a little one. It might have started broadcasting yesterday or been going for years and years. I gave the others the signal to come ahead.'

Chewbacca whined unhappily, wanting only to depart from this place. Han was losing patience. 'Chewie, I'm getting tired of this. There's receiver gear here that we can use to check for sensors and get a bearing on J'uoch's mining camp. This thing's been beaming for a whole day at least; if anybody in this miserable solar system were coming, they'd be here by now.' That made the entire installation much more of a curiosity, he had to admit; but he didn't mention it, not wanting to make his towering sidekick any more nervous than he already was.

Badure, Hasti, Skynx, and Zollux soon appeared and, when they had looked over the bogus landing field, voiced surprise and mystification.

'This isn't any part of J'uoch's operation, I'm sure,' Hasti said. Badure didn't add anything, but his expression conveyed discomfort. Skynx's antennae were waving a little erratically, but Han chalked that up to the Ruurian's timidity.

'All right,' the pilot said briskly. 'If we work fast, we'll be out of here inside of an hour. Zollux, I want to patch you and Max in on some of the equipment; one of Max's adaptor arms ought to fit. The rest of you fan out and keep your eyes open. Hey, Skynx, you feeling okay?'

The little Ruurian's antennae were waving even more pronouncedly now. His head wobbled for a moment, then he shook himself. 'Yes, I – felt strange for a second, Captain. Strain of the journey, I should imagine.'

'Well, hang in there, old fellow. You'll make it.' Han started off with the labour droid while the others began spreading out.

Then he heard a panicked squeak and whirled to see Skynx collapse in a multilegged heap, antennae vibrating.

'Stay away from him!' Han shouted.

Hasti fairly jumped back. 'What's happened to him?'

'I don't know, but it's not going to happen to us.' They had too few facts to decide with any accuracy what was wrong with him; it could be a disease, or something natural to his peculiar physiology, perhaps even a part of the Ruurian life cycle. But Han wasn't going to risk having any other living members of the party contaminated. 'Zollux, pick him up; we're pulling out of here. Everybody else, cover.'

They formed a ring, weapons ready, as the labour droid hoisted the small, limp form and held it easily in his gleaming arms. Han barked out instructions. 'Chewie, take the lead.' But as they moved out Han found his own vision becoming blurry.

He shook his head violently, which helped, but a surge of alarm made his breathing more rapid, and his heart began pumping furiously. They had only gone a few more paces when Badure, opening his flight jacket's collar, slurred: 'Whatever it is, I'm in it with Skynx.' He collapsed to the ground without another word, but his eyes remained open, his breathing regular.

Hasti rushed to him, but she, too, was already unsteady on her feet. Chewbacca would have put out a paw to support her, but Han snagged a handful of his partner's pelt and pulled him back. 'No, Chewie. We've got to get clear before it happens to us.' Han knew that they might be able to come back and help the others later, but if they succumbed now, no one was likely to survive.

Without warning, Han's legs gave way. The Wookiee, chugging like a steam engine, shifted his bowcaster to one hand and reached for his friend. His prodigious strength seemed to give him additional resistance to whatever was affecting the others. He considered running for it, for Han's statement that someone must get clear was correct. But the Wookiee code of ethics left no room for desertion. Tugging at his friend, he made a mournful sound.

Chewbacca wrestled his partner's slack body up onto his shoulder. Han, eyes still open, unable to speak, watched dully as the world spun by. Showing his fangs, the Wookiee put one broad foot in front of the other with determination. After a gallant struggle that brought him almost to the edge of the field, Chewbacca sank to his knees, nearly struggled up again, then pitched forward. Han regretted numbly that he couldn't tell his friend what a good try it had been.

Zollux now found himself in a crisis of decision – all actions and inactions pointed to members of the group coming to harm or dying. Resolving a course of action nearly burned out his basic logic stacks. Then the droid put Skynx down, and the Ruurian curled up into a ball by reflex. Zollux began the task of dragging Han Solo to safety. The pilot was, in the droid's evaluation, the one most likely to aid the others by virtue of his talents, turn of mind, and stubbornness.

As it happened, Chewbacca's fall had left Han in a position from which he could see Zollux approach. He wanted to tell the droid to take Chewbacca instead, but could form no words. Han's view of the droid was suddenly blocked by fantastic figures that leaped, capered, and circled around Zollux, gesturing and gibbering at him. They were dressed in bright costumes that were half-uniform, half-masquerade costume, and wore fantastic headgear, elaborate contrivances that suggested both helmet and mask. Even in his stupor Han registered the fact that they carried firearms of diverse types. Han thought them to be humans.

After a quick conference among themselves, the new arrivals began to push, pull, and shoo the distraught droid, forcing him out of Han's field of vision. The pilot was unable to move his head to follow the action.

A masked head thrust in close to him, examining him, but Han couldn't move back or even flinch. The globular mask bore a strong resemblance to a high-altitude or spacesuit helmet, but many of the details of instrumentation, pressure valves, hookups, and couplings were painted on. The air hoses and power-supply cords were useless tubes that dangled and swirled as the mask moved. Unintelligible words in a male human voice rang hollowly.

Han felt himself being lifted, but distantly, as if he had been packed in a crate of dunnage beads. Incidental views showed him that the same was happening to all the others except Zollux, who seemed to have disappeared altogether.

Then came a ride of uncertain duration. The lay of the land and the vagaries of the portage showed Han the rocky ground, Dellalt's blue-white sun, his companions being carried along by other captors, and then the ground again, with no predictability.

At last he saw a gaping hole in the terrain, an entrance to a subsurface area three times the size of the *Falcon*'s main hatch. The boulder that had hidden it was raised on six thick support jacks. Lowered, it would seal and camouflage the hole perfectly, Han knew, because he himself had prowled past it earlier in investigating the area.

Wide pleated hoses had been brought up from beneath the surface. Their pulsations indicated that a gas was being pumped through them, but Han could detect nothing by sight or smell. This was how they had been paralysed, then; he concluded dizzily that the fantastic headgear he had seen contained breathing filters or respirators.

His bearers moved towards the opening. Suddenly darkness swirled all around him. Either he drifted into and out of consciousness or the lighting in the underground area was only intermittent; it was impossible to tell which. He knew that once or twice he caught sight of the sources of illumination: primitive glow-rods arcing over the tunnels, like tracer trails of rockets, in soft colours of blue and green and red.

Han was carried past many rooms that seemed to serve a wide variety of functions. Once he heard sounds of adults chanting, then of children doing the same. There were the rhythms of heavy machinery, whirring turbines and banging switching panels, racing gears and the spitting crackling openings and closings of massive power bars. He smelled foods that were strange to him, and people, with all their various odours.

He tried to concentrate, either to find a way out of his predicament or to experience his last moments fully, but instead kept drifting into passivity.

His first indication that the paralysis was wearing off was when he was unceremoniously dumped onto a cold stone floor; he didn't quite let out a yelp but came close. He hurt where he had hit: his shoulder, back, and rump.

He heard someone – Badure, he thought – groan. Han tried to sit up. A bad mistake; a flare ignited in his forehead. He lay back down, knowing now what had elicited Badure's groan. He clasped his forehead, a major victory of movement, and ran his tongue over his teeth, checking to see if fungus was really growing there.

Suddenly an enormous shaggy face was hovering over him. Chewbacca hauled him up by great fistsful of his flight jacket and sat him up against a large stone. Han's faltering hand went automatically to his holster and found it vacant. That frightened him, but galvanised him as well.

He clamped both hands to his head, whispering so that it wouldn't come apart. 'Best time to escape's the soonest,' he told his first mate. 'Kick the door over and let's leg it.'

His friend *urrff*ed with a disgusted gesture to the door. Han made a major effort and looked up, setting off little shooting stars on the periphery of his vision.

The door was barely discernible, an oblong of stone fitted into the wall so tightly that barely a hairline crack showed. There was a glow-rod on either side of it, but the rest of the room was unlit. Han frisked himself – no tools, no weapons, not even a toothpick.

Badure and Hasti had been dumped together. Skynx was still rolled in a tight ball, but of Zollux there was no sign. The Wookiee plucked Han to his feet, and the pilot moved to one of the glow-rods and pulled it from its socket. The filament retained enough power to run independently for some time. Han moved farther into the chamber, waving the light as he explored; his partner trailed behind, huge fists ready.

'Check the size of this place!' Han found the breath to whisper. The Wookiee grunted. The stone ceiling arced away into the gloom beyond the light. Han came upon row after long row of low stone monoliths, about the height of his sternum, twice as wide as they were high. He couldn't see an end to them.

A voice behind them made both partners jump. 'Where *are* we?' It was Hasti, who had just recovered enough to rise and follow. 'And what are those things? Shelves? Work tables?'

'Runways?' Han added, wincing at the throbbing in his head. 'Paperweights? Who knows? Let's look the rest of this granite gymnasium over.' *At least*, he thought, *moving about would help counteract the paralysis. Best to let the others rest for now.*

But a search of the gargantuan room, which was about the size and shape of a medium spacecraft hangar, yielded no other doors, no other features at all, simply a vast space filled with the stone slabs.

'The whole mountain's probably hollow,' Han conjectured, keeping his voice low. 'But I don't see how those hopping half-wits we saw could've done it.' They started back towards the door.

Chewbacca uttered a low sound.

Han translated. 'He's saying how dry it is in here. You'd expect it to be damp, from condensation if nothing else.' Their footsteps clacked and echoed.

By that time Badure was sitting up and Skynx had uncurled. Interrupting one another with several simultaneous conversations and frequent crossovers, they established the bare facts of what had happened.

'What will they do with us?' Skynx asked, not concealing his trembling.

'Who knows?' Han responded. 'But they took Zollux and Max. I hope those two lads don't end up as drill bits and belt buckles.' He regretted now his own and Chewbacca's abuse of the aircraft mockups on the landing field, and wondered if this was the standard treatment of vandals, recalling the Swimmer Shazeen's comment that few travellers made it through the mountains. 'Anyway, they haven't killed us out of hand; that's one thing in our favour, right?' Skynx did not seem comforted.

'I'm thirsty,' Hasti announced, 'and hungry as a Wookiee.'

'I'll summon room service,' offered Han. 'Marinated range-squab for four, and a few magnums of chilled *T'iil-T'iil?* We'll get the place redecorated while we're at it.'

She snorted. 'You should get the auto-valet, Solo, and feed yourself into it; you look like a jet-juicer just off an eight-day twister.'

Amused, Han glanced at her, giving her a long-suffering smile. Then he sighed and sat down with his back against one of the stone slabs. Chewbacca lowered himself next to Han. 'Hey, partner; forward guard to your centre's flanking slot, six win-lose units.'

Chewbacca fell into deep concentration, chin on fist, envisioning the gameboard match they would be playing on the *Falcon.* Without computer assistance, playing was much more difficult and involved, but it might help pass the time.

Hasti went to stand before the chamber's single door. Han looked up and saw that her shoulders were shaking, as was the glow-rod she held in her hand. He got up and went to comfort her, assuming she was weeping, but she pushed his hand away, and it dawned on him that she was trembling in anger.

Without warning, the girl flung herself at the door, swinging the glow-rod. It burst into splinters and a shower of sparks and blazing shards. She pounded the stone with the stump of the glow-rod, kicking it and beating it with her free hand, ranting maledictions she had learned in a life among the mining camps and factory worlds of the Tion Hegemony.

Han and Badure approached her when the worst of her rage seemed spent. 'Nobody's locking me under some old mountain to rot!' she yelled. She swung randomly at the men with the battered stump of the glow-rod, and they found it more politic to duck than to grapple. 'Part of that treasure's mine, and nobody better try to cut me out of it!'

Puffing, drained, she shuffled over to where the Wookiee sat. Chewbacca had watched the proceedings curiously. Hasti dropped the glow-rod stump and sat down next to the *Millennium Falcon*'s first mate.

Han was about to say something, if only to comment on

111

the intensity of her avarice, when a glissando from Skynx's flute sounded through the room.

The Ruurian still wore his instruments. They had been cradled to his middle, concealed by his woolly coat, when he had curled up. He was tuning them in an absorbed way, shutting out his current distress, having perched on the slab against which Chewbacca and Hasti sat.

Han went to listen while Badure stayed at the door to study it with the remaining glow-rod. In the half-light Skynx played a haunting tune full of longing and loneliness. Han dropped down next to Hasti and together they listened. The music made strange play with the acoustics of the vast space.

Skynx paused. 'This is a song of my home colony, you see. It's called "By the Banks of the Warm, Pink Z'gag." It's played at cocoon-weaving time, when the cycle's crop of larvae gather to go chrysalis. At the same time the previous cycle's cocoons open and the chroma-wings come forth to exude their pheromones, which draw them to one another. The air is sweet and light then; gaiety is there.'

A large globule of emotion-secretion gathered at the corner of each faceted red eye. 'This adventuring has been educational, but most of it is nothing more than danger and hardship a very long way from home. If I were ever to come to the banks of the Z'gag again, I would never leave!' He resumed playing the sad melody.

Hasti, gazing vacantly into the darkness, was dishevelled, but looked attractive nonetheless, nearly as pretty as when she had been gowned and primped onboard the *Falcon*. Han slipped an arm around her and she leaned against him, scarcely noticing him.

'Don't fold until the hand's over,' he encouraged her quietly.

She turned to him with a laboured smile, brushing her dirty fingers against his stubble of beard, tracing the raw scar across his chin. 'You know, this is an improvement, Solo. You're not Slick now, not so smooth and careless.'

He leaned towards her and she didn't turn away. And

112

then he kissed her. There was some question as to who was more surprised. Without parting, they settled into a more comfortable embrace, and gave the kiss serious attention. Skynx's music carried them along.

She shoved herself free at last. 'Han, oh, I – stop it; please, stop!' He retreated, confused. 'The last thing I need is to get involved with you.'

Sounding wounded, he asked, 'What's wrong with me?'

'You run all over people and you never take anything seriously, for starters. You joke through life with that silly smirk on your face, so sure of yourself I want to bounce a rock off your skull!'

She kept him at arm's length. 'Solo, my sister Lanni inherited Dad's Guild book, so she had pilot's status here in the Tion. But I had to work any job I could get. Mess-hand, housegirl, sanit-crew, I've done them all in the camps, the mines, the factories. I've seen your type all my life. Everything's a big laugh, and you can charm the daylights out of people when you feel like it, but you're gone the next day and you never look back. Han, there are no *people* in your life!'

He protested, 'Chewie –'

' – is your friend,' she cut him off, 'but he's a *Wookiee*. And you've got that pair of mechanical cohorts, Max and Zollux, and that hotshot starship of yours, but the rest of us are temporary cargo. Where are the people, Han?'

He started to defend himself, but she overrode him. Chewbacca, intrigued, forgot about his next gameboard move.

'I'm sure you drive the portside girls wild, Solo; you look like you just stepped out of a holo-thriller. But I'm not one of them; never was, never will be.'

She softened a bit. 'I'm no different from Skynx. On my birthworld there's a stretch of land my parents used to own. I'm going to get my cut of the treasure, I swear on my blisters, and buy it back if I have to purchase the whole planet. I'll build a home and take care of Badure, because he took care of Lanni and me. I'll have things of my own and a *life* of my own. I'll share it if I meet the right man, but I'll live without him if I don't. Solo, light housekeeping in a starship isn't my idea of a dream come true!' She drew away from him and went to join Badure, pushing her fingers through the tangles of red hair.

Skynx finished his sad song, then lowered his flute. 'I wish I could see the home colony one more time, the air filled with the chroma-wings and their pheromones and the sounds of their wooing. What would you wish for, Captain Solo?'

Staring absently after Hasti, Han shrugged. 'Stronger pheromones.'

Skynx started. Then, sides rippling, began chortling in the Ruurian version of convulsive laughter, issuing chittering, high-pitched giggles. Chewbacca loosed a sustained howl of amusement, slapping his thigh with a huge paw, his mane shaking. That started Han chuckling ruefully. He reached up and gave Skynx a push; the Ruurian rolled over onto his back, tittering and kicking his short limbs in the air. A guffaw exploded from Badure and even Hasti, shaking her head in exasperation, shared the joke. Chewbacca, blue eyes tearing, slapped Han's shoulder, whereupon the pilot fell sideways, barely able to breathe for laughing.

In the midst of it all, the door swept open.

Zollux was ushered in and the door closed before any of them could do more than gape. In another moment they had congregated around the droid, elbowing one another, their demands for information and their questions interrupting one another's.

After a few seconds Badure shouted everyone down. They quieted, realising he would ask the same questions as they anyway. 'What's happened? Who are those people? What do they want from us?'

Zollux made the strangely human self-effacing sounds he employed in approaching a delicate subject. 'There's rather a surprising story here. It's somewhat complicated. You see, long ago, there was –'

'Come on, Zollux!' Han shouted, cutting through the cybernetic rhetoric, 'What are they going to *do* with us?'

The droid sounded dismayed. 'I know it sounds absurd in this day and age, sir, but unless we can do something, you're all about to become, er, a human sacrifice.'

XII

'By which,' Skynx said with a forlorn hope, 'we may assume you mean *only* humans?'

'Not quite,' Zollux admitted. 'They're not really sure what you and First Mate Chewbacca are, but they've concluded they have nothing to lose by sacrificing you. They're discussing the procedures now.'

The Wookiee growled and Skynx's red eyes glazed. 'Zollux, who *are* these people?' Han demanded.

'They call themselves the Survivors, sir. The signal we picked up was a distress call. They're waiting to be picked up. When I asked them why they didn't simply go to the city, they became very vexed and excited; they harbour a great deal of hatred for the other Dellaltians. I gathered that that animosity is tied up with their religion somehow. They are extreme isolationists.'

'How did you find all this out?' Badure wanted to know. 'Do they speak any Standard?'

'No, sir,' the droid replied. 'They speak a dialect that was prevalent in this section of space prior to the rise of the Old Republic. It was recorded on a language tape in Skynx's material, and Blue Max had stored it along with other information. Of course, I didn't reveal that Max exists; he translated for me in burst-signals and I conducted the conversation.'

'A culture of pre-Republic origins,' pondered Skynx, forgetting to be scared.

'Will you forget the homework?' snapped Hasti, then turned again to Zollux. 'What's all this about sacrifices? Why us?'

'Because they're waiting to be picked up,' said the droid.

'They're convinced that life-form termination enhances the effect of their broadcast.'

'So *we* stumbled in, a major power boost,' mused Han, thinking of all those people who had disappeared in these mountains. 'When's the big sendoff?'

'Late tonight, sir; it has something to do with the stars and is accompanied by considerable ritual.'

We've got just one trump card left, Han thought, then said, 'I think that'll work out just fine.'

Their captors wasted no food or drink on them, which Han loudly proclaimed an indication that they had fallen into the hands of a low-class outfit. But they still had plenty of time to question Zollux.

The mountain warren was indeed a large complex, though it apparently housed what Zollux estimated to be no more than one hundred people living in a complicated family-clan group. Asked why he had been separated from them all, the droid could only say that the Survivors appeared to understand what automata were and held them in some awe. They had been adamant about the need to go forward with the sacrifice, but had bowed to his demands that he be permitted to see his companions.

On the details of the sacrifice Zollux was less clear. Ceremonial objects and equipment were being moved to the surface even as they spoke; the sacrifice was to take place on the mock-up landing field. Although the droid had been unable to locate the confiscated weapons, the captives decided that any attempt at escape would have a better chance of success if made on the surface. Han revealed his plan to the others, vague as it was.

'There are a lot of things that could go wrong,' Hasti protested.

Han agreed. 'The worst of which is getting sacrificed, which will happen anyway. How long until nightfall?'

She consulted her wrist chrono; there were many hours yet. They decided to rest. Chewbacca barked his game-board move to Han, then settled down for a nap. Badure followed suit.

117

Han scowled at the Wookiee, whose gameboard move was extremely unconventional. 'Just because we're going to be sacrificed, you're playing a reckless game now?' The Wookiee flashed his teeth in a self-satisfied grin.

Skynx appeared to be in deep conversation with Zollux, using the obscure dialect the Survivors spoke. Hasti had gone off to commune with her thoughts, and Han decided not to bother her. He wished urgently that the group could take some immediate course of action to dispel any brooding. None was available, so he settled into that – for him – most difficult of all tasks, waiting.

The opening of the door brought Han out of a troubled sleep filled with visions of strangers doing terrible things to the *Millennium Falcon*.

Then, abruptly, Survivors wearing their extravagant costumes dashed into the quiet chamber, carrying glow-rods and weapons, making resistance sheer folly. Their weapons were a fascinating assortment: ancient beam-tubes powered by heavy backpacks, antiquated solid-projectile firearms, and several spring-loaded harpoon guns of the sort that lake men used. Han's worst fear, that the Survivors would use their anaesthetic gas again and thus preclude any action on their captives' part, was unrealised. He found himself breathing easier for that; he had no intention of ending his life passively.

With shouted instructions and gesticulations the Survivors herded their captives out of the chamber. They formed a forward and rear guard, keeping their weapons trained watchfully so there would be no opportunity for mishap. Chewbacca rumbled angrily through it all and nearly turned on one Survivor, who had jabbed the Wookiee with a harpoon gun to hurry him along. Han restrained his friend; all the other Survivors were out of reach, and there was no place to hide in the stone corridors. They had no choice but to move as ordered.

This time Han got a clearer impression of the underground warren. The corridors, like the chamber in which they had been held, were carefully and precisely cut, arranged along an organised central plan, their walls, floors, and ceilings fused solid to serve as support. Thermal plates warmed them, but Han could see no dehumidifying equipment, though he was certain it must exist. Everything implied a technology in excess of what the Survivors seemed capable of fully utilising. Han was willing to bet these capering primitives did simple maintenance by rote and that the knowledge of the original builders had been lost long ago.

He saw unhelmeted Survivors for the first time, mainbreed humans who, aside from an unusual number of congenital defects, were unremarkable. The prisoners passed heated, well-lit hydroponic layouts. The glow-rods and thermal plates in them made Han wonder about the power source; something suitably ancient, he presumed, perhaps even an atomic pile.

Badure's thoughts had been parallelling his own. 'Regression,' the old man said. 'Maybe the base was built by stranded explorers, or early colonists?'

'That wouldn't explain their unreasoning shunning of the other Dellaltians,' Skynx put in. 'They must have taken elaborate precautions to avoid notice all this time, even in these desolate –'

He was silenced when a Survivor singled him out with the end of a beam-tube, gesturing with unmistakable fury. Conversation stopped. Han saw that Zollux had been right; the warren had clearly been built for many more people than now occupied it. In some stretches light and heat had been shut down to conserve power or had failed altogether.

They passed a room from which odd, rhythmic sounds issued. For just an instant when he drew even with the doorway, Han had a view of the interior.

Coloured lights strobed in the darkness, flashing on the walls and ceiling in arresting swirls and patterns. Someone was chanting in the Survivors' tongue; underscoring the chant was the pulsing of a transonic synthesizer, as much felt as heard.

Han almost stopped short and had to step quickly to keep from being jabbed with a harpoon, thinking, *Hypno-*

imprinting! Crude version, but completely effective if you catch your subjects early enough. Poor kids. It explained a lot.

Then they felt cold night air on their faces and their breath crystallised before them. They left the Survivors' warren by a different door than that by which they had entered.

The mockup landing field was a different sight in the night than it had been during the day; it was now a scene of barbaric ceremony. The stars and Dellalt's two moons brightened the sky; glow-rods and streaming torches lit the entire area, reflected by the sides of the dummy aircraft. At the edge of the ritual field, by the steep snowfield that sloped to the valley below, a large cage had been erected, a pyramid of bars, assembled piecemeal. Its door was a thick, solid plate, its lock in the centre, inaccessible from within the cage.

Near the cage was a circle of gleaming metal, broader than Han was tall, suspended from a framework, suggesting an enormous gong. It was inscribed with lettering of an unfamiliar type, consisting of whorls and squares alternating with dots and ideographs.

Closer in, towards the centre of the light, was a wide metal table, a medi-lab appurtenance of some kind. Near it were piled the prisoners' weapons and other equipment. The implication of the table hit them at once: a sacrificial altar.

Han was ready to make a break then and there; the pyramidal cage seemed firmly anchored to the rock, so sturdy that even Chewbacca's thews wouldn't prevail against it. But the Survivors had been through this procedure before. They were alert and careful, with weapons trained in clear lines of fire. Han noticed that the muzzles and harpoons were pointed toward the captives' legs. If the scheduled sacrificees made any wrong moves, the Survivors could shoot and still not be deprived of their ritual.

This decided the pilot against any immediate action. There was still a chance his plan would work, provided Zollux and Blue Max were flexible enough to adapt to circumstances as they arose. The droid was separated from the rest of them, complying with their captors as Han had instructed him.

The other captives were chivvied to the cage, ushered to the circular door plate that swung open on oiled hinges. It took every scrap of Han's resolve to enter the pyramid; once inside he stood there closely watching the Survivors' preparations.

The strange people were decked out in their finest garb. Now that he understood a little more about them, Han could interpret the Survivors' costume. A ground-crewman's blast-suit had become, over generations, an insect-eyed getup. Spacesuit speaker grilles had evolved into pointy-fanged mouths painted on imitation helmets; communication antennae and broadcast directors were represented by elaborate spikes and antlers of metal. Back tanks and suit packs were adorned with symbolic designs and mosaics, while tool belts were hung with fetishes, amulets, and charms of all kinds.

The Survivors whirled, leaped, and tootled their instruments, striking finger chimes and drums. Two of them beat the great wheel of metal with padded mallets, the gongings resounding back and forth across the valley.

With the prisoners' arrival, things began to build towards a climax. A man mounted a rostrum that had been set near the altar. A silence fell.

The man wore a uniform festooned with decorations and braid; his trousers were seamed with golden cloth. He wore a hat that was slightly small for him, its military brim glittering with giltwork, a broad, flashing medallion riding its high crown. Two aides set a small stand on the rostrum beside him. It held a thick circle of transparent material about the size of a mealplate.

'A log-recorder disk!' exclaimed Skynx. The others competed to ask him if he was sure. 'Yes, yes; I've seen one or two, you know. But the *Queen of Ranroon's* is back in the treasure vaults, is it not? What one is that, then?'

No one could answer. The man on the rostrum regaled the crowd, delivering loud phrases that they echoed back to him, applauding, whistling, and stomping their feet. Flickering torchlight made the scene seem even more primeval.

'He's saying they've been a good and faithful people, that the proof is there with him on the rostrum, and that the High Command won't forget them,' Skynx translated.

Han was amazed. 'You understand that garble?'

'I learned it as Zollux did, from the data tapes, a pre-Republic dialect. Can they have been here that long, Captain?'

'Ask the Chamber of Commerce. What's he saying now?'

'He said he's their Mission Commander. And something about mighty forces afoot; the rescue they've been promised will surely come soon. I – something about their generations of steadfastness, and deliverance by this High Command. The crowd keeps chanting "Our signal will be received." '

With a final tirade the Mission Commander gestured to the pyramidal cage. Until now Zollux had stood to one side of the proceedings, surrounded by grey-clad, masked Survivors who chanted and rattled prayer clackers at him, descendants of techs entrusted with maintenance of machinery.

But now the droid broke out of their ring, moving quickly to take advantage of the surprise he had caused. He crossed to stand with his back to the pyramid's door. The Survivors who had been about to fetch their first victim for the 'transmission' wavered, still awed by the automaton. The droid hadn't been able to secure a weapon, a departure from Han's vague plan but felt that he could wait no longer to make his move. Even in the rush of events Han wondered about the origin of the Survivors' reverence for mechanicals. Surely there had never been a droid or robot through these mountains before?

The Mission Commander was exhorting his followers. Zollux, his photoreceptors glowing red in the night, slowly opened the halves of his chest plastron. Blue Max, carefully coached by the labour droid, activated his own photoreceptor, playing it across the crowd. Han heard sounds of indrawn breath among the Survivors.

Max switched from optical scanning to holoprojection mode. A cone of light sprang from him; there hovered in the air an image he had recorded off Skynx's tapes, the symbol of Xim the Despot, the grinning death's head with the starburst in each black eye socket. From his vocoder came recorded tech readouts from the tapes in the language of the Survivors.

The crowd drew back, many of them thrusting their thumbs at Zollux to fend off evil. Max put forth more images he had taken from the information Skynx had compiled: an ancient fleet of space battlewagons in flight against the stars; the brilliance of a full-scale engagement with exploding missiles, flaring cannonfire, and probing lasers; battle standards passing in review, displaying unit colours that had been forgotten long ago. The entire time, the droid was surreptitiously edging to the pyramidal cage's door. While the crowd was riveted to Max's performance, Zollux manipulated the door's handle behind his back.

A yell went up from the assembled Survivors just as Zollux succeeded in throwing the bolt on the stubborn lock. Blue Max had projected a holo of the war-robot's cranial turret that Skynx had brought onboard the *Millennium Falcon*. Max held the image, capitalising on their response, rotating it to show all sides. The Survivors jabbered animatedly among themselves, moving back from the frightening ghost-holo. Zollux stepped away from the cage door.

Max began running through all the other visual information he had stored about Xim's war-robots. Schematics, manual-extracts, records of the ponderous combat machines in motion, closeup details of construction, and full-length views. All the while, Zollux moved slowly forward. Step by step the crowd yielded ground, seemingly hypnotised by Max's projections. In the excitement and poor light nobody noticed that the cage door was now unlocked.

'He may not be able to hold them much longer,' Han whispered. Zollux was now at the centre of a near-circle of Survivors.

'Time to jump,' Badure said.

Han agreed. 'Make your way to the edge of the field. Nobody stops for anybody else, understood?'

Hasti, Badure, and even Skynx nodded. Unarmed, they could do little except run from the Survivors. Each individual would be responsible for his own life; stopping to give aid would be suicidal and expected of no one.

Han swung the door open slowly and stepped through. Shouting, gesticulating Survivors were still occupied with Zollux. The Mission Commander had left his rostrum to try to make his way through the crowd to Zollux, but was having trouble making headway through the press of his own people. Han waited while the others emerged.

Chewbacca slipped through the door and moved off like a shadow. Badure moved with less agility, then Hasti. Skynx exited and set off at once for the edge of the field. Low to the ground, he was nearly impossible to see. The Ruurian didn't pause or look back; he adhered to Han's directions completely, having acquired some of the necessary makeup of an adventurer. Han moved around the end of the cage to bring up the rear. He nearly backed into Hasti. 'Where's Badure?' she mouthed silently.

They couldn't spot him at first, then made out the old man as he nonchalantly strolled around the edge of the crowd, heading for the abandoned altar where the weapons lay. No one paid him any heed; all of them were transfixed by Max's holos of a war-robot being put through its paces, firing weapons, and lumbering through basic infantry tactics.

'He's going for the guns,' Han whispered. Chewbacca, who had also paused, stood with them, watching the old man's progress.

'We can't help him now; he either makes it or not. We'll wait at the edge of the field as long as we can.' He didn't know if he was happy Badure was trying for their weapons, feeling naked and helpless without his blaster, or dismayed that the old man was risking his life.

Just then a Survivor sentry, coming in off his post, stepped out of the darkness and nearly stumbled over Skynx. The

124

Ruurian chirped in fear and went into reverse. The guard's eyes bulged in amazement at the woolly, many-legged creature, then he fumbled for the flame-rifle at his shoulder, crying out an alarm.

A shaggy arm reached out and the weapon was snatched from his hands. Chewbacca's fist shot through the air and the guard was lifted, stretched out stiff as a post, to fall on the landing field, his left foot quivering.

People on the fringe of the crowd had heard the guard and repeated the alarm. Heads turned; in a moment the shout was taken up by many voices. Han ran, took the bell-mouthed flame-rifle, and slewed it in a wide, horizontal arc. A wash of orange fire streamed over the heads of the crowd. Survivors dropped to the ground, grabbing for their weapons and screaming conflicting orders at one another. Han could hear the shrieking Mission Commander trying futilely to bring order out of chaos.

Badure, having reached the altar, was out of the crowd's immediate line of sight. He shouldered Chewbacca's bowcaster and bandoleer of ammunition and began tucking weapons into his belt.

Shots were now being pegged across the field at them. 'Keep out of the way!' hollered Han, elbowing Chewbacca behind him. He backed slowly, covering the withdrawal and creating a diversion for Badure. He directed his discharges into the ground between himself and the massed Survivors, making puddles of fire to spoil their aim and sending intermittent streamers of flame over them to force their heads down. A line of tracer bullets chewed up the field a metre or two to his right, and a pale particle beam barely missed his head.

The escapees needed cover badly, but their section of the field was open and offered none. Chewbacca, with sudden inspiration, ran for the gong and, back and arm muscles swelling with effort, lifted it from its support hooks, his widespread arms grabbing it by two carrying handles welded to its back.

The slugs, beams, and flames of the firefight dissected the air. The Survivors' shots were gaining in accuracy, though they weren't used to such a pitched battle. Badure, running in a low crouch to work his way back to his companions, was spotted by the crowd. Somebody let fly with an old rocket pistol, blowing up a clod of stone in his path. In a frantic effort to change course, Badure lost his balance, and Survivors' shots began to converge on him.

Chewbacca grounded the gong in front of Han as he and the others took shelter behind it. Projectile and energy weapons splashed and ricocheted from the shield; whatever the gong was made of, it was very durable material.

Han blazed away at the Survivors to keep them from pressing the attack against Badure. He had been spending the flame-rifle's ammo recklessly and knew he might soon find himself defenceless. Badure, struggling to rise, was having trouble. The Survivors' aim was zeroing in on him now, and he returned the fire as well as he could.

I warned him, thought Han. *Life-Debt or no, it's everyone for himself.* He had trouble selling the idea to himself, though.

Then the decision was taken from him. Issuing a deafening Wookiee battle cry, Chewbacca moved off, holding up the gong to protect himself. Han looked back and saw that Hasti and Skynx were watching him. The girl, he thought, would surely run to help Badure if he didn't.

'Don't just stand there,' he snarled. 'Get to cover!' He gave her a shove towards the edge of the field and dashed off the other way, laying down heavy fire as he sprinted, zig-zagging after the Wookiee.

'You crazy fur-face!' he roared at his first mate when he had caught up to him. 'What're you doing, playing captain again?' Chewbacca took a moment from angling and manoeuvring the gong for an irritated, explanatory growl.

'Life-Debt?' Han exploded, dodging around his friend into the open to snap off a pair of quick shots. 'And who pays up if you lose us *ours?*'

But he maintained his fire, sideskipping along behind the straining, gong-toting Wookiee and bounding from cover to either side of him to get off a shot or two. Flames lit the scene, and the air was smoky and hot from the firefight. The flame-rifle's discharges were growing weaker, and its range was decreasing.

Skirting a section of field torn and ruptured by the battle, they finally reached Badure, who was pressed down flat on the ground, shooting with the pair of long-barrelled power pistols. Chewbacca heaved the gong between the old man and the oncoming shots. Han coaxed a last feeble flicker from the flame-rifle, then threw it aside. Dropping to one knee, he helped Badure up. 'Last bus is leaving now, Lieutenant-commander.'

'I'll take a one-way on that,' panted Badure, adding, 'glad you could make it, boys.'

Han snagged his own blaster from Badure's belt, and a sudden confidence steadied him. He stepped into the clear, crouched low, and let off a series of quick shots. Two Survivor marksmen who had been taking careful aim with heavy-particle beamers fell away in different directions, their wounds smoking.

Han ducked back, waited a beat, then stepped into the open again on the same side of the gong, eluding the aim of those who had been waiting to see him emerge on the opposite side. His bolts dropped two more enemies from the ragged firing line. But Survivor flankers could be seen in the wavering light, fanning out to either side in an effort to cut off retreat.

'Let's jump!' Han cried. Chewbacca began back-pedalling, still holding the gong, and headed for the field's edge as Badure and Han kept up the most intense fire they could, pinning down the Survivors facing them and impeding the flankers. Their energy weapons lit the night, answered by bullets, blaster bolts, needles, harpoons, particle beams, and gushes of flame. Han occasionally assisted the Wookiee's progress with a judicious shove.

Someone came towards them. Badure nearly burned the silhouetted form before Han batted the power pistol aside. 'Zollux! Over here!'

The droid somehow made it to the gong's cover; they withdrew step by hotly contended step. A group of

Survivor flankers was nearly in position to enfilade them, crouching by the antenna mast. Badure held both long-barrelled weapons up side by side and fired at the flankers. Men fell and the instrument shorted out; the mast's power supply was drained in a swirl of energy, and the mast fell, wreathed in crackling discharges. It crashed into the rostrum and rostrum, frame, and log-recorder disk went up in flames.

Han heard his name called. Skynx and Hasti crouched at the edge of the field. Firing and scrambling, the others joined them.

'We can't retreat down that snowfield; it's too steep,' Hasti declared, 'and even Chewbacca couldn't carry that gong down. We'd make perfect targets out there.'

Han dealt out a few more shots, pondering her reasoning and their lack of alternatives. Then Chewbacca, surveying the situation, barked a quick scheme to him.

'Partner, you *are* crazy,' Han exclaimed, not without a certain respect. But he saw no nonfatal alternative. 'What's keeping us?' He pulled the others closer and explained the plan. They readied themselves, having no time for fear or doubts.

Then Han yelled, 'Chewie! Go!' The Wookiee back-pedalled to the edge of the field, whirled, stooped, and laid the concave gong down, its curved surface indenting the hard, icy snowfield. Han fired furiously.

Badure dropped awkwardly onto the gong and grabbed a carrying handle. Zollux climbed onto the opposite side of the rim, locking servo-grips onto two more handles. Skynx swarmed aboard and clung tightly around the droid's neck, antennae flailing. Hasti braced herself next to Badure, and Chewbacca had to brace his broad feet in the snow at the tug of the gong's weight.

Han still stood, keeping up a heavy volume of fire. He shouted, 'I'll pile on last!'

Chewbacca didn't take time to argue; he swept out one long arm, gathered his friend in like a child, and threw himself onto the gong. Shots from the Survivor flankers crisscrossed overhead. The Wookiee's impetus and weight gave them a quick start.

The gong gathered speed, spinning and sliding as it cut along the icy slope. Chewbacca lifted his head and uttered a foghorn-like hoot of elation, to which Skynx added a *'Wee-ee hee-ee!'*

The gong tilted and rotated to the left as it swished across the snow. Chewbacca threw his weight the other way; they bounced and slid on a fairly even keel for a few seconds, then hit a small rock outcropping in the snowfield.

They were airborne, all hands seeking a grip and flailing to stay aboard; to fall from the gong now and slide the rest of the way without protection would mean severe laceration by ice shards and shattered bones from the hardened patches and rocks.

They came down again with a breath-stealing jolt; everyone, miraculously, contrived to cling to the bucking, jarring gong. Han grabbed Hasti, who, in helping Badure, had nearly lost her own grip. The *Falcon's* master encircled her waist with his free arm while she clenched a handful of Badure's flight jacket. Badure, in turn, had locked legs with Chewbacca, helping the Wookiee steer by leaning and tugging at the handles. Chewbacca, like the others, could barely see; their headlong speed through the icy air had stung everyone's eyes to tears and was numbing their exposed skin.

In leaning abruptly to the side, the Wookiee succeeded in guiding their mad descent around a prow of stone that would have smashed them all, but in the process he lost his balance. Zollux quickly shifted his central torsional member and secured his legs around the *Falcon's* first officer's.

Badure held onto Chewbacca, too, reaching out with a free hand to help steady the Wookiee. But in doing so he saw he was about to lose Chewbacca's bowcaster and bandoleer. He cried out, his words stolen instantly by the wind, but Han was busy clinging to a handle and hanging onto Hasti and she to Badure, while Badure and Zollux were committed to keeping Chewbacca aboard. Meanwhile, the Wookiee devoted all his attention to what could only in the most ludicrous sense be termed 'steering.'

And so Skynx, facing the fact that only he was free to act, released his grip on the droid with all but his last set of limbs. He was dragged around at once, very nearly snapped like a whip, reaching with his free extremities. Just as Badure's scrabbling efforts to hang onto the bowcaster failed, Skynx got close enough to grasp the weapon and was abruptly thrown in the other direction as the gong changed course again.

The small Ruurian now clung to his only mainstay, Zollux, by the digits of his lowermost limbs, which clenched precariously on the droid's shoulder pauldron. But he determinedly hung onto the weapon and ammunition, knowing they might be needed badly and that there was no one to catch them if he failed. With each bump and rotation of the gong, Skynx felt his grip loosening, but he hugged his burden resolutely. One by one, he began to find purchase for his other limbs. Chewbacca felt him fumbling, shifted his leg as much as he was able, and Skynx managed to fasten two sets of limbs to the Wookiee's thick knee.

They were at the steepest part of the insane plunge, shearing through the snowfield, rocking in furrows, and smashing out of depressions in the surface. Several times Han saw energy beams of various hues register hits in the snow, but always far wide of their mark. *As targets go, we must be pretty fast and furious.*

He clung doggedly, fingers, ears, and face numbed by the cold, eyes streaming a constant flow of tears. 'My fingers are slipping!' cried Hasti with unmasked fear. 'I can't feel them.'

Han knew with a sense of utter futility that he could do little to help her. He gripped her as tightly as he could, hoping that his frozen fingers would hold.

Badure yelled, 'We're slowing down!' Chewbacca bellowed pure joy. Hasti began to half-laugh, half-sob.

The gong had reached a gentler portion of the slope close to the foot of the snowfield and was losing speed moment by moment. The bumps and jolts became less dramatic, the spinning less pronounced. In seconds they were coasting.

'An excellent job, First Mate Chewbacca,' Zollux was saying, when suddenly the gong's rim hit a slab of rock that lifted it into the air like a jump ramp. Frozen hands, servo-grips, Ruurian digits, and Wookiee toes, all lost their final struggle. The gong threw them free. Human bodies, the tubular Skynx, a yeowling Chewbacca, and gleaming Zollux sailed through the air on assorted trajectories, cartwheeling, tumbling, spinning – and falling.

XIII

Han heard the whine of servo-motors over the moan of wind. From where he lay, mostly buried by the mound of snow he had scraped up on his landing approach, he could see Zollux draped belly-up over a low snowbank. The halves of the droid's chest plastron opened up and outward.

Blue Max's vocoder blustered. 'Hey! Let's get moving; we're not out of it yet!'

A drift to Han's right sloughed and erupted. Chewbacca appeared, spitting out snow and rumbling an acid remark to the diminutive computer module.

'No, he's right,' Han groaned to his partner. He raised himself on unsteady arms and gazed up the slope, foggily curious about whether his head was actually going to fall off or if it simply felt that way. A bobbing column of lights was wending its way down the snowfield from the Survivor's base. Their former captors were in hot pursuit.

'The short circuit's right on the money, folks; everybody up!' Han thrashed and floundered in the snow for a moment, then pulled himself to his feet and began beating his hands together to bring some sensation back.

Hasti was also struggling up. Han caught her hand and pulled her to her feet. She ran over to see to Badure. Chewbacca had just reclaimed his bowcaster and bandoleer from Skynx, whom he had dug free. The Wookiee growled his gratitude, patting and stroking the Ruurian's woolly back in a gruff gesture of thanks.

Hasti was chafing Badure's hands and wrists, trying to get him upright. Han moved to help and saw that the tip of the old man's nose and patches on his cheeks were whitened.

'He's getting frostbite. On deck, Trooper; time to depart the area.' They pulled him up. Meanwhile, with Chew-

132

bacca's help, Zollux was once more upright.

Counting heads before striking off, Han spied Skynx bent over the gong, which had fallen face up, a flattened dome in the snow. The Ruurian was making minute examination of the whorls and patterns on the ancient metal, labouring to see in the light of moons and stars. When Han called him, the academician yelled back, 'I think you'd better see this first, Captain.'

They all gathered around him. His small digits traced the raised characters. 'I thought I recognised these when I first saw this object, but I was too hurried to study them. All these,' a splay of digits indicated groups of characters, 'are technical notation and operating instructions. They have to do with pressure equalisation and fastening procedures.'

'Then it comes from a hatch,' Badure concluded, his muffled voice coming through hands cupped to thaw out his cheeks and nose. 'Some kind of decorative facing off an airlock hatch, a big one.'

Skynx agreed. 'A peculiar and rather ostentatious appointment, but that is the case. Those several larger characters there in the centre give the vessel's name.' He turned bulbous red eyes to them. 'It's the *Queen of Ranroon*!'

In the middle of a tumult of voices – human, non-human, and electronic – Han stood imagining the treasure of entire worlds. Though cold, near exhaustion, pursued, and starved, he suddenly found himself charged with limitless energy and a dramatic determination to live and to claim the *Queen*'s wealth.

They were interrupted. Han's thoughts and the confused conversations springing from Skynx's revelation were cut short by a long note sounding in the night, a wail from a hunting horn or other signalling device.

That brought them all up short. The bobbing lights of the pursuing Survivor's column were now well down the slope. Now and then one would drop from the line and disappear as its bearer lost footing on the treacherous snowfield and fell tumbling.

Led by Han, the escapees set out in a staggering string, helping one another as well as they could; fortunately, the

133

snow wasn't very deep. They reached down to scoop up handfuls of the stuff to melt in their mouths, trying to relieve the dehydration of their captivity. Beating his gloved hands together, Han considered what the hatch cover might mean. Were the Survivors guarding Xim's treasure in their mountain warren? What had become of the *Queen of Ranroon*?

Hasti caught up to him in the struggling line of march. 'Solo, I've been doing some thinking. The congregation back there isn't just tooting their horns to hear the echoes and let us know they're coming. I think they have patrols out and are calling the forces out on us.'

He stopped, deriding himself for having been pre-occupied with the treasure. Hasti repeated her reasoning to the others. 'We're not too far from the snow line,' Badure observed. 'Perhaps that's the limit to their territory.'

Han shook his head. 'We messed up church for them and left quite a few of them in some pain. They're coming for blood and they won't stop just because the snow does. We'd better take up a better formation. Chewie, walk the point.'

The Wookiee padded off quietly; cold and snow didn't bother him. Protected by his thick pelt, he slipped off, keeping to the cover of the increasingly frequent rocks and boulders. The others followed more slowly in his wake, slowed because they were bereft of his giant, supportive strength.

But within minutes the Wookiee was back to draw them down into the cover of a particularly large boulder and tell Han, in quick gutterals, what he had encountered.

'There's more of them, coming up this way,' Han translated. 'Chewie thinks we can hide here and wait them out. When they're past, we go on. Still and quiet, everybody.'

They waited for oppressive minutes, straining to make no noise, no shift of position or other movement that might betray them. Han slowly turned his head to check the progress of the Survivors from their base. The lights had made their way to the gentler part of the slope and fanned out for a ground search.

There was a slight sound, the smallest movement of rock and crunch of ice. Everyone tensed. A shape moved stealthily into view, keeping to available cover. The approaching

Survivor was uncostumed but wore a hood and heavy clothing. The scout's head turned slowly, searching the area carefully as he went. Moments later another sentinel appeared, farther across the valley on a parallel course.

Han thought he understood. The valley widened abruptly from here, and a few sentries, farther along, might not be able to stop the escapees from getting past. The sentries kept moving warily. When they were well past the escapees' position, Han – using hand-touches to alert his companions and dictate the order of march – slipped out from behind the boulder. The servo-motors of Zollux's body were smooth and quiet, but sounded unbearably loud to Han. He could only hope the sound didn't carry over the wind and other noises in the night.

They had wound their way among the rocks for another half kilometre and got out of sight of the snowfield and Han had just begun to let himself believe they were clear, when a yellow heatbeam flashed out of the night. It scored on a rock two metres to Zollux's right, throwing up sparks and globs of molten mineral.

Chill, shivers, frozen feet, and caution were forgotten. Everybody scattered for cover. Hasti brought her disruptor pistol up for a return shot but Han whispered, 'Don't! He'll pick up your position from the flash. Anybody see where the shot came from?' Nobody had. 'Then sit still. When he fires again, we'll nail him. Aim for the point of origin.'

'Solo, we haven't got time to sit here!' Hasti rasped fiercely.

'Then start tunnelling,' he suggested.

But instead she groped, found a stone that fit her palm, and heaved it. It clattered among the loose rocks. Another heatbeam flashed yellow from the shadows at the side of the valley.

Han fired instantly and kept on firing. The others, slower than he, joined a moment later with a torrent of blaster, power pistol, disruptor, and bowcaster shots.

'Hold it, hold it,' Han ordered. 'I think we got him.'

'Do we move on?' asked Badure.

Han didn't think the light and reports of the shots would

have been detectable back on the slopes. 'Not yet. We have to be sure we won't get backshot. Besides, I saw a gleam of metal where the heatbeams came from. Maybe there's a vehicle there, or some supplies.' He shivered from the mountain air. 'Anything'd be a help.'

'Then someone must investigate,' Skynx declared and was away before anybody could stop him, flowing between the rocks with his antennae held low, nearly impossible to see. *I'll have to warn him about those heroics,* Han thought, *he's come a long way.* To break the tense silence, he whispered to Badure, 'See what happens? First you go off medal-chasing to get our weapons back and now Skynx figures he's the valiant warrior.'

The old man chuckled softly. 'The guns came in handy, didn't they? Besides, it gave Chewbacca a chance to pay back his Life-Debt.'

Han blinked. 'That's right. Hey, what do you mean Chewbacca? We *both* came back for you!' Badure only laughed.

Just then Skynx called excitedly, 'Captain! Over here!' They went, slipping and stumbling with haste but still keeping low. They came to an overhang of rock, having to duck to pass under it. From the black regions within issued Skynx's voice. 'I found a glow-rod, Captain Solo. I'll turn up the rheostat a bit.' A faint glimmer showed them the Ruurian's face.

He had found a low, wide cave that reached in farther than they could see. The body of the single sentry was sprawled in death, hit by several of their blasts. But what excited Skynx was what had been under guard there.

'Look, a cargo lifter!' Han took the glow-rod. 'Hover-raft of some kind.' He climbed into the open cockpit of the flatbed aircraft. 'Looks like it was on down time; there're a lot of burned-out components on the floorboards, and the control-panel covers are still off.'

He brightened the glow-rod. There were two more hover-rafts nearby, access panels open, gutted and cannibalised for the parts that had gone to repair the first. Han slid the notched hover bar down; the craft rose a bit.

He flicked controls; the board was clear. 'Hop in; my meter's running.'

They rushed to comply, ducking to keep from bumping heads on the cave ceiling. With one foot on a mounting step, Badure paused. 'What was that?'

They all heard it – the sounds of running, voices, and the clatter of weapons. 'Hot pursuit,' answered Han. 'No time to punch tickets, folks: stay gripped!'

He rammed up the impeller control, red-zoning the engine. The hover-raft out of the cave, nearly losing Zollux, who had been in the process of boarding. Badure and Chewbacca dragged him aboard.

The Survivors were closer than Han had thought; they had assumed positions around the cave and were closing in on it. The hover-raft zoomed from the cave near ground level, engines complaining. One or two Survivors had the presence of mind to shoot as the raft flashed by, but most either stood frozen or sought a lower elevation to keep from being run down. The few shots went wild, and Hasti put out a few rounds at random to keep the Survivors' heads down. The raft tore through a wide arc and headed down the valley.

'Where to, citizens?' Han grinned.

'Just turn on the heaters!' yelled Hasti.

The valley widened quickly, then gave way down to an open plain carpeted with bobbing, spindly amber grass. The hover-raft was equipped with rudimentary navigational gear. Han set a course for J'uoch's mining camp. Not wanting to use the raft's running lights, he cut his speed back and peered through the windshield, thankful it was a bright night.

The wind of their passage snatched the warmth out of the heater grids. Hasti discovered a folded tarp in one corner of the cargo bed and pulled at it, but stopped and called to the others. 'Look at what they had onboard!'

Han couldn't turn from his steering, but Chewbacca, sitting next to him, pulled a handful of the tarp over the back of the driver's seat. Carefully fastened to the tarp were strands of plastic, meticulously fashioned to look like the amber grass of the plains. A camouflage cover.

'This crate comes equipped with an aerial-sensor, too,' Han noted. 'With a little warning and time to cover up, this thing would be just about impossible to spot without first-rate equipment.' And the cave had been big enough to hold more rafts like this one. But that left the question of how a group of primitives like the Survivors, on a back-eddy planet like Dellalt, had set up an operation like this.

Han slowed just enough for Chewbacca to wrestle the collapsible canopy into place. They crowded onto the short couches of the cramped pilot-passenger compartment, lit by the glow of the dashboard instruments and Zollux's photo-receptors. Outside, the moons and stars lit a sea of waving grassland as it blurred under the raft's darkened bow. Eventually the heaters made some headway, and Han opened his flight jacket.

Badure sighed. 'If that was the *Queen*'s log-recorder disk back there, we can write it off. The antenna mast destroyed it completely.'

Han posed the question: 'But how did the Survivors get it in the first place? I thought it was back in the vaults.'

'They were talking like it's been theirs all along,' Hasti put in, shifting in a futile attempt to find more room between Zollux and Badure in the back seat.

Skynx, in his best classroom voice, chimed in. 'The facts, as we know them, are as follows. Lanni somehow obtained the log-recorder disk and deposited it in a lockbox in the vaults. She evinced an interest in the mountains. J'uoch discovered her secret, or some part of it, and killed Lanni in trying to obtain the disk. And, here were the Survivors with either the same disk or one identical to it.

'Now, Lanni was a pilot, flying freight and operational missions, isn't that right? Suppose she happened to be air-borne when the Survivors were holding one of their outdoor ceremonies, and either traced their signal or saw the light?'

Han nodded. 'She could've landed somewhere, scouted, and bagged the log-recorder!' He trimmed the craft and corrected its course a bit.

Hasti agreed. 'She could have. Dad taught her to fly, and a lot about wilderness survival and reconnaissance.'

Badure picked up the thread. 'So she put the disk in the lockbox and stopped off across the lake to see if she could detect a bounce or signal leakage or find out anything about the Survivors' base, or if she'd stirred them up. I bet the treasure's back there under the mountain.'

They rode in silence for a time. Then Han spoke: 'That would only leave two questions: how to get the *Falcon* back . . and how to spend all that money.'

Han's best efforts failed to nurse much speed from the antiquated raft. He kept the airwatch sensor on, depressed as low to the horizon astern as possible, but he detected no pursuit. He was still unsatisfied, having come up with no conclusions as to what the Survivors had been doing with those cargo craft, what the hatch face off the *Queen of Ranroon* actually meant, or how it was all connected with the treasure.

Dellalt's sun set off a purple dawn; grassland disappeared under the hover-raft's bow. They had nearly crossed the basin of grassland formed by a curve in the mountain range and were bearing toward the mining camp when Zollux leaned over the driver's seat and said, 'Captain, I've been making communication monitoring sweeps as you ordered, listening for activity on the Survivors' frequency.'

Han immediately became anxious. 'Are they on the air?'

'No,' answered the droid. 'After all, their antenna mast was destroyed. But I also checked other frequencies mentioned in Skynx's tapes, and I've found something peculiar. There are transmissions on a very unusual setting coming from the direction of the campsite. They're odd because, although I can't pick them up clearly, they appear to be cyber-command signals.'

Han's brow furrowed. Automata-command signals? Mining equipment?' he asked the droid.

'No,' answered Zollux. 'These aren't the usual heavy-equipment patterns or industrial signals.'

Badure turned the raft's commo rig to the setting Zollux

had been monitoring but was unable to pick up anythin
clearly. Taking a bearing from the droid, Han change
course minutely and made a slow approach toward th
mountains. Setting the airwatch sensor to full-scan, h
readied Chewbacca and the others to pull the camouflag
tarp over the raft at a moment's notice.

He came in slowly, taking his direction from the droic
They had already walked into one trap by investigatin
signals and, though it was important that they find out wha
these new ones meant, Han had no intention of bein
ambushed a second time. He lowered the raft's lift facto
until it was bending the grass down, barely clearing th
ground.

'Signals strengthening, Captain,' advised Zollux.

They were approaching a rise in the plains, a ripple in th
landscape preliminary to the sloping of the mountains. Ha
settled the hover-raft in behind the rise and got out of th
craft. Parting the grass delicately, he and Chewbacca belly
crawled to the crest to have a look.

Less than a kilometre away the foothills began. Ha
squinted through his blaster's scope. 'There's somethin
down there, where that gully comes down to the plain.'

The Wookiee agreed. They withdrew with care and tol
the others what they had seen. Sunrise was near.

'Skynx and Hasti, take lookout on the rise,' Han directec
'Zollux and Badure, guard the raft. Chewie and I will mov
in; you all know the signal system. If you have to get out, a
least you've got a boat now.' None of them made an
objections, though Hasti looked as if she wanted to.

The *Millennium Falcon*'s captain and first mate split off t
the right and left of the rise, moving stealthily through th
tall, amber grass, each of them keeping careful count in hi
mind. They had worked together so often that the
automatically orchestrated their moves, without benefit c
chrono or signal.

Han swept left, approaching the anomaly in the terrai
that had attracted his attention. As he had thought, th
lumps at the base of the foothills were a cluster c
camouflage covers, a little too sudden and consolidated t

be a part of the landscape. He saw no sentries or patrols, nor surveillance of any kind, and so changed course to his right.

He heard something in the grass that might have been a small insect's buzz; the sound scarcely travelled a few metres. Han assumed his partner's signal had been sounding for a while.

He homed to it, parted a tuft of grass, and met his copilot with a grin. They talked in quick hand-motions; Chewbacca's recon had yielded the same results as Han's – with one addition: there was a guard, evidently a Survivor, walking a slow post. They made their plan and moved forward again. Han's first inclination was to use the stungun carried by Badure, but there was too much chance that someone would hear the discharge or see the blue light of the shot.

The sentry was dressed in common Dellaltian mode rather than in Survivor garb. He strolled along his circuit carelessly, armed with a Kell Mark II Heavy Assault Rifle. He carried the Kell at a sloppy shoulder angle. Like sentries in most of the places Han had ever seen, the man was convinced that nothing would happen and that he was walking guard for no good reason. He sauntered past, thinking thoughts of no great consequence – which was just as well. Those idle thoughts were dispelled a moment later when a hulking shape rose out of the grass behind him and expertly tapped him behind the ear with a bowcaster butt. The guard fell face-first into the grass.

Han retrieved the heavy-assault rifle, and the two partners made a hasty scout of the area. There were no more guards, but the thing that had attracted Han's attention through the blaster scope proved most interesting. All manner of ground-effect surface vehicles, all of them cargo models, were gathered there under camouflage covers, secured. A quick series of random checks revealed no cargo aboard any of them.

'What'd they need twenty flatbeds for?' Han wondered aloud as he waved his companions forward. 'Plus two or three back at the mountain base?'

The others came up behind them. Badure explained that

they had secured the stolen hover-raft with its own camouflage cover, behind the rise. They helped Han and Chewbacca in a precautionary smashing of the fleet' communication equipment. None of them could come up with a plausible reason for the strange gathering of craf either.

'There's a gully leading up into the foothills,' Han said jerking his thumb. 'How far are we from J'uoch's mining camp?'

'Straight up that way,' Hasti told him, indicating the gully. 'We can work our way along a few ridge lines and we'll be there. Or, we could go along the valley floors and washes.'

Han hefted the Kell rifle. 'Let's move out now; we'll all go. I don't want to leave anybody behind in case we get a break and get the *Falcon* back; we can raise ship right away.'

They started into the foothills, eyes darting nervously for any sign of ambush. Zollux, monitoring, picked up no evidence of sensors. The gully's floor had been sluiced by rains down to hard stone, scored and chewed as if heavy equipment had passed over it. They had seen no tracks or tread marks on the plain, but the resilient grass probably wouldn't have held them.

Zollux reported that the automata-command signals were much stronger now. 'They're repetitive,' the droid informed them, 'as if someone is running the same test sequence over and over.'

The gully cut through the first two ridges and gave out on the next, the highest they had reached. The ground here was all rock, still showing signs of the passage of what Han assumed to be machinery. That the Survivors had some special interest in J'uoch's camp was obvious; it remained to be seen if it had to do with the treasure. But uppermost in Han's mind was recovery of the *Millennium Falcon*.

They topped the ridge, advancing at a low crawl, to look down into the valley below. Hasti gasped, as did Skynx with a sound like a subdued hiccup. Zollux gazed without comment, less surprised than the others. Han's and

Chewbacca's mouths hung open, and Badure whispered, 'By the Maker!'

Now the fleet of cargo craft, the marks on the stone gully floor, the gist of the Survivors' ceremony – even the huge chamber in which they had been imprisoned – all made sense. Those monolithic stone slabs set deep in the mountain warren weren't tables, runways, or partitions.

They were benches.

And below were gathered the occupants that sat on those benches, at least a thousand of the bulky war-robots built at the command of Xim the Despot. They stood immobile, broad and impassive, mightily armoured – manshaped battle machines half again Han's height. They gleamed with a mirror-bright finish designed to reflect laser weaponry. Survivors moved among them with testing equipment, running the checks Zollux had detected.

'These are the ones!' Skynx whispered gleefully. 'The thousand guardians Xim set onboard the *Queen of Ranroon* to look after his treasure. I wonder how many trips it took to ferry them all out here? And what are they here for?'

'The only possible reason's over there,' replied Hasti, gesturing with her chin, raising up on her elbows. From their vantage point they could see J'uoch's mining camp, which straddled two sides of a great crevasse. The barracks, shops, and storage buildings were on one side, the kilometres-wide mining operations site on the other, the two connected by a massive trestle bridge left from old Dellaltian mining efforts. The camp seemed to be operating as usual, its heavy equipment tearing away at the ground.

And on the side of the site, Han saw something that nearly made him whoop out loud. He pounded the Wookiee's shoulder, pointing. There, the *Millennium Falcon* sat on her triangle of landing gear. The star-ship seemed intact and operational.

But she won't be, Han caught himself up short, *if those ground pounders of Xim's get at her*.

At that moment there was a flurry of activity among the Survivors below. Their testing sequences were done. They scurried out from among the irregularly placed robots and gathered at a gleaming golden podium that had been set up on one side of the valley. A transmission horn projected from the podium, which was adorned with Xim's death's-head emblem. The Survivor on the podium touched a control.

Every war-robot on the valley floor straightened to alertness, squaring shoulders, coming to stiff, straddle-legged attention. Cranial turrets swung; optical pickups came to bear on the podium. The Survivor on the podium spoke.

'He's calling the Corps Commander forward,' Skynx explained in a muted voice.

'I know that man on the podium,' Hasti whispered slowly. Then more quickly, 'I recognise the white blaze in his hair. He's the assistant to the steward of the treasure vaults!'

From the massed robots stepped their leader, identical to the others in his corps but for a golden insignia glittering on his breastplate. His rigid, weighty tread shook the ground, the epitome of military precision, his movements revealing immense power. He halted before the podium. From his aged vocoder came a deep, resonant question. Skynx translated in whispers.

'What do you require of the Guardian Corps?' the machine intoned.

'That with which you were entrusted is now in jeopardy,' answered the Survivor on the podium, the steward's assistant.

'What do you require of the Guardian Corps?' repeated the robot, uninterested in details.

The Survivor pointed. 'Follow the gully trail as we've marked it for you. It will bring you to your enemies. Destroy all that you find there. Kill everyone you encounter.'

The armoured head regarded him for a moment, as if in doubt, then replied: 'You occupy the control platform; the Guardian Corps will obey. We will pass in review, as programmed, then go forth.' The Corps Commander's cranial turrets rotated as he issued the squeals of his signalry.

144

The war-robots began moving, forming an irregular line, moving just as their commander had. Without cadence or formation, they grouped to one side of the podium. But as they passed it, the transmission horn's command circuitry automatically directed them to assume their review mode. From a massed group, they separated into ranks and files as they passed the podium, ten abreast, heavy feet rising and falling in step. With their Corps Commander at their head, the thousand war-robots marched, completing a circuit of the little valley.

Even the Survivors were hypnotised by it; the sight of their ancient charges walking again was nothing less than magical to them. Metal feet beat the canyon floor; arms as thick as a man's waist swung in unison. Han wondered if J'uoch's people wouldn't be able to hear their approach even over the sound of mining operations.

At some unseen signal from their Corps Commander, the robots stopped. The commander came around to face the podium with a rocking motion. From his vocoder boomed the words: 'We are ready.'

The Survivor on the podium instructed the robots to stand fast for a time. 'We go now to a vantage point, from which we will observe your attack. When we are in place you may proceed against the enemy.' He and the other Survivors hurried off to watch the carnage. Presently the air was still, the war-robots waiting patiently, the only sound the distant buzz of the mining camp.

'We've got to get to the camp first,' Han declared as they drew back from the ridge and got to their feet.

'Are you completely vacuum-happy?' Hasti wanted to know. 'We'll get there just in time to go through the meat-grinder!'

'Not if we hurry. Those windup soldiers down there will have to go the long way around; we can run the ridge line if we're careful and get there first. The *Falcon*'s our only way off this mud-ball; if we can't get to her, we're going to have to tip J'uoch that the robots are on their way, or they'll rip my ship apart.'

He wished he could figure out why the Survivors were

intent on destroying the mining camp and slaughtering it
personnel. 'Everyone keep up. I'll go first, then Hasti
Skynx, Badure, Zollux, and Chewie on rearguard.'

Han put the heavy-assault rifle across his shoulders and
set off, the others falling into their assigned places. But when
Chewbacca beckoned Zollux, the labour droid hesitated
'I'm afraid I'm not functioning up to specifications, Firs
Mate Chewbacca. I'll have to come along as best I can.'

The Wookiee was torn by indecision for a moment, then
trotted off after the rest, making it clear with hand motion
and growls that Zollux was to come along as quickly as he
could. The droid watched Chewbacca disappear from view
then opened his chest plastron so that he and Blue Max
could speak in vocal-normal mode, as they preferred.

'Now, my friend,' he drawled to the little computer
module, 'perhaps you'll explain why you wanted us to stay
behind. I practically had to lie to First Mate Chewbacca to
do it; we may very well be left behind.'

Max, who had taken in the situation via direct linkage
with Zollux, answered simply. 'I know how to stop them
The war-robots, I mean; but we'd have to destroy them al
to do it. We needed time to talk it over, Zollux.'

And Blue Max related the plan he had conceived. The
labour droid responded even more slowly than usual. 'Why
didn't you mention this before, when Captain Solo was
here?'

'Because I didn't want him to decide! Those robots are
doing what they were built to do, just like we are. Is that any
reason to obliterate them? I wasn't even sure I should tel
you; I didn't want you to blow your primary stacks in a
decisional malfunction. Wait; what're you doing?'

The labour droid's chest plastron was swinging shut as he
toed the edge of the ridge. 'Seeking alternatives,' he
explained, stepping off.

Zollux slid and stumbled and ploughed his way down the
slope to the valley floor, working with heavy-duty
suspension of arms and legs to keep from being damaged. A
last he came to an awkward stop at the bottom amid a mino
avalanche. Standing erect, he approached the war-robots
who waited in their gleaming, exact formation.

The Corps Commander's cranial turret rotated at Zollux's advance. A great arm swung up, weapons-apertures opening. 'Halt. Identify or be destroyed.'

Zollux replied with the recognition codes and authentcation signals he had learned from Skynx's ancient tapes and technical records. The Corps Commander studied him for a moment, debating whether this strange machine ought to be obliterated, recognition codes or no. But the war-robots' deliberative circuitry was limited. The weapon-arm lowered again. 'Accepted. State your purpose.'

Zollux, with no formal diplomatic programming to draw upon and only his experience to guide him, began hesitantly. 'You mustn't attack. You must disregard your orders; they were improperly given.'

'They were issued through command signalry of the podium. We must accept. We are programmed; we respond.' The cranial turret rotated to face front again, indicating that the subject bore no further discussion.

Zollux went on doggedly. 'Xim is dead! These orders of yours are wrong; they do not come from him; you cannot obey them!'

The turret swung to him again, the optical pickups betraying no emotion. 'Steel-brother, we are the war-robots of Xim. No alternative is thinkable.'

'Humans are not infallible. If you follow these orders, they'll lead to your destruction. Save yourselves!' He could not admit that it would be by his own hand.

The vocoder boomed. 'Whether that is true or not, we carry out our orders. We are the war-robots of Xim.'

The Corps Commander faced front again. 'The waiting time has elapsed. Stand aside; no further delay will be tolerated.' He emitted a squeal of signalry. The ranks of war-robots stepped off as one, arms swinging.

Zollux had to spring aside to keep from being trampled beneath them. His chest plastron swung open as he watched them go. 'What do we do now?' Blue Max wanted to know. 'Captain Solo and the others will be down there, too.'

There was a quiver of sorrow in Zollux's voice modulation. 'The war-robots have their built-in program-ming. And we, my friend, have ours.'

XIV

They had worked their way to a ridge overlooking the outer perimeter of the mining camp before Han discovered Zollux wasn't with them. Han, incensed, slipped around a spire of rock for a look at the camp. 'I *told* that low-gear factory reject we needed him to monitor for sensors. Well, we're just going to have to be extra –'

Sirens began ululating throughout the camp. The travellers all hit the ground at once, but Han risked a peek around the spire. Now that they had been detected information was more important than concealment.

The mining camp was swarming like an insect nest. Humans and other beings were running every which way to take up emergency stations. Those employees trusted by J'uoch were being issued arms and taking up defensive positions. Contract labourers were ordered by their overseers to retire across the bridge to the isolation and effective confinement of the plateau barracks area.

Han couldn't spot the sensor net he had tripped, but it was apparent that it had him pinpointed. Several reinforced fire teams were dashing to bunkers fronting Han's hiding place. Han saw that grounded near the *Millennium Falcon* and the gigantic mining lighter was another vessel, a small starship with the sleek lines of a scout.

Suddenly a response squad started up the hill to engage them, two human males with disruptor rifles, a horn-plated *W'iiri* scuttling on its six legs and bearing a grenade thrower, and an oily-skinner *Drall*, its red hide gleaming lugging a gas projector.

Half-kneeling, half-crouching by the spire, Han dragged the old Kell Mark II around by its balance-point carrying handle. Knowing of the outdated weapon's powerful recoil

148

he braced himself before thumbing the firing stud. Blue energy sprang from the Kell's muzzle, tracing a broad line across the rock wall below. He was nearly knocked over backward by the Mark II's kick, but Chewbacca braced him. The rock sizzled, smoked, and shot sparks, then cracked, fragments and shards falling downslope. The response squad sought cover with gratifying freneticism.

'That should keep them off our necks until we can talk,' Han judged. Cupping hand to mouth, he called out, 'J'uoch! It's Solo! We have to talk, right away!'

The woman's voice, amplified by a loudhailer, rose from one of the bunkers. 'Give me that log-recorder disk and throw down your guns, Solo; those are the only terms you'll get from me!'

'But she saw that we didn't have the disk,' Badure muttered. 'Didn't she guess that we couldn't get it from the lockbox?'

Han shouted down, 'We've got no time to debate this, J'uoch; you and your whole camp are about to come under attack!' He pulled back suddenly as a barrage of small-arms fire opened up. Huddling back from it, the travellers clutched their heads in protection while energy- and projectile-searching fire probed the hillside. Rocks bubbled and exploded; shrapnel and splinters flew while explosive concussion battered their ears.

'I don't think she's going to be reasonable about this,' predicted Badure.

'She's got to be,' Han snapped, thinking of what would happen to his starship if the robots overran the camp.

The firing slowed for a moment, then, at some command they didn't hear, resumed even more heavily. 'Face it, Solo,' Hasti called to him over the din, 'they want our hides and nothing less. The only way we'll get to the *Falcon* is if we can get to her while the robots are hitting the camp.'

'When they're mixing it up with J'uoch's people? We wouldn't get two metres.' At that moment the firing stopped again and a voice called his name from below.

Hasti was gazing at him in alarm. 'Solo, what's wrong? You just went pale as perma-frost.'

He paid her no attention but saw by Chewbacca's expression that the Wookiee, too, recognised the voice of Gallandro the gunman.

'Solo! Come down and negotiate like a reasonable fellow. We have a great deal to dicuss, you and I.' The voice was calm, amused.

Han realised that sweat was beginning to bead his brow despite the cold. A sudden suspicion hit him, and he threw himself up into the clear for an instant, just enough to ease the Mark II's barrel over the crest. The response squad was on the move and another was rushing to link up with it.

Han thumbed the trigger and hosed the barrel back and forth randomly. The heavy-assault rifle was a product of Dra III, made for the heavier, stronger inhabitants of that world, with its Standard-plus gravity. The Mark II's recoil forced him back a second time, but not before the play of its extremely powerful beam drove the advancing squads to cover once more.

'Spread out along the ridge or they'll outflank us!' Han ordered. His companions hurried to comply as Gallandro's voice came up again.

'I knew you wouldn't have died in something as foolish as that uneven ship-to-ship action back at the city, Solo. And I knew the *Millennium Falcon* would draw you here in time, no matter what.'

'You know just about everything, don't you?' Han riposted.

'Except where that log-recorder is. Come, Solo; I've struck a bargain with the delighful J'uoch here. Do the same, don't make things difficult. And don't make me come up there after you.'

'C'mon, what's stopping you, Gallandro? There'll be nothing left of you but those little moustache beads!' Chewbacca and the others had taken up sniping at the response squads, pinning them down for now, but Han was worried about the armed aircraft in the mining camp.

The thought had no sooner formed than, scanning the sky, he saw a quick, dangerous shape swooping down at them. 'Everybody down!'

The spaceboat, twin to the one that had been destroyed in the city by the lighter, made a quick preliminary pass at the ridge, its chin pods spitting. Anti-personnel rounds threw out clouds of flechettes; Han could feel the craft's afterblast as it darted by. He raised his head to see what damage it had done.

By some fortune the first pass, being hasty, had resulted in no one being hit. But they were badly exposed there on the ridge; the next pass might well finish them all. Han pulled the heavy-assault rifle to him with a grunt of effort, pushed himself upright, and rushed out into the open on the back side of the ridge.

At the camp below, Gallandro conferred with J'uoch. 'Madame, recall your boat; I'll trouble you to remember our deal.' He spoke with a hint of impatience, as close to emotion as he ever let himself come. 'Solo is mine, not to be killed by air attack.'

Peering out of the bunker, she dismissed the objection with a wave of her hand. 'What does it matter, as long as he's eliminated? My brother's using anti-personnel rounds; the log-recorder won't be damaged.'

The gunman smiled, reserving his retaliation for a more convenient moment. He touched up his moustachio with a knuckle. 'Solo is well armed, my dear J'uoch. You may be surprised at his resourcefulness, as may your brother.'

Han raced over the open ground, keeping one eye out for available cover. Though hindered by the weight of the Mark II, he adjusted it for maximum range and power level as he ran. He had thought about handing the weapon over to the Wookiee to let him shoot at the boat, but the *Falcon*'s first mate had little liking or affinity for energy weapons, preferring his bowcaster.

Han heard the boat begin its second pass. J'uoch's brother, R'all, dived at the exposed, fleeing man. Han threw himself into a troughlike depression in the rock, the Mark II clattering down next to him. The boat flashed past, so close that Han was in the dead area between the guns' field of fire. Flechettes burst in long lines to either side of him. R'all flashed off, adjusting his weapons for a final pass.

Han got up, braced the Mark II's buttplate against th
rock, and fired. Still the heavy-assault rifle's recoil made
jump and turn; the boat was out of range before he ha
come anywhere near it, and now was banking for a pass th
was sure to find its target.

Han hitched himself around the stone trough and pulle
the Mark II's bipod legs down. He had only one more tri
left, and if that didn't work, he'd have no more worri
about treasure, Gallandro, or the *Falcon*. Resettling so th
his knees and the small of his back were higher than l
shoulders, he wrestled the Mark II around and rested it
the incline of his legs. He set his feet against the bipod le
holding the weapon tightly to steady it.

He squinted upward through the heavy-assault rifl
open sights. The boat came at him again. He bracketed it
the sights and waited until he heard the first concussion
R'all's fire.

Then he opened up, bracing the bucking Mark II wi
hands and feet, holding it fairly steady for the first time. Th
boat's pilot recognised his danger too late; an evasi
manoeuvre failed and the heavy-assault rifle's full for
caught the light boat, tearing a long gash in the fuselag
Control circuitry and power panels erupted and a gapi
hole appeared in the cockpit canopy. The boat wallowe
and shook, out of control, and disappeared in a steep div
trailing smoke and flame. A moment later the ground shoc
with impact.

'R'all!' J'uoch screamed to her dead brother as s
clawed her way out of the bunker. The boat had explode
on impact, scattering burning debris over a long, wic
swath of ground.

Gallandro caught her arm. 'R'all is gone,' said th
gunman with no particular sympathy. 'Now, we will do th
thing as we originally agreed. Your ground forces w
encompass Solo's position, and we'll force him out into th
open and capture him alive.'

She wrenched her arm away, seething with rage. 'H
killed my brother! I'll get Solo if I have to blow the
mountains apart!' She turned and called out to h

nforcer, the hulking Egome Fass, who stolidly awaited rders. 'Get the crew to the loadlifter and warm up main atteries.' She was about to turn from him when an nfamiliar sound, rising over the fury of the boat's estruction, made her pause. 'What's that?'

Gallandro heard it, too, as did Egome Fass and all the thers in the camp. It was a steady beat, shaking the ground, he pounding of metal feet. The column of Xim's war-robots ppeared at a spot farther along the mining camp's erimeter, having finished their roundabout march from heir mustering place.

They came in glittering ranks, arms swinging, unstop-able. When their Corps Commander gave the signal that eed them from their lockstep, they spread out across the te to begin their devastation. J'uoch stared in aston-hment, not quite believing what she saw. Gallandro, ngering one of the gold beads that held his moustache, ied to remain calm. 'So, Solo was telling the truth after ll.'

Up on the ridge, Chewbacca hooted to the exhausted lan, indicating the camp. Han wearily moved to the ridge nd joined his companions in looking down on a scene of tter chaos. Their own presence had been forgotten by the esponse squads, fire teams, and other camp defenders.

The war-robots, faithful to their instructions, moved to bliterate everything in their path. First to feel the battle machines' power was a domed building that housed repair hops. Han saw a robot smash through the dome's personnel oor while a half-dozen of his comrades set to work renching off the rolling doors. Pieces of lockslab gave way ke soggy pulp, and a group of Xim's perfect guardians loved into the dome, demolishing work areas and heaving quipment, ripping down hoisting gear, and firing with the veapons built into their metal hands. Heatbeams and article discharges flashed, throwing weird shadows within he dome. The building flared, pitted in a score of places. 'he robots' fire lanced the dome, probing the sky. More of hem pressed in to tear apart everything they encountered.

It was the same elsewhere in the vast mining site. The

war-robots, with their limited reasoning capacity, wer
taking their orders literally, devoting as much attention t
devastating buildings and machinery as to attacking cam
personnel. Whole companies of the war machines wer
moving among the abandoned mining autohoppers an
landgougers, tow-motors and excavators.

The robots blasted and sprayed fire everywhere, makin
full use of their tremendous strength. One of them wa
sufficient to reduce a small vehicle to rubble in moments; fo
larger equipment, groups cooperated. Tracks were wrenche
from crawlers, whole vehicles lifted off the ground, thei
axles snapped, wheels ripped off, cabs torn loose, an
engines yanked out of their compartments like toys. A
battalion moved towards a barge shell that contained th
latest shipment of refined ore. The robots tore into i
swinging and firing, wrecking everything they encountere
and hurling the pieces aside.

Meanwhile, others engaged the camp personnel i
determined combat, turning the camp into a scene o
unbelievable chaos. War-robots flooded through th
operations site. 'They're headed for the *Falcon!*' Ha
bellowed, then charged down the ridge. Badure's shoute
warnings went unheeded. Chewbacca went racing after hi
partner; Badure took off, too, followed by Hasti.

Skynx was left alone, staring after them. Although goin
after his companions seemed a good way to insure that h
would never see the chrysalis stage, he realised that he ha
become a part of the oddly met group and felt acutel
incomplete without them. Abandoning good Ruuria
prudence, he flowed off after the others.

At the bottom of the slope, Han found his way blocked b
one of the robots. It was just finishing demolishing one of th
bunkers, kicking the fusion-formed walls to bits and hurlin
the larger chunks easily. The robot turned on him, it
optical lenses extended a bit as their focal point adjusted. I
lifted and aimed its weapon-hand.

Han quickly brought up the heavy-assault rifle and fire
point-blank, knocked back several steps by the sustaine

ecoil. His fire blazed blue against the mirror-bright chest. The machine itself was driven back a step with an electronic outburst and was ripped open. Han moved his aim up to the spot where the cranial turret was joined to the armoured body.

The head came off, flying apart, smoke and flame gushing from the decapitated body. Han shot it again for good luck and the Mark II's beam came only faintly; the weapon was virtually exhausted. But it served to topple the robot, which landed with a resounding clatter.

More war-robots were reaching that part of the camp. Chewbacca descended to level ground, trailing dust and tumbling pebbles, just as another machine came at Han. The Wookiee threw his bowcaster to his shoulder and aimed. But his fire bounced off the robot's hard breastplate; he had forgotten his weapon was still loaded with regular rounds rather than with explosives.

Han threw aside the useless assault rifle and drew his blaster, setting it for maximum power. Chewbacca stepped back, removing the magazine from his weapon and taking one of the larger ones from his bandoleer. Han stepped in front to cover him in a stiff-armed firing stance. He squeezed off bolt after bolt, deliberately and with great concentration, into the approaching robot's cranial turret. Four blaster rounds stopped the machine just as it fired in response. Han ducked the heatbeam that split the air where he had stood. As the robot fell, the beam traced a quick arc upwards.

Defenders that were sufficiently well armed were putting up stiff resistance with rocket launchers, grenade throwers, heavy weapons, and crew-served guns. Living beings and war machines were reeling back and forth in a storm of energy discharges, bullets, shells, and fire. Four robots lifted the reinforced roof off a boxlike hut as the men defending it fired frantically. Using a chattering quad-gun, the men's shots kicked up enormous clods of ground and blew away segments of the machines even as they attacked. More robots approached to join in; the crew, with barrels depressed, traversed their gun back and forth in a frenzy taking a terrible toll. But even though several crew member used side arms in a desperate attempt to keep from bein overrun, the roofless hut was gradually outflanked an disappeared behind a wall of gleaming enemies.

Not far away, a dozen of J'uoch's employees had formed firing line in three ranks, concentrating on any robot tha came near, and were thus far succeeding in preserving thei lives. Elsewhere, isolated miners worked their way amon the high rocks to exchange earnest fire with the machines which couldn't negotiate the incline.

But many of the camp personnel were caught alone o unarmed, or were surrounded. The fighting was heavies and fiercest there, the robots' implacability matche against the furious determination of the living beings Humans, humanoids, and nonhumanoids dodged, evaded ran, or fought as well as they could. War-robots simpl advanced, overcoming obstacles or being destroyed without any sense of self-preservation whatsoever.

Han saw a stocky Maltorran run up behind a robot with heavy beamdrill cradled in its brachia and press it flusl against the machine's back. The robot exploded, and th drill, exploding from the backwash, killed the Maltorran Two mining techs, a pair of human females, had got to landgouger and were making a resolute effort to brea through the automaton lines, crushing many of them unde the gouger's tremendous treads, manoeuvring to avoid thei weapons' aim. But soon the fire of many robots converge on them, finding the landgouger's engine. The gouger wa blown apart with an ear-splitting explosion. Elsewhere Han saw a robot grappling with three *W'iiri* who ha swarmed onto it, tearing at it with their pincers. Th machine plucked them off one by one, smashing them an tossing them aside, broken and dying; but in the nex moment, the robot itself toppled over, disabled by th damage they had done it.

'We'll never get through to the *Falcon!*' Badure yelled a Han. 'Let's get out of here!' More robots were approaching nd to attempt a return up the steep ridge under fire would e out of the question. The old man proposed, 'We can withdraw across the bridge and take shelter in the barracks rea!'

Han glanced across the crevasse. 'It's a dead end; there's o other way off that plateau.' He considered blowing the ridge behind them, but that would take the *Millennium Falcon*'s guns, or those of the lighter.

The latter ship was herself under attack. A ring of dozens f war-robots had formed around her, furiously firing while he huge cargo ship's engines strained to lift her off, her main batteries answering the robots' fire. Many of the robots' weapons were silent, their power exhausted, but more of the machines were gathering around the lighter very moment. Though the vessel's salvos wiped out five nd ten robots at a time, sending them flying in heaps of angled, liquefied wreckage, Xim's machines kept cluster-ng to her, weapons-hands blazing, standing their ground. oon hundreds were massed there.

Others turned their attention to Gallandro's scoutship, utting swaths in her hull. The lighter rose unsteadily, her hields glowing from the concentrated fire, her heavy guns aking back and forth. Just at the moment it seemed she vould reach safety, one of her aged defensive shields failed; fter all, the lighter was an old industrial craft, not a combat essel. The ship became a brilliant ball of incandescence, howering torn hull fragments and molten metal into the revasse. The detonation knocked combatants, living and machine both, to the ground. Han was on his feet again in n instant, charging towards the *Falcon* with his blaster in his and, determined that the same thing would not happen to is beloved ship.

So was someone else. Across the battlefield a ring of war-obots was closing in on the converted freighter, preparing o demolish her, their arms raised and weapon apertures pen. Others were shoving the wreckage of Gallandro's coutship towards the brink of the crevasse.

Another machine, far smaller than they, blocked the way

to the *Millennium Falcon*, seeming fragile and vulnerab
Zollux's chest plastron was open, and Blue Max
photoreceptor gazed forth. From his vocoder tumbled t
signals learned from tapes shown him by Skynx, amplifie
by the gear Zollux had cannibalised from the podium.

The advance stopped; the war-robots waited in co
fusion, unable to resolve the conflicting orders. The Cor
Commander appeared, the death's-head insignia of Xi
gleaming on his breastplate. He loomed over Zollux. 'Stan
aside; everything here is to be destroyed.'

'Not this vessel,' Max told him in the command signalr
'This one is to be spared.'

The towering robot studied the two-in-one machine
'Those were not our orders.'

Max's voice, directed through the podium's scavenge
horn, was high. 'Orders may be amended!'

The thick arm came up, and Zollux prepared for the er
of his long existence. But instead a metal finger indicated t
Falcon, and the command came: 'Spare that vessel.'

With signals of acknowledgment, the other war-robo
moved on. The Corps Commander still regarded the labo
droid and the computer module. 'I am still not sure abo
you two, machines. What are you?'

'Talking doorstops, if you listen to our captain's opinior
offered Blue Max.

The Corps Commander stood stock-still in surpris
'Humour? Was that not humour? What have machin
become? What kind of automata are you?'

'We are your steel-brothers,' Zollux put in. The Cor
Commander made no further comment, but continued c
his way.

The waves of robots had thwarted Han's effort to rea
his ship. One, stepping over the ruins of a crew-served g
and its slain crew, advanced towards the pilot. Han w
looking elsewhere, helping Hasti fire blaster and disrupt
shots at a machine approaching from the opposite directio
Han's shot scored the cranial turret; Hasti's less practise
sent its torso and limbs in a wild scatter. Badure was firing

still another, a long-barrelled power pistol in each hand.

Chewbacca stepped into the path of the oncoming robot and triggered his bowcaster. Its staves straightened, and the explosive quarrel detonated against the robot's chest armour, holing it but not stopping it. The Wookiee held his ground, jacking the foregrip of his bowcaster and firing twice more, this time hitting the robot's head and midsection. The machine came on relentlessly. Its weapons-hands were raised, but their power had been drained in battle. Chewbacca backed a step and came up against Han, who was still firing the other way.

Then the robot toppled forward. Chewbacca, standing in its very shadow, would have leaped clear but realised that Han was unaware of his imminent danger. The Wookiee shoved the pilot aside with a sweep of his hairy arm but failed himself to avoid the tottering automaton. It struck him and pinned his right arm and leg to the ground. Skynx raced to him and began pulling ineffectually at the Wookiee.

Another robot chose that moment to step over the one Han and Hasti had just downed. Since Hasti's disruptor was drained, Han moved forwards, then realised that his blaster's cautionary pulser was tingling his palm in silent warning that his weapon, too, was spent.

He whirled and called to his sidekick, then saw the Wookiee wriggling to extricate himself from under the fallen robot. Chewbacca paused long enough to loft his bowcaster into the air one-handed.

Han caught it, pivoted, dropped to one knee, and pressed the stock to his cheek. He squeezed, and the explosive blast blew up against the juncture of the approaching machine's shoulder and arm. The metal limb fell away, and the robot shuddered but kept coming.

Han tried to jack the bowcaster's foregrip and found, as had the man in the city, that his human strength was insufficient. He stopped himself from dodging out of the way; Chewbacca lay trapped, directly behind him. Badure, some distance away, couldn't hear Han's shouts for aid.

Hasti fired at the machine with the only weapon she had left, the dart-shooter, but emptying the whole clip at it served no purpose.

Han avoided Chewbacca's efforts to swipe him out of the way and shifted his grip on the bowcaster, preparing for a last, hopeless defence.

XV

The war-robot seemed to block out the sky, a machine out of nightmare. But abruptly its cranial turret flew apart in a blast of charred circuitry and ruptured power routing as a thread-thin, precisely aimed beam found its most vulnerable point. Han scarcely had the presence of mind to take a step back, nearly treading on Chewbacca, as the automaton crashed at his feet like an old tree.

He leaped up onto its back and scanned the battlefield. Far across it, a form in grey waved once.

'Gallandro!' The gunman gave him a bare, stark smile that held nothing Han could read. Han drew without thinking, then remembered his blaster was empty. Just then a robot appeared behind Gallandro, closing in on him, arms wide. Han never made a conscious decision, but pointed and shouted a warning.

The gunman was too far away to have heard, but he saw Han's expression and understood. He spun and ducked instinctively. The robot just missed with a blow of enormous power. With an incredible display of agility and reflexes, Gallandro seized the arm and rode the robot's recovery-backswing, at the same time putting two quick shots into its head. Letting go, he was flung clear to land lightly and put a last bolt into the robot as it fell.

Han watched the incident with awe. By far the most dangerous machine there was Gallandro. The gunman gave Han a sardonic bow and a mocking grin, then, like a ghost, was gone again in the swirl of battle.

The air was hot with the unleashed energies of the battle. With Skynx's and Badure's help, Chewbacca had squirmed free of the fallen robot, while Hasti stood nervous guard. Taking back his bowcaster, the Wookiee made a quick motion towards the robot that had so narrowly missed nailing Han and barked a question.

'It was *him*, Gallandro,' Han told his partner. 'A fifty-, maybe sixty-metre tight-beam shot.' The Wookiee shook his head in bewilderment, mane flying.

There was nowhere to go except the camp living area, across the bridge. 'Will you two stop chatting and get going?' Hasti called. 'They'll have us surrounded if we don't hurry.'

They started for the bridge at the best pace they could manage, a half-trot, each of them bearing a number of minor injuries and wounds. They moved in a defensive ring. Badure at the leading edge with his power pistols, Hasti to his right and Skynx to his left, with Chewbacca and Han bringing up the rear, back-pedalling and sideskipping. A metallic voice called Han's name.

Zollux somehow injected a note of immense relief into his vocoder drawl. 'We're so glad you're all safe. The *Millennium Falcon*'s unharmed, at least for the time being, but I don't know how long that will last. Unfortunately, it's inaccessible just now.'

Han wanted to know exactly what that meant, but Zollux interrupted. 'No time for that now. I have the means to remedy our situation, sir,' he told the pilot, resettling the signalry equipment he had taken from the robots' command podium. 'But you'll have to get to the far side of the bridge before I can use it.'

'You're on, Zollux! All right, everybody, scratch gravel!' They hastened away. The attack hadn't got as far as the bridge yet, but resistance was crumbling rapidly.

At the bridgehead Zollux paused. 'I'll be staying here, sir. The rest of you must proceed across.'

Han looked around. 'What're you going to do, talk them into suicide? You better stay with us; we'll take to the high ground on the plateau.'

With a strange sincerity, the droid refused. 'Thank you for your concern, sir; Max and I are flattered. But we have no intention of being destroyed, I assure you.'

Han felt ridiculous for arguing with a droid, but insisted,

'This is no place to get noble, old-timer.'

Seeing the war-robots converging on them, Zollux persevered. 'I really must insist that you go, sir; our basic programming won't permit Max and me to see you come to harm here.'

They departed unwillingly. Hasti walked with the tired Skynx beside her. Badure patted the droid's hard shoulder and trudged off, and Chewbacca waved a paw. 'Look after Max,' Han said, 'and don't get yourself junked, old fellow.'

Zollux watched them go, then searched among the rocks and boulders for a place of concealment at that end of the bridge.

Han and his companions slogged wearily across the bridge among others who had survived the robots' onslaught and were now falling back for a final stand. At the halfway point they came upon the body of a fallen mining tech who had died before she could complete the crossing, a *T'rinn* whose bright plumage was now charred and burned from combat. Han gently took a shoulder-fired rocket launcher from her lifeless claws, the weapon still containing a half-magazine of rockets. He was just standing up when a figure broke from the stream of retreating miners and attacked him, swinging an empty needlebeamer.

'Murderer!' J'uoch shrieked, her first blow grazing the pilot over the ear before he was aware of her onset. 'You killed my brother! I'll kill you, you filthy animal!' Dazed, he pushed himself backwards to avoid the blows she was raining on him, forearm up to protect himself.

Chewbacca would have torn the hysterical woman from his friend, but at the same moment he was struck from behind, a heavy blow from a thick forearm. The Wookiee fell to his knees, losing his bowcaster, as a huge weight fell upon him: Egome Fass, the enforcer. The two huge creatures rolled over and over, wrestling, tearing at one another. Retreating miners skirted the struggles, concerned only with staying alive.

Badure, weakened by the ordeal, waved an unsteady power pistol at J'uoch. But before he could fire, Hasti had thrown herself at the woman who had killed her sister

Lanni. They whirled and fought, hacking and kicking at each other, finding reserves of strength in their mutual hatred.

Badure pulled Han up just as J'uoch got her forearm around Hasti's throat. But Hasti writhed free of the hold, dropped and turned, put her head and shoulder against the other's midsection and drove her back with feet churning and driving. J'uoch was shoved backwards against the bridge's waist-high railing and toppled over it. She fell screaming, in a flurry of coveralls, reaching and thrashing. Hasti's momentum had carried her halfway over the rail, too.

Badure was there in time to pull her back from the rail, grabbing the material of her clothes. She sobbed for breath, her pulse pounding. Then it came to her that the roaring she heard wasn't in her ears. Chewbacca and Egome Fass had gone to war.

It had been the second time J'uoch's enforcer had struck the Wookiee from behind. What the *Falcon*'s first mate felt now could only pallidly be described as outrage. Han waved Badure off when the old man would have shot Egome Fass.

The two punched and grasped at one another while Han leaned against the rail to watch the honour match. 'Aren't you going to help him?' Hasti puffed, her face showing the scratches and abrasions of her own match.

'Chewie wouldn't appreciate that,' Han told her, keeping one eye on the rallying of robots at the end of the bridge. But he eased a pistol from Badure's belt in case the match didn't go as it should.

Egome Fass had got a choke-hold on Chewbacca. Rather than squirm out of it or apply an in-fighting trick, the Wookiee chose to lock both hands on his opponent's arm and turn it into a contest of pure strength. Egome Fass was bulkier, Chewbacca more agile, but the question of brute force was still open. Their arms quivered and muscles jumped in the straining backs.

Bit by bit the arm was levered away from Chewbacca's throat. The Wookiee showed his fangs in savage triumph, and burst free of the hold. But Egome Fass wasn't done with tests of strength. He lunged at his antagonist for a deadly hug. Chewbacca accepted it.

They staggered back and forth, first the Wookiee's feet leaving the bridge, then the enforcer's. Both applied their full brawn in fearsome constriction. Egome Fass's feet were lifted clear of the bridge and stayed that way as the Wookiee held him aloft, muscles standing out like cables under Chewbacca's pelt. The enforcer's struggle became more frantic, less aggressive. Panic crept into his movements. Then there was a crack, and Egome Fass's body slumped. Chewbacca let go, and the enforcer slid limply to the bridge's surface. The Wookiee had to rest a paw on a support to steady himself.

Han teetered over with the rocket launcher over one shoulder. 'You're getting decrepit; two tries to put away a bum like that!' He laughed and affectionately punched the Wookiee's shoulder.

'Enough, enough!' Skynx protested, tugging at Han's red-seamed trouser leg. 'The robots are ready to attack; Zollux said we must be across the bridge.'

Han didn't know how much chance the labour droid stood of stopping the steel horde, but he and the others obeyed Skynx's pleas. There was no one to stand with them at the end of the bridge. The miners who had reached it had gone either to put up barricades in the buildings or to find safe places among the rocks.

Han stopped as soon as his boots were off the bridge. He sat on the ground, looking back across the bridge. 'We might as well face it here.'

No one made any objection. Badure gave Hasti one of his pistols, while Chewbacca fitted a new magazine into his bowcaster. Hasti put one arm around Han's neck and kissed his cheek. 'That's for a good try,' she explained.

Zollux crouched in the jumble of boulders on the far side of the bridge. The mining-operations site was now completely razed. Machinery was burned and buildings were flattened, and no living thing could be seen.

The Corps Commander had mustered all his forces with

high-pitched summonses. Other resistance had been crushed; all that remained was to annihilate the barracks area on the far side of the bridge, the successful completion of their first combat action in generations.

Zollux waited and didn't try to interfere. That would have been useless, he knew; they weren't so different from him. The machines gathered around their commander by the hundreds. The Corps Commander indicated the way with a long metal arm, gleaming like a statue of death in the blue-white light. He stumped towards the bridge, and his awesome troops crowded after him. And as the war-robots drew abreast of him, about to step onto the bridge, Zollux triggered the command signalry he had brought from the podium.

The Corps Commander fell into a marching step as the signals reached him. He didn't question them; the commands were automatic, military, geared to a segment of him that didn't doubt or ponder. Such was his construction.

Behind their commander the other war-robots responded to the signal as well, falling into ranks of ten, in step with their leader. Funnelled onto the bridge, their ranks filled it from side to side. They stepped with meticulous precision. Metal feet tramped; arms swung in time.

'Will it work?' Zollux asked his friend.

Blue Max, tuned in with both their audio pickups, listened carefully, cautioning the droid not to bother him at this critical point. At Max's instruction, Zollux adjusted the marching tempo, matching the forced vibration of the robots' tread to the bridge's own natural frequency, creating a powerful resonance. The war-robots marched on to do battle for an overlord generations dead. The bridge began to quake, dust rising and forming a haze with the unified footfalls. Timbers reverberated, joints and stress members strained; the perfection of their marching made the robots a single, unimaginable power hammer. More of them poured onto the bridge and took up the step, adding to the concussions.

At last the bridge itself thrummed under them as Max found the perfect beat. All the robots were on the bridge, with no thought but to get to the other side and attack the enemy.

Han and the others rose, waiting. 'I guess Zollux couldn't pull off his plan,' Han said. The front rank, following their gleaming leader, had grown large. 'We'll have to fall back.'

'There's not much room for that,' Hasti reminded him sadly. He had no answer.

Suddenly Skynx exclaimed. 'Look!'

Han did, feeling a deep vibration through his boots. The bridge was shuddering in time with the robots' march, its timbers creaking and cracking with the punishment it couldn't absorb. Feet pounding, the robots marched on.

Then there was a rending snap; the vibration had found a member that couldn't support it. A timber bent and turned in its bed of press-poured material. The bed wouldn't accept the play and the timber twisted and split. All the supporting members at that side of the bridge gave way.

There were electronic bleats of distress from the war machines and the popping of aged rivets from the timber-joining plates. For a moment the whole doomed assemblage, robots and bridge, was suspended in space. Then all fell into the crevasse with a huge concussion, sending up clouds of rock dust and smoke and a wall of impact-noise that drove Han back from the crevasse's edge.

Wiping the dust from his eyes and spitting it out of his mouth, Han returned to the brink. Among the drifted dust and smoke he could see bridge timbers and the gleam of crumpled armour, the flare of circuit fires, overloaded power packs, broken leads, and shorted weapons. Suddenly Zollux appeared at the other side of the crevasse, waving stiffly, having divested himself of the scavenged equipment. Han returned the wave, laughing. *From now on those two are full crewmembers.*

A new sound made him look around in surprise and anger, mouthing a Corellian oath. The *Millennium Falcon* was lifting off. She rose on blaring thrusters, swinging out over the abyss. Han and Chewbacca watched in despair as they saw their ship whisked from under their noses despite all their efforts.

But the freighter settled gently on their side of the crevasse. They got to her just as her ramp-bay doors opened and the main ramp lowered, beneath and astern the cockpit. The main hatch rolled up, and there stood Gallandro. He welcomed them with a smile, his weapon conspicuously holstered. His fine clothing and beautiful scarf were soiled, but other than that, Han reflected, he looked none the worse for someone who had just waded through a horde of war-robots.

The gunman sketched a mocking bow. 'I found myself obliged to play dead among the slain; I couldn't get to the ship until the robots had all left, or I'd have been of more assistance. Solo, those droids of yours are priceless!' His smile disappeared. 'And so is Xim's treasure, eh? You're out for high stakes for a change; my compliments.'

'You tracked me all the way from the Corporate Sector to tell me that?' Chewbacca had his bowcaster aimed at Gallandro, but Han knew that even that was no guarantee against the man's incredible speedraw.

The gunman made a wry twist of his mouth. 'Not originally. I was rather upset about our encounter there. But I'm a man of reason; I'm prepared to put that aside in view of the amount of money involved. Bring me in for a full cut and we forget the grudge. And you get your ship back; wouldn't that strike you as a fair arrangement?'

Han remained suspicious. 'All of a sudden you're ready to kiss and make up?'

'The treasure, Solo, the treasure. The wealth of Xim would buy affection from anyone. All other considerations are secondary; surely that's in keeping with your own philosophy, isn't it?'

Han was confused. Hasti, who had come up behind him, said, 'Don't trust him!'

Gallandro turned clear blue eyes on her. 'Ah, the young lady! If he doesn't accept my offer, you'll be in a bad way as well, my dear; this vessel's weapons are functional.' His voice went cold, the playacting evaporating. 'Decide,' he ordered Han crisply.

The defenders were beginning to emerge from the barracks, having seen the bridge collapse and the ship land. In another moment, escape might be much more complicated. Han reached out and pushed down Chewbacca's bowcaster. 'Everybody onboard; we're back in business.'

In moments they had lifted off with Han at the controls, uttering angry maledictions at the techs who had torn the starship apart in search of the log-recorder disk and reassembled her so inexpertly. 'Why did J'uoch have the ship repaired, anyway?' Badure asked.

'She was either going to keep it for her own use or sell it,' explained Gallandro. 'She tried to sell me a lame story about her disagreements with you people, but considering the things I'd already discovered about your movements, the truth wasn't hard to guess.'

Han brought the ship in to hover over the camp. 'What about the other miners, the ones who lived?' Hasti asked.

'They've got food, weapons, supplies there,' Badure said. 'They can hold out until a ship shows up, or slog it over to the city.'

Han was bringing the *Falcon* down again on the other side of the crevasse. A gleaming metal form waited there. Chewbacca went aft to let Zollux aboard.

'Like you said,' Han found himself telling Gallandro defensively, 'they're valuable droids.'

'I said "priceless",' Gallandro corrected him. 'Now that we're comrades, I'd never offend you by suggesting you've gone soft. May I inquire what our next move is?'

'Direct collection of intelligence data,' Han declared, lifting off again. 'Interrogation of indigenous personnel for tactical information. We're going to make a couple of locals sweat and find out what all this was about.'

The Survivors who had activated the war-robots had decided to escape together in one large hover-raft rather than spread out across the plains in a fleet. A few passes and a barrage from the *Falcon*'s belly turret brought them to a halt. They threw down their arms and waited.

Han prudently left Chewbacca at the ship's controls. He and the others, weapons recharged, went to confront the Survivors. Hasti, first down the ramp, waved her gun at them, shouting and fairly dragged one of them off the raft. Han and Badure had to pull her off the man, while Gallandro looked on in amusement and Skynx in confusion.

'It's him, I tell you,' she yelled, straining to go after the frightened man again. 'I recognise the white blaze in his hair. It's the vault steward's assistant.'

'Well, clubbing him silly isn't going to help,' Han pointed out as he turned to the man. 'Better spill it, or I'll let her loose.'

The assistant licked dry lips. 'I can say nothing, I swear! We are conditioned in youth not to reveal the secrets of the Survivors.'

'Old-fashioned hypno,' Han dismissed it, 'nothing you can't overcome if we scare you enough.'

Gallandro stepped forward with a wintry smile, pulling his pistol in one fluid motion, adjusting it one-handed. A low-power, high-resolution beam sizzled into the ground at the captive's feet, blackening and curling the grass. The man paled.

Zollux had come up, his chest plastron open. 'There's a better way,' Blue Max advised. 'Circumvent his conditioning, and we can find out anything we want. We can rig up a strobe and key it to the same light pattern the Survivors use.'

Gallandro was dubious. 'Query, computer: can you duplicate the Survivors' light pulses exactly?'

'Quit talking to me like I'm some kind of *appliance!*' snarled Max.

'Beg pardon,' said Gallandro politely. 'I keep forgetting. Shall we proceed?'

XVI

The *Millennium Falcon* moved through the Dellaltian air at what was for her a conservative speed. Even so, Han was recovering the distance from the city in minutes.

Gallandro was off gathering equipment elsewhere in the ship, with Zollux's help. Hasti and Badure sat, respectively, in the navigator's and communication officer's high-backed chairs behind Han and Chewbacca. Skynx, his injuries dressed and treated, as theirs had been, was curled in Hasti's lap.

'It's hard to accept,' Hasti was saying. 'All these years. How could a secret be kept for generations?'

'Secrets have been kept for ages,' Badure pointed out. 'It was easy enough in this case; there's really two strata in the Survivors' organisation. The dupes lived and died there in the mountains, maintaining the war-robots as a religious ritual, holding their ceremonies once in a while. Then there were the others, the ones who knew the secret of Xim's treasure and waited for the time they could use it.'

'But they all got the conditioning as children, right?' Han asked.

'And when Lanni happened on the mountain base and got her hands on the log-recorder disk and put it in the lockbox at the vaults,' Hasti murmured, her voice thick with sorrow, 'she couldn't have know that the steward was part of the Survivors' apparatus.'

Such had been the assistant's testimony once his conditioning had been overcome. The steward had sent the disk back to the Survivor's mountain warren as soon as it had come into his possession, of course. And he had contrived a nonexistent voice-coder to keep Lanni, Hasti, or anyone else from claiming it. He was aware that J'uoch had learned something about the disk from Lanni before killing her, and that the woman was actively seeking it. He had passed word to her through Survivor double agents that the *Millennium Falcon* had landed, knowing he couldn't cope with the starship if force were brought to bear on the vaults. He knew J'uoch could, and hoped that Hasti and the others and their ship would be destroyed in battle, and the matter closed.

But instead, J'uoch had mounted the ambush that had resulted in the capture of the *Falcon*. Not having found the disk onboard the starship, J'uoch had made pointed inquiries at the vaults. The steward had managed to put her off but, knowing it was only a matter of time until she used force to inspect the lockboxes herself and put him to a more harrowing interrogation, he ordered the long-dormant Guardian Corps sent out against the mining camp. The war-robots, maintained through generations for just such an emergency, had come close to accomplishing their purpose.

'So why are the Survivors still sitting on their money after all this time?' Han wondered.

'The Old Republic was stable and unbeatable,' Badure answered. 'They had no hope of moving against it, even with Xim's treasure backing them. It's only now, with the Empire having its troubles, that the Survivors smelled a setup they might be able to exploit, especially here in the Tion Hegemony. I bet small-timers everywhere are getting the same sort of idea.'

'A new Xim, and a new despotism,' Hasti mused. 'How could they have believed it, even under conditioning?'

'They can believe one thing,' Han said, watching the land roll by quickly beneath them. 'The Survivors are about to suffer a capital loss.'

'Shouldn't we have a bigger ship?' Hasti inquired.

Han shook his head. 'First we make sure the treasure's there, and put what we can in the *Falcon*. Then we unship a quad-battery and some defensive shielding generators. Gallandro and I will hold the fort while Chewie and the rest of you go find a bigger ship, about the size of J'uoch's lighter, say. It won't take too long.'

'And what will you do with your share of the money?' Badure asked casually. He saw doubt and confusion cross the pilot's face.

'I'll worry about that when I've got a stack of credits so high I'll have to rent a warehouse,' Han replied at last.

Gallandro, who had just entered the cockpit, carrying the equipment he had gathered, said, 'Well put, Solo! Indelicate, but on target.' He checked their progress. 'We'll be there in a moment. I haven't ransacked a bank in a long time; there's a certain zest to it.'

Han reserved his reply and put the starship into a steep dive. The *Falcon* dropped out of the sky ahead of her own sonic boom. Dellaltians near the vaults suddenly saw the vessel appear above them, its braking thrusters thundering, its landing gear extended like predatory claws. People scurried for shelter as the shock wave of the freighter's passage caught up with her, making the ground tremble and the buildings shake. She came to rest on the roofless portico outside the vault's single door.

The *Falcon*'s external speakers whooped and wailed with emergency sirens and klaxons. Her visual warning systems and running lights were flashing at maximum luminescence. Bystanders would have difficulty seeing and hearing, much less interfering.

The ramp dropped and Han and Gallandro ran down, blasters ready, equipment and tools weighting them. Behind followed Badure, Hasti, and Skynx. The girl objected, 'Are you sure there isn't some other way to do this?' Han had to read her lips, unable to hear her in the din.

He shook his head. Chewbacca had to stay at the controls, both because he knew the ship and because Han trusted only the Wookiee with care of the *Falcon*. Zollux stayed behind as well to keep a photoreceptor on instrumentation the first mate couldn't spare time to monitor. Han wanted at least two people to hold the main door, Hasti and Badure. He and Gallandro would do the searching, taking Skynx along to translate.

The area seemed fairly secure; the Dellaltians had no way

to cope with an armed starship. Han waved to his partner in the cockpit, and though he couldn't be heard, added, 'Fire, Chewie!'

From the *Falcon*'s top and belly turrets shot lines of red annihilation, playing on the closed door of the treasure vault. Smoke obscured the door in seconds as the quad-guns traced incandescent lines across it. Red cannonfire pitted and burned through material that had withstood generations of time and weathering, cutting glowing gashes in it. No weapon of its time could have penetrated it so easily, but in moments the door had been breached, pieces of it falling away. The reports of the gunfire added to the tremendous noise level.

Han signalled again and Chewbacca ceased fire. Smoke billowed away on the chill wind to reveal a yawning hole, its red-hot edges quickly cooling. 'Armed robbery!' laughed Gallandro. 'There's nothing like it!'

'Let's get inside,' Han mouthed. They ran together and hurdled through the gaping door. Hasti and Badure followed a moment later. 'Stay here and make sure you maintain comlink with Chewie,' Han told them. Badure set Skynx down.

'Don't forget the defensive system!' Hasti called as Han, Gallandro, and Skynx raced off. Among the things their captives had revealed was the fact that the treasure vaults were equipped with defensive security devices; the presence of a firearm in any protected area would trigger automated weapons.

They went deeper into the gloom of the cavernous vestibule, abandoned by the Dellaltians, who had wisely sought other refuge. Han didn't see a man appear to one side, weapon raised, but Gallandro caught the movement, drew, and fired all in the same instant.

The steward cried aloud, clutching his middle, then collapsing to the pressure-pacted tile floor. The gunman kicked the steward's dropped disruptor away.

'You cannot, cannot,' the white-bearded man moaned, half in delirium from his wound. 'We have kept it, safe, unsullied since we were entrusted with it.' His lids fluttered and lowered forever.

Gallandro laughed. 'We'll make better use of it than you, old man. At least we'll get it into circulation, eh, Solo?'

Han, moving on, offered no answer. Gallandro came after, and Skynx rushed to catch up. They descended dusty ramps and broad staircases, the empty vaults all around them. At one point they lowered themselves by the cable of an ancient lift platform that no longer worked, complying precisely with the instructions extracted from the captive Survivors under hypno. Han marked their trail with a tint bulb. At the lowest level of the vault proper they came to a forking of the ways. Their information on the vault-complex layout went no further than this.

'It's off this corridor, one of the side tunnels,' Han said. 'Got your copy of the identi-marks? Good.'

'The little fellow can stay with you, Solo,' Gallandro replied, meaning Skynx. 'I prefer to operate alone.' He hitched up the straps holding his equipment and stalked away.

'Okay, stay sharp,' Han told Skynx, and the search began. Soon they were absorbed in the intricate business of examining side corridors for the identi-marks described by their prisoners and copied by Skynx. These lowest levels of the vault proper were stale and seemed airless, layered with ankle-deep dust, and a gloom that resisted the beam of the hand-held spotlight. They passed room after room of empty bins and vacant shelves.

At last Skynx stopped. 'Captain, this is it! These are the ones!' He was vibrating with excitement. To Han the side corridor looked no different than any other, ending as it did in a blank wall at the bottom of an obviously empty vault complex. But Skynx was right; the identi-marks matched. Han shucked his other gear and lifted a heavy-duty fusion cutter into place. Skynx, taking the comlink, tried to contact the others and inform them of the find, but could raise no response.

'The walls are probably too thick,' Han suggested as he

175

set to work. When it had been built, the wall would have withstood any assault that could have been made with portable equipment, but Han was beneficiary of a long technological gap. Chunks of the wall began to fall away. Beyond was the glow of a perpetual illumi-system.

Han set the fusion cutter aside hurriedly, anxious to see for himself. A treasure beyond spending! He could barely contain himself. He ducked and stepped through, followed by Skynx. The vault was dust-free, dry, and as quiet as when Xim's artisans had sealed it, moments before they were put to death, centuries ago.

His steps echoing in the stillness, Han smiled. 'The *real* vaults; all the time they were right here!' Hunters had scoured this whole part of space for Xim's treasure because his vaults were empty and all the time there had been complete duplicates, right under the decoys. 'Skynx, I'll buy you a planet to play with!'

The Ruurian made no answer, silenced by the weight of years hanging over the place. They followed the corridor through a few turns and came to a stretch where warning flashers blinked in their wall sockets, as they had been doing for centuries. This no-weapons zone was an antechamber to the true treasure vaults of Xim.

Han stopped, wishing neither to be burned by the defensive weapons nor to go on unarmed, aware he might face other dangers. He turned back with great reluctance. At the fusion-cut opening, Gallandro waited.

Han paused and Skynx waited uncertainly. 'We found it,' the pilot told the gunman with a jerk of his thumb. 'The real one. It's back there.' He realised Gallandro had heard Skynx's transmissions after all.

Gallandro registered no elation, only amused acceptance. Han knew without being told that everything had changed. The gunman's abandoned equipment was stacked to one side, and he had doffed his short jacket, prelude to a gun duel. 'I said, the *treasure* is back there,' Han repeated.

Gallandro smiled his frosty smile. 'This had nothing to do with money, Solo, although I postponed it until you and your group could help me find the vaults. I have my own plans for Xim's treasure.'

Han warily shrugged out of his jacket. 'Why?' was all he asked, carefully unsnapping his holster's retaining strap and rotating it forward out of his way. His fingers stretched and worked, waiting.

'You require chastening, Solo. *Who do you think you are?* Truth to tell, you're nothing but a common-place outlaw. Your luck has run out: now, call the play!'

Han nodded, knowing Gallandro would if he didn't. 'And this'll make you feel superior, right?' His hand blurred for his blaster, the best single play of his life.

Their speedraw mechanics were very different. Han's incorporated movements of shoulders and knees, a slight dipping, a partial twist. Gallandro's was ruthless economy, an explosion of every nerve and muscle that moved his right arm alone.

When the blaster bolt slammed into his shoulder, Han's overwhelming reaction was surprise; some part of him had believed in his luck to the end. His own draw half-completed, his shot went into the floor. He was spun half around, in shock, smelling the stench of his own charred flesh. The pain of the wound started an instant later. A second bolt from the cautious Gallandro struck his forearm and Han's blaster dropped.

Han sank to his knees, too startled to cry out. Skynx retreated with a terrified chitter. Swaying, clasping his wounded arm to him, Han heard Gallandro say, 'That was very good, Solo; you came closer than anyone's come in a long time. But now I'll take you back to the Corporate Sector – not that I care about the Authority's justice, but there are those who have to be shown what it means to stand in my way.'

Han gasped through locked teeth. 'I'm not doing time in any Authority horror factory.'

Gallandro ignored that. 'Your friends are more expendable, however. If you'll pardon me, I'll have to see to your Ruurian comrade before he gets into any mischief.'

177

He slapped a pair of binders he'd found onboard the *Falcon* around Han's ankles and ground the pilot's comlink under his heel. 'You were never the amoralist you feigned to be, Solo, but I am. In a way, it's too bad we didn't meet later, when you were salted and wiser. You're pretty good in a fight; you might've made a useful lieutenant.' He removed the charge from Han's blaster, tucked it into his belt, and sauntered off after Skynx, who, unable to get past the gunman, had fled back down the corridors towards the treasure vaults.

Gallandro moved cautiously, knowing the Ruurian was unarmed but counting no being harmless when it was fighting for its life. He rounded a corner to see Skynx cowering against the wall some distance along, gazing at him with huge, terrified eyes, paralysed with fear. Around the far turn of the corridor he could see the reflected warning lights of a no-weapons zone.

Gripping his blaster, Gallandro smirked. 'It's a pity, my little friend, but there's too much at stake here: Solo's the only one I can afford to take alive. I shall make this as easy as I can. Hold still.'

Drawing a bead on Skynx's head, he stepped forward. Energy discharges flashed from hidden emplacements; even Gallandro's fabulous reflexes gave him no edge against the speed of light.

Caught in a flaring crossfire of defensive weapons, the gunman was hit by a dozen lethal blasts before he could so much as move. He was the centre of an abrupt inferno, then his scorched remains fell to the corridor floor and the smell of incinerated flesh clogged the air.

Skynx uncoiled from his spot at the corridor wall bit by bit. He threw aside the warning flashers he had removed from their sockets along the corridor's wall. He gave silent thanks Gallandro hadn't noticed the empty sockets; a prudent Ruurian probably would have.

'Humans,' remarked Skynx, then went off to rescue Han Solo.

★

'Not much left of him, is there?' Han asked rhetorically an hour later as he stood over Gallandro's blackened remains. Like the others, he had left his gun outside the no-weapons zone. Badure and Hasti had made temporary repairs to his shoulder and forearm with one of the ship's medi-packs. If Han received competent medical attention soon, there would be no lasting effect from Gallandro's blaster bolts.

Chewbacca was just finishing a careful examination of that corridor and the one beyond, running a thorough check along the walls to search out each weapons emplacement. He had opened each one with hand tools and deactivated it. Satisfied that there would be no danger in bringing power equipment and tools inside, the Wookiee barked to Han.

'Let's get busy; I don't like the idea of the *Falcon* being unmanned.' When Skynx had returned with news of the gun duel, Chewbacca had moved the star-ship so that she blocked the main door, her ramp extended down through it. He had warped the ship's defensive mantle around and set her guns to fire automatically on sensor-lock should anyone come too close, one warning volley and then the real item. The Dellaltians trapped inside on the starship's arrival had already surrendered and been permitted to leave; the *Falcon* would protect the treasure hunters for the time being, but Han didn't want to press his already over-extended luck.

They gathered their gear and moved on. At the end of the next corridor was a metal wall bearing a Wookiee-high representation of Xim's death's-head symbol. Chewbacca lifted the fusion cutter to it and began slicing, splitting the insignia in two amid flying flashing motes. Then he began carving in earnest. Heat washed back across him.

In short order there was a wide opening in the door. Beyond, bathed in the glow of illumi-panels that had been keeping the place bright for generations, was the glittering of gems, the gleam of metals, piles of strong-boxes, and racks of storage cylinders in warehouse-sized shelf stacks that stretched from floor to high ceiling and away into the distance as far as they could see.

And this was only the first of the treasure rooms.

Skynx was quiet, almost reverent. He had made the find of a lifetime, a discovery out of daydreams. Badure and Hasti remained solemn, too, as they considered the size and wealth of the place, the impact it would have on their lives, and the memory of what they had gone through to stand here.

Not so Han and Chewbacca. The pilot jumped through the gap in the door, wounded arm held to him by a traction web. 'We did it! We did it!' he shouted in glee. The Wookiee lurched after him, tossing his long-maned head back with an ecstatic '*Rooo-oo*!' They slapped each other, laughter echoing away into the piles of treasure. Chewbacca's huge feet slapped the floor in a thumping victory dance as Han laughed with joy.

Skynx and Badure had gone to open containers with Zollux's help, to examine Xim's spoils. Chewbacca offered to assist them. 'Spread it out here!' Han enjoined him. 'I want to roll around in it!'

He paused when he noticed Hasti nearby, eyeing him strangely. 'I always wondered what you'd be like,' she told him, 'when you found your big win, you and the Wook. What now?'

Han still rode the wave of elation. '*What now*? Why, we'll, we'll –' He stopped, giving the subject some serious thought for the first time. 'We'll pay off our debts, get ourselves a first-class ship and crew, uh ...'

Hasti nodded to herself. 'And settle down, Han?' she asked softly. 'Buy a planet, or take over a few conglomerates and live the life of a good man of business?' She shook her head slowly. 'Your problems are just beginning, rich man.'

His joy was receding fast, replaced by a tangled knot of doubts, plans, the need for forethought and mature wisdom. But before he could berate Hasti for being a spoilsport, he heard Chewbacca's angry roar.

The Wookiee held a metallic ingot, frowning at it in disgust. He dumped a handful of them onto the floor in a chiming avalanche and gave the pile a kick that sent ingots skittering every which way. Han forgot Hasti and went to his friend. 'What is it?'

Chewbacca explained with frustrated grunts and moans. Han picked up one of the ingots and saw that his copilot was right. 'This stuff's *kiirium*! You can get it anywhere; Skynx, what's it doing in with the treasure?'

The small academician had located a vault-directory screen at the end of the nearest shelf stack, an old televiewer mounted on a low stand. He brought it to flickering life, and columns of ciphers and characters raced across the screen as Skynx answered distractedly.

'There would seem to be a great deal of it here, Captain. And a huge quantity of mytag crystalline vertices and mountains of enriched bordhell-type fuel slugs, among other things.'

'Mytag crystals?' Han repeated in puzzlement. 'They run those things off by the carload; what kind of treasure's this? Where's the *real* treasure?'

A belly laugh distracted him. Badure had found a canister of the mytag crystal and flung a double handful into the air. The crystals rained down around him, catching the light, as he convulsed in laughter. 'This *is* it! Or was, an age ago. Don't you see, Slick? Kiirium is artificial shielding material, not very good by modern standards but a major breakthrough in its time, and tough to produce to boot. With quantities of kiirium to shield heavy guns and engines, Xim could field war-craft that were better armed and faster than anything else in space at the time.

'And mytag crystals were used in old subspace commo and detection gear; you needed lots and lots of them for any spacefleet or planetary defences. And so forth; all this was critical war matériel. With the stuff in these vaults, Xim could have assembled a war machine that would have conquered this whole part of space. But he lost big at the Third Battle of Vontor, first.'

'That's *it*?' Han bellowed. 'We went through all this for a treasure that's *obsolete*?'

'Not quite,' Skynx commented mildly, still bent over the screen. 'One whole section is filled with information tapes, art works, and artifacts. There is a hundred times more information contained here than everything we know about that period altogether.'

'I'll bet the Survivors have long since forgotten just what it was they were guarding,' Hasti put in. 'They believed the legends, just like everyone else. I wonder what did happen to the *Queen of Ranroon*?'

Badure shrugged. 'Perhaps they plunged her into the system's primary after she offloaded the treasure, or sent her off with a skeleton crew to arrange misleading sightings of her and create a false trail. Who knows?'

Skynx had left the viewscreen and started a delirious dance, first on his hind limbs, then on the front ones, hopping and capering much as Han and Chewbacca had a moment before. 'Marvellous! Miraculous! What a *find*! I'm sure to get my own chair funded – no, my own *department*!'

Han, leaning against a wall, slowly sank to a squatting position. 'Artworks, hmm? Chewie and I can just stroll into the Imperial Museum with a bunch under our arms and start haggling, right?' He rested his forehead on his good arm. Chewbacca patted his shoulder solicitously, making mournful sounds.

Skynx gradually stopped cavorting, realising what a disappointment all this was to the two. 'There *are* some things of intrinsic value, Captain. If you choose carefully, you could fill your ship with items you could dispose of relatively simply. There would be some profit.' He was fighting the urge to hoard the entire find, knowing that the *Millennium Falcon* could bear away no more than an insignificant part of it. 'Enough, I suppose, to get your ship repaired properly and have your wounds looked after in a first-class medicentre.'

'What about us?' Hasti interposed. 'Badure and I haven't even got a starship.'

Skynx pondered for a moment, then brightened. 'I can write my own ticket with the university, and unlimited budget. How would you two like to work with me? Academic pursuits will be dull after this, I suppose, to a pair of humans. But there'd be generous pay and retirement benefits and quick promotions. We'll be years and years working on this find. I'll need someone to look after all the workers, scholars, and automata.' Badure smiled and put an arm around Hasti's shoulders. She nodded.

That made Skynx think of something else. 'Zollux, would you and Blue Max care for positions? You'd be of great help, I'm sure. After all, you two are the only ones who interacted with the war-robots at any length. There's certain to be an effort to study their remains; we have a great deal yet to learn about their thought process.'

Blue Max answered for them both. 'Skynx, we'd like that a lot.'

'*If* the locals don't march in here and take it all away from you,' Han reminded them, as Chewbacca helped him to his feet. Seeing their concern, he added, 'I guess we'll leave you a portable defensive generator and some heavy weapons and supplies out of the *Falcon*. That'll give us more cargo space.'

Badure sounded uncharacteristically angry. 'Han, how gullible do you think the rest of the universe is? You always want to do the right things for the wrong reasons. Well, what will you do the day you run out of excuses, son?'

Han pretended not to hear. 'We'll punch through a distress call just before we make our jump out of this system. There'll be a Tion Hegemony gunboat here before you know it. Come on, Chewie; let's break out the handtruck and get the ship loaded before anything else happens.'

'Captain,' Skynx called. Han paused and looked back. 'Here's a funny thing: I still think this adventuring was basically just danger and hardship a long way from home, but now that it's ended and we're parting company, I find myself saddened.'

'Look us up for a refresher course, any time,' offered Han. Skynx shook his head. 'I have much to do here; all too soon I'll be called away by my blood, when it's time to go chrysalis, then live a brief season as a chroma-wing. If you wish to see me then, Captain, come and look on Ruuria for the flyer whose wing markings are the same as my own banding. The chroma-wing won't recognise you, but perhaps some part of Skynx will.'

Han nodded, finding no adequate way to say good-bye. Badure called, 'Hey, Slick!' Han and his copilot looked to him and he laughed. 'Thanks, boys.'

'Forget it.' Han dismissed the entire incident. He started off again with his sidekick, both of them moving with some pain due to their injuries. 'After all, a Life-Debt's a Life-Debt, isn't it, *partner*?'

On this last note, he poked a knuckle into his copilot's ribs. Chewbacca swung angrily but not too quickly. Han ducked and the Wookiee backed off. 'Look,' Han said, 'that's it for missions of mercy, all right? We're smugglers; that's what we know and that's what we're good at and that's what we're sticking to!'

The Wookiee growled concurrence. The others, surrounded by the endless shelf stacks of Xim's treasure, heard the discussion echo back from the corridor. Han broke into Chewbacca's rumblings with, 'When the *Falcon*'s repaired and this wing of mine's fixed, we're going to try another Kessel spice run.'

The Wookiee croaked an irritated objection. Han insisted. 'It's fast money and we won't have to look at any dirt! We'll get Jabba the Hut or somebody to back us for a cut. Listen, I've got this plan ...'

Just as they were moving out of earshot, Chewbacca's protests stopped. He and Han Solo shared some joke that made both laugh slyly. Then they returned to their schemes.

'There,' Badure declared to Hasti, Skynx, Zollux, and Blue Max, 'go the *real* Survivors.'

THE HUMANOID TOUCH

Jack Williamson
author of THE HUMANOIDS

More than thirty years ago Jack Williamson
created one of the finest science fiction novels of
all time – THE HUMANOIDS. In this new
novel he returns to his classic subject: the final
confrontation of man and machine. THE
HUMANOID TOUCH is a new peak for a
master of science fiction.

'Decades before the current headlines about
automaton, computers and robots, Jack
Williamson was examining the relationship
between humankind and machines in his stories
of the Humanoids. Now, in THE
HUMANOID TOUCH, the Grand Master of
Science Fiction carries that saga to its final,
irresistible step. This is science fiction at its best:
thoughtful, thought-provoking, and thoroughly
engrossing.' *Ben Bova*

SCIENCE FICTION   0 7221 9195 2   £1.75

A selection of bestsellers from SPHERE

FICTION

PACIFIC VORTEX!	Clive Cussler	£1.95 ☐
REALITIES	Marian Schwartz	£2.25 ☐
CHAMELEON	William Diehl	£2.25 ☐
THE CAMBODIA FILE	J. Anderson & B. Pronzini	£2.25 ☐
THE STONE FLOWER	Alan Scholefield	£1.95 ☐

FILM & TV TIE-INS

E.T. THE EXTRA-TERRESTRIAL	William Kotzwinkle	£1.50 ☐
THE IRISH R.M.	E. E. Somerville & Martin Ross	£1.95 ☐
INCUBUS	Ray Russell	£1.50 ☐
THE GENTLE TOUCH	Terence Feely	£1.50 ☐

NON-FICTION

NELLA LAST'S WAR	Nella Last	£1.95 ☐
THE NUCLEAR BARONS	P. Pringle & J. Spigelman	£3.50 ☐
THE HEALTH & FITNESS HANDBOOK	Ed. Miriam Polunin	£5.95 ☐
ONE CHILD	Torey L. Hayden	£1.75 ☐

All Sphere books are available at your local bookshop or newsagent, or can be ordered direct from the publisher. Just tick the titles you want and fill in the form below.

Name _____

Address _____

_____

Write to Sphere Books, Cash Sales Department, P.O. Box 11, Falmouth, Cornwall TR10 9EN

Please enclose a cheque or postal order to the value of the cover price plus:

UK: 45p for the first book, 20p for the second book and 14p for each additional book ordered to a maximum charge of £1.63.

OVERSEAS: 75p for the first book plus 21p per copy for each additional book.

BFPO & EIRE: 45p for the first book, 20p for the second book plus 14p per copy for the next 7 books, thereafter 8p per book.

Sphere Books reserve the right to show new retail prices on covers which may differ from those previously advertised in the text or elsewhere, and to increase postal rates in accordance with the PO.

Sven Hassel

The Commissar

Translated from the Danish by
TIM BOWIE

CORGI BOOKS

THE COMMISSAR

A CORGI BOOK 0 552 12686 1

First publication in Great Britain

PRINTING HISTORY
Corgi edition published 1985
Corgi edition reprinted 1985 (twice)

Corgi Books are published by Transworld Publishers Ltd.,
Century House, 61-63 Uxbridge Road, Ealing, London W5 5SA,
in Australia by Transworld Publishers (Aust.) Pty. Ltd.,
26 Harley Crescent, Condell Park, NSW 2200, and in New
Zealand by Transworld Publishers (N.Z.) Ltd., Cnr. Moselle
and Waipareira Avenues, Henderson, Auckland.

Made and printed in Great Britain by
Hunt Barnard Printing Ltd., Aylesbury, Bucks.

Many have suffered in war — from hunger, from
    wounds and from frost
But they suffered most who bore no arms, who
    died unseen — lost.
Those who suffered at human hands. Their
    torturers saw each heart,
And around them the land they sprang from —
    then — tore them slowly apart.

                Nordahl Grieg
                (freely translated)

This book is dedicated to my old friend
the Scandinavian film producer Just Betzer
who has thrown himself enthusiastically
into the filming of my books.

Sven Hassel

CONTENTS

* The Soviet Secret Police, now the KGB

> A soldier's conscience is as wide as
> Hell's gate.
>
> William Shakespeare

The Gauleiter was in a hurry. He drove recklessly, taking no heed of the refugees choking the roads. His triple-axled vehicle was heavily loaded. He was the first to have left the city. The vehicle had been loaded for several days. Then, the sound of tank-guns in the distance persuaded the Gauleiter that the time to start on his travels was now. The only member of his large staff whom he took with him was his young secretary. She believed in the Führer, the Party and the Final Victory.

She pulled her mink coat closer about her. It had once belonged to a rich woman who had died in Auschwitz.

They were stopped four times by the Field Police, but the Gauleiter's golden-brown uniform was as good as a password. At the last stop the guards warned them against proceeding further. The next sentries they would meet would be Americans. Their road-block was where the road turned off from Hof to Munich.

A coarse-faced sergeant of snowballs* stuck a gun-barrel through the vehicle window. The Gauleiter had changed into civilian clothes.

'You ain't gone hungry, have you, sausage-eater?'

'He is a Gauleiter,' smiled the secretary, who no longer believed in the Führer, the Party and the Final Victory.

The snowball sergeant emitted a long, low whistle.

'Hear that boys?' He turned to his three-man MP guard. 'This civilian sausage-eater's a Gauleiter!'

They all laughed.

'Come on,' said the MP sergeant, prodding the Gauleiter with his gun-muzzle. 'Let's take a stroll into the woods, and see how the spring crocuses are coming along.' His breath stank of cheap cognac.

---

* Refers to the white MP helmet

The secretary heard three bursts of automatic fire. White helmets appeared again from the woods. She was halfway across the fields towards the farm, and never heard the next burst of fire which came from behind her. She was dead before her face hit the ground!

'What the hell *you* shoot *her* for?' shouted the sergeant, in an irritated voice.

'Escapin' wasn't she?' said the corporal, cheerfully. He cracked a fresh ammunition clip home with the heel of his hand.

Soon afterwards the next loaded vehicle arrived.

PANZER ATTACK

'Section, halt!' The Old Man's voice comes hoarsely over the radio. He throws up the flap of the turret with a metallic crash, and pulls his battered old silver-lidded pipe from his pocket in one and the same movement. Hard-boiled as our Section Leader is, he is still a carpenter at heart. An aura of sawdust and wood-shavings hangs about him.

'Blast these bloody things!' he swears, turning round with difficulty in the narrow turret aperture. The new, heavy winter underwear makes a man twice his normal size round the waist. 'Where's Barcelona and his lot got to?'

I open the side hatch and peer tiredly down the long column of tanks rattling along the cobbled road. They are our heavy tanks, mounted with flamethrowers. There must be something very well-defended up in front of us, or the heavies wouldn't be in the lead.

'Noisy lot o' bleeders ain't they?' growls Tiny, showing his sooty face cautiously at the loader's hatch. 'Jesus'n Mary!' he shouts, ducking quickly inside again as the muzzle flames of a pair of *degtrareva** spit from the windows of some business premises further down the street. Our machineguns begin to chatter back immediately. The clatter of running feet is heard on all sides, mixed with shouted orders and screams. It sounds as if the gates of hell had suddenly been thrown open.

A figure in an earth-coloured uniform, carrying a T-mine, comes scrambling up over our front apron. Tiny sweeps him away, with a burst from his machine-pistol, before he can place the T-mine under our turret ring.

* *degtrareva*: Russian machine-gun

11

Suddenly the street is swarming with Russians. They come flooding out from every door and window.

I catch sight of a Russian helmet on our open side. Reflexively I empty my pistol into a twisted face. It shatters like an egg.

'Grenades,' shouts the Old Man, ripping a stick-grenade from its clip.

I pull personnel grenades from my pockets, and throw them through the hatch. The little eggs explode, cracking sharply in our ears. Human screams split the darkness.

A 20 mm coughs angrily from an attic window. The small, dangerous shells ricochet between the house walls. It is as if devils were playing ping-pong with exploding balls of fire.

Without awaiting the Old Man's order I swing the turret, and aim our gun at the building from which the 20 mm and the *degtrareva* are spitting their pearly rows of deadly light.

Our long gun roars, violently.

With a certain feeling of pleasure I see two uniformed figures whirl down from the third-floor windows. They catch for a moment on the overhead wires of the tramlines, then fall to the cobblestones, landing with a soggy thump.

I send three more rounds of HE into the building. Flames commence to roar up from the roof. Tiles fall in the street like enormous hailstones. They splinter on the cobblestones.

The fire runs quickly along the houses. In the twinkling of an eye the whole row becomes a sea of roaring flame. Terrified men spring from the windows, preferring death on the cobblestones to burning alive.

'Who ordered you to open fire?' rages the Old Man, hitting out at me with a stick-grenade. 'Fire when you're ordered to, an' not before, you powder-mad sod, you!'

'They'd have done us up for sure, if I hadn't fired,' I defend myself, hurt. 'The gun's to shoot with, isn't it?'

'That building you've just disposed of so thoroughly was 1 Battalion's billet. Get *that* through your thick skull! *You* just shot it all to hell!' shouts the Old Man, despairingly.

'Sabotage, that's what it is,' says Heide, triumphantly, 'or I don't know what sabotage is! Kick him in front of a court-martial so we won't have to look at *him* any more!'

'Must 'ave rotten eggs where 'is brains ought to be,' barks Tiny, jeeringly. 'Shit on 'is own doorstep when 'e could've done it in the snow'n only shit icicles. Let's blow 'is 'ead off!'

'Shut up!' snarls the Old Man. He puffs fiercely on his pipe.

'See that sky-pilot over there,' grins Porta. 'Runnin' like mad with a bible under his arm, and a crucifix banging on his navel. The speed he's going you'd think the devil had his pitchfork up his arse!'

'I cannot ever understand why chaplains is just as scared of gettin' knocked off as all us ordinary shits,' Tiny wonders. 'Them lot 'as got *connections* to the 'igher regions!'

'The holy and righteous are just as scared of blowin' their last fart as we heathens are, my son,' philosophizes Porta. 'In reality only very good people indeed can permit themselves to become religious.'

'*Panzer, Marsch*,' orders the Old Man, pulling his headphones down over his ears, and settling his throat microphone in place. '2 Section follow me!' From old habit he lifts his clenched fist over his head. The signal to move forward. Maybach engines howl up into whining upper registers. Broad tracks churn forward over the dead and wounded lying in the street.

A Panther tank stops over a foxhole, where two Russian soldiers have taken cover with an LMG. The tank waggles on its axis, like a hen settling on to her eggs. There are screams, sharply cut off. The Russians have been crushed to a bloody pulp.

The noise of the tanks is deafening. The guns and automatic weapons drown out every other noise.

'*Anna* here! Here *Anna*,' the Old Man says to the radio. '*Bertha* and *Caesar* make safe on flanks. Fire only at clear targets! I repeat: fire only at clear targets. And I'll want an exact ammo' count from all of you. Now, fingers out, an' get

13

moving, you sad sacks!'

Flames lick at the houses. Bullets rattle and clang on the sides of the tanks. Machine-gunners fire at them, in the wasteful hope that they can do the steel giants some damage. Poisonous yellow smoke penetrates the tanks, making the crewmen's tired eyes burn and sting.

A burning roof crashes down on top of a P-III. Flames shoot up, and in a few seconds it becomes an exploding ball of fire. Reserve petrol drums lashed to its rear shield turn the tank into a travelling bomb.

The cold, damp night air stinks of explosion fumes, blood and dead bodies.

'Here Hinka, here Hinka,' comes from the scratchy loudspeaker. The steely voice of the regimental commander cuts through the racket in the tank. '5 Company will do clean-up. Prisoners will be sent back to grenadier battalion. I warn you! No looting of any kind! Breach of this order will be punished most severely!'

'Always *us*,' grumbles Porta sourly, speeding up his motor. 'It's bloody wonderful! They chase us poor bloody coolies, till even our soddin' socks are sick of it. Why am I so rotten *healthy*, and why do all them lovely Commie bullets go *round* me? I'm never, *ever* goin' to get away from this shitty war, and into a lovely, clean hospital with lovely clean, anti-septic nurse's cunt all round me just longin' to get across a wounded, bloody Ayrab like me!'

''Ot shit!' growls Tiny, bitterly. 'Risk your bleedin' life, every day in every way, for a fucked-up mark a day.'

'It's the rotten German army,' snarls Porta, angrily. 'Why, oh why, was I ever born in a war-crazy country like Germany!'

I feel dog-tired, but a rage of energy still courses through my weary body. They've filled us up with benzedrine. For the last six days we have been unable to snatch more than a few minutes of sleep at a time, and we walk around in a queer sort of haze. The worst of all is that every time we have almost fallen asleep we wake up with a start, and the

14

bitter taste of fear is in our mouths.

Tiny hangs over the guard rails. His eyes are wide open, but see nothing. From one loosely hanging hand dangles a P-38. He's like the rest of us. He dare not fall asleep. Now we are close to the danger point. The point where we can no longer be bothered to keep a watch for approaching death. It's waiting out there for us somewhere; perhaps in the form of an explosion; perhaps in a hysterical hail of machine-gun bullets.

Shells come whistling over the town in great arcs, despatched from invisible batteries to strike at distant targets far behind us.

Tiny jerks awake and cracks his head against the roof of the tank. He swears bitterly and long. Dark blood runs down beside his left ear. He dabs at it, irritably, with an oily cloth.

''Oly Mother of Kazan, what a bleedin' dream,' he mumbles. 'I was walkin' around in a wood tryin' to find the Red bleedin' Army. Up comes a commissar an' shoots the shit out o' me.' He looks around at us, quite out of touch. 'Stone the crows,' he says, feebly, 'now I *know* I don't like gettin' shot up.'

The tank stops. Mud and remnants of bodies drip from the tracks. Its white camouflage paintwork is a dirty grey from powdermarks and filth.

We stretch ourselves in our steel seats, and throw open the shutters to let in some fresh air. But all we get is poison-yellow smoke and the stink of death.

Tank grenadiers sneak along the house walls. They have the dirtiest job of all. Not a bit of glory. Their reward is more often than not a bellyfull of machine-gun bullets. They start in cleaning out the cellars for fanatics, crazy fools who fight to the last man and the last bullet. Their reward is a throat slashed open. Brainwashed idiots filled with Ilya Ehrenburg propaganda. The same kind of people as ours. The ones who die whispering 'Heil Hitler' from between crushed lips.

From where we are lying in ambush, we can see a long

way out over the steppe. It is like a whitish-grey sea, fading away into the distant horizon. Far, far behind us, towns and villages, set on fire by shell-fire during our savage attack, burn fiercely.

Wherever we look, fiery red and yellow flashes split the darkness of the night, marking clearly the deadly path of the armoured attack.

Halfway down some cellar steps hangs a US Willy's jeep with five headless bodies in it. They sit to attention as if on parade. It seems as if a huge knife has slashed the heads from the four Russian officers and their driver in one enormous sweep. There is something strange about the headless bodies. They are not wearing battle khaki but dark green dress uniforms, with broad shoulder distinctions which glitter in the flames from a burning distillery nearby.

'See now. Sights like that,' says Porta, spitting accurately out of an observation slit, 'make a man glad to be alive, even when life is monotonous and weary.'

'Where you think that lot was off to, togged up in them uniforms an' all the cunt magnets they c'd get their 'ands on?' asks Tiny, interestedly. He leans out of the turret opening. 'They must've lost their way to end up 'ere where there's a war goin' on.'

'My guess is they were on their way to a party with some field mattresses,' says Porta. He licks his lips at the thought.

'Let's give 'em a goin' over,' suggests Tiny, jumping down from the tank. 'They're goin' to a 'ores' party, they'll 'ave some pretties on 'em. Count on it!'

Porta inches up through the turret opening, eagerly, and bends over a headless first lieutenant with a row of ribbons on his chest.

'A hero,' he laughs, putting the ribbons in his pocket. Buyers for them are easy to find behind the lines. His quick fingers go through the officer's pockets, regardless of congealed blood and crushed bones.

'Not a lot o' gold teeth in *this* lot,' remarks Tiny disappointedly, nosing around in the blood-spattered vehicle.

'Perfumed officers' cigarettes with paper mouthpieces,' says Porta, putting some blue packets into his specially-made poacher's pockets.

'Any *see*gars?' asks Tiny, turning over a body, with an unpleasant squelching sound.

'Are you out of your mind, man?' answers Porta. 'Stalin's officers don't smoke cigars. That's capitalistic!'

'Lucky for us then we're bleedin' capitalists,' Tiny laughs noisily, picking up a bottle of vodka, one of the finest kind with the old Russian czarist eagle on a royal blue label. A vodka which only the top party leaders get supplied with.

Two grimy panzer grenadiers come along, dragging a screaming, half-naked woman with them. She tries desperately to tear herself loose, but they only tighten their grip on her.

'You're goin' with us, you little cat, whether you want to or not,' grins one of them, lasciviously. 'You're gonna get the chance to enjoy the war in our company. We're gonna 'ave an orgy, with sighs'n everythin' else as belongs with it.'

But the terrified girl obviously does not want to take part in an orgy. She kicks one of the grenadiers on the knee. He lets out a chain of shocking oaths, and grips her roughly by the throat with one filthy, wet fist.

'Listen to me, you little wildcat,' he snarls, wickedly. 'Get civilized or I'll smash your pretty little face in. *Panjemajo**, you Bolshevik bitch? It's a long time since me'n my mate've had any fresh goods. *Panjemajo*, Bolshy? You're goin' to an orgy, an' you're gonna be the main attraction. *Panjemajo*?'

'*Da*,' she whispers, in terror, and seems to give up all attempt at resistance.

'The party's over,' snarls the Old Man, swinging his mpi muzzle round to cover the three. 'Let 'er go! Now! Or would you rather we had a fast little court-martial?'

---

* *Panjemajo*: Russian for understood?

17

'Now I've heard it all,' shouts the biggest of the two panzer grenadiers, pushing his helmet to the back of his head. 'Been chewin' on wood, 'ave you? Belt up, you puffed-up excuse for a dragoon, you!'

They have let go of the girl and fumble for the machine-pistols hanging across their chests. They have not seen Tiny and Porta standing behind them.

'Get 'em up! Let's see you try to tickle the angels' foot-soles, my sons,' trumpets Porta, grinning happily.

Both panzer grenadiers swing round with mpis at the ready. Bullets snarl angrily past Porta's face.

Reflexively, Tiny cuts the grenadiers almost in two with a scythe-like burst from his *Kalashnikov*.

One goes down, internal organs flopping from his open gut. The other is thrown onto his back, and tries to crawl under the tracks of the tank.

'Bye-bye, then,' grins Tiny. 'See what 'appens to little boys as gets caught tryin' to pinch a piece o' cunt!'

'*Was* that necessary?' asks the Old Man, fretfully, pushing his helmet up from his face.

'What you bleedin' want us to do, then? Them two blue-bollocked bastards was gonna shoot us to death,' protests Tiny, outraged.

'The way of the world,' sighs Porta. He pushes at the nearest body with the toe of his boot. 'Him as shoots first lives longest!'

The Old Man takes a deep breath. As he crawls back down through the turret opening he breaks into a mad burst of laughter. He knows very well that this war is eating us all up. To protest against the cruelty of death is completely useless.

'Where'd the bint get to,' asks Porta, looking searchingly around him.

'There she goes, runnin' like mad,' laughs Tiny, pointing. ''Ad enough of us Germans, seems like.'

Bullets from an MG whip along the fronts of the houses, throwing earth and mortar over the jeep. The big, soft lump

18

of fear is back in our throats.

'Come on,' says the Old Man. 'Let's move!'

'Can I borrow that big feller's uniform?' asks Tiny.

'What the devil do you want with that?' asks the Old Man, wonderingly. 'Haven't you got uniform enough in the one Adolf's lent you?'

'You ain't forward-lookin' enough,' grins Tiny, cunningly. 'When "*Grofaz*"* 'as lost 'is war, and we get enrolled in the other FPO's lot, it'll be a good thing to 'ave a uniform of your own to start off with.'

'You're lookin' for a miracle, son,' laughs Porta.

'Are we to understand then,' asks Julius Heide, his eyes narrowing to slits, 'that you're turning your back on the Führer and the Reich, and no longer believe wholeheartedly in the Final Victory? I wonder what the NSFO'll† have to say to *that* when I hand in my report.'

'What a shit that Julius *is*,' Tiny bellows with laughter. 'The turd o' the world, an' never goin' to get no cleverer.'

'He's what he is,' Porta takes it up. 'A real man o' the new times. A well-trained German soldier who shits an' eats by numbers, an' turns his toes in an' feels happy as a sodding lark long as he's in company with patriotic nuts'n close-cropped generals with a window in one eye. Heil Hitler!'

'I've got all that written down, mark my words, Obergefreiter Porta,' snarls Heide, affrontedly. 'You'll have to repeat every word of it at your court-martial. The day you dangle'll be the happiest day of my life!'

'Better get crackin' then, my boy, 'fore the *untermensch* turn up. Or it'll be me, Obergefreiter by the grace of God Joseph Porta, who'll be puttin' his weight on the *other* end of the rope,' answers Porta, blowing down the barrel of his mpi.

'Up, you lazy men!' the Old Man scolds them. 'Here comes Löwe. Get your thieving fingers off them Russian

---

* *Grofaz*: Greatest Leader of All Time (nickname for Hitler)
†NSFO: Nazi political officer

bodies! It's a court for you, else! You know what *that* means?'

'Bye, bye napper,' says Tiny, patting his own cheek lovingly.

Porta has just time to lift the Russians' identification papers.

'Also saleable,' he grins as he sidles down through the tank turret opening.

'When this German world war's all over, there'll be coppers in personal documents. Everybody'n his brother'll be standing in line to get a new start in life.' He chuckles away to himself at the idea.

'Jesus, but I'm *tired*,' groans Barcelona, when the section makes a halt, a couple of hours later, in an open square. They are all hoping the halt means a rest period for them.

Suddenly the square is swarming with Russian soldiers. Some are armed to the teeth, others only half-dressed under their long khaki cloaks, which stream out in the wind. They have one thing in common. Their hands are stretched up above their heads and they are shouting: '*Tovaritsch**', the universal appeal for permission to remain alive. Strangely enough life seems only to begin to be really valuable to us when we have given up all hope and all ambition.

The Old Man swings down wearily from his turret onto the slush-covered cobblestones.

Hordes of Russian infantrymen, with grey, hopeless faces, push and shove their way past him. Only with difficulty can he keep himself from being carried along with them.

'Think they were rushin' to get in an' see the latest porno movie wouldn't you?' crows Porta. 'Mind *you* don't get taken prisoner along with them, Old Un. We don't want to lose you like that!'

Tiny's huge body blocks the side hatch of the tank. Mouth agape, he stares at the khaki-clad flood of humanity streaming around the vehicle. It fills the whole street from side to

---

* *Tovaritsch*: Russian for comrade

side. There is the burnt-out wreck of a tramcar in its path. The stream goes over, not round, it.

''Oly Russian mum o' Kazan,' cries Tiny, in amazement. 'It's the 'ole bleedin' Red Army, it is. Never 'ave I ever laid eyes on that many Russians at one time in all me German bleedin' life!'

'Hold on to your maidenheads, my sons,' says Porta, dropping back down into the tank. 'If that lot o' tired heroes gets to thinkin' how many *they* are an' how few *we* are, then our heroic participation in this fucked-up war'll be over 'fore we know it.'

'Stone the crows,' howls Tiny fearfully. He slides rapidly back into the tank and clangs the shutters to. 'Let's get *out* of 'ere!'

Barcelona's eight-wheeled Puma armoured clean-up waggon slides to a crashing halt. Its long, 75 mm gun juts threateningly from the low turret. It sideswipes the burnt-out tramcar with a screech of metal. Some Russians are caught under the heavy wheels. They scream heart-renderingly. Other soldiers pull them free and help them away. We hardly notice. This is everyday fare for us. There are too many prisoners anyway. Who cares about a few more or less?

Barcelona leans from the turret, pushes his huge dust-goggles up onto his helmet, and shouts something indistinguishable.

Albert's black African face bobs up out of the driver's aperture.

'Bow-wow!' he barks, with a flash of shiny, white teeth at the Russian prisoners. They jump back in alarm at the sight of a German negro.

'They think he's goin' to eat them,' grins Porta in Berlin gamin style. 'It'll all be in *Pravda* in a few days' time. Capitalist foes using cannibal troops!'

'Stop that cursed motor,' the Old Man boils up, irritably. 'You can't hear yourself think!'

'You *are* in a bad mood,' says Barcelona, with a broad

smile. 'Liven up! This war's only the start of something much, much worse. I've got a little message of greetings with me from Staff HQ. Get your arses in gear, boys, an' fast. Up front you go, and knock off some of the godless heathen, so those who're left alive can sneak off back where they came from. This is what we're getting paid for, you know. I'm to follow on as number three.'

'Who's two?' shouts Porta from his driving-slit.

'The "Desert Wanderer" in his P-IV,' giggles Barcelona, happily. 'He's used to lookin' out for camels, from his apprenticeship in the Sahara.'

'*Camels?*' asks the Old Man, blankly. 'There's no blasted camels in this war? *Are* there?'

'You'll see,' answers Barcelona. 'Before you know it you'll have a camel's nose up your jacksey, my friend. Ivan's sent over a whole camel division from the Kalmuk steppe.'

'Holy Mary, mother of Jesus,' shouts Porta, delightedly, 'then I can do us camel steaks. I've got a wonderful recipe for them that was given to me by a Bedouin, in grateful appreciation of my not running him over when we invaded France. Listen . . .'

'Not a blasted word will I hear out of you about food,' states the Old Man.

'What shiny-arsed bastard's found out it 'as to be *us* again?' asks Tiny, peeping cautiously over the edge of the hatch. The pure number of Russian prisoners going past us is still making his blood run cold.

'The Divisional Commander,' answers Barcelona, with a look on his face so haughty you'd think that he himself was the Chief of Staff. 'Herr General Arse-an'-Pockets wants some new silver to hang round his neck, an' we're the boys who're goin' to put it there. By the way, I hear Gregor got four threes in the black hole for smashin' up Arse-an'-Pockets Kübel. The general ended up in a tree, boots, cap an' all, an' frightened the black ravens half to death. Gregor's got the boot, and'll soon be back with us.'

The Legionnaire's P-IV can be heard starting up behind

the tram terminus. The Maybach motors stall again and again. Ignitions whine time after time. Then thunderous explosions crash down the narrow side street. The horse-power of the mighty engines begins to take hold. The roar of exhausts splits the air and fills the whole street.

Our motor catches immediately. A stench of petrol and hot oil spreads on the slush-damp air. The steel giants rattle up the steep alley, the earth shaking under their treads. Barcelona waves happily from the turret of his clean-up waggon, then disappears down inside and clangs the hatch shut behind him.

With a swing, graceful as a skater's figure-of-eight, the heavy eight-wheeled armoured vehicle disappears down the alley, slush spurting up from under its wheels.

We roll recklessly on, behind us the Legionnaire in his P-IV. Cobblestones and earth fly up from our tracks. They tear grey wounds in the poorly-paved road surfacing.

'Jesus, Jesus!' cries Tiny, banging his fist down on a shell. 'What a bleedin' bill we'll get if we ever 'as to pay for all the damage we're doin' in this country. Reckon it'll be clever to keep out o' sight for a bit, when we've lost the final bleedin' victory!'

'What a lot of *shit* you talk,' hisses Heide. He hammers viciously on the communicator, which has gone on strike again.

'Listen to it,' Porta laughs, jeeringly. 'The Führer's soldier's goin' sane. He's calling *Grofaz*'s radio programmes a lot of shit.'

'It's no fault of the Führer's,' Heide corrects him. He shakes the radio. 'It's sabotage to install a pre-war radio in a brand-new Panther tank!'

'Complain to Speer, then,' Tiny suggests, grinning broadly. 'It's 'im as is doin' the sabotage! Bleedin' barmy to give a soddin' 'od-carrier the job o' runnin' the 'ole war-industry, any road!'

'Idiot,' snarls Heide, beginning to dismantle the radio with quick, sure fingers. It begins to splutter, suddenly, and

23

a babble of excited voices fills the tank. The whole network is overloaded with the voices of hysterical tank-commanders. They have all sighted the enemy positions at the same time, and guns begin to go off unordered. A 75 mm siege gun is hit by a German shell and goes up. Red-hot metal rains down.

All at once we are wide awake. Tiredness disappears from our bodies. In a tank battle the fastest crew wins.

I pump the foot-pedal and ready the gun. Then I see Barcelona's Puma come roaring back toward us. Heide's MG rattles nastily, sending a rain of tracer bullets across the river, which is covered with a heavy gruel of thick broken ice.

'Get your finger out,' shouts the Old Man, impatiently, banging his fist on my shoulder.

'You've got your target! Fire at the muzzle-flash. Get *on* with it, man, *if* you don't mind! Or do you *want* to get roasted alive?'

Nervously, I rotate the turret a few degrees, but can still see nothing. Nothing but darkness and whirling snowflakes. Snow lies on the edges of the viewing-slits like wet cotton-wool.

'Fire then, you blasted idiot,' shouts the Old Man, angrily. 'D'you want to get the lot of us killed?'

The brutal hammering of the two MGs fills the tank. Tracer tracks fumble about, with long silvery fingers, searching for enemy flesh.

Barcelona's Puma zig-zags back down the wide avenue, now cleared completely of Russian prisoners.

Its three MGs spit out a heavy, rapid rain of tracer towards the grey-white river banks. The Russian infantry over there send back a storm of fire at us.

'Give 'em three HEs,' orders the Old Man, brusquely. 'That'll give the gun-crazy bastards something to think about!'

A huge spout of mud, blood and snow goes up, as the HEs land between a couple of machine-gun nests. Tracer comes back at us, ricocheting in a mad dance between the trees lining the avenue.

Two P-IIIs and a P-IV go up in a roaring sheet of petrol-explosion flame. The crews hang from their turrets, bodies crackling and bubbling like torches dipped in fat.

A new sound mingles with the cacophony of this devil's concert. The hollow, whining howl of Stalin organs.

Forty-eight rocket shells come sailing through the air towards us. Long comet-tails of flame stretch behind them. Then, like clowns in a circus, their tails tip forward, and they drop vertically to the earth. They give us no feeling of being dangerous, but seem more like some strange kind of firework device. When they strike the earth our impression changes. The holes they make are tremendous, and the blast from them presses the air from our lungs.

Cutting through the roar of the Stalin organs comes the shrill scream of an armour-piercing shell on its way towards us. With a deafening crack it strikes, boring through the front shield of Feldwebel Weber's P-IV. It goes through it at an angle, and up into, and through, the turret, taking Weber with it. He lands, with a soggy splash, out in the road. The lower part of his body is completely crushed. Blood pours from his shattered face.

Two blood-spattered crewmen scramble from the P-IV, which has burst into flames. The driver has his hands over his face. He runs in circles, screaming like a madman, then collapses into the slushy snow.

A P-III comes rumbling along at top speed. It passes over the driver, leaving nothing but shreds of flesh and bloody rags of uniform.

'Come death, come sweet death,' croons the voice of the Legionnaire from the radio speaker.

The other crewman goes down across a heap of twisted metal rods, pierced through and through by a burst of tracer which seems to last for an eternity.

Roars and howls fill the air like mad organ notes. The long tram terminus collapses in on itself like a house of cards. Nothing remains of it but twisted girders and an enormous cloud of brickdust and pulverized mortar. In the middle of the desolation a tramcar stands comically on end. I stare fiercely through the optical sight, but can still not find the target. I feel like tearing open the turret hatch and running, running as fast and as far as my legs can carry me.

'Let's take 'em,' rages the Old Man, impatiently. 'Can't you see they're rangin' in on us? If you're tired of life, then for Christ's sake *die* an' get it over with!'

'I only wish the devil had that rotten swine who invented smokeless powder,' I curse, furiously, and rotate the turret a further couple of degrees. 'You used to be able to *see* when they fired their shit at you.'

'Stop your complaining, son,' says Porta. 'World wars are as world wars have to be, and not the way *you* want 'em to be. Now we have smokeless powder, and that is what we have to live with.'

'You can't explain any bleedin' thing to 'im,' rumbles Tiny. ''E thinks with the tip of 'is old John Thomas, 'e does!'

I stare until my inflamed eyes hurt with staring. I turn the sights slowly and catch sight of the muzzle-flash of an 85 mm. Without removing my gaze from it for a second I adjust the sights. Lines and figures dance before my eyes. The long barrel of the gun sinks, as if it were nodding a greeting to its target.

The Old Man steadies his night-glasses on the rim of the turret.

'Heaven have mercy on us,' he mumbles. 'It's a whole PAK* battalion!'

'Shovel shit at 'em, then!' shouts Porta from the driving seat. 'Else *we'll* get shat on, an' from a great height. Gettin' shot up ain't nice, let me tell you.'

All my attention and energy is concentrated on the busy gunners on the far bank. Four muzzle-flashes illuminate the small bushy-topped trees with a ghostly blue and blood-red glare. For a second I see the PAK gun-crews clearly. Shells whine across the flat terrain and explode in the avenue, tearing up blue-grey cobblestones and sending them flying

* *PAK*: German abbreviation for anti-tank gun

to all sides like new, runaway projectiles.

Explosions roar, thunder and crash. The few remaining windows tinkle to bits.

A human shape whirls up into the air. It looks like a woman, but the incident is merely an intermezzo in the hell of explosions.

'What a trip *she* got,' sighs Porta. 'Qualified her for the air-to-land forces, that did.'

I am only half-listening to Porta, so taken up am I with my target.

The long gun-muzzle, with its new smoke-shield, turns slowly and silently. I make a fine adjustment of the sights, and zoom in on the bustling men over there. Now I can see the Russian battery commander quite clearly. He looks like an actor on stage, illuminated by blue light-beams, rather like spotlights.

'Weird,' I mumble, unconsciously, almost enjoying the sight of the tall, slim officer in his ankle-length grey-brown cloak. His fur cap is cocked cheekily over one eye. He corrects the fire of his battery, completely unaware of our new optical sighting device which can see through fog and darkness as if it were clear daylight. 'Weird,' I repeat, and feel wildly exultant over the fact that I am the one who is going to decide just how long the tall Russian officer will remain alive.

'What d'you say?' asks the Old Man, leaning down inquisitively from the turret hatch.

'Dreamin' about 'is field-marshal's baton 'e is,' jeers Tiny, with a hoarse laugh.

'Gone to sleep, have you?' asks the Old Man angrily, hitting me hard on the shoulder with his night-glasses. 'What're you waitin' for, then? Why don't you fire? Fire, I said! Fire, damn your eyes! Shoot their arses off!'

I grip the firing release with unnecessary force . . .

With an earsplitting crash the gun goes off. A yard-long flame licks from the muzzle. The enormously heavy vehicle is pressed back on its tracks, as if it were bobbing a curtsey to the projectile which leaves its gun-muzzle.

'Loaded, safety off,' rumbles Tiny, as the breech clangs shut. The hot shell casing clatters over the steel deck plates.

With an oath Tiny kicks out at it, sending it flying toward Julius Heide. It hits him in the back of the neck. Heide jumps to his feet, violently angry, and rushes at Tiny with a stick-grenade swinging in his hand.

'I'll smash your skull for you some day, you stinking Hamburg sewer-rat,' he hisses, white with rage, and strikes at Tiny with the grenade.

'Stop that and shut up,' orders the Old Man. 'When this lot's over you can *kill* one another for all I care. Until it *is* – stay soldiers. Why, *why* did I ever let them wish 2 Section on me? God curse the day!'

'You love us really,' grins Tiny, pleased. 'If we was to take you serious an' leave you, you'd be dead as a smoked 'errin' 'angin' in the chimney-place 'fore we was out o' sight. Drowned in tears you'd be, an' never see 'ome no more.'

I press my eyes to the sight, and follow the course of the shot. A gout of snow and flame goes up close to the bushy-topped trees.

Khaki-clad forms fly up into the air. A gun-carriage is thrown away to one side, taking a whole row of bushes with it.

The Old Man is firing orders into the radio, to the other vehicles of the section. Panthers and P-IVs stream into the broad avenue, and down the side streets, with popping exhausts. Broad tracks scream and clatter over the blue-grey cobblestones. Sections Three and Five halt on each side of the street. They are so close to the walls of the great houses lining it that they scrape plaster from them, with a tearing, nerve-wrecking sound.

A window on the second floor opens. An old woman with a comical old-fashioned nightcap on her head screams with hysterical rage, and shakes a clenched fist at us threateningly.

'*Ssvinja*,' she shouts, and throws some object down at the

nearest tank. It explodes with a roar. A blinding sheet of flame goes up.

'The mad bitch is throwin' grenades,' shouts Porta. He shakes his head at the fact that anyone could be so foolish.

'Soon put a stop to that,' snarls Heide, murderously. He throws open the radio hatch and presses his mpi butt into his shoulder. Coldly he sends three short bursts at the furious woman in the green nightdress.

With a rattling scream she falls from the window and splashes onto the snow-wet cobblestones. As she falls her old-fashioned nightcap comes off. It flutters down a little behind her body and lands, like a wounded bird, on our gun-barrel.

'Jesus,' yelps Tiny, stretching his neck up, 'that's a lucky omen. I remember when me and the Yid furrier's son David from '*Ein' Oyer Strasse*' was beltin' along one time on delivery bikes with a load o' fur capes. As we passed Zirkus Weg, some sod slung a used pro' out a third-floor winder. 'Er drawers come off on the way, float down light an' pretty an' land, neat as you please, right smack on me ol' nut. There was a couple dizzy coppers on bikes breathin' down our necks. They'd seen us "borrowin'" the capes from "Alster 'Ouse". Any rate as soon as the cops saw this fuckin'-machine comin' down from the third floor they drop us an' we get away clean. So that bleedin' nightcap's gonna bring us luck!'

Barcelona's Puma opens fire. In the next few minutes 2 Section sends a storm of high-explosives into the Russian anti-tank position.

A cloud of dust and all kinds of debris lifts on the far side of the river. The earth has been literally shaved clean of everything standing up.

The countless Maxims fall silent. As the cloud of dust dissipates, we see a huge pile of scrap where the PAK battery used to be.

'That's that,' says the Old Man, lighting his silver-lidded pipe. He pushes his helmet back tiredly, and rumples his shock of greying hair.

'Hell, I'm *itchy*,' he swears, scratching his head violently with both hands. 'It's these blasted leather helmets.'

Tiny rubs a grimy hand across his soot-streaked face, and fishes a fat cigar from his gas-mask pouch. With the flamboyant gesture of a movie gangster he lights it and blows the smoke down Heide's neck.

Porta passes the vodka bottle over his shoulder. Tiny takes the first long pull at it. I have hardly set the bottle to my lips when there is a deafening explosion. A 120 mm at least.

''Oly Mother o' Kazan, Jesus'n Mary!' coughs Tiny, dropping his cigar in alarm. 'That musta took 'arf the bleedin' world with it!'

'KW-2,' says Heide, superciliously.

The Old Man whirls round in the turret, searching for the source of the threat.

The night is ripped open again by a crashing shot from the KW-2's 120 mm gun.

One of 3 Section's P-IVs is hit. It is thrown like an empty cardboard box along the street. There is a gaping hole in its flank. Two of the five-man crew tumble from the wreckage; they are living torches. The P-IV goes up into a huge fireball. Chunks of tracks and armour rain down on us.

'Where the hell *is* that Commie bastard?' comes Barcelona's hysterical scream over the communicator.

The Puma come whirling up over the hill and into cover behind the rubble of a former cannery. The rest of the section scatters in all directions. The KW-2 is slow-moving but its shells make scrap-iron of anything they hit.

Porta is the first to grasp the situation clearly. There is reason behind the selection of the quickest-minded men in a tank company for the job of driver.

'Back o' that house,' he shouts, speeding up his vehicle. 'The shit's down there. Jesus what a gun. A Cossack with a jack on could lie on his back in comfort in the muzzle of it!'

'Yes, devil take me,' cries the Old Man, in alarm. 'There the beggar is. Standing there lookin' at us. Gun round 70

30

degrees. Pointblank at 80 yards. Turret five o'clock. Got it? *Move* man, damn you!'

'Got him,' I whisper, feeling a cold shiver run down my spine as I make out the giant, grey-white silhouette, with its bulldog-like gun sticking out of the huge turret.

'Holy Mary, Mother of God!' Barcelona's voice comes over the radio. 'Lookit that bastard there? If he gets us, with just one, our feet won't touch till we hit the *Potsdammer Platz* in Berlin 'n get scraped off it by the Eytie street sweepers.'

I hold my breath anxiously as I sight in on the armoured monster. Its clumsy turret is beginning to turn slowly. There is no doubt it is us he is after.

'Fire!' I give myself the order.

Before the muzzle-flash has died away our shell strikes the KW-2. It explodes on its armour in a shower of glowing splinters. Harmlessly! We have forgotten we were loaded with HE.

'I give *up*,' shouts the Old Man furiously, banging his fists on the turret ring. 'That greenhorn trick'll get you a court! I've no *time* for you lot any more!'

'Oh, great!' Porta bellows with laughter. 'Hit 'im bang up the jacksey, an' you're loaded with HE, an' don't even tickle his piles up for 'im. Try hittin' him with a marker this time, an' splash some paint up his arse. He'd like that I reckon!'

'Jesus'n Mary, what's up then?' asks Tiny, chewing violently at the butt of his dead cigar.

'I've had it! I've bloody well *had* it!' screams the Old Man, blue in the face with rage. 'What's *up*? You loaded with HE, you habitual criminal oaf, you! You mad-brained, illiterate, anti-social ape! HE he throws at the world's biggest bloody tank! I *won't* stand it any more!'

''Old up now Old Un'. You'll 'ave a stroke an' drop dead if you go on like that,' says Tiny in a fatherly tone. 'Anybody can make a mistake. Even in a world war small mistakes can 'appen. 'Ere's an armour-piercin' S-shell, *see*? We can get it off at 'im 'fore 'e's woke up. The neighbours ain't all that quick off the mark where 'eadwork's concerned. We seen that plenty o' times. It's us Germans as 'as got it up top in this man's war!'

'I'll get you a court-martial,' the Old Man promises him, white with rage, '*and* I'll take you to Germersheim personally, when they give you life!'

'Arse'oles to that,' grins Tiny, carelessly. 'They'll let me out anyway when Adolf's lost the final victory. *An'* they'll probably make me *Bürgermeister* in some funny town somewhere or other.'

'If that should come about I'd like to live in the town you get to be *Bürgermeister* in,' grins Porta. 'It'd be fantastic! An' it'd certainly go down in history as the best practical joke ever played in Germany. Send him to Germersheim, Old Un', so we can get to see a *Bürgermeister* nobody's ever seen the like of before.'

Barcelona and I fire together. Our S-shells strike the huge vehicle simultaneously, tearing the turret half-off. The commander appears in the hatchway just as the gun of the Legionnaire's P-IV spits out a long muzzle-flash. The Russian is cut over as if by a circular saw.

'*Panzer, Marsch!*' orders the Old Man, and stamps impatiently on the steel plating of the floor.

Our tank swings out and rumbles thunderously after the Panther. We leave behind us a hell of flame.

We crunch over furniture thrown from the houses by blast. A body lying spread-eagled across the tramlines, with a Schmeisser gripped in one hand, is minced under our tracks. Two turkeys dash from a pen, and run in front of us, heads bobbing.

'Jesus Christ and all the prophets,' shouts Porta, in a strangled voice. 'There goes, God help me, our Christmas dinner! Suspend the world war a minute. Those two *tovaritsch* turkeys are more important!' Before anyone can stop him he has pulled the tank to a halt and has the driver's hatch open. 'Come on Tiny, leave them shells be! Roast turkey's in the offin'!

'What's in what bleedin' oven?' asks Tiny, opening the side hatch without considering the bullets which are flying around outside. 'Jesus'n *Mary*!' he shouts happily springing out of the tank.

Before the Old Man has time to react, Tiny's huge, filthy ackboots are splashing up mud as he chases after the terrified birds.

'This beats everything,' shouts the Old Man, in a rage. 'Leaving their post in the waggon during battle! This is the worst thing they've done yet!'

'I'll swear to it for you,' offers Heide, his face lighting up. 'Desertion in the face of the enemy. That's the charge!'

'You shut your trap, you!' orders the Old Man, grinding his teeth together. He puts his head up cautiously over the rim of the turret to try to get a sight of the turkey hunters.

'It is your duty to charge them, so that those two can go before a court-martial,' shouts Heide, his bloodthirsty non-com mentality coming to the fore.

'I told you to shut up,' hisses the Old Man. He draws his P-38 from its holster. '*Do* it, or I'll shoot your head off for refusing to comply with an order.'

'You gone nuts over there?' comes Barcelona's voice scratchily over the communicator. '*Cojones**, they've got 'em! Let's get this caper over with quick so we can get our chops round some roast turkey!'

'Beg to report two prisoners taken,' cries Porta, jubilantly, as he crawls back through the driver's hatch with the maddened Russian turkeys dangling from his hand.

In a moment the whole interior of the tank seems to be filled with panic-stricken turkeys. Wings flap across our faces like whip-lashes. Blood is running down Tiny's cheek from a turkey's pecking beak.

''Elp!' he howls. 'The sod's tryin' to *eat* me. *Shoot* 'im!'

The terrified turkey flies up onto Heide's back and begins to hammer away at the back of his head as if it were trying to peck its way through to the other side. He screams in shock

---

* *Cojones* - Spanish for balls (testicles)

and pain, and thrashes at it with his fists.

'Fanatics, that's what these two are,' cries Porta, desperately. He aims a blow at one of the turkeys, which seems to be running completely amuck.

'I can't stand any more of it,' sobs the Old Man, bending over the turret rim despairingly. 'Dear God above, help me to go far, far away, far away from 2 Section! What have I done to deserve so hard a punishment?'

The communicator scratches and howls.

'What in the name of heaven have you stopped for, Beier?' comes the company commander, Oberleutnant Löwe's, angry voice. 'Get on, damn it, man, or you'll be for it. It's always your cursed section that's out of step. Clear that road-block away at the bridge, and clean out the nests. Take care, now. The area's mined. But *get on* with it, gentlemen!'

He pauses for a moment to get his breath. 'You're the lead, Beier. You and that shitty section of yours, that I'd like to see slowly roasting in hell. Your job is to go – and to *keep on going*. You stop and everything else stops. The Divisional Commander wants this job over fast, repeat fast!'

'Rotten rat-race,' mumbles the Old Man angrily. He peeps cautiously over the turret rim. 'The bridge,' he hisses. 'But fast!'

'Two more dead un's for the list,' grins Tiny, proudly, holding up the two dead turkeys.

'2 Section follow me,' the Old Man says into the communicator. He is so angry we can hear the sound of his teeth grinding.

'What you mad at?' asks Tiny, looking up at him with his head on one side. 'You're gonna get 'ot roast turkey with all the trimmin's, just like it was *really* Christmas. Enjoy the war, the peace'll be terrible! There won't be no parties 'eld in the synagogues for us thousand-year soldiers.'

Porta pulls to a halt just before the bridge and falls back resignedly in his seat.

'The tour makes a temporary stop here,' he says, with a

34

short laugh. 'The neighbours've dropped half a forest across the road. Call the Pioneers. That's what *they're* for.'

'They don't give a damn for us,' snarls the Old Man. 'Two of you get out and sling a wire round those tree-trunks so's we can pull 'em out of the way.'

'Not me,' cackles Porta. 'The driver is not to be used for any work other than driving, and is to be rested on every possible occasion. I'm bein' rested!'

'Julius and Sven! Outside! Quick's the word, *please*!'

Super-soldier Heide is out of the tank in a flash. I hesitate before opening the hatch and leaving the protection of the tank's steel walls. There one is safe from the bullets and hand-grenades of the infantry at least. The air outside hums with the sound of them, like a nest of angry wasps.

'What if the neighbours attack us?' I ask nervously when I am outside.

'That's an easy one,' grins Porta, racing his motor. 'We go into reverse. The 1000-year Reich didn't entrust us with this valuable tank to let any silly sod of a neighbour go smashin' it up. Far as you two are concerned you can be proud an' happy. You'll fall like heroes, an' *Grofaz*'ll send your families a postcard. *Heil*! *Sieg*!'

We look up fearfully at the rough sides of the tank as Porta crashes the hatch cover shut.

'Cowardly swine,' hisses Heide bitterly, as the Old Man follows Porta's example and closes the turret hatch.

'The vaunted heroic death comes to us in a dirty snow-drift,' I whisper to myself.

'What the hell are you mumbling about?' snarls Julius, staring at me. We take cover behind the huge tree-trunks, and work feverishly to get the wires into place.

I cannot be bothered to answer him. He would never understand, anyway, with his *herrenvolk* mentality.

Tracer from the turret MG whines over our heads, drawing firefly chains into the Russian tank defence positions. In a hail of whistling shrapnel fragments we finally manage to make the tow-wire fast around the first of the tree-trunks. We haul the wire after us to the tank and loop it over the tow-hooks. Our hands are cut to pieces, and blood drips from our fingertips. I drop the wire for a second to blow on my mutilated hands. Heide explodes into a howl of rage.

'You lazy pig. Letting me do all the work.' He rips his pistol from its holster, and points it at me with outstretched arms, like a film actor. 'Get up, you cardboard soldier, or I'll shoot your head off!'

At that moment I hate him so much it hurts, the puffed-up shit. How annoyingly pompous he looks, standing there tall and slim, with lips so thin they are almost invisible, and icy-cold, blue eyes. Not even the newest war-mad recruit could be so regimentally correctly dressed as Julius. When it came to it what did he know more than a recruit does? Nothing!

Raging I climb back onto my feet, murderous thoughts whirling through my brain. I know Heide is crazy enough to really shoot me if I don't get up quickly. And worst of all he would get away with it.

The Maybachs howl in top output, and the wire is drawn tight as a violin-string. After several attempts the logs begin to roll. We jump like madmen to avoid being crushed by them.

A Russian MG sweeps the road with a short burst. Bullets ricochet, howling, from the steel sides of the tank. It sounds as if a group of drummers have suddenly run amuck on their instruments.

We have almost finished clearing the road-block, and look forward to getting back to the safety of the tank when Heide gives a yell, and goes down into the ditch in one long spring. He slides like a bulldozer through the gruel of ice and water in its bottom.

'Mines!' he screams.

I stand gaping, out on the road between two enormous logs, without understanding a word. I see a large grey-red box with cyrillic lettering on it. A lever sticks up vertically into the air. The mine is armed and ready to explode. For a moment I am completely paralysed.

Our tank is rolling backwards at full speed. Porta has obviously also seen the wicked piece of machinery which is waiting to spread death and destruction on all sides.

Suddenly I am on my own in the middle of a tangle of great tree-trunks and wrecked trucks. I stare, as if hypnotized, at the flat grey-red instrument of death. Then I come alive again.

'Mines!' I yell, 'mines!' As if they didn't know it. When the lead vehicle runs into mines, the news travels back fast.

I throw myself face-down into a large, half-frozen puddle, and hardly notice the water running down into my felt boots. Soon it will turn to ice and my feet will begin to burn like fire.

'God help me,' I pray. 'Help me! Don't leave me to die here!'

There is complete silence. Even the heavy Maxims have ceased firing. It seems as if the whole world has stopped dead. As if the war is holding its breath and waiting for the mine to go off.

An eternity goes by, and still nothing happens. It should have exploded long ago. A count of five is usually enough. I have already counted to thirty-five.

The turret hatch opens slowly, and the Old Man's head appears.

'Get off your arses, you weary warriors. Get rid of that mine.'

'You must be off your rocker,' Heide shouts back furiously. 'You can see the bastard's got delayed-action fuses.'

'Shut up, and obey my order,' shouts the Old Man, impatiently. 'Get that thing out of our way, and I mean *now*. I don't care if it's got *ten* delayed-action fuses. I want it out of the way! D'you think they'll stop the war just because you lot trip over a mine?'

Porta peers cautiously through the driver's observation slit.

'What're you playin' at? Don't you *want* to get your heroic names on the big porous stone in front of the barracks at Paderborn? Very big honour that is, let me tell you. A great, national reward!'

I lift my head and take a look at the strange menacing thing. The lever points up in the air like a warning finger. I take a grip on the insulated pliers in my pocket, and ready myself to crawl over to the mine and dismantle it. It is at times like this that a man feels he never should have taken that bomb-disposal course.

The next moment everything disappears in a roaring jet of flame. Pieces of logs whirl through the air and rain down everywhere. I am totally deaf for several minutes, and feel as if my insides have been squeezed by a giant hand. Two minutes later and there would not have been a shred of me left. But the road-block has gone.

We jump up onto the tank as it comes rattling past.

'Nice job you did, there,' the Old Man praises us, with an approving smile. 'Speed up, Porta, give it more gas. We've a long way to go yet!'

'Yes, if it's China we're headed for that *is* a bit of a way off,' grins Porta, exuberantly.

'China?' mumbles Tiny, racking shells in the ammunition locker. 'Ain't that the place where they eat with sticks an' fatten up on rice? Let's get movin'. I can't think of anythin' better'n boiled rice with tiny 'errings.'

'I can give you the address of a good eating-house in Pekin,' grins Porta, putting on speed.

The armoured division rolls relentlessly on, pushing deeply into the Ukraine. Many fall, more are mutilated. The landscape is grim. The grey coldness of a Russian winter is approaching. Tanks rattle and roar through sooty-black villages, plough past huge piles of coal. We do not see a single tree. Vegetation, grass, all green things are gone. Not the least trace, even, of the much vaunted sunflower fields is left. The wild madness of war has eaten up everything in its path. Omnivorously.

The company halts for an hour before a middle-sized provincial town. We have never heard the name of it before. A Russian armoured division has taken it over and turned the town into a hedgehog defensive position. Then our Stukas come roaring out of the grey, snow-filled clouds with sirens howling relentlessly. Heavy bombs whirl down through the air. One swarm of dive-bombers follows the other. The town disappears from the face of the earth – *ausradiert* as they say in the propaganda programmes.

Then the tanks pass over what is left of it, killing everything left alive and crushing the dead to pulp under their tracks.

When we reach the next town the Stukas have already visited it, and prepared it for the taking. The dust of pulverized bricks and mortar hangs like a red-grey cloud in the air. Artillery and Cossack horses lie in the shattered streets, stiff-legged and with swollen bodies. Guns lying on their side, wrecked lorries and mountains of tangled equipment, are scattered amongst heaps of bodies. Dead and wounded Russian soldiers lie against walls, or hang from gaping window openings.

Dispassionately we stare at the bloody scene. It has become an everyday sight. In the beginning we puked and felt sick to our stomachs. It is a long time since any of us puked.

'That's the way to take a town,' shouts Julius Heide, enthusiastically. He leans triumphantly out of the forward hatch. With a jeering smile he stares at a Russian soldier sitting up against a wall and looking blankly at his crushed legs.

'You're wearin' the wrong uniform,' says Porta. 'You talk like those puffed-up arseholes in the shit-brown uniforms, an' the yellow leather equipment to hold their fat guts in. You're a shit of shits, you are, Julius! You're blinded by your crazy belief in the Führer. I really think you'd be glad if one of the shit-brown sods knocked on your mother's door one day an' screamed: "Heil Hitler, Frau Heide! Your son,

Unteroffizier Julius Heide, has fallen for the Führer and Greater Germany! We feel for you in your proud sorrow, Frau Heide! The Führer thanks you!"'

'Old Man, you are my witness,' explodes Heide, in a rage. 'This is an insult. I will not stand for it!'

'Sit down then,' says the Old Man, indifferently. 'There's a lot of things *I* won't stand for. Come on, *Panzer Marsch*! And keep your traps shut, too! I can't stand the sound of your voices. And you, Porta, stop insulting Adolf!'

The night is dark. Snow and rain fall at the same time. It is cold on the way to Nikolajev.

We stop in the middle of a huge factory. It is Porta, of course, who discovers it to be a vodka distillery. Half an hour later we are stoned out of our minds. We reel around, falling over one another, pour vodka over our own heads and lick it into our mouths like cats lapping up cream. We dip our bread in vodka, and become more drunk than ever.

A Feldwebel dies of alcohol shock. A Gefreiter sets fire to himself, to convince a friend that vodka can be ignited just as easily as petrol. We try to put it out by throwing more vodka on him, and laugh foolishly at his screams of pain.

Some of 3 Section come along, dragging four women with them. They throw them across a packing table.

An infantry Feldwebel threatens them with a court-martial. Even in the madness of war there has to be some order and discipline. The punishment for rape is hanging. This is the case in every reasonably civilized army. Nobody listens to him. He is pushed to one side, and drunken soldiers threaten to cut his throat.

'Pricks at the ready!' orders an Obergefreiter with a bloodstained bandage round his head. He throws himself lustfully on top of a half-naked screaming woman, old enough to be his great-grandmother. '*Cunt!*' he roars, and collapses, helplessly drunk, between her thrashing legs. Others pull him away from her and fight to take his place.

We wake up next morning depressed, and with the most horrible hangovers. Soon the military police arrive with their shiny helmets, and the crescent emblem dangling on their chests.

The court-martial is over in four and a half minutes. Eight soldiers dangle, each at the end of his rope. The whole battalion is paraded to see the show. The dead men hang there, with strangely elongated necks, wearing only their uniform trousers. Greatcoats and boots have been taken from them. There is a shortage of such things. They hang there still, turning and swinging on the end of their ropes, as we rattle past, mud churning up from our clattering tracks, on the way to Nikolajev.

'*C'est la guerre*! Come death, come sweet death,' hums the Legionnaire, sardonically, from the turret of his vehicle.

'A dear fuck that was,' sighs Porta. 'Better to pay for it in coin of the realm, if they won't do it for love.'

'There's more'n you'd think get it for takin' cunt what ain't theirs,' growls Tiny, looking thoughtfully at the hanged men.

Raindrops spatter on the armoured sides of the tanks. It is a cold and miserable day. The air reeks with death, and stinks of wet clothing and leather. The clouds are dirty grey. They seem to be rushing towards the west, away from the melancholy Russian day. It is no longer really day. More a kind of twilight.

The little Colonel-general is standing on a thrown-up mound of earth, observing his 4th Tank Army. As usual he is wearing his battered silk field-cap, with its short peak pulled well down on his forehead. Beneath it his eagle nose juts out like a beak from the middle of his narrow skull of a face. His boots seem unbelievably long on his short legs. He stands, stiff as a statue, with his map-case under his arm. A hugh pair of binoculars dangle from his neck, partly covering the red tabs on his cloak. To look at this tiny man, with the oversized binoculars and the almost comically high-topped riding boots, you would never dream that he is the greatest tank general who has ever lived.

The Old Man gives the Army Commander a regimental eyes right.

'If only the neighbours'd send a 150 mm down on his napper,' Porta wishes, with an abrupt laugh, 'an' send him up to give the angels a big smackin' kiss on the arse.'

'We'd only get another of the same sort,' says the Old Man, tiredly, '*and* most likely one worse'n little short-arse there!'

'He's standing right on top of a busted shithouse,' laughs Gregor Martin, who is now back with us. He is turret-gunner on Barcelona's Puma.

'Wish 'e'd drop down through the top an' fall into it,' growls Tiny, 'so 'im an' 'is fancy silk cap'd get drowned together in Russian shit.'

Barcelona both salutes and gives the eyes right at the same time. The sight of the Army Commander has made him nervous.

Colonel-general Hoth lifts his hand an inch or two.

'Who's that fool?' he asks his Adjutant, who is standing to attention at his elbow as usual.

'I will find out, sir,' barks the Adjutant, smartly.

'Don't you know your men?' asks the General, irritably. 'My Adjutant ought to know every man in my army.'

'Mad bastard,' thinks the Adjutant. 'There's 80,000 men in 4th *Panzer*. I don't know every silly sod on the staff, even.' He is, however, an old hand. He barks out the first name to come into his head.

'Oberfeldwebel Stollmann, sir!'

'Charge him,' snarls the General. 'He can be punished for unregimental saluting. I've never seen anything like it! Saluting! As if the fool was on parade. I want you to look after that man. Properly, understand!'

'Very good, sir!' replies the Adjutant, scribbling in his notebook.

As Barcelona's Puma swings round at the entrance to the long connecting road, the General catches sight of Albert's black face in the open driving hatch.

'Why's that man's face black?' he asks the Adjutant.

'*Black*, sir?' mumbles the Adjutant, in surprise. He puts

42

his glasses to his eyes, to get a closer look at Albert. 'Looks like a negro, sir!' he says, doubtfully.

The entire staff put up their binoculars. For a moment 4th *Panzer* is forgotten, and all interest is concentrated on Albert in the clean-up waggon's driving-seat.

'A *negro*?' snarls the General, irritably. 'What nonsense! Germany's had no colonies for the last twenty years.'

'Twenty-five, sir,' the Chief-of-Staff corrects him, 'and the last of the colonial troops were retired years ago.'

'Charge that man for having blackened his face without orders,' snaps the General, brusquely. 'I don't want my army turned into a lot of circus clowns!'

The Adjutant writes feverishly: Driver in Puma 524 to be punished for blackening face. He adds, on his own initiative: and for laughing.

In the course of the day we push on through stretched-out villages lining the sides of the roads. White sheets hang from every window as a sign of capitulation.

The inhabitants stand pressed up against the walls of their houses, unsmilingly, faces marked by the fear of the future.

Late in the afternoon we make a halt. We refuel, ammunition is issued, and benzedrine tablets are handed out to each man. There is still no time to waste on sleeping.

Porta and Tiny are long since inside the houses, ransacking boxes and cupboards. They do not really know what they are looking for, but are just sniffing around like inquisitive dogs.

'Funny things they drink out of in this country,' says Tiny, gazing in astonishment at a large pink irrigator and holding it up. 'Couldn't empty that bleeder very often 'fore your bleedin' brains blew out through your ear'oles. What's the tube in it for though?'

'Anybody can see *that*,' answers Porta. 'Ivan's a practical feller. He lies on his back when he drinks, so he doesn't hurt himself when he falls down. We Germans can learn a lot here in Russia.'

'I gotta try that,' says Tiny, enthusiastically, hanging the irrigator from his belt like a second gasmask pouch. 'Think o' lyin' flat on your bleedin' back an' gettin' the biggest drunk on the world's ever 'eard of! Maybe a bloke ought to turn Russki an' forget all about old Germany?'

'Holy Virgin Mary's Mother,' cries Porta, in surprise. 'Here's a dead woman, and she's wearing a hunting cap with a feather in it. Going travellin' perhaps when she died. Did go too, only a bit longer trip than she'd reckoned on.'

'Smells like murder,' he murmurs, after taking a closer look at the body. 'Took one in the guts, she did. Can't have been an execution, or she'd have got the pill in her neck. That's how they do it in this country.'

''Ow dreadful!' says Tiny, turning up his eyes. 'Such wicked bleeders ought to be put in jail!'

'Here's her handbag,' Porta goes on. He picks up a lady's bag made of reindeer skin. He shoves his nose right into it, and rummages round.

'Out of here immediately! That's an order!' yells Heide in his best NCO's voice. He positions himself in the doorway with his hands on his hips and bobs up and down on his toes.

'Up you, Moses,' says Tiny, unimpressed.

The blood flashes up into Heide's arrogant Teutonic face.

'I'm warning you, Obergefreiter Creutzfeldt, call me Moses one more time and I'll shoot you! It's dishonouring!'

'Dis'onourin'? Gettin' shot?' laughs Tiny, swinging his *Nagan*.

'*Moses*! You look like the feller as falls on 'is arse at the village fair.'

Heide fumbles furiously for his pistol, but luckily for Tiny it sticks in its holster and he has to use both hands to get it out.

'*Moses*! You'll never get to be a big cowboy star in the pictures,' Tiny screams with laughter. 'The bleedin' rustlers'd've shot you fulla 'oles 'fore you knew what was goin' on!'

A salvo of howling rockets from a Stalin organ drops in the next street, and sends a wall crashing down across the roadway.

'Jesus'n Mary,' cries Tiny, throwing himself down into cover close by the wall. 'Ain't them barmy bleedin' neighbours *ever* goin' to get tired of shootin' at us?'

A German SMG begins to bark in wild, hysterical bursts.

'Hell man, stop that!' the Old Man's voice rings through the noise. 'The tracer'll tell 'em our position!'

'Julius 'as 'ad it,' shouts Tiny, pointing with the muzzle of his mpi at Heide's body stretched out on the floor.

'The Führer lost a faithful soldier there,' says Porta, sadly.

'Hold his forehead while I take his three gold teeth. I've had my eye on 'em for a long time now!'

'You gonna do that? 'E *is* a kind of a mate when all's said an' done!' says Tiny, suddenly turning moralist.

'How's he to know what's happening? Dead isn't he?' answers Porta, bending over Heide. He is just about to take a grip on one of the teeth with his forceps when Heide comes to with a shout. 'Damnation!' cries Porta, in astonishment, 'I thought you were dead!'

'Corpse robber,' screams Heide, gazing with open disgust at Porta's rusty dental forceps.

'Corpse robber?' says Porta, blankly. 'Couldn't *be*! Not dead yet, are you?'

'I'm going to charge you,' snarls Heide, furiously. He dabs at his neck, where a shell-splinter has dug a deep furrow.

'Outside!' shouts the Old Man. 'Get this area cleaned up and quick about it. It's full of aspiring heroes looking forward to dyin' for the great Stalin!'

'I'm on my way,' shouts Porta. He runs off along the houses with the LMG in his hand, supporting grip out.

A clumsy Russian hand-grenade comes flying through the air and falls, smoking, at Tiny's feet. With a resolute kick, worthy of a soccer international, he sends it flying back. Not for nothing is he the regiment's top goal-scorer.

Porta sends a couple of short bursts up at some gaping window-openings, and jumps to cover behind a burnt-out transport vehicle.

'Either them shits're down in the cellars,' yells Tiny, falling full-length in a shower of mud and half-melted snow, 'or else they're upstairs.'

'Where?' howls Porta, crossing in long jumps to the opposite side of the street. He goes down, like lightning, flat in the gutter as he hears the feared mooing of a 'cow' on the way. A row of cobblestones flies into the air.

'Get down, damn you,' shouts the Old Man to the section, signalling with his arms.

Albert is behind a pushcart lying on its side, firing away with an MG-34 as if he were aiming at breaking the world war record for disposal of most ammunition in the shortest time.

Barcelona drops down beside him, panting. 'What the hell are you shootin' at, you black ape? We got to *account* for that ammunition!'

'Shit on that, man!' wheezes Albert, grey-faced with terror. 'No fucking Commie bastard's gonna pull the carpet out from under *my* fallen, fuckin' arches!'

'Stop it, you mad sod,' shouts Barcelona, giving the LMG a kick which sends it flying out of Albert's hands. Shaking his head from side to side, Albert leans up against the wet wall of a house and stares with a lost look at his LMG, which lies hissing in a drift of filthy snow.

'What're you sitting here moping for?' asks Porta, emerging from a house behind two prisoners with hands raised above their heads. 'You look like Frankenstein playin' the part of the Mummy.'

'Now I'm not supposed to shoot any more,' grumbles Albert. 'This is the shittiest war that ever was, you know that, man!'

''Course you can shoot,' answers Porta. 'Bang away at 'em, son. That's what the army's paying you for.' With a broad grin on his freckled face he disappears round the

46

corner with his two prisoners. He will sell them to a prisoner collection squad, out looking for medals.

'Mount!' orders the Old Man. '*Panzer Marsch*!'

'The Führer has won the war,' declares Heide, proudly, as we roll past long rows of Russian soldiers standing with raised hands. They have a lost look about them.

'There'll only be room for two kinds o' people, now,' grunts Tiny, bitterly. 'Them peacocks as does the orderin' about, an' all the other bleedin' idiots as stands to attention, in the sacks as 'olds their bones in place, an' screams 'Eil 'Itler!'

After a short, bloody battle we push forward straight through Poltawski. At the edge of the roads lie corpses clad in grey prison uniforms. All of them have small bullet entry holes at the back of their necks. Cheekbones jut sharply through the thin parchment skin of their faces, and their teeth are bared in ghastly skull-fashion.

'Liquidated,' confirms the Old Man. He sends a long, brown stream of tobacco-juice over the rim of the hatch. 'They're as bad as our rotten lot.'

'Not long since,' says Barcelona, leaning out of the clean-up waggon's turret to get a closer look. 'Blood's still fresh and drippin'.'

'But why've they shot 'em?' asks Gregor. 'And right out here on the road, where we're coming bashin' along.'

'Couldn't keep up,' says Porta, knowledgeably, 'caused trouble and slowed down the rest.'

'They bloody well can't do *that*,' says Gregor, bending over the body of a woman. 'They bloody, fuckin' *can't*!'

'You'll see worse than that,' answers Porta, laconically. 'Wait till the pendulum swings back, an' it's us who're on the run with the neighbours snapping at our arses. Then you'll see what *we* can do!'

The Old Man lights his silver-lidded pipe in silence, and wishes inside that he could get his fingers on the man who had carried out this massacre.

The rows of dead seem never-ending, but no more than

47

an hour later the maelstrom of war has driven the episode out of our heads, like many other things.

Physical death lies in wait for us round every corner. We cannot choose death, but must live, and carry on as well as we can. War is a disease, and it is best not to think of it too much, but to forget the impressions its symptoms leave on us. If we didn't we would all very soon go raving mad.

The section takes up position alongside a small river, which runs, yellow and cold, down to the distant sea.

Porta has placed the SMG behind a heap of potato-sacks. Potatoes are as good as sandbags for stopping bullets, he says. Barcelona wants the vehicles ready to go, so that we can move off at short notice if necessary, but meets with wild protests when he demands that the drivers remain in their seats.

'There's not gonna be much time,' he tries to explain to the angry drivers, who are afraid of remaining alone in their vehicles. 'I want those bloody waggons ready to move while there's still *time*!' he orders, raging.

'Up you and your time,' shouts Porta, disrespectfully. 'Sit in your sardine-can yourself if you want to. I'm staying here with the popgun. When the neighbours come knockin' on the door'll be time enough to take off. I'm gonna be one of the survivors of this world war. I'm not goin' to get fried in me own fat, if some Commie sod or other gets the idea of tacking a magnetic onto my backside.'

In the light of a huge fire, which is raging down at some grain storehouses, Tiny comes crawling out of a window opening dragging a large chest behind him.

A Maxim sends a line of tracer bullets at him.

'Stop that bleedin' waste o' bullets,' he yells, waving a threatening fist at the invisible Russian positions. 'Got earth where your brains oughta be? Or shit, is it, maybe?'

'I'll smash you to bits, if you don't leave that chest lie,' shouts the Old Man, furiously. 'Get back to your rotten squad. I see you looting one more time an' you're for a court!'

A flare goes up. A slowly sinking comet with a colourful

tail of smoke behind it. Everyone stands completely still in the blinding white light. There are sounds all around us. Heavy boots tip-toeing, nervous hands cocking weapons, battle-knives ringing, bullets being pushed into breeches. The mumbling noises of death. We see nothing, hear only the noises coming from the darkness. We are never quite sure whether they are real or whether our nervous imaginations are deceiving us.

Porta raises his head and sniffs like a tensed-up hunting dog.

Slowly, unbelievably slowly, the cursed flare sinks down towards the earth.

Without making the slightest noise I turn the LMG.

'Holy Saint Agnes of Bielefeld,' whispers Porta, in open excitement. 'If what I'm smellin' is right, I will burn a candle in the synagogue of my heart for the God of Germany for the rest of my life.'

There is a sharp cracking explosion above our heads, and we press ourselves down into the mud. One of the very largest flares flowers against the night-dark heavens.

'Life ain't nothin' but one wide-open, stinkin' black arsehole,' curses Albert, his teeth chattering, from a deep cellar opening. 'Tonight my girl'll be dancin' at the *Zigeunerkeller*, an' they'll all be starin' straight up her clean-shaven black cunt every time she swings her legs. After that she fucks with the whole rotten garrison. *That's* what a man has to put up with!'

'She black, too?' asks Gregor interestedly, his eyes watchful above the MG barrel. He is certain there are several companies of Russians sneaking around out there in the darkness, getting ready to storm our positions and cut all our throats.

'I'm a paleface compared to her,' mumbles Albert, running his hand over his face. 'She's black as only God's own people *can* be!'

'She a whore?' asks Porta bluntly, showing his face over the top of a sack of potatoes.

'You say that once more, man,' snarls Albert furiously,

49

'an' I'll pull that maggoty white skin of yours down over your stinkin' German face! She's an *artiste*, man! She dances French in the *Zigeunerkeller*. And she's got her name on the posters outside! An' I love that girl, man, even though she *is* a French nigger woman.'

'Holy Mary, Mother of Jesus,' shouts Porta. 'Can I believe my ears. Get that flare out quick. Sucking pigs, God dammit, *sucking* pigs!'

As soon as the flare dies, Porta and Tiny race off like hungry hounds on the scent with tongues hanging out. They take no notice of the Old Man's angry shouts ordering them to come back to the unit.

'It's desertion,' shouts the Old Man into the dark. 'I've had it now. My patience is at an end!'

'They smell food, *mes amis*,' the Legionnaire chuckles merrily. He lights a long cigarette from the butt of the previous one. 'The whole of the Red Army, even, would not be able to stop them now!'

Tiny falls only once during his mad rush forward, but tumbles twenty yards on down an incline, and brings up against a tilted tractor. Soon after he runs across a Russian answering a call of nature behind a bush.

The Russian's pistol has only half cleared its holster when Tiny's close combat knife thuds into his chest. 'The good die young,' growls the big man, as his knife goes home.

> 'I was so lonely,
> You were so charming,'

sings Porta, happily, in a hoarse Louis Armstrong voice, as he bends over a litter of six grunting sucking-pigs. One of them rubs itself lovingly against Tiny's jackboots. He lies down in the mouldy straw, and begins to play with the piglets.

'Cut that out, now,' warns Porta, 'or it'll be the same game as with that big sow we got fond of. The one that died of old age!'

'Why d'you sing that foreign stuff?' asks Tiny, wrinkling his brow.

'*I* dunno,' answers Porta. 'I think it sounds nice. I love Louis Armstrong. Nobody can sing like them darkies!'

'Adolf's black-listed 'im too,' says Tiny, sadly. 'I 'ad a good record of 'is. They knocked the shit out o' me once up in *Stadthausbrücke 8* for 'earin it. Gawd, 'ow they did belt me. Then they made me eat the bleedin' record afterwards, just so I'd understand that that kind o' *untermensch* shit wasn't what us Germans listened to.'

'Adolf's mad as a hatter,' says Porta, 'but we'll get him some day. Be patient, my son. The sun always comes out again after the storm.'

'I can't stop thinkin' about it,' says Tiny, scratching one of the pigs thoughtfully behind the ear. 'I reckon we ought to shoot 'is Austrian bonce off. But break 'is left leg first. Then 'is right. Then both arms from 'is finger joints upwards, so 'e'll know we mean it serious. In between times we 'it 'im in the balls, if 'e's got any. Then we wind up by pourin' petrol all over 'im an' puttin' a match to 'im like a bonfire. That's exactly what *I* think we'd 'ave to do to 'im to make everythin' even steven!'

'Take it easy, we'll fix him when the time comes,' promises Porta. 'He'll be sorry he ever took on the job of Führer. Vote for Adolf and die young,' he laughs out into the night.

A shell explodes, with a crash, somewhere inside the town. A couple of machine-guns rattle viciously, but soon go silent. The plopping of a mortar sounds as a finale.

The Old Man bursts in on them in full battle-kit. He is covered with mud from helmet brim to boot-tops.

'You gone stone bonkers? What the hell are you up to?'

'Take a look,' grins Porta, pleasantly. 'We're engaging some Commie pigs.'

'Heavenly Father,' groans the Old Man, despairingly. He throws his mpi, clattering, across the mud floor. 'What have I done to be made leader of such a lot of crazy sods as 2 Section? The neighbours are attackin' along the whole front, and close to rollin' us up, an' what are *you* doin'? Sitting here playing with some bloody pigs. You go on report for this, blast your eyes, you do!'

'Why're you always so mad at us?' asks Tiny. 'You think too much about the army an' the bleedin' war, you do. Enjoy life. It's short enough as it bleedin' is!'

'Shut your trap, you,' hisses the Old Man, viciously, pointing at Tiny with a stick-grenade.

There is the heavy thudding of distant shell-fire. In between the sharper crack of tank guns can be heard.

'Maybe it's about time a feller got 'is valuable arse movin',' says Tiny, listening critically to the guns.

A couple of Maxims start up a crossfire, but it is nervous shooting and does us no damage.

Porta tucks a kicking piglet under his arm. Tiny slings his mpi and takes one under each arm.

'You take one too,' he says to the Old Man. 'We ought to 'ave enough to be able to give everybody a bit, so they won't get snotty!'

'You can't run about carrying pigs in the middle of an attack,' rages the Old Man, copper-coloured in the face. He strikes at one of the piglets.

Porta peers out of the door, but quickly closes it again.

'What's up?' asks the Old Man, his face twitching nervously.

'Nothin' special. Only a Russian colonel, with a machine-popper under his arm, and his eyes full o' German corpses!'

A rain of bullets strikes the walls of the house, almost tearing the door off its hinges.

'Nice way to knock on a door,' growls Tiny, getting behind a heavy supporting tree-trunk, still with his squealing piglets under his arms.

The plopping of mortars sounds continually. The whole area is bombarded with earth, stones and shrapnel from the explosions.

'Let's get out of here,' says the Old Man. 'The neighbours'll be here before we know it!'

'Jesus'n Mary,' shouts Tiny. 'Them crazy neighbours is shootin' with 'eavy stuff! You'd think they was tryin' to kill us poor bleeders or somethin'!'

One of the piglets intensifies its squeals. Its side has been cut open by a piece of shrapnel. Tiny is covered with blood.

'Kill that blasted pig,' shouts the Old Man. 'They'll hear it all over Russia.'

Tiny slits its throat quickly. The squealing dies away in a few small final grunts.

'To die so young,' he says, compassionately.

It is a heavy, icy-cold morning, and fog lies like a blanket over the landscape.

Porta stops behind the cover of some bushes. He withdraws the flare-pistol from its canvas holster.

'None o' that shit,' the Old Man warns him, nervously. 'We can't see anything by it anyway.'

'*I* know *that*,' answers Porta, stretching his arm upwards at an angle with the flare-pistol clutched in his hand. 'It'll just make Ivan know we're awake an' ready. Then, while the silly sods are sittin' there afraid they're gonna get their arses shot off any minute, we sneak quietly away from the party.'

The flare hangs, for a few short minutes, over the terrain. Then it is dark again, and we can see nothing at all.

'At the double, that way, along the old position,' the Old Man orders me.

Panting with effort, I rush along the narrow trench, in mud up to my ankles. I stop for a moment at a corner. I need a cigarette. I see Russian faces under funny-looking helmets. They are looking straight down at me from the parapet of the trench. Everything happens faster than my eyes and brain can register it. The dark morning fog is filled with flame, smoke and wild cries. Behind me and in front of me there are Russians who have jumped down into the trench. The muzzle-flash of a *Kalashnikov*, going off just in front of my face, blinds me for a second. Maddened with the fear of death I fall over backwards, come up again and engage a Russian who is just as frightened as I am. I strike at him blindly with my combat knife, and feel it get home in his guts. In a close embrace we fall to the muddy floor of the trench. I wrench my knife out of his body, and stab at him

53

again and again. Hot blood spurts into my face. Then I am up again, and run in panic, without knowing which way my feet are carrying me.

The Russians behind me throw hand-grenades. The night lights up with their explosions.

Porta and Tiny come rushing towards me. I throw myself down to avoid their rattling machine-pistols.

The Old Man is behind them. Close behind him come others.

A wild, bloody hand-to-hand fight begins. I rip a *Kalashnikov* from the hands of a dead Russian lieutenant, and begin to fire blindly at whatever is in front of me.

We thirst for blood and revenge. We *want* to kill. We are happy to have hit the hated enemy in the back.

A bare-headed Russian corporal stands in front of me, with both hands above his head. I empty half of my magazine into his chest, and smash the butt of my weapon into his face.

Suddenly everything is still. The fighting is over as suddenly as it began. Some minor skirmishing, the report will say.

Porta has a bottle of vodka in his hand. He pulls the cork with his teeth, takes a long, gurgling swig at it, and gives out a long, rolling belch. The blood comes back into his thin cheeks, and his eyes begin to look more lively. He wipes his mouth with the back of his hand. Then he bends down and picks up a rifle-grenade. He screws off the cap, and puts the grenade into his pocket. Ready for use, if we run into any more surprises.

With mpis at the ready, and fingers on their triggers, Porta and I jump through a street-door, ready to mow down anything moving. We know that those left behind in such towns are crazy fanatics, totally insane, completely regardless of their lives as long as they take some enemy soldiers with them.

Silently we sneak along the walls of the houses, straining our eyes to pierce the dust hanging in the air. I strangle a cough, afraid to give away our position to some madman waiting with his finger on the trigger.

The first room is empty. The next one, too.

Quietly, I catfoot up a narrow spiral staircase. My heart seems to stop beating for several minutes when a heavy hand falls on my shoulder. Luckily I am so frightened that I forget the weapon in my hands.

'Mustn't shit in Adolf's trousers, now,' whispers Tiny, calmingly. 'It's only me! If it'd been Ivan you'd 'ave been kissin' the angels in the arse by now!'

'Lord preserve us! You nearly frightened the life out of me,' I stammer, knocking his hand away, roughly.

'Look what I found,' he says, happily, holding up an oblong box filled with cigars for me to see. 'A bleedin' colonel belongin' to the neighbours was sittin' there dead with 'is 'and on top of it when I come by.' With a flourish he places one of the fat cigars in his mouth and lights it with a lighter made out of a bullet casing.

'You must be mad,' I whisper fearfully. 'With everybody out there lying in wait, ready to shoot our heads off, you . . .'

'Worth dyin' for a good cigar,' says Tiny, calmly. He holds his primitive lighter above his head like a torch, and looks inquiringly around him.

The staircase creaks treacherously, as we tiptoe on up it.

'Rotten old shit,' he rages, kicking noisily at a loose plank.

Porta is waiting for us on a landing with a half-empty vodka bottle in his hand. He takes a long swig at it, before handing it on to Tiny, who leaves only a drop for me.

'Anybody here?' I cough, nervously, from the fiery spirit.

'How should I know?' asks Porta. 'Think I'm a bloody clairvoyant or somethin', p'raps?'

'We'll soon find out,' says Tiny, taking a couple of heavy drags on his cigar, and sticking his head out of the door-opening, like a Red Indian trying to look round corners. 'Hey, Ivan there!' he roars in a voice which echoes through the house. 'Come on out you *tovaritsches*. We got somethin' nice for you.' He thumbs off the safety on his LMG and waves the muzzle about. 'Not as much as a limp prick,' he chuckles and enters the room with long, confident strides. It is a mess of shattered furniture. Shards of porcelain and glass crunch under our hob-nailed boots.

A doll, of the kind which can open and close its eyes, lies in the middle of the floor. Porta picks it up and places it carefully on what is left of an old-fashioned sideboard.

The sweet, sickly stench of death hangs over the whole house.

An LMG rattles wildly out in the street. Two others start up. Mortars plop. The sounds die away again into a waiting silence in which death watches from every hiding-place.

'Hell, my arm hurts,' I complain, trying to roll my sleeve up.

'Where?' asks Porta. 'Let's have a look at it.'

'Gawd, you're bleedin',' says Tiny, opening his eyes wide. 'Who's cut you, then?'

'Must have been down in that rotten trench, when those murderous swine jumped down on me,' I answer.

Porta puts on a dressing, first washing the wound with some beer from an opened bottle standing on the sideboard.

'That's quite a slash they give you there,' says Tiny, pityingly. ''Ave a officer's cigar will you? It 'elps.'

I shake my head, and bite my lips with pain as Porta scrapes the long knife-cut clean.

We continue slowly on through the house with machine-pistols at the ready. In the attic we find a double bed with a body lying on it. It is swollen up and lies with staring, glazed eyes.

Tiny pushes at it inquisitively with his bayonet.

'You nuts, or somethin'? Head full o' earth, is it?' Porta scolds him. 'Put a hole in him, an' we get corpse-gas straight up in our faces. We won't be able to stand ourselves. Take a look if he's got any gold teeth, but careful! *Don't* bloody puncture him.'

Tiny opens the dead man's mouth, with the mien of a professional dentist.

'Not a sod,' he says, shaking his head, sadly. 'Proletarian shit with steel teeth. Them bleedin' Commies knows 'ow to do the people in the eye, all right. The bosses gets gold in their kissers, an' the coolies 'as to make do with bleedin' iron. An' that's what they call equal rights? I ain't never goin' to turn Commie. You can put that in the soddin' 'eadlines!'

Most of the roof has been burnt, and we can see the dark sky through it. A flare explodes into a spreading white flower of light. Immediately, the heavy guns begin to thunder. A row of red fireballs blinks into existence.

'Jesus'n Mary,' shouts Tiny clattering rapidly down the narrow spiral staircase. 'The neighbours are comin'!'

Plops and crashes intensify, as a rain of shells falls on the town.

I almost fly through the door and throw myself flat down into what I hope is cover, but turns out to be the remains of two Germans. My stomach rolls over and I puke heartily. I beat at my clothing in a hysterical attempt to rid it of the human rubbish.

'Take it easy, *mon ami, c'est la guerre*,' drawls the little Legionnaire. In one long jump he is beside me. 'It is only more human offal on the muckheap of the war.'

After a short while the artillery fire dies away. Only the mortars continue to plop away, dropping their shells around us.

A couple of Maxims bark angrily, sending lines of tracer along the street.

'Where the hell they shooting from?' asks Gregor in wonder. 'Can't see their muzzle-flash anywhere.'

'The wicked sods are shooting through tent canvas,' Porta explains, knowledgeably.

Three tank grenadiers come running noisily, weighed down by field equipment, and throw themselves down, panting, alongside us.

'Feldwebel Groos,' one of them introduces himself, putting his new-looking steel helmet straight.

'Obergefreiter, by the grace of God, Joseph Porta,' grins Porta, raising his yellow topper slightly.

'Fuck off, you silly sod,' snarls the Feldwebel, inching away as if Porta had the plague.

The sucking noise of a mortar bomb sounds again. It falls a little way in front of us. A spout of water goes up and a red fire hydrant goes spinning across the street to smash against the wall just behind Tiny.

I hunch down behind the LMG, my stomach cramping with fear. I drop my head and rest the rim of my helmet on the stock of the weapon, afraid to look up.

Another flare wobbles into the sky. The sound of the shot rings in my ears. It is the Feldwebel of grenadiers who has sent it up.

'What in the name of all the devils in hell are you up to, you dopey idiot?' rages the Old Man. 'D'you want the whole of Ivan's blasted army on our necks?'

''Ead-full o' rotten, bleedin', cat-shit's what 'e's got,' growls Tiny, looking wickedly at the grenadier Feldwebel. 'Want my advice, Old Un', you'll cut 'is balls off!'

'Who do you think you're talking to, Obergefreiter?' explodes the Feldwebel, in a fury. 'Can't you see *these*? You're talking to a Feldwebel. I'm putting you on report for speaking improperly to a superior!'

'Shut your arse, mate. Tie a knot in your prick,' Tiny suggests from the darkness, cackling with laughter.

'I won't stand for this,' bellows Feldwebel Grooss. 'I demand that this man be punished.'

'Get out of here 'fore I shoot you,' hisses the Old Man, irritably. 'Nobody invited you. This is 2 Section, and you've nothing to do with us here!'

'This *is* the same war,' Feldwebel Groos says, defensively, staring furiously at the Old Man.

'Got cloth ears have you? Didn't you hear the man? He said to beat it,' shouts Porta, happily. 'Are all Saxons as hard to dance with as you? To hell, Fido! Get back in your basket an' go to sleep!'

'Don't you let 'em talk to you like that, sir,' says a tall grenadier with a voice as thin as his body, and a uniform still stinking of depot moth-balls.

'Ivan'll be here any minute an' shoot your backsides off,' says Gregor with a long, happy whinny of laughter.

'Up on your feet! We're moving,' decides Groos, sharply. He gets to his feet with the air of a leader of men, and does not hear the treacherous whine in the air. We hear it and press ourselves down as close to the ground as we can get. 'Cowardly pigs,' he just manages to get out, before an 80 mm shell explodes right in front of him.

His body is silhouetted briefly against the glare of the explosion. The shell blast cuts him in two, and sends the upper half of his body, with binoculars and steel helmet, far off to one side and through an open door.

'Christ a'mighty!' shouts Tiny. ''E was lucky that bleedin' door was standin' on the jar. 'E *woulda* got one on the nut if it'd been shut!'

'What do we do now?' ask the other grenadiers, looking uncertainly at the Old Man.

'Find yourselves some good Russian cunt,' suggests Porta, pleasantly, 'and fuck yourselves out of this world war. That's the best way, short of gettin' out of it alive!'

'Get back where you came from,' orders the Old Man, brusquely. 'I don't want you here with my section!'

Grousing, they get to their feet and disappear into the darkness.

Quite slowly the firing dies away, and a waiting, threatening silence falls over the ruined town.

Swearing and grumbling we pick up our automatic weapons and our heavy equipment, and trudge on.

I swing the LMG up onto my shoulder, and wipe melting snow and mud from my face.

'God love us, but it's cold'n wet,' says Gregor, as he folds up the tripod legs, and blows on his fingers, which are blue with cold.

With his machine-pistol in the crook of his arm, like a man carrying a shovel, and his wet helmet pushed back on his neck, the Old Man rolls along bow-leggedly in front of 2 Section.

'Come on, my sons! Let's see if we can't find the Red Army an' get the war over quickly,' Porta emits a death's-head laugh. 'That's what we left home for!'

'What a bleedin' life,' sighs Tiny, tonguing his cigar over to the other corner of his mouth, and shaking the snow from his light-grey bowler with a great sweep of his arm. 'No sensible bloke ought to be forced into livin' through everythin' as goes on in a fuckin' world war like this'n,' he moans, pessimistically.

'Know what I'd like?' asks Gregor, impulsively, as he trudges along close to the walls of the houses. 'I'd like to visit General bloody Arse-an'-Pockets, and stick a grenade into his fucking bed. God rot him, I would! Then I'd stand outside an' watch the fun when the little sod hit the ceiling along with the *Kraft durch Freude** whore he was sleepin' with.'

'Get on, get on,' the Old Man pushes along impatiently. 'What the devil d'you think you're getting paid a mark a day by the Army for?'

Some Russians get up and come to meet us with arms stretched above their heads. But others, who were with them, disappear into the darkness, throwing grenades behind them as they run.

Tiny kills eight men in one long burst which seems to go on forever. He crushes the skull of an officer, who is screaming, '*Stalimo!*'

The section halts near a burnt-out corn silo. It is still smoking a little, and it is nice to warm oneself at it.

Soon we begin to feel alive again.

I throw myself down behind the LMG in a heap of blackened corn. Gregor lies alongside me, flat on his back. His eyelids flutter. He blows a tiny pin-feather away from his face.

The Old Man stares gloomily into space. He knows there are thousands of kill-crazy men all around us, out there in the darkness.

I watch him through half-closed eyes. As long as we have the Old Man as our Section Leader we still have a tiny chance of getting out of this madness reasonably unharmed.

* *Kraft durch Freude:* Strength Through Joy (Nazi holiday organization)

He doesn't want to see any of us killed uselessly in some idiotic caper devised by a madman a long way behind us, who is only looking for medals and a new row of salad dressing on his chest.

A 37 mm strikes and ricochets off with a howl, but does no damage.

Porta leans tiredly against the still-warm ruins of the silo and spits foolishly into the wind.

'Holy Saint Agnes, is there anything as beautiful as a fucked-up world war which loses its breath for a minute, and has to take a break? What d'you say to coffee with somethin' a bit stronger in it?'

'Got beans?' asks the Old Man, lighting his silver-lidded pipe.

'What do you take me for?' Porta laughs, hoarsely. 'The day I *haven't* got beans enough for a cup of coffee, that'll be the day they pull the world from under my feet.'

'We haven't really got time,' says the Old Man, puffing away at his pipe. 'But to hell with it, make it anyway. We're not the blasted Moscow Express, we're only 2 Section!'

With nimble fingers Porta rigs up his American petrol-burner.

'The people who sailed across the Polar Sea with this nice little thing couldn't ever've dreamed that Obergefreiter by the grace of God Joseph Porta'd be makin' coffee on it some day,' he grins with satisfaction.

'That blasted silence,' mumbles the Old Man, blowing into the metal cup attached to his water-bottle.

'Nothing like a "little black"* on a cold morning,' says Porta, adding a dash of vodka to each cup.

Albert takes a big gulp of his coffee, to leave more room for the vodka.

'If I do thirty years in this war, I'll never get used to them rotten flares,' he says, thinly, cupping his hands and blowing warm breath up along his cheeks. 'They make me think of corpse candles. Life ain't nothin' but one great big shitter,

---

* A cup of black coffee with a dash of schnapps (or vodka).

man, an' it gets blown out from under you 'fore you even know it, an' they still say "God is good!" Enough to make you grin your tripes into knots! In all my black life I never learnt as much about bein' scared as since I got into this rotten excuse for a war, and always soakin' wet I am, too! If only a man could get pneumonia, at least he'd have a temperature an' all that, but the good God has decided otherwise and here a feller's got to go creepin' around on the stinkin' face o' the earth and waiting till the neighbours shoot his black arse off!' He takes a slug at the vodka coffee, and looks around him mournfully. 'Sometimes I wish they'd just come and kill me an' get it over with. When it comes to it, man, life ain't worth livin' with, anyway!'

'*C'est la guerre, mon ami*,' sighs the Legionnaire, the eternal *Caporal* bobbing between his lips. 'You are no more than the garbage which goes to make up the military muckheap. That is as Allah has willed it!'

Porta laughs quietly and pours more coffee and vodka into our cups.

'Heide's Führer certainly took us for a ride when he promised us eternal peace and *Kraft durch Freude* with all the trimmin's!'

'Shall we place the machine-guns?' asks Barcelona, stretching out in the warm corn.

'No, sod everything,' says the Old Man, uncaringly. 'Let the neighbours come and beg us to shoot at them for once. I couldn't care less!'

It is still dark when we turn out again, and wriggle into our wet capes. They smell of mud and ancient sweat.

The Old Man is standing outside in the clammy morning mist, waiting for us. The flaps of his field-cap are turned down over his ears, and the silver-lidded pipe hangs slackly at the corner of his mouth. It is one of those miserable mornings, which Russia has such a wealth of. A morning fit to draw both the soul and marrow out of a man.

Grumbling and moaning at one another we pull our equipment together. We seem, by now, to have assembled a fantastic collection of gear. Light and heavy machine-guns, clumsy gun mountings, machine-pistols, combat knives, collapsible spades; cartridge belts criss-crossing our bodies, grenades filling our pockets and stuffed into the tops of our jackboots. Add to this, wire-cutters, magnetic charges, batteries and signal telephones, field-lamps, map-holders and compasses.

'God what a load of shit,' pants Porta, struggling with his gasmask pouch. 'Stay here, while I bring up the limousine!'

'That's in order,' answers the Old Man. 'Drivers pick up their waggons, but quick's the word, mind! Let's get this lousy war over with, so we can go home again!'

'Let's hope the neighbours' nasty boys haven't pinched the chariots out from under us in the course o' the night,' chuckles Porta, as he goes off whistling with the other drivers of the section at his heels.

'If anybody wants my opinion,' says Tiny, importantly, 'I reckon we ought to set a guard on them waggons when we're in the sack. If we don't the insurance won't cover us. Well that's up to you fellers. I'm goin' to go down an' get the bleedin' pigs.'

'You'll stay here,' the Old Man flames up, furiously, but Tiny doesn't hear him. He is already out of sight, with a grenade in one hand and an mpi in the other.

After a while the days and nights flow together into one grey blur. We cannot remember the difference between one town we have stormed through and another, and it is a long time since we stopped counting the dead. There are too many of them for us to keep up any interest.

Out in the fields lie the carcasses of piebald cows blown up like balloons and with legs jutting upwards stiffly.

Porta almost cries at this insane waste of good food, and embarks on a lecture on the correct preparation of *Osso Buco* with rice and a piquant sauce.

27 Panzer Regiment is withdrawn from the attack. Most of its companies have shrunk to reduced section size. Our company has three vehicles left. The rest are junk.

*When we left the soil of our father-
land, they told us that we were
going out to defend the holy rights.*

Marcus Flavius

*It was early in the morning. He ran wildly down through the valley.
He was the last man of his section. Most of his comrades had
already fallen, crossing the stream, when a Russian SMG which
was covering its banks opened up. The water rippled a deep red
behind him. He reached the top of the hill, and felt a burning pain in
his side. It had been ripped wide open. Everything went black.*

*Well into the afternoon he came to himself again. The air was
shimmering with heat, the sun burning down on him. He attempted
to turn his head away from it. His greatcoat was torn open. Buttons
gone. His right side was one bloody mash; minced flesh, crushed
bones and tatters of uniform.*

*'Water,' he groaned. 'Water,' he repeated, but nobody heard him.
The battlefield was silent.*

*A short distance from him lay two Russians. One of them had
died several hours ago. His face was a mask of blood. The other
soldier still moved slightly now and then, and a rattling sound came
from his ruined mouth. His stomach had been slashed open.*

*A swarm of flies crawled busily about on the protruding entrails.
'Water!' he mumbled again. 'Thirsty!'*

*The whole of the long valley was a jumble of empty cartridge
cases. Down by the bank of the stream stood a burnt-out T-34. A
little further off lay the shot-away turret of a German P-IV. The
lush, green grass had been flattened by the tread of countless heavy
boots; tank tracks had slashed open the soft earth.*

A swarm of flies buzzed up, suddenly. Some of them lighted on

64

his face, crawling between his parted lips, and up into his nose. He tried to raise his hand, and then to shake his head, but the orders from the brain resulted in no more than a slight tremor of his body.

'Water!' he thought. He kept on thinking about water until the moment he died.

Two weeks later his mother, a war widow of World War I, received the obligatory postcard:

In the name of the Führer, Adolf Hitler, we regret to inform you that your son:

     Lieutenant Georg Friedrich,
     Platoon Commander of Infantry,
has fallen fighting bravely and in line of duty for Führer, Volk and Fatherland.

The Führer thanks you. Heil Hitler!

THE FAT LEUTNANT

The town which has been chosen for us to recuperate in looks neat and clean. The war has moved through it quickly, leaving only a few wrecked houses to mark its passage. The gasworks had been blown up, of course. Gasworks are always blown up during a retreat. But we don't care. Who wants gas, anyway? Not us!

The Hotel *Ssvaeoda** hums with activity. The owner, Tanya, stands behind the bar, dressed in an ancient mauve party dress, and flanked by three attractive, short-skirted waitresses, ready to welcome the German liberators. She has an interesting, and very ripe, vocabulary which she has picked up from the Mongol troops who were stationed here before we arrived.

Porta and Tiny start immediately to teach her the equivalent expressions in German. Two days later she is welcoming everyone who enters the bar with a pleasant:

'Lick my arse?'

Tiny has his hand up under the mauve party dress. He is trying to persuade her to tell him where the commissars hid their vodka and caviare when they left.

'Fuck?' he tempts her, lasciviously, in a whisper which makes the rafters ring, and the stuffed bear by the fireplace blink its blood-red eyes.

With the proud gait of a Czarina, Vera Konstantinovna comes through the door. She keeps her expensive fox fur on indoors, despite the heat of the room. She is said to be a woman of rank, married to a high-up commissar, who has

* *Ssvaeoda:* Russian for freedom.

gone off with the Red Army. The others address her, jeeringly, as 'Your Grace', but cannot hide the fact that they are really not a little afraid of her.

'Shag, then?' suggests Porta, making the international sign for copulation with his thumb. 'A trip on the old pork dagger? *Panjemajo?*'

On their way upstairs Porta already has both hands searching about under Vera's skirt.

'I will just wash *ma petite soeur*,' she murmurs, pouting her lips for a kiss. 'My husband installed a bidet here, before he had to leave. You know what bidet is?'

'A trough to wash out ol' Porky Pig's kennel in,' laughs Porta. 'They're all over the place in France, but they fuck more there too.'

While she is in the bathroom Porta takes off his clothes. He throws his heavy Russian pistol clattering on to the dressing-table, but, as usual with him, retains his yellow topper and his boots.

From down in the bar Barcelona's heavy bass voice can be heard:

Wir, im fernen Vaterland geboren,
nahmen nichts als Hass im Herzen mit,
Doch wir haben die Heimat nicht verloren,
unsere Heimat ist heute vor Madrid . . .*

She has nothing on but her shoes and stockings when she returns to the room. Her reddish-golden hair swings loosely around her shoulders.

'What a peach,' shouts Porta, admiringly, smacking his tongue. 'Come with me to Berlin. You could make a fortune

* Very freely:
We're from many a distant homeland,
But we feel no loss in our hearts.
For we have not lost our homeland
It is here before Madrid . . .

68

in the *Zigeunerkeller*. They pay 200 for a single, and 500 for a round trip there!'

She comes slowly toward him, her lips parted in a sensual smile.

'Oh Jesus, Jesus,' he mumbles in a hoarse voice, his small eyes rolling round in his head. 'You're enough to make a dead man get it up again!'

'You are a sweet man,' she whispers, seductively. 'But why you wear the boots?'

'Helps in a quick getaway,' he grins. 'Think now if your husband, who has gone on his travels, was to put his commissar's head in here with a *Kalashnikov* in his hands. I'd be quicker over the cobblestones with me boots on!'

She kisses him. Small, feather-light kisses, which tickle his face. She falls back on to the bed taking him down with her.

'Like my old stick o'rock, do you?' he asks, after a while. 'It's all the way from Berlin, an' can do most anything!'

'You are nice, man,' she whispers, enticingly, and runs her fingers over the bristly hairs at the back of his neck.

When Porta comes back down to the bar, several hours later, he is met with cries of admiration.

'What'd it cost you?' asks a Wachtmeister of artillery, interestedly. He is wondering if the 25 marks he has saved up is enough.

'She did it for love!' Porta brags. 'But *you*, you can count on slipping a grand at least for the pleasure.'

'Fuck her then. She ain't my type,' snarls the Wachtmeister disappointedly. He goes over to chat up one of the short-skirted waitresses.

'Take cover!' shouts Tiny, swaying drunkenly to his feet. 'I'll shoot the bleeding cocks off the lot of you, else!'

The machine-pistol seems to go on chattering forever. A huge mirror carrying the old Czarist eagle shatters to pieces. Bottles fall from behind the bar. Ricochets leave splintered tracks in the floor. When the magazine is finally empty he stands for a moment swaying uncertainly on widespread legs.

'Are you dead?' he asks the empty bar-room, changing magazines. 'Maybe you know now 'oo it is as 'as invaded this bleedin' country?' With another long burst he blows all the windows out, shoots a cow in a landscape painting hanging on the wall, and makes a colander of the plank wall screening the bar from the kitchen. Then he falls to the floor, clutching the machine-pistol lovingly in his arms.

A quartermaster with only one boot on exits rapidly through the door. He thinks the Russians have come back.

Tanya helps Tiny to his feet, embraces him and tells him with false friendliness that she has always loved Germans.

'A world war's not all wickedness,' says Porta to Vera, straightening her garter. 'Does that commissar feller of yours know you dish out his private crumpet to the German liberators while he's away? He might send you to *Kolyma* for unRussian behaviour if he found out. But p'raps you'd like the work, down in the state mines?'

'We've got visitors,' yells Gregor, happily, as a Kübel comes skidding sideways through the slush of the square with tyres whining.

Five military policemen spring eagerly from the Kübel. Carefully as ballet dancers they pick their way through the melting snow, to avoid marring their mirror-bright jack-boots. Their helmets sparkle, throwing flashes of light to all sides. As they cross the square they draw Walther pistols from their new, yellow holsters. They tramp heavily and with assurance across the planks of the floor, chests well out to display their brightly-polished headhunter insignia for all to see. They are big, well-nourished men, who enjoy the fear they are accustomed to engendering.

The guard commander, a brutal-looking, beery Saxon

with the Blood Order* over his right breast pocket, marches round in a circle and sends field court-martial looks at us.

'You don't know *me*, you sons of pigs,' he roars, with a self-satisfied air, spitting on the floor. 'But God help you when you do!' He draws a long police truncheon from its special pocket in his trouser-leg, flexes it like a rapier with both hands, and swishes it menacingly through the air. 'Let's see the bastard who was shootin' in here without orders!'

'I'm the bloke you're lookin' for, Herr Wachtmeister, sir,' grins Tiny, round a fat cigar. As he answers he presses the muzzle of a heavy *Tokarew* pistol hard up under the MP's fat jowl. 'Look, you stinkin' excuse for a 'uman bein', you sod off, an' take your bleedin' shower of coppers with you! 'Cos in just one minute I'm goin' to start shootin' again.'

'You're bloody *mad*!' stammers the Wachtmeister, nervously, falling slowly back toward the door.

'No I ain't,' grins Tiny, sending a bullet into the floor between the man's feet. 'I'm Frankenstein's bastard, bleedin' son, I am, an' I drink blood every mornin' for breakfast!'

'Arrest that man!' gabbles the Wachtmeister, chalk-white in the face. There is no reaction to his order. His four MPs have fled out of the door. He gives out a shrill scream, as Tiny closes in on him with a deep snarl, and hammers his helmet down over his nose with a closed fist. He gets out of the door so quickly that he falls over his own feet and slides a long way on his face in the slush.

'There'll be trouble *now*,' predicts Barcelona, darkly. 'They'll *kill* us, when they come back with reinforcements.'

'Pick up your gear, and let's get out of here,' orders the Old Man, squaring his cap on his head.

'We are closing now,' says Tanya, decisively. 'Get off

* The Blood Order: An early *SA* decoration

with you. We see you again tomorrow. This is a *nice* place, I must tell you arse-licking Germans!'

She rattles the iron venetian blinds shut, and turns off the stuffed bear's wicked red eyes.

On the way out Tiny smashes his fist through one of the remaining window-panes. He shakes his hand, which is covered with blood, and licks at it like a cat lapping up cream.

'What the hell did you do *that* for?' the Old Man scolds him, angrily.

'It was a Commie bleedin' window, that's why,' yells Tiny. He kicks out at an empty bucket, which rolls noisily over into the opposite gutter. 'You're always grumblin', Old Un'. You don't want us poor, lonely soldiers to 'ave any fun. I *love* smashin' windows. 'Ave done since I was a nipper. If I 'ad to pay for all the windows I've busted, I'd need a big, bleedin' loan in the National bleedin' Bank to do it. You ought to 'ave been there the night me an' the Jew furrier's son David from '*Eyn 'Oyerstrasse* busted all the windows in the David Station, an' showered the bleedin' coppers all over with busted glass. It was their own fault, really. They was 'avin' a gaspipe repaired, an' the silly bleeders 'ad piled up all the cobblestones just ready to 'and for us when we come out o' the "'Appy Pig"!

'"'Ere we go, then!" shouted the Yid's kid, an' 'e threw the first stone. It landed smack bang on Superintendent Willy Nass's bleedin' desk, knockin' over 'is personal coffee-pot an' smashin' 'is inkwell, so a 'ole lot of documents important to the soddin' state gets covered with coffee an' ink. Nass went bleedin' barmy, an' went off 'Amburg-style so all the Schupo coppers started puttin' on their armour an' artillery. On their way out o' the door leadin' to the *Reeperbahn* they got stuck, there was that many of 'em. David an' me borrowed a couple o' bikes, as was leanin' waitin' for us, up against the wall of the variety theatre, an' spurted off down the road with a posse o' blue-lights chasin' our arses. Jesus, but they was narked when they copped us. Me that is, 'cos I was the only one they copped. The Yid's David 'e'd gone off to Buxtehude. Said 'e 'ad to 'elp 'is auntie with 'er tomatoes. Nass, 'e threatened me with 'eavy punishments for pinchin' bikes an' wanton destruction of property while escapin'. There was somethin' too about old women an' a paperstand. I tried to explain to 'im, best I could, as it couldn't 'ave been me 'cos I couldn't ride a bike.

'"It's a *lie*," 'e screamed, an' smashed the top of 'is desk in two with 'is truncheon. But we'll soon find out what's what, 'e promised me, an' pushed me out the door an' down the bleedin' stairs. Out in the street they give me a national police force bike, which Nass 'ad to give a receipt for. We started off from *Davidstrasse*, as goes down on the slope into the Elbe.

'"Get on!" said an Oberwachtmeister with a moustache the spittin' image of Adolf's.

'I pretended to fall off a couple o' times, an' they beat me up a bit to make me understand as 'ow this bike trip was important to 'em. They set me up on the saddle then an' give this national bleedin' bike an 'ell of a push.

'"Ride, you stinkin' cycle thief," Nass ordered me, out from under 'is 'at-brim.

'"Very good, sir," I yelled and 'eld me feet out to the sides. The bleedin' bike did the rest. It went like a bat out o' bleedin' 'ell down *Davidstrasse*, an', 'angin' over on one side, round the corner o' *Bernhard Nocht Strasse*, as is pretty steep. I nearly kissed a number 2 tram on the way, as it come pissin' up the 'ill there where all them 5 mark 'ores from *Fischermarkt* does their business.

'Down by *Landingsbrücke*, I 'ad to leave the police bike, which carried on on its own down into the bleedin' Elbe. You should've 'eard 'im, Nass, go on when 'e found out 'is bike was drowned. I 'eard later as 'e 'ad to pay for it. It was 'im as 'ad 'is name on the receipt.'

'Stop all that shit about *Davidswacht* and Nass,' sniffles Porta, who has caught a cold. 'We'll be shot before we know where we are. That commissar bint I had social

73

relations with, told me there was a mob of NKVD who'd gone underground here when the Red Army lighted out.'

'Latrine rumours,' says Gregor Martin, off-handedly. 'Our friends have lost their courage. We have won the war. All we've got to do is make our way straight across Russia, and meet up with the rice-eaters on the other side o' the earth.'

'I want to see the MO first,' sneezes Porta. 'My feet are killing me *now*, an' what a walk *that'll* be! Have you any idea just how big Mother Russia *is*?'

'Know what I think,' trumpets Tiny, banging himself on the chest. 'We ought to burn the arses out from under them NKVD bastards, so's we could get a bit of bleedin' peace for once in a while!'

'*Up* you,' groans Porta hoarsely, clearing his nose between his fingers, noisily. 'I'm about tired of fucking about on the crust of this sodding earth at everybody's beck an' call. Think of all the things that're going on in Berlin while I'm wastin' my time out here playing soldiers!'

He blows his nose again, and takes a big swig of vodka. 'Our German God ain't all that smart. If He'd been clever He'd of took out a Bohemian Gefreiter named Adolf Hitler in the First World War!'

'Watch your mouth, Obergefreiter Porta,' Heide warns him, sharply. 'It is my duty to report you to the NSFO. I have no doubt of what the result of that will be.'

'See into the future, can you?' asks Porta, ironically, wiping his nose with the back of his hand.

A revealing click sounds in the quiet night, and we go to cover alongside the wall.

'An mpi, a bleedin' mpi,' whispers Tiny, as he goes down.

Like a wise old tomcat Porta moves straight across the street and forces his way down some wrecked cellar stairs, where half a door hangs swinging.

As he moves, explosions erupt from another cellar opening.

'A *Balalaika*! God rot me, a *Balalaika*!' howls Gregor excitedly, and fires reflexively at the flash.

Just as reflexively I tear the ring from an egg-grenade, and sling it towards the cellar. There is a hollow thump, and a yellow-red flame blooms in the darkness. Its reflection comes back at us from wet steel helmets.

Tiny rushes straight through a glass door, with a deafening crash. Glass splinters fly around his ears. His *Schmeisser* explodes, chatteringly. It takes only a few minutes. He comes back out through the door-frame, kicking glass out of his way. He sneezes twice, violently.

''Ere's the bleedin *Balalaika*,' he shouts, holding a *Kalashnikov* up above his head. ''Im as played it's dead!'

'The bloody neighbours are that fucked up by this war, they ain't able to do much more'n get in the way,' coughs Barcelona. He has a cold, like the rest of us. He coughs up phlegm, and spits on a dead horse, which is lying in a pool of frozen blood.

'Don't you be too sure of that,' sniffles Porta, taking another swig from his vodka bottle. He regards vodka as an alternative to vitamin C, and thinks it will help his cold. 'Never trust the neighbours. Before we know where we are those rotten lice'll have started up all over again, and we'll be back where we kicked off!'

'Know what I think?' shouts Tiny, from inside the remains of a delicatessen. 'This war is a new Thirty Years War, like the time Jesus landed 'Is army in the Red bleedin' Sea to give the Turks a beatin' up.' His biblical knowledge is, as usual, slightly off-centre.

Heavy infantry fire sounds from the far end of the town.

'They've got shit between the ears,' sneezes Gregor. 'War-mad bastards. Why they got to always be shootin'? I wish I was back with my general. With him, war was *fun*!'

'Not allowed to shoot MPs, is it?' says Porta, mysteriously, and scrapes frozen snow from his boots.

'Too true it ain't,' laughs Barcelona, swallowing a whole

handful of throat pastilles. He has 'found' them on a body.

'There's a lot o' things as ain't allowed,' shouts Tiny. Angrily, he picks up an unexploded hand-grenade and throws it through a window. 'Fuck 'em all!'

Jesus, Jesus, why is everybody always sneezin' and freezin' in this God-awful country,' sniffles Porta. 'Anybody know a cure for it? I feel as if hair's growin' out of the sides of my head, an' the germs've built a barbed-wire entanglement in my throat!'

'A Russian grenade up your backside, or perhaps a *Kalashnikov* burst straight into your napper'd clear that cold away in a second,' says Gregor, with a less than humorous laugh.

'They're a certain cure, at least,' the Old Man admits, scraping at his silver-lidded pipe with his combat-knife. 'Colds are hell, and worst of all they're not enough to put you in sick-bay.'

'You're right there,' puffs Tiny. 'I saw the MO yesterday. Threw me out 'e did, an' threatened to 'ave me jailed for bleedin' sabotage o' the war effort.

'"I got a fever sir," I said. "52 degrees at least."

'"Up your arse, man," 'e yelled.

'"Where else, sir," I answered, and then 'e went funny an' started shoutin'. Off I went then, 'fore anythin' irregular could start 'appenin'. I did manage to sneeze straight in 'is face, though. Give 'im somethin' to think about when '*is* thermometer registers 52°C.'

'Whose people are you?' barks a monstrously fat Leutnant, with a monocle flashing in his fleshy, white face.

'Who the fuck's askin'?' comes, anonymously, from Porta, off in the shadow of the houses.

The Leutnant goes into a rage, and demands to know their unit.

'Push a gun-barrel up his arsehole,' cackles Gregor, hidden in the darkness. 'He'd love it! He looks like one o' them as likes to get their shitters reamed out now an' then!'

'You're insulting a superior officer,' rages the Leutnant, his face tightening. 'Who are you, you filthy man?'

''E's a colonel in the Chinese bleedin' Army,' roars Tiny, happily. '*Panjemajo, grabit**'*

'Shut it!' warns the Old Man, well aware that their joking can have serious consequences.

'Yes, but he *is* a Chinese colonel,' roars Porta, whinnying with laughter. 'In command of two regiments of Pekin paratroops, but all very secret, Herr Leutnant, sir. Even the Chinese ain't been told, sir!'

''Ey there, Leutnant!' Tiny bellows with laughter, and bangs his hands on his knees. 'You gone the wrong way, you 'ave. Any minute now ol' Ivan Stinkanovitch is gonna shoot that bleedin' winder-pane out o' your fat bleedin' kisser, an' send you flyin' up to 'ave a fuck at the angels!'

The Leutnant tears his pistol from his holster, cocks it theatrically and aims it at Tiny, who is lighting a big cigar with the air of a captain of industry.

The Legionnaire swings his mpi down from his shoulder and sends a burst into the ground at the Leutnant's feet. Bullets ricochet in all directions.

The Leutnant drops his monocle. It smashes to pieces on the cobbled road surface.

'*We'll* get you a glazier, sir!' offers Porta, as the Leutnant's squad disappears down the street in disorderly flight.

'You're under arrest!' screams the officer hysterically, grasping the Old Man's arm.

'Take your hands off me!' snarls the Old Man, pulling away angrily. 'You're not in garrison here, Herr Leutnant, and we're not your recruits! This is a front-line unit, and I'm its commander. You have nothing to do with us. We don't *know* you!'

'I'll have you stripped,' whines the Leutnant hysterically. 'This is mutiny. I'll get you a field court-martial!'

---

* *Panjemajo, grabit.* Russian: Understand, arsehole?

77

'Do as you wish, sir,' answers the Old Man, his eyes slitted with rage.

'Knock 'is bleedin' teeth out,' suggests Tiny with a wicked laugh, 'an' kick 'is arse'ole up round 'is ears afterwards!'

An amphibian comes rushing down the street and skids to a halt in the slush, its nose pointing back in the direction from which it came.

Oberleutnant Löwe springs lightly from the vehicle and walks, with long strides, towards the Old Man, who is standing with dirty, soaking wet boots and looking very sour.

'So here you are,' smiles Löwe. He touches his helmet brim with a large, mittened hand. He stares inquisitively at the fat Leutnant. 'What are you doing here?' he asks harshly, fishing a bent cigarette from his breast pocket.

The Old Man gives him a light, and nods his head in the direction of the fat Leutnant.

'This officer came rushing down here, and started to tell me what to do with the section, sir,' he said. 'I've just been explaining to him that I would prefer him not to do that.'

Oberleutnant Löwe blows out a cloud of cigarette smoke, takes a quick look around, and understands the situation immediately.

'Come with me,' he orders the Leutnant, who is just about to open his mouth and give vent to his repressed rage. Löwe is already back in the vehicle alongside the chief driver, Obergefreiter Brinck. The Leutnant is hardly in his seat before Brinck stamps the accelerator down and is off in a shower of mud and snow.

'Single file. Follow me!' growls the Old Man sourly, moving off at the head of the section.

'There 'e goes again. *Rotten*!' says Tiny, with a hopeless gesture. 'It ain't *my* fault this time, any road. It was that bleedin' officer as started it an' then couldn't take a bit o' fun!'

'It's always the officers,' says Porta, blowing his nose on

his fingers. 'They can't keep their mouths shut when we're talkin'. That's *their* trouble.'

Gregor finds a furniture store, and we take up temporary quarters inside it.

'Inspect for booby-traps?' asks Heide, zealously, looking under a sofa.

'Don't change the positions of the furniture, an' don't, repeat don't, touch the pictures,' advises Porta. 'If there's a picture of Stalin, let it be. Our treacherous enemies like to plant small surprises under furniture and behind pictures. Turn Stalin's face to the wall, my sons, an' you'll get the surprise of your young lives!'

'Gawd, yes!' cries Tiny. ''Member the time we moved that dead bleedin' pig, an' the entire village went up in the air, an' took a motorbike platoon with it. The neighbours 'ad tied the pig with a lead to the ammo' depot. It was like the soddin' world went off its axles, an' I went up an' kissed the soles of Jesus's bleedin' feet. There wasn't nothin' left o' the pig, either. Not even a bit o' pork to add some life to a fried egg!'

'Anybody got any rifle oil?' asks Heide, who is dismantling his machine-pistol.

'Rifle oil?' grimaces Gregor, contemptuously. 'Pull your fucking pud, brother, an' use what comes out of it. That's what the rice-eaters use. Their army don't let anythin' go to waste!'

'Shut up, you rotten swine,' snarls Heide, in a rage, sending him a wicked look.

'That's enough,' orders the Old Man. 'I don't want any more trouble. Shit between your ears, that's what you lot've got! Every one of you!' He throws himself down on to an embroidered sofa, and stares emptily at the ceiling.

A distant rumble brings our heads up.

'Tanks,' says Porta, reaching for his topper.

'Train goin' through a long tunnel,' says Tiny, stretching himself out comfortably.

'Train? You must be wrong in the head,' shouts Gregor,

throwing himself down on the floor in terror. 'It's a shell. A *big* un!'

There is a deafening explosion.

'Jesus'n Mary,' yells Tiny, rolling himself into a ball and laughing madly. 'Little bit closer this way, an' we'd never've ever seen 'ome again. An' poor ol' Julius's gun'd never 'ave been cleaned, neither!'

'Fucking *shit*!' screams Gregor, pushing his turkey-cock face through the broken window. Suddenly, he goes completely amuck, and empties a whole magazine into the darkness. 'Shoot me!' he yells, throwing a hand-grenade. 'It takes twelve men to shoot one rotten, lousy soldier who don't want to fight no more in this man's army!' He waves his machine-pistol in the air. 'Get *to* it! I've *had* it! Fuck your rotten fuckin' war! Stuff it! Stuff it up your arseholes, an' shit it out again in a load of South American revolutions. Then stuff it down Adolf's fuckin' throat an' make him thank you for the gift parcel.'

The Old Man and Barcelona wriggle across the floor to get hold of him. He is standing on the spring mattress of a double bed, hopping up and down. He has a fresh magazine in his hand, but cannot get it into his machine-pistol. 'Oh God!' he screams. 'There's none of us ever goin' to get home again! The neighbours'll shoot our fuckin' German arses off!'

The Old Man slaps him hard, twice, across the face.

'Nazi bastard,' shouts Gregor, his eyes rolling madly. He swings the muzzle of his mpi round in circles. 'You don't know who I am. Me an' my general's took out a patent on this war. You lot's only here to get shot at!'

'Battle strain,' says the Old Man, slapping him again across the face. Barcelona twists his arms up behind his back, and forces him to drop the machine-pistol.

'Get your traitorous hands off me!' howls Gregor. He kicks a steel helmet from one end of the furniture store to the other.

He fights furiously with the Old Man and Barcelona. He

thinks they are a firing squad come to carry him off to execution.

'Death makes a man want to meet death!' he screams out into the room. His eyes are bulging wildly. 'But it's easier if you take some of 'em with you, an' can get down there where God an' the Devil's barterin' souls!'

'Always the bleedin' same,' sighs Tiny, from his resting place in a broad four-poster bed. His grey bowler is pushed down over his eyes, and a fat cigar hangs from his lips. 'Goin' under together is also a kind o' pleasure, as Moses said to the soddin' Gyppos, when they all drowned in the Red Sea!'

'Up my fuckin' black arse,' yells Albert suddenly, jumping to his feet with a long howl. He rushes across the floor of the furniture store and bangs into Porta who falls across Heide, scattering the parts of the machine-pistol across the floor.

Heide lets out a roar, and tackles Albert just as he is about to go through the door.

'You stinking black rat,' he rages. 'Nobody gets away with that with me!'

A new, giant shell comes roaring over, and we all go down on the floor. The night becomes one long, shuddering, thunderous explosion.

'What the hell's happening?' shouts Barcelona hysterically, as the great concrete building begins to shake like a sapling in a storm. Shrapnel splinters come from all directions. They hammer against the walls, showering us with mortar dust.

The grey office windows at the far end of the long storehouse tinkle to pieces in a rain of glass shards.

'Halt! Who goes there?' roars the Legionnaire, releasing the safety catch on his machine-pistol.

'The Beast of the Apocalypse,' answers Obergefreiter Brinck, happily, coming crawling in through a shattered window. 'You hide yourselves real good. Took me two hours to find you.'

81

'You must be mad,' the Old Man scolds him. 'You could've got yourself shot!'

'War is a risky business,' grins Brinck carelessly, starting to rig up a field telephone on the floor.

'What's this, then?' asks Porta, wonderingly.

'Army field telephone model 1932,' declares Brinck happily. 'The Signals coolies've put down a cable. I've suggested code name "*Sauerkraut*" for you. Command's got code name "*Eisbein*". If Ivan gets on to it he'll think we've opened up a chop-house. Try to ring an' order a table he will, I shouldn't wonder. Don't get too worried, though. The neighbours're shooting off like mad, and the cables are gettin' shot up quicker'n Signals can repair 'em!'

A little later Gregor goes amuck again. He is halfway through the shattered window before the Old Man and Barcelona get hold of him. They give him a going-over with their fists. It is the only effective treatment for front-line madness.

They have hardly finished with him before Albert starts up again, howling like a wolf. He runs his head into the wall. Then he draws his combat-knife, and begins to stab and slash madly at a sofa. Screaming wildly, he cuts it to pieces. Springs fly up and hit him in the face, driving him even crazier. In the end he becomes so entangled in wires and furniture webbing that we have the greatest difficulty in freeing him.

'That black monkey's gone out of his mind,' rages the Old Man. 'Take away his weapons, before he kills some of us!'

The scream of a shell makes itself heard from out in the darkness. The flash of the explosion lights up the night. It is followed by another explosion, and then another. Shells continue to hammer down, seemingly endlessly. Beams and tiles crash around us. A large door comes flying across the room and cuts off the head of an infantryman who is on his way up the stairs.

'And they tell us this shit of a town's been cleared,' yells

Porta, wriggling further down in the four-poster bed alongside Tiny.

'I think they're gonna attack,' says Barcelona, listening carefully. 'Listen, that's 75 mm!'

'Jesus'n Mary,' mumbles Tiny, burying his head under a pillow. 'Those bleedin' shells drive a feller barmy!'

From the street comes the clatter of rushing boots.

The Legionnaire peers cautiously out of the broken window.

'*Par Allah*!' he cries, fearfully, 'it is Ivan! He is all over the street, out there!'

'Ivan?' asks the Old Man. 'Impossible! That means the whole division's been turned back!'

Porta's constantly surprised, birdlike face peers carefully from the window niche in the end wall. The hair seems to stand up on his head. He closes his eyes and emits a grunt of fear.

'The devil, it's the whole neighbour's army,' he shouts, gripping his LMG, and dashing straight across the store-room towards the street door.

We take the plank fence almost together. Hand-grenades explode, hollowly, behind us. From the darkness comes the muzzle-flash of an mpi.

I throw a hand-grenade at the flash, and take a row of empty dustbins in my stride. They go clattering away into the night.

A figure whirls up into the air, and seems to hang for a moment on the top of the flame from an explosion.

We throw ourselves flat, as their artillery lays a carpet of fire over the large park.

With fear gripping at my entrails I press myself down into a small stream, without knowing how I have got there. I don't even feel the coldness of the water, or hear the ice cracking under me. Huge shells fall behind me. A burning house crashes in on itself.

I realize I must get away from the stream. The artillery will centre in on the burning row of houses behind which I am lying.

Immediately after the next rain of shells I jump to my feet and rush straight across the road through the park. I throw myself down, senselesly, into a shell-hole which still stinks of iron and powder smoke. The shelling rises to a furious crescendo. It is as if the entire world is being turned inside out.

They are using everything they've got. Field-guns, howitzers, mortars, tank and infantry weapons. The mortars are the worst. They come almost silently and explode with a wicked sound. I am so frightened I feel like screaming, and running away as fast as my legs can carry me. But I have been long enough in this filthy war to know it would be certain death if I did. I force myself further down into the narrow shell-hole, making myself as small as possible. I rest my chin on the butt of my machine-pistol.

A shell falls not far away from me. My steel helmet is pushed back by the blast. I am unconscious for a second. The helmet strap has almost strangled me. My brain feels empty. My hands are cold as ice. It seems an eternity before life flows slowly back into me.

Now the tanks come. They are not far from my shell-hole. I hear the rattle of their tracks. T-34s and the enormous KW-2s speed through the park. The screams of men dying under their treads cut through the noise.

I hear German machine-guns firing madly, sending glowing lines of tracer through the darkness.

Five or six flares explode in the heavens, and turn the night to a ghostly, pale sort of day.

I look up cautiously and catch sight of the T-34s on their way through the park, alongside the path. Infantrymen can be clearly seen sitting up behind on the tanks.

Now the anti-tank guns start up. When the 88 mms go off, the sound is that of a huge steel door clanging shut.

A T-34 explodes in a ball of fire; another one goes up.

I hear tracks rattling close to my shell-hole, and the ticking ring of an Otto engine.

A T-34 stops close by, and I feel the warmth of its exhaust

blow down over me. It is so close I could put out my hand and touch its tracks.

My heart almost stops beating from fear. Shivering with terror I bore my fingers into the earth and try to get even closer to it. The T-34's gun goes off, and it feels as if my head is about to burst open. The force of the explosion is impossible to describe. A tank-gun is the devil's own personal invention.

An Unteroffizier from 3 Section arrives at a run. A machinegun burst from the T-34 rips across his chest. He is smashed over backwards. The LMG flies from his hands, his steel helmet following it.

A Fahnenjunker runs, limping like a winged bird. He stops, and stares in panic at the huge, armoured colossus. The tank-gun flames again. The Junker falls forward like a log.

I think for a moment that he is dead, but there is still life in him. His fingers claw at the earth and he begins to crawl slowly towards my hole.

'No,' I whisper. 'Not here. If the tank sees him, we're *both* finished!'

Engines howl, and the T-34 begins to move forward slowly, the earth shaking under its steel tracks.

The tracks come slowly towards me, cowering there in my shell-hole. Feverishly I tie two grenades together to make a heavier charge.

The T-34 swivels halfway round. Its tracks throw earth and stones high in the air. They rain down on me.

The tank slides sideways down into a ditch. I am about to throw the grenades, when it turns half round again on its own axis, and rattles toward the Fahnenjunker. He presses himself down, desperately, behind a large round stone, then gets halfway to his feet. The tank knocks him back down and crushes him under its tracks. A bloody pool is all that is left of him.

The T-34 makes off with a thunder of engines. It smashes over a wooden bridge, which collapses under its weight in a rain of splintered planks and beams. Two infantry men, who were hiding under the bridge, are crushed into an unrecognizable mass.

How long I run before I come to a halt I never know. I have lost all idea of the passage of time. My knees tremble under me; my thigh muscles are hard and knotted. My mouth feels as if it were full of sand. In a panic I spring across the ditch, and push my way through the bushes lining it.

Porta catches me by the ankle, and I fall forward.

'Calm down,' he says, easily. 'It's not *that* bad. The neighbours are just pointin' out to us that they're still around. They don't want us to go thinking we've won the war just yet!'

'Where's the Old Man?' I ask, breathlessly.

'Lying over there, enjoying the cool of the evening together with the rest of the boys. We didn't get off too badly, but there's not a button left of 3 Section, and they say the division's got its balls shot off. Arse-an'-Pockets has made a real mess of this one!'

The Old Man comes sliding down between the rose beds, with Gregor at his heels.

'We've got to get through now,' says the Old Man, breathlessly. 'Ivan's over on this side with all his pots an' pans. Half the division's got the shit shot out of it. Let's move. Go down behind that furniture factory. There's a bit more room there.'

'There's tanks behind us,' I put in. 'Both T-34s and KW-2s, and they're banging away like mad.'

'Sod *them*,' snarls the Old Man. 'Don't look at 'em. We've *got* to get through.'

'Tiny,' he calls, softly.

''Ere I am!' answers Tiny, avalanching down past the rosebeds.

'Got the stovepipe* still?' asks the Old Man.

'Too right,' grins Tiny, '*an*' a packet o' acid drops for it. Its Dad's Day in Russia y'know!'

---

* Stovepipe: Bazooka

Barcelona looks over the top of the roses. 'Adjutant's just been here. Wants us to work our bloody way up to the sunk road.'

'That clever sod could make a pancake without breakin' eggs,' snarls Porta, furiously. '*This* feller's not goin' anywhere near any sunken, rotten road. All the bloody Red Army'll be goin' that way an'll shoot us full of holes. Those people from the officer factory'll kill the lot of us before they've done!'

'We're going back,' says the Old Man, getting to his feet with his mpi at the ready.

'Follow me!' he orders, jumping over the roses.

Suddenly I begin to feel the cold, and the water which has seeped into my boots.

'Heavens above, but I'm *cold*,' I mumble, pulling my collar up around my ears.

'You'll soon get warmed up,' grins Porta.

'Spread out, blast your eyes,' commands the Old Man. 'How often do I have to *tell* you. Don't crowd together!'

Behind us we can hear the rumble of the field-guns, and, in between the sharp crack of tank-guns.

Two tanks are on fire. Tall flames shoot up from them. One of them explodes in a rain of red-hot steel splinters.

A Russian in a flapping brown cloak rushes past us with his long queerly-shaped bayonet fixed.

I raise my machine-pistol and send a short burst into his back. He gives out a long, ululating scream, and his rifle and bayonet fly from his hands.

I follow the others down a partly overgrown path, jump over a wrecked anti-tank gun and go head over heels down a steep flight of steps.

'Keep your distance,' shouts the Old Man. 'You want to all get killed at the same time? Spread out, you rotten sacks, spread *out*!'

'Mines,' shouts Barcelona, warningly, stopping short as if he had run into a wall. 'Mines,' he says again, standing as if rooted to the ground. He is in deadly fear of mines, having been blown up by them several times. Even though these

87

experiences occurred a long time ago, he has never forgotten them.

The whole section has stopped. It is best not to think too much about mines. It can stop you moving forward altogether.

'Get on, get on,' the Old Man shouts, giving me a push.

A flare bursts above our heads. The 25 men of our section turn into 25 statues. We stand, for several minutes, defenceless, bathed in its deathly white glow. Protecting darkness falls around us. The night seems to be filled with running, leaping figures; everywhere is confusion. We run around in the dark, Russians and Germans together. Hand-grenades are thrown into houses. Wounded and dying soldiers scream shrilly.

In the middle of the street a T-34 spins wildly round. It explodes in a blinding flash of light.

From the centre of the town come explosions and the noise of battle.

'Hope they don't smash up Tanya's place with all their shooting,' says Porta, worriedly.

'P'raps it's the commissar, on his way to pick up his woman,' says Gregor, with a short, sad laugh.

'It's all a fart in a colander,' sighs Porta. 'The longer I live the more I realize that the only thing of value anybody's got, is his own poor, rotten life.'

We throw ourselves down, tiredly, behind a small hillock.

'Ducks!' cries Porta, assuming his pointer attitude. He is right. The quiet quacking of a flock of ducks can just be distinguished.

'If we can get hold of a couple of 'em, I'll do you duck an' Portuguese rice,' he promises, licking his lips hungrily at the thought. 'It's a feast for the Gods! First you take some rice – that *is* when you've got your ducks – then some onions they're easy enough to find – and so is a bunch o' carrots. Finally some tomatoes, oil, salt an' pepper. The rice has to be boiled in duck-fat, adding water slowly as it comes to the boil, says the recipe, but I prefer wine to water. Smooth out the rice nice an' even, an' lay your portions of duck carefully on top of it. Then, chop your tomatoes fine together with the onions and spread 'em out over the whole thing. I tell you, my sons, the aroma is that beautiful you'd think it was a Christmas Eve before the war.'

'Shut your trap, man,' snarls Albert viciously, from the darkness. 'You make everybody more hungry than he is, just listenin' to you talk.'

'Shut it the *lot* of you,' snarls the Old Man, in turn. 'Ivan's smack in front of us!' He takes his cold pipe from his mouth, and beckons me over to him. 'Listen good, now' he whispers. 'You go first over the stream, but quietly as possible, understand? The rest of us'll wheel round in an arc behind the ruins over there.'

'Why me?' I protest, nervously.

'Because I say so,' answers the Old Man, nastily. 'Get off with you! But keep your ears open and send up a green flare if you run into the neighbours.'

The ducks scatter, quacking, in front of me, as I wade cautiously into the cold water. The icy teeth of it bite into me. After a few minutes I can no longer feel my fingers. I stop for a moment by a deserted MG position, and pour water out of my boots. They're the most stupid boots in the world, these German leather dice-cups. I wish the devil had the genius who invented them. The Russian puttee over a shorter boot is a thousand times better. Our boots are only good for goose-stepping in.

Behind a large farmhouse I meet the section again.

'Spread out,' orders the Old Man, waving his mpi at us as if we were a flock of hens he was shooing out of his way.

Cursing we crawl between bramble hedges. The thorns tear our skin, and it hurts more than ever because we are so cold.

'You two stay here,' the Old Man turns to Gregor and me. 'But don't, for God's sake, start shooting all over the place. Fire only at muzzle-flashes. Albert! Crawl over to that turnip heap, and cover the house, but God help you if

89

you make a noise! They're here, an' we can count on 'em being frightened all to hell. Frightened people've got sharp ears an' sharp eyes, and they let off at any sound they hear.'

'I'm frightened all to hell, too, man,' whines Albert, piteously. 'Jesus but I'm frightened! Think of gettin' knocked off here. And the little I've got out of my short life.'

A hoarse, stifled cough, out in the darkness, makes us start and listen shakily.

Like a couple of snakes the Old Man and Barcelona glide away over the wide field.

Porta presses his face down into his cupped hands to stop himself sneezing, while Albert puts both hands to his ears in terror.

Porta draws his breath in deeply a few times and smiles happily, at having succeeded in stifling his sneeze. It would have been a catastrophe. It doesn't need much to set the guns going off at you, when you are lying right under the noses of the other army.

A loud sneeze comes from the pig-sty. It is followed up by three or four more, sounding loud as gunshots in the night.

'Ivan's as snotty-nosed as we are,' whispers Porta pityingly. 'Shame for him, it is.'

'It's this rotten war that's to blame,' mumbles Gregor sourly. 'If you don't get your turnip shot off, you catch all sorts of aches an' pains. I hurt all over, and I can't get a pill even for any of it. And they talk about human rights. A feller's hardly started living before they get hold of him and knock every single, individual trace of a thought out of his head. I'll never forget Paust, the Feldwebel I was a rookie under. He'd got a face as red as a lobster, and his breath stunk like a shithouse. He had gaps between his teeth, an' the teeth were yellow as ripe cheese. I was dumb enough to jump to one side instead of catchin' a fuckin' dummy gun he threw at me.

'"I'll remember you," he screamed, breathin' cheap beer and stinking fish straight into my face.

'Later in the afternoon I complained that the helmet

they'd issued me with was too little, the greatcoat was too big, and the boots pinched my toes. That started something, all right. For the next three weeks we had our gasmasks on from morning to night. We only 'ad 'em off when we were eating. In the latrine we still had 'em on. When the rest of the company got fifteen minutes rest, Paust nobbled me.

'"Atten*tion*!" he screamed, "gasmasks *on*! Forward *march*! Double *march*! One-two, one-two, one-two!"

'I'm doubling straight for the barracks wall. Then comes the next order.

'"Down! Forward crawl! Get that arse down. Prick an' balls into the ground, you wicked little shower o' monkey's afterbirth, you!"

'Straight through a pool o' mud he drove me, an' down through a water-filled tank trench like I was some kind of a submarine.

'"Back an' start again," he shouted, disappointed that I'm still able to breathe.

'When we'd got to the middle of the day and the sun was so high there wasn't a single patch o' shade anywhere on the parade-ground, I wasn't runnin' any more, I was staggerin'. The rubber facepiece of the gasmask was going in and out like a bellows. My rifle felt heavy as lead and was slippery all over with sweat. The heavy uniform you could've wrung out like a dishcloth, an' God help you if you so much as loosened a button of it. In the afternoon they took us for a walk in the country. I got promoted, straightaway, to number one on the MG. Paust chased me on an' on over them ploughed fields with that fucking machine-gun on my back. When he shouted "*Down*!" I went down like a log, never caring where I landed. Then we practised advancin' in short rushes. I tell you, sometimes I'd run straight into a tree and the machine-gun'd give me a real welt across the back o' the neck.

'Then one day I gave up.' Gregor throws his arms wide, and stares, cautiously, towards the long wing of the farmhouse where we know the Russians are taking cover. 'That afternoon, when I went down I stayed down. I'd got it into my head that I wasn't going to take any more of it.'

'Feldwebel Paust came rushing over to me, blowin' on his whistle for dear life. I didn't see him, but I could hear him. I'll never forget that voice. I've often prayed to heaven to let me meet him out here somewhere.

'"So you won't get up then, machine-gunner Martin?" he howled at me. "By God, I'll smash you, man, I'll finish you right off! I won't leave you be, till you're nothing but a lump o' quiverin' jelly, beggin' to be let die!"

'I lay there in the middle o' the ploughed field, and got my strength back with the help of hate. I didn't know then, that that was just what he wanted. To be a good soldier you've got to be a good hater! If you don't hate with all your might you can't kill. Hate's the strongest source of human energy. But there I was now, lying in the middle of a fuckin' Westphalian field, outside the old Papal town o' Paderborn. My whole face felt like a glowing, bubbling pancake, and I was near drowning in me own sweat inside the gasmask. The glasses of the eyepieces was so wet you couldn't see through them. The heel'd fallen off my one boot. My uniform was torn to ribbons. My knees hurt, and blood was pouring from them. I think I'd sprained an ankle, but I forgot that when Paust an' three others got me up and chased me on.

'I threw myself down beside a tree, and could hardly hear Paust's voice screaming at me. I knew he wouldn't stop 'til tank-soldier Gregor Martin was crushed like a fly on the wall. I'd really wanted to be an officer, that's why I'd volunteered, but that day by the tree on the bank of the river decided me that I'd never be an officer.

'"Into the river," he ordered me. "Forward, *march*! One-two, one-two, you sad sack!"

'I got halfway to my feet, but fell again. My legs were simply unable to carry me.

'The whistle shrilled.

'Then I crawled. He wanted to see me before a court-

92

martial for refusing to obey an order, and you know how frightened we all are at the thought of a court-martial. Better the traditional Hell of the priests than Germersheim. I got to the water and crawled out into it like some fucked-up kind of crocodile. On the way I lost my steel helmet, but Paust kicked it in after me.

'"Helmet, *on*!" he bawled. "*I'll* tell you when to take it *off*!"

'I crawled on the river bed, followed it down, I hadn't strength enough left to swim. Two Unteroffiziers had to pull me out. An ambulance picked me up a little later. At first I thought it was taking me to the mortuary! The MO asked me who'd done it to me. But I knew the answer to that one. I said I'd fallen out of a window.

'Eight days I was in hospital, and ten minutes after I got back with the rookie company they started again where they'd left off. I was out there goose-steppin', with instep stretched, in the Westphalian bloody fields.

'"Chest out! Tighten your arse!" screamed Feldwebel Paust, his voice echoing back from the woods. The instep had to be up at the level of your waist-belt.

'Yes, we learnt it, and so effectively that we could have marched straight to our deaths with our insteps *still* pointing at the sky.'

'*C'est la guerre*, we are the human offal of the war,' whispers the Legionnaire, quietly. 'It is our fate, so has Allah willed it, and this we must accept!'

We lie silent for a while, thinking over his hopeless soldier's philosophy.

'What's this, what's this, now,' the Old Man scolds, softly. 'Still lying here?'

'We're gone,' says Albert, and disappears quickly into the bushes.

Gregor is at my heels. It is so dark we can only see a couple of yards in front of us.

I stumble over something which proves to be a tipped-over wheelbarrow. I curse quietly. A battered helmet with a comb on top comes up on the far side. Faster than thought Gregor throws his bolas. It wraps itself round the Russian's throat. He manages no more than a hoarse rattle before he goes down.

'What the hell are you up to?' asks Albert, nervously, pressing himself to the ground in fear.

'Oh, Jesus, Jesus!' he cries as he catches sight of the dead Russian. 'I'm soon gonna get a nervous breakdown! The devil take that ol' pappy of mine as just *had* to beat the drums for the Prussian Hussars! He shoulda stayed home in his grass hut, he should, and not gone gettin' the best son he had mixed up in this terrible German war of revenge.'

'Hell's bells!' shouts Gregor, in terror, as a colossal red flame splits the darkness. Like a fiery spire it shoots up towards the heavens. It folds out into a huge mushrooming cloud, like some horrible mirage, suddenly appearing from nowhere.

Half-blinded and deafened we stare into the devilish redness. It grows and grows, and becomes a brilliant carmine umbrella of enormous proportions. It spits out yellow and white spurts of fire, like flaming sprays of roses. Slowly the giant, raging fire-flower becomes millions of licking tongues of flame. The whole of the heavens and the battleground around us are coloured red.

Porta and two Russians come running out from the glowing redness; it is one thunderous, indescribable inferno.

'Run dammit!' cries the Old Man, desperately, tugging at my shoulder.

With a feeling of unreality I follow him. My feet move automatically.

A Russian, with a *Kalashnikov* slung across his chest, runs past us. A blast of heated air throws us to the ground.

In shock, we run and creep our way out into the ice-cold water of the stream. It is beginning to warm up, slowly. I dip my field-cap in the water and hold it over my face for protection.

'*Tovarisch!*' screams a terror-stricken Russian, as we run

94

into one another out in the middle of the stream. 'Idiots!' he yells, pointing to the roaring sea of flames. Then he dashes on, the water splashing up around his running feet.

After a while the rest of the section begins to collect around the remains of a shattered fountain. The granite Cossack on it has now not only lost his head, but also the rest of his torso. Only his stone trousers and boots are left standing in the basin.

'What the devil was all that?' I ask, dabbing burn ointment on the blisters which seem to be eating into my flesh.

'It was that madman Porta who pulled the chain on us,' snarls the Old Man, sending Porta an angry look.

'But who the hell could've guessed it was a bloody great petrol dump,' pants Gregor, pouring water over his red, blistered face.

'I thought it was the handle of a safe I was turning,' Porta excused himself. 'It *looked* like one. You *know*, a bit of a turn to the left an' a bit of a turn to the right and you're a rich man. In this case, however, the result was a little different. I got a bit of a shock there, when I found myself in the middle of the world's biggest bonfire, together with a coupla Ivans!'

'What a lot of lying, rotten sods they all are,' whines Gregor despondently, creeping down into his coat-collar against the icy cold. 'They said we were coming here for a rest, and we fall into nothing more or less'n the worst kind of a shit-heap. They keep on tellin' us the enemy's crushed, and then what happens? Half the rotten Red Army's pissin' around back of the German lines. Oh god, what a rotten war! They've all got nothin' but crap where their brains ought to be!'

Albert comes sauntering along, with his machine-pistol dangling from its sling round his neck. He is wearing a lady's fur coat, a crazy-looking, gingery object, with fox-tails hanging down from its lapels. He has lipsticked his heavy mouth, and drawn big red circles around his eyes. He looks like a painting from the brush of a mad, surrealist artist.

95

'What *do* you look like?' asks the Old Man, open-mouthed.

'I look like what I look like, man,' he answers. He snatches a piece of bread from the fingers of a corpse and takes a bite of it, but spits it out again immediately.

'Why can't those mad geniuses back there send some Stukas over, an' put those blasted guns out of action?' asks Barcelona. He begins to kick a punctured football about.

The battle noises of tank-guns and field artillery can still be heard from the outskirts of the town.

It is easy to tell the sharp crack of tank-guns from the heavy boom of the field artillery. In between comes the characteristic sound of a bazooka, and when the heavy guns pause for a moment, the hysterical hammering of machine-gun fire.

'Two men! Over to the park!' the Old Man orders, pointing with his silver-lidded pipe.

Albert and I plod away. We have not gone far when we catch sight of a coal-black cat, crossing the road slowly and self-importantly with its tail erect.

'We stay here,' says Albert, decisively. 'That's bad luck, that is, a black cat crossin' your path. Death and destruction'll hit us, an' *hard*, if we go on!'

'You're right. We'll wait here a bit,' I say, shivering in my wet clothes. 'Then we'll go back and tell the Old Man we've been all through the town and haven't observed anything.'

'He'll just about kill us, man, if he ever finds out we've took the piss out of him because of seein' a black cat,' chatters Albert, trying to think of a way out.

A house crashes down, tall fingers of flame shooting up from it. Not far away we hear the confused noise of hand-grenades exploding.

As we turn a corner we see Porta, tiptoeing down a narrow alley, bent over strangely and grunting all the time: 'Oink! Oink!'

We halt in amazement and stare inquisitively after him, as he clambers up over a huge pile of rubble, and bends down to look through a hole in a wall.

'Oink! Oink!' he grunts, just like a real pig.

'Gone mad!' whispers Albert, his eyes round and shining whitely in the darkness. 'I knew it'd happen. He's been queer in his ways lately. Believe you me, man, it's that cat that's done it. The devil's in every black cat.'

'Must be a lot of devils then,' I answer him. 'Because there's certainly a lot of black cats!'

'Don't you know that ol' devil can turn himself into thousands of little devils if he wants to? Gotta be able to. Else how could there be a German devil an' an American devil, an' one in this place too?'

I shrug my shoulders, and watch Porta disappear, still grunting, behind the rubble-heap.

'He thinks he's a pig that's been issued with an mpi,' mumbles Albert, shaking his head despondently. 'I see darkness, when I think what this war is on the way to turning us all into.'

When we get back the Old Man has no time to listen to our report. He is too busy giving one of the new men a talking-to.

'I'm goin' to look after you,' he shouts, angrily. 'Why'd you shoot those three prisoners?'

'Isn't that what we're here for?' asks one of the new boys, a Fahnenjunker-Gefreiter.

'Get them heels together,' rages the Old Man. 'Stand up straight when you talk to me, you lazy man. And remember it's Herr Feldwebel!'

The Fahnenjunker-Gefreiter clicks his heels together, and places his hands rigidly down along the seams of his trousers.

'Very good, Herr Feldwebel,' he replies, with a look of hate.

'Why'd you shoot those prisoners?' repeats the Old Man, in a penetrating voice. 'They'd got their hands up, and they were unarmed, and you shot 'em like lousy rats. That's *murder!*'

'I never saw their hands were up, Herr Feldwebel, and I

97

believed they were armed.'

'Liar!' hisses the Old Man. 'I was further off from them than you were, and I saw them clearly coming out of the house with their hands up!'

'I saw 'em an' all,' shouts Tiny, from a corner.

'You shut up!' the Old Man snaps. 'I can do without your help. Hand over that machine-gun,' he turns to the Fahnen-junker-Gefreiter. 'You're no longer number one machine-gunner, you're a runner for Command Group. I'll make your backside so red-hot it'll *burn* that killer streak out of you. If I did what was right I'd turn you straight over to a firin' squad, you filthy murderin' little swine. Now get out of my sight! The very sight of you makes me want to spew!'

Albert sits by the window, wrapped in his crazy ginger fur coat. He looks tired.

'Lay down and get some sleep,' I say, giving him a push.

'Sleep?' he cries, staring cautiously out through the window. 'You must be crazy, man! That black cat was a warning to us. The neighbours are comin' over tonight. Count on it. I don't want to get *my* throat cut the way that Section 4 lot did.'

'Cool down. Get that black blood of yours off the boil,' I comfort him. 'Nothing's going to happen. The neighbours are just as tired as we are.'

'I don't know,' he answers, 'but I got a funny, creepy feelin'. Those wicked sods've got somethin' brewin' for us. Take a look down that rotten long street over there. Before we can blow a fart they can be coming at us from hundreds of holes an' corners.'

'You're soft in the head,' I answer him. 'Come on, now! Let's get some shuteye!'

We roll up close together, like two dogs, for warmth. It takes only a few minutes for us to fall into a deep, troubled sleep, plagued with nightmares.

A long, scratchy, nervewracking howl brings us to our feet, clutching at machine-pistols and hand-grenades. The whole of one wall disappears in a thick cloud of dust, and a

98

blast wave throws us across the room. An upright piano comes flying through the air and breaks up with a confused jangle of notes out on the landing.

I am rushing for the door, when Julius Heide grabs me and pulls me flat on my back to the floor.

A giant orange-yellow tongue of flame shoots up. The double door to the street flies off its hinges, and goes twisting away over the housetops like a piece of paper in the wind.

'The fuckin' neighbours are lettin' us know they're still alive,' gasps Barcelona, spitting out mortar.

Albert goes down on his belly by the window, and sends wild bursts down the street.

'Who the devil's that black idiot belting away at now?' rages the Old Man. In two long strides he is over to Albert and pulls him away from the window. The LMG clatters to the floor.

'It was a Russian,' Albert defends himself, wiping the back of his hand across his mouth. 'A mad sod in a topper just like Porta's!'

'Rubbish!' says the Old Man, angrily. 'You shoot that thing off one more time just because you're shit-scared, and I'll blow the black head off you, you shakin' sack o' bones! Understand me?'

Slowly we begin to relax again. Cigarette ends glow in the dark. We try to get back to sleep, but none of us can.

'Where *is* Porta, anyway?' asks the Old Man, looking searchingly around.

'He thinks he's turned into a pig,' answers Albert, pulling the ginger furs closer about him. 'He's goin' round grunting!'

'Grunting?' asks the Old Man, unbelievingly. 'Has he gone off his rocker? What's he grunting for?'

A salvo of 155 mms falls close to us, and the noise drowns Albert's reply.

'God help us, aren't they ever gonna stop that racket?' asks Gregor, pulling his cloak up over his head. 'Any of you ever thought what a shell like that *costs*? It's bloody expensive I can tell you, and most of the ones they shoot don't do any good. Christ in Heaven, they *must* all be mad!'

'You believe in God?' asks Albert suddenly, from over by the SMG, popping up his head from the depths of the ginger furs.

'You gone mad too, 'ave you?' asks Tiny in a hollow voice. He is down inside a large chest which he has taken over for a bed. He has pulled the lid down after him and left only a narrow crack through which we can just see his eyes.

'Believe in God yourself?' asks Gregor, looking at Albert with a crooked smile.

'If he does it's gotta be a darky God,' says Barcelona, with a short laugh. 'I once saw a picture of a black God in an American magazine. He was an old feller with a big white beard, and went round with a stick and a top-hat.'

'God's always old, whether He's black, white or yellow,' says Gregor, gesturing with his machine-pistol. 'He's simply *gotta* be old. Think of all the things He's been through to get all that experience.'

'If God's the way they say He is, then He must be very tiresome an' not very tolerant,' philosophizes Albert thoughtfully, polishing away at the machine-gun as he talks. 'He must be an officer or he wouldn't expect us all to bow down before Him, and always be prayin' to Him for somethin' or other!'

'What God does is not a subject for discussion,' says the Legionnaire who is sitting reading his Koran, as usual. 'What Allah does is right and must be accepted!'

'"*Gott mit uns*", it says on our belt-buckles,' Albert goes on stubbornly, after a short silence. He seems quite fascinated by his thoughts on the subject of religion. 'Why ever should God be with *us*? The English an' the Yanks go to church a lot more'n we do, an' what about all the atheists? God's helping them, seems like, just for the minute! It's enough to make a man laugh his head off!'

'Why in the name of all hell're you bothering us with all that God rubbish? Change the subject or shut up!' explodes the Old Man, puffing furiously at his silver-lidded pipe, and sending up billows of smoke.

'Religion is a kind of opium,' Gregor trumpets, importantly. 'Me an' my general were always agreed on that. It makes people soft. Parsons should be refused admission to Heaven, my general always said. They ruin all the hard-headed people with their preaching, and all that's left are the soft-headed ones.'

'Oh I don't know,' says Albert, thoughtfully. He pulls his head back down inside the ginger-coloured furs, like a snail going back into its shell.

'What the devil do you mean by that?' asks Heide, looking up from the LMG which, as usual, he has dismantled and is cleaning.

'I mean I don't know whether there's a God, or there isn't,' answers Albert. 'An' I mean too that I don't understand a word of any of it, man!'

'Now I'm *ordering* you to decide on what you really believe in, you black monkey,' the Old Man foams, removing his pipe from his mouth. 'Either you *believe* in God, or else you *don't* believe in God. Make up your mind *now*, an' then shut up!'

'I have done,' says Albert, stubbornly, pulling his head in again. 'I made up my mind a long time ago that I was gonna believe I didn't know whether there was a God or there wasn't a God, an' that's what I believe in. And now you get mad at me because of me admitting "I don't know" is what I believe in.'

'You will have some explaining to do at any rate, *mon ami*, when you one day stand face to face with Allah,' laughs the Legionnaire, heartily.

'I don't think I will, you know,' says Albert assuredly. 'I'm a nice, decent sort o' feller, who's only killed people he's been ordered to kill, and not pinched anything if he didn't really have a need for it!'

'Shut it, shut it, shut it!' shouts the Old Man. 'A bit more of this and they'll shoot you without needing an order to do it!'

'Oink! Oink!' comes from out in the street.

'It's Porta,' laughs Gregor, looking out of the gaping window opening.

'Seen a pig go by?' asks Porta, from the opposite side of the street. 'One with black patches on it, and light blue eyes just like mine?'

'Now I've heard that, too,' the Old Man breaks out, fiercely. 'God help us, he's running about the place looking for a pig with black patches on it, while the neighbours're knocking the whole damn place down round our ears! Come back. Come bloody *back*!' he roars through the broken window. 'That's an *order*!'

But Porta is lost in the darkness, still hunting for his black and pink pig with the pale blue eyes.

More and more soldiers from other units arrive, and sit down round the fire Tiny has started in the middle of the floor.

Tiny shakes a tin of signal powder into the blaze, and the flames turn bright red.

We chuckle with pleasure at the brilliant sight.

Porta comes barging noisily through the door.

'That rotten pig must've been at the commando school,' he yells. 'I've been on his tail all night, and every time I called to him he answered me. Then, just when I thought I'd got him, down by the suspension bridge, he goes over to the attack an' dashes off across the river to the neighbours. They're sitting there chewin' on him now, I shouldn't wonder!'

'That fat Leutnant with the monocle. He's the cause of all this,' says Barcelona, staring into the red flames.

'I thought he was in jail,' says Gregor. 'That was the cook-waggon gossip.'

'Latrine rumours,' Barcelona shakes his head. 'That shit's got his feet under the table with the red-tabs. Two hours after they'd turned the key on him they had to bow him out again with an apology.'

'Better shoot his blubbery chops off him, then,' says Porta, drawing the heavy *Nagan* demonstratively from his holster, and aiming it at Heide, who ducks instinctively. 'Well, I'm off,' he goes on, returning the *Nagan* to its holster with a flourish.

'Where the hell d'you think *you're* goin'?' growls the Old Man, pushing tobacco down into the bowl of his silver-lidded pipe. 'I won't have it. I won't *have* you running around over the whole of Russia. I want you here where I can keep an eye on you.'

'Be back in two shakes,' promises Porta, elevating three fingers vertically. 'Just off to have a look-see if the war hasn't come to a stop all of a sudden. It's that still.'

Gregor flips the cards round with practised fingers. We play quietly for a while.

Suddenly Tiny crashes a petrol-can down on Albert's head. Albert is sitting opposite him in his ginger fur coat, looking as if he had stepped straight out of a coloured cartoon strip.

'That black ape's more of a twister'n a 'ole Jew colony,' rages Tiny, swinging the heavy can round his head. ''E keeps stickin' them klepto-bleedin'-maniac fingers of 'is out over the coppers, but 'e don't drop no soddin' money into the pool.' The can lands on Albert's head, for the second time, with a reverberating clang. He falls out of his chair and knocks over the card-table.

'Stay where you are, so's I can kill you dead, you stinkin' Congo German you,' screams Tiny furiously, lifting the petrol-can for the third time.

'You *have* killed me,' bleats Albert, holding both hands protectively over his head. 'Can't you see I'm dead already, and I'm *bleedin'* man!'

'Get up, you black soddin' corpse,' shouts Tiny, kicking out at him.

Oberleutnant Löwe bangs through the door, followed by the monocled Leutnant.

'Where is Obergefreiter Porta?' asks Löwe, with a steely glint in his eye. 'Where *is* that wicked man?'

'Pluckin' geese, sir,' says Tiny, with a sloppy attempt at a salute.

'*What* is he doing?' asks Löwe, gaping at Tiny.

'Pluckin' geese, sir,' explains Tiny, making feather-plucking movements with his hands.

'I've got some geese to pluck with *him*,' snarls Löwe, straightening his dirty field-cap. 'He's to report to company immediately, and tell him to keep away from Oberst Hinka. The CO doesn't want to *know* him any more. He's for a court-martial and Germersheim!'

''Ow about division then, sir?' asks Tiny owlishly. 'The General an' Porta's good friends, sir!'

'I'll look after you too, Creutzfeldt,' splutters Löwe. He turns on his heel and disappears, with the monocled Leutnant close upon his heels.

'What the hell's Porta doing now?' asks the Old Man, bitterly. 'That crazy sod's enough to drive a man up the wall. He goes on as if he owned the whole blasted army. Now I'm gonna tell you *all* somethin'. You're nothing but a shower of shit, the lot of you! I won't be finished with you till you've all seen the inside of Germersheim with lifers on you *an'* a death sentence laid on top of 'em!'

He is interrupted. The door crashes open and in comes Porta, dragging a squealing pig after him.

'He came back, after all,' he grins, happily.

'A few hours of that Commie lot was enough for him. Pretty, ain't he? That squealing's just an expression of how happy he is at having managed to defect!'

'You're to report to the OC,' says the Old Man, tiredly. 'That means now!'

'Who says you've laid eyes on me?' asks Porta, casually. 'Löwe's only a sodding officer. That lot can wait till I've got time for 'em, and time's what I haven't got enough of just now!'

'You're to report to company,' sighs the Old Man, 'whether you've got time or not! Call company,' he orders Gregor, who has communications duty.

'Connection broken,' Porta shakes with laughter, as he wrenches the telephone cable loose. 'Come on Tiny, we got to get food on!'

We eat and eat - for four hours together. Grease runs down from our mouths on to our chests. In between we take a trip outside to make room for more. We are so ravenously hungry that we are unable to stop eating.

Gregor almost chokes himself. Porta recommends that we hang him up by his heels. He coughs up a large chunk of pork.

We do not stop eating until only the gnawed bones remain. Gasping and belching, we sprawl on the floor, totally gorged with food.

War is a disease.

Sven Hassel

The train was struck by a bomb only a few yards away from the shelter of the tunnel. The railwaymen and the torn-off boiler of the locomotive were thrown 400 yards away into the ripe corn.

The leading carriage stood up vertically in the air. The next in line had been squeezed into the semblance of a closed concertina.

The Jabos came back. The leading machine dropped phosphorus bombs. Incendiary sticks skipped across the Red Cross cars. In seconds they had become a roaring sea of flame. Most of the patients burned to death in their beds.

The Jabos turned and swept the cornfield with their machine-guns. Before leaving they dropped the last of their incendiaries. The corn blazed up.

The black smoke of the conflagration was visible all day, even from many miles away. Not a single man or woman on the hospital train escaped alive.

VERA KONSTANTINOVNA

'I don't *like* this joint,' grumbles Porta, pulling the cork from a bottle of vodka with his teeth. He takes a long swig of the fiery spirit and wipes his mouth on his sleeve. 'Is this a billet to give *us*? Not even a rotten stove! It's cold as an Eskimo's arsehole! An' they call us the *herrenvolk*! Don't make me die laughing!'

'Section leaders to OC,' sings out the clerk, Gefreiter Voss, sticking his pointy nose in to us through a broken window.

'The devil,' growls the Old Man, sourly, buttoning up his long winter cloak, and slinging his machine-pistol over his shoulder, muzzle down. 'Look after the shop while I'm gone,' he turns to Barcelona, 'and I want that SMG in position. Those wicked sods could be on us again before we knew it!'

His breath clouds out around him, as he wheels away on his clumsy bow-legs through the deep sludge. His hands, contrary to all regulations, are pushed down deeply into his pockets. Anyone seeing him rolling along with his cap pulled down on his head, round-shouldered, bow-legged and wearing clumsy infantry boots, would think him no more than a stupid yokel. But they would be terribly wrong. In reality he is a deadly dangerous, battle-trained soldier, with a quite superhuman faculty of calmness, despite his frayed nerves. His face resembles a squashed orange, but still, somehow, engenders confidence. He is an old trench-rat, who doesn't trust many people; and that is one of the most important reasons for his having got us out of the dirtiest corners imaginable. And with amazingly few losses.

A little grey cat follows him, meowing, part of the way.

He kicks the door of the company office open disrespect-fully. Here Hauptfeldwebel Hoffmann reigns, fat and vain as a South American dictator. He is wearing a tankman's black uniform, despite the fact that it is reserved for line troops and is not for echelon.

'You're supposed to knock three times before you come in here,' says Hoffmann angrily, swinging half-round and then back again in his American swivel chair. 'This isn't a brothel, man, it's Company HQ. This is where the brains live!'

'Brains?' grins the Old Man, in an insulting tone. 'You're sitting on 'em! Don't get too blown up, will you! Just remember we're short of men up the line. I might just ask for you down there with me, so you'd get busted to an ordinary Feldwebel an' lose your two silver stripes!'

'*You* get *me* out in your lousy section?' jeers Hoffmann. 'No Beier, I'm this company's Hauptfeldwebel, and I'm gonna stay being that as long as there *is* a 5 Company. They need an empty-headed key-swinger to look after the prison-ers at Germersheim. Fancy the job?'

'Shit!' growls the Old Man, tramping on in to Oberleut-nant Löwe without knocking.

'*Grüss Gott*,' Löwe greets him, leaning back in his rickety, creaking chair. 'Like a "little black" to warm you up?'

'Yes, *please*,' answers the Old Man, filling a mug half-full with coffee and topping it off with vodka. He throws his helmet down on the trampled earth of the floor, sits down on a hand-grenade box, and stretches out his legs and his filthy boots in front of him. He leans his machine-pistol up against a table leg.

'You look tired, Beier,' says Löwe. 'Been rough the last couple of months, hasn't it?'

'We've had our hands full,' says the Old Man, blowing on his coffee. 'That bloody 2 Section'll soon have me climbin' up the wall. No sooner we've got away from the blasted war than I'm standin' there with me mpi at the ready keepin' the rotten lot away from the temptations of the soddin' flesh.

108

Sometimes I can't hardly understand what's going on. About a week ago Unteroffizier Julius Heide goes raving, an' mows down a couple of hundred civvies with his machine-gun. Even if I was to charge him for it nothing'd happen, except me gettin' a bawling-out from the NSFO. That spit an' polish follower o' the book, Unteroffizier Julius Heide's a valued member of the party, so why shouldn't he get his funnies murdering a few women and children! They're only *untermensch*, anyway. Soon as we're finished with the murdering an' killing, Porta and Tiny enjoys themselves with a couple of willing Russian girls. What happens? They get punished for fraternizing! The laws in this war are really *strange*!'

'I didn't hear what you just said, Beier,' smiles Oberleutnant Löwe. 'Neither of us wants a court-martial, do we?'

The four other section commanders enter, and bark out short reports.

'More than half the company's gone up in smoke,' Löwe says, looking at the casualty lists in front of him. 'So! Until further notice we remain inactive. There's fresh supplies and replacements on the way to us. But don't take that inactive business too seriously. There's strict orders from regiment to keep the men constantly on the move. Otherwise they'll get up to all sorts of monkey-tricks. Herr Oberst Hinka wants no complaints, either civil or military.' Löwe throws a glance at the Old Man, who is still sitting on the grenade box, warming his hands on his coffee. 'And I'm thinking of 2 Section in particular, Feldwebel Beier, and also in particular of those two madmen Obergefreiter Josef Porta and Obergefreiter Wolfgang Creutzfeldt. And, while we are on the subject of 2 Section, we've received a long message from Army HQ.' Löwe throws three closely-written folio sheets over to the Old Man.

'That's to do with Gefreiter Albert. They want us to wash him white!'

The four other section leaders double up with laughter.

Only the Old Man and Löwe remain serious and straight-faced.

'There's nothing to laugh at,' Löwe tells them, buttoning his greatcoat. 'This is a very annoying business. Answer it Beier, in a manner which can bring them to understand that a negro cannot be washed white. Before I forget it, there's another annoying matter between the NSFO and Joseph Porta. I thought I'd be able to stop it, but, unfortunately, it's already gone to regiment. Division's heard about it too. If the worst happens it could cost Porta his head. A bitch of a case. You *must* keep your people in order, Beier. I'm punishing your section by giving them burial duty. Don't forget, now, Germans and Russians are not to be buried in the same grave, and civilians are to be buried on their own. *Don't* make the same mess of it as you did last time, when they mixed officers and other ranks together. Officers get their own individual graves, and such graves are specially decorated. The men go into a common grave, and may be buried in three layers, as long as there is a 30 cm layer of earth between them.'

'Lord help us!' mumbles the Old Man, grinding his teeth. He fills up his mug again with hot coffee.

Almost an hour later, his pipe billowing smoke, he tramps back down the muddy, tracked-up road.

The cat meets him again, and stand up on its back legs, pawing at his trousers.

'All right for *you*,' he says, scratching his neck. 'You haven't got 2 Section! You've only got yourself. Shit, that's what it is, pussy!' He becomes more and more angry with the section, the closer he gets to the billet. 'I'll *bury* 'em!' he promises himself. 'God damn it, if I don't. I'll make 'em crawl round the world three times, an' it'll be over the North Pole an' the South Pole. *That* ought to cool 'em down a bit!'

Fuming inside, he kicks open the door, throws his machine-pistol down in a corner, and looks angrily around. He sees immediately the almost unbelievable disorder in the great hall.

Untermensch Albert is having a furious verbal battle with *Herrenvolk* Heide. 'You're always after me, Julius, but now I want to know the reason why,' snorts Albert. 'Even if I *am* black I'm just as much a German as you are, and I've got all the rights of a German. So if you're after me for bein' a Reich-nigger then I'm gonna report you for it!'

'If *you're* a German, then *I'm* a Chinaman,' rages Julius, contemptuously. 'I'll tell you what you are, you black ape! You're a charcoal cartoon of a human being, a trained, performing man-eater, who chews bones for dinner like a hound-dog!'

''E's more'n that!' trumpets Tiny. ''Is gran'dad was a French Yid from Senegal, with a bleedin' great 'ook of a snitch, an' the skin of 'is cock cut off. 'E used to clean up in the synagogue every Thursday!'

'It's a lie,' howls Albert, insultedly. 'It was my *great*-grandpappy was a French Jew, and he *married* a girl from Senegal!'

'Now I've heard everything,' gasps Heide. He is on his feet and over by Albert in three long strides. He stands over him with legs straddled and fists planted on his hips, stinking of Unteroffizier.

'*Are* you a Yid? Answer, you black mongrel, or I'll crack your skull wide open, as I have the right to do!'

Albert creeps further down into his ginger furs, in terror.

'My great-grandpappy was a French Jew. I'm a German,' he whines, fumbling for his machine-pistol. Before he can get hold of it Heide kicks it clattering out of his reach.

'*French* Jew!' sneers Heide. 'There are no *French* Jews. Either you're a Jew or you're not a Jew. You've sneaked your way into the German *Wehrmacht* under false premises. God knows what the Racial Commission'll say when I report this.'

'They'll kick you out,' grins Albert, assuredly, 'an' they'll tell you, man, to go wipe your Nazi arse on your report! I've *been* in front of 'em, an' they've looked down my throat an' up my arsehole, an' measured my face, an' held me by the bollocks an' pulled my prick for me. And they declared me

80% German when they'd finished. I was close to gettin' put in the SS, where I might've ended up an officer!'

'What *is* all this piss you're talkin',' shouts the Old Man, irritably, pushing Heide angrily to one side. 'I don't want any trouble with you lot, whether you're Jews or whether you're Germans. You keep yourself to yourself and go polish your machine-pistol, Julius! You're nothing but trouble to me. And you, Albert, go out and wash your face and make sure you rinse it several times! That's an order from Corps HQ, and you come back in here to me after and prove your black colour's *real*! You, Barcelona, you're guard commander for the next three days!'

'Why?' asks Barcelona, his mouth dropping open. 'What've *I* done?'

'Saluted the General when you shouldn't have, you sloppy fool! Do it again and they'll put you inside! Porta! Where the hell's that madman got to?'

'Cookin' food,' answers Tiny. 'Pork chops à l'Alba!'

'I don't *care* where his blasted pork chops're from,' rages the Old Man, flinging his steel helmet down on the floor. 'He's halfway inside Germersheim, an' they'll hang him there! Nobody goes anywhere, you hear! Everybody stays here! In an hour from now you parade for grave duty, and in the meantime you clean this place up. Nails in the walls for uniforms an' equipment an' regimentally hung up. Beds made up out from the wall at equal distances. Helmets on gasmask pouches accordin' to regulations. No missing nails in your boots!'

'We ain't got any nails,' protests Gregor, weakly.

'Shit some, then,' orders the Old Man.

Tiny jumps up, clicks his heels together, and lifts his pale grey bowler courteously.

'We 'ear an' obey, 'Err Feldwebel, *sir*!' he trumpets.

'Cut that play-acting *out*!' snarls the Old Man, viciously. 'There'll be early parade tomorrow mornin'! All illegal weapons to be handed in! Anybody running round with enemy guns'll be for it!'

112

'For it!' echoes Tiny.

For a second it looks as if the Old Man is going to throw himself at him. Then he gives up. The energy of his anger seeps out of him. He drops down on to a creaking bed, runs his hands through his hair, and begins to fill his pipe.

'What a shower of shit you lot are,' he mumbles, looking round at us.

We dig the common grave in the park. There is no more room in the churchyard.

The Old Man sits on the remains of a pedestal, on which a statue once stood, and blows out great clouds of tobacco-smoke.

Porta and Tiny are sorting bodies, and talking quietly to one another.

'You as much as look at a gold tooth, and I'll shoot you!' The Old Man aims at them threateningly with the stem of his pipe.

'Perish the thought,' lies Porta, with one finger inside the mouth of a corpse. Tiny stands ready with the forceps.

'Two in this one,' whispers Porta. 'Wait till he's down in the grave before you take his savings. Then the Old Man can't see it. How many we got?'

'A lot,' answers Tiny. More than five is a lot where he is concerned.

The partly decayed body of a woman slips from my hands as I pass it on to Heide and Gregor. They are down in the grave lining up the bodies regimentally.

Heide goes amuck when the heavy corpse knocks him over into the middle of the grave. Snorting with rage he throws a torn-off arm at me.

'You did that deliberately! God help you when I get hold of you!'

I hide behind a toolshed, and stay there until he goes off the boil. He is mad enough to carry out his threat.

We have to dig two more common graves. There are many more dead than we had thought.

During the sorting process Tiny comes to an SS-Hauptsturmführer who has had the lower part of his body shot away. Since orders are that parts of bodies are to be buried together with the person to whom they belong, Tiny begins to search for a pair of legs which could fit the Hauptsturmführer's body. Not finding them, he takes two torn-off legs which, by the boots, must have belonged to a Russian officer.

Porta scratches his stiff red hair doubtfully, and looks critically at the legs, with their Russian riding breeches and high brown boots.

'Don't really fit, do they?' he says, spitting over the edge of the officer's grave. 'If they ever open this one up, they *will* be confused. They'll think it's a wrong 'un they've run across. An SS officer who was going to desert and had started changing into Ivan's uniform. No it won't do, my son. We'll have to get him a couple of German legs!'

'I'll 'ave another look, then,' grunts Tiny patiently, crawling, with difficulty, up out of the grave. He stops in a kneeling position on its edge, and turns an ear toward the low-hanging clouds. '*Jabos*!' he shouts. 'Bleedin' arse'oles, *Jabos*!'

Porta stretches his neck. His cunning, foxy face sniffs towards the east.

'*There*!' yells Tiny. He is back in the grave like lightning, and burrows down between the bodies.

They seem to jump up from behind the trees, and, with a nerve-shattering roar, they pass over our heads. Their stubby wings sparkle as they rise vertically into the sky and come back round for a return run. They open fire with all their automatic weapons: machine-guns and light cannon. Hundreds of spurts of dust fountain up from the ground, as the projectiles whip across the park. Two of the machines bank, and fly along the row of open graves. They are so low that the faces of their pilots can be clearly seen.

I drop down flat on my face behind the toolshed. A machine-cannon salvo splinters into it, throwing all kinds of dirt and muck over me. I turn my face up for a moment to

114

see where the battle-planes have gone to.

Both machines seem to rear up on their tails in the air. They describe a great arc and come roaring back at us. This time they drop bombs. The shattering noise of the explosions almost burst our eardrums. The earth shakes. Clods of earth and stones rain down on me.

Someone gives out a long, rattling scream. It drowns in the roar of the Jabos, as they attack again. The projectiles spitting from their wings seem to roll up the asphalt path like a carpet.

The machines flash over us again. More bombs fall; deafening us.

They come in twice more. Then they fly off towards the east, back to their base.

We wish everything far, far away, as we start in again collecting bodies.

Tiny finds a pair of German legs which will do for the Hauptsturmführer.

It is far into the night before we have finished filling in the graves. We sit down, tiredly, on the soft earth of one of the common graves. The vodka bottle goes from hand to hand. We are soaked in sweat despite the biting cold of the evening.

The Old Man is sitting with Barcelona, sorting dog-tags. German here, Russian there. They put them separately into large bags, and tie the service books of the dead men in bundles. There are also letters. A lot of letters. Barcelona unfolds one and reads it aloud:

My beloved boy,

It is a long time since I heard from you. Did you get my parcel? There is a woolly sweater in it to keep you warm. Don't forget to change your socks if you get your feet wet. You know how you are with colds. Claus the foreman's son who you went to school with is back from the Army. He lost one arm but they are not sending him home. When his leave's finished they are putting him on barrack

115

duty. Even the ones who lose a leg aren't getting sent home now. We had an air-raid alarm again yesterday. They dropped some bombs on the railway station and they say it's flattened. I'm going down there this afternoon with Mrs Schröder to see how bad it is. Now look after yourself won't you. Now your dad's gone I've only got you. I'm glad you're on a part of the front where there's not a lot happening. Mrs Schultzes two boys are in a place where a lot of terrible things are going on but we mustn't talk about that. Our new Gauleiter is very strict and hard on people who talk too much. They came and took our neighbour Mrs Schmidt in the middle of the night because she talked about something called *Nacht und Nebellager*. So you have to be careful what you say. My dear, darling boy, it's twelve months since you went away but thank God you'll be getting leave in two months time. I am counting the hours. Write soon. I get so disappointed when the postman goes by and there's no letter for me. I know you're not allowed more than one letter every eight days, but promise me you'll write then at the least.

See you in 58 days time.

Your loving
Mother

'Shit!' says Tiny, as Barcelona refolds the letter and places it inside the soldier's service record book.

'Up you get,' commands the Old Man, coming to his feet. 'Sling arms! Broken step! Follow me! Quick march!'

Chatting as we go, we walk in a disorderly column down a narrow path. We keep to its sides, under the shelter of the trees, in cover from the air.

'Shall I cook the grub when we get home,' offers Porta, from the darkness under the trees. By 'home' he means the factory hall we have taken over for our quarters. 'I'm going to do us "Pork Chops à l'Alba",' he goes on, enthusiastically. 'It's a dish that Kings an' Emperors prize highly.

116

Orthodox Jews do it with beef cutlets, but that spoils the effect. It needs character to do "Pork Chops à l'Alba", I can tell you. First of all it's out in the fields and find your shallot onions. These you have to chop very fine, and the right song for doing that to is the "Georgian Harvest song". When they're nicely chopped up, you sprinkle 'em, with an elegant flip of the wrist, with parsley, sage, salt an' pepper. But, for heaven's sake, *black* peppers! The man who uses *white* pepper should have the devil let down through his throat with a roll of barbed wire on his back! Then you make small cuts on each side of your pork chops with a good sharp knife. I usually use my combat knife. It's always got a good, sharp edge to it. I prefer to hum "The Song of the Volga Boatmen" during the next operation, which is rubbing the onion mix into the pork. Now we come to the next step, which can be difficult. Borrow some butter from your next-door neighbour, which, of course, you never intend to pay back. A lot of people live high on borrowing from their next-door neighbours. It's cheaper an' also saves storage space. The butter you've borrowed you then melt. Take your pork chop between two fingers, I recommend the thumb and forefinger of the right hand, and dip half of it in the melted butter. Turn it, then, on a fire-proof dish for about ten minutes. After this, you pour your wine over it, but light an' easy. *Don't* drown it! The chops only need to be slightly, but happily, intoxicated. Whip in the remainder of the borrowed butter and pour the sauce over the meat.'

'What *kind* of wine?' comes Gregor's voice from the back of the section.

'White, of course, you excuse for a driver!' snaps Porta.

'Any special sort?' Gregor enquires.

'How that fool goes on! You can see he's been around generals too long! Use what you've *got*. The main thing is it's white, and what's left of it you drink yourself.'

A despatch-rider comes round the bend ahead of us at top speed and stops in front of the Old Man, who is out in the middle of the narrow path with his arm raised.

'Russian tanks, Herr Feldwebel!' shouts the despatch-rider, straddling his motorcycle. 'Coming this way to get back to their own lines. Orders from Regimental HQ. Stop and destroy!' With a roar the motorcycle is off again.

'God damn and set fire to it,' rages the Old Man. '*Tanks*, and we've got the job of wiping 'em out! Of course! Who else?'

Tiny takes a sausage from his pocket, snaps it in two and gives Porta half.

'There's some blood on it,' he apologizes, 'but they say as blood gives a feller strength!'

'Where'd you get it? asks Porta, suspiciously.

'From a dead un',' answers Tiny, chewing on his half of the sausage.

'What kind of a dead un?' asks Porta, sniffing at his half.

'Russian bleedin' lieutenant,' mumbles Tiny, looking towards the trees.

'The sausage ought to be all right then. Officers only eat top-class stuff,' says Porta, taking a large bite.

'Come on,' orders the Old Man. 'Things'll soon be humming. Get your magnetics ready! Stovepipes in the lead! We attack from the right of the road, and don't let me see any itchy trigger fingers. Wait for the order!'

'We getting anti-tank support?' asks Heide, pompously.

'Yes, up your arse,' Porta laughs noisily. 'If they'd got anti-tank guns to spare, they wouldn't send us, now would they?'

Part way into the wood we meet a couple of sections from 7 Company. They are wildly excited, and go on about hordes of Russian tanks.

'And they've infantry with 'em,' shouts a Feldwebel to the Old Man. '2 Company's been steam-rollered to bits. Not a dry eye left in the lot!'

'Sounds pleasant,' answers the Old Man, with a short laugh. 'But that's what we're here for. To kill or be killed.'

'Down!' shouts Barcelona hoarsely, as half a dozen flares suddenly open up in the sky, making everything as light as day. The whole section is flat on the ground before he has finished saying the word.

An SP comes rushing along at top speed, bumps over the top of the hill and lands with a jangling crash on the far side.

'Up with you,' bawls the Old Man. 'Move! Open line abreast! March! March!'

The section spreads out and lumbers, panting, across the uneven ground. I have the MG under my arm, supporting it on my hip. My finger is along the trigger-guard. My heart is beating so fast it is almost painful. I go rushing straight through some bushes, which tear at my face and hands. Blood runs down.

A little way in front of me Porta is running, his idiotic yellow topper on the back of his neck. Down in the valley the SP wheels round as if the driver had gone mad. The night fills with heavy thuds and brilliant muzzle-flashes. They give light enough for us to be able to glimpse half a score of T-34s. The SP stops with a jolt, and replies to the fire immediately.

From a row of ruined houses, long bursts of Russian Maxim bullets rush at us.

Some of the rookies throw themselves to the ground, and try to creep away from the hell of fire.

'Get *up*! Get *on*!' roars the Old Man, striking at them with the barrel of his mpi. 'Who the devil told you to fall down?'

Breathing heavily we break into a run. We are now not much above a hundred yards from the closer of the T-34s.

Blue-green lightnings flame from the muzzles of Russian machine-pistols: Maxims spit wicked yellow flashes as they pepper us with their deadly, pearly chains of tracer.

I go down so heavily my face smashes into the lock of the LMG. I wipe my hand over it. I am bleeding freely, but have no time to think about that. I sight in on the muzzle-flame from the Russian SMG, press the butt of my gun into my shoulder and grip so tightly with my left hand that I almost get cramp in it. I send three short bursts at the Russian SMG. Then I'm up like lightning, run to the left and fall into new cover. I am hardly into it before a grenade goes off where I was only a moment ago.

A shell from a tank-gun passes close above my head and cuts Fahnenjunker Kolb in two with the efficiency of a circular saw. The blast from the exploding shell throws me far off to one side and tears the LMG out of my hands. I sob with terror and press my face into the ground. When the rushing in my ears stops, I put my hands out to feel for the LMG. Instead, my fingers find themselves touching a naked leg. I feel at it and cannot believe my eyes when I open them to look. A naked leg, torn off at the groin and blown out of both boots and trousers. I start to scream, and beat my fists on the ground, hysterically.

'Get *on*! Get *on*!' the Old Man chases me, bringing his mpi-butt down on the small of my back.

'No!' I protest, 'I *can't* go on!'

Heide grabs me brutally by the collar.

'Get up, you yellow swine,' he snarls, viciously. 'Where's your LMG? Don't tell me you've lost your weapon?' He throws me from him, as if I were a sack of rotten potatoes.

I fall, sobbing, on one knee, completely finished.

He points the muzzle of his machine-pistol at me, and cracks me hard across the face with the back of his hand. My helmet goes back on to my neck. Then, suddenly, it is all over. I am a normal, well-disciplined soldier again. The MG is back in my hands with the strap regimentally across my shoulder. My legs are going like runaway pistons.

I literally fly past Porta, who is in cover behind a wood-pile, readying the stovepipe.

'Hey there!' he shouts cheerily after me. 'Hang on. Don't want you getting to Moscow before us an' grabbin' all the good cunt!'

A T-34 is hit just in front of me. A blinding sheet of flame goes up, and the tank breaks up with a metallic sound, like a giant fist crashing down on a tin roof. The explosion illuminates a whole row of wrecked houses. From off to the left come the hard cracking explosions of German stick-grenades. It must be Heide's squad who've got within throwing distance.

Porta's bazooka howls, and the passage of air from the speeding rocket almost tears my helmet from my head.

A T-34 goes up in a volcano of flame. Porta's rocket must have scored a direct hit on its ammunition locker.

I am deaf for several minutes from the violence of the explosion.

'Come *on*! Forward!' roars the Old Man, his bowed legs cranking away.

I rush forward, shooting as I run at the dark figures over by the wrecked houses. Between bursts I hear the short, stammering bark of the Old Man's mpi. A couple of yards in front of me I see a shadow which resembles a mole-hill, but is really a Russian helmet with its funny steel cockscomb. I shoot so low that the tracer scorches along just above the ground, cutting the Russian's head in two.

'Forward!' the Old Man chases us on. 'Forward!' He pumps his arm up and down in the air, signalling to us.

I take cover behind a concrete balustrade, and lob a couple of hand-grenades over the rosebeds, in which leafless bushes stand closely ranked. I push forward between the flower beds.

'Back!' I scream, desperately, rolling head-over-heels down the slope.

I have run into three Russian SMG gunners, and they are sending a hail of bullets along the length of the hill.

'No, damn that,' roars the Old Man. 'Forward! We've no choice! Up with you! Grenades!' I look around me, timid and frightened, and I feel like running, dumping that cursed machine-gun anywhere, and running; running till I reach home again.

'Come *on*!' shouts Porta, waving to me. 'Let's kick Ivan's arsehole up round his ears, so he won't get to thinkin' he's winning the war!'

I jump to my feet and press on up the steep slope. A couple of hand-grenades, and the Russian machine-gun nest goes up in a fount of flame. My feet seem suddenly light, as if they had grown wings.

Tracer bullets snarl and hiss past me. It seems incredible they can all miss. Running madly I reach the opposite stone balustrade, am over it, and rolling down the slope on the far side. Round about me I hear the sharp crack of tank-guns, and the hollow droning of the stovepipes.

Another T-34 explodes in a sea of red, glowing flame.

The rest of the section comes rolling down the slope after me.

Russian MGs hammer wildly. Three or four shadows flit past.

I thread a new belt into the LMG, and smack it shut far too noisily.

'Give me some covering fire,' the Old Man demands, hoarsely. 'I'm going over that balustrade there, and as soon as I'm gone you come after me! And get the lead out!'

'Very good,' I mumble, pressing the butt of the LMG into my shoulder and sending off five or six short bursts. The Old Man struggles up on top of the stonework, rolls over it and disappears. I jump up, and rush, bent over at the waist, across the open stretch, sweeping the LMG from side to side.

A green flare goes up, hangs in the heavens, and slowly dies away.

'Done it again,' pants Porta, pulling up alongside me.

A number of Russians come slowly toward us with arms above their heads. They stare at us fearfully as we search their pockets with nimble fingers. They have nothing on them worth bothering with. A few evil-smelling *Machorkas*, one or two greasy, much-thumbed letters.

'They're poor as us,' sighs Porta, patting a shaggy *Kalmuk* on the shoulder. He is an elderly man with a large moustache, drooping sadly down over his mouth.

The last of the T-34s goes clattering off through the park. In the distance sounds of fighting can still be heard, but they ebb slowly away, and the silent blanket of night falls again over the scarred town.

The next day passes with one parade after the other. We are continually sent back to do it all over again. Which we don't of course do. Instead we sit and play cards. In the end the people who lay on parades get tired of all the work it costs them. The hidden foreign weapons come back out again. A *Kalashnikov is* really better than a *Schmeisser*. For one thing it has a magazine holding a hundred rounds, and the *Schmeisser* holds no more than thirty-eight.

After a while everything is back to normal. Porta and Tiny tramp around again in their private headgear – tall hat and bowler. Albert is packed into his ginger-coloured fur. Heide is almost normal, and is no longer indignant over Albert's racial cocktail. He does not speak to him more than absolutely necessary, however.

'He looks like a shit-fly that's burned its arse on a storm lantern,' says Porta, as Albert sits down alongside Heide and starts showing him some photographs. Heide conceals his disgust, but cannot help studying them closely.

Leave is handed out generously, but only to married men with children, so that the Old Man and Barcelona are the first to go. We follow them all the way down to the leave train, and stand, waving, long after the train is out of sight, and even the sound of it has died away.

We go back to our billets feeling like small children who have been left at home on their own. Without the Old Man we feel lost.

Then something else happens, which almost knocks our pins out from under us.

Gregor is leaving us, and for ever. We think it is a lie. Even when he is packing his gear, and sharing out the things he no longer has any use for, we can't believe it. He shows us it in black and white. Army Staff has asked for him. He is again to be driver and bodyguard for his famous general. We go with him to the train, too. He is wearing a completely new uniform. They dare not send him off to report to a general in his worn-out front line kit.

'You *do* look nice,' cries Porta, admiringly. 'They could

123

put you straight on to a recruiting poster to bullshit idiots into the Army at a mark a day!'

We take leave of him on a platform filled with holes. Gregor leans far out of the window shaking our outstretched hands. As a general's driver and bodyguard he has been allocated a seat in a real passenger compartment. He treats the MPs who examine his papers accordingly. Condescendingly, he looks the spit-and-polished MP up and down, and tells him to say Unteroffizier when he speaks to him, and stand to attention.

'Anybody can bloody well see you're General Staff now,' Porta nods, approvingly. 'Give 'em some stick, the shits, but don't forget you're still one of us! If you happen to run across anything good, don't forget Joseph Porta, Obergefreiter by the grace of God, is in the market for everything!'

The train departs and we slouch back to our regular routine. Soon, however, we are beginning to feel the need of excitement again.

We do not see much of Porta. Hauptfeldwebel Hoffmann is continually sending out office runners – hounds we call them – looking for him, but it is not often they find him. When they do find him it is because he wants them to.

He is spending most of his time with Vera, the deserted wife of the commissar. She is beginning to feel herself very truly liberated by the German Army, in the shape of Porta.

It is Sunday afternoon, and everything is peaceful and quiet. Snow falls softly and silently. There are no noises from the front line, which is by now far away and almost forgotten. Out on the parade ground Tiny is playing with a large, ugly dog, which resembles him not a little.

Hauptfeldwebel Hoffmann has his trackers out after Porta, as usual. He wants to put him on 24-hour guard duty. But Porta is lying, stark naked, on his back in a large, red four-poster bed, with angels blowing celestial horns on each bedpost. He resembles more than anything a long, thin, forked radish as he lies there on the pink bed-clothes, warming his long, bony toes between Vera's thighs. They are both dozing and seem to purr with satisfaction like a couple of well-fed cats.

· Porta is dreaming that he is lying on the shore of an azure lagoon, wearing a white tuxedo, and surrounded by a group of willing ladies wearing no clothes at all.

'*Zolloto*,' mumbles Vera, rolling over in her sleep.

Porta chuckles with laughter, and moves the tips of his fingers as if he were counting money.

'*Zolloto*,' smiles Vera, happily.

Porta sits up in bed, wide awake, and suspicious as an old, experienced alley-cat.

'What do you do?' she whispers, sleepily, ruffling his red hair.

'You said *Zolloto*!' says Porta, bending over her. '*Zolloto*!'

'I say *Zolloto*?' she asks, seemingly carelessly. She swings her long legs over the edge of the bed, and pushes her feet into a pair of high-heeled white fluffy mules. With a lazy movement she takes a Russian cigarette, with a long tubular mouthpiece, from the drawer of her bedside table. 'I can *trust* you? You villain!' she says after a long silence, blowing smoke into his face as she speaks. 'I mean – *really* trust you? Can you keep silent, if the world falls down on your head, and they stroke you and they promise you the moon and all the planets, if you play canary for them?'

'What the hell d'you think I am?' grins Porta, holding up three fingers. 'In my short but exciting life, I have brought literally scores of plain-clothes coppers to the brink of the screaming meemies. I've been chucked out of the glass-house for disturbin' disciplinary routine. One General, two Obersts, six Leutnants and a whole *army* of Feldwebels and that kind of *shit* have been driven out of their minds by me. A couple of 'em put a hole through their heads after they'd chatted with me for a bit, an' an *untermensch* like you wants to know if *you* can trust *me*? Ask instead if *I* can trust *you*? Even though you've got race, you're still an *untermensch* talkin' to one of the *herrenvolk*!'

She takes two long, thoughtful pulls at her cigarette, and

125

pinches the long cardboard mouthpiece between her fingers. 'Watch out, *herrenvolk* man. You could choke on that stupid grin,' she says, sourly.

Porta is across the floor in two jumps, and fills two tumblers with cognac.

They raise their glasses and toast one another silently. She lights a fresh cigarette, and exhales smoke slowly.

'It does not make you nervous to get into something both Russians and Germans will not like?' she asks him. 'What I talk about is so unlawful, a crook lawyerman from the Mafia even, would shake with fright just to think about what could happen to him if he got caught!'

'*Me*? *Nervous*?' Porta laughs, heartily. 'Losin' my good German life's all that worries *me*. Where breaking the law's concerned I don't give a shit for that. I work for me, *and* I know how to fix people who blabber too much. I remember one feller. Talked as much as a flock o' canaries in mating-time. We took him for a sail one day when we had a hot engine to drown. We put a rope round his neck, but that was only so's he wouldn't fall overboard and get lost at sea. But when we got out there where we were goin' to lose this engine, we somehow forgot our mate's safety line was tied on to it, and the canary went down to the bottom along with the motor. The last we saw of him was a pair of shoes, round-heeled they were, waving goodbye to us.'

They lie naked on the bed for a while, drinking rum laced with cognac, while they convince one another how grey and melancholy the world is when you haven't enough money.

'I was born to be rich,' breathes Vera, a deep, thoughtful wrinkle appearing between her eyebrows, 'so that you must understand the Soviet Union is not altogether suiting me.'

'Only fools choose a life without money,' Porta agrees, filling up their glasses again. This time he chooses *Slivovitz* to get rid of the cheap cognac taste.

'My father was Imperial officer, a general,' she sighs proudly, looking sideways at Porta. 'If Lenin stay in your damned Germany I would be at the Imperial court now.

Why you do not shoot him for the devil's sake?'

'May I just touch Your Grace?' asks Porta, rolling over on top of her.

'My mama was from the best circles,' she goes on, swinging her legs up around his skinny thighs. 'Her family was much at the palace. We all believed in God.'

'God didn't help you much though, when Lenin's boys got there an' shot your blue-blooded arses off,' says Porta, biting her nose gently.

'Everyone know my father. His division was the best. He won the St George Cross. You Germans fled from him as fast as your legs could go . . .'

'Hold it,' Porta puts in, holding up his hand. 'I wasn't in that fight!'

'My father was a wealthy man! He gave his life for the state. He sign death penalties, send criminals to Siberia, was lover of fine horses and women, the Tsar and God.'

'I've met one or two generals like that,' says Porta, laughing shortly. 'They think they were born to the job. They never get round to understanding that that's something we made 'em into!'

'You talk like a filthy *Bolshevik*,' she spits, angrily.

'You're wrong there, girl,' he laughs, emptying his tumbler. 'Don't forget you're the wife of a commissar with gilt-edged red stars all over you. The Tsar's generals are all gone upstairs an' are kissin' Ivan the Terrible's arsepart now. Stalin's commissars are the boys that're steppin' light an' easy around on the stage these days.'

'What would you say to making 30 millions? Maybe more!' she asks him, sipping thoughtfully from her glass.

Porta picks up the cognac bottle, and takes a long swallow. Then he takes up the rum and washes the cognac down with a still longer swallow. He looks at her for a long time. Then he asks, in a quiet voice:

'Did you say millions? You're not kidding me?'

'Yes. 30 *millions*!' She smiles mysteriously. 'But I think more. Much more. We have worked all out, so there is nothing to get worried about. It is what you call a sure thing. We are already rich!'

'You've no idea,' he says, in a knowing voice, 'just how many clever chaps I've met who've told me just exactly what you're telling me. And what they were talking about was small potatoes compared to your millions. But they're all tucked away behind bars now, and wondering what it was went wrong with their sure thing!'

'You are frighten, then?' she jeers at him. 'I am wrong about you? Take your rags and get out of here. I don't know you any more!'

'No my dear, it ain't that easy,' he grins fiendishly. shaking the empty rum bottle. 'When Joseph Porta, Obergefreiter by the grace o' God, gets on the trail of a job with 30 million iron men, he wants to hear 'em chinking! I've dreamt about something like this all my stinkin' German life. You realize how long it'd take just to *count* 30 millions? A hell of a long time I can tell you. It'd make even the Yids in the state bank sweat just to think of it.'

'You go with us in sledge, and are ready to run a little risk to be rich and independent of politicians and other foolish people?' she asks, taking a deep pull on her cigarette.

'You can bloody well believe it I'm ready.' He roars with laughter. 'An' if your sure thing *is* a sure thing, then I swear by the Holy God above I'll burn seven candles for you forever in the synagogue of my heart!'

'Light them now, then,' she smiles, offering him her cigarette-lighter. 'You can get helpers? Good men? Not stumbling bums?'

'Too true I can,' he nods with assurance, lighting one of her cigarettes. 'I have a kind of friend in Berlin who can open any kind of safe or strong-box, from the most advanced model to the primitive ones the municipalities buy in bundles of twelve. We called him "Plastic Man", because he usually worked with plastic explosives. I once saw him open a safe that belonged to some people who didn't trust the banks after Adolf moved in to Berlin. He stuck a coupla little balls of plastic explosive on the door of it by the hinges. We stepped into the next room, where he set it off with a natty little radio an' "BOOM!" it said. When we went back inside there's this impenetrable armoured door lyin' on the floor inside out. All we had to do was empty the box. That door couldn't have been opened quicker with the proper key.'

'This has nothing to do with safes,' she corrected him. 'It is much bigger than such things!'

'Do we have to send somebody off in a natural manner, then?' he asks, with a pleased expression. 'I can fix that, too. My adjutant, Tiny, is a very handy fellow with a garrottin' wire. People drop dead from it. An' if there are any really *big* problems attached to removing somebody from this world in a hell of hurry, then I've got a mate we call "Sudden Death". When I was last in Berlin, I took him with me to "talk" to a feller who thought he could put one over on me. We arrived, just when they'd got to the dessert, with a couple of Stens. It went off that quick, we hadn't even said hello before the chap had fell over from the weight of the lead in his body. The landlord of "The Half Donkey", who was standin' there waiting with pancakes on a plate, got his tie shot off by a bullet. He was that shocked he was still standing there in the same spot, with his bloody pancakes and the shot-off bit o' tie in his hand, when Inspector August an' his posse arrived to discover who it was'd got shot.

'"Shot?" he whined, dropping his pancakes. "Nobody's been *shot*!" He didn't know a thing about the body under the table. He swore to it. Said it must have got left there, somehow!

'They closed the case as bein' disorderly conduct, when they found out where the bullets in the body came from. They were from *Prinz Albrecht Strasse 3*.'

They sit back together on the bed, propped up on pillows, and drinking steaming-hot coffee.

A large map is spread out in front of them.

'Here,' she says, 'are our millions. They lie there waiting for us.'

'Prikumsk,' he mumbles, bending closely over the chart, as if he were nearsighted. 'Prikumsk! Sounds like some kind of a drink. You sure all that glitterin' Commie gold is really hidden away there? I don't like that river. There's another town over there on the other bank. Reminds me of a beartrap ready to snap shut and hold you fast while you shit yourself waiting there to get shot!'

'You can be easy,' she says. 'My husband lead the convoy, and nobody put wool on his eyes!'

'And now your reliable husband has decided to go fetch the 30 million again?' grins Porta, sceptically. 'And *you* can trust him, of course. But can *I*? Good an' faithful servants of the state who steal with both their fingers an' their toes I do not feel happy about!'

'He is a good friend to his friends, true as steel,' she declares grandly. 'He *never* cheat!'

'No! I don't suppose so,' Porta laughs, heartily. 'What kinda feller's this commissar husband of yours, anyway? Is he from Moscow?'

'Are you mad? You believe I trust a man from Moscow?' she screams, insultedly. 'He is Georgian. His mother was Jewish from Crimea. The grandfather on mother's side from Salonica. The family was Italian.'

'If you tell me now there's Irish on his dad's side,' he says jokingly, 'then I'm sorry to say your commissar ol' man's goin' to have to go through the process of natural death. A knife in his back, or somethin' like that. A cocktail like him can be a dangerous mixture.'

'What in hell you mean by that?' she asks, her eyes narrowing to slits. 'You are some kind of racist pig?'

'No, I can't afford to be,' answers Porta. 'But let me tell you I know just what goes to making a good Mafia boss. 90% spaghetti blood, preferably Sicilian. That's the beginning of the dodgiest of the dodgiest. 2% Irish, to make him a good fighter. 5% Jew juice, so he understands figures an' knows how to alter 'em to his own advantage. Spot o' Greek on top of that lot an' he'll be one o' the worst villains on earth, with the big advantage of trustin' his fellow human beings as far as politicians trust one another. D'you understand now why I have doubts about your husband's reliability?'

'You think the gold bars are perhaps not there?' she asks suspiciously.

'I believe it's there all right, and I'm in no doubt that your good husband, with all the advantages of blood the Lord has granted him, will be able to pinch it off of his mates in the Kremlin. But I'm also in no doubt of his also having found out how he can also take a silly sod of a German. It'd be nice not to have to share with *anybody*, wouldn't it now?'

'He never do that,' she shouts, insultedly. 'You must not forget that he is a Russian officer!'

'Yes, I realize that,' he laughs, heartily. 'But just you watch out you don't find yourself sitting on your bare butt in a very cold snowdrift, watchin' honest hubby making off as fast as his legs can carry him with the shekels. Why in the world would he want to share 'em with *any*body, when he could hang on to the lot with no bother?'

'He would not dare to do that with me,' she shouts, furiously. 'I would kill him completely! Step on him like a piece of shit!'

'D'you really believe all that?' he asks, staring at her. 'You couldn't do a thing to him. You weren't thinkin' now of going to the OGPU, were you? And I'd recommend you to keep far, far away from the Gestapo. *They're* not a very tender-hearted lot. If he does you out of it, you'll have to swallow the pill no matter how bitter it is. He's got the laugh on you all ways. He's *rich*! You don't get back on rich people. Not often. The best weapon in the world's money!'

'You think he would do that,' she asks, with growing suspicion.

'No trouble,' he answers, laughing shortly. 'Can't see why he shouldn't. Money can change the best of us.'

'I am his wife, whom he loves,' she protests, shaken,

looking at Porta in shocked fashion.

'When you've got a big bag of money, it's easy to get yourself a new wife. He says he loves you, does he? A man says a lot of things on his way down the thorny road of life.'

'You have evil in your mind,' she snarls, bitterly. 'I should never have told you about this thing!'

'Maybe it would've been cleverer not to,' admits Porta. 'The more people who know about the gold, the bigger's the risk of losing it. But I don't think you'd have told me your little secret either if you an' hubby weren't in need of some good old German know-how! If God won't take you the Devil must. But we'd do best to think it over carefully before we decide who else to tell where the Jew fly-paper is, or, before we can turn round, there'll be more souls outside its hidey-hole than there are waitin' at the gates of Hell. Thirty million bucks! Good Lord preserve us! Thought about the effect it'll have on the market when you let that Commie load loose on it?'

'As I have told you, there is thirty millions and probably some little more,' she assures him, tracing dollar signs with her fingernail on the sheet. 'I have calculated on it is hot money.'

'Hot, you say?' he laughs, noisily. 'If you'd said it was glowin' you'd have been a lot closer to the truth. Thirty millions! I've never set eyes on that much loot even in my dreams.' Suddenly his Slivovitz goes down the wrong way, and he begins to cough and splutter violently.

'You keep saying thirty millions all the time,' he gasps, between spasms of coughing. 'But you don't say thirty million *what*? Don't say it's Eyetie money! *Don't*! Thirty millions of them wouldn't get a German bailiff out of his warm bed!'

'It is Yankee, capitalist dollars,' she breathes, looking at him with an expression of triumph. You would think she had printed them herself.

'Dollars,' he mumbles radiantly, working out rapidly in his head what that would be in marks. 'Holy Mother of

Kazan, that's a lot of reinforcements!' Enthusiastically he grabs his piccolo, jumps high in the air, rushes round the room, like a happy fawn and hops up on top of a table. From this new eminence he begins to sing, in a ringing voice:

There was a rich man, and he lived in Jerusalem,
Glory hallelujah, hirojerum,

He wore a silk hat, and his coat was very sprucium,
Glory hallelujah, hirojerum.

At his gate, there sat a human wreckium,
He wore a bowler hat and the rim was round his neckium,

The poor man asked for a piece of bread and cheesium,
The rich man cried: 'I'll call for a policium,'

The poor man died and his soul went to heavium,
He danced with the angels, till a quarter past elevium,

The rich man died, but he didn't fare so wellium,
He couldn't go to heaven, so he had to go to hellium,

'No,' the devil said, 'this here is no hotelium,
It's just a plain and ordinary hellium,'

The moral of the story is: Riches are no jokium,
We'll all go to heaven, 'cause we are all stony brokium.

'Who teach you English?' she asks in surprise.
'*I* did,' he grins, playing a gay run on his piccolo. 'It's a song a fence I knew used to sing when he'd taken a sucker. He met that many of 'em when I knew him I just couldn't help learning it by heart.'
'He was English?'
'No, a Yid from Berlin-Dahlem. I often used to go to the feasts in the synagogue with him with a hat on. Now he's gone off somewhere to wait till the new era goes back to bein' the old era, an' me and my hat can go to parties in the synagogue again.'

'Fancy another trip in the gondola?' he suggests, licking his lips. 'The thought of all that gold's got me really worked up!'

'It's not as easy as it looked at first sight,' he goes on, thoughtfully, as they lie, side by side, relaxing after their erotic exertions. 'I'm not happy there's so many mixed up in it. Thirty millions, even, ain't much if it's gotta be shared with half a division.'

'Who *says* we share with every man of them?' she purrs, falsely. 'They get a nice tip, big enough for a good night on the town! *One* night!'

'I couldn't agree more,' whinnies Porta, in a transport of delight. 'We ask 'em to wait for us somewhere, an' let 'em sit waitin' for us till their arseholes grow icicles. When do we go?'

'As soon as I have contact my husband,' she answers, 'and that will not be a long time. He will arrange *propusk* for you. They will be *real* ones, too. Not even a suspicious OGPU would sniff at them with his flat nose. You give me good, clear photographs for every one we take with us. Not in German uniform, of course!'

'I'll mobilize the flash-artists right off,' he promises, with a grin which makes his face look like an open cash-register. 'We're to be Russians, then?'

'You did not think you would be running around like Swastika-mad SS-men? You will be changed into weary Volga Germans. That will take care of the language difficulty.'

'Volga Germans,' he asks, blankly. 'And what kind of fellers are they?'

'German emigrants, who once settled along the banks of the Volga. They are Soviet Russians today, but they live like Germans and talk German to one another. They are given various special tasks in the Red Army in wartime, but otherwise the Army will not have them. Like the *Khirgiz* people. They too are used only in wartime.'

'But good soldiers I'm sure,' he said. 'The kind they need

134

to get shot at when there's war an' disagreements on.'

She takes two oversized bouillon cups with a handle on each side. With a suitably dignified air she prepares what the Russians call a small eye-opener. Two-thirds vodka, one-third coffee, four large spoonfuls of sugar, half a preserved pear, and to top off the whole a dab of blackcurrant jam.

Porta takes half of the concoction down in one gulp, and emits an emperor of a belch, which echoes round the four-poster bed.

'Not bad at *all*,' he praises it, and pours the rest down his throat with the gurgle of a sewer passing an air-bubble.

'My husband is very quick,' she assures him, sipping carefully at her own eye-opener. 'He thinks it is now the time for Jews who want to get somewhere to leave the Soviet paradise. It is said that every fourth prisoner they shoot in the Lubyanka is a Jew. Do you not think execution is barbaric?'

'Ye-e-es,' says Porta, drawing the word out. 'But on the other hand it's not nice to be gettin' in the way of true-believers, and hinderin' them in getting home to the wonders of paradise.'

'Cynic!' she snarls, pushing back her red-gold hair. 'I do not understand why ever I have anything to do with you.'

'Matter o' taste, as the cat said when it licked the dog's arse,' he laughs, noisily.

'Believe me,' she goes on, lighting a cigarette, 'if it was not for my husband's sake I would not have involved myself in this. As I have told you I come from an aristocratic family. One of my ancestors smashed the skulls of two hundred Turks in the wars against the Huns. He did it with only a club.'

'Must've been a very quarrelsome lot, your ancestors,' says Porta, making himself up another eye-opener. 'You ever thought your old feller might be moving over to the wrong FPO? Jews aren't just the most popular lot in Germany right now. They make soap out of 'em. Funnily enough it's all right for washing in!'

'What have you against the Jews?' she jumps up angrily, and stares him rigidly in the face. 'You do not look much of an Aryan. If you run into Himmler perhaps he will make *you* into soap!'

'I've got nothing against nobody at all,' says Porta, with a long, hearty laugh. 'I'm a businessman. On Sunday I buy something from God and on Monday I sell it to the Devil – at a good profit!'

'You remind me a lot of my husband,' she laughs. 'He does not look like a Jew. People believe he is a dumb Polish yokel. Nobody dreams he can count to more than five. But what drives him is his unique greediness and longing for power. He has everything but the fuel: *money*! And money is now lying there ready under his nose!'

'Why'n't he picked it up before, then?' asks Porta, cleaning his nails with a fork.

'Picking up no problem,' she replies. 'Another thing to get it out of Russia! What is thirty millions worth if all you can do is turn it over and look at it. To get out of Russia we have to go through all of the country you have stolen from us.'

'And that's why you need Obergefreiter Porta,' he nods, emptying his bouillon-cup with a slobbering gulp. 'What about if things go wrong? Your commissar-hubby got that one sorted out, too?'

'We shall hang!' she cries, throwing her naked arms wide in a theatrical gesture. 'There is some risk in every game!'

'I doubt if we'd get off *that* easy,' sighs Porta, sadly. 'They'd have a nice bit of fun with us first in the Lubyanka, though I don't reckon it'd be us gold-robbers who'd be doin' the laughin'. And, if we were lucky enough to miss that, don't expect to find any nice-mannered boys amongst the hat-brim fellers in *Prinz Albrecht Strasse*. They'd put us in the acid bath first to soften us up, and then they'd peel the skin off of us in two-inch strips.'

'We must be optimistic. Then everything will be all right,'

she says with a brilliant smile. 'You know, perhaps, that optimists live longer than pessimists?'

'I'm a born optimist, myself,' Porta admits. 'That's why I'm still in the land o' the living. But it *might* be a good idea if we was to take a couple o' pieces of artillery and ten or eleven machine-pistols with us on this little gold robbery turn-up. And just one other important thing! Have you figured out how you're goin' to get the gold through Germany? They have a way of executing people who're found in possession of illegal gold. I don't suppose you were thinking of sendin' the glitterin' stuff by express freight, were you? One of them train chauffeurs was to get the idea there was valuables in the boxes an' it'd be: goodbye gold! If they pick us up in Germany we'd not have a chance. Be easier making sausagemeat of little girls and sellin' it to the Army for iron rations!'

'You say you are optimist!' she shouts, angrily. 'Why do you not go and let yourself get shot to small pieces for this foreign Führer of yours? You are always against me! You do not help, but leave everything to me!'

'I'm an optimist all right, believe you me,' answers Porta. 'But I'm careful, too! You don't see me dashing out on thin ice like some silly sods do!'

She is over in a corner of the room, attempting, with much effort, to drag a chest-of-drawers away from the wall. She looks angrily at Porta, still recumbent on the bed.

'You do not think of helping me?' she shouts, gritting her teeth.

'Sure,' says Porta, without moving.

'Shit!' she snarls, tugging at the heavy piece of furniture. When she finally has it a couple of yards out from the wall, to the accompaniment of a shower of Russian curses, she removes a panel, and takes a map from the recess revealed. Still swearing she throws herself on her stomach alongside Porta.

'It's easy to see you're tellin' the truth about your aristocratic ancestors,' he grins, slapping her hard on her naked behind.

'Tanks and trucks are the only safe transport possibilities, when we are to get through these forest stretches around Minsk,' she explains, pointing to the map.

'Oh, *yes*,' says Porta. 'I don't really understand why we don't stay in your part of Russia, lady? You know who's *in* those woods? The whole rotten Red Army, that's who! Guerillas all over! You do what you like, but not with Obergefreiter Joseph Porta in tow! Where's your armoured transport column goin' to wind up, anyway?'

'Liepaja,' she says pointing to a spot on the map.

'Libau, you mean,' Porta corrects her. 'On the Baltic. And from there we take the boat direct to America, luxury class, I suppose?'

'No! To Sweden! Karlskrona!'

'I'd rather go to Stockholm,' Porta wrangles. 'I've never had a girl from Stockholm. I suppose you an' hungry hubby know that those Swedish half-Eskimos keep a hell of a close watch on their harbours? They've found out 95 per cent of the Wehrmacht's looking out for a chance to get in there, with mpi's as passports. Your plan's no good, girl!'

'As you wish,' she smiles, sweetly. 'I look after my side of the front and you fix it with your German friends.'

Porta sucks his army teeth long and thoughtfully. 'All right, I'll look after things, but there's just one point. We go 50-50.'

'You are out of your mind,' she shrills, furiously. 'Why you should have half? You think I am crazy? That a German crematory rat like you can swindle me? I have crushed bigger rats than you will ever be! You do not know me, I think?'

'You're a poison viper, you are,' Porta snarls, sulphurously. He throws his empty bottle violently at the ceiling.

'Your German greed has turned you mad,' she spits at him. 'You talk like a Greek brothel-owner!'

'Give in, you stinking Commie bitch,' fumes Porta. 'You might just as well. Your polished Soviet manners won't get you far with me! Fifty-fifty! Want me to chisel it out for you in Nazi letters ten foot high?'

She storms to and fro, spitting and frothing. Chairs are knocked over, glass smashes, a shoe flies out through the window. She stops, but only to throw a large lamp at Porta, who is still lying in the four-poster, drinking *Slivovitz* from the bottle.

'I was not wrong about you, you puffed-up male whore!' she screams, shaking with rage. 'Heaven be thanked that I have seen through you, you wicked German tramp. I will have you shot, and your head chopped off, both at the same time! God help you when my husband gets hold of you!'

'Make me die laughing, you do,' shouts Porta, sending a mouthful of spittle after her. 'I can fuck up your little gold-diggin' game for you, easy as winkin'! It'll be prick up the arse for both of you.'

In the end they throw themselves at one another, and break up everything left in her boudoir to break. They crawl out from under the wrecked four-poster and finally agree on how the gold is to be shared.

The next twenty minutes pass quickly. They literally rape one another. They go at it so energetically that two Russian soldiers hiding down in the cellar choke on their vodka at the sounds getting down to them. One of them climbs a tree outside their window to see what is happening. The sight makes him fall out of it and break an ankle.

'Better get my German glad rags on, and step along over to His Grace Chief Mechanic Wolf,' Porta decides.

'Who he?' she asks doubtfully.

'A link in the chain we can't do without, unfortunately,' he replies. 'He's an illegal transport an' arms dealer company all on his own. I've also got to wake up the "War Minister" in Berlin!'

'War Minister!' she coughs, as her cognac goes down the wrong way. 'Are you crazy? We want no minister mixed up in this! God the Father preserve us! If such a one get the slightest hint of what we are doing we will be executed *immediately*!'

'Executions?' smiles Porta. 'Maybe some'll get executed, but it's not bloody well going to be us. Only dummies let themselves get knocked off that way, and you an' me ain't dummies!'

From down in the street come the sounds of loud singing, and shrill police whistles. A couple of pistol shots crack.

'Hell!' she cries, in fright, 'what happens?'

'That'll be Tiny, celebrating the day his mother come close to losing her life,' laughs Porta, looking out of the window.

A couple of hours later he wades, panting, through the powder snow, with a photograph of a gold ingot in his hand. Without taking any notice of the large, colourful signboard:

TRANSPORT SECTION WOLF
ENTRY STRICTLY FORBIDDEN

he vaults over the barrier and goes on down the narrow pathway.

'Can't you read?' yells an Unteroffizier with a face only Frankenstein's monster would have envied him.

'Can *you*?' asks Porta, continuing calmly on his way.

'No entry for unauthorized personnel,' howls the monster-faced Unteroffizier, tearing his machine-pistol down from his shoulder.

'*I'm* not unauthorized,' answers Porta, without bothering even to turn his head.

At the next road-block he meets a notorious Feldwebel who was posted away from Germersheim for cruelty to the prisoners. He works for Wolf now. Bodily injury is his field of endeavour.

'Halt!' he roars, standing squarely in Porta's path. He looks the size of a tank block.

Porta pushes him fastidiously to one side, with the air of a man opening the door of a railway station toilet.

'What d'you mean pushin' me, rat? Can't you see these? I'm a Feldwebel!'

'Can't *you* see *these*? The highest rank in the *Reich*! Oberge-freiter, same as your Führer was. Tell Wolf I'm here, shit-head, an' quick about it!'

The Feldwebel runs to the telephone to sound the alarm,

but Porta is already in the next workshop shed before he can get through. He treads cautiously over a trip-wire which would have set a T-mine off under him.

Two grey-brown wolfhounds come towards him, growling savagely.

'Hello boys!' he smiles. 'Find somebody else to tear a piece off!'

The dogs bare yellow fangs, and continue to advance towards him, threateningly.

'Hi!' he says, saluting with two fingers at the brim of his yellow topper.

'Hi!' growl the dogs, wagging their tails in welcome.

Around a strategically well-chosen corner Wolf's two Chinese guards stand with *Kalashnikovs* at the ready.

'Hi!' Porta greets them, pushing the muzzles of the *Kalashnikovs* gently to one side.

'Hi!' reply the Chinese guards, slapping their weapons.

'You look like death on crutches,' says Porta, with a short laugh.

'We death all right,' they say, laughing an Asiatic laugh, and lifting their *Kalashnikovs*. 'You like try?'

'Some other time! I haven't a moment just now,' he replies, sidling past another booby-trap.

'I thought the neighbours'd turned you off,' says Wolf, sarcastically. 'I was looking forward to a good wake, but you've disappointed me as usual!'

There is a P-38 with a full clip lying on the desk in front of him. A *Schmeisser* hangs on the back of his chair. His desk drawer is booby-trapped. The charge is big enough to blow up a seven-storey apartment house, if anybody is foolish enough to open the drawer. On a camouflaged shelf over the door is a bottle of petrol packed in three stick-grenades, in case the unbelievable were to happen and somebody get past the first three traps. As an extra bit of security the yard-door is connected to a surprise packet for anybody who might go out that way after doing something wicked to Wolf. The uninvited guest would be turned into a lot of tiny pieces and thrown a long way up toward Heaven.

Porta makes himself at home with a bottle of whisky, which he knows is kept behind Army Service Regulations and an unread copy of *Mein Kampf*. 'Skole!' he laughs, and almost empties the bottle.

'Don't mind *me*,' says Wolf, sourly. 'You'll never learn manners. What do you want anyway? I don't recall havin' invited you?' He flaps a grain of dust from his hand-sewn Bronzini boots, which cost 1,400 marks. He has them sent from Rome by special despatch-rider. He regards highly-polished riding boots as the most important part of a highly-placed man's image. Porta says it is because he had to wear clogs from the Poor Children's Fund when he was a child.

'Can those things keep out water?' asks Porta, pointing to the glittering riding boots. Wolf wears spurs on them, in defiance of all regulations. They jingle every time he moves his feet. Wolf would never dream of mounting a horse though. He is, in fact, rather afraid of them.

'How'd I know,' asks Wolf. 'I never go out in the rain!'

'Let me just have a ride on your Jew machine,' says Porta, reaching out for the calculator. He takes some currency rate of exchange lists from his breast pocket, and puts on a thoughtful expression.

Wolf looks inquisitively over his shoulder. When he sees the size of the figures Porta is working with, he begins to shiver all over. His face changes colour several times, and his piggy, yellow-green eyes begin to light up greedily.

'*Mama mia*,' he whispers. He crosses himself religiously three times, bends down, and kisses Porta on both cheeks.

They close the steel shutters and lock them from the inside. The whole, complicated alarm system is set ready for action. Nobody is going to get away alive from an attempt to enter Wolf's lair.

'I may have been mistaken about you,' Wolf says, in a flattering tone, clinking his glass against Porta's. 'Your health, you wicked old villain!'

'Ditto, ditto,' smiles Porta, throwing the drink down with

142

mouth agape, like a man emptying a bucket into a sewer.

'To think I have always regarded you as a wicked criminal swindler, who would sell his own mother if it suited him,' says Wolf, shaking his head sadly.

'For*get* it!' says Porta refilling his glass. 'Anybody can make a mistake now and then!'

For some time Wolf sits leaning back in his generals-only swivel-chair, and enjoys the sight of the photograph of the gold ingot.

'God save all thirteen of us,' he whispers. 'With lumps o' this stuff socked away, the rest of our lives'd be without worries. We could let the rest of 'em stand in water up to their necks, and most of 'em'll wind up poor after the war. *We'll* be laughing, and enjoying the feel of fine clothing next to our skins!'

During the next few hours highest priority express messages fly backwards and forwards between Wolf's HQ and the War Ministry at Berlin.

Far into the night the plans for the most important and top-secret action of World War II are complete. They are given the codename RICHES.

Oberfeldwebel and departmental head Sally, of War Ministry 4th Office, is on his way to Russia two hours later in a JU-52 mailplane with highest start and landing priorities.

In a three-axled Mercedes, with a General Staff flag fluttering from the front fender, businessmen Porta and Wolf drive to the airport to receive His Excellency 'War Minister' Sally. Sally swaggers, like another Frederick the Great, down the steps from the aircraft standing some way out on the landing strip. He is wearing a tailor-made cavalry uniform, highly-polished boots and a big, insincere grin. Around his neck is the War Service Cross, Knight's Class, which has been arranged for him by his many shady connections.

The Luftwaffe men salute him stiffly. He nods kindly to them. A Field-Marshal could not have done it better. He tiptoes across the wet asphalt. He does not want his highly-polished boots to be smirched by the Russian mud.

'What a country to live in,' he says, shivering, as he creeps into the large Mercedes. 'Why couldn't you have chosen a warmer country to liberate?'

'Nobody asked us,' grins Wolf.

'How's the outside world looking these days?' asks Porta, tucking the almighty 'War Minister' up in a bearskin to prevent him from the aching cold. He is unused to the Russian climate.

'They're dropping bombs on us all the time. The Brits by night and the Yanks by day. It's hardly possible to lift a glass to your lips any more. Half of it gets spilled by the constant shaking everywhere. Wherever you look there's misery. The Home Front shuffles around in old clothes, and everybody's hungry. Don't think you lads out here are the only ones having a rough time. We are also suffering badly at home. But we do our duty uncomplainingly, and willingly go hungry to save old Germany!'

'Well, you don't look as if *you're* suffering much from the shortages,' says Porta, with a knowing chuckle.

'I didn't say I was, did I now?' the 'War Minister' replies. He offers American cigarettes round, and French cognac from a silver hip-flask.

'"The Lame Gendarme's" still where it was, for God's sake?' asks Porta, worriedly. 'If those bloody British and Yanks have dared to as much as scratch the paintwork they'll have me to reckon with! And *that* won't suit them one bit.'

'I'm sure they're aware of that,' smiles Sally. 'The only thing left on the square *is* the "Gendarme". I looked in there this very morning, and was asked to pass on everybody's regards. They asked if you weren't tired of fighting for Führer, Folk and Fatherland. I don't understand myself how you lot can stand living here.'

At the last second Porta manages to swing the heavy Mercedes round the still-smoking wreck of a lorry. Round about lie soldiers, their faces to the ground.

'What's your opinion, as "War Minister", of this war we were forced into starting?' asks Porta, turning his head to look at Sally, sitting there shivering. 'No danger of us winnin' it, I hope?'

'Be easy,' says Sally, knowledgeably. 'The other lot's got its collective finger out, so we will lose the last battle just as we usually do, and will be able to use the usual excuses of ambush and treachery as the cause of our losing!'

'That's the German way,' says Wolf. 'It's in the tradition. We win our way straight into defeat!'

'Thank the Lord,' Porta breathes more easily, dragging the Mercedes around another wrecked lorry. 'Sometimes I get nightmares thinkin' we might win!'

Porta treads on the accelerator. He gives the car everything it can take. The Divisional Commander's standard on the front fender makes everything else on the road give way.

'See that fat chap there, with the narrow shoulder-straps an' the silver braid,' he remarks with a laugh. 'Don't often see a salute that smart out here!'

'They all get the shits, when they see the flag of General "Arse-an'-Pockets" on the front of a car,' says Wolf, condescendingly.

'We're more'n "Arse-an'-Pockets" is,' says Porta. 'He's only a general! We'll soon be *rich*. We can buy and sell generals, if we want to!'

Three MPs start screaming and waving their arms to clear the way for them.

'Going nicely, now, ain't it?' grins Porta, in satisfaction. He pushes down even harder on the accelerator.

'Keep to the right, you dogs!' roars Wolf in his well-oiled voice of command.

Two Unteroffiziers and a squad of soldiers jump for the ditch, and sink up to their necks in snow.

'*That's* the way,' nods Wolf happily.

'I'm givin' it all it can take,' says Porta. 'Livens up the day for the coolies!'

A bottle of Napoléon cognac goes the rounds.

'This just arrived from my French Connection,' remarks Sally, taking another big swig at the bottle. Half of it comes spurting out of his mouth again as Porta bangs his foot down on the brake pedal with all his might. The heavy staff-car goes into a spin on the slippery surface of the highway. With the touch of a master he directs his vehicle between the trees, jumps a tall hedge and stops it with its nose buried in a haystack. It was at the eleventh second of the eleventh minute of the eleventh hour.

Two RATAs with red stars on their wings come roaring out of the clouds. They rush along above the road, the muzzles of their machine-cannon flashing.

'Good Lord preserve us,' stammers Sally, his eyes rolling nervously. 'They do go to it in this country. The reports say the front is steady, and all's quiet!'

'Those devil's children come over like that every day,' explains Porta. 'You can set your watch by 'em. We call them the traffic police. They can get the traffic jams out of the way like nobody else can!'

'I lost two ten-tonners last week, right in the middle of church service on a Sunday,' says Wolf, looking sad. 'That's what you have to put up with when you're fightin' the godless. I only lost the crews, thank God! The waggons could be repaired!'

'Those devils won't be back again, will they?' asks Sally, looking nervously up at the grey clouds. 'Thank the Lord I'm only visiting here. I was born to wear a uniform, but not in wartime. Lord above, no!'

'Yes,' smiles Porta, 'it's impossible to imagine how the history of the human race might be changed, if you was to come out here and take an active part in the battle.' He laughs so much he doubles up over the steering wheel, and comes close to crashing into a wrecked gun. The bodies of its six horses lie dead in the road.

'Do they go on like this every day?' asks Sally, staring at the dead horses, lying there stiff-legged with mouths agape.

146

'As I said, you can tell the time by 'em,' answers Porta, indifferently. 'When they've done five missions they give 'em a medal. Pulls in the cunt, y'know. The flak gunners shot one down the other day, a puffed-up sod who'd only talk to officers. He had eight bars on his ribbon, so he must've knocked out a good few of truck-owner Adolf's rolling-stock!'

'What happened to him?' asked Sally.

'SS strung him up,' answers Porta, carelessly. 'He was too much of a hero for 'em to call him an *untermensch*. Alive he'd have been bad for propaganda. Fellow with a bit of a headache there,' he goes on, pointing, as they go by, to an old supply-soldier, sitting in a pool of blood with his steel helmet upside down on his head.

'By the way, did you ever hear any more of that chap they called "Polka Porky"?' asks Sally, maliciously. 'He took you to the cleaners all right. There wasn't much of your 80 per cent left after he'd been there, was there?'

'He's turned over a new leaf,' says Porta, spitting out of the window. 'Stopped stealing from people. One of my pals, feller who cleans the windows for the Gestapo at *Prinz Albrecht Strasse*, took him to the dentist to have his teeth looked at. There was some trouble so my pal borrowed the dentist's drill to fix it for him. Slipped a bit now an' then and made a hole or two in his tongue.'

'Don't suppose "Porky" liked that?' laughs Sally, wickedly.

'No, he didn't, to be sure,' answers Porta, with a hard laugh. 'There weren't any teeth left, and the holes in his tongue make him stammer. He has trouble asking for other people's 80 per cent now. People get tired of waitin' for him to finish what he's saying.'

'Yes, he boasted a lot about his having put one over on you,' says Sally, handing Porta the cognac bottle. 'Remember that fellow "Fat Pino", who used to be always boasting about how big he was? Well, a fellow steps out of a car on the *Hohenzollerndamm* right in the middle of the day. He throws

147

his arms round "Pino", gives him a big, smacking pansy kiss right on his mouth, and pushes a knife into his back at the same time. Straight to the heart, and all finished very neatly. He was off, knife and all, before people had finished staring at what had been happy "Fat Pino", only a moment before.'

'They call it the kiss of death in Sicily,' explains Wolf. 'I've used it a couple o' times here in Russia. Makes the opposition pull in its horns for quite a time, an' gives a bloke room to work in!'

Porta swings off the highway, and edges the heavy staff-car through narrow, snow-covered streets, sounding his horn continually. Pedestrians dodge to all sides. With a flamboyant swing he stops outside Wolf's residence with its forest of 'No Entry' signs.

The Chinese goons open the double doors to allow plenty of room for Wolf and his two companions to enter.

Two Russian POWs stand ready to polish Wolf's boots. They are graciously permitted to polish 'War Minister' Sally's boots as well.

Porta sits drinking cognac while these operations are carried out. 'Time enough to polish your boots when the war's over,' he thinks.

Chairs clatter as they enter the main office, and the clerks spring to attention.

Chief Mechanic Wolf touches the tip of his swagger-stick to his cap-peak. He has seen British officers do this in films. Things like that give a man class, he feels. His two book-keepers, specialists with erasers and forged signatures, put thoughtful expressions on their faces as 'Field-Marshal' Wolf goes by. He tramps heavily on each step of the iron staircase on his way up it, making his spurs jingle merrily.

'Hi!' he greets his two wolfhounds, who are lying with fangs bared, ready to attack. 'They had a swamp German for dinner last week,' he laughs. 'Wasn't a lot left of *him*! The idiot came in here, somehow, without warning, and said he'd pinched something or other from King Michael's army. Or whatever it is their boss's called down there in Rumania!'

'Now then! Let's get down to business,' says Sally, when they are seated at an extremely well-furnished dinner table. Wolf's bodyguards have been thrown out, and the door locked behind them. 'After what I've heard I doubt very much whether this deal can be carried through. It fairly stinks of *untermensch* treachery and Jew-boy traps!'

'Now don't come here puffin' yourself up, as if you *were* somebody,' shouts Porta angrily, pointing his fork at Sally. 'You do what I say. You don't need to do no more or no less to put this job through. *And* you get 5 per cent for doin' it. Personally I'd have thought half that was enough.'

'You *don't* think it's too much,' Sally smiles acidly. 'That's enough for today! You going to drive me to the airstrip, or do I have to take a taxi?'

'Have a good trip,' grins Porta, 'an' see you soon!' He helps himself, with apparent indifference, to a plateful of pickled pigs' trotters.

Wolf goes mad, and explodes with rage. He knocks the pigs' feet out of Porta's hands and rushes after Sally, who has his hand almost on the door knob.

'Hands off, you dope,' he screams. 'Want to blow us all to bits? You're not back in your bloody vicarage now. You're in a headquarters that's important to the war effort. An' I'll tell you something else, too, you brain-fucked little pygmy. We don't care a streak of piss what you do or don't have doubts about. You do what we tell you, or you'll soon be finished with creepin' around playing War Minister. We've knocked off bigger meatheads'n you, you imitation, operetta shagbag you! *Panjemajo?*'

'Very well, then,' grumbles Sally, sitting down again at the table, but keeping his silk cap on. Angrily he snatches a piece of black pudding, spoons sugar over it and then syrup. 'I usually play along with the people whose bread I have eaten,' he says, stuffing his mouth with the black pudding.

'What a shit you are,' says Porta, round a mouthful of

trotters. 'Don't you try to shove me around like that. When it comes to it you're not a real War Minister, you're just a bloody clerk in a lousy office. Any prat can be one o' them!'

'Oh, to the devil with it,' Sally gives in. 'Good health, boys! And let's get on with it! We'll all end up in shit creek anyway, sooner or later.' He takes a swig at his glass, and gives out a long, ringing belch. 'But why in the world,' he goes on, thoughtfully, 'don't you just pick up that gold yourselves. Nice and quiet. It'd be cheaper and easier for you, surely? By what they say in Berlin, Russia's fallen on its backside. There's nothing left to do but a routine clean-up, so, as far as I can see, the gold's just normal spoils of war!'

'An' you call yourself "War Minister"?' Porta shouts, contemptuously. 'Man, you sound more like a pregnant virgin in a Turkish knocker!! This kinda job can only go through with the help of sensible Russians, who, like us, don't give a shit for the Fatherland an' its need for *lebensraum*! We can stick together like shit to a blanket. Look, the plan's worked out an' ready. I'm fuckin' a bint just now as has been parked here by her feller. He's a commissar. She's got that fond of my joystick she's told me all about this Kremlin gold that her commissar husband had the job of hiding away till peace breaks out again. He's got the brilliant, genius-type of idea of goin' on his travels and taking the gold with him. We put together a combined German–Russian battle group. The commissar fixes things up back where he is, and we look after things here. Fits like a prick does up Lizzie. We drive off to Libau with the liberated gold, and from there we sail to Sweden. Goodbye to the Thousand Year Reich and the Soviet Paradise both!'

'The Swedes no longer have customs and passport checks then?' asks Sally, taking another mouthful of black pudding. Syrup dribbles from the corners of his mouth. 'You're out of your minds. Bullshit, the lot of it! I have to deal with paperwork acrobats every day. We run into a couple of inky-fingered coolies in the wrong place, and they've had it. That kind of thing's too easy!'

'Sven's looking after all that! He talks the lingo,' says Porta, confidently. 'All he does is tell the Swedes we're resistance. And it ain't even a *lie*! That's what we're doing, leaving Adolf and Joe's armies. Social Democrats, we bloody are!'

'Two thousand three hundred and twelve kilometres and four and a half metres,' says Sally thoughtfully, looking at the General Staff map spread out over the food on the table. 'That's only to where the gold is hidden! We also have to get back again. A Panther goes 100 kilometres on a full tank, and then there's the lorries. Got to have *them*! You can't carry the gold in your pockets. Where's the petrol coming from? They say the petrol pumps're all closed down in the neighbours' area.'

'You *worry* too much!' shouts Porta, waving a sausage around angrily in the air. 'This commissar whore o' mine guarantees all that. They've got a petrol reserve big enough for an armoured division, if you've got one to spare. All you've got to do is cover us with the sodding Prussians, so they don't go pissing around the world looking for us. *You* get us departure orders, battle orders, movement orders, and all the rest of the paperwork shit we need to get around in this bloody war. And the orders've got to be top priority. Get that straight, Mr "War Minister"! We don't want every barrack-square bastard with a brain the size of a walnut, an' coloured rag on his hat, tryin' to stop us!'

'Is *that* all you need?' replies Sally. 'That's easier than wiping your backside and shaking the drops off your cock afterwards. You'll get papers. Papers signed by Field-Marshal Keitel with all the usual loops and squiggles. No asexual iron-hat'll start shouting at you. He'll just salute, and pass you on!'

'Well then,' smiles Porta, 'why all the nonsense? All you do's what you used to do when mum sent you down to the shops with a list in your hot little hand!'

Wolf fills their glasses quickly, and shouts 'Skole!' before Sally realizes what Porta has said to him.

151

'We'll also want you to have a flat-bottom lying in Libau,' Porta goes on, emptying his glass in one gulp. 'The Navy job, with the propeller that goes round twice as fast as any of the other grey-painted bathtubs. I've got a feeling we're going to be in a hurry, just about then.'

'Small stuff for me,' declares Sally self-confidently, adding a new note to his long list. 'It's only a question of finding the right papers and stamping a red GEKADOS* across the lot. With the right documentation those Navy pricks'll sail you where you want to go, and never ask what's in the boxes. But who's going to help us in Sweden? My stamps and signatures have no force there!'

'The Swedes?' grins Porta, easily. 'I'll buy 'em. They're only Social Democrats. They stopped using their brains long ago.'

'Social Democrats!' mumbles Wolf. 'We got to share with *them*? Don't they believe everybody should have the same pay?'

'You're stupider than you were the day you were born,' bubbles Porta. 'When it's money you're talking about, the secret's to keep the share-out to as few as possible! The commissar's bint an' me have got everything worked out. In the end we do the lot of 'em in the eye and off we go with all the loot.'

'You were perhaps thinking of pissing us in the eye, too?' asks Sally in an obviously threatening tone.

'What the devil do you take me for?' asks Porta, with a deceiving laugh. 'You two are with *me*. The others *ain't*!'

'Sounds very nice, I'm sure,' says Wolf, sceptically. 'But the fellers we leave behind on the quay, waiting, are going to be very annoyed when they realize what's happened. And they'll start looking around under all kinds of bushes and stones, to have a little talk with the chaps who've done it to 'em!'

'Are you really that stupid?' asks Porta. He dips a frog's

* *Geheime Kommandosache*: German for Secret Command Matter

152

leg carefully into jam. 'I'll cut it out in cardboard for you, then, so both you *and* your Mongols can understand it. When we get to Libau with our load marked SECRET all over, we start straight off shouting and giving orders. Tiny an' me puts on long leather coats and trilby hats with the brims pulled down over our eyes, so's any squareheaded German can see we're tough tecs from *Prinz Albrecht Strasse*. No smiles from us. Who's goin' to dare question us?'

'That reminds me, by the way, of one Herr Barsch, who used to live in *Phasanenstrasse*. He was an estate agent, with a diploma, and he knew how to take people, if anybody did. Everything went fine for him until he was unlucky enough to hit on one of these surefire certainties, which more often than not get a chap inside the box with the key turned three times and the door bolted from the outside. Some time previous Herr Barsch had met a Jew Stockbroker who he considered to be a sucker. The Jew had bought a villa in Dahlem from him that was that full of creepy-crawlies an' all sorts of rottenness, it was a wonder it hadn't walked off on its own out into the Spree. Herr Barsch had been going round for some time with the feeling that he was lettin' the Jew get away with something by not taking him again. He had a word with a couple of his pals about it, at last, and they agreed with him it'd be money for jam for people like them. They arranged a meeting with the Jew, at an office they'd rented for the day, and after a bit o' natterin' to and fro and fro and to they agreed on a new deal. The Jew puts 500,000 marks on the table, and so did Herr Barsch an' his two mates. Their ducats were, however, in the form of forward-dated cheques on a newly-opened bank account. They'd never even *seen* that much money all at one time. After that they went out and took a gander at some hot industrial buildin' areas. It was raining so the Jew-boy stayed in his car, smokin' a cigar. He didn't want to get his Paris-tailored coat wet.

'After a good dinner at Kempinski they said goodnight to one another. Herr Barsch and his two scoundrelly pals took

153

a long time getting home that evening. They kept breaking down into screams of laughter all the way home, at the thought of all the ducats they had picked up. The old Jew went off innocently to Bad Gastein to have himself a roll in the healthy mud they've got there. Four weeks later Herr Barsch & Co were invited to a little chat at "Alex". They were taken into department 9B which looks after fraud, swindle and rubber cheques. The interview with the three friends ended with them inside Moabitt where they sat counting their toes till they were brought into court. They were shackled at their wrists and ankles, so's it was quite clear they really *were* criminals.

'The judge was a woman they called "the Devil's Sister", because of her wicked nature and the heavy sentences she handed out. She stared at the three tycoons, when they were escorted into court in their rattling chains.

'"Why are these prisoners not chained by the neck, so that they could have been dragged in here like the dogs they are?" she snarled, wickedly. She bent over the indictment on the bench in front of her, and rattled through it at such a pace that nobody could understand a word she said. She raised her head and stretched her neck like a hungry vulture, staring the three estate agents down.

'"According to paragraph 900, section 3, part 4B, the punishment for the crime which you have committed, i.e. grand fraud and illegal sale of the property of third person, is imprisonment for a period of from two to ten years. In aggravated circumstances the sentence may be increased to hard labour for up to fourteen years." She banged three times with her gavel, covered up her permanent-waved hair, and announced the sentence: "In the name of the Führer and the German people I sentence you to fourteen years hard labour! I only regret that I cannot sentence you to life imprisonment," she added with a smile which resembled that of a shark turning on its back to strike.

'The three former geniuses of finance rattled their chains out of the court, taking their dead cert with them. Nobody

154

outside *Bautzen** has seen them, since they jingled off through the courthouse gates in the Black Maria!'

'Yes,' sighs Wolf, 'money can be a source of wisdom. But what were you trying to tell us?'

'Well, you see,' smiles Porta, pleasantly, 'I wanted you to understand that you must never undervalue anybody! Even though there's only a few around with more'n sand in their heads, most've 'em have still got enough up there to take you for a sucker, if you don't keep on your toes all the time.'

'Yes, anybody can buy a Jew's gun an' a piece o' paper, but usin' it right's a different kettle of fish,' mumbles Wolf, writing down a figure on the tablecloth.

'What's the Old Man going to say to this trip?' asks Sally, practically, pursing his lips. 'Won't we have trouble with him?'

'Yes, he'll be our big problem,' admits Wolf, showing all his gold fillings in a ghastly, hyena grin. 'He'll call it bank robbery, and won't like us havin' planned to leave most of the mob in the lurch.'

'Oh, come *on*,' protests Porta, shovelling the remains of the blackcurrant jam into his mouth. 'You're making it into something ugly and criminal. To my way of thinking it's completely legal. Commie theory says everything belongs to the people, and aren't we the people? So all we're doin' is going off to pick up our own gold!'

'It limps,' hisses Sally, contrarily. 'The gold belongs to the Soviet people, and that's not us!'

'In a way you're right,' Porta says, triumphantly, 'but my bint an' her commissar husband *are* Russian Commie people, and they are going to share their gold with us! And very Social Democratic of them too, I say.'

'Know what,' Wolf suddenly begins to laugh noisily and wriggles happily in his generals-only swivel-chair. 'I'd love it if we could just leave Tiny behind on the quay at Libau. I

* *Bautzen:* A notorious German prison

155

still owe him for that time he wanted to blow me to bits with this radio.'

'You must be out of your mind,' cries Porta. 'Don't make any mistakes about Tiny. Maybe he does call the letter H a rugby goal and Y a catapult, but he's still the cunningest sod that ever slunk down the Reeperbahn. If we were stupid enough to leave him at Libau, and do him out of fulfilling his dearest wish: black silk underclothes and alligator-skin shoes with pin-holes in 'em, he'd be mad enough to drink the bloody Baltic dry, an' then we'd never get to sail to Sweden.

'I remember once when he was batman to the Commander of 9th Army at Hamburg, General of Cavalry von Knochenhauer. One of the wicked sods from Sankt Pauli put the word in about Tiny having done something Herr General von Knochenhauer didn't like one little bit. In went Tiny for interrogation, and they knocked him about something dreadful, but didn't get anything out of him. Still, when he got out on the Reeperbahn again, he was limpin', reduced to the ranks and a lot thinner than when he went inside.

'"That Kurt's a wrong un," he explained to the Jew furrier's son David, when they were sitting down in "The Headless Nag" drinking beer. "A louse's what 'e is, a filthy rat, *donkey* shit! Let's me'n you go an' talk to 'im a bit an' persuade 'im to stop shoppin' people!"

'"He's a dirty, rotten, bastarding lump of afterbirth," shouted David, angry on Tiny's behalf. He'd never met Kurt really. "He's nothin' but a chopped-off pair of Kaffir bollocks!" he wound up, wrathfully.

'When they'd finished gettin' one another all worked up, they got "Pickpocket Petra" to ring over to "The Cow With Three Udders", where Kurt was sittin' drinking raspberry juice'n rum.

'"Who'm I talkin' to?" asked Kurt.

'"Me o' course," said Petra, which was true enough.

'"Who's me, then?" squealed Kurt, suspiciously. "Got a

name, haven't you love?"

'"Fräulein Müller, Petra Müller."

'"Go *on*! Now ain't that nice of you to ring, Petra? How's it goin' then? 'Ad it off lately, 'ave you?"

'"Hello Kurt! Listen to me now, I got a hot one for you! Can you be at *Zirkusweg* in a half-hour's time? It's your lucky day, dear! You'll be jumpin' for joy, you will!"

'"Go on with you. You don't say so? I'm on my way already!"

'A quarter of an hour before the agreed time there was "Kurt the Nark" standing on the corner of *Zirkusweg* an' *Bernhard Nocht Strasse*, steppin' around like a black Yankee as had something hot to dispose of.

'"Pickpocket Petra" popped up out of a watchman's shelter, and whispered something into Kurt's ear. While she was talkin' she slipped one hand into his fly-opening and tickled him up, at the same time helping herself to the wallet in his arse-pocket with the other. Second nature to her it was. It was the way she made her livin', anyway.

'Out from *Kastanie-Allée,*, where the street lamps was out, come Tiny, the Jew's David an' "Ready Money Paul", in a beer-waggon they'd borrowed for the occasion.

'"We're pickin' up a 'ot load. Wanna come along?" rumbled Tiny's bass voice from the dark of the driver's cabin.

'Soon as "Kurt the Nark's" up in the waggon, which was one o' them with a canvas back, Tiny an' "Ready Money" are up there with him. "Ready Money's" twistin' his balls up to nearly round his neck, an' Tiny's got him by the throat, an' is bendin' him over backwards so his backbone's making crackin' noises. He was soon making the kind o' sounds people do when they're gettin' close to being strangled to death.

'The Yid furrier's boy David was tryin' to aim a Baretta at him. He wanted to plug him between the eyes, but every time he was ready to pull the trigger Kurt's head was somewhere else. So when the first shot went off it only creased the top of his ear, and went out through the truck's canvas and through a third-floor window. There it nearly frightened the life out a farmhand from Soltau who was gettin' ready to have a go with "Gallopin' Gerda". The next shot ended in the same place an' Gerda's visitor was that frightened he broke an arm tryin' to run down stairs an' put his trousers on at the same time.

'By this time the "Nark'd" found out he was starring in a real live liquidation scene, which you otherwise only experience in a horror film!

'"Jesus Christ!" he screamed, and God must have given him the strength of ten at least, 'cos he managed to butt "Ready Money" in the face, an' bring his American-made boot up in Tiny's tingle-tangle with full force, at one an' the same time. Then he burst through the canvas o' the waggon head-first like a delayed-action shell, knocked Petra arse-over-tip, and found himself standing on the pavement, shaking like a leaf from the nervous tension of it all. Petra was screaming for dear life, and Kurt was spinnin' round on his own axis tryin' to find out whether he was still alive or if he'd been killed.

'"*Get* 'im!" howled "Ready Money Paul", and crawled across Tiny, who was sitting, nursing his maltreated privates.

'"Holy Synagogue," moaned the Jew furrier's David, "that shit's makin' that much noise, you'd think somebody was trying to kill 'im!"

'"Choke 'im off, then," roared Tiny. "'E's already stayed breathin' too long!"

'Kurt had found out by now that he wasn't dead after all, but would be soon if he stayed where he was. So off he goes, fast as his legs can carry him, down towards *Davidsstrasse* so he can get into *Herbertsstrasse* where he'd be safe. He was king down there. God help those three if they were mad enough to go in there after him.

'"The yellow swine's runnin' for it!" roared Paul. "*Get* 'im!"

'The beer-truck roared down through *Hopfenstrasse* right on Kurt's arse. He was running like a hare with the sparks flyin' up from his American boots. He was just about to slip into safety behind the iron fence at *Herbertsstrasse* when the truck caught up with him, and crushed him flat against it. He looked like a great splash of beer-mash some crazy sod had chucked up against the fence. The beer-truck backed off to get away before the coppers arrived. You could usually count on them getting hung up by their truncheons and pistols in the swing-doors leading from *Davidsstrasse* Station.

'They left their bumper behind, mixed up with the remains of Kurt, and disappeared down the *Landesbrücke*, fast as a Rabbi with the SS breathin' down his neck. Next day everybody in Sankt Pauli was talkin' about how "Kurt the Nark" had been taken out by a hit-and-run driver. All the coppers from *Davids Wacht* were out looking for a beer-truck, but it had been lyin' on the bottom of the Elbe, the stink of beer washed out of it a long time since.

'"Mulatto Louis", so-called because he wasn't a real, pure German, was a kind of a viceroy on the Reeperbahn at that time, and decided who it was did what! But he kicked the bucket about a year after, from natural causes. They found him hangin' by the neck in the bus terminus. He'd got worried when he heard about Kurt's sudden departure, and got some people to find out what had really happened. It soon got around who was the hit-and-run driver, an' all the bosses on the Reeperbahn were goin' round whisperin' to one another:

'"Him there, Tiny, *you* know. Him an' his mate David, the feller with the astrakhan collar. They're a coupla hot numbers, they are. *They* know how to fix things!"

'The easy removal of "Kurt the Nark" from the asphalt of Sankt Pauli made Tiny an' David, the Jew's boy, very famous. They were well on the way to becoming wealthy specialists in the removal of unwanted citizens of Hamburg. But this lucrative business they were buildin' up came to a stop, unfortunately, when Tiny got posted to the bicycle dragoons at Breslau, an' the Jew's kid David took a single to England in the bilge of a collier, 'cos he didn't get on all that well with Adolf.'

'How you do go *on*!' says Sally, irritably. 'Why waste our time with all that shit? Who the hell cares what Tiny's done on the Reeperbahn?'

'You don't understand what I'm saying, do you?' asks Porta, throwing his arms wide. 'It's because I want to get it into your thick skulls that it'd be very *un*healthy to leave Tiny gapin' after us on the docks at Libau, *and* it might also shorten our lives considerably!'

The sun is rising over the melancholy Russian landscape when they take leave of Sally at the airstrip.

'Hope he don't fuck it all up,' says Wolf, pessimistically, as the JU-52 disappears into the clouds carrying the 'War Minister' with it.

'He's no stupider than he was on his birthday,' Porta comforts him. 'He knows where the pickings are, and he'll stay on his toes!'

The Old Man turns the plan down immediately. He does not want to spend the rest of his life in Germersheim, or somewhere in Siberia. But Porta will not give up. He chatters on and on about ownership by the people, and in a couple of days time he has the Old Man convinced that the gold is really ours, and that there is nothing criminal in our going to fetch it. The plan begins to take shape.

Sally's two specialists in alterations and signatures arrive with the mail-plane from Berlin. They are each carrying two large briefcases, decorated with the German eagle. In the following days, Chief Mechanic Wolf's sanctum sanctorum is in a state of white-hot alert. TOP SECRET documents are all over the place.

After the Old Man has examined the TOP SECRET orders for a while, he gives in, with a bark of laughter.

'Never in my life have I seen anything like this! It *can't*

160

go wrong. There's even an Order of the Day from the Führer!'

Porta is sitting beside Vera, telling her about their progress since Sally's visit. Proudly he shows her the Führer's Order of the Day, signed with his own hand. It's all there. The special eagle and everything.

'Let's get moving,' he says. 'The orders for a special partisan-type action are already on the desk of the divisional commander, General "Arse-an'-pockets".'

'What if some weak-minded, walnut-brained person was to check this with the Führer's HQ?' asks Vera, with healthy suspicion.

'Don't be silly, girl,' laughs Porta. 'No German dope in uniform'd dare ring Adolf'n ask if his orders were really what he meant! Think your hubby'd ring up Joe'n ask *him* if he knew what he was up to, liquidatin' a load o' fellers who'd poked their noses in too far?'

'No, you may be right,' Vera gives in, thoughtfully.

'Up my arse, how I do look forward to bein' a civvy again,' says Porta, dreamily. 'A life without danger, where anybody can run around free, with any invitin' loot he likes in his pockets.'

'Do not start laughing too soon, my friend,' she mumbles. 'You have no idea how complicated the life of a civilian can be. There, they have no regulations written down to follow!'

'*And* there's nobody who's got to give anybody the first salute, is there?' says Porta. 'Any shit can just walk past any other shit, just staring blankly at fuck-all. But I do believe it'll be different for us who're travelling first class. They'll lift their lids to us, an' kiss our arses if we want 'em to. It's better to have money in your pockets'n a bundle of stick-grenades!'

'Yes, God knows you are right,' breathes Vera.

Porta sits waiting, with a bottle of cognac and a pot of coffee while Vera goes to find a telephone to try to get in touch with her commissar husband. She is mad enough to spit when she comes back.

'I've had enough of it,' she screams, throwing herself into an armchair. 'If those shits and my clever husband do not pull themselves together we have had it. We are for the shit-heap!'

'Yes, I thought we'd have trouble working with a bloody policeman,' says Porta, worriedly, pouring more cognac into his coffee. 'I *know* 'em! They can do anything, long as somebody's tellin' 'em what to do. If there *isn't* anybody, they flap round in circles like a lot of old maids who've had a bucket o' cow-piss thrown all over 'em. If we don't find out something that can get your twit of a husband moving, PDQ, we'll soon find ourselves on the receiving end of a lot more shocks!'

'That all you've got to say, you limp German prick?' she scolds him, forgetting she is a highly-placed, aristocratic lady. 'What've you got a head for? *Do* something! Give your orders! You *are* a German, aren't you? Just sit there swilling coffee and cognac!' She goes on furiously for some time, spitting out the foulest oaths in the language. Words she certainly did not learn in her aristocratic home.

'Yes, it is a bit shitty ain't it?' Porta admits. 'I must say it's nice and pleasant having a bundle of cash in your pants, but it does bring a lot of excitin' situations with it. Tell me, girl, does your feller drink?'

'No, never,' she says. 'But why do you ask?'

Porta sucks on a tooth, and pulls at the lobe of his ear.

'Does hubby work hard?'

'Indeed he does. I guarantee you that. He has worked like a horse all his life for the lousy state. It is only seldom he drinks, and then he gets really drunk.'

'That does ease my mind,' nods Porta. 'People who drink too much, y'know, see things through rosy spectacles an' everythin' goes easy. I must admit I was scared of the lot of it being just drunken dreams. Let me talk a bit of my Russian German to your hubby. Where's your radio? We'll soon get things on the right track an' be wealthy people with houses an' fishin' rights in Sweden. D'you like salmon, girl?'

> *It is easy to keep clean when you do not engage in trade or mix with other people.*
>
> *Henri de Montherlant*

'Let me go,' babbled the old Jew, trying to tear himself away from the brutal grip of the three young men.

'Where've you hidden the stuff?' shouted the big stormtrooper, hitting the old man in the face.

The woman screamed and tried to help her husband. She was thrown back into the dark corridor. She screamed again when the SA man's boot sank into her. She screamed for the last time when a rifle butt smashed into her face. Then they looted the shop.

When the police arrived they found the old man lying weeping across his wife's body. They turned him in to the collection point at Old Moabitt, and hanged him for wife murder eight days later. That was the day Dr Goebbels decreed:

Ordnung muss sein!

It was 3 April, 1936.

THE BURIAL OF GREGOR'S GENERAL

The men who have been on leave are beginning to return. They come plodding down the long straight highway. Some have managed to thumb a lift, but most of them have had to walk the fifty kilometres from Svatogorskaja. The leave train didn't go any further. It is easy to tell which of them are town boys and which come from the country. The farm lads are giving way at the knees from the weight of all the good food their families have loaded them down with when they left. The townies have only their equipment to carry. One thing they all have in common. They are unbelievably sorry for themselves, and under their influence the whole regiment is very soon in the grip of the blackest kind of depression.

We snarl at one another, punch-ups are started for the slightest of reasons. Tiny had already beaten eight men up so viciously that he has been tied to a tree as if he were some kind of watch-dog. We have no guardhouse to keep him in. The Unteroffizier-cook, a fellow we call 'Fried Egg' because he looks like one, gets himself scolded almost to death when two men back from leave throw him into the soup cauldron. All he'd done wrong was to say: 'Welcome back to the joys of the Eastern Front.'

Porta is slouching grumpily down the broad main road, when he runs into Sonia Pushkova, her round fat face shiny with sweat as usual. She believes herself to be very attractive, although she would be none the worse for a close shave. She crashes into Porta with all the grace of a fully-loaded truck, and throws both her fat arms around his neck.

'Like to come into my chicken coop an' have a look at

the new hen?' she asks him, licking the inside of his ear with her fat, wet tongue.

But Porta is far too low in spirits to be interested.

'Shit on your new hen,' he mumbles, and gives her broad rump a hearty smack. 'I'll come an' fuck you some other day, and your hen can sit on her perch and cackle in time to the beat!'

All alone, Gregor comes limping into what was once a fine hotel, before the war, but is now a half shot-up heap of ruins. A primitive sort of bar has been opened in it, but the kind of bar which is only for people with money – and a lot of it.

'What a shithouse of a place,' Gregor says, sitting down alongside Porta on a rickety bar-stool. 'Beer and champagne,' he orders, sourly.

'What the devil are you doin' here?' asks Porta, and stares questioningly at his stick. 'And what's happened to your leg?'

'Sprained my ankle at the funeral,' explains Gregor, swallowing half the contents of his tankard in one go. He stares at the girl behind the bar.

'You are pretty man!' she says in Russian.

'I know that,' he replies. 'I don't believe in the German God any more,' he turns and says to Porta. 'When you've had it good for a bit, and then come back to this godforsaken country, *then* you really understand for the first time what kind of a bucket of shit the German High Command's offerin' its tired heroes! Hell's *bells*!'

The Old Man comes in, followed by Tiny and Barcelona.

'Now I've seen the lot,' roars Tiny, exploding into a shout of laughter at the sight of Gregor. ''Is 'Ighness the Chauffeur-General 'as come back to the poverty-struck!'

'You been decorated?' asks Porta, pointing to the colourful KVK* on Gregor's chest.

---

* *Kriegsverdienstkreuz* (War Cross for Merit)

'My general awarded it to me on his deathbed,' answers Gregor, assuming a sufficiently sorrowing expression.

'Well, well. So *he's* gone to Valhalla too?' says Porta, sadly. 'The Fatherland certainly does require sacrifices from us. I know the family of a colonel that's sacrificed three sons an' two daughters on the altar of the Fatherland, and God help me if they don't still wave paper flags on all the national holidays!'

'Yes, it's rough enough,' sighs Gregor. 'My general'd stayed alive, my fate'd have been different.'

'No doubt about that,' admits Porta. 'The winners would probably have strung you up alongside your general!'

'Could be,' agrees Gregor. 'But what's worst? Rolling round in Russian muck with a pound o' lead in your guts an' dyin' slowly, or dropping down a couple o' yards through a hole with a rope tied round your neck? Oh well! I had some good times with the General Staff. Me an' my general, an' our monocle, had some fine manoeuvres together. In the beginning it was like the day after a Harvest Festival!

'"All we need here to make the similarity perfect," said my general, polishing away at our monocle, "is the smell of cowdung. That would be *it*! We've got to get this crowd in line," he trumpeted through his eagle-beak of a nose. "Unteroffizier Martin, you will move into staff quarters," he barked, semaphorin' with our monocle. "In twelve minutes we drive to church and remind God that it is His duty to give German arms the victory!"'

'I took over the quarters of a Leutnant who'd been reduced. They stunk of perfume worse than a whore's scent factory. This Leutnant'd been a brown-holer, so they'd made him a slave in Germersheim. On the way I met my old mate the Adjutant, the rotten swine. When he saw me he stopped dead as if somebody'd hit him between the eyes with a club.

'"You," he groaned. "God in Heaven, *you*! And I hoped and prayed you'd been shot to bits and spread all over the Russian steppe." He glared at me like an admiral out on the high seas just before he gives the order to open fire with a full broadside. Then he stuck his face up close to mine and opened his mouth so I could see his tonsils. "You know what, Unteroffizier Martin," he squealed, like a tom-cat that's got its balls trodden on. "You are the nastiest, and most repelling individual I have ever met. You're a barracks *rat*! That's exactly what you are! A meaningless shout on a wet barrack-square! But you're not going to fool me! I've seen through you! Your conduct can be compared to that of a money-grubbing Jew, but I imagine I've told you that before."

'"Yes sir, Herr Rittmeister sir!" I smiled, crashing my hobnailed heels together twice. "I realized a long time ago, sir, that the Herr Rittmeister did not regard me with the same warm affection as he would a son!"

'You should've seen that lousy bicycle dragoon,' Gregor goes on. 'He made a face for all the world like a travellin' salesman dealin' in moth-eaten rabbit skins. On the way to the mess my general got annoyed because some blokes didn't salute us, even though the divisional flag was waving merrily on the front mudguard. The Staff Padre got a rocket straight off, 'cos his dog-collar wasn't as clean as my general wanted. This made the dope of a sky-pilot nervous, of course, and he got mixed up in his bible text and told us Jesus was at the Battle o' Carthage, and handed out Hannibal the Iron Cross.

'"You need a rest, my good parson," barked my general right in the middle of the prayer, and banged him with eight days confined to quarters, before he'd got to the "Amen". But it wasn't till we got to the war game in the afternoon my general really went up the wall. He'd got a message from Führer HQ, you see, that told him that it wasn't us who'd be gettin' *53 Panzer Corps*, but some shit of a South German who'd got his party book in order. My general an' our monocle took that very near. We'd been looking forward, you see, to smashin' up an armoured corps and shedding a bit of good German blood on the battlefield.

'It was a deep secret, but we were really jealous of a

Russian colleague they called "the Butcher of Khiev", because of his remarkable efficiency at finishing off the troops he was put in command of. My general wanted to be talked of as "the Butcher of the Ukraine". Things like that look great in the history books!

'"There are dark times on the way," predicted my general. "No war game today!"

'Well, the message from Führer HQ went into the waste-paper-basket, we polished our monocle, and took a stiff drink. We were in such a bad mood we even forgot to mark the bottle so we could check if anybody had taken a swig on the sly.

'When I helped him on with his uniform, at exactly 23.00, he looked funny. It was as if his eagle nose had begun to droop a bit. He didn't check his bedtime with the three watches he carried around with him. He'd been hit pretty hard by them havin' given our armoured corps to some fat-gutted party dope from the Bavarian beer-halls.

'"Soon the ravens will come to fetch us," he said, through his nose, and sent me a steely glance through our monocle.

'"Yes, Herr General, sir!" I replied, banging my steel-shod heels together. "It really looks dark! The civilians have stolen our uniform and us gentlemen for God and the Kaiser've got to stand in the corner with our monocle in our hand! Yes sir, Herr General, sir, these are wicked times. We can expect nothing good from the civilians. They are the spawn of the devil. They will spit in our beer!"

'We were silent for a while, thinking things over.

'"Play a little for me, Unteroffizier Martin," he ordered, lounging down in the large general's chair he had had made from the skin of his late horse, Baldrian, which was so German it even topped the mares in Wagnerian rhythms.

'I sat down at the mechanical organ and sang:

> Even I, a strong man,
> Have felt the fiery
> Heat of love . . .

'My general didn't like that one much. It was too tame. So instead I sang:

> The horses race
> Like a storm along –
> A shot through the head –
> The Rittmeister's dead!
> We smash the enemy –
> Chase him home . . .

'Then my general wouldn't hear any more. He sat there and seemed to shrink in on himself on his dead horse.

'"Unteroffizier Martin, you have a spot on your mess-jacket," he said, a little irritably, pointing to a spot no bigger than a wart on a fly's arse.

'"Do you think I am going to die?" he asked, placing our monocle in his eye.

'"I'm sure of it, Herr General, sir," I answered. "Those the heavenly warrior loves he calls home to his table."

'"Yes, we all have to go some time," he sighed, with a hopeless glint in the eye wearing the monocle.

'After this sad discovery, he had to take another cognac, a double one. Between the second and the third glass my general found out that the whole of life was only a preparation for death.

'"Unteroffizier Martin, since you are only an Unteroffizier, and in no way a learned man, I conclude that you have never thought about how sad everything is. Alone we come into the world, and still more alone we march out of it again."

'We were silent for some time, each of us alone with his thoughts. I was standing there thinking how great it would be if the old clown'd pull the cheeks of his arse together and slide into the world of dreams, where everything was all splashed over with German and Russian blood. I had a bint waiting for me, you see, at the Bismarck statue that's all covered over with pigeon-shit. *Blitzmädel** she was an' fucked with the whole regiment. When she got into top gear she could make a corpse come.

'My general took another nip from the bottle of Corsican optimism. "You are firmly believed then that I am going to die, Unteroffizier Martin?" he starts up again with the verbal diarrhoea, between a couple of well-satisfied grunts.

'I was permitted to take a little one, as a reward for my honest answers, a very unusual thing where my general was concerned. Of course I had to drink it standing at ease, which is the way things are done in general officer circles.

'Then him and our monocle started marching backwards and forwards in the room. Our spurs jingled real Prussian-like. When we had our night uniform on we always wore boots and spurs till we climbed into beddy-byes.

'The way he looked walking up an' down there he reminded you of a whole regiment of hussars going at the throat of Germany's enemies, and knockin' 'em on the head with sabres. It was typical of my general, and our monocle, that they always marched about when they had to get the blue blood to run out of their heads an' down into their arses so's they could think.

'After some time of this, when I was getting dizzy from turning round all the time to keep facing my general, he finally stopped and stared at me for a long while. He looked like an executioner takin' an eye measurement of the neck of a bloke, who's due to turn up his toes.

'"I am going to give you an order, Unteroffizier Martin, and the devil will come and take you if you don't carry it out punctually and properly!" After a lengthy pause, while he rubbed his eagle-nose thoughtfully: "If I have to go off to serve in the great army, which will probably be before you dismiss for all time, you must see to it that the band of 5

* Army Signals girl

171

Hussars blows *Rote Husaren** at my funeral."

'"Very good, Herr General, sir," I replied, cracking my heels smartly. "All shall be arranged as the general orders. The buglers of the Hussars shall blow until their trumpets are red-hot!"

'"I'll trust you with that then, Unteroffizier Martin! But you also see to it that Stabsmusikmeister Breitenmüller of 5 Hussars places two *Leibhusaren* in full parade uniform with sabres in the mourning position at the head of my coffin. Two more hussars from 5 Regiment's corps of buglers are to play *Der Tod reitet auf einem kohlenschwartzen rappen†*. To be played *andante* of course. But should we be so unfortunate as not to be able to get 5 Hussars bugle corps, because they are out fighting for old Germany, then you are to see to it that a well-trained choir of soldiers is commanded out, not less than 25 men, and you, Unteroffizier Martin, will sing the solo. Is that understood?"

'"Yes sir, Herr General, sir! Beg to report sir, I'm already singing!"

'Then my general gets up into his pit at last. He was that taken up with kickin' the bucket that he'd got all the way down into bed before he found he'd still got his boots and spurs on. He got a bit rotten about that. But we got his boots off, and after I'd read him a bit about Old Fritz he went off into a deep sleep.

'Next morning we gave inspection a miss. Instead we went off an' inspected the flowers in the castle park. The Cavalry bed with the yellow tulips pleased him, as they usually did. They stood there straight as a string, bowing their necks just like the sodding horses of the 7 Uhlans in Düsseldorf, our regiment. They were the ones who rode straight to hell in a crazy cavalry attack at Cambrai in 1915, with my general in the lead. We were Oberstleutnant then. We always got ourselves very worked up when we talked

* *Rote Husaren:* Red Hussar
† *Der Tod reitet auf einem kohlenschwartzen rappen:* Death rides on a coal-black horse

172

about that ridin' trip. Sneaky as the English always are, they'd spotted machine-guns all over the place, so it wasn't easy to launch a nice-lookin' cavalry charge. If it'd been *them* that'd sent out their dragoons to charge *us* we'd have met 'em in the stirrups, face to face, with drawn sabres and lances at the ready. When we got to the white lilies my general got wrinkles all over his forehead, and started cursing like a whole gang of seamen in an Arab knocking-shop!

'"Typical infantry," he trumpeted, "look like a flock of nuns who've just been raped by French sailors. See that stupid lily there? Two centimetres out of line. Remove it, Unteroffizier Martin! On to the muckheap with it! If we're not careful, everything will go to pieces."

'At the red roses – the artillery bed – our humour went up a couple of degrees and our ice-blue eyes lit up, joyfully. The roses stand there, battery by battery. They look really soldierly.

'"That's the way!" said my general, and took the monocle out of his eye three times, as a sign that he was well-pleased.

'We walked backwards and forwards a bit, enjoyin' the sight. But it clouded over when we got to the supply troops, the blue cornflowers. Good Lord, what a mess! But that's the way it always is with echelon troops. Yokels, the lot of 'em. They don't even know the difference between right and left. You give 'em a bit of hay round one ankle an' straw round the other and then you shout "Hayfoot! Strawfoot!" Their horse detachments can't find a girl who'll have anything to do with them, and have to have a go at the horses when they get the chance.

'My general sentenced the whole cornflower bed to be executed, so at dawn I ran our hand lawnmower through the lot of 'em.

'The panzer troops, the pink roses, made a better showing. What a straight-backed lot! I felt proud to be a Panzer Unteroffizier. We stayed a long time looking at them

173

and in the end we'd convinced ourselves things weren't as black as they looked.

'"Takes balls to be a panzer soldier," my general said, rattlin' his false teeth.

'We nodded in passing to the engineer troops, black tulips. They're the coolies of the army anyway. But when we got to the catering lot, the cabbage bed, we got a shock. The Moses dragoons were standing there droopin' like so many gonorrhoea-infected pricks.

'My general sentenced them all to death on the spot. "To the gas-chambers with them," he snarled, without a thought in his head of how important a catering corps is.

'Everything went wrong when we got down to the orchards, and inspected the scarecrows. They were wearing Russian uniforms. My general got a funny look on his face when we found the first one with unpolished boots. The two next had their coats buttoned crooked, and the last was wearin' his cap back to front.

'My general nearly swallowed the gardeners, who come on the run. We chased 'em up through the orchards with that many threats, and so fast, their tongues were hanging out of their arseholes an' their piles were up around their ears.

'An old, white-haired feller cracked open like a maiden-head on a summer night, an' threw up all over the general's boots. My general pulled out his pistol and aimed it at this *untermensch*, and, of course, he fainted from fright. They sent him to the front the day after, to spend the rest of the war with a corpse-collection unit.

'We were in a black humour, as we marched back to the castle. The Angel of Victory received only a perfunctory salute in passing. The sentries slammed the doors open, but one of them made a mess of it and his door swung back and hit my general right in the face. You should've *heard* him. He didn't shout, like some stupid Unteroffizier, but what he did say, through his nose, sat right in the bullseye. He literally shot those two guards down with his words.

174

' "Never beat around the bush with people of that sort," he twanged down his nose.

'Yes, my general did just what he liked with every man in our division. He signed death warrants without even reading 'em. We didn't waste much time on that sort of thing, anyway.

'In the corridor we ran into the Catholic padre, who was so fat he had the shakes permanent. Every part of him shook like a jelly. My general stopped in the corridor without acknowledging the fat padre's salute.

' "Well, it's you is it, reverend padre? It's not often you put in an appearance, but you are, perhaps, busy preparing the way for the many soldiers who fall for the Fatherland?"

' "Very good, Herr General!" mumbled the sky-pilot weakly, looking as if he was about to drop dead on the spot.

'My general had pulled his long neck down into his collar at the sight of the Staff Padre, but now he suddenly shot it right out again, and screwed his monocle more firmly into his eye.

' "Yes, you must be very busy, reverend father," he spat out. The nostrils of his eagle-nose vibrated as if he were smelling a corpse. "Your boots are not polished, but there are perhaps other clothing regulations for the gentlemen of the Corps of Padres, with which I am not familiar? Three days confined to quarters, reverend padre, and you will report every other hour to my Adjutant with well-polished boots and equipment. It is possible that you have been allowed to slouch around in a state of unregimental filthiness in the division you came from, but *not* here in my division!"

'So we left the Jesus dragoon standin' there to think over things. After we had slashed at our riding boots with our riding whip a few times we ordered war games for the whole garrison. That's what we always used to do when the officers were goin' to get some stick. They were all there when we arrived. My general understood this sort of thing. He was always master of the situation. Nobody ever took *him* for a sleigh-ride. My job was to look after the cardboard clock, so I had a good view of what was goin' on, and I stood so's I could have a good grin now and then without 'em seeing it. Our division had the best terrain model of anybody in the whole Army. My general'd looked after that. There was dozens of streams and rivers, and guns and tanks; and bridges all over the place that we could blow up just before the enemy got to 'em.

'My general stood there for a long time, glarin' nastily at all the nervous faces round the war table. Then he gave 'em a long speech about what was going to happen if Germany, as usual, got its arse kicked up round its ears by our rotten enemies.

'"This time they will drink their ale from our skulls," he predicted. "Our sexual organs will decorate the walls of their officers' messes." But, he swore by our monocle, before it gets that far – and may God forbid it, he added, in the tone of an archbishop – we must see to it that our enemies get to know us. "We shall bombard them with fire from our long-range artillery," he explained, waving his pointer backwards and forwards over the simulator table. "Then our armour will roll forward in a destructive flying V formation. Our heavy Tigers will take away their appetite for war. Those who are left we will smash under the tracks of our self-propelled guns, and those who have gone into hiding we will blast with our flamethrowers." He hammered his pointer down on a village, destroyin' it with one blow.

'All the officers turned their eyes sadly towards the shattered village. The terrain was a German landscape, you see, with German cows and our fat German peasants on it!

'"Germany will never capitulate, gentlemen, mark my words," hissed my general, lettin' our monocle fall out of his eye. Suddenly he realized what a terrible lot of nonsense he was talking. When he had taken a break, in which he punished a couple of Leutnants by postin' 'em away to the infantry for gigglin' at a dirty story, he nodded to the Chief-of-Staff. "The Wild Boar", a dried-up stick of a

Major-General with a stiff leg and a patch over one eye, took over, and the war stimulation was on the go.

'The first who got the hammer was a Rittmeister who was going too fast. He mistook his own lines for the enemy's and let a couple of Stukas smash up his own armour that was waiting in ambush for the neighbours' T-34s. That Rittmeister was letting his tears fall in a front-line regiment the very same night. My general didn't even give him the regulation three days leave. Nobody could feel himself safe with us. Just when they were enjoying things with the staff and countin' on an uncomplicated life, off they went, all of a sudden, to a front-line unit, the anteroom to the Valhalla mess.

'A bit later a Major and three Leutnants got themselves removed from division's protectin' arms, for goin' the wrong way with the enemy's tanks.

'My general got more and more annoyed, and his eyes were shooting out wicked ice-blue flashes!

'I could see what way things were going. Before these simulated games were over the division'd have a noticeable shortage of officers. It was lucky though, I thought, that they weren't *real* officers but only reserves – war surplus shit so to speak. But our German God had kept the best to wind up with. Every bit of our concentrated anger fell on the Adjutant, the rotten swine. He got himself that infiltrated in Ivan's infantry that he lost a whole battery of SPs. My general shot his scraggy neck half a yard up out of his collar, like a submarine commander who was tryin' to sink a battleship. The adjutant feller got a fit of the Andalusian shakes, and started his AA batteries shooting down our own air support. They came down over the whole simulator area like a shower of confetti.

'I was grinnin' like mad up there alongside my cardboard clock. It was a lovely sight to see that lousy Adjutant in trouble. He looked like a constipated rat. My general told him a lot of things in a voice that nearly cut the boots away from under him, and he slunk off looking like a half-drowned suicide candidate.

'Then my general stopped the war game before the incompetent officers ruined our army completely. He made a long speech to those remaining, in which he told them what his feelings were with regard to civilians in uniform. He wound up by telling them that Attila had been much better off than the general of today. He wasn't encumbered with reserve officers, but had born warriors around him who knew how to swing a club and split the skulls of other tribesmen.

'Off we went then, and banged the door after us. I left the cardboard clock at five minutes past twelve. Just to give the clever fellers something to think about.

'Then we changed uniform, and put on our battle kit with our hand-artillery on our hip.

'"To work," ordered my general, and out he goes through flocks of cacklin' geese and poultry that thought they owned the road.

'"Hell's bells," I thought. Time to pray. I knew my general, and had a pretty good idea of what he might get up to when he was in one of his black moods.

'Just after the birds' tattoo we get up in our staff car, and drive down through the darkened villages with our divisional standard on the front mudguard and blue slits on the headlamps, so's nobody'd be in doubt of who was coming. My general muttered away darkly during the whole of the trip. "Honour be to God in the highest and peace on earth," I thought.

'My general had decided to inspect the coolies stationed round about in the civilian quarter. We dropped down on the divisional gaol like delayed action lightning on the Day of Wrath. The guards were sitting around playing cards with the prisoners and their weapons were hanging on the coat-racks out in the latrines. You should've heard my general, and seen those guards and prisoners jump around like cockroaches on a red-hot fryin' pan. In the end when they'd all been ordered into the cells, I was commanded to

178

lock the doors an' bolt 'em. When I handed the keys over to my general, he threw 'em as far as he could over on the other side of a muckheap.

'Finally we dismantled their machine-pistols and spread the parts all over Westphalia, so they'd be *really* busy when they got the order to parade for inspection with mpis. Yes, my general knew how to turn civilians into reasonable imitations of soldiers.

'The next place we rolled up at, the officer in charge appeared on the doorstep in pyjamas and slippers. My general made a terrible noise.

'"The enemy is in the outskirts of the town," he roared, pushing his beaky nose almost into the sleepy major's face. "The enemy is on its way into the town!" he repeated.

'"That's not so good," mumbled the major, and offered my general cognac for an eye-opener.

'"My dear man, have you not just heard that the enemy is here with his armoured spearhead almost standing on your toes?" said my general, with shattering calm.

'"Well I suppose there's only one thing left for us to do." The major smiled, and pulled his pyjama trousers up around his waist. "And that's to get off out of here, before we get the shop all smashed up! But what the devil's the enemy want here?"

'Now we practically jumped out of our riding boots. We dropped our field-monocle, which got smashed, but thank God we always had an extra one in our breast-pocket.

'"You give the alarm!" roared my general, in a rage.

'"Very good, Herr General, sir!" answered the major, and he shuffled out an' put on his tin helmet. Then he put his head out of the door, and shouted "Alarm!" three times into the night-still village street.

'Nothing happened for a while, and then the telephone rang, very angrily. My general picked it up.

'An angry voice asked what kind of idiot it was who shouted "Alarm!" here in the middle of the night.

'"It's me," shouted my general, in a voice which made

179

the telephone mouthpiece shrink in on itself. "An alarm has been ordered, because paratroopers have surrounded us!"

'"You must have eaten an old boot an' it's disagreed with you," laughs the voice at the other end of the line. "Go in and get some sleep, you war-crazy idiot, and wait with all that shit till daylight. No paratrooper in his right mind'd dream of landing here with us! We're not doing anybody any harm!"

'My general threw the telephone from him in disgust, and sent the major a destroying general's glance.

'"You'll hear from me," he promised him, darkly.

'"Very good, Herr General, sir," piped the major, saluting with the wrong hand to his steel helmet. He had only now realized who his guest was.

'"What a spineless individual," snarled my general, as we crashed through a new village," he'll end up wishing that it *had* been enemy paratroopers who visited him rather than us!"

'We came down like two emissaries from outer space on some quarters where a rifle regiment had found protection from the night damp, and were lolling in broad peasant beds.

'A tall, thin beanpole of a Feldwebel, with his steel helmet turned round backwards on his head, coughed out a kind of report. When he had finished and was standing and wondering what else he could find to report, he realized that he had forgotten to call the room to attention. The coolies were lying around with their heads on the tables, snoring, an' not givin' a damn for standing guard.

'"Sound the alarm, man," screamed my general. "The enemy is on its way into town!"

'"What?" grunted the Feldwebel, fearfully, breathing cheap schnapps straight into my general's face. "What?" repeated this sketch of a soldier, scratching himself violently on the backside.

'"Sound the alarm, for hell's sake," screamed my general again, nearly frightening the life out of the company cat, which was lying fast asleep alongside the stove. It sprang straight up in the air, and came down standing stiffly on all four legs.

'"*Servus*, Herr General, sir!" it meowed.

'The tin-hatted beanpole began thinking so hard, dents appeared in his helmet. He reached for his belt and pistol, which were hanging on a hook. Then he pissed off over to one of the sleepin' beauties an' began to shake him awake.

'"Herbert," he yelled. "Wake up, damn your eyes!"

'"Sod off!" answered Herbert, throwing a sleepy punch at him.

'"It's important, Herbert! Come on! Get up!" the beanpole implored him.

'"Go over'n wake up the OC, and tell him the enemy's here with tanks an' all sorts of ironware!"

'You should have seen my general! He looked as if his favourite football team'd lost an' he was goin' to have a Greater German stroke any minute. Then he went green, an' finally blue in the face. He simply couldn't get a word out for several minutes, something which only happened infrequently. But then he got his voice back, with a vengeance.

'"We're at war, man," he screamed. They must've been able to hear him down in the south of France. "Any minute now the enemy's tanks will roll in and tear the flesh from our bones. Sound the alarm. *Stufe 3**, man, damn your eyes!"

'"Very good, Herr General, sir," mumbled the Feldwebel, scratching his head, thoughtfully, under his steel helmet.

'"Get your fingers out, Herbert! Sound the alarm *Stufe 3*! Wake up the section commanders. Tell 'em the British are here with their tanks. They'd better get their gear together, too, so's we can get off out of it before we get took prisoner. Jump to it, Herbert. Ain't you found out there's a war on yet?"

* *Stufe 3*: German: Stage 3 alarm

'"Me gun," muttered Herbert, still half-asleep. He puts out a hand to fumble after his rifle, which is hanging on a hook by the window and looking just as sleepy as its owner and the rest of the guard.

'"And they dare to do this to me," wheezed my general, pushing the whole of his eagle-face up out of his collar. "They are all mad as hatters and think they're here to live off the fat of the land! Unteroffizier Martin, show them how to sound the alarm when the enemy is knocking on the door!"

'I picked up a "guitar", smacked a full magazine into place, and burnt off the whole load. Then I changed magazines and, just to be on the safe side, sent another load off up the long village street in the opposite direction.

Lights went on in some of the houses, and sleepy voices shouted protests.

'"Good Lord preserve us," groaned my general, taking our monocle out of his eye. "This gang don't even respect the black-out regulations!"

'After about ten minutes had gone by, a fat reservist came rattling up on an Army motorbike Anno 1903.

'"What the hell are you crazy loons playing at?" he yelled furiously, coming close to falling off his bike with rage. "Firing off weapons here in the middle of the night. There'll be a court-martial out of this, devil take me!"

'"Yes, you can count on that, my good man," snarled my general.

'The reserve officer let his bike fall to the ground when he saw the general's red tabs and oak leaves. He was struck dumb on the spot, and remained standing quite still in an attitude which good-natured people might even have called the position of attention. It took us some time to get out of him that he was the regimental Orderly Officer.

'"Enemy armour is on its way into your billet area," thundered my general, as if he were Marius himself on the Raudian fields.

'"What kind of armour?" asked the fat cycle dragoon, moping at us.

'"British tanks, Herr Oberleutnant, sir," grinned "Bean-pole", hitching up his pistol belt which had slid down round his backside over the hips he hadn't got any of.

'"God have mercy on us," cried the fat man, in terror, and shifted his weight from one leg to the other.

'"I'm sure he will have," barked my general. "But you had better help yourself a little first, my good man."

'A leutnant came sailing along just then, dressed in riding breeches, slippers and a pyjama jacket with red stripes.

'"The CO requests to know what the devil's going on, and why all this shooting in the middle of the night?"

'My general stared in amazement at this strangely-clad officer.

'"Tell me now, my good man. Is this a messenger service or a Prussian infantry regiment?" and I can tell you he gave that Leutnant in slippers and pyjama jacket a goin' over it was a treat to listen to! Oh, but it *was* a lovely rocket.

'When he ran out of curses and threats he went spur-jinglin' over to an anti-tank gun that was standing, getting bored to death, in between some bushes. Without glancing either right or left, and without a thought for the consequences, he released the firing mechanism and pulled the lanyard.

'"BOOM!" thundered the 75 mm.

'"There goes auntie's rock cakes off of the plate," I thought, as the shell went screamin' off into the night, waking up all the German birds in their cosy nests. Germany is used to gettin' into wars, but it's still not all that often they fire guns off back home. The shell went through three houses in a row, causing quite a bit of rearrangement of the furniture. It finished up inside a *Panzer Spähwagen** inside the ammunition locker. Lord what a row the ammunition made goin' off. That scout car got itself spread out over half of Westphalia! Some bits went into the Rhine, and some splashed into the Weser. But what else happened was that

* *Panzer Spähwagen:* German: Scout car

the life came back into that sleepy regiment. How they did mill about. Most of 'em ran for their lives, but a few war-mad sods wanted to fight back. What a sight the German sun did see when it finally came up. It came close to goin' back down again, I can tell you! An armoured company battled bravely for two hours, an' only gave in when the house they were defending was reduced to ruins. Then they discovered, to their horror, that the enemy was their own motorcycle battalion.

'My general's alarm exercise cost 88 wounded an' 9 dead. Two committed suicide an' three were reported missing. That three caused a lot of scratching of heads, until it was realized that they just couldn't have been taken prisoner by the British, because there wasn't any British. That was something my general was just playin' there was.

'"Those men have, devil take me, deserted," growled my general. He called the MP boss to him, a big, brutal Haupt-mann with eyes that wicked the Devil himself'd have envied him 'em. "I demand, my good man," he began, looking daggers at the chief headhunter, "that deserters from the flag and shirkers be treated ruthlessly! No slightest con-sideration is to be shown to dirt like that. Out with it!"

'The dummies got caught of course. They landed up in Germersheim, where a firing squad of Pioneers shot the cowardly lives out of them.

'"Can't make an omelette without breaking eggs," said my general, satisfied, as we drove back home to breakfast.

'My general used to like that kind o' service. Make 'em shiver all over! Get a move on! That was his proper element. Nobody ever could do it as good as he could, my general.

'In the afternoon we took a look at the Engineers. They threw bridges over streams, an' then they took 'em down again. My general timed 'em on his three watches. A few eggs got broken here, too, to my general's great satisfaction. A dope of an Unteroffizier got his legs crushed. He was too heavy in the arsepart when a crane we'd pinched from the Frenchies broke up. Two other fellers got drowned, caught

184

between the pontoons. Not regulars, thank God, only compulsory service blokes. But my general got browned-off about it anyway, and had the rest of 'em, and their NCOs, crawlin' on their guts with rifles at full stretch an' noses down on the ground. They got their teeth cleaned good enough to last 'em the rest of their lives. It was a pleasure to see how he made soldiers out of that lot of monkeys. People who'd soldiered with us never, ever forgot the experience.

'When we'd worked our way through the evenin' trough – we used to call it "dinner" 'cos my general liked using stylish foreign expressions, specially English. It came of his having been on detachment with the 11th Hussars, the lot that've got "Moses in Egypt" as their regimental song – we took off our evening uniform an' pulled our white gloves down again on the glove form we had for the purpose. Then we put on our garrison uniform and went to church so's Field-Marshal God'd get what he had comin' to him in that direction. But when we got back again there was a nasty surprise waitin' for us. The staff was rushing about all over the place. They were due East every man of 'em, and the reason wasn't to station them closer to where the sun rises.

'"They're mistaken, those dressed-up dummies at Führer HQ," shouted my general. "I'll teach 'em! I give the orders here! Nobody's going to move any of my division as long as *I'm* in command!"'

'The Chief-of-Staff danced round as if he'd pissed himself and was now goin' on shittin' himself. Without saying a word he handed a nicely folded and creased letter over, signed by Adolf in person. My general's face looked like Mayday. His chin dropped right down over his Knight's Cross. The Chief-of-Staff shrugged his shoulders sadly, and stared out of the window.

'"Relieved of command," stammered my general, spelling his way through the letter again. He wouldn't believe it really said what he'd read in it.

'"Those whom the Gods will destroy they first strike with blindness," he thundered. "Now the Bohemian corporal's

185

gone too far. The dice are thrown!"

'Keitel came on the phone a bit later. He got a few home truths to pass on to "the man from Brunau".

'We'd hardly got our night uniform on before the telephone started to ring fit to break all records.

'"Must be important," said my general, straightening his regimental nightcap so the gold-embroidered bird and the cockade sat in line with his eagle nose.

'It was *General der Infanterie* Burgdorff, head of personnel, who wanted a little chat with us. In the hierarchy he was known as "the Black Eminence".

'My general's face changed colour several times, and his beaky nose turned quite cobalt blue during that "little chat".

'I was in no doubt what was goin' on. The shithouse was flaming away madly, and my general was goin' to get all the fine little delicate hairs round his arse singed off. After General Burgdorff had put down the phone we sat there for a long time, quietly, thinking things over. I could almost hear the crackin' noises comin' out of my general's skull. Whatever, it seemed to have come over him that it wasn't always very clever to go round saying out aloud what you were thinking. There's a lot of Germans've died of doing that since 1933.

'Before we marched into the land of dreams, we changed back into our light duty uniform, and we wrote letters.

'When the sun popped up to see what had happened to good old Germany in the course of the night, we'd signed the last letter, and everything was laid out straight in the middle of the blotter, which is the Prussian cavalry's way of doin' things.

'"My service pistol," said my general in a severe voice.

'I chased off after the hand artillery, wiped it off quickly with a polishing-cloth, loaded it and took off the safety catch. Then I handed it to my general.

'"Goodbye then, Unteroffizier Martin," he snarled, and extended his hand to me for the first time. "Do your duty by our beloved Fatherland! I will follow your progress!"

'"*Zu befehl*, Herr General," I replied, clicking my slippers twice. "May our honourable monocle remain unsullied!"

'Then he put the gun to his forehead, while I stood off out of the line of fire at the salute, and we shot ourselves. The *way* my general could carry it off! He was fan*tas*tic, he was. But he was also my general. Three bullets went through his field commander's cranium, and only *then* he dropped our monocle. Oh, but it was dignified. If I hadn't been a little bit stinko from tasting our cognac I think I would have cried.

'I arranged him nicely, an' put his cap on him, and, after a lot of trouble, got our monocle in place regimentally. After that I alarmed the staff.

'They came along, clicked their heels and saluted and arranged their faces in regulation folds of sadness. Even the Adjutant, the wicked sod, shook his head so sorrowfully all the *mensur* scars on his jowls wriggled like eels in jelly.

'The following days were taken up with the arrangements for my general and our monocle's funeral. We inspected the goodbye-boxes, and picked out a heavy block of a coffin in ancient German oak with a long row of iron crosses cut into it all round. I had to search half Germany for a scarlet velvet cushion to lay out my general's fruit salad on. He'd done all right in the two world wars, and hadn't been backward in coming forward in peacetime either.

'The company clerk spent five hours polishin' up our parade sabre before the Adjutant was satisfied with it. It was a hell of a fine sabre we'd got. A sword of honour from the *Leibhusaren*. I often thought about swoppin' it for a cheap Solingen steel job. Some crazy collector'd certain sure pay a pretty penny for it.

'The company's Chief Mechanic paint-sprayed my general's tin helmet, so's it could reflect back the flames from the torches.

'Two Staff Padres came from Berlin, with the Padre General in the lead. They were all glittering with phoney gold crucifixes and things to help to pilot my general up to

Valhalla. Everythin' possible was done to make it a really lovely funeral. The only thing that went wrong was the buglers. Those bloody hussars were hiding out some place or other on the Eastern Front, letting themselves get shot to bits by the neighbours, and, worst of the lot, the kettledrum nag'd gone off an' deserted to the enemy. *And* it'd taken the kettledrums with it. Well, a cavalry regimental band without kettledrums isn't worth a shit! I really hope the MPs get hold of that rotten horse some time, so they can hang it up alongside all the rest of the lousy deserters. It could, at least, have left the kettledrums behind it. They're German property. It ain't fittin', the neighbours banging away on 'em!

'Every arm was represented by a Leutnant, standing guard of honour. Six they were. They stood there, stiff as statues, round my general, who was lying there enjoying himself in the Knights' Banqueting Hall. He was in full dress uniform with all his orders. *Blaue Max**, and Iron Cross with "knife an' fork", and he was wearing fine patent leather boots with silver bar spurs. I can tell you he was the loveliest body you could ever imagine. Dressed like that, my general could fly straight up to Valhalla and start an alarm exercise going as'd make the floor of Heaven red-hot under the feet o' the angels.

'There was a hell of a row about his headgear. I wanted him to have his steel helmet on. That's why I'd had it spray-painted. But the Adjutant wanted the garrison cap with gold oak leaves an' everythin'.

'"Steel helmets are out of place with dress uniform!" he screamed, wriggling all his *mensur* scars at me.

'His chops were going like a runaway howitzer. He was that mad he could've cracked Brazil nuts with the cheeks of his arse and sucked the kernels up the wrong way. In between times he told me what he thought about me. I felt like giving him one in the kisser, but it wasn't worth it. He

---

* Pour le mérite (a high WWI order)

was a Rittmeister and could've had me in the black hole without my feet touching if I'd hung one on him.

'"May you be struck with every kind of pest we've got in this country," he hissed. "If I saw you caught in a beartrap I'd leave you there to bleed to death. I can tell you, Martin, there's a terrible fate waiting for you. As soon as the general's in the ground, off you go, straight to the Eastern Front, so fast the dust and dirt'll be spurting up in clouds from your boot-soles. And I'll find the worst, stinking unit in existence to send you to! A unit that operates behind the enemy lines in *their* uniforms, and does all the things that are forbidden by the conventions of war, might be *just* the thing. Look forward to it Martin, even your sick mind couldn't imagine what the Russians do to swine like you who hide behind their uniform!"

'"Oh I know all about what they do, Herr Rittmeister, sir. First off the neighbours' boys have a bash at your balls with a good, heavy hammer. Then they put an electric wire up your arse, so's your worms are dancin' a polka round your piles before you know it. I've had a dose of it before, sir, but I've got away with it every time so far. I would, however, like to thank the Herr Rittmeister, sir, for all his good wishes, and express the hope that we shall have a pleasant reunion in the heroes' common grave."

'He wriggled his *mensur* scars at me then like a bag of snakes. He looked for all the world like a prematurely born wild boar. Lord, what a row he did make, until the Chief-of-Staff came in and told him to shut up.

'"You'll be waking the general again if you keep on like that," he said, warningly.

'My general lay there takin' it easy, while the whole garrison came and said goodbye to him. They came from near and far, clicked their heels together, rattled their sabres and turned their sorrowing faces towards the ground. Some of 'em cried, so's we could really understand how much they'd loved my general. Lies and falsehood all of it. There wasn't one of 'em who wouldn't have been glad to see my general bubbling in his own fat in hell.

'Then one morning along came the artillery, with a great rattling gun-carriage and six black horses. Commands were shouted, sabres pointed at the ground and standards sunk. Six officers strutted stiff-legged over to my general, who was lying there looking lovely and expensive in his vampire-box.

'"Funeral procession! Slo-o-ow March!" screamed the Chief-of-Staff. An' off we went towards the garrison church.

'I went to get up in the staff-car, but there was some yokel sitting back of the wheel. I'd been relieved!

'"I'll get you for this, first chance I get!" I promised him, stupidly. He was a Feldwebel, even though he was only infantry.

'"You can crawl," said the Adjutant, "believe me you'll get used to it!"

'"Shit," I thought. "We'll meet again out East perhaps!"

'In the garrison church, fat, six-foot-tall wax candles were burning, and the infantry band was playing sorrowful march music. Goethe or Chopin it was. I don't know, but it was very sad. If it'd been me that was my general and had to go off to Valhalla, I'd have had hot rhythm and a black feller from America to howl out a solo. A blues, that's a thing you can get your teeth into an' understand. It's something that can put some gunpowder up a body's arse on its last trip!

'There was a whole mob of people in uniforms and civilian clothes dancin' a war-dance round my general's wooden uniform. There was even Navy there. A couple of crooked-eyed Japs, too. If the war hadn't been forced on us there'd have been British and Russians as well. They were all mates of my general.

'The war flag was draped over the vampire-box. On top of it was the red velvet cushion. I'd got it from an old woman in Bielefeld. It was her cat's bed. All the fruit salad lay glitterin' on it. The sword of honour and the steel helmet shone like catshit in the moonlight of a spring night. My general's horse, Magda, had also been invited to the party.'

'In *Church*?' the Old Man breaks in, in amazement.

'No, damn it. She stood outside chattin' with the six artillery horses.

'Then it started up properly. An honour guard from the Panzer Grenadiers pointed their guns at the sky and loosed off a volley at Valhalla. The signal to open up the gates, I reckon, so's there'd be plenty of room for my general when he got there. When the flags went down, off went the organ at top decibel level. It roared and groaned so that even the biggest dummy present must've understood that a general's burial was a very solemn affair.

'Then the Staff Padre spoke up. He talked about God, explained how God had always been a Prussian and that that was the reason He'd always been on our side. He got a bit mixed up and got the British God tangled up with our chap. There were some who growled a lot about that. In a world war it can be a very serious matter to go fraternizing with the other blokes' God.'

'Yes,' puts in Porta, 'where the devil'd we all be if half us German dummies lay talkin' in the night with the English God? And the Scots were prayin' to the German bloke? What a mess it'd make of a world war where that sort of thing went on!'

'The Staff Padre was getting close to high treason with all his natterin' about the English God,' Gregor goes on. 'Until the Padre General got the dope smartly away from the German God's altar. I think he's off somewhere on the East Front already, and has forgotten all about the British God.

'This Army bishop really gave my general what he deserved. I've always known we were big, but I never thought we was as big as that Padre General made us out to be.

'"May the general live in the memory of the German people as the brave and duty-loving leader in the field that he was," brayed this top sky-pilot, bangin' his fist down on the edge of the pulpit. "The general was loved by his men; they followed him through thick and thin, and died with a smile at his feet."

'I could have told him a bit different. Them *I* saw kick the bucket weren't smiling. No, they were gnashin' their teeth!

'"The most beautiful death a man can have," crowed the high-flyin' sky-pilot, "is to fall in battle for the Fatherland. The general, who is now leaving our ranks to march up and join the great army in the sky, was from his earliest cadet days a shining light for German youth, a fearless and undemanding warrior!"

'For more'n half an' hour he ranted on about beautiful, lovely death. Then the next Staff Padre came on. He was kind of a parson Hauptfeldwebel.

'"Let us all pray," he roared, in a voice that'd have blown the wings off half the Heavenly Host. "On your knees for *prayer!* Helmets *off!*"

'So we knelt down with the neckpiece of our steel helmets placed regimentally alongside the third tunic button from the top. Exactly according to Army Regulations, military church service section. A Feldwebel and two Obergefreiters got put on orders by the Adjutant for laughin' when in prayer position.

'"Amen!" thundered the padre.

'"Coffin *lift!*" the Chief-of-Staff ordered, and six Leutnants spit on their hands, hoisted the goodbye-box up on their shoulders, an' staggered off out of church.

'It was snowing. There is no doubt that the German God wanted to remind my general of wicked Russia where his first Army Corps got a couple of good beatin'-ups. The gun-carriage rolled off with my general, but it couldn't drive him all the way to the hole. The garrison churchyard was on the top of some hills, you see. Up there was all the top ten, an' a few more too, of the German leaders. Some of 'em had marshals' batons with 'em in their wooden suits. But the six horses weren't enough to pull the gun-carriage up the steep hills. Magda was the only one who could manage it. She struggled up, but only with a whole lot of puffing and panting. Now an' again she'd blow a fart, and soon the whole funeral procession stank of horse-shit. A couple of times she slid down on her haunches and covered all the pretty uniforms with slush. Bushes and weeping willows bent under the wet snow, and the steep churchyard paths were slippery. The Leutnants carrying the vampire-box had the greatest difficulty in getting up.

'"Couldn't that fucking sabre-swinging bastard have arranged to get himself buried on a sunny day?" snarled an infantry Leutnant, angrily.

'"He always was a shit, a creeping Jesus," whispered the officer behind him, a Leutnant of the motorcycle corps. "He never let us alone when he was alive, and now, even when he's dead, he keeps us at it!"

'"The bad fellow down in Hell'll make it hot for him," promised an artillery Leutnant on the other side of the coffin.

'The pock-marked marble eagles stared blankly at the procession, and the angels with Prussian profiles looked around them proudly. Here in the garrison churchyard there could be no doubt of who was somebody and who was only a coolie. The last-named had only a miserable tin or wooden cross. Some had the honour of a steel helmet perched on top of the crazy cross. A company commander had a stone pillar with an Iron Cross engraved on it, while staff officers were awarded a granite stone with the bird on it, and a short note of the places in which they had played hero for the greedy Fatherland. Generals had tons of marble on their graves and cornerpieces decorated with lions or eagles with the wickedest faces a man could imagine. But the Field-Marshals broke all records. Granite was rolled over them in huge blocks, with batons chiselled out of marble and piled on top of a giant Iron Cross. What a trip we did have up that cemetery hill! Snow slashed across our faces, and melted snow trickled down our uniform collars, and played Ice Age games down our spines.

'On the first stop in the side of the hill I suddenly remembered that my general had ordered me to sing before they let him down into the hole. To get into the right frame of mind I took a couple of good swigs of some *Slivovitz* I'd brought along in a hip-flask.

'An Oberst from Führer HQ fell on his bum and slid back down the hill. When he finally got back on his feet again and had untangled his spurs, he got his sabre caught between his legs and went down again.

'I was walking a long way back in the procession. The Adjutant had ordered that. He said the higher officers would suffer from shortage of breath if they had to breathe the same air as me. On the seventh swig of *Slivovitz*, a belch a bit *too* loud came back. An Oberstleutnant turned round and looked at me in surprise. It was one of these Staff shits with red stripes down his pants. He said somethin' or other to a shaky old Major-general who was tip-toein' along as if his boots were full of shit. Now they both stared at me, with court-martials in their eyes. But by the time they'd got the paper in the machine an' started to dictate I'd have been a long time back in Russia, and who the hell can find *anybody* in Russia.

'The civvy top hats had all put up their umbrellas. God, how it did snow! My general and our monocle had certainly picked an ugly day for the last sleigh-ride. Under the snow-laden birches some leather-coated chaps in trilby hats were slinkin' about, lookin' as if they didn't belong. A blind loony could've seen they were keeping an eye on things. Even my general's Mazda could see that "the Devil and the Gestapo were listenin'". Nobody said a word so long as the melancholy birches and the leather-coats were still in sight. A smell of corpses hung around us long after we'd passed 'em.

'Part way up the steep path, where we could see the birches from above and only just catch a glimpse of the leather-coats, a high-born lady in black and wearin' a veil, fell on her arse. She went all the way down like a bobsleigh out after a new world record, and straight in under the birches where the leather-coats were waiting, just longin' to make an arrest. The black-clothed lady with the veil didn't

194

come back to the procession any more. When we staggered past the war memorial for 1870–71, I happened to give another belch. It was quite painful, really. I should never've ate *Eisbein mit Sauerkraut* before going on the Valhalla march.

'It was when we started up a very narrow path, more like a sort of staircase, made of logs and slippery as all hell, things really began to go wrong. A cavalry Leutnant amongst the bearers got into trouble with his spurs, and let out a screech. Then he went down, with the result than an engineer Leutnant doin' the dead march just behind him went on his arse too. The whole procession halted wondering what was going to happen next, and I can tell you a lot *did* happen, an' in a hell of a quick time. The bearer officers tried desperately to hang on to the wooden box, but it got away from 'em and off it went thunderin' down the path with the six Leutnants after it.

'"Stop him! Stop him!" they were all shoutin'. You'd have thought my general was a shoplifter spurtin' off with his loot out of a supermarket.

'A Lieutenant-general, a mummy from 1914, who was standin' there rubbin' his toothless gums together, got knocked over. He gave out a shrill howl, as if the whole of Verdun, and the Siegfried Line after it, had been dropped on top of him. His *pickelhauber* went up in the air, and was never seen again. It probably ended up danglin' by the point from St Peter's backside. The prehistoric sabre with its silk tassels flew off to one side as the general-box steamrollered over the uniformed mummy. The whole procession, with veils and top-hats and dress swords under their arms, went running off at top speed in front of my late general, to avoid getting their bones broken by the coffin coming rushing down from the heights. Magda was in the lead, spooked to death by the runaway coffin. Right to the end my general showed everybody he was a tanks officer who fully realized the value of a surprise attack. It was only when he got over on the other side of the tree-lined alley that he dropped down through the gears. It was lucky the gate with the helmets on the pillars was open, or God knows what mightn't have happened.

'Down there the devil got into the six black artillery horses, who had been standin' thinking over what Magda had told 'em about my general. Off they went with the gun-carriage, and the two postillions who were sitting slumped half-asleep on the backs of the two lead-horses went flyin' off into the ditch. Where the hell the six blacks and the gun-carriage wound up I've no idea, but they made a nice thunderin' noise away in the distance.

'The Padre General and the Staff Padres sent up a quiet prayer, while the Adjutant wobbled his *mensur* scars, and the Chief-of-Staff talked to the bearer officers in a manner which left them in no doubt that they were on their way to a front-line battalion. It isn't *done* to throw a general around, on his way to the hero's table in Valhalla, like *that*!

'"They were holdin' that wooden jacket like a nun holdin' a seaman's," I said to an infantry Feldwebel, who was standing there alongside me chuckling with laughter.

'The Adjutant gave us a shellackin' and promised us we'd get to know him. A reserve bearer from tanks took the place of the artillery nance. He'd broke his foot, and was still lyin' up there in a privet hedge groaning.

'"Coffin, *lift*!" commanded the Chief-of-Staff. "Funeral *party*! Slo-o-ow *march*!" And off the procession started again with the regulation sad faces in place. The drummers from the Infantry Band rattled out that thing "*Argonner Wald um Mitternacht*"*. You could literally hear all the chalky military skeletons rattlin' to attention in their graves!

'Even in death my general showed his sense of style. He'd planned the whole burial himself, and it was certainly a funeral that'd be remembered. I've only heard of one that was better. That was an admiral's funeral where a bridge broke in two and the whole procession, box, sailors an' all,

---

* *Argonner Wald um Mitternacht:* The Argonne Forest at Midnight

fell into the Kiel Canal. Fifteen of 'em drowned an' the admiral sailed off out into Kiel Bay. There he run into a surfacin' submarine. The sub's crew was that frightened they fired on the admiral, thinking he was some new kind of secret weapon they'd collided with. The admiral went down with his coffin.

'"Call this a funeral?" groused the Divisional Chief Clerk, an overweight Staff Feldwebel. "It's more like a battle course with all the trimmings!"

'The procession had thought that my general would have selected a grave plot on the first hill, but they were wrong. After a short rest and an inspection of a view of snow-covered misery we struggled down the first hill, and up the next. Two of the mummy warriors had strokes on the way.

'The Pioneers from the *Landesschützen* stood to attention with shouldered spades and drawn faces. The hole they'd dug for my general was enormous. A special detachment had decorated the grave with oak branches and flowers in the national colours. The wreaths were enormous too; the biggest of them from *Grofaz*. The red scarf on it said: "The Führer thanks you!" It seemed a bit funny somehow, when you think it was the Führer that'd sent him suicidin' off to Valhalla by his own hand.

'The funeral procession ordered off according to regulations. Top hats to the left, and uniforms to the right.

'Up came the Padre General again. He waved his fingers at us, and made a kind of a salute. Then he ranged a firm, both military and religious eye, in on the dark clouds.

'"Our God in the highest," he began, folding his thievin' fingers on the hilt of the sabre, "receive this . . ." He didn't get any further. By then he'd begun to slide down into my general's hole.

'The Orderly Officer, a creeping Jesus, who we suspected of bein' a brownie, tried to stop the servant of God. Instead the perfumed officer went down into the hole with him. "Bang!" went the oak coffin. My general probably thought the artillery was usin' him to sight in on.

'The Pioneer soldiers began to laugh, but their laughter died away quick when the Adjutant booked the lot of 'em for front-line service.

'"So long mate!" I whispered to the bloke standin' nearest me. "You've lived most of your life! Enjoy what you've got left of it!"

'He whined a bit, and said it was all a load of shit. I wouldn't deny it.

'The Padre General'd got his balance again, and the Orderly Officer had been fished up. So the bishop started off on his sermon again. My general had been a very great soldier, he said. An example to us all. He had always been ready to pile up a heap of bodies on the altar of the Fatherland, and the bullet-riddled heroes were all waiting to receive their great leader at the gates of Valhalla. "I bet they've got their hands full of some hefty clubs, ready to welcome him with," I thought, kindly. But, of course, I didn't say it out loud.

'"This German warrior," bawled the Padre General, sanctimoniously, in a voice which frightened all the church-yard pigeons to flight, "was a truly believing person, who followed the words of the Gospel. He was an officer of the Kaiser as he was of the Führer! Oh, Jesus Christ!" he went jabbering on, saluting, "here we bring to You a soldier, a man of steel, who without thought of self carried out the heavy orders which were laid upon him by the Supreme Warlord. Oh God, receive him as the hero that he is!"

'All the generals nodded in satisfaction. The Chief-of-Staff rattled his sabre applaudingly, and the Adjutant showed all his teeth in a grin, and ordered his *mensur* scars by the right.

'The God of the Germans'll open his peepers all right when he meets my general, I thought. It won't be long before the whole of Paradise is made over into a tank manoeuvre area with all the trimmin's. God and His Son'll be hauling targets an' acting as markers; St Peter'll be on the cardboard clock and St Paul keeping check of the ammo, so's none of the angels get away with a couple of live 'uns. Well, anyway, now I know how I'll be spending my time in the Heavenly Halls!'

'How?' asks the Old Man, without understanding.

'It's obvious,' grins Gregor. 'I'll be my general's chauffeur again, of course, and get promoted to Feldwebel, soon as I kick it. I pinched the Divisional flag by the way, before I took off for the front. My general'll be really glad when I turn up with it as a dead 'un. I'm sure he'll forgive me, even, for once having washed an' ironed it.

'"On your knees in prayer," commanded the Padre General, and off we went praying, the lot of us. The Adjutant still managed to catch a couple of the bicycle fellers who weren't prayin'. They were amusing themselves talking about a game the Finns play called "the grenade game". A lot of Finns stand round in a ring and one of them pulls the pin of a grenade. Then they throw it from hand to hand. The bloke whose hand it explodes in has lost. It's a most exciting game, but you have to be a Finn to really get bit by it.

'With a lot of sweating and whispered cursing the Pioneers had managed to get the coffin up out of the hole again, so it could be let down properly with whirling drums and ranting bugles. Ta-ta-ta-ta! But there was no luck being handed out that day. The bugles were frozen stiff and all that came out of them was some hoarse noises, like owls make. They frightened the cemetery crows nearly to death.

'The Chief-of-Staff whispered something viciously, and the poor musicians got orders to swop their bugles with hand-grenades an' rifles. Off to the front for them, too!

'Well, they finally got hold of some warm bugles, that could be played on, and down went my general into the cold ground to the tune of "*Alte Kameraden*"*. Everything looked as if it was going all right, until some dope of an infantry Leutnant wanted to rub his hands together because the rope was chafing him.

---

* *Alte Kameraden:* Old Comrades

'BANG! came the hollow sound, and the box tipped up on its end down in the hole. The worst part was that the end came unjointed, and there was my general's pale face starin' up at us complainingly out of the bust-up coffin. The most amazing thing was our monocle, that it still remained in his eye. It must have been good glue I'd used.

'Some of the top-hat and black veil brigade crossed themselves, and the Padre General gave the Staff Padres a rollockin' as if it was their fault the coffin'd broken up.

'Down the Pioneers had to go into the hole again to get my general out, while the coffin was repaired. We laid him out on top of a granite memorial of some place or other where German blood had been poured out in rivers.

'Three carpenters from the Engineers under the command of a Field Works Supervisor came dashing up in a *Kübel*. They splashed out slush all over the *pickelhaubers*, the polished tin-hats and the silk cylinders. First the supervisor had to make a drawing. This was done all very shipshape and to scale, while the procession stood around dancin' up and down on their freezing toes. Most of 'em had lost their burial faces by now, and just looked thoroughly brownedoff. Still it was a funeral nobody who took part'd ever forget.

'I laid a blanket over my general. He looked that cold lyin' there on the granite slab in dress uniform without a cape. I saluted him. Our monocle glittered and it was as if I felt a heavy blow on the top of my head. It must have been my dead general giving me an order.

'Finally the supervisor was finished making his plan, and the carpenters could get on with the repairs to the good-bye-box.

'While the infantry musicians rattled away on their drums they piloted my general back into his last quarters, and suddenly I realized what it was that was annoying him. I'd forgotten to *sing*! Oh, Hell! I thought and off I went to the head of the oak coffin where they'd placed the sword of honour and the cushion with the medals back in position again. And then I started off, and sang all five verses about

Death rushin' off on his black steed. It raised quite a bit of a commotion. Yes, even the leather-coated lot slunk a bit nearer. Everybody stared. The tin hats, the *pickelhaubers*, the black veils an' the silk toppers. I reckon they thought I'd gone off my head, but to be perfectly honest I don't think I sang it too badly, even though it had to go through a cloud of *Slivovitz*, and I may have swayed on my feet a bit now and then.

'The Adjutant and his *mensur* scars were standing there ready to jump on me, but I got through the five verses all right. When I'd got through 'em I managed to wait with the next swig of *Slivovitz* till I'd saluted and reported to the open coffin.

'"Orders executed, Herr General, *sir*!"

'Then I did a half turn in proper regimental fashion, and saluted the Adjutant and all his scars.

'"God's Peace!" I said.

'You should've seen his expression. His scars wriggled like a load of eels. Just for a minute I thought he was goin' to cut me down with his dress sword.

'Then I sneaked off, back of a privet hedge, and took a gulp of *Slivovitz*, to get me back to normal.

'My song caused a bit of a commotion in the big funeral procession.

'I could clearly hear they were talking about me. There was no doubt I'd gone into first place, with my solo song.

'"Shovels *up*!" the Chief-of-Staff commanded, but before the Pioneers could start shovelling a G-Staff Oberst went over and whispered in his ear.

'"Stop!" shouted the Chief-of-Staff. The Pioneers dropped their shovels as if they had become red-hot. The *salut d'honneur* had been forgotten, and up my general had got to come again out of his hole.

'After a bit everything was ready again, with the exception of the soldiers to fire off the salute. They'd gone off home in the meantime. An orderly doubled off to the grenadier barracks, and after a long, cold waiting period up comes a squad under the command of a Leutnant.

'There were a couple more minor accidents. A Gefreiter fell down into the grave, and his rifle went off and wounded a veiled lady. He got sent to the front too. Finally a volley went off with a bang, and down went my general into the hole. The Pioneers started shovellin' dirt, and it rattled down on to the lid of my general's coffin.

'I bet my general's thinking he's getting fired on by the enemy, I thought.

'"Almighty Father! Eternal German God!" sobbed the Staff Padres, "We Germans are yours for ever and ever. Amen!"

'And at last it was all over. The procession sloshed back through the wet snow. They left their funeral expressions behind them. All they were thinking of was hot coffee, fresh pastry and a drink to wash away all that sorrow.

'Some of 'em went on their arses on the way down the slippery path, but nobody noticed that but the ones it happened to. The funeral service was over. The leather-coated lot mixed in with the procession to pick up any loose talk that might help the enemy. They didn't want to get back to *Admiral Schröder Strasse* without somethin' to report.

'I saluted a German hedgehog that was sneaking over a couple of graves. "God's Peace," I said.

'Lord, how it did snow, and now it started to blow up too. I got a lift from the Field Works lot. Nobody on the staff'd have me along. I was a pariah!

'Down at the mouth, I went in to "The Red Duck", to wet my singin' organ again, and while I was having a highly treacherous talk to the landlord I suddenly realized my general had disappeared out of my life altogether. Everything was over between us. Never again would he give me a rollockin' for washing and ironing the flag, or whatever it was I'd been up to between our trips in the staff-car.

'The very next day I got my movement orders. The Adjutant came and handed them to me personally.

'"See you again, Unteroffizier Martin," he barked,

hypocritically, as I crawled up on the lorry to the other candidates for death who'd made a balls of it at my general's funeral.'

'Lord save us,' sighs the Old Man, 'there's not all that ceremony when one of us lot kicks the bucket for the highly beloved Fatherland!'

Letters arrive, and we forget the general's funeral. There are three letters for the Old Man. His wife, Liselotte, has been promoted to Chief Tram-Driver. It's a safer job during the air-raids, since there are more shelters close by. When you're an ordinary tram-driver you're not always close to a shelter when the bombs start falling. All this talk about alarms going off in good time is nothing but propaganda. Usually the sirens do not start to howl until the bombs begin to fall, and the way they bomb now there is not much chance of reaching a shelter alive. Earlier they just dropped their bombs anywhere. Nowadays they pick out an area and flatten it to the ground. Even the rats get wiped out.

Heide is astonished to find that there is also a letter for him.

'Heil Hitler,' he mumbles, reverently, when he realizes it is from the Gauleiter of the Rhineland himself. He holds it up for us to see the over-dimensioned shiny party eagle. With the reverence of a Pope leafing through the Bible, he opens the envelope.

'At last! At last!' he is jubilant. 'They've given me the Black Eagle! And about time, too!'

'Black Eagle?' asks Porta. 'Where the devil we goin' to keep an eagle?'

'Idiot!' snarls Heide. 'It's a Party Order, one of the highest, too.' He holds up the document triumphantly in front of Porta's nose. 'What d'you say to that? Like one, wouldn't you?'

'No, thank you very kindly,' says Porta. 'It could cost me a snapped neck when the neighbours turn up an' Adolf and his party's part of the past!'

'I'm warning you,' hisses Heide, like an angry cat which

has had its tail trodden on. 'With this order I'm letting nothing pass! Anybody who insults the party goes on report!'

'The salad come with it?' asks Tiny, leaning forward inquisitively.

'No, that'll be along through regiment,' answers Heide, proudly. 'The CO'll decorate me with it personally!'

'I've heard they're hard at work, stamping 'em out day and night,' grins Porta. '25 marks for 100 kgs, an' the Gauleiters can shove 'em out in bucketfuls.'

'Obergefrieter Creutzfeldt!' shouts the clerk, throwing a letter over to Tiny. 'Gawd struth!' cries Tiny, holding the letter as if it was a grenade with the pin out, and sniffing at it cautiously. 'Who in the name of 'Ell'd be crazy enough to write to *me*?'

'You'll find out easy enough if you open it,' laughs Porta.

With a thick, dirty finger and tears the envelope open clumsily, and unfolds the greasy bundle of writing-paper inside it. For some time he sits staring at the pencilled scrawl on the cheap paper.

''Ere, you read it for me, will you?' he asks, handing it to the Old Man. 'My eyes aren't all that good today. All the shit there is in the air in this Commie country ruins a man's eyesight.'

The Old Man packs his silver-lidded pipe phlegmatically, and lets his eyes run along the closely-written lines. He shakes his head. 'What a family you *have* got!'

'Who's it from?' asks Tiny, staring at the letter.

'Your sister,' answers the Old Man, beginning to read aloud:

Obergefreiter loader Wolfgang Ewald Creutzfeldt
FPO no 23645
The German Defence Forces
Russia.

Dear Brother,

You mustnt think I like you because I start my letter with Dear and Brother. You are a drunk-Wolfgang – everybody says so. I am writing this to let you know you have no reason to go round happily thinking your youngest sister Emilie Louise Bock-Creutzfeldt as used to be – has been killed dead by some of the stuff the English and the other *untermensch* lot are dropping on Hamburg just now.

Mom's still alive too. You can bet your boots on it but she dont know you any more and I wasnt to send you none of her love. I know how hard it is for you to read letters. So Im writing this one very slowly sos you wont get confused when you read it. Im looking forward to it coming back sos Ill know your dead.

Your a rotten dirty pig thats what you are. Everybody here says the fightings hot in Russia and theyve all had somebody in the family shot. Mom was dead certain youd got blowed up too by one of them shells they shoot all over the place out there. But as usual you do us in the eye. We have not forgot the time you pinched all the money out of the gas meter and the coppers came from Davids Station along with the gas collector and were going to arrest Mom.

We was very disappointed I can tell you when the NSFO as has moved in to the old cloth museum back of the Main Railway Station you know it that big grey place with the old Kaisers eagles on it where you and David pinched the curtains when we wanted to do the place up a bit – when he told us you had not come to any harm in the war. Mom collapsed with disappointment when she heard and she cried an awful lot too. Shed been working out what her pension would be after you. The NSFO comforted her and said he was sure youd soon get yourself shot and he gave her an extra butter ration and some bread coupons.

I am sorry to have to write this letter me being your sister and all to tell you your a no-good that nobody really ought to write to at all. If you ever come to Hamburg again and ride the U to Altona – as I hope you never do do – you wouldnt never know our place again. Were moved out to Langenhorn on the other side of the SS barracks. Theres always a lot going on there. If we look out the windows early in the morning we can see them shooting traitors and such-like to death. When there aint any traitors to shoot they practise at cardboard figures so we dont need an alarm clock any more which is a lucky thing because our old one has stopped going. They begin shooting at five every morning and thats our time for getting up.

I am still cleaning on the trains and getting a free ride while Im cleaning. I have been made a State Railway Cleaning Assistant second class and have blue braid on my shoulder. I am allowed to eat with the five that work in the post waggon now.

I was in Dusseldorff last week. I had it off with a Supply Corps bloke as give me 20 marks to do it with him. We went into the toilet in the first class. You wouldnt believe how posh they are. Herbert Bock my husband and your brother-in-law – though I have to tell you from him that he wont have it your being his brother-in-law – so remember that. Theres that many blots in your copybook that nice people wont belong in the same family as you. Well anyway my husband Herbert Bock has got a new job with a uniform and two stars on his collar and a navy blue hat with a cockade on it and a lot of people under him. Hes looking after a churchyard. There is not a lot to do even though he is the only one there. All the people he used to work with have been called up and have gone off to help win the war.

Do you remember Limpy Egon? It was him you and the fur Jews son David was always with when you were on the streets doing unlegal things. Hed got a new job at the Hansa Breweries and then he died. Drank himself to death they called it. He got dizzy looking down into one of them big beer vats and fell into it. But he couldnt never keep away from the drink. They do say the beer tastes better since Limpy fell down into it.

You havent ever in all your life seen as much rain as weve been having in Hamburg for the last nine weeks and three days and all the accidents that have happened. Here they are then. The Elbe went up over the red line and thats you and your mates fault. We have got no lifeboats. You took them all with you to Russia. It isnt right you taking everything off to Russia with you and us having to do without at home. Were Germans too you know and just as good as you soldiers. The Führer keeps on saying were a *Herrenvolk*. Up you Jack. I reckon Germanys the arsehole of the universe and theres a lot more as says the same. To be honest with you Wolfgang you ought to get up and show theres some good in you. Tell your mates to stop this stupid war. You can do it if you want to. The parson said you could. You know him, the bloke that goes knocking on doors with the word. I can't remember what hes called. Something foreign but who cares anyhow. Stadthausbrucke 8 picked him up so we wont be seeing or hearing his Bible words no more. But it was barmy of him to be a traitor. The Führer dont like that kind of thing.

The other day me and Emma found one of them secret papers the ones your not supposed to read but we read it anyway. A persons only human after all. It said in it that the German soldiers ought to just go over and make pals with the Russians and the whole world war would be over. Remember now to tell your mates about it. But dont let nobody from the party hear you saying it. Now the secret paper dont come any more. Them who was writing it have got picked up by Stadthausbrucke too.

They got their legs broke before they got shot. It must hurt a lot to get your legs broke. Do you remember when I broke my little finger? It did hurt and it must be a lot worse to break a whole leg. You have to watch your tongue here if you dont want your legs broke and your head cut off after. Im going to be careful to say Heil Hitler to everybody. Then they cant say I aint faithful.

Things are happening all the time here in Hamburg and so we dont have to worry about what to do to pass the time with. Last night we had five warnings and the Martens that live in Altona got a bomb right in the middle of their bed. Lucky for them it was cause the Gestapo turned up an hour later to pinch them. They were very annoyed that there wasnt nobody to pinch. Them English ought to have been a bit more careful.

Our sister Eva says too its better to get killed than picked up alive by the Gestapo and our sister knows what shes on about. Shes gone up in the world she has and has got a job wiping the dust off the desks at Stadthausbrücke 8 where she sees things your not supposed to. She saw a bloke being interviewed they call it the other day. First they broke all his fingers then they pulled the nails off his toes. Then they whipped him with steel wire and put electric current through him that he had to pay for himself. They put everything on the bill says Eva so it must cost a bit to get arrested. Then this bloke fell out of the window from the fourth floor. He must have come down head first cause it was all bashed out of shape and nearly crushed. He got to pay for the window he broke too.

Our sister Trudy – you know her that was born in the milk shop – shes had a nipper but she cant remember whose it is. She never said if it was a boy or a girl so I cant tell you if your an aunt or an uncle.

The Baumüllers over in Altona have had a wedding. We went to it and never sobered up til after Easter. It was their lodger Long Hans that got married but the Gestapo came for him and they say hes dead now. His name was on the red posters they stick up all over the place when somebody gets his head chopped off at Fuhlsbüttel. It was the funniest party I ever went to. Long Hans never got married but he had a lovely *Polterabend*. Hed have been happy about it still if he hadnt got his head chopped off in the meantime. We all went off on bikes to the Louise on the Reeperbahn. Us girls sat on the crossbars cause there wasnt enough bikes to go round. There was two that got run over by a tram. They got killed. Then there was one that fell down a cellar stairs on his bike. He got killed too. His bike was ruined but lucky for him it was one he had pinched. One of them got himself caught in the door of the elevator to the Elbe tunnel. He wasnt really with us just a gate-crasher he was. But he was lucky. He was going that fast he went straight into the Elbe elevator. His bike hadnt got no brakes on it. If hed stopped a No 1 tram that was coming rushing down the hill from Fischmarkt would have killed him stone dead.

We was over at The Louise about seven. I know Ive got the time right cause my gent had his wristwatch on and said it was seven and it was a good watch as had once belonged to a Jew.

Us ladies got champagne and cherry wine. I drunk a whole bottle and got that happy I forgot about Wolfgang and all my other sorrows. The gents drunk Bummelunder* and beer from the time they come in the door til the coppers turned up from David Station.

Jensen from Hansa Platz 7 got into a row with the bridegroom. They pulled their knives and the bridegroom cut Jensens nose off. How he did bleed but we were that happy we didnt care. Then Jensen cut the bridegrooms hair off and he bled even more.

Then we had a bit of a dance and had some more champagne and cherry wine. Then the knives come out

* Bummelunder: South Jutland schnapps

again. Emmy her with the glass eye got her ears cut off. It didnt suit her a bit. The bridegroom went right off his nut after hed drunk a whole bottle of Bummelunder with beer in it. He lost his mind altogether and started swinging a long knife round over his head. Hes some kind of a foreigner from Austria. You must excuse me but if I was to meet the Führer Id ask him if he couldnt keep all these foreigners out of the country. They do nothing but make trouble. But we probably wont ever meet. People who get up on top of the tree dont remember where they came from.

Then the bulls come running from the David. Theyd got helmets on with straps under their chins so we couldnt knock them off. What a row there was. There was no windows left in The Louise after cause a lot of the coppers and guests left that way and all the chairs was broken cause of people sitting down too hard on them. Then they started throwing the tables at the tecs but the Flying Squad turned up and put a stop to the party. The kitchen was all smashed up and there was never a pot or pan left without a dent in it. So then they arrested us and took us all over to David and there we sung that loud they could hear us down at Landungsbrücke and people come running down to see what was going on. There *was* a crowd.

Detective-inspector Nass called us all sorts of things and nearly went crazy. Outside the whole Reeperbahn was singing and inside the wedding party was singing but nobody was singing the same song. If you dont all shut up soon Im finished with you lot shouted Detective-inspector Nass. Then they took us in in groups and questioned us.

You got no nose said Mr Nass to Mr Jensen. The man who cut that off must be punished. Thats been seen to inspector said Mr Jensen. It was that Austrian bridegroom but its all fixed up. Ive got his prick in my pocket.

Well later on the whole wedding party met in the jail. It wasnt too bad. They still have single cells but nobodys in them on their own. The prisons are that full up there aint hardly room for the warders. We got *ersatz* coffee with powdered milk and some army bread. Two slices apiece with a spoonful of turnip jam. There was a lot there could tell about things you never heard of usual. Well we got out again but not all of us. I dont know where them as didnt get out went to but nobodys heard of them since. Everybody at home sends their good wishes and Mom says your to do something brave for the Führer and the Fatherland. If you get a big medal your pension will be bigger when you get shot. You could at the least do that much for Mom and dont forget your not part of my husbands family.

> Goodbye for now
> Your sister
> Emilia Louise Bock born Creutzfeldt
> State Railways Cleaning Assistant
> Hamburg/Altona

'That brother-in-law as is married to my sister Emilie an' won't be related to me can just wait till I get 'ome,' growls Tiny viciously. ''E'd do well to count 'is bones, so's 'e'll know which of 'em's missin' afterwards!'

We have only been asleep a short while when the company orderly comes rushing in to tell the Old Man he's to report to the OC immediately.

'Heavenly posting for you,' he grins, maliciously. 'This time you're going to get your backsides burnt proper. The order's from right up top, and it got TOP SECRET stamped all over it, back and sides.'

'What the devil's up now?' growls the Old Man sourly, pulling on his ankle-length winter cloak, and swinging his machine-pistol over his shoulder.

'Clear as mud,' grins Porta, scratching at his pigeon breast with both hands. That's where the lice have a tendency to hold their get-togethers. 'It's Sally at the War

Ministry who's pushing all the buttons needed to get us off on our private gold-prospecting mission. Put your warm woollens on, my boys! It's goin' to get very cold, cold as all Hell, before we get home again with our gold.'

'Here goes the curtain for the first act,' says the Old Man, when he comes back. 'The official order says we're to cause disturbance and create panic behind the enemy lines, and we're to bring a General Skulowsky back with us, whoever the guy is!'

'Create panic! We'll do that all right,' says Porta, laughing shortly. 'But who the devil's this General Stink-anovitch? We can ask our way, anyhow. Maybe my bint's feller knows him!'

'And remember. All this stuff's TOP SECRET,' the Old Man goes on. 'Our heads an' necks both are on the line if anything leaks out! We're not even to talk about it amongst ourselves. "War Minister" Sally must've used up all the ink in the ministry stampin' TOP SECRET on everything. Field-Marshal Keitel's name's on the bottom of the order, only he don't know it, and the plan's been made by Field-Marshal Walter Model, who doesn't know anything about it either.'

'*Cojones*! They'll shoot us three times over if they ever find out,' sighs Barcelona, nervously. 'But they do say the cheekier you are the better things go for you!'

'If this goes the way we want it, I'm goin' to buy a big medal for Sally,' roars Tiny, slapping himself happily on the thighs.

In the course of the night we were issued with Russian uniforms, and the tanks painted with red stars and cyrillic lettering.

'If Ivan Stinkanovitch gets his claws into us, we'll have had the most of our lives already,' says Barcelona, gloomily.

It is snowing heavily, and visibility is no more than a couple of yards, when we load the tanks on to runners. Horses are to draw them through the Russian lines to avoid the rattle of tracks and the noise of the motors.

Snarling MPs keep everybody away from the secret transport.

'Miserable way to go,' sighs Porta, watching a couple of MPs drag off a civilian who has been a little too inquisitive.

It is only when we have got a good way over on the far side of the river that we remove the German transfers and the Russian signs come into view. DEATH TO THE FASCISTS is written in large cyrillic letters on the Panther's turret.

'*Job Tvojemadj*,' grunts Tiny, sticking out his chest like a second Ivan the Terrible.

'Watch out now. NO Commie fists!' the Old Man warns them. 'Here they salute just like we do. They're very touchy about that in the Red Army. It's only civilians who clench their fists and shout Red Front!'

*Wir waren einfach, weil das Volk einfach ist.
Wir dachten primitiv, weil das Volk primitiv
denkt. Wir waren agressiv, weil das Volk radikal
ist.*

Joseph Goebbels

He opened the breech, threaded in a new belt of cartridges, and smacked the cover back on.

'Bloody shit,' he said. 'Can you hear 'em.'

'Tanks,' answered his no 2. 'You got any bread? I'm hungry as hell. Haven't had a bite for the last two days. Bloody, rotten war!'

'Ate the last I had this morning,' replied the machine-gunner, 'and that was a bit I found on a body!'

'We're not even worth a crumb of bread,' growled the no 2. 'They chase us like we were rats. Tell us to hold out! What for? So's those shits can save their own lives!'

'Shit the lot of it' said the machine-gunner, staring at the rows of ruins. 'Now they don't even give us grub any more. We have to steal it where we can find it. It's a wonder we got a bit of ammo dished out this morning!'

'That's the way it always goes,' answered the no 2, pulling his coat collar up round his ears. 'Ammunition they can give us, but food's quite another thing!'

'What do you say we knock off for good? Now! Change FPOs! Ivan can't be as bad as they say. Anyway it can't be worse over there than it is here!'

They both got to their feet, threw their MG into a stream, and went crouching forward slowly across the stubbled field.

An MG snarled in short bursts.

The no 2 was hit first. Then the machine-gunner was thrown across the wreck of a vehicle. A flock of crows flew up from the ruins, cawing harshly.

---

* *We remain simple, while the people remains simple. Our thinking is primitive, when the people's thinking is primitive. We become aggressive, when the people become radical.*

MEETING WITH THE COMMISSARS

The wind howls miserably through the stretched-out ruins of what has been, not long ago, a whole new *kolchos**. Now it is an untidy heap of collapsed walls and grotesquely bent steel girders. The frozen, half-burned bodies of its animal stock lie scattered about. War in all its wild ferocity has swept over the *kolchos*, and razed it to the ground with one satanic breath.

Three soot-blackened T-34s stand in the flattened orchard. Icicles cover them. Their crews are hanging half out of the hatches, blackened and burnt.

The Old Man is first out of the section personnel carrier. He looks about him, carefully. It is dangerous to feel oneself to be safe. Death lurks everywhere.

'Drive the waggon well in under the trees,' he orders Porta, who has his foxy, freckled face up out of the hatchway, sniffing the air.

'Jesus, but it's *cold*!' he says, his teeth chattering. He blows warm breath up along the sides of his face. 'It's colder than a polar bear's arse!'

The snow squeaks under the Old Man's boots, as he goes teetering up the icy path. He pulls the fur collar of his coat up around his ears, and turns his back to the biting wind, which tears at the stiff material of his camouflage jacket. He has a couple of stick-grenades in the tops of his boots, but this is no cause for suspicion. Russian front-line troops like to get hold of German stick-grenades. They throw better, even though the absence of a safety attachment

---

* Russian collective farm

makes them more dangerous. Once the cord has been pulled there is no way back. You've got just seven seconds left before it goes off, whether you like it or not.

The Old Man stops at the edge of a steep cliff and tugs the broad yellow leather belt with the long *Nagan* holster into place, irritably.

'Oh, how bloody *cold* it is,' whines Porta, banging his blue hands together. 'I'm glad I'm not a Russian and have to live here all my life.'

'Get the map out,' orders the Old Man. 'This has to be the rendezvous. The white *kolchos* has got to be those ruins, though there's not much white about 'em any more!'

'Who the hell *did* do that?' asks Porta, wonderingly. 'The war hasn't got to these parts yet! The enemy's a long way off! We're the first Germans here, and we're not the real enemy. We're just here to pick up something which legally belongs to us!'

'Flying bombs, I guess,' says the Old Man. He puts the heavy artillery glasses to his eyes. Silently he stares up at the long winding mountain road, which disappears in mist and driving snow high up amongst the storm-bent trees.

'Want us to put the tea-waggon in under cover?' shouts Tiny. His voice echoes in the ruins and rings back a hundred fold from the mountains.

'Shut it!' shouts the Old Man, nervously. 'They'll be able to hear you in Moscow!'

'Yes, but listen 'ere,' shouts Tiny, even louder. 'If we let this fartin'-box stand 'ere puttin' down roots d'you think Ivan Stinkanovitch will believe we're some of his mates?'

'Leave it there,' snarls the Old Man, irritably. 'But hide everything else and camouflage it. *Thoroughly*!'

Heide swaggers around importantly in the uniform of a Russian lieutenant, but despite the uniform nobody can have the least doubt that he is a German. He is far too correct. No Russian in his senses would think of going around looking like him. He has even cut away the long hairs in the grey-brown fur of his cap so that the large red star with its gold edges can be seen to greater effect.

'Get a sight of Ivan?' asks Porta, rubbing the snow from his eyes.

'Shut it, for God's sake,' snarls the Old Man sourly, polishing the lenses of the artillery glasses before again putting them to his eyes.

'There's a three-axled truck up there with a 76 on the back of it. There's something wrong with this set-up. It smells like a trap!'

'They wouldn't bloody be bothered,' says Porta, indifferently. 'Who in the world'd want to trap shits like us?'

'You never know with Ivan,' mumbles the Old Man, thoughtfully, continuing to stare intently through the glasses. 'Those devils don't think the way we do. They're an unaccountable lot of sods!'

'Give me that!' says Porta, tearing the glasses out of his hand. 'What the hell's the matter with you, letting an old Ford truck scare the shit out of you?'

'I know that gun,' answers the Old Man pessimistically. 'It's got a muzzle velocity like all get-out, and its shells can penetrate any armour in the world.'

'Weep on my shoulder,' suggests Porta. 'An explosive shell from our new 75 mm an' that peashooter can stick its muzzle up Stalin's arsehole, velocity an' all, and shit the casings out in granny's apron.'

'When we gonna start creatin' confusion?' asks Tiny impatiently, throwing a lump of ice over the edge of the cliff.

'What do you think we *are* doing?' answers Porta. 'You're screaming loud enough to give 'em earache in the Kremlin! And stop talking German in the neighbours' backyard, will you! It's dangerous!'

'Go shit! Everybody talks what 'e's born to,' snarls Tiny. 'I can't talk foreign!'

'Got us out here on a wild-goose chase again have you?' says Heide, with a malicious triumph. 'What did I tell you?'

'*I* can tell *you* that this caper's bang on,' says Porta,

raising the glasses to his eyes again. 'It's a dead certainty this time! And the prize is that big it's worth taking a risk for.'

'Last time it wound up as usual, with us empty-handed and standing there staring like a herd of dumb cattle,' says Heide, cantankerously.

'Was that my fault?' protests Porta, sourly. 'We ran into a couple of bits of bad luck. My plan was genial!'

'The plan was all right,' Heide admits, 'but all we got out of it was disappointment. All that was needed was for us all to have got shot. But this time the risk is considerably greater.'

'No battle, no victory!' says Porta, swinging the binoculars demonstratively in the air.

'If it goes wrong this time, I'll never listen to a plan of yours again,' snarls Heide.

'Listen here. Every sensible feller's goin' round waiting for the real big un'!' explains Porta.

'There's always something that goes wrong with your plans,' hisses Heide, angrily.

'You make me tired,' says Porta, giving him a wicked look. 'If you want to spend the rest of your life in Russia in company with a machine-pistol, all you need to do is to withdraw from this party.'

'Try, for the devil's sake, to keep your mouths shut for once!' the Old Man scolds them, viciously. 'A man can't hear himself think with all that crazy chatterin' goin' on!'

'Let's get under cover, *amigos*,' says Barcelona, shivering in the icy wind. It comes howling down from the mountain-tops, whipping razor-sharp crystals of ice into our uncovered faces. The cold bites through even the thick felt boots, making our toes ache.

The bitter wind is getting up to storm velocity. A deadly dangerous Russian winter storm may be on its way.

'We'll have to make snow-masks,' decides the Old Man. 'Make 'em out of camouflage stuff. Ordinary cloth gets wet and is worse than nothing. Barcelona, you put out sentries!'

'Why's it always have to be us?' protests Barcelona, stamping his feet in the snow to get the circulation going.

'Because I say so,' replies the Old Man, brusquely.

'Shit an' shankers!' barks Barcelona angrily. 'If I hadn't been through a real Prussian unteroffizier school where they teach you to eat old socks and look as if you like 'em I wouldn't bloody well accept this, I wouldn't!'

'What a lot of piss!' grumbles Albert. He is piling large blocks of snow one on top of the other. 'Why don't we just get inside the waggons and let the motors warm us up instead of workin' ourselves into the ground buildin' igloos?'

'You must have hit that black head of yours when you fell out of the tree,' sneers Porta. 'It costs fuel to keep the motors running, and if Ivan lets us down, we won't have all that much of it left to get home on again.'

'Start up every fifteen minutes,' orders the Old Man. 'The Devil help the driver whose motor freezes! It's 44 degrees below!'

The starting motors are already dead. All they give us is a long, hoarse, complaining moan. Even with the big starting handles we cannot get a response from them. Everybody helps to collect brushwood so that we can start a fire under the vehicles. The frost has turned the oil to a thick, doughy mass. The Old Man does not need to chase us. The thought of going back is in itself enough to speed us up.

'You idle pigs,' he rages. 'How often haven't I told you rotten lot to start your motors up at least every thirty minutes? Do I have to do every bloody thing myself? What the hell are we going to do if we have to take off in a hurry?'

'Grab on to the exhausts, an' slide on our bleedin' elbows,' laughs Tiny, noisily. 'It's slippy enough 'ere for it any road!'

Albert goes down flat on his face, and two large blocks of ice slip away from him. Only a stunted bush prevents him from going over the edge of the cliff. Furiously he gets up and kicks out at an invisible enemy. His feet slide from under him, and he goes down again.

'Don't count on me much longer,' he whines, and crawls up into the T-34 to make another attempt to start. To his great satisfaction the heavy Otto motor roars into top revolutions immediately. 'When you know your way around motors . . .' he boasts, looking triumphantly over at Porta, who is having trouble with the Panther's Maybach.

'German *shit*,' he hisses. 'Pretty enough to look at, but shit-all good on the job.' He kicks the instrument panel in vicious rage. After a long period of trying the motor finally begins to roar.

'What about the sentries?' asks the Old Man, as we huddle up together in the igloo.

'All in order!' declares Barcelona, snuggling down between the Legionnaire and Albert.

'Funny thing, but I happened to think of a certain Major-general Rottweiler just now,' says Porta, shaking a Juno cigarette out of its green packet. 'Not to be mixed up with the very well-known Herr Rottweiler from Hannover, who bred the Rottweiler police dog. The general wasn't even related to the dog-Rottweiler feller. They didn't either of them even know the other existed, and the general couldn't stand the sight of a Rottweiler police dog, because one of the black beasts had bit him once. It all started with a bicycle, one of the well-known Opel bikes from Bielefeld that only the upper classes roll round on. This Opel bike was standing up against the wall of the general's house one day, doin' nothing at all, and taking no notice of a big sign which said:

PLACING OF CYCLES HERE
STRICTLY FORBIDDEN

'Well, when the general got back from a court-martial he'd been holding where he'd condemned a deserter to death, and saw this bike, he was so angry he had an attack of hiccoughs. He screwed his monocle fast in his eye to make quite certain there really was a civilian bike parked up against his general's wall, and when he realized his military eye hadn't been foolin' him, he give out a lot of funny noises and changed the colour of his face. Then he made a quick strategic decision, attacked the bike, and threw the civilian shit into the park on the other side of the road. Back it came straight away. It was a park inspector who'd bunged it back again. You could just see his uniform cap above the top of the wall.

'"What the devil?" roared the general and he gave that park inspector a rollockin' of dimensions.

'With a lot of cursing and swearing he got the bike up into the regulation position for bicycles, and gave it a hefty push that sent it rolling along riderless down the hill towards the Soester crossroads. There it crashed into one of the post office's red bicycles, which was carrying reserve postman Grünstein, so that both of them were on duty. Grünstein wasn't carrying ordinary post that day, but secret post, sealed and registered and goin' from one Gestapo office to another. Herr Grünstein fell on his backside with a crash, and a treacherous gust of wind took all the letters and blew 'em all over the place. But it was much worse what happened next. Out of the park came a black-an'-brown Rottweiler police dog with its jaws lollin' open, just as the general was on his way in through his garden gate, which had eagles decorating it.

'"Bow-wow!" went the dog, an' brought its well-furnished jaws together on the general's fat rump.

'The general gave out a shrill scream, which did not quite fit in with all the medals for bravery which decorated his broad chest. He lost his grip on the gate and sprang into cover in the garden faster than any recruit. The cast-iron gate banged to behind him with a crash which almost made the Prussian eagles' beaks fall off.

'He looked cautiously out into the road to see who it was

that had taken out half the seat of his trousers, but there was nobody in sight. As you probably know, these Rottweilers're dreadfully cunning devils, and this one was not a backward member of its race. It'd nipped smartly in by the back door to continue its attack from a more strategically advantageous point.

'This time the battle was rougher. Not only the rest of the arsepart of the general's trousers went, but also a nice chunk o' the general's rump. Everything stopped though, as suddenly as it had begun, when the dog's owner turned up and called it to him with a whistle.

'"*Good* dog!" he said, patting the black devil. The general got slowly up on to his riding boots. "This is going to be an expensive matter for you, sir," he fumed. He rubbed his wounded rump: "That wild beast there is going to be *shot*!"

'"You don't seem to know who I am," roared the dog-owner, straightening himself up, "but you soon will do! I hope you're not off to the front line right away, general?"

'The general began to shout an' scream then, and asked what business it was of a civilian's what the German Army's generals did.

'"Who knows? Perhaps you are also an enemy spy?" he said, threateningly. Whole regiments of execution squads started glitterin' in his eyes, and a smile curled his lips: "I can tell you, sir, that that kind of question is one which often gives away the enemy espionage system. Let us take an example. If I was careless enough to tell you that I was going to the front on Tuesday the enemy would know immediately that 191 Jaeger Division was going into the line. One or two more of such innocent questions, and the enemy General Staff would know exactly where that division would be employed." The general pointed accusingly at the dog's owner: "And because of your regular activities, Herr Mole, the enemy already knows all about the 191st. That the men are from Sibengebirge, from which district come useful soldiers, faithful and dutiful, born infan-

222

trymen, who could be called to the flag as fifteen or sixteen-year-olds if need be. They do not have a lot of brains, but for that very reason they make extremely good infantrymen. To be sure there are not many of them left alive after a war, but that proves that that part of the country produces good soldiers. When the enemy General Staff gains possession of information of that nature, they immediately strengthen their lines, not with *one* division but with *three* elite divisions. If it had been a Berlin division, or a beerbarrel crowd from Munich, then firing off their mortars a little would have been enough to send such asphalt cowboys back to their beer-halls.

'"I saw through you straightaway, Herr Spy," he continued. "I am the Chief of the Military Counterespionage Service here in VI Military District, and I have sent a great many of your kind in front of the military courts. One careless question, and you villains stand tied to the execution post. *You* are under *arrest!*"

'"Now you've gone too far, general! You're not going to get away with that," shouted the dog's owner. "I'm a party member in good standing, and with a low number! I was in Munich." He banged himself on the chest. "I have sat alongside the Führer *twice* in *Bürgerbrau.* What d'you say to *that?*" He gave the Nazi salute, with fingertips exactly aligned with his right eye. "In 1923 I marched in the third row behind His Excellency General Ludendorff! I am a holder of the Blood Order! I'm not that easy to muck about with! I'd also like to know since when Army generals have started stealing bicycles? Do you know what it costs to steal a bike?"

'"Are you stark, staring mad?" roared the general, rattling his sabre and spurs.

'"No, but you are," said the dog-owner, with a sardonic smile.

'By this time a crowd had collected outside the general's eagle-decorated garden gate. The inquisitive stretched their necks to see what was going on, and laughed with pleasure.

'This disturbed the combatants, of course, so the general invited the Rottweiler and its owner inside, to continue the discussion without outside advice and interference.

'The dog's owner wasn't a normal, stupid person, and could talk nicely about most anythin'. He dealt on the Stock Market, too, and knew a good deal about foreign currency. He thought it would be only polite to introduce himself.

'"Strange," he bowed, clicked his heels and lifted his right arm. "Potato wholesaler, and barley exporter; party member; holder of the Blood Order. Heil Hitler!"

'The general growled a bit, but didn't consider it was necessary to introduce himself. He thought that any bloody fool, including a potato wholesaler living in that Westphalian hole in the ground Paderborn, ought to know who he was. It was people's duty, he believed, to know him!

'"Be so good as to take a seat, Herr Strange," he barked, with false friendliness, offering a gold cigarette-case with the German eagle engraved on it.

'Party member and potato wholesaler Strange scrabbled a cigarette out of the case, but had to light it himself.

'Anybody can understand that,' smiles Porta. 'Where'd we all be if this dog-lovin' spud-basher was only a demobbed Leutnant of the reserve who'd been sent home because he had his party-book in order. Or, maybe, an Unteroffizier, or even a lousy rifle-carrier? That low, a German Army general couldn't ever sink. Better make it look like forgetfulness on his part.

'For a bit everything was quiet. Like the lull they talk about before the storm. They just sat there watching the smoke spirallin' up from the general's cigar and the party member's cigarette.

'"Have you thought, general," the potato feller started off at last, "that it's about time we got moving and *won* this war? We can't go on overlooking slackness. Potato exports've practically stopped." He looked challengingly from the

224

general to the Rottweiler. The dog had stretched itself out comfortably on a lionskin in front of the fire. It was all that was left of a poor rheumatic lion the general'd shot in Africa while he was hangin' around waiting for World War II to start up. "Things look black to me, general, *very* black. Out of the few loads of potatoes one can get hold of, from good connections, 50 per cent have to be handed over to the damned Army, who pay bottom prices. Prices set by a group of sour-gutted civil servants in the Ministry of Food. People who can't even write proper German, but use a kind of idiotic civil servant language of their own. They should leave everything to the SS Reichführer and throw the remains of the rotten monarchy on to the muckheap! It makes a man despair of life, general! I have written to the Führer, but received no reply. We win and win, but none of our victories *get* us anywhere! Barley I never see any more and potatoes are fewer and fewer. Give us a great, blood-soaked victory, and get it over with so's a man can begin to do business again. Like we were forced to do by Jewish high finance before the war. Look at the great victory we're winning just at present! The whole of 4 Panzer Army's sitting down in the woods along the Oka, where they're letting themselves get shot up by the Bolshie guns, and regiments, battalions and companies are being smashed to bits and spread out all over the delta marshes. And d'you know what people say? They say that no matter which way you look the whole sky is on fire. In every direction. Villages and towns are being laid waste too, so as there's nothing left of them but piles of ashes. But that's not what I'm really bothered about. War's *like* that. Tough and manly. Not for namby-pamby people! I learnt all about that in my twelve months at the volunteer school!" As he said this the party member an' spud dealer jumped to his feet and bowed politely to the general.

'"Beg humbly to report, Herr General, sir, one-year volunteer Strange, Leonhard, 33, Prussian Infantry Regiment, 6th Brandenburgers, discharged from active service by reason of potatoes and barley!" He fell back into the leather chair, a gruesome, antique monster with a back so uncomfortable that it was something only a masochist could love.

'"I don't complain at guns being fired off, towns being burned and people being killed. That's what war's *about*!" "Spuds an' barley," he went on, waving a fresh cigarette around in the air, "but the worst thing is those accursed artillerymen, that go shooting one distillery after another into ruins. What have the distilleries done to *them* to make them turn their rotten cannons on the *distilleries*?" He lugged a thick note-book from his pocket, shaking with anger. "Listen to this, general. I'm beginning to feel this whole world war is aimed specially at ruining me!" He wets his fingers and turns the pages. "'Red Star' at Kiev – took 185 tons of potatoes – razed to the ground; 'Fatherland's Oasis', Minsk – 200 tons potatotes *and* 100 tons barley – shot to bits. These *untermensch* owe me for the last two deliveries! What about the insurance? *Force Majeure*! Not a sausage back for all those high premiums!

'"Will the mighty German Army cover my losses? Excuse me, general, it was just a passing thought. Here's the 'Golden Eagle', Kharkov – good solid business – runs night and day the year round – the manager was a lovely chap. His wife's name was Wilma – always off to some spa she was. Nerves, general. Easy for *them* to get shot – nerves I mean – when you live in the Soviet Union, where the state can decide what colour your bedroom wallpaper's got to be, and can dip its greedy fingers into your pockets whenever it gets the fancy. Almost as bad as it is here!" Herr Strange put his hands to his mouth in fear, as he realized what he had said. He jumped from the masochist chair in confusion, stuck out his right arm and roared: "Heil Hitler!"

'The general gave a forced smile, and looked out of the corners of his eyes at the Rottweiler on the lionskin. It seemed to be amused at its master's disloyal remark. All its teeth were showing.

'"The day before yesterday I found, to my dismay, that eight distilleries had been burned to the ground. Honestly, general, if it goes on like this much longer, we'll *all* go bankrupt, and *I'll* be totally ruined. Who in the devil's name'll buy potatoes and barley when there's no distilleries left?"

'"Aren't you looking a little too much on the dark side of things?" asked the general, and suggested their taking a glass of something. "Our position is quite good just now. The German divisions are rolling victoriously over the Russian steppe. I will admit that a distillery goes up now and then, but we must all make some sacrifices to achieve the final victory."

'"It's time it arrived; preferably before those Red dummies shoot the last distillery to pieces!" sighed the potato-dealer sorrowfully.

'With a commanding wave of his hand the general ordered his visitor over to the war-map which decorated the wall alongside the fireplace.

'"See here, Herr Strange. Here we have the Dniepr and a little further back the Volga, the lifeline of Russia. We have only to get a short way over on the other side of *that* and our punishment expedition to the east is over. And here we have Africa. As you can see, it is no great distance to Cairo!"

'"How many kilometres?" asked Strange, practically. He picked up a match-stick, which represented about a thousand kilometres on the map.

'"*That* is of no importance," shouted the general, furiously, knocking the match from his visitor's hand. "As I say, it is not far, and now at this very moment Field-Marshal Rommel is preparing to make a decisive strike through the weak British lines. The German war banner will soon wave over the minarets of Cairo. The rest is merely a question of local mopping-up operations. The

227

Egyptians and the Arabs have always sympathized with us Germans. It can be only a matter of hours before they turn openly against the British terror regime and place themselves under the protection of our just, German leadership. Throughout Africa you hear the call '*Heim ins Reich!*'*" He sweeps his pointer from Cairo to the mountain ranges of the Caucasus and describes a graceful loop around the whole of Georgia. "Here the German war-machine rolls forward, crushing all that stands in its path." The pointer hops over to Burma. "And here the Imperial Japanese Army is smashing the British and American forces. The day is fast approaching when the victorious German and Japanese forces will join hands across the northern border of India. A masterstroke of strategy. What do you say to that, Herr Strange? Can you now see the Final Victory?"

'The potato-dealer cleared his throat, passed his hand across his face and ran his eyes over the large war-map. At the same time he couldn't help remembering all the wrecked distilleries.

'"Yes it looks all very nice, general," he admitted. "We're going forward a lot!" He seemed to consider a little, judging the distance between Burma and the Caucasus. "But we've retreated in a lot of places, too," he remarked, weakly. He put out a stiff, cautious finger and touched the chart. He ran his finger backwards and forwards at the western end of Georgia. "The Georgian Army road is unfortunately no longer in our hands," he said, speaking as if he himself had personally pulled the road out from under the feet of the German Army. He was getting close to high treason. "And what about Moscow, general? Even with the best of German eyes I don't think anybody could see a lot of Moscow from where our boys are at!"

'"And *you* have been a volunteer?" roared the general, purple in the face and sending the Rottweiler on the

---

* *Heim ins Reich!*: Back to the Reich

lionskin a severe military look. "We have had one or two small setbacks recently in unimportant sectors of the front. But what you call retreat, my good man, is no more than regrouping and straightening of the front. A necessary tactical operation which demonstrates the cool-headedness of our Supreme Commander. At this very moment our tanks are crashing along the Russian roads. Machine-guns rattle and German artillery pieces roar. Our shells rain down on the heads of the *untermensch*, who are now beginning to realize who makes the decisions. A good army leader can do great things with the German soldier!" He crashes his pointer down on the map. "In these forests we have amassed an army with a striking power of which neither God nor the Devil has ever seen the like. Once it begins to roll nothing will stop it until it is east of Moscow. Look, man! We have stormed from victory to victory. We have rolled up Jugoslavia and Greece, and thrown them into the ashcan. The crowing Gallic cock has lost his feathers, and been sent head over heels to defeat in just 40 days! Holland, Belgium, Denmark and Norway smashed and thrown on the scrapheap. They can only do what we order them to do. And here are Finland, Rumania, Bulgaria and invincible Hungary, our brave European allies. We could, if we wished, hand over the whole conduct of the war in the east to them."

'"The general forgot Italy," the potato-dealer put in.

'"Yes! We must also take Italy into account," admitted the general, letting the pointer wave a few times up and down the Italian boot. In reality he couldn't stand the Italians, or their spaghetti.

'"Can we *really* trust these Bulgarians and Rumanians?" asked Strange, thinking of all the money owing to him in those two countries. "I've heard they desert to the enemy by the battalion and they won't speak German any more?"

'"That's *enough*," roared the general. "I won't have high treason talked in my house! Understand *that*, you – you *volunteer*!"

'Now things began to develop at a pace nobody could have foreseen,' smiles Porta, happily. 'All the accusations they could think of, from cycle-stealing to high treason, flew to and fro in the room, accompanied by barked comments from the Rottweiler.

'"They can stuff this world war for all I care," roared "Spuds", scarlet in the face. "I don't give a damn who wins. All I want is for a few distilleries to be left standing by the artillery shits and the mad bombers, so that I can get my potato and barley sales back up again when it's over!"

'"I've seen through *you*," screamed the general, planting his fists on his hips. "Do you understand me? You – you bottle-lover!" He grabbed the potato-dealer by the shoulders and shook him like a rat.

'Unfortunately he carried out this unbridled attack on a party member right in front of the Führer's melancholy likeness.

'The potato-feller tore himself out of the general's grip, and took the opportunity of giving the Führer's picture a stretched-arm salute.

'"I warn you, general," he howled, insultedly. "I am not just a uniformed booby dancing round with a tin sword at his side! I am a holder of the Blood Order! I am a party member, I have a permit to carry a gun, and I'm not afraid to use it!"

'"What do I care about that," shouted the general, who had by now forgotten all he had learnt at Potsdam Officers' School, and was back on the parade-ground again. "I shit on your Blood Order, believe me, you schnapps burner, you! And where your party's concerned there won't be much of that left when the war's over! Ha!" he barked, whiffling his pointer through the air. "Do you and your Führer think that *we*," pointing a finger at his own chest, "the Prussian Army, which sprang from the earth at the command of Frederick the Great, will give your seventh-rank party the time of day? A party that's only able to think in terms of swivelling swastikas! D'you

230

think we Germans can be led astray by foreign idealogies?"

'The potato-dealer couldn't believe his ears. He was close to going over to the wall and knocking his head against it to clear his thoughts. A *foreign* idea! Shit on the party! This uniformed fop must have had his brains boiled from too much sun on his *pickelhaube*! Swivelling swastikas? What interesting thoughts those generals had! But the red-tabbed dope had it all wrong. They weren't curtseying round a semi-crippled Kaiser any more. A Kaiser whose only positive result in life was to lose a world war. They'd got to learn what the new era was all about! He opened his mouth several times to say something. His brain was overflowing with ready answers. But the general didn't give him time to speak.

'"Look at that," roared the general in a well-trained voice of command. He pointed to a large, dark painting which represented German justice. A giant oak, decorated like a rich family's Christmas tree. From every branch dangled a malefactor with a good German rope round his neck. It was a well-balanced composition. Women, children, young and old, even a skinny dog, were hanging there. "Look you potato-dealer, *look*!" he roared. "Here ends every German scoundrel, mongrel, *schweinhund* and plague-rat, who dares to besmirch the Fatherland with word or deed. Take note of it, schnapps-burner! We Prussians deal harshly with villains who think they can go their own way. A rope round their necks, and up with them. The thought, my man, is father to the deed! Consider that!" He emphasized his harsh words and dark warnings by pointing to a number of beautifully framed pencil drawings, showing smiling SS-men carrying out executions after the Army's victorious march through Poland and Russia. Carrying them out completely in accordance with Army Regulations. "I had begun to regard you as being a good person, but now I have seen through you. You are a beast of the field, an *untermensch* swine! Get out of my house! You wicked scoundrel! *March*! And take your mongrel with

231

you! It too will get to know what facing a German court-martial means!"

'The potato-dealer almost fell out of the door, followed by his dog. The dog turned its head and stared, with grinning jaws, at the raging general. "You can just wait," it thought, "till we two party members've been down to have a word with our Gauleiter!"

'Herr Strange jumped on his bicycle and pedalled off. He almost fell off again, when he turned in his saddle to spit a few farewell curses and threats at the general. *He* was still standing in the doorway, slashing holes in the air with his riding-whip.

'"That uniformed queer's going to learn what it's all about," the potato-dealer confided to his dog as they spurted down *Soest Weg*.

'"Bow-wow!" barked the dog, in agreement.

'They didn't stop till they arrived at the Gauleiter's pompous residence. Outside it the blood-red swastika flag waved lazily in the summer breeze.

'"The flag," said the potato-dealer, raising his right arm. "Heil! Sieg!"

'The Gauleiter came all the way out on to the steps to greet him. They had been friends ever since they worked together as farmhands on the estate of a baron who had since been executed.

'"Asphalt disease, Leonhard?" asked the Gauleiter in his thick, beery voice. "You look as if you'd been eating tar!"

'"A general," panted Strange, "an Imperial Prussian sod!"

'"Hope you didn't bite him?" laughed the Gauleiter noisily. "That could give us problems, you know!"

'"I didn't, but Wotan did! He ate off half his arse when he said he'd shit on the Führer, and the party was only a foreign idea!"

'"The devil! I didn't know your dog could talk," cried the Gauleiter in surprise. He straddled his legs and stared threateningly at the dog. "Be careful what you say, you black villain!"

"'No! Hell, Bruno, it wasn't Wotan who said it, it was that fop of a general!'"

"'Shit on the Führer, would he?" asked the Gauleiter, a threatening tone coming into his beery voice. "We'll *flatten* him! No trouble! By the way, you owe me 500 marks from last Thursday. Not forgotten it, I hope?'"

"'You'll get 'em tomorrow. Word of honour! I'll get 'em from the woman who hasn't got her divorce yet from the Yid we sent to the concentration camp!'"

"'Mind you don't get yourself mixed up in anything smelly," the Gauleiter warned him darkly, scratching the dog behind the ears. "The good times, when us party comrades could do what the hell we liked, are passing away! The bloody Army's got too much say in things, these days. All the police shits are scared of 'em. Watch out for the front line, Leonhard. As you know there's a need for gun-fodder, and, unfortunately, the Army decides who's to be the targets! Once get posted there and even the party couldn't get you back home again!'"

"'Don't say things like that, Bruno. *You* can get *me* out of it if they suddenly drop on me? I've been in one war for Germany. That's enough for me.'"

"'Let 'em reach out after you first," the Gauleiter comforted him, opening his arms wide. "Your job's still deferred. The country can't do without schnapps. We need it to keep our spirits up under all these hard and testing experiences we're going through.'"

'They sat down happily at the Gauleiter's large desk, which once belonged to a Social Democratic Minister for Justice. He's been rehabilitated since and now works on the rock-pile at Buchenwalde.

'Well, they sat there drinking cognac and putting a long report together. They were both holders of the Blood Order and the party emblem in gold, and they knew exactly which way to march to get somewhere. They'd played cards together every Thursday for years. They even had the same mistress, the sausage and delicatessen shop-owner Kelp's wife, Gertrude, a tall, black-haired, slightly plump lady whose ears stuck out. She wore size 8 in shoes, and could walk any infantryman tired on Winter Help Day, when they all marched to Pader Halle in a torchlight procession to drink beer, after rattling their collection-boxes all day. Gertrude was Herr Kelp's third wife, by the way. The first one died a natural death by drowning. Jumped into the Pader River with a lump of iron tied round her neck. Her name was Ulrikka, a very Christian, believing lady. She jumped in the river from the bridge behind the cathedral. Probably thought the Lord'd forgive her if she gave up her life near a holy place.

'If God did forgive her I've never heard about it,' smiles Porta, waving his arm in the air. 'Still there's not much gets out about what happens up there! Or down in the other place, for that matter!

'The sausage and delicatessen man's second wife's name was Wilhelmina. Feminine of the Kaiser's name. Her father sold cheese off the barrow. Mrs Wilhelmina was Aryan all over. Flaxen hair pulled back tight over her skull and braided. Looked like a frayed rope that had been left out in the rain. Down deep in her horsy-lookin' face a couple of wicked, German hen's eyes glittered. She always wore flat-heeled soles, and white stockings with black and red bobbles, that went halfway up her leg. This Aryan lady was not a sexually exciting creature. Quite the opposite! A man who got inside her would have got his prick broken up and ground into sausage-meat! They used to say she had a couple of rotating swastikas mounted up in it goin' both ways.' Porta suggests the motion with both hands. 'This Himmler-style woman took the mail train to Dortmund one day to buy curtain remnants at Liebstoss's shop in *Hindenburg Strasse*. An ancient liver sausage had exploded in the hands of the Kelbs' Polish servant girl, and has

234

spurted out all over the curtains. It cost the servant girl a spell in Ravensbrück, by the way. But Frau Wilhelmina had better have stayed home that day. She started her trip by visiting the baker, Otto, in *General Ludendorffstrasse*, who had a combined coffee-house and bakery. There she got four large cream cakes down her. She exchanged news with a couple of other party wives, who also had flaxen hair and buns at the back of their necks.

'When she was crossin' *Adolf Hitler Platz* a couple of hours later they began to toot a red alert. Bombs started to fall immediately. It howled, whistled and crashed all round her German bat-ears, and dust and dirt came down on her flaxen hair. Her Aryan braids came loose. She looked like a witch that'd been through a thunderstorm, on her way down from Norway to have a look at what was happening in old Germany under the national awakening!

'BANG! A bomb went off in front of her. It seemed as if the world had gone up in flames. BANG! Another went off behind her, and it seemed as if Satan was stoking up the fires of Hell! She became, of course, completely, Teutonically confused. First she ran one way, then she ran the other way.

'"Get under cover, you soppy idiot," screamed a bare-headed policeman. His helmet had been blown off his head.

'"*Wachtmeister! Wachtmeister!*" she screamed. "Tell me where to go!" She just managed to get her flaxen poll out of the way when a number four tram came flying through the air. The helmetless policeman didn't, though. The tram took him with it into Schultze's furniture store. Luckily for Schultze he had closed down two days before to wait for better times. Now he got rid of his stock, anyway, and only had to clean up after the tram and the policeman.

'Frau Wilhelmina ran round in circles, screaming. Then she saw a safe place: the National Socialist Constituency Office. But before she got there a 1,000 pounder bulls-eyed in on her. It tickled her all down her back and then went off. Frau Wilhelmina went with it!

'I've heard they shovelled her remains up, with the others, and they're all together in a mass grave in Döbliner Cemetery. RIP they put on the stone over 'em.'

'RIP? What's that?' asks Tiny, blankly.

'Rest in pieces,' answers Porta. 'But they didn't give her much rest under that flashy stone. A day or two after, one of those air gangsters dropped his whole load of 1,000 and 500 pounders in the wrong place. They landed bang on the cemetery, and he followed 'em up with a few thousand incendiaries for dessert. So now nobody knows what's become of Frau Wilhelmina's earthly remains. But this didn't faze the good Kelp. He married for a third time. This one was Müller's daughter, the well-known pig-dealer from Münster. She was a good-lookin' piece who knew what to use it for. She'd been working for Kelp for some time in the sausage section, making over old sausages into new ones.'

'Hey, now,' the Old Man breaks in, with a crooked smile. 'Aren't you forgetting your potato-dealer? He was on a visit to the Gauleiter?'

'Of course, damn it,' shouts Porta. 'You know how one story leads you into another. Where'd I got to?'

'They were laying plans, across the desk of the former Minister for Justice,' smiles the Legionnaire, lighting a *Caporal*.

'Oh yes! Well the telephone began ringing over at the Gestapo on *Ringstrasse*,' Porta continues. 'The Gestapo boss was one of their Thursday card-school mates.

'A *general*,' he roared happily, drawing his Walther 7.65 mm from his shoulder-holster. He was pleased as a bailiff who finds something worth money at a client's place.

'There wasn't almost anything the general wasn't accused of but *he* hadn't been wasting his time either. He'd had a ninety-minute talk with the Corps Auditor, Kurze. Everything went on report. The dog, the bicycle, the potato wholesaler, the wrecked distilleries and the long-awaited Final Victory.

'"We'll take *him*, all right," Kurze promised, self-confidently. "A crummy spud-dealer can't say what he likes to the German Army. He must be out of his mind! I suggest we start with the minor crimes, which give only fifteen years imprisonment: insulting the army, damaging military property, threatening the armed forces, jeering at the military uniform. Then we can go over to the ones punishable by death: defeatism, disseminating enemy propaganda, sabotage of the will to resistance, espionage."

'"What about the dog?" asked the general, vengefully.

'"We'll get to *him* all right," promised Kurze, letting out a bellow of court-martial laughter. "Sabotage of military equipment, and attack on a highly-ranked officer. Both hanging offences! Even the best of defenders couldn't save him from the rope. I'll use paragraph 241, section 5 of the military penal codex. That paragraph got me the War Service Cross First Class with clasp. Soon as the executioner hears that one, he starts off readying the scaffold for use."

'Things began to move the very next day, and I mean *move*! It could all have been settled by a good beating-up, and a German kick in the arse for the dog. Anyway! Department IV/2a picked up the general for a short interview, while GEFEPO* Department VIIb picked up Herr Strange. He was put in irons with collar and lead-chain immediately, according to Army Regulations.

'After some chatting about the weather, and dogs, the "interview" with Strange became more – what they call rigorous. The potato feller was given a few MP taps on the nose. He was lucky it wasn't the 30 Year War he was bein' interrogated in. In those days they used to nip people with red-hot pincers, and make 'em drink melted lead mixed with hot tar. This often used to help them to remember what it was they'd done.

'All afternoon funny sounds kept getting through from the interrogation office. People thought they'd got hold of

---

* GEFEPO: The Secret Field Security Police

a pig on the black, an' were slaughtering it. The noises didn't stop until the three GEFEPO blokes went down to "The Lame Duck" to freshen up for the second part of the interrogation.

'The potato feller didn't look too good by then. Unteroffizier Schulze, who'd been thrown out of Torgau for cruelty, and seconded to GEFEPO, had broken two of his ribs and had managed to turn his nose permanently upwards. Troublesome it was in rainy weather.

'The third day Herr Strange confessed to everything, and this made the GEFEPO quite human and friendly toward him. His wife brought him food parcels and they all sat round the table together and tanked up on West-phalian country ham and drank schnapps with eggs beaten up in 'em. Between meals they smoked the cigars and drank the cognac.

'The potato wholesaler signed a confession gladly. He was, in fact, by now so pleasant and easy to get along with that he was allowed to rubber-stamp it himself, and put it in a large Army envelope, which was then sealed with the bird and all the trimmings. And off it all went to the Judge Advocate General at Münster.

'The good times with GEFEPO were soon over, however. One grey, rainy day, "Spuds" got put into an asthmatic DKW, and sent off to 46 Infantry Regiment's barracks, where the Paderborn glasshouse was. They had rationing there. Two thin pieces of bread and a little blob of mar-garine. Even a hungry sparrow wouldn't have been attracted by the menu. On national celebration days they got a square of pâté de foie horse!

'His wife brought him plenty of extra food. Stabswacht-meister Rose of 15 Cavalry Regiment checked it in very carefully. Then the guards ate it all, down to the last crumb; after, of course, the potato-man had signed for receipt of it.

'They shot Strange in Sennelager early one August morn-ing. They did it on target range 4, which wasn't used for practice any more.

'The general ended up up shit-creek without a paddle. I don't know the details. There were a lot of rumours. Hung himself by his boot-laces, one of 'em said. It can't be true. He never wore lace-up boots in his life. Always swaggered round in long riding boots. A friend of mine in interrogation told me three apes from Fort Zittau came with an order for him to be handed over to them.'

Porta throws out his arm despairingly. 'Fort Zittau *eats* people. You go in, and you never come out. Even the Devil and his great-grandmother wouldn't dream of puttin' their heads inside Zittau's gates.

'This dog business was bad for a lot of other people too. There was the matter of the Gauleiter's toilet-rolls. They turned into a political matter. The paper was red, you see, and . . .'

Porta's story is cut off. Gregor Martin puts his frost-stubbled head in through the igloo opening.

'We've got visitors,' he says, rubbing the frost from his face. 'Hurry up and get outside!'

It is an icy night. The sky seems to drop icicles. The temperature is down below 45°. The storm howls along the steep cliff-walls. We feel as if our very souls are freezing to ice.

We stare anxiously towards the north-east, from where we can hear the noise of motors. Shadowy motor-sledges move rapidly down the winding mountain road.

Two sharp reports sound, sending us headlong to cover behind the snowdrifts. We get back on our feet again when we realize that it is only frost splitting the trees growing on the side of the mountain.

The motorized column is now clearly in sight, up by the gulch. An armoured motor-sledge is leading it, followed by an armoured car and a half-track transport waggon.

Suddenly a flare wobbles up into the air. It explodes with a hollow sound, sending three green stars out to one side. Shortly afterwards another one goes up, this time red.

'The Devil fuck my great-grandmother,' howls Porta, dancing round like a madman. 'It's bloody *him*! Where the hell's that signal pistol?'

'In the waggon,' answers Tiny, already legging his way over to it in a shower of snow. He is back in a flash with the pistol and hands it to Porta. 'It's loaded,' he grins.

'I should hope so,' replies Porta. 'You didn't think I was going to throw the bloody thing up in the air did you? We've got to get our answer back quick. Else that hell-hound out there'll be on his way back where he came from again.' He breaks the pistol open and examines the cartridge. 'We don't want to send up a wrong 'un,' he says. 'It ain't every day people are out pinchin' Stalin's gold out from under him. That boy'll be nervous. They'll cut him into tiny pieces if this job goes wrong.'

'Yes, and us with him,' comes drily from the Old Man. 'I must've been crazy to get mixed up in this caper!'

'Don't shit your trousers yet,' says Porta, pointing the flare-pistol up into the air at an angle. The flare goes up and explodes hollowly in a burst of red stars. He reloads with a green flare and sends it up to burst alongside the red one.

Exactly sixty seconds later a green, and then a yellow, flare goes up.

'Fits like a prick in Lizzie,' grins Porta, satisfiedly. He smacks the lid of the stopwatch shut.

'*C'est le bordel*,' mumbles the Legionnaire nervously. 'That firework show must have been seen the devil of a way off!'

'Yes, before we know where we are alarm units from all over'll be on their feet looking for us,' forecasts Heide, darkly.

'I was beginning to get a bit nervous of whether that commissar bint hadn't taken my arse,' says Porta, tucking the signal pistol into his belt. 'She'd have been bitterly sorry for it if she had. Wolf's got a little rocket surprise for her if anythin' funny should happen to Joseph Porta on this trip.'

'Open out,' orders the Old Man, 'ready your arms! You never can trust Ivan!'

'We shoot first and ask questions after?' asks Tiny, readying his *Kalashnikov* noisily.

'None of that Chicago by night stuff here,' explodes Porta, furiously.

With a breakneck swerve a heavy armoured sledge comes roaring down the winding road, skids sideways across the clearing, and stops so close to Barcelona's T-34 that it would be impossible for him to bring the gun to bear on it.

'Bloody hell!' mumbles Gregor admiringly. 'That's some trick they've got there!'

There are a couple of minutes of excited waiting. The only sound is the whirling of the sledge's propeller. The wind from it tosses snow into the air. The hatchway of the vehicle opens slowly and a grey-white commissar cap with its large red star comes into view. For a moment two hard grey eyes stare over towards our two tanks. Then the newcomer turns his gaze up to the clouds, which hasten, darkly threatening, towards the east. He jumps lithely down into the snow, spews out a number of Russian oaths, and rubs his knee, which he has knocked on the hatchframe. A *Kalashnikov* is handed out to him. In silence he hangs it across his chest in the Russian manner. He puts his left hand down into his deep fur pocket. It is so deep that his arm goes down into it right up over the elbow. When he withdraws it he is holding a bottle in his hand. He puts it to his lips, takes a long pull, wipes his mouth with his furry mitten, and gives out a long, satisfied snort, like a cold horse which has come home to its warm stable. His cold grey eyes examine Porta, who is leaning nonchalantly up against a soot-blackened tree, playing with a bundle of hand-grenades tied around a petrol bottle.

'Joseph Porta?' he asks with a wry smile, tipping his machine-pistol slightly forward.

'The Golden Commissar, I presume?' smiles Porta, lifting his yellow topper respectfully.

'Right you are,' smiles the Commissar, offering Porta the vodka bottle.

'*Stolichnaja*,' nods Porta, sniffing appreciatively at the neck of the bottle. He puts it to his lips and enjoys the silky taste of the Russian luxury vodka. He feels it go right out into his fingers and toes. They pass the bottle back and forth between them until it is empty.

'You arrived late,' says Porta, 'but you *did* arrive!' He accepts a perfumed Russian officer's cigarette, offered him from a gold cigarette-case.

'It's been a tough trip,' answers the Commissar. 'We had to go the long way round, more than once. How was your trip, *tovaritsch*?'

'Apart from the hellish low temperatures you run to in your country, and the snow that piles up on what you call your roads, I've no complaints,' replies Porta.

After a while we are all standing in a circle round the two 'Mafia bosses'. More vodka comes out. This time a cheaper brand.

Tiny snatches a bottle from the hand of a little Siberian sergeant, who is preparing to take a swig from it.

'*Herrenvolk* first,' he protests, downing almost half the bottle. He licks his lips appreciatively before handing it back to the sergeant.

'Pull in your tongue,' says the Siberian. 'Sticking out like that, it makes you look as if they'd just strung you up!'

A new bottle of *Stolichnaja* had been brought out, but only for Porta and the Commissar. The rest of us have to make do with the cheaper *Raj*.

Before very long even the Old Man is looking on the brighter side, and beginning to kick up his heels in a few dance steps. It is 6 January, the Russian Christmas, to which everyone looks forward the whole year.

The sledge-driver fishes out a balalaika and Porta his piccolo. To their accompaniment the Commissar sings in a deep bass:

'Snow covers hill and plain.
From longing's bitter deep
Our souls cry out in pain.'

We forget our mission here, and no longer feel the icy cold; no longer see the moon with its frosty, barren light; no longer hear the trees cracking, with reports like rifle shots.

A bony corporal, in the olive-green uniform of the frontier troops, starts up an ancient Slavic song to the melancholy strumming of the balalaika:

'Bless Thee, O Lord!
Look down with grace upon us . . .'

It is more than the Commissar can stand. He cries out. A wet drunken snort, like the barking of a dog with a heavy cold. His face reddens, and tears run down his cheeks. His wet, carroty hair hangs down over his watery eyes.

'Ssss Rozh deniem Khristvym,' he gulps, deeply moved. He grasps Porta in his arms, and he too begins to weep, in his drunkenness. 'I get so terribly sad at Christmas-time,' he sniffles, with such a sorrowful expression on his tear-wet face, that the rest of us are close to crying with him.

'A feller can't *stand* it,' sniffs Tiny, wiping his eyes with a filthy mitten.

'Look down with grace upon us, Eternal Master,' intones the corporal of frontier troops, taking a swig at the vodka bottle. 'Look down with grace upon us,' he repeats, handing the bottle to Tiny.

'We're goin' to need it, too,' sighs Porta, blowing his nose noisily. 'This is no ordinary criminal caper we're going on.'

'Bet it's the first time in history anybody's ever used tanks and guns to bust open a bank,' Gregor laughs loudly.

Tiny goes down on his haunches and tries to dance *prisjodka* with the frontier corporal, with the result that he

243

comes close to breaking his back. On the advice of the corporal we tie him to two motor-sledges and pull in opposite directions. His vertebrae go back into place with a sound like a splintering plank.

'Bet that bloody well hurt,' says Gregor, wincing.

With a piercing howl the Commissar jumps high in the air, cracks his heels together a yard above the ground and begins to whirl round in breakneck circles:

> 'I am always drunk
> and fear no man or beast!'

he sings in a ringing voice.

The frontier corporal is hopping round with a full glass gripped between his teeth and his hands clasped behind his neck. The Commissar falls over with the vodka bottle still clutched in his hand. He looks at it in amazement.

'So *there* you are!' he hiccoughs. 'Thought I'd seen you around.' He staggers back on to his feet with great difficulty. Through a vodka haze his eye falls on Tiny, and he hands him the *Stolichnaya*.

'Take care of that till I get back. Drink any of it and you'll wind up in Kolyma! *Panjemajo?*'

'Trust me,' grins Tiny, looking thirstily at the bottle.

'A man's more stupid than the Pope, if he trusts anyone,' slavers the Commissar, staggering dangerously. 'You know Tomsk,' he asks a snowdrift, trying to embrace it. 'You can hear yourself walk there. When you're on your way back from the brothel "The Merry Bed" your footsteps *echo*! They've laid the roads with wood in Tomsk! Only thing they've got plenty of in Tomsk. If you've been in Tomsk, *tovaritsch*,' he tells the snowdrift, 'the rest of the world you won't bother with. You won't be able to manage it, see! Tomsk is the arsewhole of the universe!'

Finally Porta manages to get him back on his feet. They kiss one another on both cheeks in the old Russian fashion. Arm in arm, and singing at the top of their voices, they stagger towards the remains of the soot-blackened *kolchos*'s main building. They fall several times on the way.

They are almost there when the Commissar remembers the *Stolichnaja*. He turns back, swearing viciously, and after colliding with several trees on the way he reaches Tiny. He puts out a demanding hand towards him.

'I'm sorry,' says Tiny falsely, handing him the empty bottle.

'The devil!' roars the Commissar, staggering threateningly. 'I'll be damned! And I thought it was only Russian corporals who stole from their officers! What am I to do with you?' He hiccoughs and emits a long, long belch. 'I'll send you to Kolyma!'

'Gimme a bottle of vodka then, first?' asks Tiny, belching in his turn.

'You know all the tricks, do you?' says the Commissar, blinking his watery eyes.

"Give him a bottle,' he turns to the frontier corporal. 'Now we're having a party it might as well be a good one. It's only Christmas once a year.' He looks prayerfully up at the clouds and mumbles: 'Look down in grace upon us, Lord!'

'That Tiny, he's a wicked chap,' Porta confides to the Commissar, as they stagger arm in arm towards the main building. 'He was hardly born before the Children's Aid took him. Nobody can *stand* him, down at the David. He goes round with Jews too!'

'Does he really?' asks the Commissar, stopping to salute a tree, which he seems to think is a rabbi. 'It's not all Jews who're suitable company for weak people,' he says, giving out a thunderous belch.

'You're right, there,' says Porta, putting the wrong end of his cigarette in his mouth.

'Look down in grace upon us, Lord,' pants the Commissar, throwing a snowball at an imaginary enemy. 'This cursed war will lead to nothing good! Before we know where we are properly, all our ideals will have been destroyed, and our banners trampled into the mud!'

'I just want to tell you one thing,' shouts Porta, letting himself down on to an up-ended bucket. 'They're whores an' pimps the lot of 'em, no matter how high up you go. They fuck one another's wives to get an advantage out of it and do it backwards and forwards too.' He stares at the Commissar, with streaming eyes. 'It's bloody immoral! You can't do that an' *stay* moral! You ever fucked anybody else's wives?'

'You are my friend,' screams the Commissar, in drunken happiness. He throws his arms round Porta, so hard that he falls backwards off his bucket. 'And you have fucked my wife,' he laughs, cunningly. 'How is she, by the way?'

'Last I saw of her she was playin' monkeys up a tree with some counter-jumper from supplies, but he had the clap and the MPs picked him up.'

'Red Front!' shouts the Commissar in a ringing voice, clenching his fist. 'When you're driving in a waggon you cannot get off,' he breathes, mysteriously.

'The trick's in the deal,' explains Porta, with drunken honesty. 'Everything's based on buying and selling, and what you've *got* to have is your head screwed on straight. The dearest thing you've got to sell is yourself!'

'Who the devil'd buy me?' asks the Commissar, doubtfully.

'A lot more people than you'd dream of would,' answers Porta.

'As ugly as *I* am?' smiles the Commissar, mirthlessly.

'If you can't get what you want you have to take what you can get, as the ostrich said when he tried to have a fuck at a duck.'

'Look down in grace upon us, Lord,' sighs the Commissar, throwing his arms wide despairingly.

'Nobody move!' roars Gregor in a high, screaming voice. 'This is a hold-up!'

'He's practising for when we get to the gold,' Porta tells the Commissar.

Drunk as we are we can see there is a storm coming up. One of the feared mountain storms which, in a moment, change everything to a raging hell of snow, with winds strong enough to send a twenty-ton truck flying over the edge and down the mountainside like a piece of loose paper.

We crawl into the igloos and roll up close together to protect ourselves against the terrible cold. Sausages and legs of mutton are passed from hand to hand, and after some brief, mumbling talk we fall into a heavy sleep. Only the machine-pistols lying around us indicate that there is a war on.

Tiny grunts in his sleep and smiles like the cat who has eaten the goldfish.

The Commissar sleeps with his cap turned round on his head. Now and then he makes strange noises and sobs in his sleep.

With a scream he suddenly sits up and clasps his head with both hands. It feel like one huge inflamed boil. He groans aloud, as he tries to turn his body and realizes that his backbone creaks like a door hanging on rusty hinges. He cannot discover where he hurts most. He is in pain from the tips of his toes to the roots of his hair. He finds out his head is the worst. It feels like a basin of gruel made with old, sour milk. 'Look down in grace upon us, Lord,' he sobs, and falls, groaning, back down amongst the rest of us.

'*Gauno**,' snarls tank-driver Ermolov, turning angrily away from the unhappy Commissar, who mumbles again, weakly: 'Look down in grace upon us, Lord!'

'*Guano*,' repeats the driver, viciously.

'Don't be too hard on me,' whines the Commissar, drunkenly maudlin. Then he throws a wicked look at Ermolov. 'Arsehole,' he growls, offended at a miserable Staff-sergeant permitting himself to say 'shit' to a Commissar of the Army, the highest ranking authority at Corps

* *Gauno:* Russian for shit

HQ. Where the devil's it all going to end if this filthy war goes on much longer? Never heard anything like it. A lousy NCO throwing a word like 'shit' at *him*. A Commissar of the Army! He falls back down and snores his way straight into an alcoholic nightmare.

> 'I'm goin' to Maxim's
> Where all the girls are dreams . . .'

sings Porta happily in his sleep.

It is more than Albert can stand. He springs up excitedly and begins to shake Porta roughly.

'What the hell are you up to, you black shithouse?' rages Porta, punching at him. His beautiful dream has been broken into and he is angry.

'You were singing!' snarls Albert furiously, diving under the canvas again and burrowing down between Gregor and me.

'Singin'?' gapes Porta. 'I was bloody well sleepin'! The Bible's softened your brain, you black apeman!'

'Shut it!' roars the Old Man from his corner. 'Go to sleep! That's an *order*!'

Quiet falls again on the igloo, and we all dream of what it is going to be like to be rich. None of us have ever tried that before.

It is still dark when we get up, and all around us is a blinding hell of snow. Ice crystals drive at us like bullets, tearing our skin so that the blood comes.

Tiny starts a violent argument with Staff-corporal Oscar Rowitsch, called 'Frostlips', because he always looks as if he is freezing to death.

'You 'eap of Caucasian camelshit,' screams Tiny angrily, and begins to swing his arms, threateningly.

'Frostlips' ducks like lightning, and just manages to avoid Tiny's devastating punch.

'Stand still, so's I can get at you,' roars Tiny, rushing forward like a bulldozer.

'Frostlips' lands an iron-shod infantry boot on the tenderest part of Tiny's instep.

He lets out a roar which a lion would have envied him and grabs at his injured foot. A serious tactical error. He barely sees the heavy Russian infantry boot coming at him until it thuds into his face. With a scream of pain he falls on his back, blood spurting from nose and mouth. Now he is really angry. Like lightning he rolls himself into a ball, kicks his feet into the air and straightens out like a released spring. With the force of a steamhammer, his forehead crashes into 'Frostlips's' broad Mongolian face. Then he spins round and kicks out backwards like a crazy horse.

For a moment he seems to hang in the air. Both his size 14 boots hammer into 'Frostlips's' chest, knocking all the breath out of his lungs. The next kick sends him back several yards and he slides towards the edge of the cliff. We see him already on his way over into thin air, but his dangerous slide is stopped unexpectedly. Warrant Officer Stepanov comes round a corner of the ruins, with his arms full of fried sausage and mutton, and gets in the way.

Stepanov lets out a roar as his feet are swept from under him, and sausage and mutton fly up into the air.

He is on his feet first with his *Kalashnikov* gripped by the muzzle and on his way to split 'Frostlips's' skull with the butt. The Commissar's quick intervention saves the man's life.

'Stop those crazy games,' he growls. 'Wait to play 'em until you've all become Swedish Social Democrats!'

But Stepanov, whom they used to call 'Whorecatcher' when he was serving on the Moscow Vice Squad, is so angry they have to tie him to a tree until he simmers down.

It is well into the afternoon before we get away. There are problems with several of the vehicles, since their drivers have been in no condition to turn their engines over during the night. We have to tow the half-track behind the T-34.

We are totally exhausted when we stop, well into the night, for a couple of hours of rest. We have laboured

249

through oceans of snow. A couple of times we have come close to losing the trucks. Ice broke under their wheels on the way across rivers not yet frozen through.

The Old Man has to threaten us with his machine-pistol to get us to build an igloo. But it gets built at last, and we huddle together, freezingly cold, inside it. Now we come suddenly awake again. Porta gets the cards out. He shuffles and deals with practised fingers.

'Tell me,' he asks 'Whorecatcher', 'what did you Moscow fellers do with rapists when you got hold of 'em?'

'Sent 'em to Kolyma,' the former Vice man says, making a clumsy attempt at palming the ace of spades under cover of the talk.

'Better have that one, too,' says Porta, sweetly, holding out his hand.

'That's funny,' answers 'Whorecatcher', looking innocent.

'Yes *very*, bleedin' funny,' rumbles Tiny, angrily. He draws his .*Nagan* from its place in his boot-top. 'You just watch somethin' funny don't 'appen to you, mate. Like you suddenly growin' a couple extra 'oles in you somewhere or other!'

'I can't see there's any risk grabbin' a bit o' free cunt now an' again!' Tiny laughs noisily and scratches his crutch. 'If you get picked up for it all you got to say's the bag's a bleedin' liar!'

'You don't get away with it that easy, lad,' says 'Whorecatcher' sadly. 'The Vice Squad knows all those games. Keep off rape! Any caveman of a copper can prove it's you that's been inside it easy as winking. Cunts're like guns. The rifling tells you what's been through 'em, and even the most corrupt judge'll take that kind of thing seriously. I can only remember two cases where the sod got away with it. There was this Anna Petrovna who'd accused some limp prick of having raped her. Well, the report revealed that she'd let 946 high-born gents get across her. They used to contact her by telephone. Not too clever of her that, 'cos our telephone bugging service

250

checks all telephones. We had a serious talk with her, and she told all. Rape, that was just a bit of fun she was having. The real reason was he wouldn't share his black money with her. They both wound up in Kolyma!'

'But you said he got away with it,' protests 'Frostlips', disappointedly.

'I said he got away with the rape charge,' answered 'Whorecatcher'. 'He went to the mines for having black money. Three years later he committed suicide with an ice block.'

'What was the other case?' asks Porta, interestedly, raking in the pool. It is the fourth time he has had twenty-one!

'It was a Chinese bint,' smiles 'Whorecatcher', lifting up the corners of his eyes with his fingers to show us what she'd looked like. 'She found out one day that her belly was growing at a surprisingly rapid rate. So she stepped off up to the social worker, who was one of them that was born in the bottom of a laid-up barge, an' believed every word the slit-eyed bint told her about rape and being misused and that. So if the yellow bitch could get a prick tacked on to her coming nipper then she was certain of getting a bag full of roubles from the social lot. We had a bit of a talk with her and read what she'd said to the bull she'd got on the board as being pappy. Luckily for him our sex experts were able to prove that what this Pekin duck was saying was not on. They sent her to Kolyma, together with what she was carrying around in her.'

'What about the feller?' asks Porta. 'He go to Kolyma, too?'

'No, not for that,' answers 'Whorecatcher', sorrowfully. 'He went up for a different job, couple of years later. He'd been celebrating the first of May, and got drunk. While drunk he'd talked a lot to a bloke who didn't agree with him. You know what I mean, I reckon? He was picked up before he'd even got rid of his hangover!'

'Jesus,' cries Tiny, impressed. 'You reckon the German

Vice bleeders are as good as your lot?'

'*I* dunno,' says 'Whorecatcher', playing a jack, on which Porta promptly drops an ace for another 21, 'but I can guarantee not much gets past 'em, and I know that when there ain't a war on they visit one another and pass on the news!'

'What a bleedin' world we do live in!' sighs Tiny, letting his cards down, thoughtlessly, so that 'Frostlips' gets a look at them.

'Twenty-one,' chuckles Porta. He has immediately picked up the signal from 'Frostlips', who is his partner.

Tiny is speechless. With a silly look on his face he stares at the ace and two queens lying in front of Porta. He has two jacks, and a king on the side. If it hadn't been for all that talk about the Moscow Vice Squad he could have bid 'Twenty-one' long ago. But he is still so shocked at what he has heard that he does not even get annoyed.

'Are you really telling me,' he asks, bending absorbedly forward across the table, 'that you Vice cops can find out if I've been having a bit of illegal crumpet off with some bint or other? Sounds like a bleedin' fairy tale, to me!'

'Well, it's still a fact,' says 'Whorecatcher', putting a king in place. 'And the sentence is thirty years. After twenty years you've got a chance of transfer to a labour camp. Oh, and don't forget, if you like a bit o' rape, that most of those chaps get sent to the *Pjopre* prison on the Tomsk river. I was there once on an escort job for two blokes who hadn't committed rape, but who'd had a couple of "frigates" cruising the *Nevski Prospekt* for 'em. They'd got twenty-five years for it. They were both of 'em in good humour all the way, making plans for the future and such, but you should've seen their faces when we come up over the hills and got a sight of the place they were headed for on the other side of the river. It was still a good way off, but it felt just like a wicked, cold fist being smashed into your face. We three that was escorting them, we took a good firm grip on their leading chains. We knew they only had one thought in their heads: to get away from us in any way they could. Those "ship-owners" had just realized what a long time twenty-five years really is.'

'Holy Mother of Kazan, but it *is* a long time,' Porta comes in thoughtfully. He strokes his chin, consideringly. 'A whole Porta lifetime. Lord save us. It's a *long* bloody time!'

'Shut *up* for Christ's sake,' mumbles Tiny. 'It'd knock over the wickedest black monkey as ever lived. Twenty-five years! Just for 'avin' a couple of biddies out workin' to put a bit more butter on your bleedin' bread. And I suppose there *could* be twenty-five years more 'angin' fire in the re'abilitation camp?"

'You can count on it,' says 'Whorecatcher'. 'I never heard of nobody who came straight home when he was finished with a stretch. Whether it was prison or punishment camp. There's always a "surprise" for dessert. They call it expulsion to Siberia anyway.'

'Jesus,' groans Tony, putting his hand to his head, so that 'Frostlips' can see all his cards again. 'Be better to *pay* for it, and get a receipt too. Fifty years, just for a shag! Bleedin' 'ell no! I'm going into a monastery!'

'Bet there's a lot of those cunt-crazy sods in gaol on the Tomsk who wish they'd been born without goolies,' remarks Porta, bidding twenty-one triumphantly for the twelfth time.

> *You don't have to be in a war for more than five*
> *minutes to find out how stupid it all is. There must*
> *really be a better way of doing things!*

> *Porta to Tiny on the outskirts of a burning Russian*
> *town*

The great, cool church hummed with the voices of people in prayer.
They prayed aloud for the things they were allowed to pray for, but
in the silence of their thoughts they prayed for peace. For an end to
the hellishness of war; never to see soldiers or tanks any more; never
to experience bombs and incendiaries again. They prayed that the
man in the grey party uniform might be amongst the dead in the next
bombing raid. They begged in their prayers that they might soon be
granted the sight of British and American soldiers.

Suddenly the mumble of prayer stopped. Panic grew in the eyes of
the congregation.

The priest rose from his knees and stared fearfully towards the
closed door, heard the hard tramp of jackboots and the hoarse, brutal
song:

> *Wir werden weiter marschieren,* *
> *wenn alles in Scherben fällt,*
> *denn heute gehört uns Deutschland*
> *und morgen die ganze Welt!*

'SS,' mumbled the priest and let his folded hands fall down to
his sides.

Everything was in ruins already. Berlin was a pile of
rubble. Stuttgart burnt. Hamburg pockmarked like a lunar
landscape. Leipzig a hell of fire. Breslau fighting to the last
man and the last bullet. In Cologne the ruins of the cathedral
loomed above wrecked houses; but the Führer's guard marched
on, crunching the ruins under their heavy boots.

---

* *We will march on*
When all is in ruins,
Today Germany is ours
Tomorrow the whole world!

THE PARITIP

The Commissar's armoured sledge leads the column. But then, he is the only one who knows the way to the hiding-place of the gold.

The narrow, winding path grows steeper and steeper. The higher we go the more our spirits sink.

Time and again the tanks slide backwards, and risk going over the edge and down into the depths below us. Looking down, it reminds one of a cauldron of water at the boil. Driving snow spouts up from it in jets like those of a fountain. Only the drivers remain in the vehicles. The rest of us put on Siberian snow-shoes and run along the inner side of the path, close in to the rock wall where there is less risk of being blown over the edge by a sudden violent puff of wind. Close to the tree level, where the eternal winds have hardened the snow, we change to short skis.

The tanks and motor sledges can now increase speed and we have difficulty in keeping up.

At breakneck speed Porta's Panther goes into a hairpin bend, slides sideways and hits the mountainside with a crash. It spins completely round on the icy path, slides backwards and comes rushing down towards us, with ice and frozen snow showering up around it. We throw ourselves headlong to one side to save ourselves from being crushed by the 45-ton monster.

The rear T-34 is in the middle of the first hairpin when the Panther comes rushing down on it in a giant cloud of snow.

'Holy Christ!' screams Albert, grey-faced with terror.

'Turn the waggon, you bloody black fool,' shouts Barcelona, desperately, but Albert is completely paralysed. He glares, wild-eyed, at the death coming roaring down at him.

The Old Man is up on the T-34 in one long jump, but before he has got down through the turret the Panther has arrived. Steel clangs against steel, and both tanks rush on down the slippery path.

Somehow Albert gets the tracks to go the opposite way, so that the T-34 slides into the wall of the cliff and stops the wild race. How, is a mystery. The Panther rears up, mounting halfway up on the T-34. Through the clashing of steel we can hear Albert calling wildly on God. The Old Man brings his hand across the black man's face twice, hard. Albert stops shouting, and begins to grin foolishly.

'No man can stand up to this sort of thing,' he whines miserably. He is standing out in the snow, a little later, staring down into the abyss below.

'Shut your black trap!' shouts the Old Man furiously. 'Get back up in that tea-waggon of yours, so's we can start up again.'

'I bloody won't,' protests Albert, grey-faced. 'I don't want anything to do with that gold! I'm satisfied with bein' a poor, black Obergefreiter in the German Army, I am. What good's a load of gold to me, man, if I'm lyin' smashed up in my tea-waggon at the bottom of a rotten cliff?'

'I ordered you to shut it,' rages the Old Man. He turns his mpi on Albert. 'Up with you!'

Whining softly to himself Albert shrugs his way down through the hatch and bangs it to behind him.

There is wild discussion as to which of us are to go with the drivers in the vehicles. We all refuse, and then Porta arranges a driver strike. They won't drive without an observer in each waggon.

It is hard to tell whether it is the Old Man or the Commissar who shouts the loudest. But it all ends as it usually does, with the weakest going to the wall. Resignedly, swearing in an undertone, I climb up to Porta and edge my way down behind the instruments.

'You look like my pal Rodeck the day they picked him up on a 30-year rap!' he grins.

'I don't *know* your bloody friend Rodeck,' I answer him, sourly.

'He was a nice, pleasant chap,' Porta goes on happily. 'They called him a car-thief, and it *was* cars he stole. But he was really a painter, and he was that good at it he could repaint any size of car you liked to come with, in 1 hour and 11 minutes flat. There was usually some paint left over, too, so the owner of the car and his family could sniff themselves silly for a week after. He lived, free and happy, in the company of his paints and his sprayers, until one Wednesday mornin' between 3 and 5 o'clock. Then the door-bell rang so long and loud you'd have thought it was the Devil arrived to pick up a lost soul.'

'"Who the hell's that?" shouted Rodeck from his side of the door. He was naturally a bit narked at being woke up at that un-Christian time of the day.

'"Give you three guesses," creaked a voice out from the landin', and then the door gets smashed in on him, and two snap-brims are asking for a view of his wrists. "Click" go the cuffs and there he is with his pyjama jacket fitted with steel extensions.

'So off he went with all his paint-pots, and nobody outside the "Alex" tec-shop has seen him since.'

The road has begun to improve, and everybody gets back up into the vehicles. Before we cross the pass, the Commissar orders us to rope the waggons together with double towing-wires. The path will become so steep that there is danger of the vehicles toppling over backwards. Their theoretical angle of climb we have long ago exceeded. The new T-34 is in the lead with Albert driving. It is a tank which has everything the others ought to have but haven't. It can climb like a chamois on its incredibly wide tracks, and Albert knows how to drive it; but we have to fill him up with plenty of liquor to make him forget his constant fear of death. When he has got half a bottle of vodka inside him he is on top of the world. Only Porta is a better driver.

'Take it easy now, black-arse! No further'n the edges,'

Porta warns him from the Panther's turret. 'Don't get to thinkin' that Russian thunder-box can scramble down sheer rock faces!'

Albert gives him the international 'Up you' sign, with a slap of his hand on the inside of his bent elbow.

The tow-wires break twice, as if they were cotton, and the Panther slides back down towards the dizzying abyss.

'Don't we soon get a break?' says Barcelona, dog-tired. 'Hell, it's black as the inside of your hat!'

'A break? Here? At three in the afternoon?' shouts the Old Man angrily. 'You must be off your rocker!'

The Commissar orders us to tie outselves to one another with our climbing-ropes, in order that nobody get lost in the roaring hell of snow.

'I just can't go on any more,' moans Gregor. 'You can have my share of the gold! If this had been a legal job, they'd have had to strike a new medal for it. We deserve one!'

'An' if it goes wrong,' laughs Tiny, raucously, shaking chunks of ice from his shoulders, 'they'll tie 120 years on our back, with a little bit of a chance of gettin' out on parole when we've done 80 of 'em an' 'ave forgot entirely what cunt's all about!'

'Save your breath!' snarls the Old Man sourly. 'Stay here,' he orders, shortly, releasing himself from the safety-rope. 'I'm going forward a bit to have a look. Don't blow me away when I come back!'

With his binoculars bumping against his chest, he climbs on up, and is hidden, in a few seconds, by the driving snow.

'He's that bloody careful, he wipes his arse an hour before he goes to the shithouse,' snarls Porta irritably, taking a big bite of frozen brawn, and washing it down with a swallow of vodka.

'There isn't a chance of Ivan Baggytrousers laying an ambush for us. It's overcareful sods like that who slow down the war effort. If it was up to me it'd be off we go for Uncle Joe's gold as fast as the tracks'd let us! That'd soon make the neighbours take off, if they really *were* crazy enough to be sitting nursing their frost-bitten pricks and waitin' for *us*.'

'How cold *is* it?' asks Gregor, shivering.

'*Je ne sais pas, mon ami*,' answers the Legionnaire despondently, beating his body with his arms. 'But I have never been through anything like it!'

'48 below,' reports Heide, arrogantly.

'You're barmy,' protests Tiny, hopping on the spot and swinging his arms. 'You mean 148 below at least! My toes've turned to icicles inside these felt boots, and my blood thinks it's become part of the bleedin' Arctic Ocean!'

'Oh, no!' groans Barcelona, brushing icicles from his face. 'It's not worth it. Who the hell'd ever believe it could *get* this cold?'

'Pack yourselves out with paper,' orders the Commissar, throwing down some bundles of old newspapers which he and 'Frostlips' come up with. 'Rub yourselves down with snow all over first, then pack yourselves in a layer of newspaper!'

'You must be round the bleedin' bend,' screams Tiny. 'Take our clothes off at 148 below? We'll go off bleedin' bang like the soddin' trees!'

'Wait till it gets *really* cold,' laughs the Commissar. 'This is only the beginning!'

'If it's goin' to get colder'n this then my share of the gold's goin' cheap,' declares Tiny, through chattering teeth, while he packs a few copies of *Pravda* round his stomach.

'No, not like that,' 'Whorecatcher' warns him. 'First you've got to rub yourself down with snow. It's not near as bad as you think. Feet most of all. Rub 'em till you feel they're glowin'!'

'Oh Jesus!' sobs Gregor, rubbing snow all over his naked body. 'Some ski tour this is. And we're doing it as volunteers!'

'Yes, you don't 'ave to go to the soddin' psychopaths to be certified as a bleedin' super-idiot,' rages Tiny, struggling with his frozen fur jumpsuit.

'Who the hell would've thought it could get this cold any place on earth,' pants Porta, pushing an extra copy of *Izvestia* down round his chest. 'I'm cured of winter sports for the rest of my life!'

'I can't help wondering, man, whether that fuckin' gold's really worth all this trouble?' chatters Albert. 'You want to hear what I think, we'd turn back now, before the new Ice Age overtakes us!'

'*I'm* not givin' up *my* gold,' shouts Porta. 'If I have to roll on my bollocks through ice an' snow all the way to where it's hidden, an' do it on my own, I'll still do it! But if you want to go on living your little lives out in lousy, stinkin' poverty, then step off now before you've got too far into the Ice Age!'

The Old Man comes back, blue in the face with cold.

'Why the devil didn't you take me with you?' asks the Commissar, smearing frost salve on his face. 'Never do that again! You don't know how easy it is to get lost. You can't count on the compass. The mountains make the readings go wild!'

'Give me a drink,' says the Old Man, brusquely, reaching for Porta's water-bottle.

'D'you know this area?' he turns to the Commissar.

'No, I've never been here. But we save about 400 kilometres by going over the pass. Everybody says it's impossible from October to the end of May. I chose it for safety. Nobody would dream that anybody would try it in winter-time.'

'The devil,' curses the Old Man. 'Let's get out of here. We've got to get through that pass quick as possible. There's a storm on the way. Just on the far side of the pass, there's an old fort, or a monastery or something, where we can tank up and get a breather for the night.'

When we are halfway up the pass, one of the half-tracks skids off the path and we have to dig it out of the snowdrifts.

Porta wants to push it over the edge, and is on his way

with the Panther, but the Commissar protests violently. The truck cannot be done without, if we are to bring back the gold.

Then the older T-34 gets stuck. We weep with rage and despair and are ready to give up completely. Finally we get the new T-34 backed into a position from which it can pull its elder brother out of the snow. The tow-wires stretch and hum.

'Back!' shouts 'Frostlips' warningly, jumping behind a snowdrift.

'Somebody comin'?' asks Tiny, confusedly, staring from behind a large tree.

The wire snaps with a whining crack and the pieces fly close by Tiny's head. A fraction of an inch to one side or the other and he would have been beheaded. A madness of rage grips him. With a shovel in his hands he rushes towards the T-34, where Albert's black face is just visible above the turret coaming.

Like lightning Albert has the hatch slammed to and dogged fast from the inside. Tiny smashes the shovel down on the closed hatch cover in a mad rage.

'Come outside, you black cannibal, so's I can kill you!' he roars madly.

'Knock him out!' shouts the Old Man. But none of us dare go near him when he is like this. A mad grizzly is a lapdog compared to him.

'Come out, you black ape,' he screams, pulling the cord of a grenade and swinging it round his head.

'Hell! Get rid of it,' warns Porta from the Panther's hatch.

''Ere then!' shouts Tiny, throwing the grenade at Porta, who is down under cover inside the tank with the speed of a ferret.

The grenade strikes the top edge of the hatch coaming, but the antenna causes it to change direction and it goes off with a sharp crack.

'The devil take me if I'm going to stand for this any longer,' rages the Old Man. He grabs his *Kalashnikov* by the

261

barrel and swings it round his head. The butt comes down with a hollow thud on the back of Tiny's neck. With a long, hoarse exhalation of breath he goes down in the snow. His arms and legs jerk a few times, then he lies still.

'Shoot him,' foams Albert from inside the T-34, 'shoot that mad bastard.'

'Where *did* you catch *him*?' asks the Commissar, shaking his head wonderingly. 'He ought to be kept in a strait-jacket for the rest of his life!'

'Tie him up,' orders the Old Man, grinding his teeth together. 'Tie him up like a Christmas tree! When he wakes up he'll be worse than a ton of HE. Tie him to the gun. Even he can't shift that!'

'What was up with him?' asks Porta, putting his head up again cautiously through the hatchway.

'He nearly got his napper chopped off when the wire went,' explains Gregor, with a laugh. 'Now he thinks Albert did it on purpose. They had a bit of an argument over some black puddin' earlier on.'

'It's what I always say,' laughs Porta. 'He's too touchy, that boy!'

It is well into the night before we are through the pass and go slipping and sliding down the far side. The huge fort rises before us, dark and threatening. It is built of great, shaped blocks of stone, piled upon one another without any kind of mortar. If mortar had been used it would have crumbled away long ago. Frost has bitten deeply into the corners of the blocks.

'That's what I call building blocks,' cries Heide, for once really impressed. 'How on earth did they manage to get them up on top of one another?'

'Slaves,' replies 'Whorecatcher', as if it were the most natural thing in the world. 'Never been a shortage of them, here in Russia. They're willin' and effective, and there's plenty of 'em. People can be made to do most anything, if you know how to apply a knout to 'em, or cut 'em a bit with a Cossack knife!'

'I've always been a great admirer of your humanitarian

principles,' says Porta, sarcastically.

The Old Man wants us to tank up before resting, but he has to give in to our wild protests.

'Frostlips' and Gregor get a huge fire going inside the great hall.

'Stinks o' dead men in here,' says Barcelona, sniffing the air.

'To hell with that,' hisses the Commissar. 'Dead men aren't dangerous!'

'You're that ugly a feller could spew up just lookin' at you,' shouts Tiny angrily. He hits out at Heide with his machine-pistol.

'Stop that everlastin' squabbling,' shouts the Old Man. 'Now I want quiet! One word more and you get guard duty!'

'That Nazi shit looks like 'e's on 'is way to a funeral,' roars Tiny, pointing at Heide with his mpi. ''Is own funeral, too!'

'Shut up and come over here. Let's have a game of idiot bank,' suggests Porta, shuffling the cards. 'How many's in?' he asks, looking around him.

'I'm too bloody tired,' moans Barcelona, dropping down heavily on the packed earth on the floor.

'There's two things a man's never too tired for,' says Porta, cutting the cards into talons. 'Gambling and shagging! I can tell you a story about what can happen to people who think they're too tired to fuck!'

'The very widely-known *Wachtmeister*, Alois Fresa from the "Alex" station, got temporarily posted, one Palm Sunday it was, to the plain-clothes branch. He put on his good pin-striper, and then got himself an Afro hair-do – that's a typical symptom of paranoia. When he found it not so easy to pick up a bit o' the other, he got hold of a couple of yellow leather shoulder-holsters an' stuck a couple of P-38s into 'em. He'd seen that was how the tough cops on the films did it. Of course, this made a hell of an impression on the shield-struck floozies. He let the word go round he was Gestapo, but that was a lot of balls. He was on the bicycle-theft flying squad, really. Then his lucky day rolled round. He met three villains comin' out of the *Commerzbank* in *Hohenzollern Damm*, each with a bagful of shekels in his hand, and he blew 'em away with his hand-artillery. This blood-bath got itself talked about all over Berlin, and the women were soon standin' ten-deep round Alois. After a bit of this, though, he found it was more'n he could manage and wished they'd all get to hell out of it and leave him be. So there he was, late one night, sitting in "The Crooked Cop", head down, an' fucked all to pieces. Up came a little made-up doll from the Wedding district, totterin' along in heels like stilts, an' began touching him up for starters.

'"How'd you like to show me your *other* gun?" she whispered, passionate as all hell. "I've heard a lot about *you*! You know you look the way Clark Gable always wanted to look!" She touched him up a bit more then, and got one of her long, painted nails inside, and started working direct on John Thomas with the roll-collar. But Johnny T. wasn't havin' any. He was limp an' wrinkled as a 90-year-old eunuch.

'"Sod off!" snarled Alois, giving her a push. "If I was to really get hot for you, you'd have to look a lot different!"

'This Wedding bint started givin' him mouth then, which Wedding bints have a way of doin'!

'"An' *you're* the feller they're all talking so much about," she yelled. "You ain't even got hair on your balls. You don't get away with turnin' *me* down!" And before anybody knew what she was up to, there she stood with his two P-38s in her hands. She'd flipped 'em neatly out of his shoulder-holsters. Then she cocked 'em with her thumbs the way the cowboys used to do when they walked into Prairie Town bank to arrange a loan.

'"God! No!" he screamed, holding out his hands in front of him. As if that was goin' to help!

'The one-legged bartender choked on his drink. He was tryin' to shout "Heil Hitler!" an' swallow at the same time.

'"Understand me! Please! Darlin'! I'm too *tired*!" babbled

Fresa. But he'd gone off the bar-stool on to the floor before he even knew he was dead.

'The bartender tried to scream, but all he got out was a sound like a sea-lion with asthma.

'So there you see what can happen to a feller who's too tired to fuck! Anybody else want in?' asks Porta, looking around again.

'Twenty!' shouts Gregor, slapping twenty marks on the nearest talon.

But the game soon peters out. We are far too exhausted, and hardly care whether we win or lose. The two last players are Porta and 'Frostbite'. Then they, too, give up.

Tiny has hardly got his head down before he breaks into a roar of laughter. He is one of those lucky people who can laugh for hours at their own jokes. His unbridled laughter takes the rest of us with him. Soon laughter shakes the whole room.

The Commissar whinnies, tears running down his cheeks. Every time we look over at Tiny, sitting with his pale-grey bowler cocked at an angle on his head, we explode into laughter again. We simply cannot stop. The only serious face is that of Heide. Each of our roars of laughter seems to tighten his face into an even stiffer mask of severity.

Finally we fall into a sleep of exhaustion. Suddenly Tiny is there again. He stands over the Old Man with legs apart, jabbing at him with a machine-pistol.

'What the hell now?' curses the Old Man.

'You're under arrest!' says Tiny with an MP look on his face.

'Arrest? Are you mad?' hisses the Old Man, angry at being pulled back out of dreamland. 'What the hell're you talking about? Don't you know I'm your Section Leader?'

'That's why,' growls Tiny, darkly. 'In mine, Adolf's an' the German people's name you are under arrest. You have illegally laid hands on a subordinate!'

'Now I've heard that one too?' protests the Old Man, blankly.

'It won't 'elp you to deny it, Oberfeldwebel Beier,' says Tiny, with the strict air of an interrogator. 'Did you, or did you not, crack me on the bonce with an mpi butt? You see? Now I'm going to shoot you for it! I will not stand any more of it!'

'He's mad as a hatter,' whispers 'Frostlips'. He edges over towards Tiny, who has released the safety on his weapon and whose finger is already curling dangerously on the trigger.

The Old Man sits there paralysed, staring at him.

'Frostlips' jumps forward and bores three stiff fingers into Tiny's diaphragm. Air leaves the big man's lungs with explosive force. He bends over forward.

The Legionnaire lifts his arm and brings the edge of his hand down with all his strength on Tiny's neck. He falls unconscious.

'What the devil's wrong with him?' gasps the Old Man, wiping the sweat from his brow. 'It's not the first time I've knocked him cold with a butt-stroke. I'm getting fed up with the bloody idiot!'

'*Bien sûr*, he is dead drunk,' says the Legionnaire. 'That is the trouble! You can see it on him!'

The Commissar begins frantically to rummage in his pack. He pulls out two empty *Stolichnaja* bottles.

'I'll say he's drunk,' he says, throwing the bottles disgustedly from him. 'The swine's drunk two litres of vodka!'

'Let's kill him,' suggests 'Whorecatcher', as soon as he discovers there is not a drop left in the two bottles.

'A beating is what he needs,' says the Legionnaire. 'A good whipping with our belts would make him think twice!'

'No good,' answers Porta, shaking his head. 'He's a double-nature. One of 'em, when he's drunk, is completely unaccountable for his actions; then there's the sober feller, who can't remember a single thing the drunk did while under the influence. When he's not drunk he's right enough.'

'Then we'll have to see to it he don't get drunk, won't

we,' says 'Frostlips'. 'He's a danger to all around him!'

'That's nothing to what he's like if you *refuse* to give him anything,' laughs Porta, heartily.

I don't know how long I have been asleep when the others awaken me. Soundlessly I grasp my machine-pistol, and strain my ears in the darkness.

Porta sits up alongside me and is about to give a shout. I put my hand on him to indicate silence. Instinctively he covers the glowing embers of the fire with a tin bath. The room is in total darkness.

'What is it?' whispers the Old Man, nervously.

'I don't know,' I whisper back, my hands tightly around the mpi. 'Something woke me up!'

'Skis,' mumbles Tiny, who has ears like a weasel. He claims he can hear a fly rubbing its legs together five miles away. Against the wind, too!

'Are you sure?' asks the Commissar, in a voice which shakes a little. 'It's not the wind, fooling you?'

'Don't you believe it!' answers Tiny. 'Me an' my flappers don't make mistakes! When you been a slave in Torgau, you can 'ear the lice dancin' a tango on the belly of a Chinese whore in Shanghai!'

'Skis!' mumbles the Commissar, thoughtfully. 'Then they're after us! But how the hell can they have found us here?'

'Impossible!' whispers 'Frostlips'. 'Can't be us they're after. Must be somebody else. There's manhunts on in Russia all year round!'

'Well, they ain't come out here in this hellish snow for the fun of it, you can bet your boots,' says 'Whorecatcher'.

'Let's get outside!' orders the Old Man, nervously. 'We're like rats in a trap in here!'

Unfortunately, it has stopped snowing. A full moon has come out from behind the hurrying clouds, and the snow glitters in its pale beams.

We huddle together, freezingly cold, behind the frost-weathered stones, and stare out over the snowy distances.

We can see nothing, only hear the wind, howling.

'Jesus'n Mary!' cries Tiny suddenly. 'The 'ole Red bleedin' Army's on its way up 'ere after us!'

The Old Man turns his glasses in the direction Tiny is indicating, but can see nothing.

'You're still bloody drunk, and seein' things,' he snarls angrily.

'*Job tvojemadj*,' cries the Commissar. 'Siberians! A whole company of 'em, and they're coming this way!'

Soon after, the rest of us can see them too. They come racing down the mountains on skis in one long line.

The Legionnaire slides down behind the MG-34, inserts a belt, loads, and closes the cover with a tiny click.

I draw my pistol from its shoulder-holster, cock it and let the hammer down carefully on the round. It's the best way with a *Nagan*.

'What the hell d'you think you're goin' to get up to with that popgun?' asks 'Whorecatcher', with a gesture of resignation. 'Do you realize what those fellers'll do to us when they get hold of us? I hurt just thinking about it. We'll never see the light o' day again! And when they've finished with us we'll only be able to crawl!'

'Shut up,' I snarl, holstering the pistol again. 'They won't take *me* alive!'

'You're wrong! If they want us they'll take us, however much you bang away with that pistol of yours. The sun's gone down for us. We're *dead* men. Think I'll just stroll down there and get it over quick!'

'You stay here,' commands the Commissar, in a voice sharp as a knife. 'Damned if we're going to give up just because a couple of slit-eyed NKVD coppers come sliding down on boards!'

'I'm not givin' up either,' swears 'Frostlips', readying his *Kalashnikov*.

Gregor cracks a magazine in the LMG. He too is ready to fight things out.

The Legionnaire puts a *Nagan* in his boot-top, and draws his Moorish combat-knife.

'What the hell good'll it do, bangin' away now, man?' sighs Albert despairingly. Still he loads himself up with hand-grenades.

'You look like a lump of black pudding left behind in a shithouse,' grins Porta.

'That's what I feel like,' admits Albert sadly.

'Shall we give 'em a dose up the arse with stovepipe Lizzie here?' asks Tiny, battle-hungry. He handles the heavy mortar as if it were made of cardboard. 'We can blow them shits away like confetti, when they come on to that long flat bit.'

'You must have been reading our propaganda leaflets again,' Porta scolds him irritably. 'They'd hear it a million miles off in these shitty mountains. Then we'd have the whole rotten OGPU on our necks!'

'*Njet mortira**,' warns sledge-driver Ermolov, hugging his *Kalashnikov* closer to him. He has loaded with explosive bullets which smash anything they hit.

'Is it the OGPU?' asks Albert with wide-open eyes. Even the thought of the OGPU or the Gestapo makes him shiver like a blancmange.

'Yes! Who'd the hell you think it was?' asks Porta, with a short laugh. 'Think it was a load of Salvation Army blackbirds, out picking up loose souls?'

'*Ssatana*,' curses the Commissar. 'Of all the fucking patrols to run into! Siberian bloody OGPU. *Ssatana*!' he repeats, banging his fist down viciously on the *Kalashnikov*'s round magazine.

'What the hell difference does it make if they're Siberians or whatever?' asks the Old Man, blankly. He keeps his eyes on the long line of snow-camouflaged skiers on the far side of the mountain slope, as he speaks.

'Hell of a difference,' growls the Commissar. 'Siberians are the best manhunters in the world. They're on their feet night and day all year round, in peace or war. They range the country from the Polar Sea to the Black Sea, from the

---

* *Njet mortira:* No mortars

269

mountains of China to the forests of Finland and Poland, and they get a *bounty* for every single body they bring in.'

Staff-corporal Dalin comes rushing down the ice-clad path, completely out of breath, throws himself down alongside the Commissar and fishes a crumpled cigarette from his pocket. Hungrily he sucks smoke into his lungs, and lets it come slowly out through his nostrils.

'Igor's still up there,' he explains, pointing to the mountain top. 'There's a whole company of OGPU special service troops on the way up and they've got a short-barrelled mountain gun with 'em. Igor thinks they've picked up our trail.'

The cigarette burns down one side. He looks at it, sadly. '*Tovaritsch!*' he says, giving the Commissar a pleading look, and scratching his head under his fur cap. 'Let us go home, and leave the gold where it is! A man who has never been rich will never miss it!'

'Shut up, you mangy cur,' says the Commissar angrily. 'There *is* no way back. Take a swig of vodka, maybe it'll swill the cowardice out of you!'

'Get your pecker up, mate.' Tiny puts his arm, comfortingly, round Dalin. The man looks like a sick hen, whose eggs have been taken from her. 'Buck up, now! You're gonna be rich, an' can pick out your own wall-paper.'

'Have we got any chance at all of getting out of this?' asks Gregor desperately, looking up at the snow-capped mountains.

'I'm no prophet,' growls the Commissar impatiently. 'But first of all we've got to get up through that gulch before they start cackling on that bloody radio of theirs!'

'We can soon blow that lot away,' cries Porta, optimistic as always. 'We've got two tea-waggons, the PIV and the Panther *and* that armoured sledge. We're a whole bloody army. They've only got a pissy little mountain gun, and for sure not a single armour-piercing shell for it. They can't do more'n scratch our paintwork a bit!'

'The *radio* dammit, the *radio*!' shouts the Commissar

furiously. 'Before the noise of our first explosive shell has died away they'll have alarmed their base and we'll have a whole division on top of us – supported by Jabos! There'll be headhunters swarming all over these mountains like flies on a hot midden!'

'Who says we use guns?' asks Porta. 'We just go quietly up to 'em with open hatches so they think we're on their side. Then when we get close enough to start up on 'em with balalaikas an' guitars. Goodbye the slit-eyed shits!'

'*Njet!*' answers the Commissar, shaking his head negatively. 'Anybody can tell you don't know the headhunters. Immediately they sight us a radio report goes off, and somewhere or other somebody starts finding out who we can be. Nobody can *move* in Russia without the OGPU having been informed, and what d'you think'll happen when they can't obtain radio contact with the company we've liquidated? I promise you. Everything comes to the boil!'

'You don't think, then, that it's us they're looking for?' asks the Old Man, doubtfully. 'Who the hell else can it be?'

'It's *certainly* not us,' answers the Commissar, decisively. 'They're one of those blasted tracking patrols who're not looking for anything in particular. Patrols like that are permanently on the hunt for anybody wandering round without a *propusk**.' He pushes his fur cap thoughtfully back on his head.

His grey eyes suddenly begin to glitter cunningly. 'I think I've got it,' he says after a long pause. 'A natural disaster! Their base could accept *that*!'

'You don't call it a disaster being rocked into eternity with lead guitar music?' asks Porta, with a short laugh, and patting his mpi.

'Certainly,' answers the Commissar, 'but we can't use that kind of disaster in this instance.'

'If you want to know what I think, man, then I'm for pissin' off out of here in one hell of a hurry,' whines Albert,

* *Propusk:* Permit

in a hoarse voice. He pulls his snow-mask further down over his face.

'What kind of weak sisters are you?' roars Porta angrily. 'Here I'm trying to make you rich, so you can wave goodbye to the stinking army for the rest of your lives, and lie on the beach playin' with the luxury whores. When you've started something then you finish it. *Panjemajo*? The earth's round, and if you ain't smart you can risk falling off it. And it *ain't* smart to give up now just because a party of Sweatyfoot Indians come slidin' along on planks. Let's get on with it. There's daylight up ahead!'

'Und wenn die ganze Erde bebt,*
und die Welt sich aus den Angeln hebt,
da kann doch einen Goldsucher nicht erschüttern!
Keine Angst, keine Angst, Rose Mari . . .'

hums Tiny thoughtfully, drumming his fingers on his *Kalashnikov*.

'Could we get along that windin' trail there that goes up alongside the ruins?' asks Barcelona, pointing.

'Yes, you could if you were a mountain goat that'd lost its wits,' answers the Commissar. 'This time of the winter nobody gets through without going through the gulch, and after that there's the *Paritip*†, but we can leave that for now. I can tell you it's not for people with weak stomachs, and in a high wind even the strongest-nerved get the shits!'

'*Paritip*? What the hell's a *Paritip*?' asks Porta.

'Wait till you see it,' grins 'Frostlips'. 'It might make

---

* Freely translated:
  And should the whole earth tremble.
  And the world roll off its tracks.
  That cannot shake a prospector.
  Never fear! Never fear! Rose Marie . . .
† Russian: roughly 'the Floater' or 'Glider': a suspension platform over a gorge

even you wish you'd stayed home. That is if you ain't one of these religious types who thinks death's better'n life!'

> 'Und noch bei Petrus wollen wir*
> den Würfelbecher schwingen . . .'

hums Tiny, and kisses a hand-grenade.

'Shut bloody up, you half-witted idiots,' rages the Old Man, banging the butt of his machine-pistol into the snow.

'Won't even let us sing any bleedin' more,' grumbles Tiny.

The Commissar goes down in the snow between the Old Man and 'Frostlips' and draws a sketch with the tip of a bayonet.

'An avalanche,' cries the Old Man, in surprise, studying the sketch with a sceptical mien. 'Think it can be done?'

'Our one chance,' answers the Commissar. 'There's tons of snow up above ready to come down if we just help it a bit.'

'Shut *up*, then!' cries Porta, licking his frost-chapped lips cautiously. 'The light begins to flicker out there. An avalanche! Fuck *me*! Those headhunters down there'll get rolled straight into Paradise. Both St Peter an' Jesus'll go arse-over-tip when they arrive up there with all that snow!'

'How much gel' we got?' asks the Old Man, getting to his feet.

'Three full boxes,' answers Barcelona. 'Enough to put the Kremlin up on the moon!'

'One box o' ten's enough,' says the Old Man.

'Catch!' shouts Tiny, throwing a package of explosives into the Old Man's lap.

'Are you completely mad?' shouts the Commissar, in terror, throwing himself down like lightning behind a

---

* Freely: And up with Peter we will make
             The dice-cup shake and rattle . . .

weathered stone block. 'In this temperature? Anybody knows it'll have degenerated by now and can go off at the slightest touch.'

'Take it easy,' smiles Porta. '*We* don't have to abide by the patent laws, so we've changed the formula round a bit. What we've done'd send the inventors crawling up their own arseholes for fright, but we found out, when we were soddin' about up there where it'd freeze the balls off a brass reindeer, that a bit of nitroglycerine in the dough and a freshener of nitre made it more stable in cold weather. If we'd used what the eggheads at Bamberg'd told us to we'd have been on the moon by now playin' hide and seek with the Mars-men!'

Tiny fishes a whole bundle of loose primers carelessly out of his pocket, and hands them to him. Any ammunition expert would have jumped out of his boots at the sight. Primers have to be treated with great care. The least shock can send them off.

'Shall we blow off all the soap, then?' asks Tiny, eagerly, beginning to make preparations.

'Hell no!' answers the Old Man crossly. 'Five or six ought to be more than enough!'

'*Mon Dieu*! Where are the pincers?' asks the Legionnaire, excitedly. 'We must hurry! They are coming towards us quickly!'

'Pincers?' asks Tiny. 'They've gone missin', but who needs 'em? You can bite 'em on to the cable. I've done it often. Quicker, too! Don't 'ave to bite too 'ard though, else your teeth fall out – *an*' your old napper goes with 'em, too!'

'*Merde*!' says the Legionnaire, shaking his head. 'Only a man who is tired of life bites on those things!'

Unworriedly Tiny pushes the wires into the primers and bites them fast.

'He's too stupid to realize the danger,' grins Porta. 'Not even the dumbest dog'd even *sniff* at a primer!'

'He's raving mad,' says 'Frostlips'. '*We* have to put on rubber shoes when we go into the depots where they keep that shit. That sod *eats* 'em!'

'It's because he's a Sunday's child, born on Christmas Eve,' laughs Porta. 'Nothing can happen to *him*!'

Tiny is already chewing on the fifth primer. When he has finished he connects the explosive mass in a way that sends shivers down our spines. Then he puts the whole lot down into his deep pocket. The dangerous primers stick up on their wires and bob about like the bells on a jester's cap.

With Dalin in the lead we make our way towards the mountain-top. When we have got some way up we have to change from skis to snowshoes.

'You're goin' to have to learn to stand on those planks a hell of a lot better,' Dalin criticizes us, with the irritability of the expert, 'or you'll never manage this job!'

Up under the small conifer trees, we fumble our way in pitch darkness, and have to use our handlamps in short flashes. There are narrow, deep crevasses everywhere. To go down in one of these is certain death.

The storm howls, in long, miserable moans. Frost explodes in branch and trees with the sharp crack of rifle-shots.

Cursing and fuming we try to protect our faces against the short stiff branches of the trees. They whip across our faces, drawing blood when the skin breaks.

Dalin pushes us along, angrily, jeering at us for our clumsiness.

'Even an old, worn-out Cossack grandmother could catch up with you,' he rages, impatiently. 'Dopes like you lot'll never win this world war!'

'Wait'n see, you bowlegged Jewboy,' screams Tiny, throwing his mpi at Dalin, but not succeeding in hitting him. 'You don't know us Germans yet!'

After two hours of inhuman toil we reach the open slope above the tree-line. Tired out we drop down. The wind is not merely icy, it is a roaring hurricane. We can see the peak, like a great, threatening colossus, a little way in front of us.

'*Ssatan*,' Dalin curses. 'Up on your feet! In half an hour

the moon'll be out, and they'll be able to see us 100 miles off.'

'Jesus'n Mary,' groans Tiny. 'I can feel them OGPU *Kalashnikov* explosive berries borin' their way into my good German guts already!'

Suddenly I stumble, and begin to slide down the slope. I am rolling like a snowball at constantly increasing speed when a large rock gets in my way. For a moment I think I have broken, or sprained, an ankle, but the fear of being left alone soon gets me back on my feet, even though I can feel the pain right up through my back.

'I can't go on!' groans Gregor, dropping like a felled tree to the snow.

'Up you get!' snarls Porta, giving him a brutal kick. 'Think of your share of the gold and you'll *want* to go on!'

'Shit on the gold,' pants Gregor, worn out. 'If it's all the gold in the world you can keep it! Let me *sleep*! I want to die! *Now*!' He presses his face into the snow, and his whole body shakes with hysterical sobs.

Together we get him back up on his feet, and drag him between us like a sack. He shouts, and calls us every name he can think of. Finally Porta cannot stand it any longer. He gives him such a beating that all his frost-sores break open like ripe boils. It helps for a while.

Ermolov is lying in the shelter of a projecting shelf of rock staring through his night-glasses. Silently he points down the mountain. We can see the OGPU company, like small, moving, black spots below us.

'We've got to get further up,' says Dalin. 'But get some speed on now! There's not much time to lose! But don't look down,' he warns us. 'Look up!'

'Good Lord deliver us,' Porta breaks out, in amazement, when we are all the way up, and see the enormous masses of snow which are resting on only a relatively small rock-shelf.

'When once that starts to roll,' says Barcelona, 'that band of murderers down there'll do well to move arse in one hell of a hurry!'

'Four charges ought to be plenty to set that snowball rolling down on their nuts,' says 'Frostlips', scratching his head thoughtfully under his fur cap.

'Let's use five. Better safe than sorry!' suggests Porta, looking up at the huge lip of snow. 'But now the devil are we goin' to position the loads without settin' the avalanche going too soon? If it starts before the neck-shooters have got into the wide bit there, they'll get back with their balls intact and we're in the shit up to our necks!'

'We'll have to get over on the other side,' says Barcelona. He leans over the steep cliff-face and draws back, shivering. 'That's impossible! Take an eagle to do it!'

'Leave it to me,' says Tiny, pushing energetically forward. 'I ain't no eagle, but I'm clever'n one. You lot ain't got no idea of 'ow to blow anythin' up! *I'll* show you how to do it!'

'Don't do it,' warns 'Frostlips'. 'You'll break your neck!'

'Don't give me that piss!' sneers Tiny, contemptuously. 'Take a look at the way a bloke from 'Amburg does it! I'll be up on that mantelshelf and 'ave the fireworks in place quicker'n a bull up a butcher!'

'He's right,' says the Old Man, convinced. 'The shelf's bound to increase the force of the blow an' make even more snow come down on 'em. The noise of the charges'll get damped down by the snow, and the slits down there won't get frightened and do the devil out of a nice fresh delivery!'

'Why not?' asks Porta, shrugging his shoulders, indifferently. 'Try it! Tiny's always gettin' away with things other fellers'd break their necks trying!'

'D'you think it's *dangerous*?' asks Tiny doubtfully, peering cautiously down into the dizzying abyss.

'Not a bit of it,' lies Porta impudently, pointing up to the snow-cap hanging threateningly out over the lip of the shelf. 'If all that weight of ice an' snow can't fall, how'll you be able to? Just be careful not to spit on both hands at the same time!'

'Let's do it then,' says Tiny, decisively, wrapping the

277

rope around him. 'Gimme that ice-axe. Keep a tight hold on the string now so's you can pull me up again if I go on me arse!'

Gregor sits down, presses his heels well into the cliff and passes the rope out slowly, as Tiny moves across the icy slope.

'He'll never make it,' whispers Barcelona nervously.

'More rope,' shouts Tiny impatiently. 'I got to go round a corner, for Christ's sake! It's black as up Albert's arse down 'ere!'

'He'll kill himself,' says Gregor, darkly, paying out more rope.

Frostlips sits down beside him and helps him hold on to it. It is literally Tiny's lifeline.

'Jesus Christ!' howls Tiny, in a voice which sounds as if it is coming to us through cotton-wool.

'Anything up?' asks Porta, looking up, but unable to catch sight of him.

'Fell on me arse,' comes faintly from the cliff-face. 'It's blowin' like 'ell over 'ere. My prick's turned into a bleedin' icicle.'

'This is madness,' mumbles Barcelona. 'He'll never *make* it!'

'Wait and see,' says Porta. 'I know Tiny. If he gets really angry there's nothing can stop him!'

We can hear the sound of the ice-axe, which he is using to cut steps in the rock and ice. Gregor and 'Frostlips' pay out more and more rope.

'How the hell's he *doing* it?' asks 'Frostlips', shaking his head. 'He needs all his strength to even hang on to the cliff-wall, and he must already be frozen through and through!'

'Yes, and don't forget he's got his pockets full of explosives,' says Barcelona. 'And like the dope he is it's primed! Don't need much of a knock for him to blow himself and half the mountain to bits.'

'Did he ever take an ammunition course anyway?' asks 'Frostlips'. 'Nobody who's ever had anything to do with explosives treats 'em the way he does!'

'He *was* on a course at Bamberg,' laughs Porta, carelessly. 'But they threw him off it before he managed to blow the whole place up. He did kill off a few ammo experts though, without getting as much as a scratch himself. Even though he went up there on the Milky Way a time or two, he still came down licking the cream off his chops!'

If we lean out over the edge of the cliff we can just see Tiny's dark shadow moving slowly upwards, veiled in billowing clouds of snow.

'He looks like one of those stuntmen climbing up a skyscraper,' mutters the Commissar nervously.

'Bit short of windows to nip through, though, if he gets tired,' says Porta, drily.

'If he slips now,' mumbles 'Frostlips', 'he's got 5,000 feet under him. The rope'd cut him clean in two!'

'Damn an' set fire to it,' curses Tiny from out in the snow. 'This bleedin' ledge ain't no wider than a fly is between the eyes.'

'Hang on with your toes,' suggests Porta. 'Bend 'em like the birds do!'

'What do you think I *am* doin'?' comes Tiny's voice from out on the mountain-side.

'Get on with it,' shouts 'Frostlips' nervously. 'Those headhunters'll be in the valley in a minute, and at our throats before we know where we are!'

A nasty crash and a rain of powdery snow cuts him short. The rock-shelf has given way. With a howl of terror Tiny goes out into thin air but in some miraculous manner manages to hang on with his ice-axe.

Cursing and swearing he begins to work his way upwards again. We lean out and see him hanging and swaying where the ledge was before.

He hacks viciously at the snow and finally makes a hole large enough for the charges. Spitting with rage he rolls the cables a couple of times more round the explosive and forces stones and pieces of ice into the hole to wedge the charge in place. It wouldn't be smart if we were to take it with us when we moved the wires.

A strong gust of wind takes off his fur cap and nearly sends him down into the gulf with it. He slides down hazardously, but finds a foothold on the second ledge, which is somewhat broader.

Even though he is bear-like in size, he looks small against the tons of snow which hang, suspended, above his head. He checks the charges once more and gives the primers an extra crimp with his teeth. Balancing on the edge he takes a swig from his water-bottle. Then he starts back across the vertical, wind-blown, rock wall. A huge eagle flaps close by him. Furiously, he throws a punch at it, loses his grip and slides some way down the mountain face.

Gregor, alone on the safety rope, had become unobservant from cold and exhaustion and does not feel Tiny's tug on the rope. It is hanging so loosely that it has become dangerous. The big man has no more than just rounded the sharp corner when the eagle attacks again. He strikes out at it and loses his footing. His hands claw at the ice, blood spurts from long gashes and nails rip away. His axe curves out over the edge of the cliff, and goes sailing on down in a cloud of snow.

The eagle gives a hoarse, triumphant scream, and dives to the attack again.

Porta lets out a terrified shout, which warns Gregor just in time. He manages to press himself in between two vertical rocks, before he is taken over the edge by the terrific pull on the rope.

'What the devil are you up to?' asks the Commissar, wriggling his way over to us. 'Good Lord Almighty. He must have been killed!'

Far below we can see Tiny swinging back and forth on the rope with the raging eagle flapping around his head.

'He's lost his axe!' says Porta.

The Commissar lowers his own ice-axe down to him, quickly, and he manages to grasp it after several attempts.

Slowly we tighten the rope. If we go too quickly we can risk it snapping.

As we pull him up higher and higher we can hear him cursing and swearing.

'Got a full head of steam up,' says Porta. 'Gregor'd better get going till he's gone off the boil!'

'I'm off,' says Gregor firmly, beginning to buckle on his skis.

None of us has noticed that Tiny is already up over the edge, foaming with rage. The Commissar gives a warning shout as he comes rushing towards us through the snow, looking for the guilty party.

'You drop Tiny's bleedin' rope?' he roars accusingly, pointing his ice-axe at me.

'No, *no*!' I yell, to avoid certain death. 'It was Gregor! He dozed off!'

'Dozed off, did 'e?' roars Tiny. He bulldozes through the snow, towards where Gregor is sitting buckling on his skis.

The Old Man throws an mpi at him. It hits him right in the face, but he carries on, without even a second's pause.

Gregor just manages to turn around. Tiny grabs him by both skis and swings him round above his head like a hammer-thrower. When he has got speed up he lets go of him. With a crunch his body strikes a rock, his skis splintering. Then Tiny is on him again, hammering at him with his fists. They seem to be rotating as fast as propellers. Gregor knows he is fighting for his life. With the courage of desperation he succeeds in kicking upwards and hitting Tiny on the knee. Now the big man goes really crazy. With a scream he jumps up into the air, turns, and comes down on Gregor with such force that the man's body is literally pressed down into the frozen snow.

'Back!' hisses the Commissar, white with rage, and pressing the muzzle of his *Kalashnikov* into Tiny's throat. 'Back I say, or I'll shoot your head off!'

But Tiny is deaf to everything. Foaming at the mouth with rage he goes on beating the unconscious Gregor.

'Let me,' says Porta, bringing his machine-pistol down on Tiny's neck. With a tired grunt he falls down and lies motionless across Gregor.

'Chuck him over the edge!' suggests 'Frostlips' furiously, giving Tiny a brutal kick. 'The mad bastard's *dangerous*!'

'Take it easy,' says Porta. 'Who wouldn't be annoyed at some idiot lettin' him take a 300-yard sprint down the side of a mountain, and gettin' his whole bag o' bones knocked sideways?'

Shortly afterwards Tiny regains consciousness, shaking his head like a duck which has just been down to have a look at the bottom of its pond.

'I couldn't help it,' Gregor excuses himself weakly, wiping blood from his battered features.

'We'll discuss that later,' Tiny promises him with a wicked look, and lumbers off towards the edge of the cliff.

'Where the devil are you going?' asks the Old Man, running after him with his machine-pistol at the ready.

'Ain't we gonna roll that snowball?' asks Tiny. 'Ain't that what we crawled up on this Commie bleedin' mountain to *do*?'

Cursing and swearing furiously he begins to climb the icy granite wall again. He is so angry that he has forgotten to attach his climbing-rope.

'If he slips now,' says 'Frostlips', 'he's had it! Mad as they come, he is!'

'Don't for God's sake tell him it's dangerous,' warns Porta, 'then he'll be sure to fall!'

It seems an eternity before he finally finds the cable. It is still attached to the explosive charge. As carefully as if it were made of glass he pulls it over to him, and winds it around his elbow.

'God have mercy on us all!' groans the Commissar. 'Never in my life have I seen anything so insane!'

Twice, on his way back, he slips on the slope. Only a frozen snowdrift which is accidentally in his path stops him from going over the edge and down into the abyss.

'What about if it's a dud?' asks Barcelona, nervously, when Tiny is back and has gleefully connected the wires to the batteries.

'We'll be paddlin' up shit-creek,' answers Porta. 'Nothing left but to go straight at 'em with hand-grenades, balalaikas and guitar music!'

'The radio,' says the Commissar. 'That blasted radio. They always station it at a distance from them under cover! The signaller will be screaming for help as soon as we make a move, and up'll come the Jabos!'

'I'm against this battery shit,' rumbles Tiny. 'An old-fashioned fuse, what splutters off to where you can *see* it goin'. That was better'n more fun too! Used to remind me of Christmas Eve, when old Mr Creuzfeldt used to get drunk an' make us sing:

> And when they came to 'Erod's 'ouse,
> 'E was there in the window, an' lookin' out . . . .'

'Come *on*!' orders the Old Man, lowering his field-glasses. '*Use* the batteries! It's a matter of minutes! Send it off when I give the order!'

'What you talkin' to me like *that* for?' Tiny flares up, angrily. 'Think I live in a bucket with a 'ole in it, and've got me brains where me balls is, do you? I can tell you the psychopaths give me intelligence gradin' 0.7, which is very 'igh!'

'Depends which end of the table you start at,' grins Porta. 'But steady on with those leads and that battery. *Would* be funny if we got the lot of it down the back of our necks ourselves. Those bloody assassins down there'd kill themselves laughing, and we'd go down in world history as the biggest dopes ever to have taken part in *any* war!'

'*Job tvojemadj*,' mumbles 'Frostlips'. 'Here come those devils!'

The moon comes out like an explosion. We can clearly see a line of soldiers moving upwards on skis. They stop several times, and stare up at the peaks as if they knew we were there.

'Must be time we sprinkled a bit of snow down on 'em,' says Porta. ''Fore it's goodbye gold an' the life of Reilly!'

'Wait!' warns the Commissar. He examines the terrain through his binoculars. 'We've got to take them *all*! If one gets away, up goes the alarm!'

'There's, guests on the way up the cliffs,' says Tiny, listening tensely. 'I can 'ear their climbin'-irons!'

'Balls,' says 'Frostlips'. '*I* can't hear a thing!'

'No, but I *can*,' says Tiny, wiggling his nose like a rabbit in a cabbage-patch.

The officer leading the column stops and turns his field-glasses up towards the brow of the cliff behind which we are hiding.

'Keep *still*!' whispers the Commissar, his voice shaking. 'The slightest movement, those bastards'll *see* it!'

'I'm ready to move this mountain,' says Tiny, grinning broadly.

'Hell!' whispers the Old Man. 'No shit now, or we're finished!'

The OGPU soldiers below us have fanned out. They have their skis on their backs and push themselves up by their staves. We can now hear, too, that there are more of them on their way up the face of the cliff.

'What we bleedin' waitin' for?' asks Tiny, impatiently. 'Ivan'll *be* here in a minute, shakin' 'is bleedin' balalaikas under our noses!'

Nervously, I screw the cover off a stick-grenade, and put my finger through the ring. I am ready to throw it as soon as the first Russian face appears above the edge of the cliff.

Most of the soldiers in the long single column have now disappeared along the side of the mountain, where we can no longer see them. Their voices become more and more audible, however, through the wild howling of the storm. Suddenly the tail of the column – five soldiers – stops. They point field-glasses towards the top of the great mass of granite. Some instinct must be warning them of an unknown danger. They are not recruits. They are manhunters of the most experienced kind.

'Shall I *do* it?' asks Tiny, moving the wires even closer to the battery. So close that we cannot understand why the

284

charge has not gone off.

'Not yet!' whispers the Commissar. 'We've got to have those five come closer!'

Porta is down behind the LMG, the butt pressed into his shoulder, and his finger on the trigger.

I open the covers of the cartridge boxes, and hold the long belts ready for use.

'*Now!*' hisses the Commissar, bringing his fist down in the snow.

Tiny gives out a scream of pleasure, and makes the contact.

For a moment it is as if the world stands still. Then the icy quiet of the night is split open by a series of thunderous explosions. They roll across the mountains and die away in far-distant echoes.

'Ought to give the headhunters something else to think about,' grins Porta with satisfaction, bringing the night-glasses up to his eyes. The OGPU soldiers have been gripped by panic, and are scattering to all sides.

It seems as if the huge overcap of snow has remained untouched by the explosions. Several minutes go by in which nothing happens.

The OGPU soldiers have also seen this. They stop, and begin feverishly to buckle on their skis. A little officer waves excitedly with his *Kalashnikov* and shouts hoarse orders.

'Roll then, you bleedin' snow, you!' mumbles Tiny, shaking his fist up at the snow-cap. 'I'm going up to see what's wrong,' he says, getting up on one knee.

'Crazy sod!' snarls the Old Man. 'You're staying *here*!'

There is a sound like that of distant thunder, swiftly coming closer. The first of the colossal snow-masses whirls up in a huge white cloud. For a moment it seems to hang suspended in the air; then movement commences. Hundreds of tons of frozen snow hit the opposite slope and are thrown up again as if from a new explosion. Then the first gout of snow thunders against the rocks further down the mountain.

Faster than thought countless tons of snow are on their

way down the mountain, sweeping away everything in their path.

The nearest of the OGPU soldiers are whirled by the snowy masses into nothingness. A couple of soldiers on skis are racing in front of the tumbling snow, and seem as if they may have a chance of getting away from it.

'*Vive la mort*,' snarls the Legionnaire. He picks up a sniper's rifle and adjusts the telescopic sights.

'Not at that range,' says the Old Man.

'*Bien sûr*,' replies the Legionnaire. He presses his cheek against the butt and fires rapidly three times.

The leading skier falls forward, and continues on down the slope with his head down like a figurehead between his skis. The soldier bringing up the rear turns to see where the shot came from. Then he makes a fatal mistake. He makes a half-turn but is caught by panic. Turns again, and is overtaken by the avalanche, which thunders over, and buries him.

Trees whirl in the air before the advancing masses of snow. A whole forest is torn off the face of the mountain.

'What a bleedin' snowball *that* was!' shouts Tiny happily, when we are down at the vehicles again. The others have been waiting for us down there, getting more and more nervous.

'Those headhunters certainly lost their skis,' says Porta. 'What a roller-coaster that was!'

'I'll take it,' offers Tiny, crawling into the radio-room, from which we can hear a howling call-tone.

Tiny fiddles with the receiver, and bangs it a couple of times impatiently on the side of the tank before it works.

''Ello!' he says into the microphone. 'Who am I? I'm me, that's who I am!'

'Idiot! What's your position?' fumes a sharp, annoyed voice.

'Down round the arse'ole o' the universe,' answers Tiny, with a little laugh. 'We just threw a snowball at the neighbours' kids!'

'Where are you speaking from?' asks the voice, impatiently.

'From 'ere!' answers Tiny. 'Where else?'

'Are you out of your mind? I want to know where you are?' snarls the voice.

'You're a dumb 'un! We're in bleedin' Russia, of course!'

'Now you watch yourself, soldier!' The strange voice shakes with rage. 'You don't seem to know who you're talking to?'

'Think I'm a fortune-teller or somethin', do you?' answers Tiny, bursting into a roar of laughter.

'Are you laughing at me?' The voice becomes dangerously calm. 'I want to know who I'm talking to?'

'You're talkin' to me, you dope!' shouts Tiny, beginning slowly to come to the boil. 'Ain't you realized that yet? You're about as useful as a prick that's been touched up by a circular saw!'

'You are speaking to the communications officer,' snarls the voice, angrily. 'Now I want a straight answer from you: rank, name and unit!'

''It your 'ead on somethin' 'ave you?' explodes Tiny. 'We're only allowed to talk secret! The neighbours ain't got to be able to know what we're goin' about, see! You ain't gonna get a thing out of me! You could be one of these bleedin' spies they talk such a lot about. *Panjemajo*?'

'God help us to have patience! D'you know the code word?'

'No, why should I?' Tiny laughs noisily. 'It ain't me that's the sparks. I'm just standin' in for Julius that's gone for a walk!'

'Listen now, soldier,' hisses the communications officer, his voice shaking with rage. 'You're mopping up. Now I want to know *what* you've mopped up!'

'You coulda said that straight off, 'stead of askin' where we are,' answers Tiny. 'We just threw a bleedin' great snowball at Ivan, as is now on the way to Paradise fast as 'is skis can take 'im!'

'Give me your section commander and get off the radio, you madman! I'll give you bloody snowballs!'

'Old Un'!' screams Tiny in a ringing bass baritone. 'There's some sod of a psycho on the radio as wants to know what we've mopped up! Watch out for 'im though, 'e might be one of them bleedin' spies as is sneakin' around all over the place listening in! Says 'e's an officer but I think 'e's probably lyin'!'

'What the devil have you done now?' asks the Old Man, looking worried, and edging down in front of the radio.

A long conversation follows, which, for the Old Man's part, consists of: 'Yes, sir! Yes, major! Yes, sir!'

'You know what I fancy, now?' asks Porta, when we are again on the move. 'Hard-boiled eggs and shrimps in lobster sauce, then a large helping of pork with *sauerkraut* and preserved pears.'

'Shut up,' hisses the Old Man, crossly. 'Shut up about food! And I'll shoot you, Tiny, if you ever go near that radio again!'

A grey dawn has broken through when we reach the *Paritip*, which we hope, with a good deal of luck, can take us across the ravine. It is an odd-looking construction.

'Bottoms up, St Peter!' says Porta, looking down into the depths. 'Can that thing carry a tank?'

'So they say,' answers 'Frostlips' with a shrug of his shoulders. 'And we've got to hope they're right, because we ain't got a bit of choice in the matter! We've got to go over! We've blocked the pass ourselves with that avalanche!'

'Doesn't look all that solid,' says the Old Man, eyeing the contraption sceptically. It is a heavy platform, which hangs, swaying, suspended from thick cables.

'Come along! Let's get on with it! Who's going first?' shouts the Commissar, impatiently.

'You can go first, Albert,' says Porta, with a graceful wave of his hand.

'Not me, man!' says Albert, after he has been out on the rocking platform. It has to be propelled over the chasm by the turning of a hand-winch.

'You'd rather go last, perhaps, when the cables are a bit more worn?' asks Porta, sarcastically. 'You grab that offer of mine in a hurry, my son, and take off first!'

Albert gives in, and edges his way down through the T-34's turret hatch.

Cautiously, as if he were driving on glass, he edges the

heavy tank out on to the *Paritip*. The platform rolls like a ship in heavy weather at the overload. Slowly it begins to glide over towards the far side, its cables singing with the strain.

'Slowly,' the Commissar warns. 'Only slowly!'

Silently, and with butterflies in our stomachs, we follow the swaying platform. Despite the weight it is carrying, the violent blasts of wind still move it from side to side.

'Looks bloody dangerous, that,' mumbles Gregor. 'And think, we've volunteered for it!'

'Kind of thing a man only does once in his life,' grins Porta, carelessly. 'We'll have a story to tell when we're all Swedish Socialists!'

The heavy Panther goes over last. The logs of the platform creak warningly and the cables sing as they take the strain of its weight.

Porta runs his hand through his red hair, spits into the ravine, and he and Tiny take the winch.

'I daren't watch,' mumbles the Commissar, turning his back. 'It can't be long before those cables go!'

As he speaks the words there is a sharp crack, and one of the cables breaks. The platform begins to heel over to one side. The Panther slides slowly backwards.

'*Par Allah*!' cries the Legionnaire, nervously. 'It's going off. It's all over with them!'

'Hell!' howls Porta, in terror. He throws himself at the winch. 'The whole shithouse is goin'!'

The platform heels more and more. One gust of wind and they are finished.

'Grab the cables!' shouts the Commissar. 'Move! Bring up the T-34!'

Albert backs the tea-waggon into place. Working against time we get a wire to the platform and haul it on to firm ground before the other cable breaks.

'God the Father preserve us!' says Porta. He is up on the edge staring at the *Paritip*. The platform now hangs at an angle of 45° down towards the bottom of the ravine. 'That was *close*! A feller needs a good bit of luck to get through a world war still breathin'!'

Brutality creates respect.

Adolf Hitler

They ran across the playground, jumped the fence and went on down
Wundt Strasse, panting heavily. They heard the shouts from behind
them:

'Halt! Stehen bleiben!'

But none of them stopped. The hard staccato bark of a machine-
pistol sounded.

The first man to go down, with his face in the chuckling, spring-
flushed waters of the stream, was the Section Leader, an old Feldwebel. He had already lived through one world war and had been
firmly determined to live through this one as well.

The next to fall was the youngest. He was just sixteen. He crawled
some distance on his knees, his face down close to the cinders. A long
trail of blood marked his path. He was still alive when the military
police reached him. They put a bullet through the back of his neck.

The rest of the section reached the race track and disappeared into
Scheibenholtz Park. They hardly noticed the Leutnant, dangling by
the neck from a tree with his hands tied behind his back.

A little further on an Oberst and a Gefreiter were hanging.

All three had a sign around their necks:

ICH BIN EIN FEIGLING,
DER DEN FÜHRER VERRATEN HAT!*

Two hours later the military police picked them up crossing
Johannes Parkweg.

All nineteen were hanged on the nearest trees as a terrible warning
to other deserters.

This happened on 3 March 1945 at the Leipzig race track. The
bodies of the deserters were not cut down until six weeks later.

* I AM A COWARD
  WHO HAS BETRAYED THE FÜHRER

THE MAD OGPU CAPTAIN

The Commissar raises his hand in the signal to halt.

In the middle of a round market-place, half-covered with powdery snow, a number of motorcycles stand parked. They all have side-cars on which machine-guns are mounted.

'Queer they don't take the guns inside with 'em?' Porta wonders.

'Not a *bit* queer,' sneers Heide. He is, as usual, annoyingly well-informed. 'As long as they're outside they're ready for firing. That's due to their effective frost lubricant. Take them inside and the temperature variation would make them freeze up and they'd be useless.'

'Watch out that swivellin' swastika in your *'errenvolk* prick don't freeze to ice,' Tiny roars with laughter at his own witticism.

'Not a sign of a sentry,' mumbles the Old Man, putting his head cautiously up over the edge of the turret hatch. 'These chaps must feel pretty bloody safe round here!'

'Over behind that house there's an old lorry,' says Porta, pointing.

'Then there'll be a lot of Ivans, count on that,' warns Tiny, craning his neck inquisitively.

The Commissar jumps heavily down from the motor-sledge. With his long cloak billowing in the wind he tramps towards us through the deep snow.

'Stay on your toes,' he says, bending his head back to look up at the Old Man in the Panther's turret. 'I don't understand this! There's not supposed to be any military personnel here! I'm afraid they may have got wind of us. Drive up through that street over there! I'll make this place safe with the T-34s and the sledge. Don't fire unless absolutely necessary. The dark'll help us. These yokels can't tell the

291

difference between a tank and a tricycle. If anybody asks, tell them you're transporting muck. They can understand *that*!'

Porta starts up, with a roar which makes the nearest houses shake. He speeds the 700 HP Maybach up to maximum revolutions to show what it can do. Typical driver showing-off. It is something he will never grow out of.

'What'll I put in the peashooter?' asks Tiny, patting a shell.

'HE, dammit! What did you think?' snarls the Old Man, irritated.

'I thought markers'd be all right,' grins Tiny, happily. 'We've still got some with red paint! Ivan'd be pleased as punch to get twenty gallons of red paint plastered all round 'is chops! Red's the colour o' the season in this country, they say!'

'Good God Almighty!' the Old Man breaks out. 'Have we still got those cursed markers? I've told you to chuck 'em out! They'll be the death of us if you make a mistake some time!'

'I never make mistakes,' boasts Tiny, in a superior tone. 'An' I don't want to lose those shells! Sooner or later we can 'ave some fun with 'em!'

Porta swings the Panther into a narrow street, which only leaves it fractions of an inch on each side.

'Get out and steer him,' the Old Man orders Tiny.

'It's always me,' protests Tiny, sourly. 'Why can't it be Sven? 'E's a volunteer an' wants to be an officer! Let 'im give the orders, then!'

'Shut up,' snarls the Old Man, 'and do as I say!'

With a lighted cigarette Tiny steers Porta down the narrow alleyway. When we have got some distance along it the Old Man orders a halt.

'Where the devil're we going to end up?' he mumbles, resignedly.

'In a boozer,' grins Porta, indifferently, and points to a large sign KUKHMISS – TAERSSKAJA* *Bajomaj*. 'They

---

* Restaurant

got rooms to let, too! Let's go in and sign the book. I can't remember what it's like any more to sleep in a proper bed.'

Tiny is already on his way up the broad steps leading to the restaurant.

'Where the hell're you off to, you crazy sod?' explodes the Old Man, pulling himself up on to the edge of the hatch.

'Goin' to order coffee an' 'ot Danish,' shouts Tiny, with his hand on the door-knocker.

'Idiot!' roars the Old Man. 'D'you want to get us shot?'

'No, I want a cup o' coffee,' chuckles Tiny, with a grin like a split pumpkin.

'You steer Porta, and nothing else,' snarls the Old Man, not far from boiling-point.

'Slowly, very slowly,' warns Tiny. 'Just a bit to the left an' you'll knock the 'ole bleedin' 'ouse down. The landlord wouldn't like *that* a bit!'

'Hell!' groans the Old Man, wiping the sweat from his brow. 'That was *close!*'

Suddenly Tiny dashes back to the tank and goes in through the side-hatch with the celerity of a rabbit disappearing down its hole.

'What's up?' asks the Old Man, in amazement.

'The *entire* Red Army's standing there just round the corner, scratchin' its arse,' pants Tiny, out of breath. 'If I 'adn't been careful stickin' me bonce round the corner of the 'ouse, they'd 'ave shot me up far as the other side of the bleedin' moon!'

The Old Man looks through the night-viewer, but can see nothing. The street lies dark and deserted.

'You've been drinking again, as usual, I suppose,' he says, sending Tiny a nasty look.

'Oh, you think that, do you?' shouts Tiny, in an insulted tone. 'Well then, You take a trip up there yourself an' stick your own nut round the corner!'

'What now?' asks Porta, taking a quick nip at the vodka bottle. 'Shall we rock along and take a look at these Commie soldiers? Or shall we give 'em an acid drop so's they'll know we're coming?'

'Slow forward!' orders the Old Man, shortly.

The heavy tank bobs a deep curtsey when Porta treads cautiously on the accelerator. Its near-side track takes the pediment of a house with it.

'That whatsit over there on the corner. Ain't that one of the flowers of the neighbours' army?' asks Porta, stopping the tank with a jerk.

'Slow forward!' orders the Old Man, in a low voice. 'He'd never be standing there, gaping, if he had any suspicions of us. He'd have screamed an alarm long since and woke up the half of Russia.'

'What about givin' 'im a pot o' paint?' asks Tiny, with a little laugh.

'The gun safe?' asks the Old Man, nervously.

'Too true she is,' answers Tiny. 'Think I'm barmy enough to be steppin' along in front of a tin-can with a readied gun pointing at my backside?'

A guard with a *Kalashnikov* is standing at the street crossing and staring with interest at the tank rattling towards him. If he gets suspicious, we're caught in a trap. We can't use the gun in this narrow street. They can put us out with hand-weapons without the least bit of trouble.

'What the hell's that clown thinkin' about?' whispers Porta, staring out through the driver's slit at the dark form standing planted like a statue a couple of hundred yards in front of us, with both hands buried deep in its pockets. 'Must be one of those Cossack abortions they've picked up on a midden and given a gun in exchange for his muck-rake!'

'And it's all gone that quick the army's forgot to give 'im the course on tank silhouettes,' grins Tiny. 'so 'e thinks we're a mechanized shit-barrow!'

Just before we reach the guard, Porta's eye falls on a narrow side street. With a great noise of falling bricks he turns the Panther into it, only to brake suddenly.

'They after us?' asks Tiny, taking a comforting swig at the vodka bottle.

'No. but we're in a blind, bloody alley.' snarls Porta. 'Why the hell can't they put up signs? We'll bloody well complain about this!'

'Couple of Commie squaddies from the neighbours on the way towards us,' warns Tiny, peering cautiously out of the side hatch.

Porta takes a quick look in the mirror. 'The devil! And they look like a couple of real public enemies!'

'Damnation,' curses the Old Man, nervously. 'Back! To hell with the consequences! Let's get out of here, before we get our arses singed!'

Nervously I take down an mpi from its bracket, and cock it. There is a whine of metal biting into concrete.

'Watch those tracks,' warns the Old Man. 'Bust one, and we've had it!'

''Ere comes another public bleedin' enemy,' says Tiny, stretching his neck.

Porta throws the tank round to the right so sharply that the shells come out of their open racks and clang about on the steel deck.

The Old Man lights his silver-lidded pipe with shaking fingers.

'Drop your speed, damn it!' he shouts, desperately.

'Fuck all to be frightened of,' howls Porta, switching on the forward spotlight. Too late, he sees two four-wheel-drive Tempos parked so close to one another that nothing wider than a bicycle could get past them. 'Everything's under control,' he screams, presses home the accelerator and rips the Tempos in two.

The Old Man drops his pipe, and covers his face with his hands.

'I trust you,' he says. He has no other choice. He gives up, leans back in the tank-commander's seat, and watches the night come rushing towards him.

The motor is thundering at maximum speed. Round about in the houses, lights come on without consideration for the black-out.

'Oh hell!' cries Porta. 'Now we're stuck! Elevate the gun! I'm going straight on!'

'You're not bloody well going straight through that wall, are you?' asks the Old Man, in fear. '*That* ought to make 'em realize we're not on their side!'

A balcony comes down, raining bricks and mortar on the tank. A motorcycle is flattened under its tracks.

Three Russians come towards us waving their arms.

'Shall I give 'em a pot o' paint?' asks Tiny. 'That ought to make 'em think a bit!'

'*Stoi, stoi idjiotsetvo*,' they shout and make threatening gestures at the tank, which goes roaring on down the narrow street smashing everything in its path.

The three Russians stop, and stare in terror at the onrushing tank. The next moment they are thrown up into the air, fall again to the cobblestones and two are crushed under its tracks. The third is back on his feet, and rushes off madly down the steep street.

'Get *him*!' shouts the Old Man. 'He mustn't get back and give the alarm, or all hell'll be loose!'

'I'll *eat* 'im!' shouts Tiny, and is already out of the side hatch with his garrotting-wire in his hand. He falls, of course, on the icy road. '*Ruki verch*!*' he screams after the fleeing Russian, who is out of his mind with terror. He stops and spits angrily towards Tiny, and bends down and picks up a lump of ice which he throws at the tank. Then he sprints off again with Tiny thundering at his heels. They go down in a heap in a snowdrift.

Tiny jabs with his combat knife, but slips on the ice and misses his stroke.

The Russian gives out a scream of terror and disappears at top speed round a corner before Tiny can get back on his feet.

Careless of what he hits, Porta backs out of the narrow street at such a speed that you'd think the whole town was coming down round our ears.

A woman screams, hysterically, somewhere out in the night.

'Where the hell's that woman?' asks Porta, craning his neck. 'Screamin' women make me nervous!'

* *Ruki verch!:* Hands up!

'She's moved in with us. Up on the turret!' answers Tiny, laconically.

'Moved in?' asks the Old Man, blankly.

'Yes, and she's brought 'er bed an' blankets with 'er, too,' grins Tiny. He puts his head out of the side hatch.

The girl lets out a couple of strange long gulps at the sight of Tiny's sooty face. Then she gives another rattling scream.

''Eavens above. She's fell off,' he says, rubbing the palms of his hands together.

'Jesus *no*! Didn't hurt herself I hope?' cries Porta.

'Don't think so,' answers Tiny, who is hanging half out of the hatch opening. 'She's running that fast you'd think she'd got a wildcat in 'er pants!'

'Did she take the bed with her?' asks Porta, interestedly.

'No, it's still 'angin' there,' chuckles Tiny.

'Great! We can take it in turns to sleep in it!' Porta turns the tank in the direction of some old wooden houses with balconies and loggias projecting out over the street.

'Be careful, you're too close,' warns the Old Man. There is a sound of splintering wood and the tinkling of broken glass.

'The devil!' curses Porta, treading on the brake.

'What's wrong?' asks the Old Man nervously, bending down from the turret. 'Brakes gone?'

'*They're* all right!' snarls Porta, tramping away at the pedal. 'It's this rotten can. It keeps skidding, and smashing into these shitty houses!'

'Looks like the bleedin' 'ouses are tryin' to overtake us!' shouts Tiny, throwing half a loggia off the side hatch.

'That's what they *are* tryin' to bloody do,' answers Porta. He continues his attempts to brake lightly, but the tank only goes faster down the icy road. 'Somebody must be pushin' us. Shoot the bastard!' he shouts.

'Are we in difficulties, then?' asks Tiny.

'Difficulties?' answers the Old Man. 'We've been in bloody difficulties ever since this fuckin' world war got started!'

'What about goin' outside an' 'avin' a look at things?'

suggests Tiny. What he really wants to do is to get his feet on solid ground again. The atmosphere inside the tank seems to have become very hot all of a sudden.

Porta steers us in between two apartment blocks built of reinforced concrete. We are stuck there, quite helplessly.

'By all the devils in hell!' curses the Old Man, tensed like a spring. 'What the hell did you want to come in here for?'

'I'm tired of bustin' up houses,' answers Porta, resignedly, 'and, as you know, all roads lead to Rome!'

'We gotta go to Rome now?' asks Tiny, in amazement. 'Them Commies moved our gold to Rome, then, 'ave they?'

'Idiot!' snarls Heide. 'You *are* as stupid as you look!'

Tiny is about to go for him, when a yell is heard above from a first-floor window. A big Russian in shirt-sleeves with a steel helmet on his head leans out and waves his arms furiously.

What happens next is really a reflex movement.

Tiny's machine-pistol spits blue flame at the gesticulating figure. It rolls out through the window, slides down the front shield of the tank and lies still in the snow.

'*Dis*-mount!' orders the Old Man, jumping down from the turret. 'Let's get back to the market-place and see what's happening there! It sounds as if all hell's broke loose!'

At full speed I run headlong into Albert coming the opposite way past the baker's shop on the corner. He lets out a hoarse yell, and stumbles over a dead dog.

'If I get out of this alive I'll go to church every single Sunday!' he whines miserably. 'I'd rather be a sausage-man in Africa!'

'Who's firin'?' asks Porta, dropping down behind the LMG.

'Neighbours,' shouts Barcelona, taking cover behind a road-sweeping machine.

The market-place is a scene of wild confusion. Muzzle-flashes blaze from all directions.

'Take cover, for Christ's sake,' shouts 'Frostlips', as Gregor dashes recklessly across the square with tracer whistling around him.

'What's going on?' he asks in terror. He goes over the fence in a long arc and lands alongside 'Frostlips' in a cloud of snow. They are only a foot away from one another, but shout at the top of their lungs, covering one another with spittle.

'They shooting?' Gregor asks excitedly, readying his machine-pistol.

'Yes, you dope,' spits 'Frostlips'. 'That's what they're doin' nothin' *but*!'

'Why don't you shoot back at 'em?' roars Gregor, sending a waterfall of spittle into 'Frostlips's' face.

'That's what we *are* doin'!' answers 'Frostlips'. He sprays a rain of bullets out in front of him without taking any kind of aim.

'Think we can make it?' shouts Gregor in a voice which echoes between the houses.

'How the fuck should I know?' squeals 'Frostlips', sending an idiotic burst through a plateglass window. It breaks up into a million pieces and sets a burglar alarm going.

'Burglars!' shouts Gregor. 'They've got a nerve with both the German an' the Red Army in town!'

'Shut your stupid bloody mouth!' rages the Commissar, wiping spittle from his face.

The snarl of a *Kalashnikov* cuts him short. The windows on the far side of the market-place disintegrate, and all six tyres on the lorry parked under cover of the long house, go off with deafening explosions.

In the confusion I throw two hand-grenades. One of them goes into the cabin of the lorry which immediately catches fire.

'What the 'ell's goin' *on*?' shouts Tiny, staring round him in confusion. 'What kind of bleedin' idiots are shootin'? An' who the bleedin' 'ell they shootin' *at*? We're *friends*!'

A long, raging burst from a pair of machine-guns answers him.

'This is bloody well *enough*!' shouts Porta resentfully, losing his yellow topper.

'Those bastards have mounted guns up there on the third

floor,' screams Albert, pointing wildly. 'I don't think they know we're friendly!'

'I'm not taking any more of this shit,' shouts Porta, lifting his machine-pistol.

The shutters splinter. Snow, ice and shards of glass fly in all directions, as he empties the *Kalashnikov*'s entire magazine into the window in one long burst.

A very fat and very angry lady in a bright yellow night-dress, and with a red nightcap on her head, appears at the shattered window.

'Sons of bitches!' she screams, furiously. 'You're going to have to pay for every bit of what you've smashed! Cowardly mongrels! Go out and shoot Germans, and leave us Russians in peace!' She lifts a large pottery floor-vase above her head, goes back a little way and runs forward to get more distance on her throw. Unfortunately for her she gets too much distance. She forgets to let go of the vase and goes with it out of the window. With a shrill scream she lands in a snowdrift. The vase flies out of her hands and hits 'Frostlips' on the head. He gulps, and goes out like a light.

'Wow!' cries Tiny.

'Right on the coconut!' laughs Porta, happily.

'Wow!' repeats Tiny. 'Was that lady *mad*?'

'I should think so, too,' replies Barcelona. 'Who wouldn't be, with a gang of gun-crazy bums going round shooting people's windows up in the middle of the night?'

'Was it 'er as shot off the gun?' asks Tiny.

'No, we must've been wrong,' says Porta, shaking his head. He cranes to get a better view of the fat lady, who is crawling round swearing in the middle of the snowdrift. 'God, what a lovely creature! Just my style! Between her legs the Thirty Years War wouldn't seem a minute too long! Hej! Olga!' he yells, 'come on over here and let's have a jump together!'

'Let's try shootin' the other way and see what happens,' suggests Gregor, his fighting blood up.

A long MG burst kicks up the snow along the whole length of the market-place. A bullet burns a furrow in

Porta's left boot.

'Ow-ow-ow! Blood!' howls Albert. A ricochet has slashed his cheek.

'Frostlips' has regained consciousness, after his meeting with the floor-vase. He jumps back and takes cover behind Porta. He holds out the heavy *Nagan* in front of him, clenched in both hands. Unwittingly he is aiming it directly at Porta.

'Jesus, Son of Mary!' cries Porta, turning round and looking straight into the black muzzle of the *Nagan*. He can see the rifling clearly, and can sense the round-headed 11 mm bullet waiting down there to be fired.

'You're *dead*!' howls 'Frostlips', quite out of his mind with fear.

Porta ducks just as the gun goes off. The bullet passes only a fraction of an inch from his cheek. His eyes turn up, showing the whites, and he falls backwards into the snow. He claims he is dead.

'Hell, man! That bullet went straight through me! I never heard a bang like that before in all my life!'

We have to show him his face in a mirror, so that he can see there is no entrance hole, before he realizes he is still alive and that 'Frostlips' has missed. It takes him a while to get over the shock.

'Reminds me a lot of a fight I was in once in Wedding in Berlin,' he says, ducking under a burst of machine-pistol fire. 'Me old dad comes home blind-o an' thinks the long-haired's been having a bit on the side! While he was punishing her for that, he finds out the pork roast has got itself burnt. So he makes up his mind to smash up the whole street, *before* he goes back to knocking the old woman about. Well, then the coppers turn up and *they* start in beating *him* up and everybody else with him. They never thought to ask where the blame lay!'

'Let's get over there,' shouts Tiny. He grabs a *Schmeisser* and starts off at top speed across the market-place, careless of the bullets that are flying round his ears.

The crazy Maxim gunner on the far side of the houses

knocks snow into the air again with a new long burst. He is traversing the square.

Porta rushes down the street, stops at a cellar window and sends a whole magazine through it. Suddenly the machine-gun stops firing, and everything becomes strangely still.

Tiny goes up the long cement stairway in two big jumps. He crashes the door in with his boot.

'Shut the door, you fool,' roars a voice. 'There's a crowd of madmen out there shooting at us!'

Tiny grips the long magazine of the *Schmeisser* firmly, and presses the stock in under his elbow.

A captain with green OGPU shoulder-boards gives a shout, and goes down behind a desk with both hands clamped down on top of his head.

A big figure stands in the middle of the room, waving a '45 around. A single shot sounds, but from another direction. Tiny believes for a moment that he is dead, so shocked is he. He swings the snub-nosed German machine-pistol in a half-circle.

The big Russian with the '45 gives a shout, as he looks down the black barrel of the *Schmeisser*. He drops his pistol and raises his hands in the air.

Along the filthy wall stand a group of half-dressed supplies soldiers, staring in astonishment at Tiny and the *Schmeisser*.

A corporal goes forward a couple of steps, and blinks his eyes. Realizing that what he sees is really there, he stops and pulls his head down between his shoulders like a tortoise.

The *Schmeisser* chatters like a runaway circular saw. Blue flames spit: long gashes appear across the walls. Chalk-dust comes down like heavy snow.

A little soldier, who is very drunk, zig-zags across the room at top speed, dives across a table and crashes headfirst into the floor. He stays down there, with both hands protectively covering the back of his neck. Cautiously, he turns his head to see if what he thought he saw was really what he did see. It was.

A group of Russians sit there staring, quite paralysed by

302

the number of things which have happened in such a short space of time. Then they fall over backwards, the legs of their chairs shot out from under them.

A funeral party, armed with black umbrellas, comes running up the stairs to see what is going on. They need a little amusement after the melancholy atmosphere of the churchyard, and push forward behind Tiny to peer over his shoulder. Those in the lead catch sight of the *Schmeisser* with its bulldog snout and long magazine. Then they see the ugliest face they have ever set eyes on, and quickly realize that something is happening which should *not* be happening. They fall over one another's feet to get away; slip on one another's hats and galoshes, which have fallen off, and involve themselves inextricably in wet black umbrellas, some of which have turned inside out.

A large, damp, unbelievably ugly dog lollops over and sniffs at Tiny. It looks up at him and licks his hand. It seems as if it is smiling at him. It closes its eyes when the firing starts. Splinters of glass fly through the air and are pulverized into powder. Woodwork splinters. Stray bullets gouge into walls. The dog opens its eyes again, and is so happy its tail seems ready to fall off.

Roars and hysterical screams are heard, in time with the flaying, raging stutter of the German mpi. Bullets ricochet and fan out, whining across the room. A waterpipe bursts, and water spouts in all directions.

A large oval object rolls to rest in front of Tiny's feet.

The wet dog sniffs at it cautiously, and backs away.

'Holy Mother of Kazan,' howls Tiny, in terror. 'A rifle-grenade, a bleedin' rifle-grenade!' With a well-aimed kick he sends the dangerous thing into the furthest corner of the room. There is an earsplitting explosion. Then a 6-foot tall, red-hot stove comes flying through the air.

Tiny and the dog duck in unison as the stove passes over them, and stare after it fearfully as it goes crashing on, taking the double doors with it, and making the civilian funeral party run even faster. They think the red-hot stove is the devil himself out collecting souls to take back down to hell!

A hand-grenade comes flying through the air, hits the door-post and screws back again like a billiard ball which has been given wrong side. It explodes on top of a buffet. Blood flows everywhere. It resembles a butcher's block.

A sergeant, wearing only one boot, and with his helmet on the back of his head, comes rushing along with wildly staring eyes and throws his arms round Porta, who is on his way through the swing doors.

'*Tovaritsch, Tovaritsch*, do something or other!' he screams, beside himself with fear.

'We *are* doin' something!' answers Porta, tearing himself from the man's embrace.

'You're all wrong,' roars the sergeant at the top of his voice, although he is only an inch or two away from Porta. 'We are Russians! We are *friends*!'

'That's just what we *thought*,' screams Tiny, equally loudly. 'We're *Germans*, man!'

'I know it,' roars the sergeant. 'You belong to the Volga Brigade!'

'What're you shooting at us for then?' asks Porta, in a ringing voice. 'We thought you were counter-revolutionaries that we were supposed to shoot the heads off of?'

'No, no! You're wrong!' shouts the sergeant. 'We are all in a service and supplies company! We never do nothing to *nobody*!'

'Come on out then,' shouts Tiny, waving invitingly with the *Schmeisser*. 'It's all over. All a mistake!'

'Mistake?' sighs the Old Man, his eyes widening as he looks at the wreckage around him. 'Preserve us! What a mess you've made out of this place!'

'It was their own fault,' Porta defends himself. 'It was them that started with grenades!'

A Russian with his fur cap right down over his eyes and his cloak fluttering out from his shoulders, comes rushing down the steep street as if the devil were at his heels.

'Paratroops, paratroops,' he screams in panic fear. He misses his footing and slides a long way on his stomach. When he finally gets up enough courage to look up from the snowdrift in which he has ended he stares, paralysed, into

Albert's coal-black face. He makes some strange noises, and then his heart stops beating. He has, quite simply, died of fright.

'Well I'm damned,' cries Porta in amazement. 'Before we know where we are Albert'll be our secret weapon. We hold him out in front of us and they all die a natural death. Their hearts stop beating at the sight of him!'

'*Job tvojemadj*!' curses a sergeant, picking bits of glass from his face. 'And one *Schmeisser* can do all that! If I hadn't got down behind that cupboard quick that fucking machine-shitter'd have cut me in two. Shot every bit of rotten life I've got out of me, it would have!'

'I was close to shitting myself, when that sod started up with the *Schmeisser*,' admits a corporal, his face chalk-white. 'If I hadn't fell down the stairs it would've been all up with me.'

A white-haired warrant officer is sitting in a heap of broken glass and wall tiles. He is holding his leg, which has been slashed open from the instep to above the knee.

'My leg! My leg!' he gasps in despair, 'and those cursed liars told me it was a piece of cake in supplies! I'd never hear a shot fired in anger, they said. In the last five minutes I've heard more shots fired than ever there was in the whole of the First World War!'

Suddenly a new burst of fire rakes across the market-place, and a guttural voice rings through the night:

'Pull in your heads, you pigs! Here comes Michael Yakanashi! And he's not coming alone!'

A long shimmering salvo from a *Kalashnikov* terminates the threatening message.

'It's that crazy captain again,' explains the pale corporal, crawling under a bench. 'I wish the devil'd crawl down his throat with a sack o' dynamite on his back! He won't give up till he's killed the lot of us. He can thank his good connections he hasn't been strung up long since. It was "shiverin' pig" that caused it all!'

'"Shiverin' pig"?' asks 'Frostlips', blankly.

'Jellied pork,' nods the corporal, solemnly, throwing his arms wide. 'The crazy bastard *hates* "shiverin' pig"! They say he killed his wife for givin' it him every day.'

A very young soldier with a heavy blood-soaked bandage round his neck, and with eyes which bug out like a frog's, drops down, out of breath, between Porta and Tiny.

'I've got such a headache,' he moans. 'All that *noise*!' He lifts his *Kalashnikov* and empties its 100-shot magazine at the spot where he thinks the mad captain has taken cover.

'Come on! We'll take care of him,' shouts the Old Man, furiously. 'I want to get some *peace*, dammit!'

Singly, in short crouching rushes, we move towards the building. In between the chatter of the mpis and MGs we hear shouts coming from the third floor.

'Down with the counter-revolutionaries! Death to the Trotskyite traitors!'

'That mad bleeder's got shit where 'is brains ought to be!' growls Tiny angrily. He runs across the market-place at top speed, tracer whistling around him.

'You meet these flag-waggin' idiots everywhere these days,' says Porta, hitching his equipment to a more comfortable position. 'They've got the national rag hangin' out of both their ears and their arseholes, just so's nobody'll make the mistake of thinking they don't love the lousy Fatherland!'

In a shouting, confused mob we land in a deep gutter which gives us some cover.

'This the first time you been on a job like this?' asks 'Frostlips', with a grin. 'Ever been with the cops?'

'Only arrested by 'em,' answers Porta. 'I've never been out shooting with them!'

'Then you've missed a lot,' grins 'Frostlips', sending a couple of shots from his *Tokarev* up at the third floor. 'Blokes like him up there I know all about! See here, the end of the show's nearly always the same! They bang away till they get tired of playing. Then they put the cannon in their mouth and send it off with their big toe!'

'That one with the big toe ain't easy,' says Porta, knowingly. 'Usually goes wrong and they live on with half their nut blown off.'

'Right!' grins 'Frostlips', 'and then they're on a forced diet for the rest of their lives! No pork! No blinis!'

'Down with Trotsky,' comes a roar from the top of the stairs. The captain has opened the battle for control of the house.

He keeps us pinned down on the landing for over an hour.

'He must have enough ammo for a whole corps,' mumbles Porta, shaking his head. He presses himself close to the wall as a salvo from above smashes in the door of an apartment.

'Why the hell did we have to stop here, anyway?' the Old Man turns to the Commissar. 'If only we'd gone on! This caper is pure madness!'

Now the situation has got completely out of hand. 131 gun-crazy German and Russian soldiers literally shoot to pieces the building which the mad captain has chosen for the scene of his last battle.

'He's switched on the lights,' screams the young corporal with the bug-eyes. 'Let's get the hell out of here! That mad bastard's put the lights on!'

'He's got us now,' shouts 'Frostlips', in terror. He tries to creep down the stairs backwards, but a couple of shots from above pin him down where he is.

'He can stay there and put holes in the lot of us, easy as pie,' roars Porta, getting even closer to the wall.

'Put the bleedin' light out,' shouts Tiny, 'before that dummy shoots our 'eads off!'

21 automatic weapons are aimed at the staircase light. On the films one shot would have been enough. But it is not like that in real life, and we feel the fear of death creeping up to the very roots of our hair.

Several hundred shots are fired. The ceiling and walls hang in shreds. We cough at the chalky powder filling the air and the acrid smell of cordite.

'You're all mad!' says the Old Man, getting to his feet and stepping across Porta and the Commissar, who are lying with their machine-pistols in firing position.

'The lights,' babbles the young corporal. 'That crazy bastard can *see* us!'

'God help him when I get hold of him,' promises a fat sergeant, picking at a jammed cartridge.

'We'll 'ave to cool that barmy bleeder to get 'im out of

'ere,' hisses Tiny, his finger curling itself reflexively on the trigger of his mpi.

The Old Man edges along close to the battered wall, keeping a careful eye on the staircase opening. When he reaches the fuse-box he calmly reaches up and screws the fuses out of their sockets.

'Wow!' says Porta, in surprise. 'Why didn't we think about that long ago? That's the army for you! Why do it the easy way when there's a hard way?'

There is a bang and a flame shoots out of the primitive fuse-box.

The young corporal gives out a high screech, and almost falls down the stairs. He thinks they are throwing grenades.

A hysterical burst sprays the staircase. Bullets chisel away at the handrail.

21 mpi muzzles are directed at the madman. Muzzle-flashes light up the stairs. The noise is terrific.

A heavy object whirls down from the top landing, taking the handrail with it. With a sickening thump it lands at the bottom of the stairwell. Blood splashes up on to us.

'Looks like a plate of "shiverin' pig" himself now,' says Tiny. He stand up and swings his mpi up on his shoulder.

'Get him out of here!' orders the Commissar, making a grimace.

There are crowds in the street. All the umbrella people are back, and have brought their children with them. The fathers hold them up over their heads to let them see the body, which is being carried out by four supply soldiers. Some give a cheer.

We go back with the Russians to the wrecked canteen. Porta has found a cauldron filled with *Bortsch-koop**. He adds a few things to it, which make it even tastier, and soon the whole canteen smells beautifully of meat soup.

Porta and a sergeant go out after supplies. There is a wild argument over a case of mutton sausages which the sergeant refuses to hand over without a requisition. The Commissar signs one gladly, and gives it all kinds of official stamps.

* *Bortsch-koop:* Russian soup

308

Now the sergeant is free of responsibility, and Porta can have anything he wants. But when he comes back carrying two large baskets of eggs the Old Man protests. He can see what could happen with eggs inside a tank.

'You're out of your bloody head!' shouts Porta, angrily. 'Wait till I do you Greek *Musaka*. Then you'll be glad I brought the eggs along!'

'Do you not use eggplants – *aubergine sautée*?' asks the Legionnaire, astonished. 'I have never heard one uses eggs!'

'There's sure to be a lot you haven't heard, while you were soddin' about in the desert shooting the arse off the Arabs,' Porta jeers. He hands the basket of eggs to Tiny. 'When I say, I make *Musaka* with eggs then I *mean* I make *Musaka* with eggs! Now all we need is a bit of minced beef, some onions and tomatoes. Butter we've got!'

The Old Man gives in, but demands that Porta clean up the waggon if the eggs do get smashed.

Tiny is having a row with a supply sergeant. First the sergeant kicks him on the ankle and then he hits him over the knee with a club. Tiny makes the V-sign. '*Pig!*' he yells and pushes his fingers hard into the sergeant's eyes. The man runs off screaming, and goes straight into a wall he cannot see.

'Bleedin' mad lot, these Russians!' says Tiny, sitting down to take the cards from Porta. ''Oo's got all the money, then?' he asks, kissing the cards. 'It ain't me, that's for sure!'

You have to hate to be a good soldier in wartime.
If you cannot hate whole-heartedly, you cannot
kill. Hate is the strongest energy source in a
human being.

Sven Hassel

'It's all up!' said the Feldwebel brusquely, pointing at the road-block
in front of them.

'Turn right!' ordered the major. His left uniform sleeve waved
emptily in the breeze.

'It's all over, sir,' grinned the driver. 'They'll mow us down if we
try to get away!'

The major fumbled his pistol from its holster, and prepared to jump
from the Kübel. He stopped with a jerk. Machine-gun fire kicked up
the dry earth in front of and behind the car. The driver and the
Feldwebel jumped out immediately, and raised their hands above their
heads.

Five Russians came out from the trees.

'Tovaritsch,' shouted the Feldwebel, and waved a piece of
something white. He fell forward on his face in the dust of the country
road.

The driver ran off to one side, but stopped suddenly and went down.
Muzzle-flashes spurted from the five Kalashnikovs.

The major was knocked out of the Kübel. His face broken in, his
chest split open in an explosion of shredded cloth and flesh.

The three wounded soldiers in the back of the car slumped down in a
fountain of blood.

'Job Tvojemadj,' laughed the youngest of the Russians, as they
poured petrol over the bodies.

When the petrol-can was empty, the sergeant threw a hand-grenade
into the car. It became a flaming bonfire. They stood for a while
watching the burning Kübel, then turned and sauntered back into the
woods.

'Germania kaputt,' grinned the corporal, and lighted a papyrus.

THE VLADIMIR PRISON

The captain, who is big, and has a face which resembles what a Neanderthal Man must have looked like, pushes us over towards the guard-room wall.

'*Propusk*,' he growls, extending a demanding policeman's hand towards us. As he does so his tongue suddenly protrudes from his mouth, and the beginning of a scream dies away in a horrible rattle.

'Come death, come . . .' hums the Legionnaire, whipping his garrotting wire from around the dead man's throat.

The Old Man hurries us on.

Silently we go up over the narrow wall, to come in from behind the other guards before they can sound the alarm.

Igor is over at the cable-box, as quick as a cat. Fat sparks shower down as his cutter bites into them. In only a few seconds of action the Vladimir prison is cut off entirely from the outside world.

With machine-pistols at the ready we dash towards the guard quarters. Tiny is in the lead. He swings a *Nagan* above his head in true policeman style.

'Come on out with your hands in the air!' he roars, in a Chief of Police voice.

'Idiot!' snarls Porta. 'It's not in the plan, the gold-robbers sayin' that! That's what the OGPU says to the robbers!'

Tiny ignores him. He has become paranoiac since we put him into a Russian warrant officer's uniform.

'Come out of there!' he shouts, even louder than before. 'Or we'll shoot your heads off!'

'Have you gone *mad*?' rages Barcelona, kicking open the door of the guard-room. 'That's queer!' he cries.

'What's queer?' asks the Old Man.

'There ain't a soul in here,' says Barcelona, in amazement.

'D'you mean we're in the wrong guard-house?' cries Porta, shakily.

'Out of the way,' says Igor, pushing forward. 'I threw a gas-grenade in here. Those boys are sleeping like never before.'

'Here they are, all snoring,' says Porta, jumping over the counter. 'Makes you sleepy, just to look at 'em!'

He yawns audibly, and drops down into a deep armchair.

'Out, out!' screams Igor, excitedly. 'Are you mad? The gas is still working!' He almost drags us out of the guard-room.

Porta brings up the rear, staggering and blowing like a whale.

'Where are the gas-cylinders?' asks the Commissar. He comes down the broad prison gangway like a second Trotsky with a *Nagan* held in his hand.

'Here!' grins Tiny quietly, pushing a serving-trolley in front of him loaded with gas-cylinders.

'Don't drop those!' the Commissar warns him. 'That gas works faster than an iron bar across the head.'

'Yes, we saw that just now,' answers Porta. 'I still feel like Snow White in the glass box!'

'I don't bloody like this,' mumbles Barcelona. 'Have you thought what they'll do to us, if they get hold of us?'

'All the things the censors cut out of the horror films,' answers Porta, with a short laugh.

A woman soldier waving a *Tokarev* rushes out of the kitchen.

Igor jumps on her and places his *Nagan* between her eyes. There is a hollow crack and the wall behind her head is covered with blood, brains and bone splinters.

Two jailers come out from the south wing of the prison, and stare blankly at Igor standing there with the *Nagan* in his hand.

'Enemy of the people,' he snarls, kicking irritably at the body.

The jailers give a Russian shrug of their shoulders, and go on without a word. It is best not to know, or see, too much in Vladimir prison. It is not unusual for people to be liquidated without explanation.

Our two lorries rumble into the prison yard, followed by one of the T-34s.

'Get your gasmasks on,' orders the Commissar nervously. '*Keep* them on no matter what happens! This whole prison's full of gas already!'

'Will they die?' asks the Old Man, worriedly.

'Not all,' laughs Igor indifferently. 'Only those who would have died in any case!'

'Come on,' says the Commissar, catching Porta by the shoulder. Porta's head bangs into a door-post.

'What the hell?' he cries, yawning like a sleepy horse. 'What's goin' on? Hell, where am I?' He leans against the door, and tries to remember where he is.

'Move it!' says the Commissar, pushing him. 'You've got a vault to open! You told us you'd been a locksmith's apprentice, and could open any lock in existence!'

'Right enough!' mumbles Porta, and wobbles sleepily down the stairs.

'Frostlips' is behind him with two large bundles of keys. He swears one of them must be the key to the vault.

'Are you sure the right key's *there*?' asks 'Whorecatcher' in a worried voice. 'You've been wrong before!'

'I'll guarantee one of 'em fits,' says 'Frostlips' in an insulted tone. He clashes the bundles of keys together.

'One's enough,' says Porta, leaning tiredly against the heavy door of the vault. He looks through the big keyhole, but can see nothing. He begins trying keys in it. None of them fit.

'Frostlips' gets a funny look on his face, and stammers something about how maybe he has got hold of the wrong bunch of keys.

'I should've known!' says 'Whorecatcher', angrily, 'the last time you were wrong you had a toothache, and this time you're suffering from nervous stress!'

'The whole bleedin' prison's asleep,' reports Tiny. He comes clattering down the stairway with a pleased look on his face and swinging a gasmask in his hand.

'I never in my life seen anybody go on their backs quick as the key-rattlers and the slaves in this cage! That bleedin' gas ought to be able to close down this world war quick as knife! I'd just love to see Adolf's an' Uncle Joe's coolies sleepin' like

313

babes in one another's arms!'

'Unfortunately it only works in a closed room,' says the Commissar. 'Otherwise, I can assure you the whole German Army would have been put to sleep long ago!'

The Old Man comes down into the cellars. He is angry.

'Don't you think we're going to get our arses singed on this one?' he asks, standing with feet apart, in the middle of the room.

'We'll manage,' says Porta, running his fingers over the armoured door. 'All I've got to do is find out how this thing works, and then we're rich!'

'How long will it take?' asks the Commissar, impatiently. 'We haven't got a lot of time! There's enough gas to put 'em to sleep just once more and then we've had it!'

'Why not liquidate them all now?' Suggests Igor, his *Nagan* already in his hand.

'Don't you ever get tired of killing people?' asks the Commissar, irritably. 'You must soon be sick of yourself. *I* get sick just looking at you!'

Igor shrugs his shoulders indifferently, and slams his *Nagan* back into its holster with a jeering look on his face.

After half an hour's work on the difficult lock, Porta sits down despondently.

'I can do it,' he says. 'But that's not the question!'

'Then be so good as to inform us, please, of what the question *is*!' says the Commissar, with heavy irony. 'I'm just dying to know!' Under stress conditions the Commissar's right eye winks involuntarily. It opens and closes as if the eyelid were on a string. It has brought him into contact with a number of ladies in the course of his life, but it has also brought him a number of scoldings from ladies who did not approve of being contacted in that manner. His right eye is winking furiously now, but there are no pretty girls in sight.

'It's a question,' explains Porta, with a dubious contortion of his features, 'of time!'

'Time?' whispers the Commissar, working his eyelid so hard it is wonderful the eye does not fall out of its socket.

'Yes, time!' Porta smiles with an effort. He sits down

314

cross-legged in front of the unapproachable vault door.

'It's going to take more time, then!' nods the Commissar, falling resignedly into a chair. 'How *much* more time?'

Porta counts on his fingers, and it seems for a moment as if he is about to begin on his toes as well.

'This is a very intelligent vault we've to do with here! The bloke who gave birth to this was no pal of safe-crackers. It's *different*! Different in every way!' He knocks, thoughtfully, on the door towering above him. 'The steel's different! The lock's an unknown make, and the bloody door itself's different! It's a real shit vault this one. Must've been a Jew that invented it!'

'Thank you!' smiles the Commissar, with a snarl in his voice.

'I've not been let in on everything, I see,' says the Old Man, pushing his fur cap back on his head. 'That's for sure! I've been done!'

'Porta,' says Gregor, bending over him, 'tell us straight, now. How serious *is* it?'

Porta grunts, as if a bullet had sunk into his midriff.

'Shitty!' he answers.

'How much shit?' asks Gregor.

'A great big bloody pile of shit!' answers Porta, lighting a cigarette. 'More shit than I'd ever have thought there could be!'

'How long will it take you to open it?' asks the Commissar, puffing nervously at his cigarette.

Porta counts on his fingers again.

'All night an' part of next day,' he says sadly, holding out his hands like a fisherman showing the size of the one that got away.

'That's *great*!' the Commissar explodes, jumping up from his chair. 'We'll have plenty of time for sightseeing, then?'

Porta gives him a long stare.

'Let me just tell you I'm no happier about this than you are. But don't forget it's a Soviet bloody vault we're dealing with, made in the USSR. No German vault would have been so mean!'

'Listen here!' says Barcelona, pushing forward. 'The fact of the matter is, put short and sweet, that you reckon you can get this rotten box open some time before next Christmas, so we can get away with the gold?'

'I've told you. There's not a lock in the world I can't get past, but it takes the time it has to take! When I was helping Egon, the best locksmith in Berlin, there wasn't a lock didn't give up when we arrived. We even used to open locks for the coppers, and we were highly respected, I can tell you. Look at those wheels there! They ain't even round like normal wheels. They look like somethin' out of a wrecked aeroplane!'

The Commissar tramps backwards and forwards impatiently, making figures of eight on the floor.

'I do believe I'm dreaming,' he says, knocking himself on the forehead. 'Yes, I'm dreaming! I'm in hospital being anaesthetized, before they cut off both of my legs!' He kicks the vault door viciously, and grimaces with pain. 'And I hope it's true, too, because this situation is much worse!'

'We goin' to live?' asks the Old Man, puffing fatalistically on his silver-lidded pipe. 'That's all that interests me. Don't tell me it's a lot to ask!'

'This job ain't for us,' shouts Tiny, resolutely. 'If you lot'll listen to me, we'll get out of 'ere quick as we can, an' find a proper bank. We go in there with mpis, scrape the beans together an' sod off out of it! Any dope can fix a thing like that! I knew a kid o' twelve as done it! He'd got to sixteen before they shot 'im!'

'An' where'd you get rid of all those roubles you'd knocked off?' asks Porta, with a sneer.

'Roubles? What roubles?' asks Tiny blankly.

'The roubles you and your chopper had picked up in the bank,' answers Porta, ironically. 'You don't bloody well think Russian banks are stocked up with dollars, do you? Roubles you can wipe your arse on, and they don't even do much of a job of that!'

'An hour from now the gas won't be working any more,' remarks the Commissar, with a hopeless look on his face.

'Give me all the tools down here,' Porta demands. 'That

rotten, shitty lock's going to get to know Obergefreiter, by the grace of God, Joseph Porta!' He pulls the vodka bottle from his pocket, and reduces its contents by a third. Then he screws the cap back on and returns the bottle to his pocket.

'You're dead sure you can open that damned door?' asks the Commissar, with the air of a Grand Inquisitor.

'I said I could,' answers Porta, annoyed.

'And you can do it before the turn of the century?' the Commissar goes on. 'I only want to know, so that I can arrange my affairs accordingly!'

'Don't get me worked up. Come and give me a hand instead! I need light! Plenty of light. Then everything'll go a lot quicker!'

'Yes, I'm sure,' says the Commissar, turning the hand-operated spotlight on to the lock.

Porta takes a few deep, long breaths to quieten his nerves. He squats down on his haunches, like an Inca warrior readying himself for breakfast.

'Normally a lock like this ought to fly open when a feller blows on it!' he says, thoughtfully.

'Blow on it,' suggests Gregor.

'The rotten thing's shaken my confidence!' says Porta fiercely.

Igor rattles down the stairs with his *Nagan* ready for action in his hand.

'Found a piece of cunt sergeant rattling off to the OGPU on the blower,' he says, holstering his *Nagan*. 'I blew her away and smashed the phone. We hadn't cut it off when we moved in.'

The Commissar presses his lips tightly together, and keeps back some remarks which he was otherwise prepared to spit out.

'What'd she tell the OGPU?' asks Barcelona practically.

'Nothing much! I was right behind her when she made the connection. I blew her brains up the wall.'

'Did anybody ever tell you what a stinking pig you are?' asks the Old Man, staring contemptuously at him.

'Only you,' grins Igor, executing a highly complicated Russian shrug.

Porta leans down toward the door of the vault. His pointed nose touches the lock.

'I can't give you more light when you're standing *there*,' protests the Commissar. He turns the spot on to Porta's right eye, which is peering into the lock.

'God dammit,' shouts Porta, spitting angrily on the lock, 'it's *mean* to make anything so bloody complicated! If all locks were like that, think of all the unemployed there'd be!'

'Unemployed?' asks 'Whorecatcher' in amazement, kneeling down alongside him to relieve the Commissar with the spotlight.

'Yes, of course! Bank robbers would have to give up altogether, and the police shut down their robbery sections! I need a drill with a diamond tip, that can get through that blasted metal!'

'Here,' says 'Frostlips', handing him a diamond drill.

'I'll fix that bloody thing now,' says Porta grimly, and presses the drill against the lock. It whines like a runaway outboard motor. Then it slips. It has hardly scratched the metal.

'You'll do it all right. Take it easy,' Igor comforts Porta, patting him on the shoulder.

Porta moves away like a dog which has been patted by a cat. He pushes a thin tool into the lock, but soon gives up again.

'Dammit,' he mumbles despondently. 'I'm *good* at locks, but this bastard's a real headache.'

'If we get taken,' grins Gregor, carelessly, 'we can write a book about it. How about this for a title: *Gold-robbers in Siberia*!'

'Oh, you *are* funny!' snarls Porta wickedly. 'You're close to making me *die* laughin'!'

'What about acid?' suggests the Commissar. 'We've got a bottle here, and a syringe!'

'Why not?' answers Porta. He empties the entire contents of the acid bottle into the lock.

It bubbles and hisses for about ten minutes. One or two drops splash on to the Commissar's uniform, burning holes in it immediately. Nothing happens to the lock.

'Rat piss!' says Porta, sending the empty acid bottle rattling across the floor with a kick.

'What about a saw?' suggests 'Frostlips'.

'If you're in need of exercise,' hisses Porta, 'then saw as much as you like. But, if it's opening the vault we're talkin' about, then sawin' at it won't do any good!'

'I can't get away from it,' says Tiny, giving the door of the vault a kick. 'It's too much trouble breakin' into a bleedin' vault! Why don't we go for a sausage factory. It's a lot easier!'

'A *sausage* factory?' asks Porta, turning his head.

'Yes,' grins Tiny. 'I know a couple of fellers who make a livin' at it!'

'Were they hungry?' wonders Gregor.

'Not on your life,' answers Tiny, grinning even more. 'They go in the day the slaves pick up their coppers. They go quietlike into the pay office, pick up the shekels an' off they go again. Easy as shittin'!'

'What about if the wages are paid by cheque? That's common practice nowadays,' smiles Porta, sourly.

'Nip down to the bank an' cash 'em, then,' shrugs Tiny.

'Try that,' suggests Porta. 'You'd be sorry for the rest of your life!'

He picks up a tool, and does something complicated to the vault lock.

'No,' he says, shaking his head. 'I'll have to drill again. This is what the trade calls a tricky box!'

'Tricky?' asks the Old Man, wonderingly. 'What do you mean by that?'

'The tricky part is that there's traps in it, and they're what you've got to give a miss to,' answers Porta, knocking on the door of the vault. 'If I make a balls of it, at least ten big, wicked steel rods are goin' to shoot out an' lock that door so's nobody in the world can ever open it. There might be one feller who could get in to the gold, and that'd be the bloke who made it in the first place.'

'Why didn't we bring 'im with us, then?' asks Tiny irritably, throwing his arms out wide in despair.

'Even if he was here, it wouldn't help a shit,' says Porta. 'When those steel bars come out you need a special machine to break the wall down. A shit of a thing like that weighs Christ knows how many tons, an' you don't walk about with it under your arm.'

'Sounds promising,' moans the Commissar. 'Time's up! The key-boys need more gas! Get your arses in gear!'

'Shall we give 'em the lot?' asks 'Frostlips', from the cellar door. 'Will it send 'em off for ever?'

'It's a humane way to die,' the Commissar feels. 'Everybody likes a good sleep!'

'Damnation!' hisses Porta, pressing his lips together. He picks up a tool. His grip is so tight that it hurts his hand. 'Hell!' he curses again. 'I know all the most advanced ways of fixing a lock, and Egon and me's tried 'em all! Give me that electronic listening thing!' He puts the earphones on with the air of a famous surgeon who is about to cut the stomach out of a patient. He turns the combination lock carefully, listening for the pawls to drop. After a moment, which feels like a week, he tears the earphones from his head.

'Somebody's comin',' says Gregor, gazing up the stairs.

'I belched,' says Porta.

'No, somebody *is* coming,' mumbles the Commissar. He picks up his *Kalashnikov* from the floor.

'Shut up, or I can't think! If somebody's comin' then shoot 'em! I want quiet!' says Porta.

'So do we,' says the Commissar, clicking off the *Kalashnikov*'s safety.

'Maybe it ain't clever to shoot 'em straight off,' says Tiny. 'I've heard it's best to greet God's local representatives with a smile!'

'An' who's God, then?' asks 'Frostlips'.

'Depends where a feller is when 'e's smilin',' grins Tiny. 'Uncle Joe 'ere p'raps?'

'I will go up and speak with our guests,' says Igor, with a Siberian grin. 'You look after things while I am gone!'

'I've made my decision! I'm going to hit that vault in every way possible,' rages Porta. 'An' I'm going to do it all at the same time. I'm not going to let a shit like that fuck me!'

'Right!' says the Commissar. 'What d'you want me to do?'

Porta gives him a funny look.

'Watch your napper now,' he warns, ''cos something's going to happen! Make some coffee! It clear's a feller's head!'

'To be quite honest I've begun to lose my liking for our planned life of luxury,' says Barcelona doubtfully. 'Maybe it ain't all that much fun owning a little island over there by Haiti, where you run everything yourself and can be king, emperor, grand duke, general or anything else you want to be!'

'Oxygen bottles and a burner!' demands Porta, brusquely.

The flame hisses, and sparks fly round our ears. Soon after, Porta gives up the torch. It was about as much use as a dull cheese-knife.

Albert backs the T-34 in, and attaches the towing-wires to the three odd-looking cogs on the door of the vault. We hope he can loosen it from its hinges, but all that happens is that a wire snaps and causes a lot of damage.

When we try again, this time with triple tow-cables and the tank moving backwards in small jerks, all three cogs come away from the door.

We sit down, despondently, and drink coffee.

'I could have made this coffee a lot better,' grumbles Porta, sniffing at the dregs in his cup. 'All I'd had to do was to make it from dried-out cow-dung!' He gets up, takes a bundle of dynamite charges and begins to affix them to the big door of the vault.

'Think that's all right?' asks the Commissar, his right eye ticking away madly.

'If it ain't,' answers Porta, 'and we don't get under cover in one hell of a hurry, then we'll suddenly be dead, and won't have to worry about this bloody door any more!'

The noise of the dynamite exploding is deafening, but when the smoke clears all that has happened to the door is that a large black spot has appeared in the middle of it.

'Well, we'll just have to get even tougher,' hisses Porta,

shivering with rage. 'Soup*, an' a few more charges! That's *got* to be able to leave that door lyin' in peace with its backside up!'

The first explosion was like a paper bag popping in comparison to this one.

The cellar looks like a split melon. We scramble over collapsed walls to get to the gold. But when the dust finally clears away we stand choking and spitting in front of the vault door, which is standing where it has stood all the time.

'I won't take this from anybody, or anything!' rages Porta. 'My honour's at stake now! I'll show 'em who's an Obergefreiter by the grace of God!'

'Get on with it, in the name of Hell!' says the Commissar, spitting out brick-dust. 'We've got to get out of here as fast as possible!' He stares at Porta with his ticking eye and blows out more brick-dust.

'Are we going to *live*?' asks the Old Man expressionlessly, withdrawing slowly up the stairs.

'I think so, yes,' answers Porta. 'It won't be all *that* much of a bang.' He presses plastic explosive on every available inch of the door. Tiny helps him, crimping the primers with his teeth.

'I think you'd all better get up out of the cellar,' Porta advises us, when he is ready. 'One or two things might start rattlin' around in here!'

'I could do with throwing a few things around, myself,' says the Commissar, running quickly up the stairs.

We wait tensely outside the cellar, while Porta completes the wiring of the door. Then he backs slowly up from the cellar with a cable in each hand.

'All clear?' he asks. ''Cos in a minute it's goin' to go bang-bang!'

'Blow that fucking shit into bits and pieces!' shouts the Commissar, going down on one knee.

'Yes!' mumbles Porta. He brings the ends of the two cables together.

* Soup: Nitroglycerine

The explosion is so loud that none of us can find words to describe it afterwards. But we feel the blast. It comes roaring out of the cellar opening, and throws us across the parade ground and through the door of a guard-room on the far side of it. The room is full of sleeping soldiers – and smashed furniture after we arrive.

We pull ourselves together after a while. When we are back in the cellar and stand staring at the unharmed steel door the Commissar begins to sob.

'The gun,' says Porta sharply, and is already on the way over to the Panther with Tiny at his heels.

'We certainly got all that rubbish cleared out of the cellar, anyway,' says the Old Man. He kicks at the one remaining piece of brickwork the blast has not taken with it.

With rattling tracks the Panther comes rolling across the barrack square. It waddles into the cellar entrance, brickwork collapsing on all sides.

Porta puts his head out of the driver's hatch.

'Better take cover before I start bangin' away! That door'd better tighten its ring, now!'

The long gun sinks down, with a humming sound, and traverses towards the armoured door.

We hold our ears and await the sound of the shot, tensely.

There is a heavy thud, and everything is suddenly blood-red.

We look at one another, and cannot believe our own eyes. We have become live, surrealistic paintings. Tiny has loaded with the wrong ammunition, as the Old Man has feared he would for some time. He has used a marker, and there is red paint everywhere.

'Unmilitary, miserable drunkard!' shouts the Old Man, trying to wipe the paint from his face.

'I'll strangle that cheeky Social Democratic son of a bitch!' rages the Commissar, hitting away madly at a dented bucket.

'Take it easy, fellers,' says Tiny, with his head out of the side hatch. 'Anybody can make a mistake! I'll soon get a couple of tins of paint remover, so you can begin to look 'alfway 'uman again.'

'We'll need new uniforms,' says 'Frostlips', who is dripping with red paint. 'We'll be arrested, soon as they set eyes on us. Red as we are nobody *is*! Not even in *this* country!'

'Back everybody!' screams Porta, warningly, from the turret. 'We'll give it one up the arse now!'

'Not *another* bloody marker!' shouts the Old Man, nervously.

The pressure wave from the S-shell is terrific. It feels as if a giant warm hand clenches itself round our bodies. The deafening noise seems to split the air apart. When the dust disperses the powerful shell appears to have done little damage. There is a small hole in the door.

'Got him!' shouts a jubilant Porta from the turret hatch, grinning all over his face. Bluish-grey smoke seeps from the hole.

'You bloody *did* it!' shouts Gregor happily.

'What's that smoke coming out of there?' asks the Old Man, in a frightened voice.

Suddenly an ominous silence sinks over the cellar. We all stare at the smoke issuing from the hole.

'Can gold burn?' asks Albert, blinking his eyes behind the mask of red paint which covers his black face.

The Commissar crosses the room in three long strides, and peers through the hole.

'Hell! That rotten German shell has started a fire inside! Quick! Get some water!'

We fall over one another on our way up the stairs for water.

'Fire!' shouts Tiny. He comes dashing back with a hose and a ladder he has found hanging outside on the wall.

When 'Whorecatcher' turns on the water, the pressure on the hose sends Tiny tumbling over backwards, and the stream of water swills the rest of us out to the sides of the room.

With much shouting and screaming of threats we finally get control of the hose and direct the jet through the hole.

'Give it two more shells,' orders the Commissar, pressing his lips together.

Twice in succession the tank-gun fires. It seems as if the entire prison is falling down on our heads. We are totally deaf for several minutes, and pains wrack us through and through.

'I'll bet we're the first people in the history of the world to have used a tank for a tin-opener!' says Porta, with a short laugh, as he jumps down from the Panther's turret.

'Let's go in and take a look at the goods,' suggests the Commissar, rubbing his hands together.

The big vault door gapes open like a peeled banana.

Porta stops to take a closer look.

'Yes, that's it,' he mumbles, 'it's quite different! Never seen anything bloody like it!'

'Jesus'n Mary!' whispers Tiny, impressed. He stares in fascination at all the gold ingots which have been thrown down from the shelves in the vault. 'I'm goin' to buy the entire bleedin' world, an' kick all the arses I feel like kickin' an' never salute nobody, never again!'

'Get moving!' the Commissar chases them. 'The gas'll soon have stopped working, and there'll be a crowd of sleepy-headed, panic-stricken idiots asking unpleasant questions! Get the Panther out, and back the waggons in so we can load up and get out of here!'

The Old Man is sitting on the big tool-chest, watching the loading with a peculiar look on his face.

'Aren't you going to help?' asks Porta, wonderingly.

'No!' snaps the Old Man, making a face as if there were a bad smell under his nose.

Everybody stops work and looks at the Old Man, who is sitting carelessly on the tool-chest, puffing at his silver-lidded pipe.

'What's the matter with you?' asks the Commissar. 'You've got to admit we did it! It could easily have been a fiasco!'

'I'm not with you any more,' says the Old man, looking angrily at the Commissar, 'and I'm bitterly sorry I ever was! It's a load of shit, that's what this is! Here we are, murdering right and left for some miserable gold! You can do what you like, but I'm *out*!'

325

'You gonna shop us when we get back?' asks 'Frostlips', his eyes narrowing.

'I don't understand your filthy way of thinking!' snarls the Old Man contemptuously.

'Don't you want *any* of the gold?' asks Tiny, practically. 'Thought 'ow much of it there'll be apiece when we get it sold?'

'No!' replies the Old Man decisively. 'In any case I don't believe any of you are going to get much fun out of that shit!'

'Shit?' Barcelona gives a forced laugh. 'You're off your head! We're rich men! A week from now we can demob ourselves, and if you want the biggest carpenter shop in the world you can buy it for yourself. That is if you want to go on planin' planks for fun!'

Porta sweeps up the gold-dust from the battered ingots and puts it in his pocket.

'What're you doin' that for?' asks Gregor blankly.

'Berlin intuition,' smiles Porta, foxily. 'Who knows, somebody might manage to take our arses at quarter to midnight, and then it'd be nice to have a bit in reserve in your pockets!'

'Stop!' comes a warning shout from Barcelona. 'The waggon can't take any more!'

''Ow bleedin' annoyin',' says Tiny, vexedly. 'There's a load of bars left yet! We can't leave them for Ivan Stinkanovitch! It makes me bleedin' ill to think of it!'

'Share 'em out between the tanks,' shouts the Commissar nervously. 'Time's run out! The gas has stopped working! They'll all be here soon, and they won't like what we've been up to one bit!'

From the parade ground two shots sound in quick succession.

Igor comes down the stairs, grinning.

'Couple of 'em woke up too soon,' he says, pushing his *Nagan* back in its holster.

'Get ready to blow up the communications centre,' the Commissar orders Igor. 'They must, above all, have no possibility of communicating with anybody outside for the next twelve hours! Set the primers for thirty minutes, and surround the lot with phosphorus cans! They'll burn like hell, and give them more than enough to think about!'

'Nothing more's going to be blown up here,' says the Old Man harshly, 'and there'll be no more killing either!'

'I'm in command here!' roars the Commissar, in a rage, 'and what I say is to be blown up *will* be blown up! Get going, Igor! What naïve fools you Germans are when it comes to it!' he jeers, his lips curled in contempt.

'Shut it! You stinking Soviet Jew shit! Shut it!' Heide swings round with his mpi at the ready.

Like lightning the Commissar has the weapon out of his hands, and slings Heide over against the wall.

'Don't call me a Jew shit, you stinking little Nazi creep!'

White with rage, Heide tears the *Nagan* from its leather holster, and aims it at the Commissar.

'Be a good boy now, little Moses, or Daddy smack,' grins Tiny, kicking the gun from Heide's hand.

Heide jumps forward as if on steel springs, and his right fist crashes into Tiny's face. There is such speed and power in the punch that Tiny goes over on his back and gasps for air.

'You 'it me, Moses!' he howls. 'I'm goin' to *kill* you!'

Battle is on. Heide rushes forward with a mad scream. Tiny is too slow in getting away from the rain of blows which come at him. A murderous punch lands on his temple, and he staggers and shakes his head like a pole-axed bull. The edge of Heide's hand catches him across the larynx and sends him to the ground. It would have killed another man.

'This time I'm going to *kill* you,' hisses Heide furiously, aiming a kick at the big man's kidneys.

Now Tiny is really angry and in that condition he is more dangerous than a whole case of dynamite. He gets back on his feet, wipes the blood from his face, and spits out a couple of broken teeth. With a noise like the splitting of skulls he crashes his forehead into Heide's face.

'Uh!' he grunts, and spits blood, as Heide's fist buries itself

327

in his middle, pumping the air from his lungs. 'Uh!' he grunts again. He turns half round and smashes a karate kick at Heide's stomach.

Heide tries desperately to jump to one side, but Tiny's size 14 boot gets home on his hip with the force of a diving Stuka. He bends forward, and Tiny brings up his giant fist, with a happy grin, into his pain-distorted face. The left fist follows the right, and lands with a sound like a ton of dough falling from a skyscraper.

'*Mama mia*! What a punch!' cries Porta, who is sitting on a pile of gold ingots enjoying the fight.

We are all taken up by the battle. We shout and encourage them, and give good advice.

His face pouring with blood, Heide tries an attack, which, by all the tenets of boxing, is suicidal. One hard blow after another crashes into Tiny's twisted face. It resembles a bowl of minced meat, blood oozing from it. Tiny takes it all with the indifference of a rock, not even guarding against the merciless punches. You can no longer see from where the blood is coming. It is pouring from the whole of his face.

'Kick him in the balls,' shouts Porta kindly, banging his fist into his other hand to show how.

'Butt him! That rotten swastika rat,' roars Igor, furiously boxing holes in the air.

'Tear his head off!' screams the Commissar. 'Kill the stinking Nazi pig!'

There is no doubt where the Russian/German audience has its sympathy.

Tiny steps backwards towards the cellar door. Kostia, the little slant-eyed Siberian with the big Cossack fur hat, opens the door. The whole prison seems to shake as Tiny falls backwards down the stairs and through the trapdoor which leads to the heating system. All we can see of him are his size 14 boots caught on the edge of the trapdoor. The rest of him is dangling over the hissing hot-water pipes which have been smashed by the explosions.

Heide gives out a victorious yell, and throws himself murderously at Tiny, who is desperately attempting to release himself from the trapdoor. Kostia and Porta help him by pulling off his boots. He somersaults up onto his feet.

For a moment the two bloodthirsty berserkers stand watching one another. Heide, the boxer, is continually on the move, and using his left. It is no secret that he has a left hand everyone is afraid of. He has learnt to use it in the same way as the Britishers. Every punch is hard and deadly accurate. He is a feared regimental boxer, and has won countless matches. Anyone but Tiny would long since have been dead. Heide is grimly determined to kill him. Years of hatred are culminating in the battle between these two.

Tiny gives a scream like a bull elk at mating time, and flails away, but without any of his punches landing. He has no thought of defending himself. A hail of hard blows makes him stagger for a moment. He spits out a couple more broken teeth. His mouth looks like a crushed tomato.

Heide gets home two karate kicks on Tiny's body. The spectators howl in disgusted protest. When Tiny manages to do the same, they cheer and clap excitedly, and all seem to feel that everything is as it should be.

Shortly after, Tiny goes down on one knee. Heide immediately kicks him in the face, with a cracking sound like eggs breaking.

Tiny is now literally mad with rage. Roaring furiously he gets back up on his feet and lands a right on the side of Heide's head which sends him spinning round like a top. He gets a few more punches home, but this time on Heide's ribs. With blood running down over his face and both eyes closed he goes in like a mad bull to crush the Nazi's face.

But Heide ducks like lightning and feints a left towards Tiny's bloody face. Lithely he springs to one side and avoids a murderous kick at his crotch which would have crushed not only his testicles but his entire pelvis if it had landed.

Heide grins satanically, and begins to hammer away at Tiny's smashed face with his ramrod of a left.

'We've got to stop this,' says the Old Man, worriedly. 'Hell, that Hamburg crook's no more than a gutter fighter. He hasn't the faintest idea of how to box. The Nazi pig'll murder him. It's like a cat playing with a mouse!'

'The big dope don't even know how to defend himself,' says Gregor, shaking his head in commiseration.

'Stop 'em!' repeats the Old Man. 'It's cold-blooded murder!'

'Have to shoot Heide to do that,' says Porta, accepting one of the Legionnaire's *Caporals*.

Heide's fists are going like drumsticks, and every time they land on Tiny's face it sounds like a butcher slapping a parcel of minced meat.

Tiny keeps hitting out, but without his punches landing.

Heide is dancing round merely flicking his left into his face, certain he has won.

Tiny gives out a ringing scream, and rushes forward like a mad bull in the arena.

The attack makes Heide step to one side professionally, and accept a couple of light blows. He bobs and feints, cool as a cucumber, takes a step forward and lands a straight left which stops Tiny as if he had run into a wall. His animal roar turns to a strangled gulp, as the air is knocked out of his lungs. He stops, in confusion, and wipes the blood from his eyes, trying to find Heide, who is dancing lightly around him on his toes. Every time Tiny throws his club of a fist at him he is out of reach. Cut to bloody doll-rags, Tiny shakes his head in an attempt to clear it. His left ear hangs down on his neck, half torn away.

'Yellow Nazi swine!' he growls furiously, and kicks out backwards like a horse.

Heide sees his chance. Two murderous blows and a kick and Tiny is staggering across the concrete floor like a dying man, with blood streaming from his nose and mouth.

Heide struts over towards the wall, brushing his hands together contemptuously, as if he had been handling something filthy.

'Butcher's offal!' he snarls, and goes to a water-tap to swill the blood from his face.

Tiny, who is lying on the floor struggling desperately to regain his breath, lifts his bloody head, and peers around. He looks like a grizzly bear awakened too early from hibernation, and he is just as vicious as one.

The babble of conversation amongst the spectators dies away. The sudden silence warns Heide, who has begun to comb his hair. He whirls and barely manages to duck under Tiny's giant fist as it comes hurtling at him in a hook which would have taken off his head if it had landed.

Heide goes to work with a whole series of professional body blows.

Tiny's lungs whistle for air, but Heide is in close, hammering at his middle. It feels as if his stomach is being smashed in, and his lungs dilate emptily in his chest.

Murder and hatred glitter in Heide's eyes. None of us doubt that he is not going to stop now until Tiny is dead.

'Adolf's little Moses,' gasps Tiny, with a horrible grin, swinging his arms in circles. He hits Heide on the chin with a punch which lifts him from the floor and throws him against a row of shelves. Machine-pistols clatter down over him. Tiny thunders forward and runs straight into the barrel of an mpi in Heide's outstretched arms. He is moving so fast it is a wonder the barrel of the weapon does not go straight through his body. He gives out a shrill scream and goes down on his knees with both hands pressed to his stomach.

With a crazy grin Heide swings the machine-pistol at him, but Tiny manages to duck away from it and the butt only grazes his head. He rolls across the floor and gets back up on his feet. On his way he too has got hold of a machine-pistol, and now the two men go at one another with the butts. Heide is the faster at this, too. Tiny remains the slow-thinking gutter fighter with no idea whatever of finesse. What takes Heide a fraction of a second to work out, takes Tiny an hour. Every time Tiny thinks he has Heide set up and swings at him, the mpi butt hits something else. Igor goes down without a sound, blood streaming over his red-painted face.

Heide has got round behind Tiny, who is standing staring blankly at the unconscious Igor whom he thinks of as a friend.

'Sorry!' he mumbles, sniffing sorrowfully. Behind him

331

Heide takes careful aim, and brings the butt of the mpi down on the back of his neck. He goes down on his face like a felled tree, his arms spread out like a man crucified.

The Old Man bends over him, worriedly, feeling for his pulse.

'Get a doctor!' he orders, harshly.

'Doctor?' the Commissar screams with laughter. 'Where the hell d'you think you are? You're in Vladimir isolation prison, man! They only use doctors here to certify death, and if there was one he'd be crazy from gas for the next 48 hours! Now it's *off*! And it can't be too soon!' He turns to Igor and coughs an order in some strange Russian dialect.

When we are a few miles from the prison, a blinding flash of light illumines the sky, and we hear the long, thundering roll of an explosion.

'Those villains blew up the prison anyway!' snarls the Old Man furiously.

'What the devil! At war aren't we?' remarks Porta, cheerily. 'And it's not only legal, it's also our *duty* to knock off the lads from the other FPO. It's only the communications centre Igor's blown up! If the commandant went with it, nobody's going to cry for him, either!'

The Old Man growls and looks angry.

A little later the differential goes on one of the trucks. We blame one another for it, and World War III nearly breaks out on the spot.

In the end Porta downs tools and refuses to do any more to repair the damage.

'I'm a bloody tank-driver,' he shouts furiously. 'Accordin' to regulations I'm not allowed to repair anything! The mechanical engineers are supposed to look after all that! Dial three zeroes and get ADAD*.'

'I'm a tank-driver, too,' bawls Kostia, his narrow black eyes glinting. 'I do no repairs either!'

'Let's go in and shoot some dice,' suggests Porta, crawling down into the Panther.

* ADAD: Equivalent to the British AA

'Why not?' grins Kostia, following him.

'No you bloody don't. I won't stand for it,' shouts the Old Man. 'I said I'd have nothing to do with your gold robbery, but I'm still the goddammed Section Leader of 2 bloody Section! Out of there, Porta, and get on that differential! That's an order!'

The only answer the Old Man gets is the smack of the hatch, closing down and being dogged on the inside.

'Frostlips' and Gregor crawl under the broken-down truck with a lot of cursing and swearing, but give up after a while, shaking their heads.

'Can't do a thing with it,' says 'Frostlips', 'it's a total write-off! The Yanks knew what they were doing when they made us a present of those rotten Studebakers! Capitalist shit!' he rages, kicking at the big tyres.

'What the hell's that?' asks the Commissar, and listens tensely.

'Crow,' cries out 'Whorecatcher' nervously, staring up at the dark sky.

As if in reply an old scout biplane appears from the clouds and circles low over us. Then it disappears again into the cloud curtain.

'If it's us they're looking for, they know where we are now,' remarks the Old Man, uneasily.

'It's not us,' says the Commissar thoughtfully. 'I had some German equipment and weapons scattered about in the prison, and the Kübel with the smashed radiator I left outside. So they're not looking for Russians. They're looking for a German Brandenburg Commando*!'

The broken-down truck is taken on tow behind one of the T-34s.

'We'll get another truck all right,' promises the Commissar, confidently. 'But until we do we'll just have to tow that Yankee shit.'

Six days after our departure from the Vladimir prison we halt in a deserted, forgotten village to make necessary repairs

---

* German special unit for raiding behind enemy lines.

to two of the vehicles. Their radiators are boiling so much that it is a wonder they have not split open long ago.

When the repairs are completed we sit down to play cards with the village mayor and the local OGPU chief, a man who got into political hot water twenty years earlier. We play in silence for a while, until 'Frostlips' accuses the mayor of cheating. When 'Frostlips' keeps on with his charges the mayor gets angry and threatens to cut off his ears if he does not stop talking such nonsense.

'May God grant you the pains and tortures of a slow death, you immoral dog,' snarls 'Frostlips' at the mayor.

The mayor goes pale, but still continues to cheat. Suddenly the light goes out, and while the mayor is gone to see what has happened, 'Frostlips' sweeps the money up from the table and hurries out into the kitchen.

When the fuse has been changed and the sleepy light again shines down over the table, the mayor discovers that his winnings have disappeared. He gives out a loud yell and looks under the table in the vain hope that the money has fallen on the floor. Of course, it has not.

'And you're the one who's supposed to see to it there's law and order here,' he screams accusingly at the OGPU chief, as he realizes slowly that he has been robbed. 'May the Evil One grant you thousands of cramps, pestilences and cankers, and so order it that these bounties not only fall upon you, but also upon your children and your children's children even unto the twelfth generation, if you do not find my money!'

'When we're finished with this lousy war,' scowls Barcelona, 'I don't want ever to see snow again! Damnation, how I *hate* snow! No matter where you look everywhere's white! The only chance you've got of seein' a bit of colour is to go out and look at your arse in a mirror!'

'What did you do before you became a soldier?' Kostia asks Porta.

'Oh, a lot of things,' answers Porta. 'Beat up the mothers' darlings from out in Dahlem, and fucked their girls; mugged a yokel now and then that'd come to Berlin to find out what it was like to ride on a tram. Had a job for a bit delivering for

334

the greengrocer on *Bornholmer Strasse*, and then went up in the world and went round with coke on a delivery bike. Used to measure up the coke in a wooden keg. That was 5 litres and cost 95 pfennigs. Every household'd buy one of them, and it was just enough to keep the place warm through the evenin'.'

'Bloody hell!' cries Kostia, in amazement, 'I always heard you Germans were high finance people and that rich, you put notes in between your sausage and your bread!'

'Don't believe all you hear,' Porta advises him, condescendingly. 'In Old Moabitt we were that poor we used to steal the bottoms out of the beer-glasses when we went past a boozer!'

'We were poor, too,' says Igor. 'I washed houses, and made just about enough so's things could go round. One little vodka of a Sunday at the most, and even though it's forbidden to be poor in the Soviet Union we were still poor anyway. But then I got a bit more rich too, and I would've been really rich if you rotten Germans had stayed where you belong. My young brother an' me hit on a really great idea. We started holding up the deliverers from the meat market, and selling the proceeds on the black.'

'Did you rustle cows then?' asks Tiny, with interest. 'That ain't no good! I know all about that 'cos me an' the fur Jew's kid David pinched one of them things once. All we got out of it was all three of us landed up with old Nass in the David Station. Since then they don't bring cows inside. They took the bleedin' thing up to Nass's office on the first floor, and then couldn't get it down again. They 'ad to 'oist it down, and when it wouldn't go out of the window they 'ad to knock a 'ole in the wall for the walking milk-shop. They made it too little, and before they'd finished the cow got that scared of 'avin' been picked up by the coppers that it shit all over Nass an' all 'is detectives!'

'No, we did not take live cattle,' explains Igor, with a cunning grin. 'We waited for the ones who came to fetch meat on bicycles. When they went in to warm themselves with a quick early morning vodka, they'd leave their bikes outside. Then we would take the lot, bikes, meat and all.

They tried to come after us sometimes, but they never caught us!'

'Did your kid brother join the OGPU too?' asks Porta, interestedly.

'No, he was eaten by lions!'

'Eaten by lions?' asks Porta, in astonishment. 'How, then? I've never met anybody who's been eaten by lions!'

'Well, it was like this,' sighs Igor, sadly. 'We never used to pay to get into the Zoo, we went in over the wall. Sometimes, of course, we made a mistake and landed in with the sea-lions or the polar bears. We always got away with it though. The polar bears were that surprised when we came chasing over the wall that they never thought of eating us until we were out of there again. After a bit we knew all the animals pretty well. And they knew us, too. It was only the keepers who didn't like us.

'Well there was one day when we hadn't had anything proper to eat for several days, and were standing there watching the big cats getting outside their dinners.

'My kid brother was standing down in front of the lions' cage watching the keepers putting great big lumps of meat in to them. When the keeper was out for a minute, my brother nipped into the cage and grabbed a big chunk of meat from right under the nose of a motheaten old lion. It gave out a terrible roar when the meat disappeared, and struck out at him. He got such a blow that he went flying up in the other end of the cage and landed on another lion that was having its lunch siesta. All hell broke loose. Round and round they went in the cage! The whole crowd of 'em after my brother. What a din! When the keepers finally turned up there wasn't much left of him. Those mangy lions had eaten him all up!'

Kostia tells us that he has always been a headhunter, and has caught many prisoners who had escaped from Kolyma.

'The *Jakaeirs* always told us when anybody had gone over the wall. They got ten roubles for the information. Bounty was a hundred roubles for every body we handed in. We were merciful. We never tortured a prisoner. We would shoot him sleeping, so that he would not experience the fear of death. Winter was the best time. We could collect the bodies and store them until we had a sledge-load. In summer we had to get them handed in before they rotted and could not be identified. We got no pay for bodies unless they were identified at Central Camp, and there was another risk in handing in rotten bodies that nobody wanted. I know several who have been hanged for an unsolved murder. In that way the police got them off their lists and had less trouble with their percentage of open-ended cases.'

'Hell's bells!' cries Gregor, spitting, as if to get rid of a nasty taste. 'What kind of company's this we've got into?'

'But it was parasites on the body of the community we captured,' Kostia defends himself.

'You've got to be a Siberian, to think like that,' explains the Commissar, and sends Kostia a wicked look. 'These slit-eyed monsters come into the world through Satan's arsehole!'

Kostia laughs long and loud, and does not appear the slightest bit insulted.

'It's snowing like all get-out,' says Barcelona, looking out of the window. 'We're not going to get any further. Those snowdrifts are thirty feet tall!'

'I'll get a snowplough,' promises the Commissar, shrugging into his long fur coat. He slings his *Kalashnikov* across his chest, and waves to Kostia who follows him with a Siberian grin.

'Snowplough!' jeers Heide, who is sitting by the stove, looking insulted.

'He doesn't mean an ordinary snowplough,' says 'Whorecatcher'. 'He means a snow*eater*!'

'Never heard of such a thing,' says Porta, shuffling the cards deftly. 'What is it?'

'It's a machine which swallows tons of snow a minute,' explains 'Whorecatcher'. 'If you let a couple of 'em loose at the North Pole there soon wouldn't *be* a North Pole any more!'

'And he's going to find one of them in this hole in the ground?' Porta screams with laughter. 'What a bloody optimist!'

'He's a three-star commissar!' says 'Whorecatcher', and does not feel that any further explanation is needed.

After some time the Commissar and Kostia return.

'Get ready,' snaps the Commissar. 'The snowplough's here, and we have to follow close up behind it. T-34 first, Panther behind!'

'Tell me,' says Porta, blowing smoke in his face, 'you always want me in the rear! Don't you *trust* me?'

The Commissar gives out a long, long laugh.

'You're a funny bloody chap,' he says, between bursts of laughter. 'Anybody who trusts you ought to be kept in a padded cell! You don't mean to tell me that the thought of doing us all in the eye hasn't even crossed your mind!'

'Oh, well! There's a lot of things a fellow can meditate on.' Porta forces a smile.

The snowplough is an enormous machine which really does 'eat' snow, as 'Whorecatcher' has told us. We have never seen anything like it. The tallest of drifts disappears in minutes when it starts work on it. But shortly after we have passed by, new mountains of snow lie behind us, making the road completely impassable.

'Makes us safe from possible pursuers,' grins the Commissar, with satisfaction. 'This was the only snowplough in town. If anyone wants another they'll have to get it from Irgorsk, and that's where we're going!'

'Smart, smart!' Porta admits. 'A man doesn't even have to pretend to be thinking about it to be able to see we're home and dry!'

A militia man shouts at us halfway inside Irgorsk. The Commissar waves him off in a manner which only people who are in a position of power can permit themselves.

'He was scared of our red-painted faces,' grins Porta, exaltedly.

A row of searchlights send their rays up into the pitchblack night. They cross one another and play nervously over the dark clouds.

'What the devil!' cries Porta, in amazement. 'An air raid? Who the hell'd bomb this place? Must be some mistake!'

The thundering roll of an explosion makes the air shake.

'That a mistake too?' asks Gregor. 'Sounds real enough to me!'

An enormous column of fire goes up, sending a sea of white-hot sparks out over the whole town. Battalions of flames dance whirling along the rooftops. Melted lead drips into the streets, and whistles and bubbles in the snow. The heavy rafters of the large buildings begin to sink down, cracking and splintering. Gargoyles, cut in granite, fall from on high, smashing everything they land on. A granite head with a long tongue hanging from its mouth rolls along the street and ends up with a ringing sound against the Panther's tracks. An old-fashioned fire-waggon with solid rubber tyres breaks up under the rain of bricks. Firemen sitting along the sides of it do not even realize what is happening.

We stare, in fascination, at a concrete wall. The building is expanding like a balloon, slowly being blown up. The huge flat roof falls down through the inside of the house, which is one seething bonfire. Sparks fly hundreds of yards up into the air; steel girders bend as if they were made of soft rubber.

Two screaming girls come running down the street, with their hair and clothes in flames. A fireman aims his hose at them. They are thrown back down the street, and stick to the boiling, bubbling asphalt.

'Get *on*! Hell, let's get out of here,' shouts the Old Man, hysterically. 'That's all we needed! To get killed by our own air force!'

A container full of incendiaries splashes up alongside us. Phosphorus splashes on to the sides of the tanks and begins to burn. Paint ignites and bubbles on the sides of the vehicles.

'Don't touch it!' the Old Man warns over the radio. 'It can only put itself out!'

We swing up a broad boulevard, and see a row of corpses lying at a cellar entrance. They have been burnt to the size of tiny dolls, and are curled up in the strange positions which burnt bodies always assume.

A General of Infantry, his cape blowing out behind him,

roars commands, and rages threats at us when we ignore his orders.

'*Job tvojemadj*!' grins Igor, grimly. 'Let him burn! Poor soldiers can't expect anything of rich generals!'

The general runs after us, shouting and gesticulating. He stops and jumps to one side to avoid being crushed by Kostia's T-34, which rushes at him at top speed. He falls into a large puddle. When he gets to his feet again his boots are burning. There was phosphorus at the bottom of the puddle and it ignites as soon as air gets to it. Desperately, he rubs his boots on the cement. It is apparently the first time he has encountered phosphorus. Otherwise he would have removed his boots immediately. Now he is spreading the phosphorus, and making it burn even more furiously. He stumbles backwards into the pool. Gripped by panic he crawls out of it, and finds himself in a worse position than ever. Tiny blue flames dance all over his back. His cloak crisps rapidly. In only a few minutes he lies on the street, a heap of flaming rags!

'That phosphorus can get anybody,' mumbles Porta, staring at the bubbling heap which was once a general. 'I've heard they've gone over to using it down in hell. It's more effective than old-fashioned coal!'

A Stuka is hit, and explodes in a ball of fire. Shrapnel and red-hot metal parts shower down, and rattle on the steel sides of the tanks.

AA-guns bang. Wherever one looks something is exploding. It is as if an umbrella of blue-red-yellow fire had been opened above the town.

Some elderly firemen with an old-fashioned fire-engine work like mad things at the handles of their pump. Not much water comes out of it, but they still keep working.

A little further on, a fat man in a green uniform stands staring, paralysed with astonishment, at his arm. It is burning and bubbling. He was foolish enough to handle an incendiary.

Fleeing people run around him. They keep well away. Nobody helps him. A heavy air attack makes everyone insensitive. They all have enough to do to look after themselves and their nearest relatives.

The fat man falls on his knees, and burns up, apathetically, in a sea of blue flame.

The infernal howling of the dive-bombing Stukas tears at one's nerves. People are gripped by panic and rush round like terror-stricken hens.

'Not a bad idea, those sirens on the Stukas,' says Porta, holding his hands over his ears. 'That howling could make a lamb take part in a steeplechase!'

Soon the whole town has become a roaring inferno. Now the big Heinkel machines roar over and drop their high explosive bombs into the sea of flames.

A heavy lorry is thrown high into the air. Soldiers fall from it like confetti, and a few moments later they too are burning, down on the bubbling asphalt.

Automatic weapons begin to go off on their own. Bullets ricochet in all directions, like rice scattered over a bridal couple.

On the great ring boulevard in the expensive quarter of the town two ambulances stand across the road, in a blaze of dancing flames. Stretchers hang out of them and unrecognizable bodies burn in a mixed-up, soot-blackened heap.

Porta has a moment of panic when a tall concrete building collapses. The outer walls crash out across the boulevard and block the street. At the same time the street behind us breaks out in a hellish sea of phosphorus flames, at the new influx of oxygen.

Confused commands stream from the radio.

'Turn that bloody thing off,' snarls the Old Man desperately. He pulls out the plug to the chest-receiver, and the communicator goes dead. 'Come on Porta! *Quite* slowly, back! Cool down and do exactly as I say! If we start going into a spin, we'll never make it!'

Finally, Porta gets the heavy tank moving, and backs. He goes straight through a baker's shop. Glass shelves, bread, and paper bags fly everywhere. In a cloud of flour the tank goes through a partition wall and finally breaks through the outer wall in a shower of bricks.

'The tracks are burnin',' shouts Tiny, in alarm. 'Bleedin' 'ell they are! An' stinkin' like 'ell too!'

'It's phosphorus!' says the Old Man despairingly. 'We've got to get it scraped off before the whole blasted waggon goes up, and us with it!'

He chases us. We leap out through the hatches, and begin to scrape away feverishly at the burning tracks and rollers.

'Watch out,' shouts the Old Man, warningly. 'Get that stuff on you and you're finished!'

He does not need to warn us. We know only too well what war-phosphorus is like. That frightful substance which attaches itself to everything and blazes more fiercely the more air it gets. The more you scrape, the more it burns!

The heat around us is terrible. Our hair singes and curls up, our skin burns. Incendiaries throw out their white magnesium glare wherever they strike.

An OGPU officer in a half-burnt uniform, but with a new, shiny *Kalashnikov* bumping across his chest, comes rushing from a side street, stops, and spits a hail of curses at us.

The Commissar comes running up like a vicious Dobermann, swells himself up in front of the OGPU officer, and lets off a stream of invective at him which makes him completely lose his breath.

The OGPU lieutenant is about to slink off, but changes his mind when a whole group of OGPU soldiers turn the corner with *Kalashnikovs* at the ready. One of them grabs Gregor and pushes his mpi barrel into his neck.

The first salvo goes over our heads and has an unexpected effect on the gun-crazy OGPU lieutenant. He is thrown a good way up into the air with his arms spread out like wings. The battle-happy officer is hit in the chest and it is as if the tracer bullets go straight through him. He manages to give out a rattling scream, before he is thrown backwards on to a burning lump of phosphorus. It flames up immediately.

Four machine-pistols spit fire at us.

Heide is in cover behind the Panther, shooting from between its burning tracks.

342

The OGPU men go down with crushed kneecaps. Heide has to shoot low from his position. He gets to his feet, and walks coldly towards the groaning OGPU soldiers. With a crooked smile, and a merciless coldness in his blue eyes, he clicks his mpi to single shots and puts a bullet into each of the pleading faces.

'Why the hell did you do that?' protests the Old Man, furiously. 'I've had enough of you!'

'The situation required it,' barks Heide arrogantly, changing magazines.

'Julius is nothing but a twisted caricature of his own beliefs,' sneers Porta. 'He stinks of dead bodies like all his swastika mates!'

'The day is not far off when I'm going to take care of you quite specially,' promises Heide, sending Porta a wicked look.

A jet of flame several hundred yards high shoots up into the air, and a long, rolling explosion sounds over the burning town.

Boris, the T-34's turret gunner, is thrown along the street and spitted on the machine-cannon mounted on the tank. He spins like a paper windmill, the long barrel of the gun projecting from his middle.

It was the city gasworks which had blown up. Everything has become an indescribable inferno. Brickwork splinters like glass. Iron rods expand and contort. Roofs are lifted from houses, as the blast flame sweeps across the town like a glowing fire-storm.

A JU-88 comes roaring in above the roofs with flames streaming from its wings. It sways and rolls from side to side, and crashes into a house. It explodes in a blinding red ball of fire.

A Willy's jeep comes towards us at a mad speed. The driver is hanging lifeless over the low metal door. With a crunching sound it hits the T-34 and is mashed to scrap under its tracks.

A long, sliding, scratching sound, like a sack of coke rolling down a ramp, sends us diving to cover. The strange sound ends in a thundering explosion, which makes our ears hurt,

343

and almost blows the sense out of our heads. A large bomb has fallen a couple of hundred yards from us. It blows away everything standing, and leaves only shaved earth around the spot where it has fallen.

'Christ on the cross,' groans Porta, putting his hands to his head. 'Devil take the rotten Luftwaffe!'

One of the T-34s is burning. Black, oily smoke goes up towards the sky. Shortly afterwards the ammunition in the tank explodes and splits it to pieces.

'Take cover!' shouts the Commissar, as a coloured marker sinks down, throwing out a cascade of green fire all around it. High explosive bombs rain down. Dancing flames shoot up from the streets, like an army of flamethrowers.

'It's the gas pipes,' says Heide, importantly.

'You stupid bastard,' hisses Tiny, with a sneer. 'The gasworks has gone up long since!'

'Idiot!' snarls Heide, 'there's gas other places!'

The sky sparkles red, suddenly. A new bomber wave is closing in. The threatening thunder of the motors grows by the second. Markers fall, making a large square of light. We are right in the middle of it.

The first two thousand-pounders go off around us. It is like a volcano in eruption, and throws steel and fire many yards up into the air. The road surface cracks and piles up in heaps, and the huge artillery barracks behind us is pulverized. It seems as if the broad boulevard is thrown up towards the sky. Trees in the middle of it fly through the air like arrows from a bow, and the night becomes as light as the clearest day.

The Legionnaire and I come to ourselves out on the barrack square amongst broken guns, artillery tractors and corpses.

The motor-sledge has been turned upside down, its turret forced down into the softened asphalt. The motor hangs out, half off its mounting.

The Commissar curses, viciously, when he realizes the motor-sledge has been turned into scrap.

A fifty-pound incendiary bomb falls a couple of yards from the Panther, which is immediately wrapped in a roaring curtain of flames.

We go at the incendiary sticks with the fire-fighting equipment we have. Without the Panther we are never going to get back alive. Desperately we throw earth and sand over the red and white magnesium blobs, which burn all over the tank. The heat is unbearable. Time and again we are forced back by it.

The red paint we have been covered with begins to bubble up, but this has the advantage of thinning it. It begins to run away from our faces. Soon we only look as if we were suffering from measles.

We drive the vehicles under cover on the far side of the barracks, where there is a park adjoining the woods.

'I'll try to get hold of a lorry in place of the one that broke down,' says the Commissar. 'Kostia! You come with me! Grab a couple of grenades! You never know what kind of regulations-crazy fools we might run into!'

Half an hour later he is back with a brand-new Studebaker.

'What d'you say to that?' he asks, throwing out his arms proudly.

'The Soviet's going to suffer a great loss, when you leave it!' Porta grins in acknowledgement.

A thousand-pound bomb drops in the middle of a flock of sheep. Torn-off limbs are thrown along the street, and a heavy rain of blood spatters down on us, again turning us red. The stench makes us retch.

When we swing off the road to take what we think is a short cut, there is a deafening explosion, and white clouds of steam come hissing up out of the earth.

'Must be steampipes,' says 'Whorecatcher'. 'They'll be goin' off before we know where we are! Let's get to hell out of here fast!'

'Get back!' shouts the Commissar, waving with both arms from the T-34's turret. 'Hell, get back! If it's what I think it is, all hell's loose!'

The road begins to sink down, as if it were being sucked away by invisible forces. Houses on both sides of the road crumble and disappear into the hole, which closes after them with a horrible, sucking sound.

'Good Lord above,' cries the Old Man, in horror. 'That's got to be more than burst pipes!'

'Too true,' shouts the Commissar furiously, 'but let's get out of here quick as all hell. I'll explain later!'

On the far side of the boulevard the road bulges up into a huge mound. It is as if the world were turning inside out. Houses fall down in whole rows, as if the earth were sucking them down into itself.

'This is bleedin' nasty,' mumbles Tiny. 'Seems like the devil's on 'is way up to 'ave a look at what's goin' on!'

In the middle of the park we are stopped by an OGPU patrol, which has driven two armoured sledges across the road.

'Get ready,' growls the Commissar viciously. 'Nothing's going to stop us now! Not the whole bloody Kremlin!'

Two nasty-looking OGPU men, dressed entirely in black leather, and with *Kalashnikovs* at the ready, stand in the middle of the road waving us down like policemen.

The Commissar jumps down from the T-34, puffs himself up and marches towards them. He shouts loudly and waves his fist in the air. A *polittruk** comes out from behind the road-block. He too seems to have puffed himself up. His broad, Slavic face promises us no good.

'Necker!' says Porta, world-wise. 'It'd be clever of us to shoot his balls off!'

'*Propusk!*' shouts the *polittruk*, holding out his hand in true policeman style.

'Up my arse!' screams the Commissar. 'I am on special duty with some Volga Germans! God help you when I report to Moscow! You're sabotaging a mission of national importance!'

'I've got my orders,' roars the *polittruk*. 'Even if the great Stalin came past, he'd have to show a *propusk*! *Panjemajo?*'

'A drink?' asks Porta, with a false smile. He offers his water-

---

* *Polittruk:* A Russian police commissioner

346

bottle from the driver's hatch with a gesture of invitation.

'Vodka?' asks the wicked-looking *polittruk*. He grabs eagerly at the water-bottle, and takes a long drink from it. He hands it on to his two leather-clad minions, who swallow it down like thirsty horses. 'Nice an' warming!' he says, and his tone has become a little milder.

Suddenly, something strange seems to be happening to his face. He goes white as a corpse, then scarlet. The red goes slowly over to a blue tint. He grasps his stomach and gives out some very strange sounds.

One of the black-leather fellows puts both hands to his mouth, and throws up like a man in the grip of seasickness.

'Hell!' gulps the *polittruk*. He feels as if the whole of his insides were being eaten away. He stares, confusedly, with eyes which seem about to fall from their sockets. The three men's bowels give way. Their legs bend under them, and they collapse to the ground with long rattling groans.

Porta puts the water-bottle back under the driver's seat, and makes a mental note to fill it up again with his special brand of grog.

The Commissar stares quite blankly at the three prostrate forms.

'What the hell . . . .' He has got no further when a sound reminiscent of distant thunder stops him. The earth under us begins to quiver.

'What the devil's that?' shouts Porta, looking around confusedly.

'Landslip!' shouts the Comissar, in terror, and comes towards us on the run.

From behind the two motor-sledges barring our way come two new OGPU men. They shout in confusion as trees begin to sway and move as if they were stems of grass.

'What the hell's happening?' shouts Gregor, with terror in his voice, as another row of trees comes crashing down.

'Landslip!' howls the Commissar, 'fucking hell it's quick *clay*! Run! Run for your lives!'

The whole forest dissolves before our eyes. A jumble of

rocks are thrown here and there. The earth begins to toss, like waves in a stormy sea. The noise is shattering.

In front of us the road begins to move like a plank caught in a whirlpool. Both of the OGPU motor-sledges slide down a deep incline which has appeared, and splash into a bubbling lake of mud and splintered trees. Through the deafening turmoil comes a new sound. A long, sucking noise, like that of a blocked pipe which can suddenly take air again. But a million times louder.

'*Run!*' shouts the Commissar, sprinting down the road with the rest of us at his heels, including the leather-clad OGPU soldiers.

The road begins to give way under our feet, and we jump up some inclines onto a narrower path which lies rather higher than the broad main road.

Apparently firm ground gives back hollow noises under our running boots. It is as if we were running in dough. Slowly the earth slips down and is churned into a muddy swamp.

Tiny gives a scream of terror when a large fir tree falls on him.

Gregor and I work desperately to release him from it, but it is only when Porta comes to our help that we manage to move the big tree.

A giant boulder comes careening down the slope and takes Boris with it. He gives one shrill scream, and is forced down into the ooze under its weight.

In desperation we run on down the narrow path, but it is like trying to cross a rushing whirlpool, which is continually attempting to suck us down into its depths. When we are only a short distance from the road fountains of mud and water spout up hundreds of yards into the air.

'Where's all that *water* coming from?' asks Porta. He is clinging desperately to an uprooted tree, which is whirling round in the bubbling mud.

'It's being pressed up out of the quick clay,' pants the Commissar. 'There's millions of gallons of it.'

'How the hell's it happening?' asks the Old Man, helplessly. 'I've never *heard* of quick clay!'

'It exists in Russia,' explains the Commissar, a little later, as we struggle through the slimy, boiling mud, slipping and sliding helplessly all over the place. 'A remainder of the Ice Age. 50 per cent of it is water, which has been trapped in pockets of clay and rubble. It can hold on to it for ever if only nothing starts it off. If something does, then what has seemed to be hard ground turns to mud which sucks down everything, as you have seen here. We've had whole towns disappear here in Russia when quick clay has started to move!'

'What silly bleeder started it off 'ere then?' asks Tiny, sneezing, and pulling himself up with difficulty from a sucking mudhole.

'Those damned German bombs did!' hisses the Commissar, savagely. 'I had an idea of what was happening down in the town, when the streets started to disappear!'

Finally we manage to work our way up to the solid road. Completely worn out we drop to the ground. We are no longer red. We have been turned into mud-coloured statues.

'*Job tvojemadj*!' shouts Kostia, pointing over at the OGPU guard barracks. It has begun to move down the road like a house on rollers. It begins to break up. Walls fall in, tiled roofs shatter, and in the winking of an eye it has been sucked down into the earth.

The whole of the slope on the far side of the road begins to slip downwards with ever increasing speed. Great trees are thrown into the air, and huge boulders crash together, splintering one another.

The water pressed out of the clay spouts up towards the sky. Millions of tons of clay are moving like a storm-whipped sea.

'It can't be *true*!' howls Porta desperately, hopping up and down. 'The Devil's come to steal our gold!'

Open-mouthed we stare at the heavily laden Studebaker truck, as it disappears quite slowly into the bubbling mud. Round about us geysers go roaring up. It is a fantastic sight, but we are too shocked to take in the splendour of the natural phenomenon which is going on around us.

A stream of mud and water roars down the road, and in a

matter of seconds both of the trucks loaded with gold have disappeared. A little later one of the T-34s slips down sideways from what is left of the road. With a deafening rattle it swings round and is sucked down into the mud. Its gun points upwards to the last like the bowsprit of a torpedoed warship.

'There goes the rest of the gold!' groans the Commissar, despairingly. He tears his fur cap from his head and tramples on it wildly, as if it were that which was to blame.

We struggle madly to get back through the seething mud to the Panther and the remaining T-34. They are jammed between two huge boulders.

Depressedly we walk round them to see how they have fared. The damage is a catastrophe. The tracks of the T-34 have been torn off, and lie spread in individual links down the remains of the road. The Panther's rollers have been torn from their beds. Several shock-absorbers have been smashed.

I climb up in the turret to look at the gun. *That* seems to be undamaged.

'*Can* these two shit-buckets be repaired?' asks the Commissar, with a look of defeat on his face. 'Without them we haven't got a hope!'

'How d'you think the foot-sloggers manage?' asks Porta, nastily. 'They've got nothing to carry their arses round in!'

'They *don't* manage,' answers the Commissar pessimistically. 'They walk till their ears are dragging on the ground!'

'Well there's not much left to talk about then, is there?' replies Porta, taking off his muddy fur coat. 'I'll forget I'm only a driver for once! Let's get the gas-cylinders out so's we can start welding! Need teaches modest maidens to fuck! Really we need a whole workshops company to get these two tin cans on the road again!'

For two days we work literally incessantly, but at last both waggons are roadworthy. Porta wipes his hands on a piece of waste and looks sadly round at the crumpled, muddy earth in which all the gold is buried.

'Well, now we know what quick clay is!' he says and throws the waste from him, resignedly.

Tiny is inconsolable. He walks around all the time jabbing a long spike into the ground in the hope of striking the gold. He simply refuses to believe that it has gone forever.

'Think we could organize an excavator?' asks Porta, looking at the Commissar. 'It must be possible to turn that forest upside down an' find our gold again?'

'Not a chance,' says 'Whorecatcher'. 'I once saw a whole town disappear in Siberia. They dug for three months with an army of excavators and didn't find as much as a brick of it. The Devil had swallowed the lot.'

'I *won't* believe it!' shouts Porta, angrily. He pulls down a pickaxe from the T-34. He starts to swing it energetically at the hardened mud. 'Think of all those dummies who dug up the whole of Alaska and half Canada in the hope of finding a handful of gold-dust! And those clowns didn't even know if there *was* anything, there where they were diggin'! We have at least got the advantage of knowin' there's a hell of a big lump of the stuff down there! Come on boys! Grab a spade or a shovel! Don't you *want* to go to Sweden and fish for salmon! It's more fun than bein' a German soldier in wartime!'

'You got somethin' there,' cries Tiny, grabbing a spade. 'When the Mafia 'ears about our gold they'll all be down 'ere! An' them white'eaded old bastards'll be diggin' too, even though it may 'ave been a long time since they used their 'ands!'

'They'd have their *spaghetti carbonara* goin' down the wrong way!' jokes Gregor, beginning to dig.

'Shut up a minute,' sighs the Commissar, resting his chin on his hands. 'I've got to think!'

'Don't do it for too long,' advises Tiny. 'It can be dangerous to think too long! When I was with the military psychopaths they said I *mustn't* think. Since then I 'aven't done it, an' it suits me down to the bleedin' ground!'

'The only way we could possibly get the gold back is with half a score of dredging machines,' says the Commissar, in a voice which sounds as if it is coming from the depths of a tin can.

'We can't get *them* down here,' protests Porta. 'They're

things that sail on *water*!'

'That's right,' answers the Commissar. He is so depressed he looks like a whole town in mourning. 'So forget the gold. We've lost it forever!'

'I got a plan!' shouts 'Frostlips', lighting up like a candle.

'Both God and the Devil protect us!' cries 'Whorecatcher', making a gesture of despair.

'We could drill for the gold the way they drill for oil,' 'Frostlips' goes on. 'I know a feller who can get hold of a drill for us!'

'Idiot!' snarls the Commissar. 'Why not a corkscrew?'

For a while we sit gazing miserably out over the dried-up sea of mud, which has swallowed up the gold which was going to turn us into good Swedish Social Democrats.

'You thought what's going to happen to us if they get hold of us, even if we're not carrying any gold?' Gregor throws out the idea. 'I don't reckon it'll be nice!'

'They'll hit us with all sorts of nasty charges and things. More'n we could count,' says Porta, heavily. 'For a start: High Treason or whatever it is they call it when you don't love the Fatherland enough! That gives you fifteen times life imprisonment, and that's a good bit of forever! The fact of our having lost the gold we pinched don't make a bit of difference!'

'They wouldn't even believe that rotten mud swallowed up the gold,' says 'Frostlips', with a mien sad enough for a man sentenced to death. 'They'd just keep on torturin' us till there wasn't nothing left *to* torture!'

'One thing we must be in agreement on,' says the Commissar, his face dark as summer thunder. 'We keep our mouths shut and forget all about the gold! If they get just a sniff of it having been us who took it we'll be chased by the lot of 'em. And they'll be tough about it. Not only the OGPU but the Gestapo, and the CIA and MI5, and the yellow thought police, and even the solitary member of the Soviet Secret Service! They'd all be on our tracks!'

'What about the Boy Scouts?' asks Tiny. 'I know a feller that's a Rover Scout!'

Two days later we stop at a crossroads where there is a whole cluster of signs pointing to all sorts of places.

Porta sits on the front apron of the Panther, chewing at a sausage and washing down each mouthful with vodka.

'What now?' he asks, glancing at the Commissar, who is hanging out of the T-34's turret hatch, looking miserable. 'You still want to go back with us? Now we're still as poor as we were when we started. Our fishin' trips in Sweden we're going to have to put off for a bit, I fear!'

'It's probably best we stay in our respective countries,' answers the Commissar, jumping down from the tank. 'I've heard a bit about what you Germans do to Commissars. And particularly *Jewish* Commissars!'

'Oh, I don't think we're as bad as all that!' says Tiny, trying to force a smile onto his dejected face.

'It's not you I'm thinking of,' says the Commissar, holding out a hand for Porta's vodka bottle. 'You're just Fritzs like our lot are Ivans. It's your Gestapo, SS and all the other rottenness I meant!'

'They're no worse than your filthy OGPU,' shouts Heide furiously.

'All Secret Police are an invention of the Devil,' says the Commissar, harshly.

'I still think you ought to come with us,' says Gregor. 'We'd get you in the Hiwis* easy, until we say goodbye to the army some day and *really* go fishin' in Sweden!'

'No!' says the Commissar decisively, shaking his head. 'Life's a game of chance! A man doesn't give up when he loses once! If I go with you now, I'm a loser! I've only gained a little time. I reckoned on it perhaps going wrong for us this time, and I've got my back covered. Another thing is I haven't got the nerve to stay around you lot much longer!'

'Moscow,' mumbles Porta, thoughtfully. 'So you'll be going via Tambow?'

'Yes, and after that Stalinogorsk,' 'Frostlips' grins without humour.

* Hilfswillige: German Work Troops

'Devil of a way you've got to go, there,' nods Porta, peering to the north-east. 'And there's bad weather coming up!'

'You can be on the other side of Kursk in four days,' explains the Commissar, 'but don't go through Voronez! Can't spit there for OGPU!'

'This is goodbye then,' says the Old Man quietly. 'It's a bit sad. We've got to know you!'

'We like you too,' smiles 'Frostlips', putting an arm round Porta's shoulder. 'How stupid war is!'

'You'll be shittin' your pants when you cross Dzherzhinski Square,' says Gregor, shivering in his cape.

'Not us. We'll get by all right,' laughs the Commissar, self-confidently. 'I'm more doubtful about you fellows! You must have something to tell 'em when you get back!'

'Our orders were to pick up some general, and invite him home with us,' says Porta, 'but where we going to find one of them?'

'Frostlips' spreads out a map on the Panther's front apron and makes a ring with a crayon.

'Here's 38 Motorized Brigade. It's been strengthened with a cavalry regiment, which is *here*! You've counted seventy-somethin' tanks of types KW-2 and T-34/85, and the usual filler of obsolete BTs!'

'Now you *are* certain that brigade *is* there?' asks the Old Man, doubtfully. 'They'll soon find out if it's a wrong 'un, and that'd be worse than coming back empty-handed!'

'Be easy,' answers the Commissar. '"Frostlips" knows what he's talking about!'

'We'd better give you something in return,' says Porta, bending over the map. 'Here, along the Merla by Solotev's 23 Panzer, and they're piss-poor! They've lost the most of their tanks. A medal-hungry general can win a couple for himself right there!'

'That's treason,' rages Heide. 'It'll cost you your head if I report you to the NSFO!'

'But you're not going to,' smiles Porta, coldly. 'Don't forget you were here! We're in the same boat, my son!'

'What about swoppin' tanks?' asks 'Frostlips', with a sneaky grin. 'We come home with your Panther, and you take in our T-34/85. They'd like *that*! The latest new creations of the tank modistes!'

'Maybe it's *not* such a bad idea,' says the Old Man, thoughtfully. 'We'd get through the Russian L of C a lot easier, and if nothing else we could lie in wait for an attack and slip through easy as winking!'

'Let us say goodbye properly,' laughs the Commissar, opening the first bottle of vodka.

Porta wipes his porcelain cup on an old sack. It doesn't make the cup any cleaner, but at least he *has* wiped it.

'Bring out our little surprise!' The Commissar turns to 'Frostlips'. He chuckles and trots over to the tank, and comes back with a case of red caviare. None of us have ever set eyes on red caviare before.

'You are all my friends,' hiccoughs the Commissar, knocking the neck off a fresh bottle of *Moskovskaja*. 'Every one of you is my very good friend, and I shall always be happy to see you again!' He takes a long pull at the bottle, shovels down a couple of spoonsful of caviare and belches loudly: 'Life is a good thing, don't you think?' he says, dreamily. 'There are always new surprises. You'll see! Some day there will be some other gold we can take off after!'

'Without me,' says the Old Man. He is half seas over by now and is explaining to 'Whorecatcher' how to make a chest-of-drawers.

'The most important thing,' the Commissar goes on, in a drunken voice, 'is to have good friends spread about all over the world! Then you can always help one another!' He lifts a finger and points it at Porta. 'Where we Russians stop thinking, that's where you Germans step in! Let us drink to friendship and the small, forbidden thoughts! It is quite wrong of us to fight one another,' he sniffles.

'A health to the Soviet people,' shouts Kostia. He rolls his black, Asiatic eyes confusedly when he realizes that there is something wrong with his toast. Although there are 250 million people in Russia, even the dumbest OGPU man knows that nobody cares to be called a Soviet citizen. He pushes a handful of caviare into his mouth and pours vodka on top of it. Then he toasts himself.

'A toast to Berlin!' suggests the Commissar, pleasantly.

'To Moscow!' hiccoughs Porta. He carries the chipped porcelain cup to his lips, and almost falls over.

'Not forgetting Hamburg!' roars 'Whorecatcher'.

'Thank you,' sobs Tiny, moved. 'You are all 'ereby invited to 'Amburg! We'll meet at the fur Jew's kid David's place at *'Ein 'Oyerstrasse* no 10, and there'll be a red alert out to all the 'ighclass 'ores from "Chéri".' He gets to his feet, swaying. 'To Tashkent!' he sobs, lifting his tin cup. It is a mystery how he knows there is a town called Tashkent, but, as always, he is full of surprises. Some people have died from them.

Heide is exercising Kostia. He is teaching him the German salute and the Prussian goosestep. Unfortunately every time Kostia gets his foot up on a level with his belt buckle he falls over backwards. In the end he gives up and sits looking sadly up at the racing snow-clouds.

'Thank God I am not a German!' he groans. 'They are far too energetic!'

It is icy cold when we wake up in the old roadmender's hut.

Porta puts both hands to his throbbing head. It is possible he may have felt worse at some time in his life, but just now he cannot remember when.

'*Job tvojemadj*!' groans Kostia, looking as if he has just been shot. 'What *have* they done to Kostia?'

Albert laughs loudly. He is one of those happy people who never have hangovers. Hangovers are always amusing – for those who do not suffer from them.

'You black cannibal,' screams Tiny cantankerously, making a face at him. 'If I wasn't sick I'd give you *such* a bashin'. You rotten apeman, you!'

The Commissar wakes up with a piercing scream. He thinks that the worst thing that can happen to a Russian has happened to him. He has been locked up in the cellars of the Lubyanka. He begins shouting at us in Odessa Yiddish, then goes over to German and claims he is chief of the SS.

'They must've put something really Russian in that *Moskovskaja*,' moans Gregor, his eyes brimming tears. 'It was strong enough to knock over a tree and turn it into sawdust!'

'It was bleedin' strong, I can tell you,' mumbles Tiny, wiping the sweat from his brow. 'I got a little bleedin' drop of it on my finger, an' now the nail's gone!' He has forgotten he has caught his fingers two days earlier in the turret hatch.

'I have suddenly realized, Josefvitschi,' says the Commissar to Porta, with a broad smile, 'that you are a crazy fellow. The most crazy fellow I have ever met! How the devil did you ever become a soldier?'

'Yes, I've wondered about that myself,' Porta laughs, heartily. 'But, as you must know, the most important jobs in the world are being a soldier or a whore!'

'There's only two kinds of bints,' shouts Tiny, with a cunning look on his face. 'The 'ores an' the dumb 'uns!'

'Let everybody think you're an ordinary, dumb twit,' explains Porta, 'an' you can stay standing upright on the crust of the earth enjoying watching the rest of 'em fall off!'

It is late next day when we finally take leave of one another. We cannot stop embracing, and agreeing meeting-places after the war.

High on a hilltop Porta stops the T-34, and we wave a final goodbye to our Russian friends who are disappearing in the distance on the road to Moscow.

> 'Sag' mir beim Abschied leise Servus,
> ist ein schöner letzter Gruss,
> wenn man Abschied nehmen muss . . .*'

Porta hums. Resolutely he starts the Otto motor up again.

As we get closer to the front line, traffic increases. We get tied up in traffic jams several times. There are Russian MPs everywhere. We are glad we are riding in a T-34, which does

* Old Viennese song

not draw the slightest attention.

We come to a halt. Papers are to be checked. Our hands grip mpis and grenades nervously. Porta shows our *propusk* and chatters in a mixture of Russian and German.

'Volga Germans,' mumbles the fat MP, and looks as if he would like to eat us.

'Right *tovaritsch*!' smiles Porta, offering him a swig from the water-bottle.'

The long column of artillery and tanks begins to move forward again.

The MP jumps down from the T-34 and waves us on.

For several hours we drive on in the middle of the column. Then Porta manages to turn off into a narrow forest path. Well into the woods he stops. We jump down and run about in the snow to thaw out our icy feet.

'I'm fed up!' says Tiny. 'I want to go home!'

'Good heavens, a general!' whispers Gregor, fearfully.

Three fur-clad forms appear from the closely ranked trees. It is a Lieutenant-general and two staff officers. They are carrying heavy briefcases, chained to their wrists.

'Who the devil are you?' snaps the general, in a deep, guttural voice. His sharp blue eyes peer at us from below white bushy brows.

'Volga Germans, *gospodin general*,' answers Porta in his best Russian.

'What the devil are you doing here?' the general goes on, suspiciously. He takes a red and white packet of cigarettes from his pocket. He lights one and blows smoke thoughtfully through his nose. 'Aren't you, rather, deserters? It seems to me very strange that you have stopped here to take a rest. You're a long way from the tank positions!'

'We lost our way,' answers Porta, throwing his arms wide.

'*Propusk*!' the general demands, putting out his hand.

A lot of things happen in a very short space of time. The general is down in the snow, stretched there by a blow from the edge of Tiny's shovel of a hand.

A short burst comes from the slim colonel's machine-pistol. A bullet burns across the side of Tiny's head. Blood

358

pours down over his face.

The Legionnaire smashes the colonel's face in with a butt stroke.

The third officer, a lieutenant-colonel turns and begins to run off through the knee-deep snow.

'*Stoi!*' shouts Barcelona, readying his mpi. '*Stoi!*' he repeats, sending a short burst of bullets whipping around the officer.

The lieutenant-colonel stops and raises both hands above his head.

'*Germanski?*' cries the general, in amazement, getting slowly to his feet. He rubs his neck and swears softly.

'Well, we did get our general!' grins Porta, happily. 'See what they've got in those briefcases!'

'Well, look at *this*!' cries Barcelona, in surprise. 'They're draggin' a whole army corps battle order with 'em out here in the forest! They won't only kiss our cheeks, they'll kiss our arses too when we get back with this lot!'

The general tries to do a deal with us. He offers us the world if we'll let him turn the tables and take us in.

'Think we're *that* stupid?' jeers Tiny, with a roar of laughter.

'Don't forget dancing's better than hanging!' says the general, with an obviously threatening tone in his voice.

A German SP section breaks through the sapling trees.

Like lightning the Legionnaire is out there, waving a snow camouflage shirt.

With a deafening crash of tracks the leading SP comes to a halt. A hard-looking major with a machine-pistol in his hands leans out of the turret and snaps, harshly:

'*Halt! Hände hoch!*'

Two artillerymen jump from the gun with mpis at the ready. They order the Legionnaire over to the major, who breaks into a roar of laughter at the very idea of our being Germans. He changes his mind, however, when he sees the contents of the Russian briefcases.

'Well I'm damned,' he mutters. He salutes the captured general, who looks like a man who has lost everything he owned at poker.

'We'll meet again,' he says to Porta, and sends him a look which ought to have sent his army teeth down his throat.

We are on our way back to regiment, and there we get a reception equal to that of the prodigal son.

Oberst Hinka is delighted. When the interrogation officer is finished with the two Russians, wild activity commences in 4 Panzer Army.

Porta is resting in Helena's brothel, getting up strength to go over and tell Chief Mechanic Wolf the sad news of where the gold has ended up.

Some of the girls are dancing closely together to the music of a balalaika. Porta is the only male guest. A Tartar girl is sitting at the bar showing off her beautifully-formed legs. Her narrow eyes regard him with interest. Soon she sways over to him and sits on the edge of the table. Her narrow black skirt rides up to well above the edge of her stockings.

'You have measles?' she asks, letting a long, slim finger slide over the red paint spots which are left as a reminder of Tiny's marker shell.

'Only German measles!' answers Porta sadly.

'German measles?' she trills. 'That is catching?'

'Only for Germans,' answers Porta, looking national.

'You are prettiest tankman I ever see,' she whispers, giving him a look which could have melted a glacier. She slips down from the table and presses her body intimately against him. 'Would you like to come and see my room?' she asks, taking his hand, and pressing it between her warm thighs.

Porta smells her. Cheap perfume and old beer mixed. A lustful gleam comes into his small eyes.

She takes a small sip from his glass.

'You like to fuck now?' she asks, sighing deeply. She takes another tiny sip from his glass. 'I am good fuck! When you go with me it will be first time in your life you really fuck!'

The door bangs open, and Chief Mechanic Wolf marches in, his spurs jingling and his Brosini riding boots flashing.

'So here you are, then. Thin and crazy. Don't give a sod about telling any of us others how things've gone off! I've

360

been lookin' for you everywhere!' He turns round and sees the Tartar girl. She is back on the table edge again with her skirt so high you can see she is wearing no underclothing.

'Buy yourself a piece o' cunt, then! Slant-eyes there's all right! Then we can get over to my place! I think we must have a lot of things to talk over!'

'You've been to the barber's,' grins Porta, running his hand over the girl's crutch. 'And you've had a shave too,' he smiles to her.

'Like it?' asks Wolf, in a self-satisfied voice. He passes his hand over his coal-black hair, which is shiny with brilliantine. 'My barber's famous, you know! Had a shop at "Kempinski". Even rich old bald bastards with no more'n five hairs left used to go to him to get permed. "War Minister" Sally sent him out here when the army finally found out they could use him in a war. As you can see he's sculptured my hair in the latest Hollywood style!'

'Well, well!' said Porta, blowing smoke between the girl's thighs. 'I prefer the professor style myself, with a couple of balls of cottonwool stickin' out over a feller's ears. Makes you look clever!'

There is silence for a while. Porta blows smoke between the girl's legs again, leans back in his chair and balances it on two legs. He pulls back his upper lip in a jeering hyena grin. It makes him look like a snarling dog. He has been practising it for a long time!

'You gonna fuck, or you goin' over to my place?' asks Wolf, impatiently.

Porta puts his hands on the girl's knees. Wolf's hand-sewn Brosini riding boots squeak.

'Don't waste my time with all that shit,' he rasps, bitterly. 'Come on! We're off! You can fuck her some other time! If you live long enough that is!' he adds, dropping his voice to a subterranean rumble. 'I can tell you Sally's on his way here from Berlin, and he's got a couple of these sudden-death fellers with him!' He stops speaking for a moment, and awaits a reaction to his sad news.

'Really?' answers Porta, looking as if he had heard nothing of any importance.

'You fuck now?' asks the Tartar girl, rubbing Porta's crotch. 'Better fuck than get shot! Come! We go this way!'

'No we don't!' roars Wolf. 'This is the way we're goin'!'

A little way down the street Wolf stops again and stands in front of Porta with his British swagger-stick lifted as if he were going to hit him with it.

'Listen 'ere, you shit, I don't seem to've expressed myself clearly enough! I said Sally was on the way! And he's determined that either he gets the gold he's got a right to, or else you go off suddenly on a one-way ticket! I'm tellin' you this as a friend.'

'Both you and that imitation "War Minister" can go and get fucked!' grins Porta, confidently.

Wolf does not answer, but contents himself with staring at Porta with a look which would have frightened away a poisonous snake.

They continue on down the street in silence, Wolf jingling his spurs and Porta banging down his hobnailed heels.

Without acknowledging either the growling wolfhounds or the icy-cold Chinese they stroll into Wolf's lair.

'Where did you put our gold?' asks Wolf, before they have settled in their chairs.

'Yes, what *did* I do with our gold?' answers Porta thoughtfully, taking a bite of sausage.

'That's what *I'm* bloody askin' *you*,' shouts Wolf, furiously. 'I saw you arseholes come in, but even with a monocle I couldn't see anythin' but a fucked-up old museum exhibit of a T-34, and I can't imagine there was space for both you lot *and* our soddin' gold in that tin can!'

'You're right enough there,' Porta forces a smile. 'There was only us and not as much as a grain of gold!'

Wolf walks slowly round the table.

'You didn't have to tell me *that*,' he hisses, and smashes his British swagger-stick down so hard on the table that it breaks in two. Raging, he throws the pieces from him. 'I've been over an' had a look inside that Russian shit-bucket, and now

I want to know where you've hid our gold? You might just as well tell me now before Sally gets here! He ain't got time to do a lot of talking with you! He's gonna just say gold, an' if you say there ain't any then you're dead! Where *is* the gold?' he repeats in a roar, spittle flecking his lips.

'Let me get a word in,' smiles Porta, in friendly fashion. 'That's what I'm tryin' to tell you!' He takes another bite of sausage and swills it down with *Slivovitz*. 'The gold! Yes! A very sad affair that was. It's gone. Been eaten up!'

'Eaten?' gapes Wolf. 'Who the bloody hell eats *gold*?'

'The earth,' smiles Porta, mildly. 'The earth ate our gold! Took it in, lorries and all! Drivers and mates went down with it!' He makes some slobbering sounds like a stopped-up sink and throws his arms so that Wolf can understand how the gold had gone down under the earth.

'I *see*,' says Wolf, pressing his lips together into a thin line.

'It sank down! You don't *say* so! D'you think I'm a complete bloody idiot? You're a lyin' bastard, an' that yarn of yours stinks of con! Jesus, I never heard anythin' like it! The earth ate the gold *all* up! You ain't the feller who wrote the *1001 Nights*, by any chance? Can't you make up a better bleedin' tale?'

Porta spreads out his hands resignedly.

'I didn't know the earth swallowed up gold, either,' he admits, sadly. 'But it *does*, though! I saw it with my own eyes, and it didn't only take the gold, it took three tanks, four trucks and two motor-sledges in the same mouthful. For dessert it took thirty-two men and a whole bloody OGPU guard barracks. If you don't believe me ask the others!'

'A right lot to ask,' yells Wolf, beside himself with rage. 'They're bigger bloody liars than you are! I might as well ask my dogs, an' be satisfied with bow-wow for an answer. But let me tell you somethin', you dirty bastardin' son of an alley cat an' a backyard bitch! If you don't tell me where you've hid that gold I'm gonna tear your lyin' tongue out an' kick your balls straight up into your rotten brains!' He gets more and more furious, crumples his favourite silk cap into a ball and tears at it with his teeth. Words come flying from his mouth like bullets. When Porta takes another bite of sausage he snatches it from his hand and throws it against the wall. 'Do you think you're in a boozer?' he screams. After a while he becomes so hoarse and out of breath that he is forced to stop.

'Finished?' asks Porta quietly, picking up the sausage from the floor. 'Then let me explain! And if you want to lash anybody with that filthy tongue of yours then take it out on the Luftwaffe! They're the shower that's responsible for it all! They bombed the wrong place! It's a wonder I came out of it alive, but, of course, you don't care a shit about that!'

'Too fuckin' true I don't!' snarls Wolf, grinding his teeth.

'Thought as much!' says Porta apathetically, slapping a large piece of sausage on a slice of bread.

'Like some rat poison to put on that?' asks Wolf, nastily.

'No thanks. Jam, though, if you've got it?' smiles Porta ingratiatingly, dipping his sausage in a bowl of redcurrant jelly. 'You ever hear of something called quick clay?'

'Never,' says Wolf. He stares blankly at Porta, whose jaws are working double time to keep the sandwich he has made from choking him.

'Quick clay,' explains Porta, gesturing with the hand which is holding his sandwich, and splashing redcurrant jelly on to Wolf's tailor-made uniform, 'is made up from silicon, sand an' a lot of other shit in clay tubes that can hold together on the outside but are full of water, a hell of a lot of water, inside. So long as it's left alone fuck all happens, but with certain kinds of disturbances, like, for example, bombs dropped by German knotheads, then all hell can break loose! The whole lot of it turns into a bloody great pool of mud when the walls of the tubes break up! The more it gets shook up the worse it gets! The whole surface of the earth starts movin' an' everythin' on it gets sucked down into hell. Trees, people, waggons, tanks and *gold*! I can tell you it was a very unpleasant experience, that lot was!'

'I wish it'd been a hundred times worse,' rumbles Wolf, viciously making himself a sugar sandwich. 'Couldn't you have hung on to our gold, *somehow*? You don't let anything valuable as that slip through your fingers! I hope, for your own sake, you can get Sally to believe your horror story! Otherwise something very nasty might happen to you!'

Sally arrives the next day. He has so little time to spare that he has himself flown from the airstrip in a Fiesler Storch which can land on the wide boulevard.

'They tell me you're up to something!' he shouts as soon as he catches sight of Porta, although still a long way off. 'But that *must* be a lie! You're not that stupid!'

'Drop dead!' answers Porta, with a disarming smile, aiming his forefinger at him.

'Let me hear it! What happened? Where's the gold?' demands Sally. 'I don't give a shit for your Grimm's Fairy Tales stuff, and I want you to know I've brought three interrogation experts with me from Berlin! When they've had you and your pals under treatment you'll confess it was you lot that nailed Jesus and the robber to the cross and stuck a spear in Him and gave Him vinegar instead of vodka like the pigs you are! What a shower!'

Arguing loudly they push their way into Wolf's sanctum sanctorum. They are so excited they come close to fighting when they stick in the door, trying to go through it all three at the same time.

Sally strides up and down the floor, foaming with rage. With a flourish he pulls the oversized pistol he carries round to the front of his belt and unbuttons the flap of the holster. He changes his expression from one of anger to deep, fatherly perturbation and then back again. He shows his teeth in a horsy grin and bends confidentially down over Porta.

'I think you're lying! And d'you know what else I think?'

'I'm no thought-reader!' says Porta.

'Shut up! I'll do the talking!' Sally roars. 'I think you and that filthy Jew Commissar have put that gold somewhere, and are just going to wait till the warring powers have knocked the stuffing out of one another. Then you'll take off and pick up *our* gold, and shit all over your good buddies here! See, that's what I think, you greedy son of a bitch!'

'Really?' smiles Porta sarcastically. 'Look at that, now!'

'Defend yourself, blast you! And shut up about that cursed

quick clay,' shouts Sally furiously. 'Not even a drivelling idiot'd believe that! And let me tell you the risk you and your Jew Commissar are running with this crazy scheme! The morons over there know you've pinched the gold from under their noses, and now they're looking for it. It's enough to make 'em forget the world war! And before you know where you are the whole world'll be after it! You'll never be able to get rid of it! Even the sneaky bankers in Switzerland or Liechtenstein won't touch it!'

'The Mafia might!' says Porta, laconically.

Sally sits down again, scowling, and digs out a large black cigar from his breast pocket, while he considers how to shoot Porta where it will hurt most.

'Let me talk,' says Porta placatingly. 'And I'll explain it to you so it can get through even that thick guard commander skull of yours! I know the gold's red-hot, so I'd never dream of goin' it alone. Believe me or not, the bloody earth's swallowed it up! And all those shits from the OGPU and the Gestapo ain't ever going to find it!'

It takes a very long time before Wolf and Sally are convinced that Porta is telling the truth.

Wolf looks as if he is waiting for the firing squad, and Sally looks as if he has already been hanged. Porta is eating jam with a spoon. It calms his ragged nerves.

'We'll need a whole lot of excavators,' Wolf breaks the heavy silence.

'I can get those!' promises Sally. 'We'll turn that rotten Russia inside bloody out!'

'You'll have to go through the front line again,' decides Wolf. 'And this time don't come back without the gold!'

'You might as well chuck it!' says Porta, disillusioned. 'The earth's swallowed it down and has digested it long ago!'

'How about that Commissar woman?' asks Wolf, after a long silence. 'We can't have her running about free! She knows a lot too much, and it can't be long before the Gestapo's here doin' a bit of gold-prospecting!'

'Funny you should say that,' smiles Porta in friendly fashion. 'That's just what the Commissar said when I asked

366

him what to do about her. Kill her, he said. Don't let her get back! She'd talk to people she shouldn't be talking to!'

'I'll send 'er a gift parcel!' Wolf smiles strangely, like Father Christmas in the snow.

'One you die of when you open it?' asks Sally.

'That's it,' answers Wolf, and goes out to give some orders to the Chinese.

'I do believe I've developed a weak heart fom all this disappointment,' says Sally, as he climbs into the Fiesler Storch on his way back to Berlin.

'Now we're on speaking terms again,' says Porta, 'I've got another plan that can get us to Sweden so's we can go fishing for salmon!'

'Another plan,' shouts Sally, looking scared. 'I get closer to a heart attack every time I hear of one of your plans. But go on, what is it this time?'

'Sable,' whispers Porta secretively, looking around him cautiously.

'Sable?' asks Sally, looking blank. 'Those things they make fur coats of for the whores? You're surely not thinking of going into the furrier line. That's Jew business. You'd do well to keep out of it!'

'It's a lot bigger than that!' smiles Porta mysteriously. 'My friend the Commissar let me in on it. There's more than one kind of sable it seems, and one of the kinds is black and very rare. It's worth ten times as much as all the other bloody sable. It's called Barguzhinski sable, and is only found in Russia and there only in very secret places! They export only a few of 'em every third year so Uncle Joe can keep the price up for the little devils. There's a death penalty for breakin' the monopoly! But I've got a plan! We nip back through the front line and pick up an armful of females and a couple of lusty males. Then goodbye the Soviet at a hell of a lick! We hide the little beasts in some safe place, and then all we've got to do is get 'em to fuck. Then we're rich! Stalin has a stroke an' his moustache falls off!'

'And then he comes and shoots our heads off,' Wolf continues, pessimistically.

367

'Maybe that idea's not so crazy after all,' Sally is thinking aloud. 'I'll have a look at it when I get back to the War Ministry. We'll see what we can find out about Barguzhinski sable!' he mumbles with increasing interest as he slams the door of the Storch.

'Come on,' says Wolf. 'Let's you and me go over and get stinking drunk. We're rollin' again some time tonight! So it probably won't be long before you go on your arse for Führer, Folk and Fatherland. I'll come over an' spit on your grave!'

'I'll come back an' pee in your tea, then!' promises Porta.

THE END